The Tea

The Locksmith

The Tearsmith

A Novel

ERIN DOOM

Translated by Eleanor Chapman

DELL

NEW YORK

A Dell Trade Paperback Original

Translation copyright © 2024 by Eleanor Chapman

Published in the United States by Dell, an imprint of Random House, a division of Penguin Random House LLC, New York.

Dell and the D colophon are registered trademarks of Penguin Random House LLC.

Originally published in Italy as *Fabbricante di lacrime* by Magazzini Salani in 2021. Copyright © Adriano Salani Editore s.r.l., Milano, 2021.

This translation is published in the United Kingdom by Michael Joseph, an imprint of Penguin Books Limited, a Penguin Random House Company, in 2024.

isbn 978-0-593-87438-7
Ebook isbn 978-0-593-87439-4

Printed in the United States of America on acid-free paper

randomhousebooks.com

4 6 8 9 7 5 3

For those who have believed from the beginning.
And until the very end.

The Tearsmith

Prologue

We had many stories at The Grave.

Whispered tales, bedtime stories . . . legends flickering on our lips in the glow of a candle. The most famous was the one about the Tearsmith.

It told of a distant, far-away place . . .

A world where no one could cry, and people's souls were empty, stripped of all emotion. But hidden far from everyone lived a little man cloaked in shadows and boundless solitude. A lonely artisan, pale and hunched, whose eyes were clear like glass and could produce crystal teardrops.

People went to him in order to cry, to feel a shred of emotion — because tears encapsulate love and the most heart-wrenching of farewells. They are the most intimate extension of the soul. More than joy or happiness, it is tears that make us truly human.

And the Tearsmith fulfilled this desire. He slipped his tears and all that they held into people's eyes. And so it came to be that they learnt to cry: with anger, desperation, pain and anguish.

Excruciating passions, disappointments and tears, tears, tears — the Tearsmith corrupted a world of purity, tainting it with the deepest and darkest of emotions.

'Remember, you cannot lie to the Tearsmith,' they would say, to finish the tale.

They told us this story to teach us that every child can be good, *must* be good, because no one is born evil. It is not in human nature.

But for me . . .

For me, it wasn't like that.

For me, it wasn't just a story.

He was not dressed in shadows. He was not a pale and hunched little man, with eyes as clear as glass.

No. I knew the Tearsmith.

1. A New Home

*Dressed in sorrow, she was still the most
beautiful and radiant thing in all the world.*

'They want to adopt you.'

These were words I never thought I would hear.

I wanted it so much, had wanted it ever since I was a little girl, so for a moment I thought I must have fallen asleep and be dreaming. Again.

But this wasn't the voice from my dreams.

It was the gruff bark of Mrs Fridge, her voice infused with the usual contempt.

'Me?' I gasped incredulously.

She sneered at me with a curled upper lip.

'You.'

'You're sure?'

She gripped her pen with her pudgy fingers, and I flinched under her glare.

'Have you gone deaf?' she snapped. 'Did all that fresh air block your ears?'

I hurried to shake my head, my eyes wide in disbelief.

It wasn't possible. It couldn't be.

No one wanted teenagers. No one wanted older children, never, not under any circumstances . . . It was a proven fact. It was like in the dog shelter – everyone wanted a puppy, because they were cute, innocent, and easy to train. No one wanted a dog that had been there its whole life.

This had been a difficult truth for me to accept, having grown up under that roof.

When you were little, they would at least look at you. But gradually, as you grew up, those looks would become fleeting glances, and their pity would carve you into those four walls forever.

But now . . . *now* . . .

'Mrs Milligan wants to have a little chat. She's downstairs waiting for you. Show her round the institute and try not to ruin everything. Keep your head out of the clouds and with a bit of luck you'll be out of here.'

My head was spinning.

The skirt of my good dress fluttered against my knees as I climbed down the stairs, and again, I wondered if this was just another of my daydreams.

Surely, it was a dream. At the bottom of the stairs, I was greeted by the kind face of a mature woman, clutching an overcoat in her arms.

'Hi,' she smiled, and I noticed that she was looking me directly *in the eyes*. That hadn't happened in a very long time.

'Hello . . .' I exhaled.

She told me that she'd noticed me in the garden earlier, as she was coming in through the institute's wrought-iron gates. She had seen me in the long grass, lit by the shafts of sunlight filtering through the tree leaves.

'I'm Anna,' she introduced herself as we started to walk.

Her voice was velvety, mellowed by age. I gazed at her, enraptured, wondering if it was possible to be electrocuted by sound, or to be so enamoured by something you'd only just heard.

'What about you? What's your name?'

'Nica,' I answered, trying to contain my emotion. 'My name is Nica.'

She looked at me curiously, and I was so keen to hold her gaze that I didn't even look where I was stepping.

'That's a very unusual name. I've never heard it before.'

'Yes . . .' My gaze became evasive and shy. 'My parents named me. They . . . well, they were both biologists. Nica is a type of butterfly.'

I remembered very little of my mom and dad, and what I could remember was hazy, as if I was looking at them through a dirty window. If I closed my eyes and sat silently, I could just about make out their faces looking down at me.

I was five years old when they died.

Their tenderness was one of the few things that I could remember – and what I most sorely missed.

4

'It's a really lovely name, "Nica" . . .' Her lips rolled around my name as if she wanted to taste how it sounded. 'Nica,' she repeated decisively, with a graceful nod.

She looked into my face, and it felt like a warm light was beaming down on me. It seemed as if my skin was glowing under her gaze, as if a single glance from her could make me shine. This was a big deal for me.

Slowly, we wandered around the grounds of the institute. She asked me if I'd been there long, and I replied that I'd basically grown up there. The sun was bright as we strolled past the climbing ivy.

'What were you doing before . . . when I saw you over there?' she asked during a lull in the conversation, pointing towards the shoots of wild heather in a distant corner of the grounds.

I quickly turned to look where she was pointing, and without knowing why, I felt the urge to hide my hands.

Keep your head out of the clouds. Mrs Fridge's warning flashed through my mind.

'I like being outside,' I said slowly. 'I like . . . the creatures living here.'

'Are there animals here?' she asked, a little naïvely, but I knew I hadn't explained myself very clearly.

'Little ones, yes . . .' I replied vaguely, taking care not to step on a cricket. 'Often, we don't even see them . . .'

I blushed a little as we caught each other's eyes, but she didn't ask me any more questions. Instead, we shared a gentle silence, listening to the jays chirping and children whispering as they spied on us through the windows.

She told me that her husband would arrive at any moment. *To get to know me,* she implied, and my heart felt so light I felt like I could fly. As we went back inside, I wondered if I could pour those feelings into a bottle and keep them forever. Hide them under my pillow and bring them out to watch them shine like a pearl in the darkness of the night.

I hadn't felt so happy in a long time.

'Jin, Ross, no running,' I said good-naturedly as two children rushed past, jostling my dress. They snickered and ran up the creaky stairs.

I turned to look at Mrs Milligan and realised that she had been watching me. She was gazing deep into my eyes with a touch of something that seemed almost like . . . admiration.

'You've got really beautiful eyes, Nica,' she said unexpectedly. 'Do you know that?'

Embarrassment gnawed at me. I didn't know what to say.

'Everyone must tell you that all the time,' she prompted tactfully. But the truth was that no, no one at The Grave had ever told me anything of the sort.

The younger children would sometimes innocently ask me if I saw colours like everyone else did. They said my eyes were 'the colour of a crying sky' because they were a strikingly light, speckled grey. I knew that many people thought they were unusual, but no one had ever told me they were beautiful.

At the compliment, my hands began to tremble.

'I . . . no . . . but thank you,' I stammered awkwardly, making her smile. I discreetly pinched the back of my hand and felt the slight pain with an infinite joy.

It was real. It was all real.

That woman was really there.

A family, for me . . . A new life, away from all of this, away from The Grave . . .

I had thought that I would be trapped inside those walls for much longer. For another two years, until I turned nineteen – that's when you legally become an adult in Alabama.

But now, perhaps I wouldn't have to wait to come of age. I had given up praying that somebody would come and take me away, but now . . . perhaps . . .

'What's that?' Mrs Milligan asked suddenly.

She was looking around, captivated.

Then I heard it too. A beautiful melody. Deep, harmonious music was reverberating through the cracks and flaking plaster of the institute's walls.

An angelic sound floated through The Grave, as bewitching as a siren's call. I felt my skin crawl.

Mrs Milligan wandered towards the sound, entranced. There was nothing for me to do but follow her. She reached the arched doorway into the living room and came to a stop.

She stood, bewitched, staring at the source of this invisible wonder.

The upright piano was old, clunky and a bit out of tune, but despite all of that, it still sang sweetly.

And, of course, those hands . . . those pale hands and those sculpted wrists, flying fluidly over the keys.

'Who is he . . . ?' Mrs Milligan breathed after a moment. 'Who is that boy?'

I clenched the skirt of my dress in my fists. I hesitated, and at the other end of the room, the boy paused.

His hands came to a gradual stop. His squared shoulders were a stark silhouette against the wall.

Then, gradually, as if he had been expecting it, *as if he already knew*, he turned around.

His hair was a dark halo, as black as a crow's wings. His face was pale, with a sharp jawline and two narrow eyes that were darker than coal.

There it was, that fatal charm. The seductive beauty of his pale lips and finely chiselled features made Mrs Milligan fall silent at my side.

He looked over his shoulder at us and his hair flopped over his lowered, shining eyes and high cheekbones. Trembling, I was certain I saw him smile.

'That's Rigel.'

I had always wanted a family, more than anything else in the world.

I had prayed that there was someone out there for me, ready to come and take me away with them, to give me the chances that I had never had.

It was too good to be true.

If I stopped to think about it, I still couldn't believe it. *Or maybe . . . I didn't want to believe it.*

'Is everything all right?' Mrs Milligan asked me.

She was sitting next to me in the back seat.

'Yes . . .' I made myself say, forcing a smile. 'Everything's . . . great.'

I clenched my fists in my lap, but she didn't notice. She turned back around to look out the window, and every now and then would point out a feature in the landscape rushing past.

But I was hardly listening to her.

Slowly, I turned to look at the reflection in the mirror in front of us. In the passenger seat next to Mr Milligan there was a shock of black hair brushing against the headrest.

He was staring indifferently out the window, his elbow propped against the car door and his head leaning on his fist.

'That's the river down there,' Mrs Milligan said, but his dark eyes did not look at where she was pointing. Through his black eyelashes, he blandly observed the landscape.

As if he'd heard my thoughts, his eyes suddenly met mine in the mirror.

His gaze was piercing, and I quickly looked away.

I refocused on what Anna was saying, blinking, nodding and smiling, but I felt his eyes burning into me, holding me captive.

After a couple of hours, the car slowed down and we pulled into a leafy neighbourhood.

The Milligans lived in a small brick house, identical to the others on the street. It had a white picket fence, a mailbox, and an ornamental windmill amongst the gardenias.

I glimpsed an apricot tree in the back garden and strained my neck to get a look at it, genuinely curious about that little patch of green.

'Is it heavy?' Mr Milligan asked, as I picked up the cardboard box containing my few belongings. 'Do you need a hand?'

I shook my head, touched by his kindness, and he led us inside.

'Come on, this way. Oh, the path is a little worse for wear . . . watch out for that slab, it sticks up a bit. Are you hungry? Do you want something to eat?'

'Let them get settled in first,' said Anna softly, and he pushed his glasses up his nose.

'Oh, yes, of course . . . You must be tired, right? Come.'

He opened the front door. I saw 'Home' written on a doormat on the threshold and felt my heart racing.

Anna tilted her head. 'Come in, Nica.'

I took a step forward and found myself in a narrow entrance hall.

The smell was the first thing that struck me.

It didn't smell like the mouldy walls or damp ceilings of The Grave.

It was an unusual smell, deep, almost . . . intimate. There was something special about it. I realised suddenly that it was Anna's smell.

I looked around with shining eyes. The wallpaper was a bit shabby in places. There were a few picture frames dotted about on the walls, and a doily on the table, next to the key bowl. It all felt so lived-in and personal that I was frozen in the doorway, unable to move a muscle.

'It's quite small,' Mr Milligan said, scratching his head in embarrassment, but I didn't even register his words.

God, it was . . . perfect.

'Your bedrooms are upstairs.' Anna started climbing the narrow staircase, and I took the opportunity to steal a furtive look at Rigel.

He was holding his box under one arm and looking around with lowered eyes. His gaze swept swiftly from side to side. His expression gave nothing away.

'Klaus?' Mr Milligan called, looking for someone. 'Where's he got to . . .' I heard him bustling away as we headed upstairs.

We each settled into our own rooms.

'This used to be another little living room,' Anna told me, opening the door to my new bedroom. 'Then it became the guest bedroom. You know, if we had a visit from a friend of . . .' she hesitated, freezing for a moment. Then she blinked and forced a smile. 'It doesn't matter. Anyway, it's yours now. Do you like it? If there's something you'd like to change, or move, I don't know . . .'

'No,' I whispered, standing in the doorway of a room that, finally, I could call all *mine*.

No more shared bedrooms, or roller blinds that let the morning sun through. No more freezing, dusty floors, or dreary, mouse-grey walls.

It was a lovely room, with wooden floorboards and a long, wrought-iron mirror in the far corner. There was a breeze coming in through the open window, softly fluttering the linen curtains, and the clean bedsheets gleamed white in contrast to the warm, vermillion bedcover. I found my fingers brushing the snow-white corner of the sheets as I approached the bed with my cardboard box still under my arm. I checked that Mrs Milligan had gone, then hurried to bend over and smell them. The fragrance of fresh laundry flooded my nostrils and I closed my eyes, taking deep, inebriating breaths of it.

It smelt so good . . .

I looked around, unable to believe that all this space was just for me. I put the box on the nightstand, opened it and reached inside. I took out my little caterpillar plushie and placed him on the middle of the pillow. He was a bit grey and tattered, the only memento I still had of Mom and Dad.

I looked at the pillow with shining eyes.

Mine . . .

I took my time sorting out my few belongings. One by one, I hung up my shirts, my lumpy sweater and my pants. I checked all my socks and shoved the ones with more holes to the back of the drawer, hoping they'd go unnoticed back there.

Before I headed back downstairs, I took a final look at my room from the doorway and wondered with anticipation if the smell of it would soon start clinging to me, too.

'You're sure you don't want anything to eat?' Anna asked later, looking at us with concern. 'Not even a quick bite . . . ?'

I declined, thanking her. We had stopped for fast food on the way, and I still felt full.

She seemed uncertain. She gazed at me for a moment, then looked over my shoulder.

'What about you, Rigel?' She hesitated. 'Am I pronouncing it right? Rigel?' she repeated, pronouncing it as it was written.

He nodded and, as I had, declined.

'Okay . . .' she gave in. 'There are cookies, and the milk's in the fridge. Anyway, if you want to go and get some rest . . . Oh! Our bedroom's the one at the end of the hallway, if you need anything, anything at all.'

She was worrying.

She was worrying, I realised, with a light fluttering in my chest. *She was worrying about me, if I'd eaten, if I hadn't eaten, if I needed anything . . .*

She really cared, and not just about passing inspections like Mrs

Fridge had, on the occasions when Child Protection came to tick off that we were all clean and had full stomachs.

No. She genuinely cared . . .

As I went back upstairs, trailing my hand along the banister, I toyed with the idea of coming back down in the middle of the night and eating cookies at the kitchen counter. It could be like the movies we used to steal glimpses of through the crack in the door when Mrs Fridge fell asleep in the armchair in front of the television.

As I reached my bedroom door, the sound of footsteps made me turn around.

Rigel appeared at the top of the stairs. He turned away from me, but I was sure that he'd seen me.

I suddenly remembered that he was also a part of this beautifully embroidered tapestry. That this new reality, however precious and coveted, was not all sweetness and light, warmth and wonder. No, it was tinged with darkness around the edges, like a burn, like the scorch mark from a cigarette.

'*Rigel*,' I whispered, and I heard his name as if it had leapt spontaneously out of my mouth. He was standing still in the middle of the empty hallway, and I wavered, uncertain.

'Now . . . now that we're . . .'

'Now that we're *what*?' he asked in a harsh, venomous way that made me flinch.

'Now that we're here, together,' I went on, looking at his back. 'I . . . want it to work out.'

I wanted all of it to work out and there was nothing I could do about it. The tapestry included him, that sooty stain. In a burst of desperation, I prayed that he wouldn't destroy the delicate stitching of this lacy dream, that it wouldn't all unravel before my eyes.

He paused for a moment, then, without a word, started walking away towards his room. My shoulders slumped.

'Rigel . . .'

'Don't come into my room,' he spat. 'Not now, not ever.'

I looked at him anxiously, feeling my hope melt away.

'Is that a threat?' I asked quietly, as he turned the door handle.

I saw him opening the door, but at the last moment he hesitated. With a jerk of his sharp jaw, he turned to glare at me over his shoulder, and just before he closed the door, I saw his lips viciously curling into a sneer of condemnation.

'It's advice, *little moth*.'

2. A Lost Tale

Sometimes destiny is an unrecognisable path.

The institute was called Sunnycreek Home.

It stood at the end of a decrepit, dead-end road, in the forgotten outskirts of a little town in the south of the state. It housed unfortunate children like me, none of whom I ever heard call it by its real name.

Everyone called it The Grave, and it didn't take long for me to understand why: everyone who ended up there seemed condemned to a fate of *decrepit dead-ends*, just like the road that led to it.

I felt like I was living behind bars in The Grave.

I spent every day longing for someone to come and take me away. For someone to look me in the eyes and choose me, over all the other children. For someone to want me as I was, even though I wasn't all that much. But no one had ever chosen me. No one had ever wanted me, or even noticed me. I had always been invisible.

Not like Rigel.

Unlike many of us, he hadn't lost his parents. No tragedy had befallen his family when he was little.

They had found him in front of the institute's gates in a wicker basket, with no note and no name, abandoned in the night with only the stars to watch over him like great sleeping giants. He was only a week old.

They named him *Rigel* after the brightest star in the constellation of Orion, which was shining that night like a diamond web spun on a bed of black velvet. With the surname Wilde, they filled the void of his identity.

For all of us at The Grave, that was where he was born. It was obvious even from his appearance that the night shone through his skin, as pale as the moon, and his black eyes stared with the steadiness of someone unafraid of the dark.

Ever since he was a child, Rigel had been the jewel in The Grave's crown.

'The son of the stars,' the matron before Mrs Fridge had called him. She adored him so much that she taught him to play the piano. She would sit with him for hours, with a patience that never extended to the rest of us, and with note after note she transformed him into an impeccable boy who shone out against the grey walls of the institute.

Rigel seemed as good as he looked. He had perfect teeth and got good grades. The matron would sneak him candy before dinner.

He was the child everybody would have wanted.

But I knew that he wasn't really like that. I had learnt to see *beneath*, beneath his smiles, his pale lips, the mask of perfection he wore with everybody else.

I knew that he harboured the night within him, and that hidden in the folds of his soul was the darkness he had been plucked from.

Rigel always acted . . . *strangely* with me.

I had never been able to explain it. It was as if I had somehow done something to deserve that behaviour, his distant, silent glares. It all started one normal day, I don't even remember exactly when. He knocked into me, and I fell, grazing my knees. I brought my legs up to my chest and brushed the grass away, but when I looked up, I saw no trace of an apology on his face. He just stood there, staring at me, in the shadow of a cracked wall.

Rigel would yank at my clothes, pull my hair, untie the bows at the ends of my braids. The ribbons would flutter to his feet like dead butterflies, and through my tears I would see his lips curl into a cruel smile before he ran away.

But he never touched me.

In all those years, he never once made direct contact with my skin. Just the hems and material of my clothes, my hair . . . He would pull me over by my sweater, and I ended up with baggy sleeves, but never bruises. It was as if he didn't want to leave any evidence of his guilt on me. Or maybe he just found my freckles disgusting. Maybe he despised me so much that he didn't want to touch me.

Rigel spent a lot of time by himself, rarely seeking out the company of other children.

But once, when we were around fifteen, a new boy came to The Grave, a blond boy who was transferred to a foster home about a week later. He immediately took to Rigel – the one boy who, if possible, was worse than he was. They would hang out, leaning against the crumbling walls, Rigel with his arms crossed over his chest, his lips twitching and his eyes shining darkly with amusement. I never saw them argue about a thing.

Then, on a day like any other, the new boy came down to dinner with a black eye and a puffy face. Mrs Fridge glared at him unkindly and in a thundering voice demanded what in God's name had happened.

'Nothing,' he mumbled without looking up from his plate. 'I fell over at school.'

But I knew full well that it wasn't 'nothing'. When I looked up, I saw Rigel lowering his face so that no one would see his expression. He had *smiled*, a thin sneer had cracked his perfect mask.

And as he grew up, he grew into his beauty in a way that I struggled to admit.

But his beauty was anything but sweet, soft or gentle.

No . . .

It scorched you to look at Rigel, but your eyes would be drawn to him, like to the frame of a burning building or the carcass of a destroyed car on the side of the road. He was viciously beautiful, and the more you tried not to look at him, the more his twisted charm wedged itself behind your eyes and got under your skin until it infected your entire body.

He was seductive, solitary, sinister.

A nightmare dressed like your most secret daydream.

The next morning, it felt like I had woken up in a fairy tale.

Clean sheets, that divine smell and a mattress with no springs poking through. I didn't know how to want for more.

I sat up, my eyes bleary from sleep. That comfortable room, all mine, made me feel luckier than I ever had before.

Then, as if a black cloud was passing over me, I remembered that that was only half the fairy tale. There was also that dark patch, that scorch mark, and nothing I could do to remove it.

I weakly shook my head, and roughly rubbed my eyes with my wrists, trying to push those thoughts away.

I didn't want to think about it. I didn't want to let anyone ruin it, not even him.

I knew how these things went well enough not to delude myself that I'd found my forever home.

Everyone seemed to think that adoption was just a happy ending, that your new family would take you home and after only a few hours, you'd automatically become one of them.

But it wasn't like that at all. It only works like that with pets.

Actual adoption was a much longer process. First of all, there was a short stay with the new family, to see if everyone got on well enough for cohabitation to be possible. This was called a 'pre-adoptive placement'. During this stage, it wasn't unusual for incompatibilities or problems to arise that would disturb the family harmony, so it was very important for the family to use this time to decide whether or not to proceed. Only if everything went smoothly, with no glitches, would the parents eventually finalise the adoption process.

That's why I couldn't really think of myself as a proper member of the family yet. This fairy tale that I had found myself in was beautiful, but fragile. It could shatter like glass in my hands at any moment.

I'll be good, I resolved. *I'll be good, and everything will be fine.* I would do everything in my power to make it work. Everything . . .

I went downstairs, determined not to let anyone ruin my chances.

The house was small, so I didn't have much trouble finding the kitchen. I heard voices, and tentatively stepped towards them.

When I arrived in the doorway, I was lost for words.

The Milligans were sitting around the kitchen table in pyjamas and slightly tatty slippers.

Anna was laughing, her fingers wrapped around a steaming mug, and Mr Milligan was pouring cereal into a ceramic bowl, a sleepy smile on his face.

And right in the middle of them sat Rigel.

It was like a slap in the face, his black hair a bruise in my line of vision. I blinked a few times to make sure I wasn't imagining it. He was in the middle of telling them something. His shoulders were softened and relaxed, and his hair tousled around his face.

The Milligans were watching him with bright eyes, then suddenly, simultaneously, they burst out laughing at something he had said. Their laughter rang in my ears as if I had been torn asunder and each part of me flung to the far ends of the world.

'Oh, Nica,' Anna burst out. 'Good morning!'

I slightly raised my shoulders. They were all staring at me and somehow I managed to feel like a spare part, even though I had only just arrived and hardly knew them. Even though it should have been me sitting there between them, not him.

Rigel looked up at me. His dark eyes found mine instantly, as if he already knew, and I thought I glimpsed the corners of his mouth curling coolly. He tilted his head and smiled angelically.

'Good morning, Nica.'

My blood ran cold. I couldn't move, I couldn't speak. I felt more and more gripped by that icy dismay.

'Did you sleep well?' Mr Milligan pulled out a chair for me to sit down. 'Come and have some breakfast!'

'We were just getting to know each other a little bit,' Mrs Milligan told me. I looked again at Rigel, who was gazing back at me like a perfect painting with the Milligans either side of him.

I sat down reluctantly. Mr Milligan filled Rigel's glass and Rigel smiled at him, perfectly at ease. I felt like I'd sat down on a bed of thorns.

I'll be good. I watched Mr and Mrs Milligan chatting with each other in front of me, and the words *I'll be good* flashed through my head like scarlet lightning bolts. *I'll be good, I swear I will* . . .

'How are you feeling on your first day, Nica?' Anna asked, so gentle even first thing in the morning. 'Are you nervous?'

I struggled to push my clamouring worries far away.

'Oh . . . no,' I tried to relax. 'I'm not scared . . . I've always liked school.'

It was the truth.

School was one of the only chances we got to leave The Grave. Walking along the road to the public school, I would look up at the clouds, pretending I was just like all the others. I would dream of getting on an airplane and flying away towards distant worlds of freedom.

It was one of the only times I almost managed to feel normal.

'I've already called reception,' Anna told us. 'The principal will see you as soon as possible. The school has got you on the register, and they've assured me that you can start lessons right away. I know it's all very quick, but . . . I hope it will all be all right. You can ask to be put in the same classes if you want,' she added.

I met her eager gaze and tried to hide my unease. 'Oh. Yeah . . . thanks.'

I sensed I was being watched. It was Rigel's dark, narrow eyes staring right at me from under his arched eyebrows.

I snapped my eyes away, as if I'd been scalded. I felt the visceral need to get out of there, and with the excuse of going to get dressed, I got up from the table and left the kitchen.

As I was putting walls between us, I felt something twisting in my stomach, the way he had looked at me infesting my thoughts.

'*I'll be good,*' I whispered to myself, shaking. '*I'll be good . . . I swear . . .*'

He was the last person in the world I wanted to be there.

Would I ever be able to ignore him?

The new school was a grey, blocky building.

Mr Milligan pulled up, and a few kids ran past the front of the car in their rush to get to class. He rearranged his heavy-framed glasses on his nose and awkwardly placed his hands on the steering wheel, as if he didn't know what else to do with them. I realised that I enjoyed watching him. He had a meek, nervous personality – that was probably why I sympathised with him so much.

'Anna will come and pick you up later.'

The idea of someone being out there waiting for me, ready to take me home, gave me a stronger surge of pleasure than ever before. I nodded from the back seat, my shabby backpack sitting on my knees.

'Thank you, Mr Milligan.'

'Oh, you can . . .' he started to say as we got out of the car, his ears a little red. 'You can call me Norman.' I stood, watching the car disappear down the road until I heard footsteps behind me.

I turned around and saw Rigel walking alone towards the entrance.

My eyes followed his slender body, the relaxed swinging of his broad shoulders. There was always a hypnotic, natural quality to the way that he moved. He strode surely and confidently, as if the ground would shape itself to his footsteps.

I entered the building after him, but my bag strap got caught on the door handle. I suddenly stumbled wide-eyed into someone who was entering behind me at just that moment.

'What the hell,' I heard as I turned around. An irritated boy jerked his arm away, clutching a couple of books.

'I'm sorry,' I whispered faintly, and his friend gave him a nudge.

I tucked my hair behind my ears. He met my gaze and seemed to re-evaluate me. The irritation disappeared from his face. He stood stock still, as if my eyes had struck him with lightning.

Then, out of nowhere, he dropped the books he had been holding.

I looked at them heaped on the floor, and when I didn't see him bending to pick them up, knelt down to retrieve them myself.

I held them out to him, feeling guilty for having bumped into him, and realised that he'd been staring at me the whole time.

'Thanks . . .' he smiled slowly, letting his gaze wander all over me in a way that made me blush, which he seemed to find entertaining, or maybe intriguing.

'Are you new?' he asked.

'Let's go, Rob,' his friend urged. 'We're really late.'

But he didn't seem to want to go anywhere. I felt a stinging on the back of my neck, a stabbing sensation, like a needle piercing through the air behind me.

I tried to shake off the feeling of foreboding. I backed away from him, and with my face downturned, I stammered, 'I . . . I've got to go.'

I got to reception, which was just down the corridor. I saw that the door was already open and hoped I hadn't made the receptionist wait. It was only after I'd crossed the threshold that I noticed the silhouette lurking to one side.

I almost winced.

Rigel was leaning against the wall, his arms crossed over his chest. One leg was bent, the sole of his shoe against the wall, and his face was slightly lowered, his eyes looking at the floor.

He had always been a lot taller than everyone else, and significantly more intimidating, but I didn't need that as an excuse to immediately take a step backwards. Everything about him frightened me, his appearance and what lay beneath.

What was he doing loitering there, right next to the doorway, when there was a line of chairs just there on the other side of the waiting room?

'The principal will see you now.'

The receptionist called us through from the principal's office, bringing me back to reality.

'Come in.'

Rigel moved away from the wall and walked past me without so much as a glance. We headed into the office and the door closed behind us. The principal was a young, attractive, austere-looking woman. She gestured for us to sit down in front of the desk while she checked our files. She asked us a few questions about the syllabus in our old school, and seemed particularly interested in what was written in Rigel's file.

'I spoke to your institute,' she said. 'I asked a few questions about your academic performance. I was pleasantly surprised by you, Mr Wilde.' She smiled, turning the page. 'Good grades, impeccable behaviour, not a toe out of line. Truly a model student. Your teachers could only sing your praises.' She looked up, satisfied. 'It will be a real pleasure to have you here with us at Burnaby.'

I wondered if there was any possibility that she knew how wrong she was, if she realised that those glowing reports didn't reflect reality, because the teachers never saw *underneath*. They were exactly like all the others.

I wished I could find it within me to say something.

But Rigel just smiled in his charming way. I wondered how people managed not to notice that his smile never reached his eyes, which stayed dark and impenetrable, glinting like knives.

'The two students waiting just outside will take you to your classes,' said the principal. 'But as of tomorrow, if you'd like, you can ask to be put together.'

I had hoped to avoid this. I gripped the sides of the chair and pushed myself forwards, but he spoke first.

'No.'

I blinked and turned to look at him. Rigel was smiling, a lock of dark hair falling over his forehead.

'There's no need.'

'You're sure? You won't be able to change your minds later.'

'Oh, yes. We'll get plenty of time together.'

'Very good,' the principal declared, seeing as I kept silent. 'You can start class. Follow me.'

I tore my eyes away from Rigel. I got to my feet, picked up my backpack, and followed her out of the office.

'Two seniors will be waiting for you outside reception. Have a great day.'

She retreated into her office and I crossed the room without looking behind me. I had to get away from him, and I would have done so, had a different urge not taken over at the last minute. I couldn't stop myself from turning around to confront him.

'What did you mean?' I bit my lip. I didn't need to see his raised eyebrow to realise what a stupid question it was. But I didn't trust his intentions, and I couldn't believe that he would turn down an opportunity to torment me.

'What?' Rigel looked down at me, his towering presence making me feel even smaller. 'You didn't *seriously* think . . . that I would want to be with *you*?'

I pursed my lips, regretting having asked. The intensity of his gaze made my stomach quiver and his stinging sarcasm scorched my skin.

Without replying, I turned the door handle and made to leave. But something stopped me.

A hand appeared from over my shoulder and pushed the door shut.

I froze. I saw his slender fingers on the doorframe, and every one of my vertebrae became alive to his presence behind me.

'You stay away from me, *little moth*,' he ordered. His hot breath tickled my hair and I stiffened. 'You got that?'

The tension of his body so close was enough to give me chills. *Stay away*, he said, but it was him who had pinned me against the door, breathed all over me, prevented me from leaving.

He moved past me, and I watched him go through narrowed eyes, without moving an inch.

If I'd had my way . . .

If I'd had my way, I'd have forgotten him forever, along with The Grave, with Mrs Fridge, and the pain that had marred my entire childhood. I didn't want to end up in the same family as him. It was a catastrophe for me. It felt as if I had been condemned to bear the burden of my past, as if I would never truly be free.

How could I make him understand?

'Hi!'

I hadn't realised that I'd robotically walked out of reception. I looked up and found myself greeted by a radiant smile.

'I'm in your class. Welcome to Burnaby!'

I saw Rigel striding confidently along the corridor, his black hair swishing as he went. The girl who was with him seemed like she was hardly paying any attention to where she was going. She was staring at him, bewildered, as if she was the new student. They both disappeared around the corner.

'I'm Billie,' my new classmate introduced herself. She held out her hand, beaming, and I shook it. 'What's your name?'

'Nica Dover.'

'Micah?'

'No, *Nica*,' I repeated, stressing the N, and she put a finger to her chin.

'Oh, short for Nikita!'

I found myself smiling. 'No,' I shook my head. 'Just Nica.'

Billie's curious gaze didn't make me feel uncomfortable, like the boy's look earlier had. She had a sincere face, honey-coloured curls, and bright, passionate eyes.

As we walked along, I noticed that she was watching me intently, but it was only when our eyes met again that I understood why. She too was fascinated by the unique colour of my irises.

'Because of your eyes, Nica,' the younger children used to say, when I would ask why they were looking at me in that alienating way. *'Nica's eyes are the colour of a crying sky, big and shining, like grey diamonds.'*

'What happened to your hands?' she asked.

I looked down at my fingertips, which were covered in Band-Aids.

'Oh,' I stammered, awkwardly hiding them behind my back. 'Nothing . . .'

I smiled, trying to change the conversation, and Mrs Fridge's words barged into my head again: 'Get your head out of the clouds.'

'It's so I don't bite my nails,' I burst out. She seemed to believe me, because then she lifted her hands proudly to show me her nibbled nails.

'What does it matter? Mine are down to the bone at this point!' She turned her hands over and started inspecting them. 'My grandma says I should dip them in mustard, "Then you'll lose the taste for them," she says. I've never tried it, though. I find the idea of spending an afternoon with my fingers in mustard a bit . . . perplexing. What if the mailman knocks?'

3. Differences of Opinion

Our movements, like the planets, are governed
By invisible laws.

Billie helped me settle in.

It was a big school, and there was a lot going on. She showed me the classrooms for all the different subjects and took me from one lesson to the next, introducing me to all the teachers. I tried not to be too clingy and weigh her down, but she said that she was actually happy to keep me company. My heart soared like never before. Billie was kind and generous, two qualities you didn't often come across where I came from.

When the bell rang to mark the end of class, we left the classroom together and she looped a long, leather strap around her neck, then shook her curly hair loose.

'Is that a camera?' Curious, I inspected the object that was now dangling from her neck, and her face lit up.

'It's a Polaroid! Haven't you seen one before? My folks gave me this one ages ago. I love photography, my bedroom's covered in photos! Grandma says that I've got to stop cluttering the walls, but every time I find her whistling while dusting them . . . and she ends up forgetting what she said.'

I was trying to keep up with her chattering and, at the same time, trying not to bump into other people. I wasn't used to such bustling crowds, but Billie seemed oblivious – she kept rattling on, bumping into people all over the place.

'I like taking photos of people, it's interesting to see their facial expressions immortalised on film. Miki always hides her face when I try to take her photo. She's so pretty, it's a shame, but she doesn't like it. Oh, look, there she is! Over there!' She waved euphorically. 'Miki!'

I tried to catch a glimpse of this mysterious friend who she'd been telling me about all morning, but I didn't have time before she started dragging me through the crowd by the strap of my backpack.

'Come, Nica! Come and meet her!'

I awkwardly tried to follow her, but just ended up getting under her feet.

'Oh, you'll really like her, just you wait!' she declared excitedly. 'Miki is really so sweet, and so sensitive! Have I already said she's my best friend?'

I tried to nod, but Billie gave me another yank to get me to move. After we'd finally barged most of the way through the crowd to her friend, she ran the final stretch and did a little leap in front of her.

'Hey there!' she trilled. 'How was class? Did you have gym? This is Nica!'

She pushed me forward, and I almost ended up slamming my nose into an open locker.

A hand appeared on the metal and pushed it away.

Sweet, Billie had said. I prepared a smile.

In front of me was a girl with an attractive, slightly pointy, heavily made-up face and thick black hair. She was wearing a baggy hoodie and had a piercing on her left eyebrow. She was chewing gum.

Miki looked me up and down indifferently, then hitched up the strap of her backpack and slammed the locker shut, making me jump. She turned her back on us and headed down the corridor.

'Oh, don't worry, she's always like this,' Billie chirped, as I stood rooted to the spot and staring. 'Making new friends isn't her strong suit. But deep down she's a big softie!'

Deep down . . . *How deep?!*

I looked at her, slightly scared, but she dismissed my concerns, encouraging me to carry on. We headed through the chaos of students, and when we got to the exit, Miki was there watching the shadows of clouds dancing on the asphalt yard, smoking a cigarette and looking deep in thought.

'What a beautiful day!' Billie sighed gleefully, drumming her fingers on her camera. 'Where do you live, Nica? My grandma can give you a lift home, if you want. She's making meatballs for dinner tonight, and Miki's coming over.' She turned to face her. 'You are coming over, right?'

She nodded unenthusiastically, taking a drag of her cigarette, and Billie smiled happily.

'So? Are you coming with –'

She was interrupted by someone running into her.

'Hey!' Billie protested, rubbing her shoulder. 'What sort of manners are those? Ow!'

Other students were rushing past us, and Billie shrank towards Miki. 'What's going on?'

Something wasn't right. Students were running back inside, some with their phones out, some with a terrifying fervour in their eyes. There was an excited atmosphere, and I flattened myself to the wall, frightened by the frenzied crowd.

'Hey!' Miki shouted to a boy who was buzzing with excitement. 'What the hell's happening?'

'There's a fight!' he yelled, pulling out his phone. 'Over by the lockers!'

'A fight? Between who?'

'Phelps and the new boy! God, he's really beating the shit out of him! Out of *Phelps*!' he squawked. 'I gotta film it!'

He leapt away like a grasshopper and I found myself against the wall, arms stiff, eyes staring into the void.

The new boy?

Billie squeezed Miki like a stress ball.

'No! Not violence, please! I don't want to watch. Who would be crazy enough to go for Phelps? Only a *moron* . . . hey!' Her eyes opened wide in alarm. 'Nica! Where are you going?'

But her voice got lost in the flood of students. I overtook people, barging past shoulders and backs, like a butterfly in a labyrinth of plant stalks. There was something crackling, almost suffocating, in the atmosphere. I heard the distinct sound of thumping, the clanging of metal and then something hitting the ground.

I got to the front of the crowd, the shouting and screaming pounding in my temples. I ducked under somebody's arm and, finally, could see what was happening.

The two students were wrestling on the ground in a blind fury. It was difficult to make out who was who in their frenzy, but I didn't need to see their faces. That unmistakable black hair stuck out like a blot of ink.

There was Rigel, the other guy's shirt gripped fiercely in his fist, his knuckles pink and raw as he thrashed the body underneath him. There was a mad glint in his eyes that made my bones tremble and my blood run cold. He dealt brutal, fast punches in a frightening rage. The other boy tried furiously to hit him back, but there was no mercy in Rigel's eyes. I heard the crunch of cartilage as screams filled the air, clamouring, chanting . . .

Then, suddenly, everything stopped.

Teachers parted the crowd, and literally threw themselves on the fighting boys. They managed to pull them off each other, and one of them tackled Rigel and tore him away by the collar, while the others swooped down upon the boy on the ground, who was now looking at him with wild eyes.

My eyes froze on him. It was only then that I recognised who he was – the boy from that morning. The one I'd bumped into in the doorway, the one with the books.

'Phelps, suspended again!' a teacher shouted. 'This is your third fight, you've gone too far!'

'It was him!' the boy cried, beside himself. 'I didn't do anything! He punched me for no reason!'

The teacher shoved Rigel aside, and I saw him looking down, his hair dishevelled and a sneer cutting across his face.

'It was him! Look at him!'

'Enough!' the teacher shouted. 'Straight to the principal! Both of you!'

The teachers pushed them by the shoulders, and I saw Rigel letting himself be escorted away, utterly compliant. He turned his face and casually spat into a water fountain, while the other boy hobbled behind him in the teacher's grasp.

'And the rest of you, get out!' they screamed. 'And put those phones away! O'Connor, you'll be expelled if you don't get out of here this instant! You lot too, go on! There's nothing to see here!'

The students shuffled off, listlessly dispersing towards the exits. The rabble quickly thinned out, but I stayed put, feeling soft and vulnerable, the shadow of him still in my eyes, relentlessly punching, punching, *punching* . . .

'Nica!'

Billie ran up, dragging Miki by her backpack strap behind her.

'Heavens, you scared me! Are you all right?' She looked at me with wide, distressed eyes. 'I can't believe it, your brother!'

I felt a strange shudder. I stared at her speechless and dismayed, almost as if she'd slapped me. Bewildered, I realised that she was referring to Rigel.

Of course . . . Billie didn't know. She wasn't aware that we had different surnames, she only knew what the principal had told her. Basically, from her perspective, we were from the same family, but the way she referred to him felt like nails scraping down a blackboard.

'He . . . he's not . . .'

'You should go to reception,' she interrupted me, agitated. 'To wait for him! Heavens, a fight with Phelps on your first day . . . he'll be in a bad way!'

I was pretty sure it wasn't Rigel who would be in a bad way. I thought of the other boy's swollen face when they had torn Rigel's fists off him.

But Billie pushed me forward anxiously. 'Let's go!' And they both came with me to the school entrance. I found myself wringing my hands. How could I pretend to be just a little worried, when I was completely disturbed by what I'd just witnessed? I remembered the rage in his eyes with glaring clarity. The situation was absurd.

Raised voices were coming through the door.

The boy who was being accused was shouting like a madman, trying to make his own side heard, and the teacher was shouting even louder than him. There was a hysterical exasperation in Phelps's voice, probably because he had got into yet another fight. But what caught my attention most was the shocked, incredulous way that the principal was speaking to Rigel. He was so well behaved, so perfect, he wasn't the sort to do this kind of thing. He would never have started anything 'as serious as this'. The other boy protested even louder, swearing he didn't do anything to provoke him, but Rigel's silent indifference screamed innocence.

After half an hour, the door opened, and Phelps came out into the corridor.

His lip was split and his face was blotchy. He glanced at me distractedly, taking no notice, but the next moment he turned back, as if he'd suddenly just realised who I was. I didn't have time to interpret his distressed expression before the teacher dragged him away.

'I think they'll expel him this time,' Billie murmured as he disappeared at the end of the corridor.

'About time,' Miki retorted. 'After the *incident* with those freshman girls he should have been thrown in a pigsty.'

The door handle turned again.

Billie and Miki fell quiet as Rigel came through the door. His veins were bulging in his wrists and his presence was so magnetic that everyone fell silent. Everything about him made him difficult to ignore.

It was only then that he noticed us.

Well, no. Not *us*.

'What are *you* doing here?'

The surprise in his voice didn't escape me. I felt him looking at me and realised I didn't know how to reply. I didn't even know what I was doing there, waiting for him as if I genuinely was worried about him.

Rigel had told me to stay away from him, had snarled it at such close range that I could still feel his voice echoing in my head.

'Nica wanted to make sure you were all right,' Billie intervened, drawing attention to herself. She gave a crazy smile and lifted a hand. 'Hi . . .'

He didn't reply, and Billie seemed intimidated. Her cheeks reddened, embarrassed by the raw magnetism of his black eyes.

And Rigel noticed. *Oh, he noticed all right.*

He knew full well how attractive his mask was, how well he wore it, the reaction it sparked in others. He flaunted it arrogantly and provocatively. It gave him a sinister charm, a seductive, devious and one-of-a-kind appeal.

He sneered, bewitching and mean. It almost seemed as if Billie shrivelled.

'You wanted to . . . *make sure*,' he mocked, looking me up and down, 'that I was . . . *all right?*'

'Nica, won't you introduce us to your brother?' Billie chirped, and I looked away.

'We're not related.' The words burst out of me, almost as if someone else had said them. 'Me and Rigel are getting adopted.'

Billie and Miki turned to look at me, and I firmly, courageously held his gaze.

'He's not my brother.'

He was staring back at me with a thin smile, darkly amused by my efforts.

'*Oh*, don't put it like that Nica,' he said sarcastically. 'You sound like you're *relieved.*'

I am, my eyes flashed at him, and Rigel looked down at me, scalding me with his dark irises.

Suddenly, someone's phone started vibrating. Billie took hers out of her pocket and stared at the screen.

'We've got to go, my grandma's waiting for us outside. She's already tried calling me . . .'

She looked up at me and I nodded.

'So . . . see you tomorrow?'

She smiled at me, and I tried to do the same, but I could still feel Rigel's eyes on me. It was only then that I realised Miki was staring at him from under the shadow of her hood. Her worried, attentive eyes were scrutinising him.

Then she turned around too, and they both headed off down the corridor.

When we were alone, his voice slid slowly and sinuously, like fingers over silk. 'You're right about one thing.'

I lowered my chin and dared a glance up at him.

He was staring at where the others had disappeared, but he wasn't smiling any more. He turned his gaze on me, a hail of bullets.

I could have sworn that I felt his eyes drilling into my skin.

'I am not your *brother*.'

That day, I decided to erase Rigel, his words and his violent glare, from my mind. I distracted myself by reading late into the night. The lamp on my nightstand emitted a soft and comforting light that drove my worries away.

Anna had been amazed when I asked if I could borrow their beautifully illustrated encyclopaedia. She had been surprised that I was interested, but I was fascinated by it.

As my eyes ran over the illustrations of the little antennae and the crystal-clear wings, I realised how much I liked to get lost in that bright, colourful world.

I knew other people thought it was unusual.

I knew I was different.

I cultivated my strangeness like a secret garden that only I had the keys to, because I knew that most people couldn't understand me.

I traced the rounded shape of a ladybug with my index finger. I remembered how many wishes I had made as a little girl, watching them fly away from my open palms. I would watch them flying free in the sky, and found myself hopelessly wishing that I could do the same, that I could burst into a cloud of sparkles and fly away from The Grave . . .

A noise caught my attention. I turned towards the door. I thought that perhaps I had imagined it, but then I heard it again. It sounded like something scratching wood.

I carefully closed the encyclopaedia and got out from under the covers. I slowly walked towards the door, then turned the handle and stuck my head outside. I saw something moving in the darkness. A shadow was flitting on the ground, quickly and stealthily. It seemed to pause and wait for me, watching for what I would do. It disappeared down the stairs, and I gave in to my curiosity and followed it.

I thought I had glimpsed a fluffy tail, but I hadn't been quick enough. I found myself on the ground floor, silent, totally alone and unable to see it anywhere. I sighed, ready to head back upstairs, but then I noticed that the light in the kitchen was on.

Was Anna still up? I approached to check, but soon wished I hadn't. When I pushed the door open, I encountered a pair of eyes already fixed on mine.

Rigel's.

It was him, sitting there. His elbows were perched on the table and his head was slightly lowered. His hair fell in long, precise brushstrokes over his eyes. He was holding something in his hands. It was ice, I realised, a few moments later.

Finding him there stopped me in my tracks.

I had to get used to this, to the constant possibility of running into him. We weren't at The Grave any more, there wasn't as much space as in the institute. This was a small house and we were living in it together.

And yet, the idea of getting used to him seemed impossible.

'You shouldn't be awake.'

His voice, amplified by the silence, sent a long shiver down my spine.

We were only seventeen, but there was something strange about him, something that was difficult to explain. A merciless beauty and a mind that could captivate anyone. It was absurd. Everyone made the mistake of letting themselves be manipulated by him. He was born for this – for bending people to his will. He scared me, because he wasn't like other kids our age.

For a moment, I tried to imagine what he would be like as an adult, and before my eyes appeared a terrible, corrosively alluring man with eyes darker than the night . . .

'Enjoying the view?' he asked sarcastically, pressing the ice onto the bruise on his forehead. He seemed relaxed now, but with that air of absolute control that always made me want to run away.

Before I could come to my senses and get away from him, I opened my mouth to speak.

'Why?'

Rigel raised an eyebrow. 'Why what?'

'Why did you let them choose you?'

His eyes stayed fixed on mine.

'You think it was my decision?' he asked slowly, watching me closely.

'Yes,' I replied cautiously. 'You made it happen . . . You played the piano.'

His eyes burned with an almost annoying intensity, and I said, 'You, you've always been the one that everyone wanted, but you never let anyone adopt you.'

Few families ever came to The Grave. They would look at the children, studying them like butterflies in a display case. The little ones were always cuter, more colourful, and more worthy of attention. But then they would see him, with his clean face and polite manners, and they would seem to forget all the others. They would watch this black butterfly, enchanted by the rare cut of his eyes, his beautiful velvety wings, how elegantly he flew above the others.

Rigel was unmatched, the prize of the collection. He wasn't dull like the other orphans, but he cloaked himself in their greyness to make himself seem all the more enchanting.

And yet, every time someone expressed the desire to adopt him, he had seemed to do everything within his power to ruin it all. He would cause some disaster, disappear, misbehave. And eventually people would leave, unaware of the magic his hands could conjure on the perfect ivory teeth of the piano.

But that day had been different. He had played the piano. He had sought attention rather than spurned it.

Why?

'You'd better get off to bed, *little moth*,' he said coolly and derisively. 'Tiredness is playing tricks on you.'

That's what he did . . . He *bit* me with his words. He always did.

He would tease me and provoke me, then crush me with a smile, until I was full of doubt and unsure about everything.

I should have despised him. Despised his personality, his appearance, how he ruined everything. I should have, and yet . . . some part of me just couldn't do it.

Because Rigel and I had grown up together. We had spent our lives behind the bars of the same prison. I'd known him since he was a little boy, and I'd seen him so many times that some part of my soul couldn't be as coolly detached as I'd have liked. I was used to him, in a strange way. You sympathise with someone you've shared something with for so long.

I had never been good at hating. Not even when I had good reason for it.

Maybe, despite everything, I still hoped that this new life could be the fairy tale I so yearned for . . .

'What happened with that boy today?' I asked. 'Why were you fighting?'

Rigel slowly tilted his head to one side, maybe wondering why I hadn't left yet. I got the impression that he was weighing me up.

'Differences of opinion. Nothing to do with you.'

He stared at me, urging me to leave, but I didn't.

I didn't want to.

For the first time ever . . . I wanted to take a step forward instead of back. To make him understand that, despite everything, I wanted *us* to move forward. To try. And when he pressed the ice to his forehead, so hard it must have hurt, I heard the memory of a distant voice inside me.

'*Tenderness, Nica. Tenderness, always . . . Remember that,*' the voice said softly.

I felt my legs carry me forward.

Rigel stared at me as I finally stepped into the kitchen. I went up to the sink, took a piece of paper towel and dampened it with cold water. I could feel his eyes drilling into my back.

Then I stepped towards him and looked at him candidly. I held out the paper towel.

'The ice is too hard. Put this on the wound.'

He seemed almost surprised that I hadn't run away. He examined the paper towel, unconvinced, as wary as a wild animal. When he didn't take it, filled with a sudden compassion, I moved to put it on his forehead.

Before I managed to get close, his eyes opened wide and he jerked away. A lock of his jet-black hair fell over his forehead as he glowered at me.

'Don't,' he warned me with a threatening look. 'Don't you dare touch me.'

'It won't hurt . . .' I shook my head and stretched my hand out further, but this time he pushed me away. I brought my hand to my chest and met his eyes with a jolt. He was glaring daggers at me, fury pulsing icily from his eyes.

'Don't just touch me like that – *ever*.'

I clenched my fists and held his punishing gaze. 'Or what?'

A violent bang from the chair.

Rigel was abruptly towering over me, and I jumped, taken unawares. I made myself step backwards, a thousand alarm bells blaring under my skin. I tripped and knocked into the kitchen cupboard. I lifted my chin, my shaking hands gripping the marble countertop.

I felt his eyes pelting me like stones. The closeness of his body made me shudder. I was hardly breathing. I was utterly engulfed by his shadow.

Then . . . Rigel bent over me. He stooped his head closer, and his breath burned like venom in my ear.

'*Or* . . . I won't be able to stop myself.'

My hair fluttered as he shoved me out of the way.

I heard the thud of ice on the table and his footsteps disappearing as he left me there, immobile, petrified against the marble.

What had just happened?

4. Band-Aids

Sensitivity is a refinement of the soul.

The sun wove threads of light through the trees. It was an afternoon in spring and the fragrance of flowers filled the air.

The Grave loomed like a colossus behind me. Lying in the grass, I watched the sky with my arms spread wide as if to embrace it. My cheek was puffy and painful, but I didn't want to keep crying, so I gazed up at the vastness above me, letting myself be cradled by the clouds.

Would I ever be free?

A little noise caught my attention. I looked round and glimpsed something moving in the grass. I got up and decided to carefully approach it, nervously twisting a lock of hair around my fingers.

It was a sparrow. He was scratching the dust with his spindly feet and his eyes shone like black marbles, but one of his wings was stretched out at an unnatural angle and he seemed unable to fly.

When I knelt down, he let out an extremely high-pitched, alarmed chirp, and I sensed that I'd scared him.

'Sorry,' I whispered, as if he could understand me. I didn't want to hurt him — the opposite, I wanted to help him. I felt his desperation as if it was my own. I was also unable to fly, I also wanted to escape, I was also fragile and powerless.

We were the same. Small and defenceless against the world.

I stretched out my hand, wanting to do something to save him. I was just a little girl, but I wanted to give him his freedom back, as if that would somehow bring mine back to me.

'Don't be scared . . .' I reassured him. I was young enough to believe that he really could understand me. What should I do? Could I help him? As he withdrew, terrified, I felt something resurfacing in my memory.

'Tenderness, Nica,' my mother's voice whispered. 'Tenderness, always . . . Remember that.' Her soft eyes were imprinted in my memory.

I gently took the sparrow in my hands, careful not to hurt him. I didn't let him go, not even when he pecked my fingers, not even when his little legs scratched my fingertips.

I held him close to my chest and promised him that one of us, at least, would get our freedom back.

I returned to the institute and immediately asked Adeline, an older girl, for help, praying that the matron wouldn't discover what I'd found — I feared her cruelty more than anything else.

Together, Adeline and I took a popsicle stick from the garbage to use as a splint, and for the next few days I smuggled crumbs from our meals to the hiding place I had found for him.

He pecked at my fingers many times, but I never gave up.

'I'll make you better, you'll see,' I promised him, my fingers red and painful. He ruffled his breast feathers. 'Don't you worry . . .'

I spent hours watching him, a little distance away so as not to scare him.

'And you'll fly,' I whispered. 'One day, you'll fly, and you'll be free. Just a little longer . . . just wait a little longer . . .'

He pecked me when I tried to check on his wing. He tried to stay away from me. But every time, I persisted with tenderness. I made him a bed out of grass and leaves and whispered to him to be patient.

And the day he got better, the day he flew away from my hands, was the first time in my life I felt a little less dirty and dull. I felt a little more alive.

A little freer.

As if I could breathe again.

I found within me the colours I didn't think I had. The colours of hope.

And with my fingers covered in multicoloured Band-Aids, not even my life felt quite so grey.

Slowly, I pulled off the blue Band-Aid. My index finger was still a bit swollen and red.

I had managed to free a wasp from a spiderweb a few days ago. I had been careful not to break the fragile weaving, but I hadn't been quick enough, and she'd stung me.

'Nica and her creatures,' the other children would say when we were younger. 'She's there with them all the time, among the flowers.' They were used to my peculiarities, maybe because in the institute, oddness was more common than normality.

I felt a strange empathy with everything that was small and misunderstood. The instinct to protect creatures of all shapes and sizes had been with me since I was a little girl. It had coloured my strange little world and made me feel free, alive and light.

I remembered Anna's words from the first day, when she had asked me what I was doing in the garden. What must she have thought? Did she think I was strange?

Distractedly, I sensed a presence behind me. I opened my eyes wide and with a start, jumped away.

Rigel's hair swished as he turned to see me jerk away. I stared up at him, still frightened after our last meeting.

He was unphased by my reaction. On the contrary, his mouth sharpened into a crooked sneer.

He stepped past me into the kitchen. I heard Anna greet him, and my shoulders shuddered. Whenever he was near, I got the shivers, though this time there was an obvious cause. I had spent all day replaying what had happened the night before, but the more I thought about those indecipherable words, the more they tormented me.

What did he mean by 'I won't hold myself back'? Won't hold himself back from . . . what?

'There you are, Nica!' Anna greeted me as I cautiously entered the kitchen. I was still lost in thought when an explosion of colour, a fiery violet, flooded my eyes.

An enormous bunch of flowers was on display in the middle of the table, their soft buds springing from a crystal vase. I gazed at them, entranced, overcome by their beauty.

'They're wonderful . . .'

'Do you like them?'

I nodded in response, and Anna smiled. 'I brought them back this afternoon. They're from the store.'

'The store?'

'My store.'

I looked at her genuine smile. I was still struggling to get used to it.

'You . . . sell flowers? Are you a florist?'

What a stupid question! I blushed slightly, but she nodded, simply and sincerely.

I loved flowers almost as much as I loved the creatures that lived in them. I stroked a petal with the tip of my index finger and it was like touching cool velvet.

'My store is a few blocks away from here. It's a bit old and out of the way, but I still get customers. It's nice to see that people still like to buy flowers.'

Anna and I were made for each other. I wondered if she had seen something in me, when she noticed me that day at The Grave, that linked us together even before our eyes first met. I wanted to believe it . . . in that moment, as she looked at me through that jubilant bouquet, I really wanted to believe it.

'Evening!'

Mr Milligan entered the kitchen dressed in a peculiar outfit. He was wearing a dusty blue uniform with heavy-duty gloves sticking out of his pocket. Various contraptions dangled from his leather belt.

'Just in time for dinner!' Anna said. 'How was your day?'

Norman must have been a gardener. Everything about his outfit seemed to suggest it, even the shears dangling from his belt. I thought that they couldn't be a more perfect couple, until Anna put her hands on his shoulders and announced: 'Norman works in pest control.'

I choked on my saliva.

Mr Milligan put on his cap, and I saw the emblem above the visor. A graphic of a massive, stiffened bug was ostentatiously overlaid with a no-entry symbol. I stared at it with icy eyes, my nostrils unnaturally flared.

'Pest control?' I bleated after a moment.

'Oh, yes,' Anna stroked his shoulders. 'You've got no idea just how many critters infest the gardens around here! Our neighbour found a couple of mice in her basement last week. Norman had to go and prevent an infestation . . .'

Those shears weren't quite so appealing any more.

I stared at the image of the beetle with its legs folded like it had swallowed something poisonous. It was only when they both looked at me that I made an effort to somehow move my lips, feeling again the urge to hide my hands.

Beyond the vase of flowers, from the other side of the room, I was sure I could feel Rigel's eyes on me.

After a few minutes, all four of us were sitting around the table. I was uncomfortable hearing Norman talk about his work. I tried to mask my discomfort, but having Rigel sitting next to me didn't calm me down at all. He towered over me even sitting down, and I wasn't used to being that close to him.

'Seeing as we're getting to know each other a little . . . why don't you tell us a bit about yourselves?' Anna smiled. 'Have you known each other for long? The matron didn't tell us anything . . . Did you get on well at Sunnycreek?'

A piece of bread fell off my spoon into the soup.

Next to me, Rigel had also frozen.

Was there a worse question she could have asked?

Anna met my eyes and suddenly, the fear that she could see

the truth made my stomach turn. How would she react if she knew that I struggled to even be near him? Our relationship was sinister and unclear, the furthest thing possible from a family. What if they decided it wouldn't work out? What if they changed their minds?

Panic took me over. Before Rigel could say anything, I blurted out something stupid.

'Of course.' I felt the lie sticking on my tongue and hurried to smile. 'Me and Rigel . . . we've always got on very well. We're pretty much . . . like brother and sister.'

'Seriously?' Anna asked, surprised, and I swallowed, as if I'd just fallen victim to my own lie. I was sure that he would do all he could to contradict me.

I understood my mistake only too late, when I turned and saw his tense jaw.

I had called him my *brother* again. If there had ever been a way to make the situation worse, to make the situation *with him* worse, it had just come out my own mouth.

With an unnatural calm, Rigel looked up and his gaze crossed with Mr Milligan's. Then, with an artful smile, he announced, 'Oh, absolutely. Me and Nica get on fantastically. We're *close*, I'd even dare say.'

'How wonderful!' Anna exclaimed. 'That is really just amazing news. You must be happy to be living here together then! Such good luck, isn't it, Norman? That they get on so well?'

As they exchanged satisfied remarks, I noticed that my napkin had fallen into my lap.

It was only after a moment that I realised that *my* napkin was actually still on the table.

The one in my lap was Rigel's, and his hand had landed on my thigh to retrieve it. He squeezed my knee and his touch had a staggering effect on me. It felt like I could feel it on my bare flesh.

My chair scraped along the floor. I found myself on my feet, with my heart in my throat and Mr and Mrs Milligan staring at me, flabbergasted. I wasn't breathing.

'I . . . I've got to go to the bathroom.'

I slunk away with my head lowered.

I was swallowed by the dark of the hallway, and carried on until I turned the corner, where I leant against the wall. I tried to calm my racing heart, to contain myself, but I had never been good at hiding my emotions. I could still feel the imprint of his fingers as if he had scorched me. I could still feel him on my skin . . .

'You shouldn't run away like that,' a voice behind me said. 'You'll make our so-called parents worry.'

In the end, Rigel was the one spinning this tale, he was the spider of this web. I saw him there, leaning against the wall. His venomous charm was infectious. *He* was infectious.

'Is this a game for you?' I burst out, shaking. 'Is this all just a game?'

'It was all your doing, *little moth*,' he replied, tilting his head. 'Is that how you think you'll win their approval? With lies?'

'Stay away from me.' I pulled away with a shiver, increasing the distance between us. His black eyes were like bottomless pits, they had an indescribable, frightening power over me.

Rigel looked down at me inscrutably, taking in my reaction.

'*That's* what our relationship's really like . . .' he muttered harshly.

'You've got to leave me alone!' I burst out, quivering. I directed all the bitterness I could find within me at him, and an unfathomable shadow passed behind his eyes. 'If Anna and Norman saw . . . if they saw . . . *if* they saw how much you despise me . . . that you just run away from me . . . that it's *not* as perfect as they think . . . they could change their minds, couldn't they?'

I stared at him, wide-eyed. It was as if he could read my thoughts. I felt incredibly exposed. Rigel knew me so well, understood my simple soul, saw in me the sincerity that he'd never had.

All I wanted was a chance, but if they knew the truth, if they saw that it was impossible for us to live together . . . they could take us back there. Or maybe just one of us. The doubt nagged at me, gnawed at my thoughts – *which one of us would they choose?*

I tried to tell myself my doubts were not reality, but it was useless. As if I hadn't noticed the adoring way that Anna and Norman looked at him. Or the wonderful piano in the living room, polished with incredible care.

As if I didn't know that they would always choose him.

I pressed myself against the wall. *Stay away from me*, I wanted to scream at him, but my doubts crushed me and my heart started racing faster.

I'll be good, drummed in my throat, *I'll be good, I'll be good*. Nothing on this earth would have convinced me to return to The Grave. I remembered the echoing screams and still felt trapped there. I needed their smiles, their looks, the fact that for once in my life I had been chosen. I couldn't go back, I couldn't, no, no, no . . .

'One day they'll see who you really are,' I whispered feebly.

'Oh yeah?' he asked, unable to hide his amusement. 'And who am I really?'

I clenched my fists and glared up at him accusingly. Quaking with anger, I looked him straight in the eyes and spat out, 'You're the Tearsmith.'

There was a long silence.

Then Rigel threw his head back and burst out laughing.

His laughter made his shoulders shake alarmingly, and I knew that he'd understood.

He was laughing at me, the Tearsmith was laughing at me, with his bewitching lips and gleaming teeth. The sound of his laughter pursued me as I walked down the landing. Even once I'd shut myself in my room, alone, with walls between us.

And there, my memories started flooding in . . .

'Adeline . . . have you been crying?'

Her blonde hair stood out against the cracks in the plaster. She was curled up on her back, small and hunched – the position she always assumed when she was sad.

'No,' she replied, but her eyes were still red.

'Don't lie, or the Tearsmith will take you away.'

She hugged her knees to her chest. 'That's just a story they tell to scare us . . .'

'You don't believe in it?' I whispered. Everyone at The Grave believed in it. Adeline threw me a worried look and I understood that she was no exception. She was only two years older, and she was like a sort of older sister to me, but some things never stop scaring you.

'I told a boy at school about him today,' she confessed. 'He's not here at The Grave with us. He told a lie so I said to him, "You can't lie to the Tearsmith."

But he didn't understand. He'd never heard of the Tearsmith. But he knows something similar . . . he calls him the Bogeyman.'

I watched her, not understanding. We had both been at The Grave since we were tiny, and I was sure that not even she knew what this meant.

'And this Bogeyman – he makes you cry? He makes you upset?' I asked.

'No . . . but he scares you, he said. He also takes children away. He's terrifying.'

I thought about what scared me. And a dark basement came to mind.

I thought about what terrified me. And She came to mind.

And so, I understood. She was the Bogeyman for me, and Adeline, and many of us. But if a child outside of the institute spoke of it too, it meant that there were others like Her roaming about the world.

'There are lots of bogeymen,' I said. 'But there's only one Tearsmith.'

I had always believed in fairy tales.

I had always wanted to live in one.

And now . . . I was inside one.

I walked through the pages, following the paper paths.

But the ink had spilt.

And I'd ended up in the wrong fairy tale.

5. Black Swan

> *Even the heart has a shadow*
> *That follows it wherever it goes.*

I was sweating. My temples were throbbing. The room was small, stuffy, suffocating . . . And it was dark. It was always dark.

I couldn't move my arms. I was scratching at the air, but no one could hear me. My skin was burning, I tried to stretch my hand out, but I couldn't do it. The door closed and the darkness swallowed me up . . .

I woke with a jolt.

I was still surrounded by the darkness of my nightmares and it took me an interminable amount of time to fumble for the light switch. I was still gripping the bedcovers.

Light flooded the room, revealing the corners of my new home. My heart was still pounding in my throat.

My bad dreams had come back. Well, in truth they'd never gone away. A new bed wasn't enough to drive them away.

I weakly touched my wrists. The Band-Aids were still on my fingers, their colours comforting me, reminding me I was free.

I could see them, when it wasn't dark. *It wasn't dark, I was safe* . . .

I took deep breaths, trying to calm myself down. But that sensation was still crawling over my skin. It was whispering at me to close my eyes, it was crouched in the dark, lying in wait for me.

Would I ever truly be free?

I pushed back the covers and got out of bed. I rubbed my face with my hand and headed towards the bathroom.

The light made the white, clean tiles shine. The mirror was bright and the towels were as soft as clouds, helping me to remember that I was far away from those nightmares. It was all different. This was another life . . .

I turned on the faucet and doused my wrists with cold water, slowly recovering my inner calm. I stayed there for a very long time, trying to get my thoughts in order, until the light came back to illuminate even the darkest corners of my mind.

It would all be fine. I was no longer living in my memories. I didn't have to be scared any more . . . I was far away, safe. I was free. And I had a chance at happiness . . .

When I left the bathroom, I realised that morning had already broken.

We had biology first thing that morning, so I made sure I wasn't late. The biology teacher, Mr Kryll, wasn't well known for his patience.

The sidewalk in front of the school was teeming with students. I was very surprised when I heard a voice in the crowd shout, 'Nica!'

Billie was in front of the gates, her curls swinging as she waved excitedly. She was smiling radiantly and I found myself staring at her, lost for words, unused to so much attention.

'Hi,' I greeted her shyly, trying not to show how happy I was that she had spotted me in a crowd of so many people.

'So, how's your first week at school going? Feeling suicidal yet? Kryll drives you crazy, right?'

I scratched my cheek. In truth, I'd been fascinated by his classification of invertebrates, but the other students spoke about him as if he'd instigated some sort of reign of terror in his classroom.

'Actually,' I started tentatively, 'I didn't think he was too bad . . .'

She burst out laughing as if I'd just told a joke.

'Sure!' She gave me a friendly nudge, making me jump.

As we walked along together, I noticed that she had a tiny, crocheted camera dangling from the zipper of her backpack.

A moment later her face lit up. She ran forward euphorically, stopping when she reached Miki, who she hugged from behind.

'Hello!' she exclaimed joyfully, her arms around Miki's backpack. Miki turned around with a zombie-like expression. She had dark circles under her eyes and her face looked drained from exhaustion.

'You're here early!' Billie trilled. 'How are you doing? What lessons do you have today? Do you want to go home together later?'

'It's eight in the morning,' Miki protested. 'Stop pummelling my brain.'

She noticed that I was there too. I lifted a hand to wave hello at her, but she didn't respond. I saw that she also had a tiny, crocheted keyring dangling from her backpack. This one was a panda's head, with two huge black patches around its eyes.

At that moment, several girls passed by us, squealing excitedly, and joined a dense throng of students outside a classroom. One of them strained her neck to look inside, the others covered their mouths with their hands to hide their conspiratorial smiles. They looked like a crowd of praying mantises.

Miki stared at the little crowd, looking bored. 'What can they be mewling at?'

'Let's go see!'

Together we headed towards them – or rather, Miki headed towards them, and Billie followed, but not before grabbing me happily by the strap of my backpack. We reached the little crowd of girls and I also tried to take a look inside, curious now.

I understood only too late that it was the music room.

I was paralysed.

Rigel was there, his profile like a perfect portrait. A dim light flooded the room, illuminating the black hair framing his striking face. His slender fingers were stroking the piano keys, producing ghostly melodies that dissolved into the surrounding silence.

He looked gorgeous.

I tried as hard as I could to push that thought away, but to no avail. He was like a black swan, an unbearable angel who could unleash mysterious, unearthly sounds.

'Do boys like him really exist?' one of the girls whispered.

Rigel wasn't even playing a piece of music. His hands were moving through simple chord progressions, but I knew what they were capable of conjuring when they wanted.

'He's so hot . . .'

'What's his name?'

'I didn't catch it, it's an unusual name . . .'

'I heard that he got away with just a detention for that fight!' they murmured with bewilderment and excitement. 'He didn't get suspended!'

'I'd take detention every day for a guy like him . . .'

They giggled a little too loudly, and I felt annoyance in the pit of my stomach. They were gazing at him as if he was a god, letting themselves be charmed as if he was a fairy-tale prince, not realising that he was the wolf. At the end of the day, hadn't the devil once been the most beautiful of the angels?

Why did no one seem able to see it?

'Shh, he'll hear you!'

Rigel looked up.

And they fell silent.

It was maddening. Everything about him was perfect, his pure, delicate features, and *that* gaze. It burned your soul, literally. Those black, penetrating, shrewd eyes stood out against his face in a way that took your breath away.

Realising that he was no longer alone, he got up and stepped towards us.

I shrivelled, looked at the floor, and murmured, 'It's late, we should get to class.'

But Billie didn't hear me. She was still holding my backpack strap, and the girls behind me didn't even move to let me through. They were all frozen, as if bewitched, subjugated by the mysterious charm that emanated from his violent beauty.

Rigel got to the door and made to close it, but one of the girls boldly flung an arm out and held it open.

'It would be a real shame if you stopped,' she said, smiling. 'Do you always play so well?'

Rigel glanced scornfully at the hand holding the door open.

'No,' he replied with a cool sarcasm. 'Sometimes I play seriously . . .'

He took a step forward, looking straight at her, and this time, the girl was forced to take a step backwards. He gave her a lingering look before moving past her. And then he left.

I looked away as suggestive glances flew around the group, refusing to participate in their collective excitement.

After that evening in the hallway, I had started doing what I had always done at The Grave – keeping as far away from him as possible. His laughter was permanently echoing in my mind. I couldn't free myself from it.

'Your brother seems like he's come from another planet . . .'

'He's not my brother,' I snapped brusquely, as if the words had burnt my lips.

They both stared at me, and my cheeks stung. It wasn't like me to respond like that, but how could they really think that we were related? We were complete opposites of each other.

'Sorry,' Billie replied hesitantly. 'You're right, I . . . I forgot.'

'It's fine,' I reassured her in a softer voice, hoping to put things right. Billie's expression turned calm again and she glanced at the clock on the wall.

'Heavens, we've got to get going or Kryll will have our skins!' she burst out, her eyes wide. 'Miki, see you later, enjoy class! Come on, Nica.'

'Bye, Miki,' I murmured before following Billie. She didn't reply, but I felt her gaze watching us leave together.

Did she see me as an intruder?

'How did you become friends, you and Miki?' I asked as we reached the classroom.

'It's a funny story. Because of our names,' Billie replied, entertained. 'Mine and Miki's names are a little . . . well, out of the ordinary. The first day of elementary school I told her that my name was quite strange and she replied that it couldn't be any more unusual than hers. We only use our nicknames now, but ever since that day we've been inseparable.'

I sensed something unusual about Miki. I couldn't really say that I knew her, but I couldn't doubt her fondness for Billie. She acted cool, but there was a shining intimacy in her eyes when they spoke to each other. Their friendship was like a pair of comfortable shoes that you've worn with confidence and familiarity your whole life.

At the end of the school day, I felt tired but happy.

'I'm coming, Grandma!' Billie said into her phone. We headed outside as our classmates piled into the yard, chatting excitedly.

'I've got to go. Grandma's double parked the car and if she gets another fine she'll be apoplectic. Oh, wait . . . do you want to swap numbers?'

I slowed to a stop, and she did the same beside me.

She giggled, waving her hands in the air. 'I know, I know. Miki says I'm a pain. Just because one time I sent her a seven-minute-long voice message she calls me a chatterbox . . . but you don't believe her, do you?'

'I . . . I don't have a phone,' I confessed eventually. I felt a burning sensation in my chest that took my voice away. I would have liked to tell her that I didn't care that she talked a lot. That she was great as she was, because when she spoke to me so familiarly, I felt less strange and different. I managed to feel *normal*. And it was wonderful.

'You don't have a phone?' she asked, gobsmacked.

'No . . .' I murmured, but the sudden honk of a car horn made me jump.

An old woman's head appeared through the window of a massive Wrangler, wearing a huge pair of black sunglasses. She screeched something at the man in the car behind, whose mouth fell open, offended.

'Oh my God, they're having a go at Grandma . . .' Billie ran a hand through her curly hair. 'Sorry, Nica, I've got to go! See you tomorrow, okay? Bye!'

She scuttled away like an insect and disappeared into the crowd.

'Bye . . .' I whispered, waving my hand. I felt incredibly light. I took a deep breath and, stifling a smile, headed along the road towards home.

It had been a long day, but all I could feel was a tingly sort of happiness.

Mr and Mrs Milligan had apologised that they weren't able to pick us up from school every day – Norman was out at work until the evening, and the store needed Anna's constant attention.

But I liked walking. And also, seeing as Rigel had detention, I had the whole house to myself in the afternoons.

I took care not to tread on a line of ants crossing the sidewalk. I stepped over the apple core they were feasting on and turned the corner into our neighbourhood.

The white picket fence soon filled my vision. 'Milligan' was written on the mailbox. I approached, calm and content, but with a pounding heart. Maybe I would never get used to having somewhere to return home to . . .

I entered the house, and was greeted by a welcoming stillness. I tried to memorise everything: the cosiness, the narrow hallway, the empty frame on the sideboard that maybe used to have a photo inside it.

In the kitchen, I swiped a teaspoon of mulberry jam and ate it near the sink.

I was crazy for jam. At The Grave they only let us have it when there were visitors. Guests liked to see that we were treated well, and we would parade around the institute in our best clothes pretending that jam was a normal occurrence.

I gathered some things to make myself a sandwich, humming a little tune to myself. I felt peaceful. Happy. Maybe I'd already made a friend. Two good people wanted to give me a family. Everything seemed light and sweet, even my own thoughts.

When the sandwich was ready, I noticed that I had a little guest.

A gecko was climbing up the wall, behind the row of cups. He must have come in through the open window, enticed by the smell.

'Hi,' I whispered to him. There was no one watching who could judge me, so I didn't feel ashamed. I knew that if anyone saw me they would probably think I was mad. But this was normal behaviour for me. Secret, but instinctive.

Some people talked to themselves, but I talked with animals. I had done so since I was a little girl, and sometimes I was certain that they could understand me better than other people could. Was talking to an animal really that much stranger than talking to yourself?

'Sorry, I haven't got anything to offer you,' I informed him, drumming my fingertips on my lips. His flat fingers gave him a foolish, harmless look, and I cooed, 'You're such a little thing . . .'

'Oh,' a voice sounded behind me. 'Nica!'

Norman appeared in the kitchen doorway.

'Hi, Norman,' I greeted him, surprised that he'd come home for lunch. Sometimes I happened to cross paths with him in the daytime, but only very rarely.

'I just came by for a quick bite to eat . . . Who were you talking to?' he asked, rummaging about for a bowl, and I smiled.

'Oh, just with . . .' but I faltered. The emblem of the dead beetle loomed before my eyes.

I quickly turned towards the little gecko and blanched when I saw him tilting his head and looking back at me. Before Norman looked up, I lunged for the creature and hid him behind my back.

'. . . no one.'

Norman looked at me, confused, and I shrugged my shoulders with a nervous giggle. I felt the gecko wriggling in my hands like a little eel, and my wrists stiffened when I felt him nibbling one of my fingers.

'Okay . . .' he stammered, as my eyes darted from one side to another, searching for escape routes.

'I've got a big job this afternoon. A client called this morning, I've got to pass by the warehouse to pick up . . . heavy artillery. If you catch my drift . . . Mrs Finch is going crazy, she swears she's got a hornets' nest in her –'

'Oh, heavens!' I burst out, pointing behind him. 'What's that?'

Norman turned around, and I took my chance. I hurled the gecko out the window. He whirled in the air like a spinning top and then landed somewhere on the lawn.

'It's a lamp . . .'

Norman turned back around, and I beamed at him. He looked at me, concerned, and I hoped that he hadn't caught on to my crazy trick. By the looks of his expression, the opposite was true. He asked if I was all right, and I reassured him, trying to seem at ease, until once again he left me alone. I heard the front door close and let out a breath, a little disheartened.

Would I ever manage to make a good impression? To be liked, despite my slightly strange and unusual ways?

I looked at the Band-Aids on my hands and sighed. My nightmares came to mind, but I pushed them away into a far corner before they could ruin everything.

I washed my hands and ate calmly, relishing every second of that normal moment, in that normal house. As I ate, I silently watched the little bowl on the floor in the corner of the kitchen.

I had heard scratching outside my door the past few nights, but when I told Anna she had just waved her hand.

'Oh, don't worry about it,' she had said. 'It'll just be Klaus. He'll decide to show up sooner or later . . . He's a solitary sort.'

I wondered when he would let me get to know him.

After washing up the plates and cutlery, I checked that everything was as tidy as Anna had left it, went upstairs, and spent the rest of the afternoon studying in my room.

I got lost in algebraic equations and the dates of the Wars of Succession, and it was evening by the time I finished my homework. I stretched, and I realised that the finger the gecko had nibbled had gone red and was throbbing. Maybe I should put a Band-Aid on it . . . *A green one, like him*, I thought, as I left my room.

Lost in thought, I headed to the bathroom and reached for the door handle. Before I could even touch it, however, it turned.

I looked up just as the door opened. I found myself pinned under two magnetic, black eyes. I shuddered in surprise and jumped back.

Rigel had calmly appeared in the doorway. Plumes of steam rose from his shoulders – he must have just taken a shower.

Once again, his presence gave me a visceral feeling of discomfort.

I had never managed to be indifferent towards him. His black eyes were two deep pits from which it was impossible to hide. They were the Tearsmith's eyes. It didn't matter that they weren't pale like in the legend. Rigel's eyes were dangerous, even if they were the opposite colour to what the tale told.

He leant his shoulder against the edge of the door, his hair brushing against its frame. Rather than moving out of the way, he crossed his arms and stood there, staring at me.

'I need to get past,' I informed him stiffly.

The steam was still billowing around him, making him seem like a demon at the gates of hell. I shuddered as I imagined stepping into that mist, letting myself be engulfed by his scent . . .

'Come on in,' he invited, showing no sign of moving.

I hardened my gaze and stared at him reproachfully. I knew what he was doing.

'Why are you doing this?'

I didn't want to play this game, I wanted him to stop it, to leave me in peace.

'Doing what?'

'You know full well what,' I said, trying to sound tough. 'It's what you've always done.'

It was the first time that I had dared to speak to him so directly. Ours had always been a relationship of silences, of things left unsaid, of sarcasm and naïvety, snaps and flinches. I'd never wasted time trying to understand his behaviour, I'd always steered clear of him. Strictly speaking, you couldn't really call what we had a relationship.

The corner of his mouth curled up into a mocking sneer.

'I can't resist.'

I wrung my hands.

'You won't do it,' I burst out, as resolutely as I could. My voice sounded loud and clear, and I saw his expression darken.

'Do what?'

'You know what!' I snapped.

I was tense, almost on my tiptoes, and I was burning with a powerful emotion. Was it stubbornness or desperation?

'I won't let you do it, Rigel. I won't let you ruin this . . . You hear me?'

I was tiny, and my hands were covered in Band-Aids, but I stared him straight in the eyes because I felt the urgent need to defend my dream. I believed in tenderness and goodness, in gentle voices and quiet movements, but Rigel brought out aspects of my personality that I struggled to recognise. It was just like in the legend . . .

At that moment I noticed that his expression had changed. He was no longer smiling, but his dark eyes were fixed on my lips.

'Say that again,' he murmured quietly.

I set my jaw, determined.

'I won't let you do it.'

Rigel was staring at me intensely. His eyes ran all over my body, and the shudder that ran through me dented my confidence. My stomach turned. Under his slow examination, I felt as if he was *touching* me. A moment later, he unfolded his arms and started to move.

'Again,' he whispered, taking a step towards me.

'I won't let you ruin this,' I said, starting to get worried.

Another step. 'Again.'

'You won't ruin this.'

But the more I said it, the closer he came.

'Again,' he insisted, and I stiffened, confused and concerned.

'You won't ruin this . . . You won't . . .'

I bit my lip and took a step backwards.

He was standing right in front of me now.

I was forced to lift my chin up and, heart in my throat, met his piercing gaze. His eyes were fixed on me. The sunset was a crumb of light that his dark eyes devoured.

Rigel took another step forward, as if to re-emphasise his point, and I tried to take another backwards, but my back was to the wall. My eyes urgently flashed up to meet his, and I saw him bend down towards me. I stiffened as he drew close to my ear, and his deep voice echoed in my head.

'You don't even realise how fragile and innocent you sound.'

I tried not to shudder, but my soul felt naked in front of Rigel. He could make me tremble without even touching me.

'You're shaking. You can't even bear to be close to me, can you?'

I suppressed the urge to put my hand out to push him away. There was something . . . something telling me that I shouldn't touch him. That if I put my hands on his chest to push him away, I would do irreparable damage to the distance between us . . .

There was an invisible wall between Rigel and I. And his eyes had always warned me not to bridge it, not to make that mistake.

'Your heart's beating like mad,' he murmured at my throat, where my pulse was racing. 'You're not scared of me, are you, *little moth*?'

'Rigel . . . please, stop this.'

'Oh, no, Nica,' he reproached in a soft growl, his tongue clicking. '*You* have to stop this. All this defenceless cooing like a little nightingale . . . will only make matters worse.'

I don't know where I found the strength to push him away. I only know that one minute, Rigel was there, his toxic breath on my skin, and the next he was a few steps away from me with his brow furrowed.

But it wasn't me . . . There was something darting around his feet, making him retreat even further. Two yellow eyes were shooting arrows through the dark, staring at us with slit pupils.

The cat hissed at him with flattened ears, then bolted down the stairs, almost tripping Anna up.

'Klaus!' she exclaimed. 'You almost tripped me up! Finally decided to show up, have you, you crusty old cat?'

She was surprised to find us on the landing.

'Oh, Rigel, he always hides in your room. He's used to curling up under the bed in there . . .'

I didn't hear any more, because I seized the opportunity to rush away.

I hurriedly shut myself in the bathroom, hoping that that would be enough to banish his noxious presence from inside of me, from the world, from everything. I leant my forehead on the hard doorframe and closed my eyes, but he was still there, with his silky voice and his destructiveness.

I tried to get him off my skin, but the steam enveloped me, infused me with his smell.

It infested me, reaching down as far as my stomach.

Taking deeper breaths was useless, it felt like I was drowning.

Not all poisons have an antidote. Some of them get into your soul, stupefy you with their scent and have eyes more beautiful than any you've ever seen before.

And there's no cure for them.

None at all.

6. Kindness

Those with springtime in their souls
Will always see a world in bloom.

Rigel had left me in complete disarray.

For the next two days, I was unable to shake the feeling of him, the feeling of him infused in my blood.

Sometimes I was sure I knew everything about him. Other times, there were so many shadows circling around him I was convinced the opposite was true.

Rigel was like an elegant beast dressed up in his best clothes. But lurking inside him was a wild and unpredictable soul, frightening, and dangerous to approach.

On the other hand, he had always done everything within his power to make sure I wouldn't understand him. Every time I got too close, he *snapped* at me, and warned me to stay away, like he had done that evening in the kitchen. And then illogical, contradictory situations would arise, and I would be unable to make sense of his behaviour.

He confused me. He disturbed me. He was sinister, and I would have done better to heed his warning and to steer well clear of him.

Aside from my relationship with him, though, I couldn't say that things were going badly. I adored my new family.

Norman was bumbling and kind, and every day Anna seemed more and more like something from my childhood daydreams. She was maternal, attentive and caring, and she was always worrying whether I'd eaten enough and whether I was doing all right. I knew that I was very thin, that I didn't have the rosy, healthy complexion that other girls my age did, but I wasn't used to receiving that sort of attention.

She was a real mom, and even though I wasn't brave enough to tell her, she was becoming as dear to me as my own mom.

The little girl who used to dream of embracing the sky and finding someone who could set her free was now beholding that reality, enchanted.

How could I avoid losing it all?

I left my room after another afternoon of homework. I studied a lot, and it was very important to me to be good at school. Above all, it was important to me that Anna and Norman were happy with me.

To my surprise, I bumped into something on the landing.

It was Klaus. He had decided to show up, once and for all. I was delighted to find him outside my room, because I loved animals, and interacting with them made me very happy.

'Hi,' I whispered, smiling at him. I thought he was a really beautiful cat. His lovely dusty grey fur was as soft and fluffy as cotton candy, and he had wonderful round, yellow eyes. Anna had told me that he was a distinguished ten years old.

'Aren't you lovely . . .' I gushed, wondering if he would let me cuddle him. He stared at me suspiciously. Then his tail stood up tall and off he went down the stairs.

I followed him like a little girl, watching his every move, enthralled, but he threw me a scowl, giving me the impression that he wasn't happy with my actions. He jumped out the window and landed on the ground, leaving me alone on the landing. He really must be a solitary sort . . .

I was about to move on when a noise caught my attention. I didn't realise straight away, but it was a rasping noise coming from the room next door. But it wasn't just any room . . .

It was Rigel's bedroom.

I realised that the sound was him breathing. I knew I shouldn't go in, but hearing him breathing like that made me momentarily forget this. The door was ajar, and I looked inside.

I glimpsed his imposing figure. He was standing in the middle of the room with his back turned. Through the crack in the door, I managed to see the swollen veins on his stiff arms and his fists clenched at his side.

They were what caught my attention. His skin was tight over his knuckles and his clenched fingers were bone-white. I noticed the tension running through his arm muscles up to his shoulders, and didn't understand what was going on.

He looked . . . *Furious*?

The floorboards creaked under my feet, betraying me before I could get a better look. His eyes darted towards me and I jumped. Instinctively, I stepped backwards, but a moment later the door slammed shut, cutting short my speculation.

My mind was whirring as I stared at the door. Had he seen me there? Or just that *someone* was there? I felt a stab of humiliation in my chest to even be wondering. I bit my lip and backed away. Rushing downstairs, I told myself to stop thinking about it. Rigel had nothing to do with me. Nothing at all . . .

'Nica,' Anna called to me. 'Can you help me?'

She was carrying a basket of clean laundry. I pushed my worries to one side and immediately went to her, as jittery as I was every time that she spoke to me.

'Of course.'

'Thank you. I've still got some things to do, if you could help me put these away. You know where they go?'

I took the basket of fragrant laundry from her, reassuring her that I'd be able to find the right drawer for her lace doilies.

The house wasn't too big, and I walked from one end to the other, stopping every now and then to fill a drawer or cabinet. I had learnt where some things went, and now I had the chance to enhance my knowledge of the house. As I put my clothes back in my room, I felt ashamed that Anna would have seen how old and threadbare they were.

When I left my room, I realised that the only things left in the basket were a couple of short-sleeved shirts.

They were men's shirts. I touched them thoughtfully. I doubted that Norman would wear such shabby clothes. In fact, I knew that he wouldn't.

They were Rigel's.

I turned towards his bedroom door. After what had happened only a few minutes before, the idea of approaching the door made me freeze. I didn't know for sure that he had seen me, but I absolutely knew that I didn't have permission to go in. Rigel had been extremely clear about that.

But I was doing Anna a favour. With everything that she had done for me, how could I refuse such a tiny gesture? I had promised her that she could trust me with a simple chore like this, and I didn't want to have to eat my words.

I hesitated, indecisive, but eventually I found myself in front of the door.

I swallowed, then lifted a hand, mustered my courage and just about managed to knock. I received no reply.

Had I knocked too quietly? The thought that maybe he wasn't in his room any more lit a little flame of courage in me. Rigel had told me not to go in, and I had done my best to listen to him, but maybe I could take advantage of his absence to leave his clothes in there without having to run into him.

I took the door handle in my hand and turned it.

I jumped when the metal slid out from under my fingers.

The door opened and all my hopes shattered.

I was caught under the spell of his dark eyes.

He was right in front of me. My legs started to tremble.

How could a seventeen-year-old boy burn you like that?

'Would you care to *inform* me what you think you're doing?' he drawled chillingly. There was nothing promising about his expression. My eyes dropped to the laundry basket, and his quickly did the same.

'I . . .' I stammered. 'These are yours, I just wanted to leave them for you . . .'

'*What*,' Rigel snapped, 'part of the phrase "don't come into my room" wasn't quite *clear* to you?'

I swallowed and felt myself withering under the indisputable rage radiating from his eyes.

'Anna asked me to,' I explained. I felt the need to assure both of us that nothing would have persuaded me to go in there but a sense of duty. I realised only too late that it sounded like a lie. 'She asked me a favour. I'm only doing her a favour . . .'

'Do yourself a favour.'

Rigel abruptly grabbed the basket out of my hands. His biting, threatening glare rooted me to the spot.

'Clear off, Nica.'

He always called me Nica, not little moth, when he was growling at me like that, as if using my name made his words seem more serious.

He was already closing the door and I wrung my hands, feeling the tackiness of the Band-Aids on my fingers.

'I was just being kind,' I said reproachfully, pointlessly trying to match his scornful attitude. 'Maybe you find that hard to understand?'

The door stopped moving.

I saw a shadow pass through his dark eyes as he murmured through incredibly still lips, 'Just being . . . *kind*?'

I stiffened. Rigel started to open the door further, and one by one my muscles tensed.

He took a step forward, and I swallowed dryly as he put his hand against the doorframe, just above my head. He was looming over me, tall and intimidating with his icy stare.

'I don't want . . . your *kindness*.' The words dripped slowly and threateningly from his lips. 'I *want* you out from under my feet.'

His deep voice moved me intimately. It was infused into my blood. I jumped away and his eyes followed me with startling precision.

I stared at him, frightened by my reaction. For once in my life, I wished I could feel anger, spite or resentment about how he was behaving, but my chest stung with something much deeper. It was almost painful.

The next moment, he closed the door and silence swallowed me up once again.

I bit down hard on my lip and found myself clenching my fists, trying to chase those feelings away. Why did I feel so wounded? He had always been like this. That was just one of many arguments we had had. I had been a fool to expect anything different.

Rigel had been *snapping* at me his entire life. He had never wanted me to touch him, to get near to him or to try and understand him. He wanted nothing from me, but at the same time, he knew how to torment me like nobody else. He consumed me. Sometimes it seemed like he wanted to ruin me, other times like he hated my very presence.

He was a wild, mysterious and shadowy beast. The wolf.

He was as alluring as the night, and his eyes were as cold and distant as the star he was named after. And I . . . I had to stop hoping that things would change.

I went back to Anna and told her I had finished, trying to hide from her how I was feeling. In response, she thanked me with a brilliant smile. She asked if I wanted a cup of tea and I accepted, my heart sighing. I ended up chatting with her on the couch, our hands wrapped around our steaming mugs.

I asked her about her store, and she told me about her assistant, Carl, a nice young man who gave her a hand. I listened to her, enraptured, trying to take in every single detail about her, and once again I was enchanted by the light emanating from her smile. Her voice was like an embrace, a glove that made me feel warm and protected. Her light hair and soft features were shining with a luminescence that I felt only I could see.

In my eyes, Anna sparkled like a fairy tale, and she didn't even know it. Sometimes, as I was gazing at her, I thought of my own mom, her sweet eyes and how she whispered to me when I was little, *'Tenderness, Nica. Tenderness, always . . . Remember that.'*

I liked Anna so much. And not only because I felt a desperate need for affection, not only because I had always dreamt of smiles and hugs . . . but also because she was more sensitive and thoughtful than anyone I had ever met before.

After we'd finished chatting, I went up to my room to fetch the encyclopaedia she had lent me. Downstairs there was a room with a bookshelf covering an entire wall. I approached it with the large book clutched to my chest, and took a moment to appreciate the light seeping in through the white curtains. The last rays of sun created a warm and welcoming atmosphere. The grand piano gleamed in the centre of the room like a throne without a king.

I approached the bookshelf and put the encyclopaedia back in its place. I had to stand on tiptoes because the shelf was a bit too high, and the book almost fell out of my hands, but I managed it in the end.

I turned round, and my heart jolted.

Rigel was leaning in the doorway, staring at me. His imposing figure cast shadows over the warm light that had been enveloping me, and instantly sent my skin crawling. His sudden, unexpected appearance made my heart race and my lips part. His gaze was alert and intense, like a cat studying its prey.

I wished I didn't always have that reaction to his presence. The intensity of the discomfort I felt was matched only by the perverse attractiveness of his angular face. His straight nose, his perfectly proportioned lips, his sharp jawline and delicate, harmonious features . . . and then his eyes. His slanting eyes shone under his arched eyebrows with a destabilising and provocative confidence.

'It's going to be like this forever, isn't it?'

I was the one who spoke. I could no longer hide the subtle note of melancholy in my voice.

'Our relationship . . . won't change, not even now we're here.'

Then I noticed that he was holding a book by Chesterton in his crossed arms. I'd seen him reading it in the last few days, so I guessed he had finished it and come to put it back.

'You say that as if you're sad about it,' he replied silkily.

I withdrew slightly, even though he was standing far away, because that tone of his had a strange effect on me.

Rigel slowly and cautiously looked down at me. 'Do you want it to be different?'

'I want you to be less hostile,' I hurried to say, and wondered why it sounded almost like a prayer. 'I want you not to always look at me like . . . like that.'

'Like *that* . . .' Rigel repeated. He always did that. Turned my statements into questions, modulating them in that slow and sinister tone, twisting my words around on his tongue.

'Like that,' I said stubbornly. 'You look at me as if I was your enemy. You know so little of kindness that when you see it, you don't even notice it.'

What I didn't want to admit to myself was that it hurt me.

It hurt me when he spoke to me like that.

It hurt me when he snarled at me.

It hurt me when he didn't give me the chance to improve things between us.

After all that time I should have been used to it, I should have recognised that I was scared of him and left it at that, and yet . . . I just wanted to fix everything. That . . . that was just how I was.

'I notice kindness. But I think it's hypocritical.'

Rigel was now watching me with serious, contemplative eyes.

'It's performative . . . useless and sanctimonious.'

'You're wrong,' I objected. 'Kindness is sincerity. And not asking for anything in return.'

'Oh yeah?' His eyes sparkled through his half-closed eyelids. 'I have to disagree. It's forced . . . especially when it's directed at just *anyone*.'

I thought I could sense something lying beneath his words, but I concentrated on what he was saying, because I couldn't understand. What did he mean?

'I don't get what you're trying to say,' I breathed, admitting my confusion. I tried to make sense of his reasoning, but Rigel stared fixedly at me, with those eyes that gave me goosebumps and pierced my soul.

I started feeling my heart thumping in every part of my body, and felt panic rising within me. I realised that it was all because of how he was looking at me.

'For you, I'm the Tearsmith,' he exclaimed. 'We both know what you meant. "Don't ruin this," that's what you said to me . . . I'm the wolf of the story, aren't I? So, tell me, Nica, what would you call kindness towards someone you just want to disappear, if not . . . *hypocritical*?'

I was taken aback by his bitterness. Kindness, for me, was a virtue, it was a form of tenderness, but he had capsized everything with a reasoning that was so twisted that it seemed to have its own logic. Rigel was sarcastic, scornful and shrewd, but I would never have thought that this was because of such an acidic way of looking at the world.

'What do you want me to be?' His voice roused me.

I was alarmed when I saw him moving away from the door towards me.

'Our *relationship* . . . how should it be?'

I retreated until I felt the bookshelves jabbing me in the back. His voice was silky, it was always halfway between a hiss and a snarl, and sometimes I found it difficult to work out whether he was trying to contain his anger or make himself as creepy as possible.

'Don't come any closer,' I ordered him, poorly disguising my agitation. 'You tell me to stay away from you, and then . . . then . . .' My words withered in my mouth. Rigel was now towering over me, with his overwhelming good looks and his eyes lowered to mine. In the sunset, his black hair looked like it was oozing venom.

'Go on. *Tell me,*' he whispered fiercely, slightly lowering his face. I hardly came up to his chest, and the air between us was throbbing like a living being. 'Look at you . . . even my voice scares you.'

'I don't know what you want, Rigel. I just don't know . . . One minute you're snarling at me and the next . . .'

You're breathing all over me, I wanted to say, but my heart prevented me from speaking. I felt it in my throat, like an alarm warning me how close he was.

'You know why fairy tales end with "ever after", Nica?' he whispered mercilessly. 'To remind us that some things are destined for eternity. Some things are immutable. Some things won't change. It's in their nature to stay as they are, otherwise the whole story falls down. You can't disrupt the natural order of things without disrupting the ending. And you, with all your daydreams . . . with all your constant *hoping* . . . you're so desperate for your happy ending, but are you brave enough to imagine a fairy tale *without* a wolf?'

His voice was a ferocious, deep whisper that terrified me.

I shivered before him, and Rigel looked deep into my eyes, watching me through his long eyelashes for what seemed like an eternity. His words created a disordered feeling in me, like dust swirling in an unfathomable galaxy.

Then, all of a sudden, he lifted his hand. He brought it close to my face and I closed my eyes instinctively, as if I was scared that he would hurt me. I sensed him stretching his arm forward and . . .

Nothing happened. I opened my eyes wide, my heart still flailing, but Rigel was already far away, disappearing through the door. In a moment of intuition, I turned around to see that he had simply placed the book back on the shelf behind me.

I tried to slow down my heart rate, but I was too confused and upset to think straight.

How should I have interpreted his actions?

And his words? What did they mean?

I noticed that a bookmark was still inside the book he had borrowed. I was sure that he had finished it, so after a moment I lifted my hand to reach for it and opened the cover.

A passage on one of the pages caught my eye.

Someone had underlined it in pencil.

As I read, my heart sank, dissolving into mist, eventually evaporating into nothingness.

> *'Are you a devil?'*
>
>   *'I am a man,' answered Father Brown gravely. 'And therefore have all devils in my heart.'*

7. Little Steps

> *Have you ever seen a shooting star?*
> *Have you ever seen them shining in the night?*
> *She was like that.*
> *Rare. Tiny and powerful.*
> *With a smile that shone so brightly*
> *Even as she crumbled.*

There was a strong wind that morning.

It bent the blades of grass and wiped the sky clean of clouds. The air was as clear and fresh as citrus detergent. February had always been mild and warm around here.

Rigel's shadow slid along the asphalt in front of me like a panther formed from molten lead. I watched how he stepped forward precisely, one foot in front of the other. Even the way he walked was domineering.

I had kept my distance from him ever since we left the house, dawdling behind warily as he walked ahead without even a single glance back.

I had not felt peace since the incident the previous evening.

I had gone to bed with his voice ringing in my head, and woke up feeling it in my stomach. No matter how hard I tried to get rid of it, I could still feel his smell on my skin.

I thought again about the quote he had underlined in that book, the words like an indecipherable song. The more I tried to make out a melody, however, the more I crumbled underneath the jarring dissonance of his actions.

A moment later, I collided into his back and yelped. I hadn't realised that he had stopped. I put a hand to my nose, and he looked at me over his shoulder, annoyed.

'Sorry,' I burst out. I bit my tongue and looked away from him. I still hadn't said anything to him since last night and it was embarrassing to blunder around him like this.

Rigel started walking again and I waited for him to get a few paces ahead before doing the same.

After a few minutes had passed, we crossed the bridge over the river. It was old, one of the first things to have been built in the town, and one of the only landmarks I'd noticed from afar the day we arrived. A few construction labourers were busy with roadworks. Norman complained every day that they made him late for work, and I could understand why.

When we reached the school gates, I noticed something on the side of the road, something that pulled at my delicate heartstrings, stirring my childlike soul.

An oblivious little snail was recklessly slithering over the asphalt. Cars were thundering past, but she didn't seem to notice a thing. She was moving so slowly that she would have been squashed under car tyres so, without even thinking, I launched myself in her direction. I would never understand what came over me, but maybe I was most myself when I wasn't pretending to be like other people. It was a necessity for me to try to help such a small creature. It was pure gut instinct.

I stepped down from the sidewalk and picked her up before she tried to cross the road and meet her death. My hair fell over my face, and when I saw that she was all right and all in one piece, my face broke into a spontaneous smile.

'I've got you,' I whispered, realising too late how stupid I'd been. I heard the rumbling of an engine. A car was speeding towards me from behind. My heart leapt into my throat. I didn't have time to turn around before something forcefully yanked me out of the way.

I found myself back on the sidewalk, my eyes wide and staring, and the furious sound of a car horn blaring in my ears.

A hand had grabbed the shoulder of my sweater and was still gripping it firmly. When I met the eyes looming above me, I stopped breathing.

Rigel was watching me with his jaw clenched, his gaze as cutting as steel blades. Suddenly, he let me go, almost with disgust, and the now baggy part of my sweater fell down to settle back on my shoulder.

'Jesus,' he snarled through gritted teeth. 'What were you thinking?'

I opened my mouth to speak, but I couldn't say anything. I felt full of disbelief and confusion. Before I could do anything, he turned his back on me and headed towards the gates, leaving me standing there.

I watched him walk away, with the little snail still cradled in my hands. There were a lot of girls standing around, watching him go and murmuring. After the fight on the first day, the boys warily let him pass, while the girls ate him up with their eyes as if hoping he'd hurl himself at them, too.

'Nica!'

Billie was coming over to meet me. Before she got to me, I hurried to make sure the snail was safe, laying her down on a low wall close to a shrub, ensuring she wasn't at risk of rolling back down into the road.

'Hi,' I greeted my friend as she passed a group of giddy freshmen. There was more hubbub than normal that day. Everyone seemed noisier, rowdier, livelier. I sensed something strange in the air, a sort of exhilaration that I couldn't quite make sense of.

'Watch out,' she warned as another overexcited group of students ran past us.

'Er . . . what's happening?' I asked as we started to walk off together. It was a Friday like any other, and I couldn't understand what could have caused such excitement.

'Don't you know what day it is on Monday?' Billie lifted a hand to wave to Miki, who was waiting in front of the gates. Billie waited for me to respond for a moment as I thought it through, trying to grasp at something that was obviously evading me.

'It's . . . the fourteenth,' I murmured eventually, not understanding.

'And that means nothing to you?'

I felt I must have been being rather dumb, because every girl of my age around me seemed to know full well what day Monday was. They seemed to know it viscerally. But I wasn't like girls my age. I had had an unusual upbringing which made even the most normal events seem alien to me.

'Oh, come on! It's the most romantic day of the year,' she said in a sing-song voice. 'Couples celebrate it . . .'

Suddenly, I understood, and blushed. 'Oh . . . the holiday for lovers . . . Valentine's Day.'

'*Bingo!*' Billie squealed, right into Miki's face. Miki threw her a dirty glare from under her hood, the smoke from her cigarette blown away by the wind.

'Did you eat sugar sachets for breakfast again?' she asked scathingly.

'Hello, Miki,' I greeted her quietly.

Her eyes met mine and I slowly lifted a hand, trying not to be too forward. She took a slow drag of her cigarette, but, like every morning, said nothing back.

'I was trying to explain to Nica why everyone's so excited,' Billie said, elbowing her. 'After all, Garden Day only happens once a year!'

I tilted my head.

'Garden Day? What's that?'

'Oh, only the most anticipated event of the school year!' Billie replied, chastely linking arms with me and Miki. 'A day that stirs up something in everyone!'

'A day that stirs up vomit,' Miki retorted, but Billie ignored her.

'Every year, on Valentine's Day, a committee sets up a special pavilion dedicated to . . . *roses*! Every student can anonymously give a rose to whoever they want, and every colour has a different meaning! Oh, you've got to see it, bouquets of all colours flying all over the place! The popular girls, the sporty ones . . . One year, even Coach Willer found his cupboard full of roses . . . some people swore that they'd seen the principal sneaking around . . .'

Miki rolled her eyes as Billie jumped about, giggling.

'Oh, it's a day of drama! Declarations of love, broken hearts . . . It's Garden Day!'

'It seems cute . . .' I said with a little smile.

'It's like a day in a loony bin,' Miki muttered, and Billie gave her a gentle push.

'Oh, won't you stop sulking? Don't listen to her, Nica,' she waved her hand. 'Last year she got four beautiful roses . . . all of them scarlet . . .'

She poked her in the ribs and sniggered. Miki squished the cigarette stub between her fingers then flicked it away. It landed close to the little wall where I had left the snail.

At that moment, I noticed a boy sitting in just that spot. I stopped, watched him for a moment, and when I realised what I had seen, my eyes widened a little.

Miki and Billie started to bicker, absorbed in teasing each other. I turned towards them indecisively, but before they could notice me, while they were distracted, I seized the opportunity.

I breathlessly headed towards the stranger. The trees behind him were swaying in the wind, casting a dancing lattice of shadows on him.

'Umm . . . Excuse me . . .' I cheeped.

He didn't hear me. He was listening to music, looking down at his phone. I took another small step forward and stretched out my hand. 'Sorry . . . excuse me?'

I saw his brow furrow and he looked up. He squinted against the sun and looked at me, a little annoyed.

'Yes?' he asked.

'The snail . . .'

'Huh?'

I interlaced my fingers under my chin, my eyes a little wide.

'I . . . well . . . can I . . . can I take the snail off your trousers?'

He blinked several times, staring at me with slightly flared nostrils.

'Sorry . . . what?'

'I want to hold the snail . . .'

'You want to hold . . . *my snail*?'

'Yes, but . . . slowly . . .' I hurried to say as he stared at me, disconcerted. 'It's just because I left her here after I'd picked her up from the road and . . . if you sit still, I just want to put her somewhere safe . . .'

'What on earth are you . . . Oh, shit!'

He noticed the slimy trail on his jeans and his headphones fell off. He jumped to his feet, disgusted, and I leapt forward as he tried to pluck her off.

'Wait!'

'Piss off!'

'Please!'

I plucked her off before he let her fall to the ground, or worse, trod on her. The boy lurched backwards, staring at her in my hands with a horrified grimace.

'Damn it! Of all the places it could have gone! Gross!'

The snail curled up into her shell and I threw him a slightly offended look. I checked that her shell wasn't cracked and sheltered her in my hands, keeping her in their warmth.

'She's shy . . .' I muttered, slightly peevish. A part of me hoped that he hadn't heard me, but I hadn't spoken quietly enough.

'Excuse me?' he asked indignantly, quickly growing furious.

'She didn't do it on purpose,' I defended her faintly. 'She doesn't understand. You know?'

He stared at me, incredulous and disgusted. I felt like an infant, small and strange, like a little girl stuck in a world that others would always look at with that same incredulity and disgust.

'She's not gross,' I continued quietly, as if I was defending a part of myself. 'She's a very fragile creature . . . she can only defend herself. She's got no way of hurting anything or anyone.'

My hair tickled the sides of my face as I stayed there with my head slightly to one side. 'Sometimes she comes out when it rains. She's a sign that rain and storms are coming . . . She feels them, you know? Before anyone else does.'

I slowly moved towards the little wall, holding her close to my chest. 'She's safe in her shell. She's at home there.' I stooped down to the bottom of a tree nearby, in the corner of the soccer pitch behind the goal, where no one ever went. 'But if her shell ever cracked, the splinters would get stuck inside and they'd end up killing her. She wouldn't be able to survive it. No way. Because it's her shelter . . . the only refuge she has. It's sad, isn't it?' I murmured, upset. 'The thing that keeps her safe is also what can hurt her the most.'

I carefully placed her down close to the roots. She was still hiding in her shell, too scared to emerge, and I moved the soil beside her a little, trying to uncover a moist patch for her.

'There we are,' I whispered, smiling slightly. I mustered all the tenderness that my mom had taught me.

I got back to my feet, slowly tucking my hair behind my ears. When I looked up, I saw that the boy had been watching me all that time.

'Nica, hey!' Billie was waving from the entrance. 'What are you up to? Come on, it's getting late!'

'I'm coming!' I tightened my backpack straps with both hands, and looked towards the boy, intimidated. 'Bye,' I said quietly, before running away.

He didn't reply, but I felt him watching me as I entered the building.

'Do you want to come over to mine for lunch today?' I heard Billie ask.

I dropped the pencil case I was putting in my backpack, and hurried to grab it, watching Billie with flushed cheeks. The invitation had caught me unawares.

'My grandma really wants you to. She saw you outside school the other day and almost had a stroke! She says you're so thin. She's been cooking all morning. I don't think she'll take no for an answer. But only if you want, obviously.'

'You . . . you're sure?' I asked uncertainly as we left the classroom. I didn't know what to say. I always felt the stinging fear that I was too much, that everyone wanted to be rid of me, that deep down they didn't really want me to be there.

But Billie was kind, waved her hand and smiled at me.

'Obviously! Grandma almost dragged me out of bed this morning, pointed at me, and said, "Tell your friend that she's our guest today!" She says you look like you haven't tasted her potato pie – what a sacrilege!' She giggled and threw me a look. 'So, you're coming?'

'First . . . I should ask permission. You know, check if it's all right . . .'

'Of course!' she replied, as I took out a scrap of paper with Anna's phone number written on it.

I headed towards reception, where I asked politely if I could make a phone call.

'To my family,' I specified to the receptionist, and when I saw her nod in response I was overwhelmed by a feeling of pride and happiness.

Anna picked up after three rings, and not only did she calmly agree, but she was even happy that I would have company. She told me I could stay out as long as I wanted and come back whenever I was ready, and my appreciation for her grew even stronger. She trusted me, she was measured and easy-going. She worried a lot, but her concern wasn't suffocating – she respected my freedom in a way that was very important to me.

'Perfect, I'll let Grandma know!' Billie trilled, tapping off a message on her phone.

I felt a surge of lightness. I was smiling so hard that I could even feel my eyes crinkling as I realised she was offering me the opportunity to spend time together.

'Thank you,' I said, and she grinned.

'Don't even mention it! It's us who should be thanking you!'

'No one has ever invited me over before . . .'

Her eyes lingered on mine, as if she'd suddenly been reminded of something important, but then she was forced to move out of the way as several excited girls ran past us. In the corridor, I saw people emptying their lockers, leaving them unlocked as they rushed away.

'Garden Day is just around the corner,' Billie smiled. 'They're setting up the pavilion for the roses in the gym. Then, on Monday, the members of the committee will go round the school handing them out.'

'But why is everyone emptying their lockers?' I asked, not understanding. 'Why are they leaving them open?'

'Oh, it's sort of a tradition! Some people deliver their roses themselves, before the event. The boldest ones, you know. Or maybe just the show-offs . . . But anyway, people can leave their lockers unlocked, so that anyone can leave them a rose between lessons if they want to. Basically, it's a good compromise for people who are a bit shy! And it's fun to find that someone's left you a rose. And to rack your brains over who it could have been, who's thinking of you, who's not thinking of you, what colour the rose is! It's like, "he loves me, he loves me not." '

'You really like this event,' I observed. 'Don't you?'

Billie giggled and shrugged. 'Who doesn't? Everyone seems drunk on it! The girls go crazy to compete over who gets the most roses . . . and the cutest boys are in high demand! It's like watching a documentary show about vultures!'

I raised my eyebrows and she burst out laughing.

She carried on telling me anecdotes about past Garden Days as we walked towards the exit.

'Wait,' I stopped her, rifling through my pockets. 'The paper with Anna's number . . . I must have left it at reception.'

I still hadn't memorised Anna's phone number, so it was the only way I had of contacting her. I apologised, embarrassed by my absent-mindedness. I promised Billie that I'd be back soon, and started to retrace my steps. I didn't want to make her wait long, so I quickly went to reception, and luckily found the scrap of paper under the counter. I stuffed it back in my pocket, relieved, and turned back around.

But I bumped into someone in the corridor. A boy. He was being really rowdy. He charged past me, and the angry tension of his body was so intense that he was drawing looks from lots of other people. I felt my stomach churning and attributed it to his blatant rage – that charged, nervous sort of anger portended violence and had always frightened me.

'*You!*' he roared. 'What the fuck did you say to my girlfriend?'

He had come to a stop outside a door. I recognised it with a gut-wrenching sense of foreboding – it was the music room. I knew that it should have been empty at that time, but I could sense *who* was inside. Several people were gathered around, drawn in by the unfolding drama. When I got close, driven by an inexplicable force, I got confirmation that it was, in fact, Rigel.

He was sitting on a bench, silent and impervious. Pianos had a strange lure for him that was difficult to understand. I wouldn't have described it as a passion, it was more of a calling that he had never been able to resist.

'D'you hear me? I'm talking to you!'

I was sure that he'd heard him, but Rigel didn't seem all that bothered. He tilted his head to one side, and looked him up and down, extremely calmly.

'I saw you, you were harassing her,' the boy got even closer to him. 'Don't you dare, you hear me?' he threatened.

Rigel's expression was impenetrable, as if he was hardly being confronted at all. But this didn't reassure me. Black angel's wings were furled around his body, hidden and invisible to everyone else. I feared the moment when he would spread them out and reveal his worst.

'Don't think you can do whatever the hell you want just because you're new. It doesn't work like that here.'

'And who says how it works?' Rigel asked sarcastically. '*You?*'

He fixed his eyes on him and got to his feet. He was taller than him, but most intimidating was the absence of any warmth in his sharklike eyes.

'If I were you, I'd have *other* worries,' he retorted. 'Maybe ask your girlfriend why she was so intent on wasting my time . . .'

He moved past him, and the boy clenched his fists in a blind fury.

'What the fuck did you say?' he snarled as Rigel turned his back to him, picking up the sheet music from the piano. 'Where do you think you're going? We haven't finished here!' he screamed, beside himself. 'And look at me when I'm speaking to you, asshole!'

He grabbed him aggressively by the shoulder, but as soon as he touched him, I wished that he hadn't. The next moment, a hand was clasped around his neck and his face was smashed into the piano with shocking brutality. A terrible noise exploded through the air. My heart was thumping in my chest and I could feel someone near me holding their breath.

My heart leapt into my throat as Rigel dug his nails into the boy's scalp and a screeching wail tore out of him. He branded his silent and icy fury into the boy's skull and the next moment, as suddenly as he had grabbed him, he let him go. The boy fell to the ground, stunned, unable to stand back up. I was frozen by how quickly Rigel had reacted, how forcefully he had gripped him and how much he had hurt him.

Rigel walked around him slowly, bending over to pick up the sheet music that had fallen to the ground. No one was breathing.

'Your girlfriend took a photo of me,' he drawled. 'She probably didn't tell you. Seeing as you're here, tell her not to do it again.'

Then he noticed that I was there too, and his eyes fixed on me.

'But make sure to do it *kindly*, of course,' he added sarcastically.

He left the room before any teachers could arrive. I stayed rooted to the spot with my pulse thumping in my wrists. I looked around me and saw several girls watching him walk away, fearful but no less bewitched by his enigmatic, violent appeal.

He had just revealed how brutal, cold and callous he could be.

And yet, every girl around me, despite everything, would still have happily let themselves be gobbled up by that dangerous mystery emanating from his eyes.

When I went back outside, shaken, there was a strange taste in my mouth. I could still see the whole scene playing out in front of me . . .

'There you are!' Billie greeted me with a smile. 'Did you find it?'

I blinked, trying not to show how disturbed I was. Rigel created unfathomable, worrying feelings in me.

'Yes,' I whispered. I bit my lip and looked away, trying not to let her see.

'We'd better get going,' she urged. The huge Wrangler was waiting right in the middle of the busy road, with angry drivers and motorcyclists lining up behind it. 'Seems like it's getting tense.'

'Hold on, are we not waiting for Miki?'

'Oh, no, she's not coming,' she replied calmly. 'She can't make it today.'

I had thought it was going to be the three of us . . .

We crossed through the gates and rushed to the car.

When I opened the door, Billie's grandma threw us a glance from behind her sunglasses.

'Hi, Grandma! How's your hip been today?'

'No chattering, get in,' she ordered authoritatively, and we obeyed. I settled into the back seat, staring at her with wide eyes.

'This is Nica,' Billie introduced me as her grandma started the engine. I lifted a hand shyly, and she looked at me in the rear-view mirror. The instinctive fear of not being liked pierced my heart. I was worried that I wouldn't live up to her expectations, whatever they might be.

'Hi there, dear,' she greeted me sweetly, making me relax.

Relieved, I smiled. I decided to finally let myself enjoy the moment, and pushed the thought of Rigel far away.

Billie's house wasn't too far from school. She lived in a quiet neighbourhood close to the river, on such a narrow street that the Wrangler could hardly squeeze through.

We had to climb up a few steps to get to a dainty little red door, beside which stood a brass umbrella stand.

Their apartment was small but welcoming, with walls that were covered with slightly crooked photos and paintings. There were wooden beams on the ceiling and the threadbare carpet created an intimate atmosphere that made me feel warm and enveloped. There was a mouth-watering smell of something sautéing in the kitchen. I ate until I was fit to burst, and discovered that Billie's grandmother, underneath her slightly grouchy demeanour, was actually a deeply affectionate, caring and maternal person.

She made sure I took a second helping of pie, and asked me how long I'd lived in the area. I replied that I came from an institute, and when I told her with a hopeful smile that I was going through the process of being adopted, a profound sweetness filled her expression. I told her about the day I had met Anna, the morning when I'd seen her at the bottom of the stairs, and the walk we'd taken around the institute grounds that sunny afternoon.

Billie's grandmother listened attentively, without interrupting me once. Then, when I'd finished speaking, she got up, came around the table and gave me another portion of pie.

After lunch, Billie took me upstairs to show me her room.

Before I entered, she lowered the blinds and flicked a light switch.

Inside the room, a hundred thousand sparkles burst across the walls, and I held my breath. Reflections of light spun around, dancing through a labyrinth of photographs.

'Oh, it's . . .'

A flash blinded me. I blinked, stunned, and saw Billie smiling from behind her camera.

'Your face was just too cute,' she giggled, lowering the camera, and pulled out the Polaroid as the image developed. She waved it in the air a few times before holding it out to me.

'Here, take it.'

I took the little white square, and watched the colours spread out across the surface, almost as if by magic. There I was, my face a little dreamy and a slight smile playing on my lips. The universe of swirling lights around me was reflected in my eyes, making them shine like illuminated mirrors.

'You can keep it! My gift.'

'Really?' I whispered, bewildered by such a wonderful present – a moment of frozen time and captured colours. There was something wondrous about holding a fragment of life in your own hands.

'Of course. I've got loads of them, don't worry! Grandma tried to give me an album to put them in, but I can't get to grips with being that organised. See?' She gestured around at the galaxy of photos. 'Photos of sunrises in the east, and of sunsets in the west. Photos of skies close to my desk, so I can feel more light-hearted when I study. And I put pictures of people around the bed, so I don't feel alone at night when I can't sleep. I look at their smiles and always fall asleep before I finish counting them all.'

'How did you get into photography?' I asked, my gaze wandering over all those faces.

'My parents.'

She told me that they had been away for months. They were internationally famous photographers who worked for renowned magazines like *National Geographic* and *Lonely Planet*. They were always travelling all over the world for work, discovering exotic landscapes and scenes in all four corners of the earth. They didn't come back home often, so Billie's grandma had moved in to live with her.

'That's really wonderful, Billie,' I told her in a whisper, entranced. I looked at the photos of her parents in the mountains of the Grand Canyon, standing next to a Mayan pyramid, and then in the middle of an explosion of butterflies, inside an old Native American tent. 'You must be very proud of them . . .'

She nodded happily, looking at the pictures of them. 'I am. Sometimes they can't phone us because they go to such remote places that there's no signal or connection. The last time I heard from them was four days ago.'

'You must miss them a lot.'

Full of melancholy, Billie stared at a photo of the two of them smiling and brushed it with her fingertip. I felt her yearning as if it were my own.

'One day I'll be just like them. I'll leave with Mom and Dad and fill the room with photos of me, too. You'll see,' she told me with silent longing. 'When I'm older, I'll be right there with them in these photos, the glossy finish won't keep us apart.'

It was lovely. I couldn't stop thinking about it the whole time I was walking home.

I felt totally at peace. I was going *home* after an afternoon with my *friend*. Was there anything better than feeling normal? Than feeling . . . *accepted*?

I passed by the school, feeling serene. It was unusual to see the sidewalk without a living soul. But I glimpsed movement out of the corner of my eye. I caught sight of someone between the open entrance doors, her back turned and her black hair swishing.

I thought I recognised her . . .

'Miki?' I called out once I'd come up behind her.

She jumped, and then suddenly spun around, her t-shirt ripping noisily.

My eyes opened wide and I stopped myself from reaching out towards her. Holding my breath, I stared at the tear in her sleeve.

'I . . . I . . . I'm so sorry,' I began, mortified.

Miki looked down at the tear and clenched her jaw.

'Well, great. That was my favourite t-shirt,' she said bluntly.

I wrung my hands, distraught. I tried to say something, but before I had the chance, she walked away without a single glance.

'Miki, please wait,' I stuttered. 'I'm sorry, I didn't mean to . . . I saw you there, I only wanted to say hi . . .'

She didn't bother replying to me. She carried on walking, and I instinctively leapt forward.

'I can fix it for you!'

I didn't want to watch her walk away like that. I knew that Miki trusted very few people, I'd grasped that she was introverted, cautious and reserved, but I didn't want her to hate me. I wanted to do something, I wanted to carry on trying, I wanted . . . I *wanted* . . .

'I'm good with a needle and thread, I can fix it if you want, it won't take me any time at all.' I stared at her imploringly. 'I live nearby. It won't take me long, believe me, it'll just be a couple of minutes . . .'

Miki slowed to a stop. I took another step forward, my voice soft and earnest.

'Please, Miki . . . Let me fix it.'

Give me a chance, I was begging her. *Just one chance, I'm not asking you for anything else.*

Hesitantly, Miki turned around.

She looked me in the face, and in her eyes, I saw a glimmer of hope.

'Here we are,' I said a little later, pointing to the white picket fence. 'This is my house.'

Miki was walking silently next to me, strangely close. I glanced at the violin case she was holding out of the corner of my eye, curbing my curiosity before the question burst out.

'Come in,' I invited her, leading the way into the house. She looked around a little warily. 'You head on into the kitchen, I'll be right behind you.'

I shrugged off my backpack then went to get the old cookie tin that Anna kept the sewing kit stashed in.

I went back to Miki, and found her staring at the cow-shaped kettle. I put down the tin and invited her to come closer.

'You can sit down here.'

I settled her down by the kitchen island so that her arm was at a convenient height. She took off her leather jacket as I rummaged around for threads of the right colours. I nodded to myself, then threaded a needle. I saw a hint of nervousness in the glance that Miki threw me.

'Don't worry,' I reassured her in a clear voice. 'I won't stab you.'

I bent over and gripped the two edges of the fabric together, then carefully began to sew. I kept my fingers underneath the fabric, so that I would feel the needle before it scratched her skin. I felt her recoil when I accidentally brushed her with my fingertips, but I didn't complain. What Miki was giving me in that moment meant a lot to me.

I only noticed a few minutes later that she was staring right at me. Her gaze moved to watch the needle precisely disappearing into the fabric then immediately reappearing, disappearing and reappearing, over and over with each stitch.

'Where did you learn to sew?' she asked neutrally, as her gaze switched to the window, and the garden beyond it.

'Oh, I've always done it. When I was at the institute there wasn't anybody who would repair our clothes for us, so I did it myself. At the beginning it was a disaster, I just kept stabbing my fingers . . . but with time, I learnt. I didn't want to go about the place in rags,' I said, speaking a little louder. I met her gaze and smiled gently. 'I wanted to be clean and tidy.'

I took the scissors out of the tin and finished my handiwork.

'There we go!' I announced. 'All done.'

She looked down at her sleeve, inspecting the tight and tidy stitching. Then she froze.

'What is *that*?'

I pressed my lips together. She had noticed something that wasn't there before. In the patch of stitching, a panda's face was now embroidered.

'I . . . well, the fabric was ruined there,' I stammered, feeling slightly guilty. 'And I know you like pandas . . . or at least, I think you do, seeing as you've got that keyring on your backpack and I . . . I thought it was cute.'

She looked up, and I lifted my hands up in defence. 'But you can always take it off! Just a quick snip with a pair of scissors and it'll come undone. It'll just take a moment . . .'

My stumbling was interrupted by the phone ringing.

'Oh, you're home!' Anna said happily when I rushed over to pick it up. She wanted to make sure that I'd got back all right. I realised once again that she was worried about me, and, like it always did, my heart fluttered. She asked me how lunch was, and told me that she'd be back soon, too.

When I hung up, I saw that Miki had put her jacket back on and had picked up her case. I really wanted to ask her something about the violin, but I didn't want to be too intrusive.

I opened the door for her, smiling, and then I saw something sneaking past us, heading inside.

'Oh,' I said contentedly. 'Hi, Klaus.'

The old cat threw me a surly glare. As I let Miki pass, I couldn't resist the impulse to stretch my hand out to give him a stroke, but he leapt abruptly out of the way and tried to scratch me.

I brought my hand to my chest, embarrassed that I'd tried to touch him without his permission, or maybe because I'd been so obviously rejected in front of Miki.

I glanced furtively at her, and saw that she was already looking at me.

'Seems he's not in too great a mood today,' I giggled a little nervously. 'Normally he's quite playful, aren't you? Eh, Klaus?'

Klaus hissed at me, baring his teeth angrily before slinking off. I watched him disappear up the stairs, suddenly feeling slightly uneasily.

'He's got a bit of a temper sometimes . . .' I mumbled. 'But deep down . . . *very* deep down . . . I'm sure he's a sweetie . . .'

'Thank you,' I heard her whisper.

Surprised, I looked up, but Miki had already turned her back on me.

She disappeared through the door, and without waiting for anything else, headed off into the night.

'*Tenderness, Nica,*' I heard my mother's voice say.

I knew no other way of interacting with the world.

But maybe . . .

Maybe, the world was beginning to understand me.

8. Sky Blue

Strength is the ability to touch with tenderness others' vulnerabilities.

I once read something that Foucault wrote: '*Develop your legitimate strangeness.*'

I had always cultivated my strangeness in secret because when I was growing up, I was taught that other people thought normality was more acceptable.

I spoke to beings that couldn't speak back to me. I rescued little animals that other people didn't even notice. I valued what other people thought was insignificant, maybe because I wanted to prove that even little creatures like me could count for something.

I lifted my hand. I was in the garden at home, and the sun was sweetly kissing the leafy branches of the apricot tree. I stretched out my fingers towards the tree trunk and helped a bright green caterpillar onto the bark.

I had found him in my bedroom underneath the window, and I was giving him his freedom back.

'There you are,' I whispered. I smiled as he crawled inside a crack in the bark. I clasped my hands together and watched him with a quiet sort of peacefulness.

I had always heard it said that it took great power, great strength to change the world.

I hadn't ever wanted to change the world, but I'd always thought that it wasn't grand gestures or displays of power that made a difference. For me, it was the little things that mattered. Everyday actions. Simple acts of kindness from ordinary people.

Everyone, no matter how small, can leave a bit of themselves in this world.

When I went back inside, I smiled. It was Saturday morning, and the irresistible smell of roasted coffee was wafting in from the kitchen. I closed my eyes, enraptured, taking in deep, satisfying breaths of it.

'Is everything okay?'

It was Anna's sweet voice. As I opened my eyes, however, I realised that she hadn't been asking me.

Her hand was resting on Rigel's head. He had his back turned to me, his black hair was messy and his hands were wrapped around a mug of coffee. He nodded, but I hardly noticed it. I was so enraptured by the sight of his fingers and the prominent veins on his forearm.

Those hands . . . were capable of both merciless violence and the most heavenly of melodies. His strong knuckles and lithe muscles seemed like they were made for subjugation, but his fingers could also caress a keyboard with such incredible delicateness . . .

I shook when Rigel got to his feet.

He stood to his full height, and for a moment, the smell of coffee lost some of its intensity. He headed towards the door, and I took a step backwards.

His eyes fixed on me.

I don't know how to explain it . . . I was scared of Rigel, but I didn't know what it was about him that terrified me so much. Maybe it was the almost violating way his eyes pierced deep inside of me. Maybe it was the way his voice was too mature for a boy of his age. Maybe it was because I knew how violent he could become.

Or maybe . . . it was because of the maelstrom of shivers he caused in me every time he so much as breathed nearby . . .

'Scared I'll bite you, *little moth*?' he whispered in my ear as he passed me.

I quickly jumped back, but by then he had already disappeared through the door behind me.

'Hi, Nica!'

I jumped, and found Anna smiling at me.

'Coffee?'

I nodded tensely, and then noticed with a rush of relief that she hadn't noticed the little exchange between Rigel and I. I joined her at the table for breakfast.

'Would you like to spend some time together today?'

My cookie fell into my coffee. I looked up at her with raised eyebrows, stupefied.

Anna wanted to spend time with me?

'You and me?' I asked to make sure. 'Just the two of us?'

'I was thinking a girly afternoon, without the guys,' she replied. 'Do you not fancy it?'

I hurried to shake my head, trying hard not to smash my mug. My heart was shining, making all my thoughts glow in its light.

Anna *wanted to spend time with me*, for an afternoon, for an hour, for however long a walk took. It didn't matter how long – the mere fact that she had asked flooded my soul with light.

The fairy tale smelt sweet when she was around. It shone like her hair and glowed like her smiles. It was imbued with the sound of her laughter and the warmth of her eyes.

And I wanted to live inside it, forever.

'Nica, how about this one? Oh, no, wait . . . what do you think of this one, instead?'

I was dazed and confused. The clothes store was massive. I had already tried on so many outfits, but Anna approached me with yet another shirt and held it up to my torso. Instead of looking at it, I gazed glassily at her. She smelt like the house, and she was so close that I was walking around, entranced, in a dream. I couldn't believe I was really here, with an array of shopping bags at my feet and someone at my side who wanted to buy me even more. Someone who wanted to spend money on *me*, even though she knew I could offer nothing in return.

When Anna had suggested spending time together, I never imagined that she would take me shopping, or that she wanted to buy anything for me, least of all shirts, skirts and new underwear.

I felt the need to pinch my hand to make sure that it was all really true.

'Do you like it?'

I stared at her dreamily.

'Yes, a lot . . .' I whispered, stupefied, and she laughed.

'You've said that every time, Nica.' She looked me in the eyes, just as I liked. 'You must have some preferences!'

I felt my cheeks flushing with embarrassment.

The truth was that I liked everything. It might seem exaggerated and hard to believe, but it was true.

I wanted to find the right words to explain it to Anna. To make her understand that I found all of her suggestions golden and wonderful.

That no one had ever given me their time before.

That when your life is entirely wishes and daydreams, you learn to enjoy the small things – unexpectedly finding a four-leafed clover, finding a drop of jam on the table, the intensity of meeting another's gaze.

And preferences . . .

Preferences were a privilege I had never been able to afford.

'I like colours,' I murmured with almost childish hesitation. 'Multicoloured things . . .' I lifted up a pair of pyjamas with happy little bees on them. 'Like these!'

'I think . . . in fact, I'm pretty sure those are for children,' Anna objected, blinking several times.

I blushed, my mouth hanging open. I quickly checked the label, and she burst out laughing. Then she put her hand on my arm.

'Come on, I saw the same design in the hosiery department.'

An hour later, I had a bag full of new socks.

I would no longer feel draughts on winter nights, or feel splinters poking through the threadbare fabric on my feet. Anna left the store, and I ecstatically rushed after her with all my bags.

'Oh, hi, honey!' she was saying into her phone. 'Yes, we're still here . . . Of course, all great,' she smiled, taking a few bags off me. 'Just a few little things . . . No . . . No, Carl's giving me a hand, but I'll have to open on Monday morning. Where are you?' Her face lit up, and she came to a stop. 'Really? By which entrance? I didn't think you'd come right here! How come you didn't . . . What?'

I watched her listening attentively. Her eyes opened wide in surprise and she lifted a hand to her mouth.

'Oh, Norman!' she burst out, thrilled. 'You're joking? But . . . but, that's marvellous, honey!' She burst into a peal of laughter. 'What wonderful news! This is your year, didn't I say so? And I'm sure it'll be really good publicity for the business!'

I stood beside her, not understanding what she was talking about, and she carried on congratulating him, radiating happiness.

'Good news?' I asked her once she'd finished the call.

'Very good! It's not really all that exciting, but Norman just got some news he's been waiting for for a long time. His firm is going to participate in an annual conference! He's been chosen along with a few others, it's really a unique opportunity. He's been waiting for this for so long!' With a smile she gestured for me to come with her. 'Come on, he's here too! The conference is in a week's time. Norman had almost given up hope . . . I'll cook a roast tomorrow! After all, it's Sunday, and we should celebrate with a nice meal, don't you think?'

I nodded, happy to hear her so excited.

We crossed the mall and Anna carried on telling me about the annual conference, a prestigious event for industry experts. We reached the other entrance and she pointed out another clothes store.

'He should be around here somewhere . . . Norman! Hey!'

He waved and came over to meet us.

'Oh, I'm so happy for you!' Anna dived into his arms, making him blush.

'Yes, well . . . you did say so, and you're never wrong. Hi, Nica,' he smiled at me awkwardly, and I smiled back. Anna smoothed the shoulders of his jacket.

'I'd be more than happy to come with you! We can chat about it later . . . But how come you're here? I thought you were going to stay at home today!'

'I'm here with Rigel . . . he also needed to buy a few things,' Norman said.

A strange feeling came over me, and my eyes started scanning around looking for him.

'I lost him between departments, I think . . .' He scratched his head and Anna smiled.

'Nica, do you want to have a look around?' She pointed towards the shelves inside the store. 'You might find something you like. Why don't you go and have a look?'

I hesitated, but decided to let them talk and slipped inside the store, looking around warily. I tried to concentrate on the clothes, but I couldn't do it. I knew that he was in there somewhere, with his unfathomable eyes and irresistible aura.

As I wandered around the store, a bag slipped out of my hands and fell to the ground. I bent down to pick it up, but then someone bumped into me. He cursed, and I opened my eyes wide.

'Sorry . . .' I stammered. 'I dropped a bag and . . .'

'Watch it!' the boy grumbled, picking up a sweater he'd dropped.

I hurried to collect my things and he held out a bag to me. I reached to take it, and felt him tugging on it slightly as I murmured, 'Thanks . . .'

'Hey . . . I know you.'

I looked up and he blinked a few times. His face looked a little familiar.

'You're the snail girl.' He looked intensely in my eyes. 'You are, aren't you?'

That's where I'd seen him before, on the little wall outside school the day before. I was surprised he remembered me. No one normally did.

'You got enough bags there?' he asked suddenly. 'One of these shopaholics, are you?'

'Oh,' I gathered myself. 'No, I, well . . .'

'A big spender,' he observed, looking into my eyes with a slightly studied smile.

'It's really just this once . . .'

'Yeah, yeah, sure, that's what they all say,' he replied. 'But the first step to overcoming a problem is admitting you have one, don't you think?'

I tried to come up with a retort, but he interrupted me again. 'Oh, don't you worry, your secret is safe with me,' he said knowingly. 'I've never seen you before at Burnaby, by the way . . .'

'I'm new,' I replied, noticing that he'd taken a step closer to me. I suddenly wondered why he was talking to me.

'Are you a senior?'

'Yeah . . .'

'Huh . . . well, welcome,' he murmured slowly. His lips curled and he looked at me closely.

'Thanks . . .'

'Maybe, snail girl, you might like to know my name . . . What do you think? So that next time you want to warn me about some creepy-crawly in the vicinity you'll know what to call me.' He held out his hand and smiled confidently. 'Tell you what, I'll make this simple. I'm –'

'*In the way.*'

An icy voice cut through the air, freezing me to the spot.

The boy turned around to find a looming presence behind him.

Rigel's black eyes were planted on him, following his every little move as he opened his mouth and glanced back at me.

'Oh, um . . . sorry,' he stammered, caught by surprise. He moved aside, flattening himself against a shelf to let Rigel pass.

Rigel slowly stepped past him, without looking away from him and without any of the haste or courtesies that you'd normally show to someone who had crammed themselves into an uncomfortable position to let you pass.

Unexpectedly, he stopped right behind me, so close that it was impossible for me to ignore him. The lure of his body was immense and irresistible. It was destabilising.

'Ah . . .' the boy murmured, looking at us. 'Are you . . . together?'

Rigel was silent, and I shifted a little uncomfortably. I repressed the urge to turn round and look into his eyes to try and see what his intentions were and clasped my hands together awkwardly.

'In a way . . .' I replied.

The boy met Rigel's gaze, almost reluctantly.

'Hi . . .' he said, vaguely, but behind me Rigel did nothing.

I was sure that he was still staring at him.

Then, suddenly, I felt his hand brushing against my hair.

A flash of icy surprise froze me to the spot. My legs were jammed, I couldn't move.

What was he doing?

Was Rigel . . . touching me?

No . . . I felt the precise touch of his fingertips. His fingers were making their way through my hair, without pulling, without brushing against me. He slowly coiled my hair around his fingers, and I turned to look up at him.

Rigel gave the boy a long look, his eyebrows arched. Then his eyes slipped down to me.

He met my tense and bewildered gaze, and I thought I could feel his fingers tightening around my hair.

'We're going,' he said in his deep voice. 'Come on.'

If he hadn't been standing so close to me, I would have already noticed that Anna was behind him. I saw her motioning for us to leave and gathered myself.

'Oh . . .' Clutching the shopping bags, I looked uncertainly at Rigel and then turned back round towards the boy. 'I've got to . . .'

'Of course,' he nodded, sliding his hands into his pockets.

'Bye then.' I gave him a little wave before moving away.

Rigel took his hand off my hair and turned around, walking in front of me. I watched his broad shoulders and realised that my throat was a little dry. I could still feel his fingers in my hair.

What had come over him?

'Find anything?'

I looked up at Norman. His thick glasses made him look like an owl.

'Oh, no . . .' I replied. 'I've already bought too much stuff.'

He nodded, if possible, more awkward than me. I took the opportunity to congratulate him on the conference. He stammered at me, embarrassed, but I noticed him smiling all the same.

He told me that he'd been waiting for this moment for a very long time. It was only the most famous firms who were asked to participate, and there would be discussions on the hottest topics in the field – rat poison, innovative insecticides, gadgets and strategies for parasites of all shapes and sizes.

After he'd been talking for a while, my head felt quite heavy. We walked past a store window, and as Norman happily chatted about the latest pesticides on the market, I noticed my complexion had taken on an unhealthy tinge. I started to feel unwell.

'Hey, are you okay?' I heard him ask doubtfully, noticing my face. 'You've gone a bit green . . .'

'Nica!'

Anna was waving, a few metres in front of us. She was beaming, and I felt extremely relieved that she'd interrupted.

'Come and look at this dress!'

It was only when I got to the boutique that I managed to see what had caught her eye.

In the window there was a pretty little pastel-coloured dress. It was plain, made with a delicate fabric that clung to the bust and hips. It had thin shoulder straps, a line of little pearl buttons down the front, and the skirt billowed out from the waist in soft pleats.

But what struck me most was the colour of the fabric. It was a light, sky blue – like the forget-me-not petals that I would rub on my clothes when I was little to try and make them less grey.

I was enraptured, like I used to be when I stared up at the clouds from the grounds of the institute. There was something about this dress that reminded me of those moments, something delicate and clean like the skies I would chase after, dreaming of freedom.

'Isn't it just the cutest?' Anna said, touching my wrist, and I nodded slowly. 'Do you want to go in and try it on?'

'No, Anna, I . . . You've already bought me so many things . . .'

But she had already opened the door and gone up to the store assistant.

'Hello. We'd like to try on that dress over there.' She pointed towards the corner of the window display, making the girl's face light up.

'Of course,' she said politely. 'I'll go get it for you right away!' She disappeared into the back.

I slowly tugged at Anna's sleeve.

'Anna, really, there's no need . . .'

'Oh, why not?' she replied, smiling. 'I want to see what you look like in it. You'll do that for me, won't you? After all, it's our day together.'

I started to stammer something, uncertain, but the sales assistant popped back into the store again.

'We're all sold out!' she exclaimed, wiping the back of her hand across her forehead. 'But you can take that one in the window!'

She went up to the mannequin and delicately slid the dress off it.

'The last one left! Here you go,' she handed it to me and I gazed at it for a moment, enraptured. 'The fitting rooms are this way, follow me!'

Anna gestured for me to follow and took the bags off me. I saw Norman coming in through the door, and behind him, briefly, glimpsed Rigel.

I followed the sales assistant to the fitting rooms, in a corner hidden from view in the back of the store. I slipped into the one furthest away from the door.

I made sure that the curtain was properly closed and got undressed. I lifted the dress over my head, getting it caught in my hair. I'd never been particularly skilled at getting dressed, maybe because the clothes I used to wear at The Grave were always too big and baggy, or maybe because the few times that I'd put on good clothes I had always been too euphoric to wear them in front of anyone else.

The dress fit tightly over my chest and clung to my body down to my waist. I got slightly embarrassed by the way that it so perfectly hugged my breasts and revealed so much of my legs. I stared at it, unable to look up.

I tried to zip it up at the back but couldn't reach.

'Anna?' I called hesitantly. 'Anna, I can't zip it up . . .'

'Oh, no problem,' her voice replied from just outside. 'Come here? I'll help you.'

She reached a hand through the curtain and pulled up the zipper. Then, before I could do anything else, she pulled open the curtain, taking me totally by surprise.

'*Wow!*' she smiled ecstatically as soon as she saw me. 'It looks amazing on you! Oh, Nica, you look so pretty!'

I cringed as she looked at me with shining, wonderstruck eyes.

'It's like it was made just for you! Have you seen how great you look? It suits you so well!'

She came to stand at my side, and I saw that my face had turned red from embarrassment.

'How's it going?' the sales assistant asked after a moment, then froze when she saw me. 'Oh!' She came up to me with her mouth hanging open, happy and admiring. 'You look incredible! Like an angel!'

Anna turned to her. 'Doesn't she just?'

'You just need the wings!' the girl joked, and I flinched when I heard other people coming into the store. I scratched my cheek, looking at the floor.

'Oh, I . . .'

'Do you like it?' Anna asked.

'Do *you* like it?'

'Nica, how could I not like it? Look at yourself!'

I looked at myself.

I lifted my face and looked at myself. I looked at myself properly.

In my doubtful eyes, there was a glimmer I never thought I would see. There was something in my gaze that even I didn't know how to interpret.

Something alive.

Delicate.

Light.

It was me.

It was me, wearing the sky like I'd always wanted. It was me, shining on the inside, as if one of my dreams had been sewn onto my skin. As if I would never again have to rub flowers onto myself to feel less dirty . . .

'Nica?' Anna called me, and I looked down.

My eyes were stinging. I hoped that she wouldn't hear me sniffling as I touched the hem of the dress. I whispered, 'I like it . . . I like it so much. Thank you.'

Anna squeezed my shoulder so softly that I wanted to feel her next to me all the time. She was giving me so much . . . too much for a soft heart like mine. I could no longer even consider the possibility of losing her. If something in the adoption process went wrong, I'd never see her again.

'We'll take it,' I heard her declare.

I headed back into the fitting room. I touched the dress with my fingers, the line of little white buttons following the curve of my chest.

It was so cute . . .

But then I remembered I wouldn't be able to take it off alone.

'Anna, sorry, please could you give me a hand?' I asked. I moved aside the fitting room curtain just enough to reveal my back. I waited patiently. She said nothing, but I could sense her presence behind me. I gathered my hair over to one side, moving it off my back so it wouldn't get in the way.

'The zipper, Anna,' I specified awkwardly. 'Sorry, I can't reach it. Can you help me?'

There was a long silence.

Then, after a moment, I heard the sound of footsteps slowly walking towards me.

One hand held the collar, the other shuffled to clasp the zipper. Slowly, she pulled it down.

My ears filled with the quiet metallic *zwip* and the dress fell open.

'Okay, thank you,' I said, when it was undone down to my shoulder blades.

But she didn't stop there.

The dress continued to be unzipped with a disarming slowness, and I felt a shiver down my spine.

'Anna, that's fine,' I reassured her gently, but the fingers tightened on the collar and the zipper continued downwards.

Right down, down to the waist, then just under the small of my back. The dress opened like a beetle's wings to reveal my skin, and my voice came out higher.

'Anna . . .'

Then the click of the zipper arriving at the bottom. The dress was completely undone. I turned to stare at my reflection with my arms wrapped around my chest to keep it from sliding off me.

I could now take it off easily. I blinked, moving my lips into a slight smile.

'Oh, er . . . thanks . . .' I murmured, before pulling the curtain closed.

I shook my head, letting the dress fall to my feet, and stood there in my underwear. I put my clothes back on and left the fitting room.

There was no one standing outside.

I looked for Anna but couldn't see her, and when I came back into the store, I found her close to the counter holding her phone. Norman was outside, looking into the store windows.

'All good?' she asked.

'Yes, thanks . . .' I smiled, clutching the dress. 'I wouldn't have been able to take it off without your help.'

Anna lifted a hand to her chest and looked at me apologetically.

'Oh, I'm sorry, Nica, I got a phone call and completely forgot! It wasn't a lot of hassle, was it? You managed to undo it?'

I looked at her with that smile still on my lips. I didn't understand.

'Yes . . . thanks to you,' I said again.

Her confusion made me feel even more alienated. A strange feeling arose inside of me, and then, suddenly, I was overcome by a sense of foreboding.

My gaze swung to look outside.

Rigel was leaning against a pillar. His piercing eyes were looking around. He looked almost bored, and his arms were folded over his chest.

No . . . What was I thinking?

'Here we are!' The sales assistant approached and looked at me happily. 'So, you're taking it, are you? Great decision.' She smiled. 'It looks so good on you!'

'Thanks,' I said, embarrassed and blushing a little. She looked at me enthusiastically.

'And it'll go with just about anything, you could even wear it as part of a more casual outfit . . . Look.' She picked something up from a hanger. 'Even just one of these . . . see how cute that looks?'

I realised only too late that she was holding a belt.

She put it around me, but my arms were still dangling at my sides so the leather brushed against my skin.

It all happened very quickly.

I felt it on my flesh.

I felt it chafing.

I felt it pressing, squeezing, closing around me, constraining me . . .

I violently tore away. I jerked backwards, eyes wide. The sales assistant stared at me, stupefied, her hands still outstretched, and I carried on moving back until I collided with the counter. My body contracted. My icy heart started beating wildly, fit to burst. I tried to control it but my hands were shaking and I had to grab on to the side to keep hold of reality.

'What's happening?' Anna asked, coming back from looking for Norman. She saw me shaking and immediately got worried. 'Nica, what's wrong?'

My skin felt tight. I absolutely had to calm down, to fight those sensations, keep them under control . . . I looked at Anna's face. I didn't want her to see me like this. I wanted her only to see me as the perfect girl wearing the pretty dress.

As a girl she'd want beside her.

A girl who would never annoy or bore her.

'Nothing,' I whispered, trying to seem convincing, but my vocal cords took no pity on me. I swallowed, trying to keep my body's reactions under control, but in vain.

'Do you feel unwell?' she asked, looking at me with concern. She came closer and her eyes looked enormous and overwhelming, like magnifying glasses.

Things got worse. I felt a visceral, pathological need to cover my body, to hide, to run far away from her gaze, to disappear.

Don't look at me, something inside of me prayed. Uncontrollable anxiety coursed through me, made me feel wrong, small, disgusting and guilty. My heart was pumping furiously, and I fell at breakneck speed into my fears, trying desperately to hold Anna's gaze.

She would throw me away.

She'd throw me out with the garbage because that was what I deserved.

That was where I belonged.

That's where people like me ended up.

I would never have that fairy tale.

I would never have my happy ending.

There were no princesses in this story.

There were no fairies, or mermaids.

There was just a little girl . . .

Who had never been *good* enough.

9. Thorns and Roses

You know what makes roses so beautiful?
The thorns.
There's nothing as magnificent
As something you cannot hold.

Light-headedness, from the heat and the emotion. The feeling that I was going to pass out.

That was how I explained what had happened in the mall, hiding my reactions the best I could.

I had tried to suppress my body's panic, I had tried with everything I had to contain myself. I reassured Anna multiple times, and in the end, she believed me.

I didn't like lying to her, but there was nothing else I could do. The idea of telling her the truth made me feel so nauseous that I couldn't breathe. I just couldn't do it.

I couldn't tell her what had caused those feelings, because they came from so deep down in me that even I didn't want to probe there.

'Nica?' I heard on Monday morning.

Anna was standing in the doorway to my room. Her eyes were still as clear as a cloudless sky. I hoped she'd never see me like that again.

'What are you looking for?' she asked, watching me rummage through my desk. I knew that she had accepted what I told her as true, but this hadn't stopped her worrying about me.

'Oh, nothing, just . . . a photo,' I murmured as she came near. 'My friend gave me one the other day and . . . I can't find it.'

I couldn't believe it. Billie had only just given it to me and I'd already lost it?

'Have you looked on the kitchen table?'

I nodded, tucking my hair behind my ears.

'You'll find it, I'm sure. It won't be lost.'

She tilted her head and tidied a lock of hair on my collarbone. As she looked me in the eyes, I felt a surge of affection for her warming my chest.

'I've got something for you.'

A small box appeared under my nose.

I came back to my senses and looked at the wrapping paper, unsure what to say. When I opened it, I couldn't believe my eyes.

'I know it's a bit old,' Anna commented as I pulled away the wrapping. 'It's definitely not the latest model, but . . . well, this way I can always know where you and Rigel are. I gave him one too.'

A cell phone. Anna was giving me a cell phone. I stared at her, utterly speechless.

'It's already got a SIM, and I've put my number in the contacts,' she explained calmly. 'You can reach me at any time. I've put Norman's number in there too.'

I was unable to express what I was feeling at that moment, with something so important in my hands.

I thought about all the times I'd daydreamed about exchanging numbers with a friend, or hearing my phone ringing somewhere, knowing that someone was looking for me, that someone wanted to speak specifically with me . . .

'I . . . Anna, I, I can't . . .' I stammered. I looked at her, enraptured, overwhelmed with gratitude. 'Thank you . . .'

It was surreal. I had never had anything of my own, except for that caterpillar plushie . . .

Why did Anna go so out of her way for me? Why did she give me clothes, underwear, such long-lasting things? I knew I shouldn't delude myself. I knew that nothing was for certain yet . . . And yet I couldn't help but *hope*.

Hope that she wanted to keep me with her.

Hope that we could stay together, that she was starting to care about me as much as I cared about her . . .

'I know that girls your age all have the latest model, but . . .'

'It's perfect,' I whispered, savouring the moment. 'It's so perfect, Anna. Thank you.'

She smiled affectionately, then put a hand on my head. My heart felt warm.

'Oh, Nica . . . Why don't you put on those new clothes we bought?' She looked at me a little sadly. 'Don't you like them any more?'

'No,' I replied urgently. 'The opposite . . . I love them!'

Too much, in truth.

When I came to put them away, I hadn't been able to see them together in the same drawer with my old clothes. So, I left them in their bags, tidy and safe like holy relics.

'I was just waiting for the right moment to wear them. I didn't want to ruin them for nothing,' I murmured quietly.

'But they're clothes,' Anna pointed out. 'They're made for wearing. Don't you want to wear all those colourful socks we got together?'

I nodded vigorously, feeling a bit like a little girl.

'So what are you waiting for?' She stroked my hair and I lowered my face.

She had given me another bit of herself, and I couldn't help but feel happy. With that conversation, once again, Anna had offered me a piece of the normality that I had always dreamt of.

That morning, I walked to school alone.

Changing my outfit had made me late, and I didn't need to see the empty hook on the coat rack to know that Rigel hadn't bothered waiting for me.

It was better that way. At the end of the day, I had promised myself that I'd keep well away from him.

When Billie had told me about Garden Day the previous Friday, I had imagined a day of pure romance. I had always thought that Valentine's Day would be intimate and personal, that there would be no need for grand, showy gestures as love reveals itself in secret, private ways.

I couldn't have been more wrong.

The yard outside school was thronging like an anthill. The atmosphere was so electric that everyone was as jumpy as grasshoppers.

I was surrounded by a gaudy mosaic swarming with yellow, pink, blue and white roses, devoid of thorns but full of meaning.

There were some students roaming around with baskets bursting with bouquets and reading the little labels attached to them. When they approached a group of girls, they all held their breath, then exploded into giggles when the chosen one was handed a rose. The others hid grimaces of disappointment or sighs of restless anticipation.

I tried to get to the entrance without ending up in the middle of some big scene. I had to agree with Billie. It was a day full of drama.

Some girls exchanged pink roses as a symbol of their friendship, while others would point fingers and hurl insults at them. Jealous girlfriends accused their boyfriends of having sent a scarlet rose to some other girl, and then forgot to say thanks for the flowers that they themselves were holding.

I recognised one of my classmates – he ran towards a dark-skinned girl and hugged her from behind, flourishing a bunch of flowers in front of her face, which made her smile.

I stood watching them affectionately, before a cheerleader shoved into me. She was furious, to say the least.

'Pink? *Pink?* After everything we've done together, that's all I am to you? Just a friend?' she raged at some guy who scratched his head awkwardly.

'Hmm . . . well, Karen . . . in a way . . .'

'*Friends,* my ass!' she screamed at him. I slipped away with wide eyes, slightly terrified.

In the distance, I glimpsed an unmistakable mane of blonde curls.

'Billie, hey,' I groaned, approaching her. 'Sorry, can I get through . . .'

Her face lit up as I practically fell at her feet.

'Nica, just at the right moment! It's all kicking off!'

I saw Miki sourly stuffing two roses into her locker. They were a beautiful, bright red.

'I hate Garden Day,' she grumbled gloomily.

'Hello, Miki,' I greeted her sweetly. She glanced at me distractedly like she did every morning, but this time I noticed a hint of tenderness in her eyes.

'Two red roses already, and it's not even first period,' Billie teased her as I opened my locker. 'I bet there are more on their way too . . . what do you think, Nica?'

She elbowed me, turning towards me with a smile.

'Hey, you're looking so colourful today!' she commented, looking at me.

I pulled at the sleeves of my new shirt, happy to be wearing something other than grey.

'Anna got me so many new clothes,' I replied, as I caught Miki's glance.

'Oh, these colours look great on you! Who knows, maybe you'll get a *flaming red* rose too . . .'

'Let's get to class,' Miki snarled with an energy she didn't normally have that early in the morning. 'If I hear another word, I swear I'll . . . *Hey*! Let it go!'

Billie jumped out of the way impishly and before I could understand what was happening, she had grabbed the padlock from my locker too.

'I'll keep these!' she exclaimed triumphantly. 'Garden Day is for everyone!'

'Not if you value your life,' Miki growled, her eyes ablaze.

'Come on, I'm just encouraging some secret admirers! Who knows how many flowers you might get by the time class is over . . .'

'I was wrong. You do want to die – *horribly*.'

Billie's lively laughter filled my ears, and then I noticed an unmistakable presence in front of reception, a figure that magnetically drew my eyes.

Rigel came through the door into the corridor. He parted the crowd like waves, his gaze fixed determinedly ahead of him.

I was staring at him without even realising it. He always oozed that disdainful confidence, as if he was aware of the world and was deliberately ignoring it. He knew how to draw attention to himself but paid no attention back. He didn't care about anyone, and yet it seemed with every step he took he asserted himself above everyone else.

When he stopped in front of his locker, I noticed a long, green stem poking through the door.

I realised I was holding my breath.

It was a shining white rose.

Someone had left it there in the hope that he'd take it.

It was beautiful. I found myself staring at it, speechless, but Rigel opened the locker and the rose fell to the floor.

It languished there among the dust and gum wrappers as he headed off, without even glancing at it.

'He didn't take it,' I heard some other girls stammering. 'He didn't even take it!'

I turned around to look at them, disorientated, and saw that they were avidly watching him leave.

'I told you, he didn't accept Susy's,' one of them said. 'She took it to him in person . . . I was sure that he'd take it, but he just walked past her.'

'Maybe he's already dating someone . . .'

I tried to ignore them. It upset me to hear him spoken about like that. All the girls wanted him ardently, as if he was a dark and distant prince from a nameless fairy tale. At the end of the day, Rigel's was a rare beauty, as sharp as a blade, and just as lethal. And when he left a room, he always left murmuring ripples in his wake.

'I'm going to class,' I muttered, ignoring the heavy weight in my chest.

I didn't know what it was, but I didn't like it.

But the idea of finding out . . .

I liked that even less.

The day went by alarmingly quickly.

Halfway through first period, two committee members knocked at the door. They entered with wicker baskets and sweet smiles, holding the power to bestow joy and tears with nothing but a wave of their hand.

I was stunned to see a girl receive a very rare blue rose.

'It's obvious who sent it,' Billie whispered beside me. 'Blue represents wisdom. Someone admires her for her intelligence. It's not a colour that some gym rat would have given her. Just look how red Jimmy Nut's gone!'

I looked over at where he was hiding behind a history textbook and smiled.

Then, a committee member stopped in front of us.

Surprised, I saw him read the name on the label. He extracted a single stalk from the others and held it out. I stared, wide-eyed.

I turned around. Next to me, Billie was smiling calmly.

'Is it for me?' she asked simply.

The boy nodded, and she took the rose off him.

'It's white,' she noted gleefully. 'Isn't that the symbol of true love? I get one every year,' she confided in me emotionally. 'I've never gotten many flowers. In fact, practically no one . . . but every Garden Day I get this . . . every year. Once, I saw the shadow of a boy close to my locker, but I've never found out who sends them.'

I noticed how warmly her cheeks were glowing and understood why she liked Garden Day so much.

'You should put it in water,' I smiled gently. 'I'll come with you after class.'

When we left class at the end of the day, Billie was still clutching her flower tightly.

'She's wilting,' she noted with a smile. 'Look!'

'It'll pick up again.' I looked at the slightly drooping petals. 'Let's go to the water fountain.'

Of course, the water fountain in question was crowded like a busy bird bath. There was a long line of girls proudly waving their own flowers about.

'There's the faucet behind the yard,' Billie suggested, 'let's try there first.'

We turned around, moving against the current. As we headed around the back of the school, she started chatting excitedly again.

'Oh, by the way, my photo? Did you keep it?' she asked me lightly.

I felt my stomach churn.

I was mortified by the idea of having lost it. Billie had shared her passion with me, and I really had appreciated her gift, but somehow, I'd still managed to misplace it. I didn't want her to think that I didn't care about it, so I found myself telling another lie.

'Yes,' I swallowed. She smiled and I promised myself that as soon as I got home, I'd find it. It couldn't have just disappeared. I couldn't really have lost it . . .

We went to the concrete yard around the back of the school. The faucet was next to the basketball hoop.

'Wait!' Billie facepalmed. 'I left my water bottle in class!'

My eyes opened wide. 'Let's hope the janitor hasn't got there yet!'

She quickly turned around, promising me she'd only be a moment.

I couldn't help but return to wondering where that photo could have gotten to . . .

Then I heard a noise. The sound of footsteps, but I couldn't work out where they were coming from. I noticed that a window of one of the ground-floor classrooms was open.

'I'm not surprised to find you here.'

I froze.

That voice.

It was indescribable to suddenly hear it so close. It was like he was right there with me, with his black eyes and his irresistible charm.

I stepped aside stiffly, and my suspicions were confirmed.

Rigel was there, in the classroom.

He was still sitting down, as if he had stayed behind to finish reading a last paragraph. He was putting a book into his backpack. Next to him was a cascade of glossy hair.

I recognised her straight away. The girl who had stopped outside the music room the day that he had played the piano. She was, to say the least, stunning. Her soft and slender body made her look like a fairy. She was standing close to his desk, and I noticed that her hands were extremely well cared for. Her nails had a light polish on them, and her fingers were perfect and slender, so different to mine, which were covered in scratches and Band-Aids. And her long fingers were holding . . .

A red rose.

'Are you expecting me to take that?' Rigel asked, aloof and derisive. He didn't turn a hair, but there was still that intimidating flame in his gaze that would make anyone feel uncomfortable.

'Well . . . that would be nice.'

That whisper had a strange effect on me. It upset me. Rigel zipped up his backpack and then got up from his seat.

'I'm not nice.'

He passed her and walked out into the corridor, but she reached her hand out and grabbed his backpack strap.

'What are you like then?' she asked, trying to get his attention. But he didn't turn around, refusing to give it to her. She took a step forward, approaching his broad back.

'I want to get to know you. I've wanted to since the first time I saw you, that first day, when you were playing the piano,' she said softly. 'I'd like us to get to know each other better . . .'

She lifted up the rose, fixing her eyes on his.

'You could take this . . . and tell me something about yourself. There are still so many things that I don't know about you, Rigel Wilde,' she said seductively. 'Like . . . what type of guy are you?'

Rigel was no longer facing the door.

He stood there staring down at the rose, his dark hair framing his perfect, frozen features, and his eyes were flat and expressionless. They were impenetrable. Indifferent. Like walls of black diamond, devoid of any emotion. They were empty, cold and distant, like dead stars.

He looked up at her. And I could tell that he was about to show his charming mask.

Rigel lifted a corner of his mouth . . . and he smiled. Smiled in his persuasive, enticing way. It was breathtaking, that crooked smile. It poisoned you with malice then lured you in seductively. It was the grin of a beast who let no one near.

He lifted his hand and closed it around the flower, resolutely holding her gaze. He squeezed it, and his fingers squashed the petals until it disintegrated. Ragged petals fell to the ground like a fistful of dead butterfly wings.

'I'm a *complicated* guy,' he whispered, in response to the girl's question.

The sound of his low, gravelly voice sent a shiver down my spine.

Then he turned around and left the room. He disappeared through the door.

But I could still hear him. As if he was still there.

His voice had carved a path inside of me.

It was like he had violently, silently, bruised the air.

I jumped as a hand touched my shoulder. I whirled around and saw Billie looking at me, confused.

'Did I scare you?' she giggled. 'Sorry! I found my bottle. I had to argue with the janitor but I got it in the end!' She showed it to me triumphantly, and I stared without really seeing it.

We filled it with water from the faucet and then turned around. Billie started talking again but I wasn't listening.

I was still thinking about Rigel.

The polite mask he hid behind.

His cynical, insolent smile, as if he thought that girl's attempt to get closer to him had been amusing and pitiful.

How did he do it? How did he manage to be that bewitching?

How did he manage to melt you with one look, and then make you freeze in terror with the next?

What was Rigel made of? Flesh or nightmares?

Billie glimpsed Miki in the crowd and rushed towards her, as radiant as a sunflower.

'Miki! Look! This year too!'

Miki distractedly, wearily, looked at the rose, and Billie smiled. 'It's white!'

'Like it is every year . . .' Miki muttered, opening her locker. One of the roses fell down and she tried not to take any notice as she shoved her books inside, amongst the tangle of leaves and stems.

Billie bent down to pick it up for her and held it out with a happy smile. Miki froze. She stared at her for a moment, then slowly took it from her. I watched her blinking, then she shoved it into the locker along with the others.

'Umm . . . do you think it will be all right with all this water? It's not too much? I don't want to drown it . . . What do you think, Nica?' Billie asked, turning to face me, and I replied that flowers could do many extraordinary things, but drowning wasn't one of them.

'Are you sure?' she asked. 'I don't want to kill her, she seems so delicate . . .'

'Excuse me?' someone interrupted.

A boy was standing behind Miki, holding something bright red in his hands.

'Excuse me?' He smiled confidently. Billie and I watched him as he fervently poked her shoulder. He suddenly went pale when Miki turned around, her eyes flashing angrily.

'*What do you want?*' she snarled, about as sweet as a raging bull.

'I just wanted . . .' The boy faltered. He fumbled with the rose and Miki's glare turned even more fierce.

'*What?*'

'N . . . no . . . nothing,' he retreated hastily, hiding the flower behind his back. He laughed nervously, then fled like his feet were aflame.

There was a moment of silence as we watched him run away.

'It has to be said,' Billie said after a moment. 'You really do turn everyone on.'

Miki lifted her hands and Billie gave an entertained little shriek.

They started bickering fervently, writhing like water snakes. I hid a smile and opened my locker.

The next moment . . .

The whole world stopped.

My smile faded and all noises were swallowed up by the black hole inside my locker.

Black.

Black like the night of a new moon.

I never thought that something so delicate could be so dark.

It was black like ink.

I was so upset I could hardly breathe. I reached in and brought it out of its metal cage. The black rose was like a bruise, thorny and wild, its petals doused with an enticing pathos.

It wasn't smooth and harmless like the others. No, its stem was covered in thorns that snagged on the Band-Aids on my fingers.

I stared at it in disbelief.

And this time, I didn't feel uncertainty, but clarity.

My heart was beating fast. Some mechanism in my brain had activated. I realised something that I should have already known. My books tumbled to the floor as I stepped backwards, holding the rose, my fingers finding purchase between the thorns.

I hadn't lost that photo.

I would never have lost it.

The more the certainty grew inside of me, the more the rose cut into my fingers, chasing away any doubt.

I turned around and started running.

The world blurred around me as I hurtled down the corridor, across the courtyard and through the gates, propelled by an unstoppable impulse.

People threw anxious looks at me, disturbed by the flower I was holding. 'It's black . . . there's never been a black rose . . .' they murmured, and the girls, slightly nervously, said, 'It's beautiful!'

It's black, black, black, kept thundering in my head as I ran straight home.

I shoved the key in the lock and dropped my backpack on the stairs, my jacket on the top step. And then I stopped in front of his door.

The thorns were still digging into my hands, scratching my skin in the gaps between the Band-Aids. It was as if I couldn't let it go.

As if it were proof. My suspicion becoming my reality, screaming *his* name.

It was crazy. Nonsensical. Illogical and absurd . . .

Had it been him? Had he taken the photo?

'Don't come into my room,' he had told me.

I vehemently turned the door handle and entered.

I hoped he wouldn't be there, because that afternoon he had detention. I closed the door behind me and looked around.

I took in the unfamiliar atmosphere. Everything was tidy and precise, the curtains were drawn, the bed made.

I couldn't help but notice the almost artificial tidiness of the room. It was as if Rigel had never slept there, despite his books on the nightstand and his clothes in the drawers.

Despite the fact that he spent most of his time here . . .

No.

I swallowed.

This *was* his room.

Rigel slept here, studied here, got dressed here. That was Rigel's shirt on the back of the chair, Rigel's towel poking out of the closet, his notebooks full of his elegant handwriting on the desk.

It was Rigel I could smell.

A strange discomfort came over me. It felt as though the thorns were even piercing through the Band-Aids now, urging me to hurry up.

I cautiously stepped towards the desk. I sifted through the stacks of paper, moved a few books, then looked in the closet, in the chest of drawers, even the pockets of his jackets.

I rummaged everywhere, taking care to put everything back exactly where it had been. I looked in every drawer of his nightstand, and found almost all of them empty, but the photo wasn't there.

It wasn't there . . .

I stood still in the middle of the room, wiping my wrist across my forehead.

I had looked everywhere.

Hold on, no. Not *everywhere* . . .

I turned towards the bed. I looked at the pillow, the perfectly tidy bedsheets, the tight corners, without a fold out of place. And then the mattress.

I remembered all the times I had hidden candy under my bed springs, so I could eat them without anyone seeing me. I remembered the popsicle sticks I put there so the matron wouldn't find them . . .

I should have heard him.

Maybe, if I hadn't reached out to lift the mattress up and found nothing underneath, I would have realised it sooner.

Maybe, if I hadn't been gripping the rose so tightly, I would have felt the icy cold that preceded his words.

'I *told* you . . . not to come into *my* room.'

I quickly fell into a darker reality.

I had walked into a trap.

Petrified, my eyes swung towards him.

Rigel was standing in the open doorway, dark and looming like only he could be.

Unbearable. There was no other word for it.

Narrow and feline, his black eyes shone like dark chasms, ready to swallow me up.

I couldn't move. Even my heart had frozen in my chest.

He looked so tall and terrible that he scared me. His tense shoulders and implacable eyes were like those of a nightmare guard.

And I had just stepped into his territory . . .

I was still trying to react when, slowly, without taking a step . . . he lifted his arm. He raised his hand and placed it on the door. Then he pushed it.

The long *click* of the latch turned me to stone.

He had just closed the door behind him.

'I . . .' I swallowed. 'I was just . . .'

'*Just?*' he snarled threateningly.

'. . . just looking for something.'

His glare was frighteningly cold. I clutched at the rose, not knowing what else to do with my hands.

'Something . . . in my room?'

'I was looking for a photo.'

'And did you find it?'

I hesitated, my lip trembling.

'No.'

'No,' he whispered emphatically, narrowing his eyes slightly.

His fearsome aura made me want to run as far away from him as possible.

'You come into the wolf's lair, Nica, and then you ask him not to tear you to pieces.'

I stiffened as he came near me.

The urge to retreat screamed at me loud and clear, but I didn't give in.

'Was it you?' I burst out, brandishing the black rose. 'Did you give me this?'

Rigel stopped. His cold and expressionless eyes fell to the flower, and he raised an eyebrow.

'Me?' he asked, failing to hide a hint of amusement in his voice. His lips curled into a mocking, spiteful smirk. 'Did *I* . . . give *you* . . . a flower?'

His words *stung* me, and all of my supposed certainties dissolved once more into doubt.

I lowered my eyes, hesitating in that way that so amused him, and the smirk on his lips glinted like a knife.

He took a few steps towards me and tore the rose out of my hands.

My mouth fell open as he grabbed the flower and started to tear it apart. A shower of black petals fell to the ground in front of me.

'No! No! Leave it!' I struggled to grab it off him. It was mine, despite everything, the rose was mine! It was an innocent gift, and now that Rigel had mocked it like that, I felt more than ever the need to defend it.

I scratched helplessly at his sleeves, but he just held it higher so that it was out of my reach.

He tore off every single petal, and in a fit of desperation I stretched up onto my tiptoes.

'Rigel, stop it!' I clutched at his chest. '*Stop it!*'

My eyes flew open as I lost my balance.

Instinctively, I grabbed on to him. He can't have been expecting it, because I managed to take him down with me.

I fell backwards onto the bed, the mattress breaking my fall.

I had no time to think anything at all before a weight landed on top of me, and the ceiling went blurry between my half-closed eyes. My vision was hazy, and I squeezed my eyes shut tight.

I felt something fall delicately on my hair and the hollow of my throat. They were petals. I barely registered them as a weight lifted up off my torso.

When my vision focused, my breath snagged in my throat.

Rigel's face was right in front of mine.

His body was looming above me.

It was all so unexpected that my heart jumped to my throat. His knee was between my thighs and the fabric of his pants was grazing my skin. His short breaths were hot and damp in my mouth, and his hands, eagle's talons, were on either side of my face.

It was only when our eyes met that I started to tremble. I noticed something in his gaze that I had never seen before, a gleam of light that made my throat go dry.

I saw myself reflected in his eyes. My lips had parted, my chest was rising and falling rhythmically and my cheeks were flushed. We were so close that it was like the heartbeat in my throat was his.

My astonishment was his.

My breath was his . . .

It was all his, even my soul.

I shivered violently. My mind was screaming hysterically and with a force I didn't know I had, I pushed him away.

I scrambled off the bed and fled from the room like a startled hare.

I stumbled into the hallway and dove into my own room, shut the door and slammed my back against it, sliding to the floor.

My heart was thumping painfully against my ribcage, I was overcome by shivers. My skin was reeling from his presence, as if I could still feel him all over me.

What was he doing to me?

What had he poisoned me with?

I tried to calm my breathing, but, inside me, something raged, burning hot.

He was whispering in my ears, playing with my heartbeat and walking through my thoughts.

He was feasting on my emotions, leaving me only with shivers.

It made no sense.

It knew no limits.

And it had nothing to do with . . . tenderness.

10. A Book

I couldn't move. My legs were trembling, my eyes blind. The darkness was too dense. My gaze was darting from side to side, as if hoping that someone would appear. My nails scraped against metal, convulsive and feverish, but I couldn't get free. I never could.

No one would come to save me. No one would answer my screams. My temples throbbed, my throat burned, my skin cracked under leather, and I was alone . . . alone . . .

Alone . . .

I woke with a stifled sob.

The room was spinning. My stomach was in knots. I sat up, gasping for air, trying to calm down, but cold sweat clung to my back, terror sinking into my skin.

Clammy shudders ran through me, and my heart threatened to burst out of my chest.

I curled up against the headboard and clutched my caterpillar plushie.

I was safe. That was another room, another place, another life . . .

But the feeling remained. It crushed me. It crumpled me up and sent me right back there, to that darkness. I went back to being a child again.

Perhaps I still was.

Perhaps I had never stopped being one. Something inside me had broken long ago, and remained small, childlike, innocent and frightened.

It had stopped growing.

And I knew . . . I knew I wasn't like the others, because as I grew up, that broken part of me stayed a child.

I still looked at the world with the same eyes.

I reacted with the same naïvety.

I searched for the light in others, just like I had searched in vain for it in *Her* when I was little.

I was like a butterfly in chains.

And maybe . . .

I always would be.

'Nica, are you okay?'

Billie was staring at me. Her head was tilted to one side, her bushy hair pushed back from her face with a headband.

I had been awake all night, trying to keep my nightmares at bay, and it showed on my face.

The darkness was unrelenting. A few nights, I had tried leaving the bedside lamp on, but Anna had noticed and, thinking I had just forgotten, came in to turn it off. I didn't have the courage to tell her that I would have preferred to sleep with a nightlight on like a little girl.

'Yeah,' I replied, trying to sound natural. 'How come?'

'I dunno . . . You look paler than usual.' She scrutinised my face. 'You seem tired . . . Did you sleep badly?'

Anxiety tightly wound itself around me. I was used to sudden, unwarranted reactions like this. I was often overcome by excessive worries that ate away at my most fragile and childlike self. It always happened when I thought back to *that*.

My palms were sweaty, my heart was so tight it felt as if it was about to burst, and all I wanted was to be unseen.

'Everything's fine,' I replied faintly. I wondered if I sounded convincing, but Billie seemed to genuinely believe me.

'If you want, I can give you the recipe for a calming herbal remedy,' she suggested. 'My grandma used to make it for me when I was a child . . . I'll message it you later!'

As soon as Anna had given me the phone, Billie had asked to exchange numbers and given me some tips on setting it up.

'I'll put a butterfly for you,' she told me as she saved my number in her contacts.

'Emojis,' she continued cheerfully. 'Grandma has a rolling pin. I put a panda for Miki, not that she deserves it. She saved me in her phone as a poop emoji . . .'

There was so much to learn. I could barely send a message without getting confused.

'Have you quite finished your conversations?' Mr Kryll said indignantly. 'You're not here to socialise. This is a classroom! *Silence!*'

The chatter faded away. Mr Kryll inspected the students one by one as we filed into the laboratory. He told us to put on protective goggles and threatened to suspend anyone caught misusing the equipment.

'Why do you write your address on the front of your books?' Billie whispered to me as I pushed my biology textbook to the corner of the desk we shared.

I looked at the label with my name, subject, year, and address written down.

'Why? Is that weird?' I asked, embarrassed, remembering how happy I had been to write my address down. 'So if I lose it, they'll know who it belongs to, right?'

'Your name's not enough for that?' she chuckled, making me blush.

Maybe it will be confusing . . .

'Are you all quite ready?' barked Kryll, demanding everyone's attention.

I adjusted my goggles and tucked my hair behind my ears.

I was on tenterhooks. I had never done a lab before!

I put on the plastic gloves and took note of how they felt against my skin.

'I hope he doesn't make us disembowel eels like last time,' someone behind me murmured. I raised my eyebrows with an uncertain smile.

Disembowel?

'All right,' announced Kryll. 'You may now place the materials on the table.'

I reached towards a small folder, which had a pen attached by a string.

Kryll continued, 'And remember, the scalpel doesn't cut through bone.'

'The scalpel doesn't cut . . . what?' I asked innocently, before making the mistake of lowering my gaze.

My blood ran cold.

A lifeless frog lay spreadeagled on the metal cutting board.

I stared at it in horror. The blood drained from my face. Two boys in front of me were inspecting the row of knives like butchers. A short distance away, a girl pulled on her gloves with a crisp snap. Near the door, someone was hunching over their frog, but it definitely wasn't to perform mouth-to-mouth resuscitation. I suddenly realised.

Help!

I turned around just in time to glimpse Kryll leaving what looked like a torture chamber: a cupboard full of jars, vials and containers filled with beetles, centipedes and cicadas.

My stomach dropped.

Billie lifted the scalpel with a smile.

'Do you want to make the first incision?' she asked as if we were talking about meatloaf.

I was sure I was going to faint.

I grabbed the edge of the table. The folder slipped from my hands.

'Nica, what's wrong? Are you okay?' she asked me.

Someone in front of us turned around to see what was going on.

'I . . . No,' I swallowed, pale.

'You're going green . . .' she observed, watching me closely. 'You aren't afraid of frogs, are you? Relax, look, it's already dead! *Dead—as–a–doornail!* See? Look!' She started poking it with the scalpel under my horrified eyes.

My goggles fogged up from my breathing, and for the first time in my life, I found myself praying that I'd be sent to go stand outside the classroom.

No, not this. I couldn't take it. I really couldn't . . .

'I can't believe it,' a voice behind me said, 'the guardian of the snails is afraid of a little frog . . .'

At the table behind mine, I recognised the guy I had met at the wall and then seen again at the mall.

He flashed a smile, his protective goggles perched on the top of his head.

'Hey, snail girl.'

'Hi . . .' I whispered. He gave me a look as if he wanted to say something, but a moment later, Kryll barked at us to get back to work.

'Don't worry, Nica, I'll deal with it,' Billie reassured me, seeing me using the folder as a shield. 'It's clear this is your first lab! You've got nothing to be ashamed of, okay? It's a piece of cake! Let's make a deal: I'll do the cutting, and you write down what happens.'

I nodded reluctantly, glancing around.

I took a furtive, pitying look at the frog and regretted it instantly. Billie grinned, brandishing the scalpel.

'All right! Now . . . don't get splashed!'

I flinched as I heard a slimy squelch. I held the folder so close to my face that all I could see was a blurry white.

'Here it is! The heart! Or is it a lung? Oh, my goodness, it's so squishy . . . it's such a weird colour! Look at this . . . Nica, are you taking notes?'

I nodded stiffly, scribbling feverishly.

'Oh, my *goodness* . . .' I heard her murmur.

I turned the page gingerly, with spidery fingers.

'Oh, it's so slimy . . . Listen to the squishy sound it makes . . . *eww* . . .'

Perhaps it was providence. Destiny. Salvation.

Whatever it was, it came in the form of a piece of paper.

I found it on the table next to me.

I opened it with trembling hands and saw one simple word written inside:

'Hey.'

Someone cleared their throat behind me. I turned around. The boy had his back to me, but I saw the torn corner of a sheet of paper in his folder.

I opened my mouth uncertainly, but before I could say anything, I jumped as: 'Dover!' Kryll shouted. 'What have you got there?' My eyes widened as everyone turned to look at me.

Oh, no!

'W-where?' I stammered.

'There! You've got something, I saw you!' He came towards me quickly, and I glanced around frantically. Panic overwhelmed me.

What would Anna and Norman say if they found out I wasn't paying attention in class? That I had been caught passing notes?

I didn't know what to do. I couldn't even think. I saw the teacher marching furiously towards me, and desperately, impulsively, I turned around and stuffed the note into my mouth.

I chewed like a madwoman, really going at it like I had few times in my difficult life.

And as if I wasn't ashamed enough, behind me was the very boy who had passed me the note. I glanced round and he was facing me, astonished. I swallowed it right in front of his eyes.

I had survived. In body, at least.

Kryll wasn't best pleased to see my hands were empty.

He looked at me suspiciously, then told me to pay more attention and get back to work.

I wondered what he would have thought if he had seen me later hurrying along the sidewalk with my arms wrapped tightly around myself as if I had a stomach ache.

When I was far enough away, I snuck a furtive glance over my shoulder.

I was by the bridge, on the grassy riverbank. I knelt down and unzipped my hoodie.

A beetle was scurrying around inside the jar in my hands. I watched it through the strands of hair that fell over my face.

'Don't worry,' I whispered to him, as if it was our secret. 'I got you out of there.'

I unscrewed the lid and lowered the jar to the ground. The beetle stayed inside, too terrified to come out.

'Go,' I whispered, 'before someone sees you . . .'

I turned the jar over and he fell out into the grass, but still didn't move.

I watched him. He was little, different. Many others would have found him disgusting, horrifying, but I only felt sorry for him. Some people wouldn't have noticed him at all, he was so insignificant. Others would have killed him because, in their eyes, he was too ugly to live.

'You can't stay here . . . they'll hurt you,' I whispered bitterly. 'People don't understand . . . they're scared. They'll squash you just so they don't have to be near you.'

The world wasn't used to freaks like us. They shut us away in institutions to forget us, to keep us far away, in the dust, forgetting we existed because that was more convenient. No one wanted us around, just seeing us made them uncomfortable.

I knew this only too well.

'Go on . . .' I scraped the ground next to him and he unfurled his wings. He took flight and disappeared from view. I sighed with relief, my heart lighter. 'Bye bye . . .'

'Oh, wow . . . and I thought it was just lunatics who talked to themselves . . .'

I tried to hide the jar. I was not alone. There were two girls looking at me with sarcastic pity. One of them was the girl who had given the red rose to Rigel. I recognised her shining hair and manicured hands.

When our gazes crossed, she smiled, still with that fake pity.

'You'll scare the pigeons like that.'

My stomach twisted with shame. Had they seen me freeing the bug from the lab store? I hoped not, otherwise I'd be in serious trouble.

'I wasn't doing anything,' I said quickly. My voice sounded feeble and too high, and they burst out laughing.

I instantly understood that it wasn't what I was doing that they found funny, but me.

They were laughing at me.

' "*I wasn't doing anything*," ' the other girl mocked. 'How old are you? You're like a little kid straight out of elementary school.' They stared at my colourful Band-Aids, and my insecurities swallowed me, just like they did when I was little.

They were right. In their presence I shrank into a little child, a stupid, weird little creature with scratched hands and dull, grey skin, like a gremlin kept indoors for too long. They had seen me when I was in my own little world, when I was at my most vulnerable.

'The kiddies in the kindergarten down the street have imaginary friends too. Maybe you could go and talk to them.' They laughed. 'You can share your juice box . . . No fighting, though. Go on, go play with your little friends,' the girl who had given Rigel the rose kicked my backpack.

I jerked it closer to me, and she stepped on my hand. I flinched in pain and watched her, bewildered, unable to understand why she was behaving like this. She looked down at me scornfully.

'Maybe they'll teach you not to eavesdrop. Didn't your parents tell you it's rude?'

'Nica!' a voice interrupted.

Behind them, a not-too-tall figure was watching us warily, fists clenched at her sides.

It was Miki.

'What are you doing?' she asked sharply.

The girl turned that mocking smile on her. 'Oh, look who's here. I didn't know this was where they were holding the freak convention.' She put her painted nails to her lips. 'How sweet! Shall I make you some tea?'

'Here's a better idea,' Miki retorted. 'Why don't you both get the hell out of here?'

Something in the girl's face shifted, but her friend lowered her gaze and hid behind her.

'What did you say, bitch?'

'Hey, let's go . . .' her companion tried.

'Don't you have some veins to cut?'

'Right,' Miki burst out. 'I've got the razor right here, why don't we start with yours?'

'Come on,' the other girl whispered again, gently tugging her friend's sleeve.

The girl looked Miki up and down with a disgusted scowl.

'Weirdo loser,' she said slowly, repulsed. Then she turned around and the two of them walked away without looking back.

When they were far enough away, Miki looked down at me.

'Did they push you?'

I looked up at her as I got up off the ground.

'No,' I replied in a fragile voice.

She searched my face warily, as if she was trying to read me. I hoped she wouldn't see how humiliated I was.

'What are you doing here?' I asked, trying to change the subject. 'Are you getting the bus home?'

Miki hesitated. She glanced towards the junction about twenty metres down the road.

'I'm getting picked up down the street,' she answered reluctantly. I followed her gaze.

'Oh . . . How come?'

I hoped I didn't sound nosy. In truth, I was just still reeling with too much shame to be tactful.

'Just because.'

Maybe Miki didn't want others to see who was picking her up or how she was getting home. Maybe she felt awkward, so I respected her silence and didn't ask any more questions.

'I have to go,' she said when her phone rang from her pocket. She glanced at the screen without unlocking it, and I nodded, tucking my hair behind my ears.

'Bye,' I said. 'See you tomorrow.'

She headed off without ceremony. I watched her walk away along the sidewalk, and then my voice got the better of me.

'Miki!'

She turned to look at me.

I watched her for a moment. And then . . .

Then I smiled. I smiled with soft, calm eyes, as the wind tousled my hair.

'Thank you.'

Miki looked at me for a long time, saying nothing. It was as if, for the first time, she was finally able to see me.

I got back home a few minutes later.

The warmth of the entrance hall embraced me like it always did. I felt held, enveloped, safe.

I froze when I saw Rigel's jacket hanging up on one of the hooks.

The thought of him suddenly overwhelmed me, and before I knew it, my heart was stirring.

Now that he no longer had detention, I'd have to get used to him being around all the time.

I had been trying not to think of him all morning. The memory of his breath on my mouth made me tremble like never before.

It wasn't normal, the effect he had on me.

It wasn't normal that I could still feel him on my skin.

It wasn't normal, the way in which the sound of his voice made my blood boil.

There was nothing normal about it, maybe there never had been.

I wished I could forget him. Wash him away. Shrug him off.

But it took nothing at all for me to fall back into those feelings . . .

The doorbell rang unexpectedly, shaking me from my thoughts.

I jumped and turned towards the front door.

Who could it be, at that time of day? Anna was at the shop, and I was sure it wouldn't be Norman — he was dedicating every spare moment to preparing for the imminent conference.

I peered through the obscure glass, then opened the door.

It was the last person I would have ever expected to see.

'Hi.' The boy raised a hand to greet me.

It was him. The lab. The mall. The snail.

I stared at him in astonishment.

What was he doing there?

'Sorry to burst in on you like this . . . um . . . are you busy?' he asked, scratching his neck.

I shook my head, surprised by the unexpected visit.

'Okay. I . . . I just came by to give you this,' he said, holding something out to me. 'I hope I'm not interrupting, but you left this in the lab.'

It was my biology book. I took it warily, surprised at myself.

Had I forgotten it? How was that possible? I was sure that the desk was empty when I left the lab. Had I not noticed it in my rush to take the jar?

'I saw the address and, well . . . I happened to be passing by . . .'

I wondered what was happening to me. I had never in my life allowed myself the luxury of being so distracted that I left my belongings all over the place. First the photo, now the book . . .

'Thanks,' I replied, holding it tightly. He stood still as my pale eyes gently met his. I looked down and touched the tip of my nose. 'I've been losing everything lately,' I joked a little nervously, trying to downplay this new, unfamiliar side to my personality. 'I really don't know where I . . .'

'I'm Lionel.'

I looked up. He seemed embarrassed. He glanced down, before looking into my eyes again.

'My name is Lionel. We haven't introduced ourselves yet, I don't think.'

He was right. I hugged the book to myself shyly.

'I'm Nica,' I replied.

'Yes, I know.'

He flashed a smile and pointed at the label with my name on it on the cover of the book.

'Oh, of course . . .'

'Well, that's certainly a step forward, don't you think? At least now you know my name, if there are any snails about . . .'

He laughed. My nose crinkled as a smile curved across my cheeks.

His kindness was like a fresh breeze. I couldn't help but think about how selfless it had been for him to come all this way just to bring me my book.

Lionel had thick blond hair and a friendly laugh that reached his hazel eyes. There was something genuine in those eyes, something that made me feel very calm.

But suddenly, his face changed.

He looked over my shoulder.

A faint shift in the air was all it took for me to understand.

The next moment, slender fingers came to settle on the door knocker just above my head. A pale hand, with a broad, well-defined wrist set off alarm bells in my mind. I froze. Every inch of my skin reacted to his presence.

'Are you lost?'

God, *his* voice. That breathy, piercing voice. It rang in my ears, so close that I shuddered fiercely.

I gripped the book, praying that Rigel would move away from me.

'No, I . . . I was just passing by. I'm Lionel.' He watched Rigel cautiously. 'I also go to Burnaby.'

Rigel said nothing, and the silence was so uncomfortable that my skin crawled and I bit the inside of my cheek. I burst out, 'Lionel brought me a book that I'd forgotten.'

I was sure I could feel Rigel's gaze on the back of my head.

'Well, how *kind*.'

Lionel tilted his head, watching him carefully. Rigel always made people feel out of sorts, caused a discomfort that was hard to explain.

'Yeah, I . . .' he said, staring intently at Rigel. 'Me and Nica have practicals together with Mr Kryll. I'm her lab partner. You?' he asked, his hands in his pockets, as if to ask, 'And who might you be?'

Rigel leant against the doorframe and stared at Lionel with brazen self-assurance, the corners of his mouth mockingly upturned. It was only then that I noticed that he wasn't wearing a sweater or hoodie. A plain t-shirt closely hugged his chiselled chest.

'Can't you guess?'

He said it in that insinuating voice of his, that characteristic way of casting doubt, as if his being in the same house as me was open to multiple interpretations.

They exchanged a look I didn't understand, but when Rigel looked down at me, it was clear that he knew he had got the last word.

'Anna's on the phone,' he said. 'She wants to speak to you.'

I took a step away from him and glanced into the living room.

Anna wanted to speak to me?

'Thanks again for this. Really,' I stammered to Lionel, not knowing what to say. 'I've got to go, see you soon!'

I made a hasty goodbye and ran towards the phone. He leant towards me and I had the impression that he was about to say something, but Rigel spoke first.

'See you, Leonard.'

'Actually, it's Lio—'

The door slammed in his face.

11. White Butterfly

There's a mystery in each of us.
It's the only answer to who we are.

I always thought that Rigel was like the moon.

A black moon who kept his face hidden from everyone, shining in the darkness, eclipsing the stars.

But I was wrong.

Rigel was like the sun.

Limitless, burning, unapproachable.

He was blazing. Dazzling.

He scorched my mind bare, cast shadows inside of me that consumed all thought.

When I got home, his jacket was already there. I wished I could have said I didn't care, but that would have been a lie.

Things were *different* when he was there.

My eyes searched for him.

My heart fell.

I could get no peace, I couldn't stop thinking about him. The only way to avoid his penetrating eyes was to stay shut in my room all the time, until Anna and Norman got home.

I hid away from him, but the truth was that there was something that frightened me much more than the cutting cruelty of his gaze and his cold, volatile temperament. Something that stirred inside me, even when we were rooms apart.

But one afternoon, I decided to set aside my concerns and go down into the garden for a bit of sun.

Around here, February was pleasant, grey and cool. Our winters had never been too harsh. For people like me who were born and raised in South Alabama, it was not difficult to imagine seasons so mild, bare trees and rainy streets, white clouds at dawn and, already, the scent of spring.

I loved to feel the grass between my toes again.

I was studying in the dappled sunlight under the apricot tree, savouring a moment of peace.

Then, a sound caught my attention.

I got to my feet, intrigued. But my high hopes were dashed when I found out what was making the noise.

It was a hornet. One of its legs was stuck in the mud. When it tried to fly away its wings made a loud buzzing sound.

Despite my usual sympathy for the plight of animals in peril, I found myself staring at it in terror. I thought bees were really cute, with their stumpy legs and furry little bodies, but hornets had always quite frightened me.

I had got stung quite badly a few years previously. It had hurt for days, and I didn't want to relive that pain.

But he carried on thrashing about so uselessly and desperately that my sentimentality got the better of me. I approached cautiously, torn between fear and pity. Tensely, I tried to help him with a twig, but I jumped away with a sharp yelp when he started that furious buzzing again. I went back with my tail between my legs, distressed. I wanted to try to help him again.

'Don't sting me, please,' I begged as the twig snapped in the mud. 'Don't sting me . . .'

When I managed to free him, relief flooded through my chest. For a moment, I almost smiled.

Then he took flight.

And I blanched.

I threw the twig away and ran like mad. I hid my face in my hands, squealing in a shamefully childish way. I tripped over my own feet and fell over. I only avoided hitting the paved driveway as someone caught me at just the last moment.

'What . . .' I heard a voice behind me. 'Are you mad?'

I whirled around, astonished, gripping the hands that held me. He was staring at me, dumbfounded.

'Lionel?'

I was surprised to see him here. What was he doing in the garden?

'I swear,' he said, embarrassed, 'I'm not stalking you.'

He pulled me up and I brushed some dirt off my clothes. He gestured towards the road.

'I live nearby. A few blocks that way . . . I was passing by and I heard you screaming. It scared the living daylights out of me,' he said, scowling. 'What were you doing, exactly?'

'Nothing. There was an insect . . .' I hesitated, casting my eyes around for the hornet. 'I got scared.'

He looked at me with a furrowed brow.

'And . . . you couldn't have just killed it, rather than screaming?'

'Of course not. How is it his fault I was scared of him?' I frowned, slightly annoyed.

Lionel watched me for a while, surprised.

'But . . . you're all right?' he asked, looking down at my bare feet.

I nodded slowly, and it seemed like he couldn't think of anything else to say.

'Okay . . .' he murmured, staring at his shoes. Then he glanced up at me. 'Bye, then.'

As he turned away, I realised I hadn't even thanked him. Lionel had caught me as I was falling, he had rushed towards me to check I was okay.

He had always been so nice to me . . .

'Wait!'

I saw him turn around. I realised I had rushed towards him a little too enthusiastically.

'Do . . . do you want a popsicle?'

He looked at me, dumbfounded.

'In . . . winter?' he asked, but I nodded, keeping my face expressionless.

He scrutinised me for a long time. Then he seemed to understand that I was being serious.

'Okay.'

'Popsicles in February,' Lionel remarked while I happily licked mine.

We were sat on the sidewalk. I had given him one that tasted like green apples.

I adored popsicles. When Anna had found out she bought me the ones with gummy animals frozen inside and I had stared at her as if struck by lightning, unable to express how much I adored her.

I chatted a little with Lionel. I asked him where he lived, if he had to cross the bridge with all the shouting workmen.

He was easy to talk to. Every now and then he would interrupt me, but I didn't really mind.

He asked me how long I had been here, how I liked the town, and as I replied, it felt as though he was stealing glances at me.

At a certain point he asked me about Rigel. I felt the tension rising, like it always did when he came up in a conversation.

'I didn't realise he was your brother at first,' he confided, after I had vaguely explained that Rigel was a relative. He stared at the gummy crocodile in his palm before eating it.

'What did you think he was?' I asked. I tried not to dwell on what Lionel had called Rigel. Every time I heard him described as my brother I felt the irrepressible urge to scratch something with my fingernails.

Lionel snorted and shook his head.

'Don't worry about it,' he evaded calmly.

He didn't ask me anything about my childhood. And I made no mention of The Grave. Nor of the fact that the boy inside the house wasn't really my brother.

It was nice to pretend I was normal. No institutes, no matrons, no mattresses with springs poking through.

Just . . . Nica.

'Wait, don't throw it away!' I stopped Lionel quickly as he started to break his popsicle stick. He looked at me, perplexed, as I took it from him.

'Why?'

'I'll keep it,' I said quietly.

He gave me a look that was halfway between amused and intrigued.

'What for? You're not one of those people who build scale models in their spare time, are you?'

'Oh, no. I use them to splint the sparrows' wings when they get hurt.'

Lionel was speechless. Then, he seemed to decide that I was joking and started laughing.

He watched me thoughtfully as I got up and brushed the dirt off the back of my jeans.

'Listen, Nica . . .'

'Hm?' I turned and smiled at him. I saw the reflection of my ocean grey eyes in his. He was transfixed, unable to utter a word. His lips parted and he stared at me, utterly bewildered.

'You . . . you . . . your eyes . . .' he stammered. I frowned.

'What?' I asked, tilting my head to one side.

He shook his head hastily. He lifted a hand to his face and glanced away from me.

'Nothing.'

I watched him, not understanding, but I forgot about it when it came to saying goodbye. I still had homework to finish.

'See you tomorrow at school.' I headed towards the walkway and Lionel seemed to grasp that it was time to go.

He hesitated, then looked up.

'We could swap numbers,' he blurted out all of a sudden, as if it had been on the tip of his tongue for some while.

I blinked. He cleared his throat.

'Yeah, you know . . . that way if I miss class, I can ask you for the homework.'

'But we're not in the same class,' I reminded him innocently.

'Y . . . yeah, well, we are for labs though,' he stressed. 'I might miss some *important* dissection . . . You never know . . . Then again, who listens to Kryll . . . But it doesn't matter, no worries if you don't want to . . . You just have to say . . .'

He continued gesticulating wildly, and I couldn't help but think he was a little strange.

I shook my head, to stop his torrent of words. Then I smiled.

'Okay.'

That evening, Anna got home earlier than expected.

There were just a few days to go until the pest control conference, and she had asked me if there was anything I needed her to buy me.

'It'll just be a day trip,' she told me. 'We'll leave at dawn, the flight's an hour and a half. We'll get back after dinner, probably around midnight. Your phone is working okay, right? You've been making calls all right? If you need anything at all . . .'

'We'll be fine,' I reassured her gently. I didn't want to ruin an important event that Norman had been building up to for years. 'We'll manage, Anna, you don't need to worry at all. Me and Rigel . . .'

But I froze. His name stuck in my throat like a shard of glass.

It was only then that I realised I would have to stay home with him for an entire day. With only his presence to fill the silent rooms. With only the sound of his footsteps and his intense eyes . . .

'Wh . . . what?' I roused myself.

'Could you go and call Rigel?' Anna repeated, putting a few packets of passata on the side. 'I want to speak to him about this too.'

I tensed. The idea of going to fetch him, of going near him, or standing again in the threshold to his room immobilised me from head to foot.

But she looked up at me. I pursed my lips.

I'll be good, a voice inside me whispered.

Anna knew nothing about the twisted relationship between me and Rigel.

And that's how it had to stay.

Or I'd risk losing her . . .

I moved almost mechanically, and without uttering a word I did as she asked.

I discovered that Rigel was not in his room. The door was ajar, but he wasn't inside.

I looked for him all over, peering into every room in the house, but I couldn't find him anywhere. Eventually, reason led me outside.

The last few glimmers of the sunset lit up the gardenia flowers. Dark branches stood out like arteries and capillaries against the beautiful orange light.

I walked along the porch, my bare feet kissing the wood. I paused as my gaze fell on him.

He was in the back garden.

He was half-turned away from me, the twilight bathed his clothes, making his dark hair glint unexpectedly, like blood.

I only glimpsed a sliver of his face. He was surrounded by such a perfect silence that I felt like I was intruding. I stayed there watching him from afar like I always had, and I couldn't help but wonder why he was standing there.

There, right there, in that quiet, with his hands deep in his pockets and that jumper that was a little bit too big around his neck, his soft shoulders and the slight breeze brushing against his wrists . . .

You're watching him too much, I chastised myself. *You shouldn't.*

But before I glanced away, a fluttering caught my eye.

A white butterfly was flying about the garden, dancing here and there. It slipped among the leafy tree branches then suddenly landed on Rigel's jumper.

It had landed over his heart, innocent and brave. Or maybe just crazy and hopeless.

My eyes rushed back to his face, and I stared at him with an urgent concern.

Rigel tilted his head. His eyelashes brushed his prominent cheekbones as he lowered his gaze to her, her wings unfurled in the fading sun, fragile and unaware.

Then he lifted his arm, and before she could fly away, he closed his fingers around her.

My heart plummeted.

With a tightness in my chest, I waited for him to crush her. I anticipated how he would suffocate her, as I'd seen many of the other
children at The Grave do.

I was so tense that it felt as though it was *me* he was holding in his
palm. I waited and waited and . . .

Rigel unclenched his fist.

The butterfly was still there. She crawled up his hand, innocent
and carefree, and he stayed there watching her with the sunset in his
eyes and the breeze tousling his hair.

He watched her fly away. He turned his face up to the sky and
before my eyes, something happened that I'd never seen before.

I stared at him. He had always suited shadows and black pits,
bruises and darkness, and so I was surprised to see him look so good
enveloped in that warm, bright light. I had thought that darkness was
almost perfect for him – an exiled angel, a beautiful Lucifer condemned to curse paradise for ever more.

But at that moment . . .

Watching him in that brightness, in such warm, soft light, I realised that he had never looked so magnificent.

You're watching him too much, my heart murmured. *You've always
watched him too much, but he destroys and he scratches and ensnares. He's the
Tearsmith, he's the ink the tale's written in. You shouldn't, you shouldn't.* I
clenched my fists, squeezed my arms, became tense all over. I was
about to break apart at the sight of him.

'Rigel.'

He lowered his eyelids. He turned and his dark eyes probed deep
inside of me.

My skin burned and I regretted all the time I had spent watching
him. I regretted that I wasn't able to hold his gaze without feeling like
he was possessing some part of me.

'Anna's looking for you.'

You've always watched him too much.

I rushed away, fleeing from the sight of him. And yet it felt like a
part of me stayed there, trapped forever in that moment.

'He's on his way,' I told Anna before leaving the kitchen.

I was a victim of ill-defined emotions that I couldn't shake off.

I tried to remember how he had destroyed the rose, how he had kicked me out of his room, how he had warned me to stay away from him. I remembered how he had always looked at me with scorn, harshness and contempt, and I got scared by emotions that, despite everything, gave me no respite.

I should have hated him. Wished he would disappear. And yet . . . and yet . . .

I couldn't stop looking for the light in him.

I couldn't give up.

Rigel was enigmatic, cynical, and as deceitful as the devil. How much more proof of this did I need before I would give up?

I spent the rest of the day in my room, tormented by my thoughts.

After dinner, Anna and Norman suggested a walk around the block, but I declined. I wouldn't have been able to enjoy their company, nor behave as cheerful and carefree as I wanted to, so I watched them leave with a hint of melancholy.

I wavered on the steps before deciding to go back upstairs.

I was climbing the stairs when suddenly, angelic music filled the air.

My legs froze and my breath caught in my throat.

A bewitching melody came to life behind me. Everything else became background for that music which accompanied the slightly frantic beating of my heart.

I turned towards the piano.

I was caught in a net of invisible spiderwebs. I should have been sensible and gone back upstairs. Instead . . . my feet carried me to the doorway of the room.

I found him there, his back turned, his black hair haloed by the lamplight. On top of the piano there was a beautiful crystal vase in which Anna had arranged a bouquet of flowers. I glimpsed his pale hands, moving fluidly and deftly across the keys, the source of that invisible magic. I was entranced, aware that he hadn't noticed me.

I had always had the impression that he was expressing something through his playing. That despite being so silent, this was his way of speaking. There was a wordless language in the music that I had never been able to interpret, but now . . . I wished I could understand what his notes were saying.

I had never heard him play lively or joyful pieces. There was always something inexplicably heart-wrenching in his music.

After a while, Klaus leapt onto the piano. He approached Rigel and sniffed him, as if he thought he knew him.

Rigel's fingers slowly came to a stop. He turned to face the cat, then lifted him by the scruff of the neck to put him on the floor. But suddenly, his shoulders stiffened. His fingers plunged violently into Klaus's fur. The cat wriggled and hissed, but it was no use. Rigel stood up and threw him away. His claws scratched the piano keys and he knocked over the vase of flowers, which crashed noisily to the ground, shattering into a thousand pieces. The violence of the scene in front of me made my heart leap to my throat.

I was scared witless. That moment of peace had been torn to shreds by blind fury. I stumbled backwards, overwhelmed, and fled up the stairs.

Panic came over me in waves, my thundering heartbeat clouded my mind, bringing back a faint, distant memory . . .

'He frightens me.'

'Who?'

Peter didn't reply. He was shy, skinny, scared of everything. But this time there was something different shining in his eyes.

'Him . . .'

Even though I was only a little girl, I knew who he was talking about. We were all scared of him, because Rigel was strange, even by our standards.

'There's something wrong with him.'

'What do you mean?' I asked uncertainly.

'He's violent.' Peter trembled. 'He hits and hurts anyone, just for the fun of it. I see him sometimes . . . tearing up fistfuls of grass. It's like he's out of his mind. He scrapes at it like an animal. He's savage and angry, all he knows is pain.'

I swallowed and looked at him through the strands of hair that had come loose from my braids.

'You've got nothing to be scared of,' I assured him in a little voice. 'You haven't done anything to him.'

'Why you, then? What did you do to him?'

I picked at the edges of my Band-Aids, not knowing how to respond. Rigel made me cry despairingly, but I didn't know why. I just knew that every day, he seemed more and more like that bedtime story.

'You don't see him,' Peter whispered in a ghost-like voice. 'You don't hear him, but me . . . I'm in the same room as him.' He turned to look at me and the expression on his face frightened me. 'You don't know how many things he's torn apart for no reason. He wakes up in the dead of night and screams at me to get out. You see how he smiles, sometimes? You know that sneer of his? He's not like other people. He's crazy and cruel. He's evil, Nica. We should all stay far away from him.'

12. Akrasia*

> The soul that snarls, hisses and scratches
> Is usually the most vulnerable.

Violent and cruel.

That's how he was described.

He manipulated when he wanted to bewitch, and was terrible on the flipside.

Rigel would show me the blood on his hands, the scratches on his face, the hardness in his eyes when he was hurting someone. He snarled at me to stay away, while his dark, mocking smile seemed to dare me to do the opposite.

He was not a prince. He was a wolf. Maybe all wolves looked a little enchanting, sensitive and prince-like, or else Little Red Riding Hood wouldn't have fallen for it.

I knew I had to accept this.

There was no glimmer of light.

No hope.

Not with someone like Rigel.

Why couldn't I understand him?

'We're ready,' Norman called out. The day of departure had come

---

* Akrasia: acting in a way contrary to one's sincerely held beliefs.

too soon, and as I placed their luggage at the bottom of the stairs, I felt a strange and inexpressible sense of sadness.

I met Anna's gaze and realised that it was because I wouldn't see her again until late that evening.

I knew I was overly attached, but seeing them leaving gave me a strange sense of abandonment that made me feel like a little girl again.

'Will you be all right?' Anna worried. The idea of leaving us for a whole day concerned her, especially in this delicate stage of the adoption process. I knew she didn't think it was a good time to leave, but I had reassured her that we'd see each other again that evening and that we'd still be here when she got back.

'We'll call you when we land.' She rearranged her scarf and I nodded, trying to smile. Rigel was standing just a short distance behind me.

'Remember to feed Klaus,' Norman reminded us and, despite everything, I lit up. I looked uneasily down at the cat, who glared at me before showing us his butt and strutting away.

Anna squeezed Rigel's shoulder and looked at me. She smiled and tucked a lock of hair behind my ear.

'See you this evening,' she said tenderly.

I stood there close to the stairs as they headed towards the door, and waved goodbye as they left.

The sound of the door locking echoed through the silent house.

Soon, I heard footsteps behind me. I only just had time to notice Rigel slipping upstairs. He had left without even deigning to spare me a glance.

I stared at where he had been for a moment, before turning around. I looked at the front door and let out a small sigh.

They'd be back soon . . .

I waited in the hall, as if they could reappear at any moment. I found myself sitting cross-legged on the floor, with no idea how I'd got there. I tapped my fingers along a groove in the wooden floor, and wondered where Klaus had got to.

I looked towards the living room and found him cleaning himself in the centre of the rug. His little head kept bobbing up and down and I couldn't help but find him cute.

Maybe he wanted to play?

I crouched down and peered around the doorframe at him. Then, without letting him see me, I approached him on all fours.

He lowered his paw and turned to look at me. I immediately froze, staring at him like a little sphinx. He gave me an irritated look, his tail flicking from side to side.

He turned around, and I continued crawling towards him.

I froze as soon as he looked at me again. We started a game of statues, with him turning round and shooting glares at me and me freezing like a skittish beetle every time he did.

But when I got to the edge of the rug, Klaus meowed nervously and I decided to stop.

'You don't want to play?' I asked, a little disappointed, hoping he'd turn around again.

But Klaus just flicked his tail a few more times and left. I leant back on my heels, a little disheartened, before deciding to go and study in my room.

As I got upstairs, I wondered when Anna and Norman would get to the airport. I was lost in my thoughts when something caught my attention. I turned around and looked down the hallway.

Rigel was standing still with his back turned to me and his head bowed slightly forward. I stopped when I saw how tensely he was leaning against the wall.

What was he doing?

My lips parted, uncertain of our closeness.

'Rigel?'

I thought I could see the tendons in his wrist ever so slightly bulge, but he did not move.

I peered around, trying to see his face. The old floorboards creaked under my feet as I slowly tiptoed towards him. When I was close enough, I thought I could see him squeezing his eyes shut tight.

'Rigel,' I called again, cautiously. 'Are you . . . all right?'

'I'm *great*,' he snarled back, without turning around. I almost flinched when I heard him spitting through his teeth like that.

I stopped, but not so much because of his hostile tone. No . . . I stopped because his lie was so disarming that it stopped me in my tracks.

I stretched a hand out towards him.

'Rigel . . .'

As soon as my fingers brushed against his arm, he flinched away. Rigel suddenly turned, retreating away from me, his eyes fixed on mine.

'*How many* times have I told you not to touch me?' he hissed threateningly.

I stepped back. I watched him with anguished eyes. I felt more wounded inside than I cared to admit.

'I just wanted . . .' I started, then wondered why, *why* I never learnt. '. . . I just wanted to check you were all right.'

I then noticed that his pupils were slightly dilated.

Then his face changed.

'Why?' His mouth was twisted with a cruel, excessive sarcasm. It was disconcerting, even for him. 'Oh, of course,' he quickly corrected himself, clicking his tongue in a way that seemed designed to hurt me. 'Because that's what you're like. That's your nature.'

My hands tensed. I trembled.

'Stop it.'

But he took a step towards me. He towered over me with that stinging, venomous, brutally cruel smile.

'It's stronger than you are, isn't it? Your desire to help me?' He whispered mercilessly, his eyes as sharp as needles. 'You want to . . . *fix me?*'

'Stop it, Rigel!' I impulsively stepped backwards. My fists were clenched but I was always too delicate, too weak and powerless. 'It seems like you do everything you can to . . . to . . .'

'To?' he prompted.

'To make people hate you.'

To make me hate you, I wanted to blurt out. *To make me, only me, hate you, as if you were punishing me.*

As if I had done something to deserve the worst part of him.

Every time he snapped at me it was a punishment, every glance a warning. Sometimes I had the impression that he was trying to tell me something with those looks of his, something that he was also trying to bury under thorns and scratches.

And while I watched him, swallowed by the shadow he cast over me, it seemed as though I could almost see something flashing just under the surface of his eyes, something that even I was unable to see.

'And do you hate me?' He was so close his voice resounded in my ears. His face was slightly downturned, to make up for the height difference between us. 'Do you hate me, *little moth*?'

I searched his eyes, destroyed.

'Is that what you want?'

Rigel slowly closed his mouth, his gaze pinned to mine, before it shifted away over my shoulder. I didn't need to hear the slow, scathing way in which he replied, almost as if it hurt him too:

'Yes.'

He disappeared down the stairs, freeing me from his presence.

I froze, his words echoing in my mind, until I heard him leaving through the front door.

I spent the whole day alone.

The house was as silent as an abandoned sanctuary. The only sound was the rain. I sat on the floor and absentmindedly watched it fall. The streaks of water running down the window cast shadows on my legs and the parquet flooring.

I wished I had words to explain how I was feeling. To pluck them from inside me and arrange them on the floor like pieces of a mosaic that might somehow fit together. I felt empty.

Some part of me had always known that things wouldn't work out.

I'd known it from the start. From my first step outside The Grave. I was tarnished by hopefulness, like I had been as a child, because deep down, that was the only way I knew how to live, polishing things, making them shine.

But in truth, I couldn't see beyond this. In truth, no matter how I looked at it, that black stain could never be polished away.

Rigel was the Tearsmith.

For me, he had always been at the centre of the legend. He embodied the torment that had so often reduced me to tears as a child.

The Tearsmith was suffering incarnate.

He caused suffering, contaminating you with anguish until you cried. Made you lie and despair. That's what they taught us at The Grave.

I remembered that Adeline didn't see it that way. She used to say that the story could be interpreted differently, from another perspective. That it couldn't be all suffering, because if tears were the price of feeling, they also meant love, fondness, joy and passion. There was pain, but also happiness.

'They're what make us human,' she had said. It was better to suffer than to feel nothing.

But I couldn't see it like she did.

Rigel destroyed everything.

Why did he stay so dark? Why couldn't I see the light in him, like I could in everything else?

I would have illuminated him gently, *tenderly*, without hurting him. Together, we could be something different, even though I couldn't imagine anything other than the way he glared at me.

But we could have been a plausible fairy tale. Without wolves, bites or fear.

A family . . .

My phone buzzed on the desk with a message notification. I sighed heavily: I was sure it would be Lionel.

He had messaged me several times in the past few days, and we had chatted a lot. He told me many things about himself, his hobbies, the sports he played, the tennis tournaments he'd won. He liked telling me about his successes, and even though he didn't ask me anything about myself it was nice to have someone to speak to without having to bother Billie all the time.

But that afternoon was different.

He messaged me, and I couldn't help but tell him about Rigel.

What happened had stuck inside me like a thorn. I told him honestly that we weren't really brother and sister. I told him there was no blood relation between us, and he didn't reply for a long time.

Maybe I shouldn't have spoken about myself so much. Maybe I had annoyed him by drawing attention to myself when he had been telling me about the latest trophy he had won.

It started to rain, and the only thing I could think about was that *he* was out there somewhere, in that sheeting rain without even an umbrella.

Because deep down, that was the only way I knew how to live. Polishing things, making them shine, even though the more I tried, the more rough edges appeared.

A ringing flooded the house.

I jumped as if a bucket of cold water had just been thrown over me.

I left the room to grab the landline, hurrying back to the living room before answering.

'Hello?'

'Nica,' a voice said warmly. 'Hi. Everything okay?'

'Anna,' I breathed, happy and bewildered. She had called me around lunchtime to let me know that they'd arrived and that it was snowing there. I hadn't been expecting to hear from her again.

Her voice sounded slightly different. The signal was bad.

'I'm calling from the airport. The weather's got worse here. It's been snowing really heavily all afternoon and it's not forecast to get any better until tomorrow morning. We're in the queue, but . . . Oh, Norman, let the gentleman pass. His suitcase . . . sorry! Nica, can you hear me?'

'Yes, I'm listening.'

'They've closed all the gates, they're cancelling flights and we're waiting for an update, but they just keep announcing cancellations due to bad weather conditions . . . Oh, wait . . . Nica . . . Nica?'

'I can hear you, Anna,' I replied, clutching the phone with both hands. Her voice was a distant echo.

'They say they aren't scheduling any more flights until tomorrow morning.' I heard Norman talking to someone. 'Or at least until the storm's over,' she concluded. I stood there, in the silent house, absorbing what she had just told me. 'Oh Nica, sweetheart, I'm so sorry . . . I never imagined that . . . Er, excuse me, there's a queue. Don't you see we're queuing here? You're standing on my scarf! Really, I know we said . . . Nica? I know we said we'd be back this evening . . .'

'Everything's fine,' I urged down the phone, trying to soothe her nerves. 'Anna, you don't need to worry, we've got enough to eat.'

'Is it raining? You've turned the heating on, haven't you? Are you and Rigel all right?'

My throat went dry.

'We're fine,' I said slowly. 'The house is warm, don't worry. And Klaus has eaten.' I turned towards the cat who was resting at the other end of the room. 'He finished his food and now he's snoozing on the armchair.' I forced a smile, sensing Anna's worry from down the line. 'Really, Anna . . . don't worry. It's only one night . . . I'm sure it will get sorted out soon, and in the meantime . . . don't even think about it. We . . . we'll wait here for you.'

We spoke for a little longer. Anna asked if we knew how to lock the door properly, and urged me not to hesitate to call her for anything. I basked in her concern until it was time to finish the conversation.

I hung up and found myself enveloped by the evening dusk.

'Just me and you then,' I smiled at Klaus. He opened an eye and threw me a scowl.

I switched on the lamp and picked up my phone, which I had left on the side table. I still had to reply to Lionel.

I frowned. He had sent me a photo. I opened the message as a flash of lightning lit up the windows.

I wasn't ready for what happened next.

I should have sensed it. Just like you can smell the rain before a storm.

I should have sensed it, like you can feel disasters, the damage they wreak before they even take place.

The front door was suddenly blown open by a gust of icy wind and I almost dropped my phone.

Rigel towered in the doorway, his fists clenched and his soaking hair dripping all over his face. His shoes were caked in mud and his elbows were red below the short sleeves of his shirt.

He looked terrible. His lips had gone blue with cold and his clothes were soaking. He closed the door without even glancing at me, and I stared at him, shocked.

'Rigel . . .'

He turned towards me. I felt a painful throb in my chest when I saw the state of his face.

The sight of his cut lip hit me like a slap in the face. Red blood mixed with rain as it trickled down his jaw. His split eyebrow stood out starkly against his pale skin. My eyes searched his face, terrified, inspecting his wounds.

'Rigel,' I exhaled, lost for words. My eyes followed him as he moved away from the door.

'What . . . what happened to you?' The sight of all that blood destroyed me. It was only when he drew closer that I noticed his knuckles were grazed, and my concern deepened into a sense of fore-boding. My phone flashed with another message, and I glanced down.

My blood froze, turned into thorns and shards of glass pricking and stabbing the bones under my skin.

I couldn't breathe. My head was spinning. The world around me was fading away.

On the phone screen was Lionel's face, bruised and bloody. His hair was dishevelled, the impression of punches blooming all over his skin. I staggered backwards on unsteady legs.

Every letter of his last message was like a needle stabbing me right in the eye: 'It was him.'

'What have you done . . .'

I looked up at Rigel's back, the photo still swimming before my eyes.

'What have you done . . .' my voice trembled a little louder, making him stop this time.

He turned towards me, his fists clenched. He stared at me through his swollen eyelids, and his gaze fell on the phone in my hands.

His lips twisted into a sneer.

'Oh, the boy cried wolf,' he jeered.

I felt something explode in my head. My blood was boiling, every inch of me was tense. I was trembling from head to foot. My temples were pounding, my eyes were wide and blinded by tears. Rigel turned and started to walk away.

I lost control. Everything fell away.

All that was left was a burning rage. An anger that I had never felt before.

Something snapped.

I lunged forwards and struck out at him. I clawed at the wet fabric of his clothes, his elbows, his shoulders, wherever I could. He moved away from the unexpected attack and tears flooded down my cheeks.

'Why?' I screamed hoarsely, trying to catch hold of him. '*Why?* What have I ever done to you?'

He pushed me away, trying to get to the stairs. He flicked my fingers away as if they were spiders, staring stubbornly ahead as I clung to his clothes with my Band-Aid-covered hands, trying to hurt him.

'What have I done to deserve this?' I screamed, my throat hurting. 'What? *Tell me!*'

'Don't touch me,' he hissed.

I couldn't even see any more. I struggled against the hands pushing me away. I raged against him and he snarled, 'I've *told you* to . . .'

I didn't let him finish. I seized his forearm and yanked it forcefully.

It was violent, explosive.

For a moment, there were only my fingers sunk into his bare, *exposed* skin, and me, tense against him.

The only thing I saw as he shoved me back with force was the angry flash of his black hair.

At the last moment, he grabbed my shoulder with a vice-like grip.

The outline of his mouth came towards me and his lips landed on mine.

13. Thorns of Regret

The first time he saw her, they were five years old.

She arrived on a day like any other, as lost as they all were, mother-less ducklings.

She stood there, framed against the wrought-iron gates. The colours of fall swallowed her brown hair and the leather of her unlaced shoes.

She hadn't been anything more than that. He remembered her as dispassionately as one remembers a simple stone: lifeless, slender, moth-like, neglected. As quiet as the silent sobs that he had seen on an endless sequence of faces.

And then, she turned to face him, leaves swirling around her.

The ground shook, the world stopped, his heart skipped a beat. He was overcome by the sight of her eyes, the like of which he had never seen before – stunningly, dazzlingly grey, more sparkling than water. Shimmering like the fairy tale, Rigel saw her otherworldly eyes filled with tears and clear as glass.

He froze when she turned her Tearsmith eyes on him.

They had told him that true love never dies.

That's what the matron had told him, when he asked her what love was.

Rigel couldn't even remember where he had first heard of this fabled love, but he spent the mornings of his childhood searching for it – in the garden, inside hollow tree trunks, in other children's pockets, in his clothes, in his shoes. It was only later he learnt that it wasn't like a coin or a whistle.

It was the older boys who told him about it. They had felt it first. The most reckless, or maybe just the most mad.

They spoke about it as if they were intoxicated by something invisible, intangible. Rigel couldn't help but think they seemed even more bewildered, lost, but happy in their bewilderment. Shipwrecked, castaways, lured by a siren's song.

They had told him that true love never dies.

It was true.

It was useless to try to shake it off. Love stuck hard to the walls of his soul like pollen on a bee's legs. It was a condemnation of poisonous nectar, smearing his thoughts, breath and words, sticking to his eyelids, tongue and fingers. There was no escape.

One glance from her had torn his chest asunder, obliterated it with one flutter of her eyelashes. She had branded his raw heart with her Tearsmith eyes, and torn it away from him before he could clutch it back.

Nica had ransacked him in the blink of an eye, leaving him with a writhing, burning sensation in his chest. Without ever having touched him, with nothing but the ruthless, devastating grace of her delicate smile and those subtle moth colours, she had left his heart bleeding in the doorway.

They had told him that true love never dies.

But they hadn't told him that true love tears you to shreds, that it roots itself inside you and ensnares you in its clutches.

The longer he looked at her, the more he couldn't tear his eyes away.

There was something about how sweetly, how gently she moved, something childlike, small and true in her sincerity. She looked out at the world through the wrought-iron gates, her hands gripping the bars, hoping, *longing*, in a way he never had.

He watched her wandering about barefoot through the overgrown grass, cradling sparrow eggs in her arms, rubbing flowers on her clothes to make them look less grey.

Rigel wondered how something so simple and delicate could have the power to hurt him so much. He pushed the feeling away as stubbornly as an obstinate child, burying it deep inside him, trying to stifle the seed of the feeling, nip it in the bud.

He couldn't accept it.

He didn't want to accept it. She was so featureless and insignificant, she didn't know anything. She couldn't get under his skin like that, without permission, breaking his heart and shattering his soul.

It was an untameable abyss. It devoured everything around it. It destroyed his control with a frightening brutality. And he hid it, Rigel, he hid it, because deep down, he was afraid of it. Articulating it would mean admitting it was inescapable, and that was something he wasn't ready to accept.

But the writhing within him grew stronger, taking root in his veins. It pushed him towards her, touching nerves he didn't even know he had. Rigel's hands trembled when he pushed her for the first time.

He watched her fall and didn't need to see her scraped knee to devour that proof, to drink it greedily. *Fairy tales don't bleed*, he urgently reminded himself as he watched her run away. *Fairy tales don't scratch their knees.* That was all it took for him to see her free of any doubt, shiver and shadow.

She was not the Tearsmith. She didn't send him into floods of tears, and she didn't slip crystal teardrops into his eyes.

But it was his heart that wept, every time he looked at her.

Perhaps she had slipped something else inside of him, he thought, a poison much more noxious than joy or sadness. A venom that burned, stung and corrupted. Something had bloomed inside of him, but its petals were like teeth. Every time she laughed, its roots sunk deeper still, plunging its claws into his mind, its fangs into his soul.

So Rigel pushed her, shoved her, pulled her hair to make her stop laughing. He was only satisfied when she looked at him with frightened eyes that were brimming with tears. The irony of seeing despair in the eyes that should have made the whole world cry made him smile.

But the satisfaction only lasted a moment, just long enough to watch her running away. And then the pain returned, as ferocious as a wild animal, clawing, imploring for her to come back.

She was always smiling.

Even when there was nothing to smile at. Even after he had grazed her knees again. Even in the morning, with the matron's punishments still smarting on her wrists and her hair cascading over her shoulders.

She would smile, and her eyes would be so pure and sincere that Rigel felt them chafing against his darkness.

'Why do you keep helping them?' another child asked her just a few years later.

Rigel had seen her from the first-floor window. Sat with all her little creatures, her deer-like legs immersed in the long grass. She had saved a lizard from the children who had wanted to stab it with sticks, and in return, it had bitten her.

'You help all these creatures . . . but they only hurt you.'

Nica looked at the other child candidly, blinking steadily.

The sun shone as her lips parted. There was a bright light, an incredible splendour, and the writhing inside him went still, defeated, as she lifted her outspread fingers covered in colourful Band-Aids.

'*It's true,*' she had whispered, with a warm, genuine smile, 'but look at all these beautiful colours.'

Rigel had always known there was something wrong with him.

He was born knowing it.

He had felt it for as long as he could remember. That was how he had justified to himself that he had been abandoned.

He didn't work like other people, he wasn't like other people – *he watched her, and as the wind tousled her long brown hair he saw bronze wings on her back, fluttering, then fading away, as if they'd never existed.*

He didn't need to see the matron's glances, or the way she shook her head when families said they wanted to adopt him. Rigel watched them from the garden, and saw on their faces a pity he had never asked for.

He had always known that there was something wrong with him, and the more he grew, the more he felt that writhing feeling spread monstrously through his body.

He hid it bitterly, suffocated with anger and stubbornness. It got worse as he got older. More thorns erupted, because no one had told him that that's how love consumes you. No one warned him that love takes root in your flesh and grinds you up, *that it boundlessly wants and wants and wants* – a glance, *just one more glance,* the hint of a smile, a heartbeat.

'You cannot lie to the Tearsmith,' the other children would whisper at night. They behaved well so they wouldn't be taken away.

Rigel knew it. They all knew it. Lying to the Tearsmith would be like lying to yourself. The Tearsmith knows everything, knows every feeling that makes you tremble, every emotional breath.

'*You cannot lie to the Tearsmith,*' Rigel tried to stifle the phrase echoing round his head.

He didn't want to think about how she would look at him, her soul so clear and pure, if she knew about the wretched illness he carried inside him.

Love, for Rigel, wasn't butterflies in the stomach or a world of blissful sweetness. It was a *hungry swarm of moths, a devastating cancer*, absences that scratched at him, tears he drank from *her* eyes. It was a slower death.

Maybe he just wanted to let himself be destroyed . . . by her. By that deadly poison she had injected into his veins.

He sometimes thought of surrendering to that feeling, letting it invade him until he could feel nothing else. If only it weren't for that fierce, terrifying tremor shaking his bones, if only it wasn't so painful to dream of her running into his arms, instead of away.

'It's scary, isn't it?' whispered a child one day when the sky had turned a savage black.

Even he, who never looked at the sky, raised his gaze. In the vastness, he saw dark, sometimes reddish, clouds, like a stormy sea.

'Yes.' He felt it blooming inside him and closed his eyes. '. . . But look at all these beautiful colours.'

When he was thirteen, girls looked at him as if he were the sun, unaware of the insatiable monster inside of him. When he was fourteen, girls were like sunflowers, turning to watch him wherever he went, their gazes ever more yearning and adoring. He remembered how much Adeline had longed for him, even though she was older than him. How devotedly she touched him, the way she bowed before him, *and how all he could think about was long, shiny brown hair and grey eyes which would never look at him with that desire.*

At fifteen, it was the girls who became the insatiable monsters. They blossomed in his hands like flowers, and Rigel staved off the writhing inside of him with girls who bore some resemblance to her, a spark or a fragrance.

But it only led to disasters. Do not doubt love, when it burns so violently, when it makes your heart beat in time with another's. His need for her became more and more unbearable. Rigel felt bitterness sour his thoughts and sharpen the thorns and shards inside his chest.

He took his frustration out on Nica, twisting her name into 'little moth', as if he wanted to minimise the effect that she had on him. He wounded her with his barbed words, hoping to cause her just a fraction of the pain that she inflicted on him. She destroyed him, every day. She didn't understand the impact she had, *she would never be able to understand it.*

She was so pure and serene that she would never choose to linger in that chaotic, dirty place that was his heart.

The more he grew . . . the more Rigel noticed her devastating beauty. It kept him awake at night, clutching at the sheets with repressed desire.

As Nica got older, he burned with an ever more agonising passion, that felt more and more like a thicket of thorny teeth, which, when she cried, no longer smiled.

But he was terrified that she could see it with those Tearsmith eyes of hers – the way he yearned to touch her, how he needed to feel the warmth of her skin.

He desperately wanted to imprint himself on her as she had imprinted herself on him. Just one look from her had made him crazy with desire to touch her, but just the idea of holding her made the writhing inside him ever stronger.

It had been during that period that a new boy arrived at The Grave.

Rigel didn't pay him that much attention, too busy fighting against that disturbing, overwhelming love.

But that boy was out of his mind. He was mad enough to try to come near him, to not fear him. Deep down, Rigel didn't mind crazy people, their irrationality entertained him. It was a good distraction.

They might even have been friends, had they not been so alike.

Rigel might even have cared about him, if only he didn't see himself reflected in his narrow smirk and darkly sarcastic glances.

'Do you think Adeline would do with me what she does with you?' the boy said one afternoon, the hint of a smirk in his voice.

There was nothing Rigel could do. He had felt that smirk on his own lips.

'You want to give it a try?'

'Why not? Her or Camille . . . they're all the same.'

'Camille's got fleas,' Rigel jibed, with a crude and derisive amusement that momentarily replaced the burning sensation in his chest. The writhing within him quietened, guarding against scratches and sighs.

'Nica, then,' he heard. 'Her innocent face makes me want to do so many *things* to her . . . you can't even imagine what she does to me. Do you think she'd wriggle? *Oh*, that would be fun . . . I bet if I put my hand between her legs, she wouldn't even have the strength to push me away.'

He didn't feel the cartilage under his knuckles. He didn't feel his hands violently flying through the air and ruining that sunny afternoon.

But he would always remember the red blood under his nails as he yanked him down by his hair.

He would never forget the way she had looked at him the next morning. He had never seen eyes flash from so far away, a silent scream of terror and accusation that bore into the void inside of him.

Facing the bitter irony of his fate, Rigel found himself smiling. Smiling because it hurt too much.

Deep down, he had always known there was something wrong with him.

When they had been adopted together, Rigel felt a noose tightening around his heart.

Staying with her was better than the unbearable prospect of watching her leave. Playing the piano had been one last, desperate attempt to keep her with him, tied to him by those deep, soulful binds. She would cruelly, ignorantly, delicately destroy those connections with her first step away from The Grave.

He knew he would be paying the price for this forever. He could never have imagined a condemnation more painful, not in his most tormented nightmares, than the hell of being so close, entwined, and yet divided by the same family.

The only way she felt like a sister was because she was in his blood, like a poison with no remedy.

'Did you see how she looked at me?'

'No . . . How did she look at you?'

Rigel didn't turn around. He continued placing the new books inside his locker as he listened to the conversation.

'As if she was begging me to bump into something else . . . Did you see how quickly she bent down to pick up my books?'

'Rob,' his friend said from the adjacent locker, 'you don't want a repeat of the freshmen incident.'

'Trust me, it's written all over her face. It's screaming from her eyes. It's always the quiet ones.'

He heard them again.

'Oh, come on, let's bet on how long it takes,' Rob joked. 'I say a week. If she spreads her legs before that, the next round is on me.'

Rigel caught his reflection in the closed locker door and wasn't surprised to see a smile carved across his cheeks like the blade of a knife, his lips curling thinly over his teeth.

He was still smiling when he turned and saw his reflection in the boy's eyes. He couldn't hide his satisfaction as he pummelled him to the ground.

He would never forget how she looked at him.

With that irrepressible force that occasionally shone through her delicate nature, how her eyes gleamed like a fallen angel's.

'One day they'll see who you really are,' she whispered. Her voice had tormented him for as long as he could remember. He hadn't been able to quell his curiosity, anticipation, not with her so close.

'Oh, yeah?' he pressed her. 'And who am I really?'

He couldn't take his eyes off her. He was only breathing to hear Nica deliver her final verdict, because even in the dimness she shone with a unique light, clear and true. It drove him mad.

'You're the Tearsmith.'

And Rigel felt the writhing swell inside him. A shudder, a tsunami. The laughter that burst from him was like a heart spurting blood as black as oil.

His chest was tight. It hurt so much that he could only feel bitter relief. As he always did, he disguised his suffering with a sneer, swallowing it with the brash resignation of the vanquished.

Him . . . the Tearsmith?

Oh, if only she knew.

If she knew . . . *how she made him tremble, suffer and despair . . . If she had any idea of it* . . . Perhaps he felt a shred of relief, a warm spark flickering in the dampness and the dark, but it was instantly extinguished by a gust of icy fear.

He flinched away from hope as if burned by it. Rigel couldn't imagine anything more terrifying than seeing her pure eyes stained by those turbulent, thorny, untameable feelings.

It was already too late when he realised that he loved her with a dark, wicked love, a slow poison that gnaws at you until your last breath. He felt the writhing inside him intensifying, daring him to say certain things, to do certain things. Sometimes he could barely keep it at bay.

She was too precious to be spoiled by it.

He watched her walk away, and in the silence she left behind her, there was another abyss: the absence of the final glance she didn't grant him.

'Was it you?'

Thorns.

'Did you give me this?'

Thorns and teeth, teeth, *teeth* – before his eyes was the proof of his weakness, the rose that he couldn't help but give her, that now deafeningly screamed of his guilt.

He discovered that black was the colour of the end.

Of anguish, of a love that was destined to never see the light. It was such a tragically appropriate symbol that Rigel wondered if it was a black rose that had grown in the contaminated soil of his heart.

It was a stupid, impulsive mistake, a crack in his resolve to keep her away from him. He regretted it immediately, as soon as she came into his room bearing that accusation of leaves and ribbon.

He quickly put on his mask, balancing it on such an artificial smile that it threatened to fall.

'*Me?*' He hoped she wouldn't see how tense he was. 'Did *I* give *you* a flower?'

He said it with as much disgust as possible, spat it out with sarcasm and disdain, and prayed she would believe it.

Nica was looking down, she wasn't able to see the terror in his eyes. For a moment, Rigel feared she had understood. Just for a moment, doubt gnawed at his soul, he saw his life of tremors and lies shatter into pieces.

He responded to his fear the only way he knew how: wounding and attacking, dispelling any doubt before it could take hold.

A part of him died as he snatched the rose from her hand.

He ripped it to shreds before her eyes. He tore off each petal and wished he could do the same to himself, to the flower of emotions inside him.

They fell onto the bed and the world stopped.

His flesh screamed, his heart thundered so ferociously that it felt like it was shooting sprouts and roots.

He saw his reflection in her eyes for the first time.

A terrifying desire blurred his vision. He was overwhelmed by a surge of bare, blind hope, *astonishment*. Nica's hair, Nica's hands, Nica's eyes, Nica's lips.

Nica, just a breath away, her body under his as he'd only been able to dream of.

He felt uprooted. He madly wanted to tell her that he saw her every night, that in his dreams, they were still children, and she was always shining, perfect.

She was perfect. He couldn't imagine anything purer than her.

He wanted to tell her that he hated her for how kind she was, for how she smiled at everyone, for how her moth-like heart could care for anyone, anyone at all, even including him. *That she pretended to care for him,* but that was actually just how she was, how she treated everybody.

He wanted to tell her so many things. Things that were burning on the tip of his tongue, a tangled mass of words and emotions, fears and stabs of anguish. His love was like thorns in his throat, brambles caught in his teeth.

But before he could say a thing, she had pushed him away.

Everything shattered into a shower of shards. He exploded into fragments of glass and regretted every crumb of hope.

He knew she would never want him; *he knew it.* Deep down, he had always known it. He had made sure of it.

He closed his eyes, to spare himself the agonising suffering of watching her leave.

He had to get out of there.

He had to get away from her, from that house. If he had to hear her voice again, or feel her fingers through his clothes when she tried to touch him in the hallway, he would go crazy.

His clothes were drenched, the rain had soaked his every emotion. Rigel clenched his fists and gritted his teeth, pacing back and forth like a caged beast.

'You!'

A shout broke through the thunderstorm.

Rigel saw someone approaching him furiously. It didn't take much to recognise him, even through the rain.

He suppressed the writhing feeling as the figure came closer.

'Leonard?' he asked hesitantly, an eyebrow raised.

'It's *Lionel*,' he snarled, now just a few steps away from him.

Rigel thought to himself, at the end of the day, whether his name was Lionel or Leonard, it didn't matter. Both names annoyed him. Everything about the guy annoyed him.

'And is there a reason, *Lionel*, why you're roving around the neighbourhood like a maniac?'

'Maniac?' Lionel stared at him, his face scrunched up with anger. '*I'm the maniac?* How dare you?' He approached, burning with tension. 'If there's a maniac here, it's sure as hell you!'

Rigel looked at him mockingly, curling the corner of his mouth.

'Oh really? Too bad I live around here.' He saw flashes of anxiety in Lionel's staring eyes. 'Can't say the same about you. Now *beat it.*'

Rigel attacked him like he attacked everyone else, but as sarcastically, as derisively as possible. He sunk his teeth in, wanting to cause him *pain, pain, pain.* Lionel clenched his fists in anger.

'Your tricks won't work on me,' he snarled, soaked to the skin. Rigel found him so intensely annoying. 'You think I don't know? You think she hasn't told me? You're not her brother! You're nothing, absolutely nothing. You've got no right over her, she's not yours!'

The writhing inside him reared up. He clenched his fists, crackling with anger.

And him? What rights did he have? What did he know about the bond between him and Nica? What did he think he knew?

'Oh, but *you* do, do you?' He leant forward, furious, reeling at the idea of Nica being treated like an object to possess. 'You've known her for all of a day, but you've got rights over her?'

'Yes, I do,' Lionel replied. Rigel made out the curl of his smile through the sheets of rain. 'She's been messaging me all day, saying she can't bear to be near you. She wants me,' he said emphatically, and it felt to Rigel like a slap in the face, a stab in his heart. It burned, it felt like his stomach was being corroded away, and he had to strain to not reveal just how painful that revelation was.

Lionel beamed with satisfied triumph.

'She wants me, and all she does is tell me how much she can't stand you. She despises having to live with you, having to see you every day. She hates your guts! And . . .'

'Oh, she talks that much about me?' he shot back venomously. 'Shame. She never mentions you.'

He clicked his tongue.

'*Never*,' he repeated forcefully. 'Are you sure she knows you exist?'

'*She sure as hell does!*' Lionel hurled at him. The air between them was crackling with anger and tension. 'She's always messaging me, and when you're finally out of the way . . .'

Rigel threw his head back in gruff, angry, contemptuous laughter, that ached with a black, all-consuming pain. It hurt like hell. Those words – her hatred, her closeness with this guy – shook with an undeniable truth that damned him for all eternity.

Rigel had always known it, that thorns would beget more thorns. That what he carried inside was so soiled and damaged that a soul as pure and gentle as hers would never want him.

He had always known, but hearing it spoken aloud destroyed whatever was left of him. It was stupid, paradoxical: he was disillusioned, but he could still find pricks of hope among the thorny bushes. It was those that hurt the most.

Among the ruins, the only light he could see was the one that haloed her.

It was a light that kept him awake at night. That made her glow in all of his memories.

She was like a shining star. A star that, in the devastating loneliness of that feeling, did nothing but bring him comfort.

It was even shining in that moment, that light.

A warm glow – *her, she who always smiled.* Rigel wished he could extinguish it, free her from his cruel love.

He would have if he could but, as always, there was nothing he could do to smother the flickering light of his feelings for her. He clung to it with all his might, grasping, desperate, unable to let go.

'When you're out of the way . . .'

'Yeah,' he sneered caustically, sheltering the memory of Nica within himself. 'Keep dreaming.'

The first punch split his lip.

Rigel's blood mixed with the rain. He couldn't help but think that, all in all, the physical pain was more bearable than how he had just felt.

The second punch missed, and Rigel turned back to Lionel like an incensed beast. His fist hit Lionel's jaw with a blood-curdling crunch, louder even than the thunder.

Rigel didn't let up, not even when Lionel punched back, splitting the skin over his eyebrow. He didn't let up when his knuckles were red raw, and strands of wet hair pierced his eyes like needles.

He didn't let up until he was the last one standing, and Lionel was rolling on the ground grimacing in pain.

He looked down at him. Lightning flashed and an ocean of black clouds loomed above them. He spat a mouthful of blood onto the asphalt.

He didn't want to think about what her face would look like if she could see him now.

'See you, *Leonard*,' he snarled and walked away.

He left him curled up in the rain, reeling from his own mistake.

He saw his wretched, miserable guilt in Nica's always shining eyes.

It was more prominent than ever before, a dark stain on her beautiful, pristine purity. When she lifted her eyes, full of condemnation, from her phone to his face, it was like a wave violently hitting his chest.

He would remember the way he felt like he was dying for the rest of his life.

He looked into her Tearsmith eyes, and knew he would never be able to lie to her.

He couldn't deny it. His knuckles were bloody and grazed, and Lionel had already told her it was him. Rigel understood then, that her disappointment was the price he had to pay for every single lie he had ever told.

For having lied and hidden, for having pushed her away before she had a chance to understand.

He smiled a thorny smile, but felt himself wilting inside. His chest tightened sharply, agonisingly.

He had only given her what she expected. He had worn the mask that was tattooed on his face. He only did what he always did because, deep down, he knew that that was how she saw him: irredeemably vile.

'Oh, the boy cried wolf!'

What happened next, Rigel would remember only in part.

Confused, blurred fragments — *her eyes, her light, her hands all over him. Her hair and scent, and her lips* forming words he couldn't hear. He was too busy trying to escape the sun-like heat she radiated.

Her Band-Aid-covered hands dug into his arms, and inside he writhed and growled and yearned. *She was close, so close, so angry and close* that it made him tremble.

And as he desperately, urgently tried to move away from her, Rigel couldn't help but notice that even despite her burning rage and distress, Nica was devastatingly beautiful.

Even with all those Band-Aids and bruises on her fingers, Nica was devastatingly beautiful.

Even as she struck him, tried to hurt him, to scratch him, to return to him everything that he had only ruined, Nica remained the most beautiful thing his eyes had ever seen.

It was his fault, and the fault of the spell she carried unknowingly within her, that he couldn't stop himself in time.

She had gotten too close, and when he pushed her away, the writhing within him spurred him on and his mouth landed on hers.

. . . And for the first time . . .

For the very first time in his life, he surrendered to all that beauty and pain. He let it consume him, died with an exhausted sigh of relief, threw himself into the abyss and landed on a bed of rose petals, after having spent his life among the thorns.

He surrendered himself to her warmth and could feel nothing else.

He yielded to her, to the peaceful light shining sweetly inside her, lighting up every corner of that endless battlefield.

Perhaps, our greatest fear
is accepting that someone can truly
love us for who we are.

*   *   *

I staggered backwards.

I had pulled away from him so abruptly that the room was spinning. My phone fell to the ground and I continued retreating, stunned, staring.

I couldn't breathe. I shuddered as I touched my lips with trembling fingers.

I stared at the face before me with devastated eyes, the taste of blood, *his blood*, on my aching mouth. I felt a small cut on my lips.

He had bitten me.

Rigel had finally really bitten me.

I stared at his heaving chest. He wiped the blood from his glistening, red lips and I thought I saw a fleeting bright spark behind his veiled eyes.

In his eyes, for a moment, I thought I glimpsed a memory reflected back at me.

The same silent, accusatory way in which I had looked at him, one evening long ago:

'One day they'll see who you really are.'

'Oh, yeah? And who am I really?'

'You're the Tearsmith.'

Rigel's jaw clenched. '*You're* the Tearsmith.'

His voice was sharp, he spat it out involuntarily as if it was poison he had held in his mouth for too long.

I was reduced to a heap of astonished shudders. He quickly turned around and disappeared up the stairs.

14. Disarming

There are some types of love you cannot cultivate.
They are like wild roses:
They rarely flower,
And their thorns are like tenterhooks.

I remembered her, my mom.

Her curly hair and her sweet scent of violets, her eyes as grey as a winter sea.

I remembered her warm hands and her kindness, how she would always let me hold the samples she was examining.

'Be gentle,' I remembered her whispering as she handed me a beautiful blue butterfly.

'*Tenderness, Nica,*' she said. '*Tenderness, always . . . Remember that.*'

I wished I could tell her that I had held her words inside of me, that they were the foundation upon which I had built my heart.

I wished I could tell her that I'd always remembered, even when the warmth of her hands had disappeared and mine were covered in Band-Aids, the only colour left in my life.

Even when my nightmares were tainted by the sound of creaking leather.

But in that moment . . . I just wanted to tell Mom that sometimes tenderness wasn't enough.

That not all people were butterflies, and that no matter how gentle I was, they'd never let themselves be handled with care. That I would always be covered in bites and scratches, that I would end up covered in wounds I was incapable of healing.

This was the truth.

In the darkness of my room, I felt like a forgotten doll. My gaze unseeing, my arms hugging my knees.

My phone screen lit up again, but I didn't get up to reply. I already knew what it would say, and I didn't have the courage to read any more. Lionel's messages were an unending sequence of accusations:

> Look what he did to me
> I told him to stop
> He started it
> It's his fault
> He punched me for no reason

I'd already seen it happen too many times. I no longer had the strength to question whether it was true.

Deep down, this was how Rigel had always been.

Violent and cruel, that was how Peter had described him. It didn't matter how hard I tried to write him into the pages of this new reality: he would never fit there.

He would always crush me, defeat me. Day after day, I would end up losing more pieces of myself.

I wished that Anna and Norman had never gone away, that Anna was here, telling me that nothing was beyond repair.

This would have happened anyway, I thought to myself. *Whether they'd stayed or not . . . it would have fallen apart, sooner or later.*

I sighed heavily, swallowed and noticed I was very thirsty.

I decided to get up. I had been there for hours and night had fallen.

Before leaving my room, I made sure there was no one on the landing. Bumping into Rigel was the last thing I wanted.

I moved through the darkness. It was no longer raining, and the moonlight shining through the clouds and illuminating the shapes of the buildings outside allowed me to find my way.

Downstairs was immersed in shadows. I stumbled into something in the kitchen and almost fell over. I gasped, grabbed on to the wall and stared at the floor, blinking.

What . . .

I quickly reached for the light switch.

The light hurt my eyes. I took a sharp breath in and instinctively stepped back.

Rigel was lying face-down on the floor, his hair spread out over the parquet flooring. His white wrist stood out against the wood and the sides of his face were covered by a fan of black hair. He wasn't moving.

I was so stricken by the sight of his immobile body that as I took another step backwards, I realised I was shaking. The vision before me clashed with the image I had of Rigel, his strength, his ferocity, his unshakeable self-control.

I stared at him, wide-eyed, unable to make a sound.

It was him. On the ground. Not moving.

He was . . .

'Rigel,' I uttered in a strained whisper.

Suddenly, my heart thudded against my ribs and reality crashed around me all at once. With a violent shudder, I came back to myself. Breathing frantically, I crouched over him.

'Rigel,' I breathed, grasping the fact that there was a human being lying at my feet. My eyes ran over his body, but my hands were shaking too much to touch him. I didn't know where to put them.

Good God, what had happened?

Panic rushed over me. A flurry of thoughts crowded my mind and I stared at him weakly, my chest tight.

What should I do?

What?

I reached my hand out far enough to touch his temple. Feeling him through my Band-Aids, I jumped.

He was burning hot. God, he was burning like a furnace.

I threw him one last glance before running into the living room. I leapt like a cat onto the armchair and grabbed the house phone.

Never before in my life had I found someone lying on the floor like that. Maybe out of panic, or maybe simply because I couldn't control my panic, I found myself dialling with shaking fingers the number of the only person who came to mind in that moment of need. The only person I knew I could count on, though I didn't have anyone to compare her to.

'Anna!' I burst out before she could say a word. 'Something's happened . . . something . . . *Rigel!*' I gripped the receiver. 'It's Rigel!'

I heard a groan and a rustling of bedsheets.

'Nica . . .' she replied sleepily. 'What . . .'

'I know it's late,' I said hurriedly. 'I'm sorry, but . . . it's important! Rigel's on the floor, he . . . he . . .'

I heard Anna's breathing suddenly closer.

'Rigel?' There was more worry in her voice. 'On the floor? What do you mean on the floor? Is he okay?'

I rushed to get my words out. In a ramble, I explained that I had gone downstairs and found him there, lying in the kitchen.

'He's got a high fever, but I don't know . . . Anna, I don't know what to do!'

Anna panicked. I heard her throwing back the bedsheets and waking Norman. She said they'd take a coach, or get home any other way they could.

I regretted how scared my ineptitude was making her. Maybe, if I'd been able to keep my head, I could have called an ambulance, or I might have realised that it was just light-headedness from the fever that had made Rigel pass out.

But instead, I had panicked and called her, while she was thousands of miles away and could do nothing. I was so ashamed of my stupidity I wanted to bite my hands.

'God, I knew we should have come back, I knew it,' her voice trembled. 'I could have made sure he was in bed by now . . . I could have been looking after him . . . and maybe, *maybe* . . .'

Anna seemed beside herself. I wondered if she was maybe over-reacting, but then again, there had never been anyone who worried about me, so I had no standard to compare her to.

Maybe she wasn't overreacting, maybe it was like this in other families. Maybe if I hadn't been so rash . . .

'Anna, the fever, I can . . . I can deal with it.' I wanted to fix my mistake, to make myself useful in some way. I felt the need to try and calm her down. 'I can try to get him upstairs and into bed . . .'

'He'll need an ice pack,' she interrupted me anxiously. 'Heavens, he'll have got so cold on the floor! Medicine! There's drugs for fevers in the bathroom, in the cupboard beside the mirror, they're the ones with the white lid! Oh, Nica . . .'

'Don't worry,' I said, though it was clear that she was beyond worried. 'Now . . . now, I'll sort it, Anna! If you tell me exactly what I need to do, I . . .'

She rattled off instructions and I etched them into my brain. I hung up, promising that I'd understood and that I'd call her back.

I went back into the hallway, stopped a metre away from Rigel and took a deep breath. There was no time to lose.

I would have liked to say that I lifted him onto my shoulders and carried him in a dignified manner up the stairs. But this was far from the case.

I placed a hesitant hand on his shoulder blade and noticed my fingers were shaking.

'Rigel . . .' I lowered my face towards him and my hair tumbled over his back. 'Rigel, now . . . you've got to help me . . .'

I managed to turn him onto his back. I tried, in vain, to get him into a sitting position. I put my arm around his neck and lifted his head. His black hair fell over my forearm and onto the floor. His head flopped backwards and his white skin was tense over his throat.

'Rigel . . .'

The sight of him so defenceless knotted my stomach. I swallowed, and threw a nervous glance at the stairs before looking back at him. I was very close to him, and didn't realise that I was gripping him tighter than I needed to.

'We've got to get upstairs,' I told him quietly, tender but deter-mined. 'The stairs, Rigel, that's all . . .' I pursed my lips and lifted his chest. 'Come on!'

Well . . . these were fighting words.

I was used to tending injured sparrows and rescuing mice from traps – creatures of much smaller size.

I tried to convince him to put a bit of effort in, but he showed no sign he could hear me, so I started to drag him along the floor. I blew a strand of hair off my face and my feet slipped on the parquet floor-ing. Somehow, I managed to get us to the foot of the stairs.

I gripped Rigel's t-shirt and managed to pull him up enough to prop his back up against the wall. He was terribly tall and powerfully built; I was miniscule in comparison.

'Rigel . . . please . . .' My voice strained with the excruciating effort. 'Get up!'

It was a colossal task. With an exhausted groan, I nestled his head against my abdomen to stop him from falling to the ground again. I buckled under his immensely heavy weight, my legs shaking.

I gritted my teeth and we struggled up the stairs, Rigel barely managing to stay upright. His arm was looped around my neck and I felt his jaw against my temple.

I sighed heavily in relief as we approached the top of the stairs, but on the last step, I slipped. My eyes flew open, but it was too late: the walls spun and we crashed down.

My hip collided with the edge of one of the stairs and I bit my tongue in pain.

'Oh God . . .' I trembled, the metallic taste of blood in my mouth.

Could I really be this much of a disaster?

I crawled towards Rigel. I put a hand to the stabbing pain in my hip and anxiously checked his head for injuries.

I couldn't get him upright.

Hobbling, I finally managed to drag him up the stairs and into his room, and with a superhuman effort, I heaved him onto the mattress and pulled the covers over him.

I wiped my forehead and allowed myself a moment to catch my breath. His arm was dangling off the side of the bed, his hair was strewn all over the pillow.

Exhausted, I ran to the bathroom and filled a glass of water. Then, I opened the cupboard and found the right medicine.

I heard the springs of the mattress as I sat back down on the bed and took a pill from the tub.

I lifted his head, cradling it in the crook of my elbow.

'Rigel, you've got to take this . . .' I said, in the vain hope that he could hear me, that just for once he would let me help him. 'It will make you better . . .'

He didn't move. His face was alarmingly pale.

'Rigel,' I tried again, balancing the pill on his lips. 'Come on . . .'

His head was pressed to my side. His forehead came against my ribs, just under my breasts, and the pill fell from my flustered fingers.

I frantically hurried to retrieve it from the folds of the bedsheets, feeling my nerves burning under my skin.

I clumsily shoved it into his mouth. His lips fell apart limply under the pressure of my fingers, and I only just managed not to brush them with my index finger as the pill disappeared into his mouth.

I reached for the glass of water with shaking hands.

I managed to get him to take a little sip and finally he swallowed the pill.

I lowered his head onto the pillow and jumped up. My cheeks were irritatingly hot.

I dashed down into the kitchen and prepared an ice pack as Anna had told me to. Then I returned upstairs and pressed it to his burning skin.

I stood still, close to the bed, thinking hard.

Had I forgotten anything?

I tried to recollect Anna's instructions, when suddenly I heard my phone ringing. I glanced at Rigel then ran to pick up. It was Anna's name on the screen.

Despite the fact that the situation was more under control, I could sense her agitation even more acutely. I reported that I'd done everything she had told me, to the letter, not forgetting a thing. I told her that I'd closed the curtains and put an extra blanket on Rigel. She told me that they were about to take a coach that would get them home in the early hours of the morning.

'We'll be there as soon as possible,' she promised anxiously. All her concern gave me a warm, unfamiliar tightness in my chest.

'Nica, if you need anything at all . . .'

I nodded vigorously, but then remembered that Anna couldn't see me.

'Don't worry, Anna . . . if anything happens, I'll phone you straight away.'

She thanked me for how diligently I had taken care of him, and after giving me a last few pieces of advice and promising to see me soon, she hung up.

I turned around and went back into the bedroom, closing the door behind me to keep the warmth in.

I silently stepped towards the bed, placed my phone on the bedside table, and slowly lifted my eyes to Rigel's face.

'They're coming back,' I whispered.

His face remained as still as polished alabaster. I couldn't move either, I was frozen beside his bed as if held hostage by the sight of his face.

I don't know how long I stood there watching him, worried and indecisive. Finally, I perched carefully on the edge of the mattress, scared that the sound of the bedsprings would wake him.

I couldn't imagine how furious he would be if he knew that not only had I come into his room, but I was even sitting on his bed, watching him as if I wasn't scared of the consequences.

He would have snarled at me. Chased me away. Glared at me in that scornful way that cut me like a blade.

'*You're the Tearsmith.*'

I thought back to his accusation with a bitter, indefinable pain. Me? How could I be the Tearsmith? What did he mean?

I gazed at his sleeping face with the wariness of someone tiptoeing towards a wild, unpredictable beast.

And yet . . .

And yet, watching him in that moment . . . I felt something inexplicable. An indescribable peace.

His beautiful face was relaxed. His long lashes cast shadows on his elegant cheekbones and tranquil lips. His proud features were marked with a serenity that I had never seen in him before.

He had never let me see him like this. His lips were always twisted into a sneer, his gaze darkened with malicious intent.

I swallowed. Unfathomable feelings seized my heart. I watched his broad chest gently rise and fall, his heartbeat pulse in his throat . . . he had never looked so beautiful. His hollow cheeks and the shadows under his eyes, far from detracting from his harmonious beauty, lent him the charm of corrupted, faded youth. No matter how ashen, he would always be enchanting, and there was no scratch, cut or wound that could dim his light.

He was so beautiful when he was peaceful.

How could such radiance hide something so . . . dark and unfathomable?

How could the wolf look so graceful, when he was supposed to be frightening?

Suddenly, Rigel took a gasping breath and his mouth fell open. He limply moved his head and the cold compress fell to one side. Without thinking, I leant over him to pick it up. I held my breath and my anxious eyes urgently flicked back to his face, but he . . .

He was still immobile, just a breath away from me. I stared at him, on the brink of an intimacy he had never allowed me. I saw him as if he wasn't the Tearsmith. As if he was just . . . Rigel.

Just a young man, sleeping, ill, with a heart and soul like many others.

An indescribable sadness came over me. I felt crushed, crestfallen, powerless. Covered in bruises he had given me without ever having touched me.

I hate you, I wanted to whisper, as anyone else would have in my place. *I hate you. I can't stand your silences, nor anything that you say to me.*

I hate your smile, the way you don't want me near you, all the ways you've hurt me.

I hate you for how you always ruin beautiful things, for how violently you leave, as if it was me who had deprived you of something.

I hate you . . . because you've never given me any other choice.

But I didn't say a word.

I didn't voice the thoughts. Let them dissolve my heart. I felt drained by a sense of resignation. I was suddenly utterly exhausted.

Because it wasn't true.

I didn't hate Rigel. I would never hate him.

I just wanted to understand him.

I just wanted to see that there really was something down there in the shadows of that heart just like any other.

I just wanted to convince the world that it was wrong about him.

'Why do you always push me away?' I whispered in anguish. 'Why don't you let me understand you?'

I would never hear answers to those questions. He would never give me the answers.

I felt myself slowly slipping down onto the mattress, increasingly foggy with exhaustion. Darkness enveloped me.

And in the end, all I could do . . . all I could give him in exchange for what he had always given me, was just a deep, slow sigh.

15. To the Bone

You can scratch love, you can renounce it,
you can wrench it from your heart,
but it will always know where to find you.

Everything was burning around him.

It was a soft, boiling prison.

Where was he? He couldn't hear anything. He could only make out a diffused pain, it was almost as if the fever had melted the bones under his muscles.

And yet, even in that dense, unnatural sleep, *she* came to him like a dream.

Nica's outline was so blurry that no one else would have been able to tell it was her. He only could because he knew every glimmering corner of her by heart.

Even feverish and disorientated, he could picture her perfectly. It seemed like she really was there, close to him, radiating warmth.

Oh, how wondrous were dreams . . .

162

There was no terror, no limits. He didn't have to restrain himself, hide away, hold himself back. In his dreams, he could touch her, feel her, be with her without having to explain a thing. Rigel might have been able to love this unreal world, if he didn't always wake from this fleeting happiness with such deep scars on his heart.

Nica's absence burned him. It dug furrows in him as tenderly as she caressed him in his dreams, and he felt each and every one of these cuts when he woke up in the morning in his empty bed, without her.

But in that moment . . .

It almost seemed as if he could touch her. Circle her narrow waist with his hands and hold her until he felt complete.

He managed to move. Despite being delirious, he felt conscious. But was he? No, it was impossible. It was only in his dreams that he found her next to him.

But she was so real . . . He held her and buried his face in her hair, as he did every single night.

He wanted to burn in the smell of her. He wanted the eternally bittersweet comfort of Nica not running away from him, but cradling him in her arms and promising to never let him go.

It was as if . . . oh, it was as if . . . as if her tiny body really was breathing near him, quivering against him . . .

*   *   *

Something tickled my chin.

I moved my head, burying my face into the cool pillow.

Outside, the birds were singing and the world was waking up. I waited a few moments before opening my eyes.

Narrow beams of light blurred my vision. I blinked sleepily and reality slowly took shape around me. As my eyes were focusing, I became aware of the strange position I was lying in. It was very warm. Why couldn't I move? And why wasn't I in my own room?

Something black filled my eyes.

It was hair.

Hair?

My eyes flew wide open.

Rigel was pressed against me.

His chest was a burning wall of flesh and muscle. I was nestled against his broad shoulders and his arms were wrapped loosely around my waist. I couldn't see his face, it was tucked deep in the hollow of my neck. I could feel his warm breath fluttering against my skin.

Our legs were entangled and at some point the covers must have been kicked off the bed and onto the floor. For a moment, I forgot how to breathe.

Suffocating, I noticed that one of my arms was under his neck, the other was softly draped over his head.

My head exploded. A sudden claustrophobia tightened my throat and my heart thudded against my skin.

How had we ended up like this?

When? When had I got in his bed?

And the covers? What had happened to the covers?

I felt his hand trapped between the mattress and my body, holding me tenderly and firmly at the same time.

Rigel . . . Rigel was embracing me.

I felt his breath on me.

He, who had never let me touch him, had his face in my neck and was holding me so tightly that I couldn't make out where I started and he ended.

I was astounded.

I tried to squirm free, but then my nostrils flooded with the intense scent of his hair.

His fragrance hit me like a forceful, vibrant shadow. I didn't know how to describe it. It was . . . powerful, insidious, and wild, just like him. I remembered the rain and the thunder, the wet grass, the full clouds and the crackling storm.

Rigel smelt like a storm. *What does a storm smell like?*

I moved my face to the side, trying in vain to get away from those sensations.

I liked it. I liked how he smelt . . . I found it irresistible, almost familiar. I had the horrible feeling that it was *mine*. That it was me who had got soaked in the rain, me who had smelt freedom in the wind, me who had embraced the sky so many times. It was exhilarating, maddening.

It couldn't be real.

It was lunacy.

I closed my eyes, trying not to tremble in the arms I had always fled from . . . I tried to move away, and strands of his hair flopped over my Band-Aids.

I froze.

Rigel was still fast asleep. My heart was in my throat as I moved my fingers to brush the hair at the base of his neck.

It was . . . it was . . .

I touched it gently, carefully. And when he didn't move . . . I slowly moved my hand through his hair. It was so soft and silky.

I studied him, my heart aflutter. Every breath, every touch was new, lethal, destabilising. The moment imprinted itself in my memory forever.

As I caressed him as gently as I could, I thought I heard him let out a quiet sigh. His breath was like a warm, invisible wave on my skin. It soothed me.

Slowly, reality melted away. All that was left was Rigel's heart beating steadily, gently, lullingly.

What did that heart hold?

Why did he keep it caged away like a ferocious beast, if it beat so sweetly?

I desperately wished I could touch it, as I was touching his skin. His heartbeat resounded in my stomach with a disarming softness. Defeated, I rested my cheek on his head.

I gave in . . . I didn't have it in me to fight something so tender.

I half-closed my eyes and, with an exhausted sigh, I surrendered myself to the arms of the only boy I should have stayed far away from. I let myself be cradled by his heart. *And for a moment . . .* for a moment, lying there close to him, far away from the world, from what we'd always been . . . *just for a moment, heart to heart, I wondered why we couldn't stay like this forever . . .*

I woke again to the sound of a vibrating phone. I opened my eyes in a daze and the room wobbled into view.

I turned over in Rigel's arms and stretched my arm out.

I couldn't reach the phone.

'Rigel,' I whispered quietly, unsure what to say. 'The phone . . . it might be Anna . . .'

He didn't hear me. He was still fast asleep, his face burrowed in my neck.

I put a hand on his shoulder and tried to loosen his grip on me, but it was no use.

'Rigel . . . I've got to pick up!'

The ringing suddenly stopped.

With a little sigh, I leant back down on the pillow.

It was Anna, I could tell. Maybe she wanted to let me know they were nearly there. Heavens, she must be so worried . . .

I turned over again. Rigel's breath warmly caressed my skin and I placed my hand on the top of his head.

Clearly but gently, I said, 'Rigel, I've got to get up now.'

Some part of me was scared to wake him. Scared of his reaction. Scared that he'd push me away again.

'Rigel,' I murmured reluctantly. 'Rigel, please let me go . . .' I whispered gently in his ear, hoping that my soft voice would somehow reach him.

Something happened.

My voice seemed to melt into his dreams. He exhaled against my throat and gave a low moan before pulling me closer. His seductive smell enveloped me.

'Rigel,' I repeated weakly. His muscular body wrinkled the bedsheets. He gripped me tighter, his body feeling hotter and hotter.

I was sure I could feel him rubbing his nose against my skin.

My stomach contracted and my cheeks burned. I thought he must be dreaming, because he was making slow movements that drew me even closer to him.

Maybe I had to move even slower, even more *tenderly* . . .

I brought my lips even closer to him. My fingers sweetly pushed his hair away from his ear and I whispered softly, *'Rigel . . .'*

It just made things worse. He opened his mouth, and his breathing became heavier, longer, slower, almost intimate, as if it was costing him to breathe.

And then, suddenly, his angular jaw tilted towards me.

And his lips landed on my neck.

My heart skipped a beat. I couldn't breathe. Shivers of surprise ran down my entire body and my fingers pressed into his shoulders.

Frozen, I felt his arms tighten around me. Rigel's lips moved on my neck, kissing me so tenderly that I wriggled and recoiled.

I was so shocked and tense that I didn't even protest. Crazy sensations were consuming me from the inside and I felt thousands of little infernos blazing over my skin.

I turned and urgently pushed at his chest.

'*Rigel.*' His name stuck in my throat. His mouth opened and his teeth sleepily grazed my skin. I realised then that he wasn't asleep, but was in a semi-conscious state because of his fever. Delirious. He must have been delirious.

A moan escaped from me as he gave me a gentle bite. I clenched my jaw and prayed he'd let up. His tongue, his mouth, his bites – *all of it* – it was mad, a storm of shivers so powerful I couldn't bear it. It was too much for me.

The situation took a turn for the worse when I heard a door slam and movement in the house.

I was overcome with panic. *Anna and Norman.*

'Nica!' Anna called. I plunged my fingers into Rigel's shoulders. *Oh God, no, no, no . . .*

'Rigel, you've got to let me go.' My heart leapt like an agitated insect. 'Now!'

His mouth overwhelmed me. I was stiff and burning, it felt like *I* was delirious. When his knee slipped between my legs, all my muscles contracted and my heart skipped a beat. I instinctively tightened my thighs and a raspy breath shook his chest.

'Nica!' Anna called again, and I gasped sharply. I threw an anxious look at the door. She was close, she was there, she was . . . *she was . . .*

In a fit of panic, I grabbed a fistful of Rigel's hair and pushed him away.

He gave a low moan as he fell back onto the mattress and I slipped out of the bed.

I flung the door open and there was Anna, her hand outstretched ready to grip the handle.

She stared at my reddened, panicked face in surprise.

'Nica?'

'He's doing a lot better now,' I stammered madly, while Rigel slept under the pillow I had thrown right at his head.

I swept past her, pressing a hand to my neck.

I fled from the room on trembling legs, dazed and confused, my heart trapped back there with him, where Rigel's mouth still burned in a way I would never be able to forget.

Several hours later, I still couldn't shake that feeling. I felt it crawling over my skin. It burned me. It obsessed me. It throbbed all over me like an invisible bruise.

I touched my throat with my fingertips as I went downstairs. When I had looked in the mirror, I had seen a little red mark on my neck, and hoped against hope that if I wore my hair down it wouldn't be noticeable.

But however hard I tried to hide it, what disturbed me most wasn't on the surface. Something was roiling deep inside of me like a ship caught in a tempest and I still had no idea how I could save myself.

In the late afternoon, I went into the kitchen to get some water. I came to an abrupt halt in the doorway.

Rigel was sat at the table.

He was wearing the blue jumper which was slightly baggy around the neck. His face still looked paler than usual, but nonetheless alluring. His thick, messy black hair stuck out in the afternoon light and his eyes were staring right at me.

My heart leapt to my throat.

'I . . . Oh!' I bit my tongue nervously. I looked down at the little box in my hands. 'Anna told me to bring you your medicine,' I explained, as if I didn't know how else to fill the silence. 'I was . . . well . . . I came to get some water.' I noticed the glass he was holding and pressed my lips together. 'I guess there's no point now . . .'

I slowly looked up, hesitant, and my cheeks started tingling when I saw that Rigel's eyes hadn't moved a millimetre from my face. They were incredibly bright and shining, not even tiredness seemed to dull the depth of his gaze. His irises stuck out against his skin like black diamonds.

'How . . . are you feeling?' I breathed after a while.

Rigel looked to the side, furrowing his dark brow, and arranged his lips into a sarcastic smirk.

'Marvellous . . .' he pronounced slowly.

I turned the package over in my hands, embarrassed. My eyes followed his.

'Do you . . . do you remember anything from last night?'

It was stronger than I was. I needed to know. I needed to know if he remembered. Any tiny detail, however insignificant . . .

Every piece of my soul prayed that he would remember. I felt engulfed by the question, as if the fate of the world depended on it.

Because . . . something had changed for me.

For the first time, I had seen Rigel's vulnerability. I had touched him, brushed against him, been close to him. I had taken care of him. He had been human and disarmed, and even the little girl inside me had had to abandon the idea of the invincible Tearsmith and see him for what he truly was.

A boy who pushed the world away.

A solitary, rough, complicated boy who wouldn't let anyone touch his heart.

'Do you remember anything about what happened?' I asked again. He held my gaze.

Anything . . . Anything at all . . . Anything rather than see him go back to being that wolf who always pushes me away . . .

Rigel stared at me, reticent, confused.

He leant back in his chair and his domineering aura once again prevailed.

'Oh, well . . . someone must have taken me to my room.' He looked around the kitchen before planting his eyes insolently back on me. 'And I imagine I've got you to thank for the bruise on my shoulder.'

The memory of our fall flashed before my eyes. I was silenced by a sharp stab of guilt.

But still, I didn't move. Rigel had just implied that the wall between us was still there, but I didn't give in. I didn't step backwards, I didn't hide behind my hair. I stood in the doorway of the kitchen staring at the box of medicine. There was something scant but bright flickering inside me – hope. That candid, uncrushable hope that I had carried inside me since I was a child. Hope that I now had for him, and had no intention of giving up.

Instead of pushing me away, an unfamiliar force pulled me into the kitchen.

I approached the table where he sat, opened the box and took out a pill.

'You've got to take two of these,' I said softly. 'One now, and one tonight.'

Rigel stared at the white pill. Then, slowly, he lifted his gaze to mine. There was something elusive in his eyes. Maybe it was the knowledge that I had come close to him despite how sarcastic he had been with me. Maybe it was because I was no longer scared of him . . .

For a moment, I thought he would chase me away.

For a moment, I thought he would mock me or lash out.

But instead, he tilted his head and looked down.

In silence, without uttering a word, he reached out his hand and took the pill.

I felt a warmth in my chest as he lifted the glass. An unrestrained happiness percolated through me, pushing me forward.

'Hold on, you need more water.'

My fingers brushed his.

It happened all of a sudden.

His hand flinched away and he jumped to his feet. The sound of the chair cut through the air and the glass shattered on the floor, shards scattering everywhere.

I stumbled backwards, stricken by how forcefully he had recoiled.

I stared at him breathlessly. He had flinched away from me with such repulsion that it felt like I'd been stabbed by a shard of glass.

When his eyes met mine, I felt a sharp stab of disappointment. I felt it spreading through me like the roots of a dead tree, snuffing out the hope that had been there before.

And . . .

It was a little bit like dying.

* * *

She was burning.

Her breath was *burning*.

He should have been able to control himself, but that unexpected contact made his heart quiver. Rigel felt a heat much fiercer than the fever.

He bit back a curse. In a fit of panic, he wondered whether she noticed he was shaking as he jerked away.

When he found the courage to look up, he sensed an emptiness. He saw the disappointment in her incredulous eyes, and felt pain devastating every inch of his soul.

Nica slowly looked down and every second of that little movement was like a splinter jabbing under his skin.

He saw her bend over. Her tiny hands collected the shards of glass that were shining like jewels in the afternoon sunlight. If he let her touch him, Rigel wondered, would she ever do the same with the pieces of his shattered heart?

Even though they were so black. And dirty. Even though they were dripping with all the despair he had always thrown at her. Even though they cut and scratched and grazed, and each shard was the colour of her silvery eyes, each one a smile that he had snatched from her lips.

He knew he just had to say thank you. He owed her much more than he had let her see.

He knew this, but he was so used to hurting and scratching that by now it was instinctive. Or maybe, he was simply incapable of anything other than the wickedness stitched within him.

He was terrified by the thought that she, so pure and clean, could know about his desperate feelings.

'Rigel . . .' he heard her whispering quietly.

He didn't move; she had turned him to stone. He froze every time he heard his name in *that* mouth.

'You . . . you really don't remember anything?'

Doubt clawed at him. *What was he supposed to remember? Was there something he had forgotten?*

No, it was fine, he told himself urgently. Just the idea of her hands touching him as she helped him up the stairs was enough to make him lose his mind. And yet, the thought that he could have forgotten that touch was far worse.

'What does it matter?' he heard himself asking. Bitterness seeped from his mouth before he could stop it, and he regretted it as soon as he saw her look up into his eyes.

Her gaze pierced him so sweetly. Her freckles shone on her

delicate, graceful features and her lips stood out like forbidden fruit, like some sort of punishment.

She watched him in that way of hers, like a defenceless nymph, a forest fawn, with an innocence that took his breath away.

Rigel suddenly became aware that she was kneeling in front of him. He felt the burning sensation again, but this time, much lower than his chest. He quickly looked away. Torment rendered him speechless, he felt the need to get away from her. He clenched his jaw and moved away.

He would have left had she not grabbed him by the heart.

He would have left if she hadn't chosen precisely that moment to utter his name again, stopping the earth from spinning under his feet.

He would never forget what she said next.

'Rigel . . . I don't hate you.'

★ ★ ★

I had just told him the truth.

It didn't matter how many times I had run away.

It didn't matter how he continued to bite me.

It didn't matter how hard he had tried to push me away.

None of it mattered . . .

I couldn't bring myself to snap that thin thread that had always bound our lives together.

I couldn't go back . . . not after he had given himself up, defenceless in my arms. Not after that morning, when he had marked me in ways that were more than skin deep.

I had *seen* him.

Not as the Tearsmith I thought he was, but as the boy he had always been.

'And do you hate me?' I remembered our conversation in the hallway. *'Do you hate me, little moth?'*

No . . .

Rigel lifted his chin.

It was like watching the conclusion of something that had been foreseen, that was planned, painfully inevitable. But that didn't make it hurt any less.

He turned to me and stared. After a while, he smiled.

'You're lying to the Tearsmith, Nica,' he mocked, slowly and bitterly. 'You know you shouldn't.'

There we were again: me, the little girl from The Grave, and him, the Tearsmith, with that wall still between us.

We were back to where we had started as children.

History was destined to repeat itself.

Fairy tales always followed the same rule: you get lost in the woods and vanquish the wolf. That was the only way to reach a happy ending. After all, fairy tales end with 'ever after'.

Could we be the exception?

16. Behind Glass

Love that is silent is the most difficult to touch,
but under the surface, it shines with a sincere,
incredible immensity.

He held on as tightly as he could.

He wasn't hurting him enough.

Fingernails dug painfully into his supple skin, but Rigel didn't loosen his grip.

'I told you to give it me,' he hissed again, in that tone that always drove fear into everyone's hearts.

'No! It's mine!'

The other boy thrashed about like a wild dog. He tried to scratch him and push him away. Rigel pulled his hair violently, making him whine in pain and anger. He crushed him with all his strength.

'Give it me,' he snarled, furiously digging his nails into the boy's skin. 'Now!'

The other boy obeyed. He opened his fist and something fell to the floor. As soon as Rigel saw it at his feet, he let the boy go and pushed him away.

The boy tumbled to the ground, his fingers grasping at the dust. He shot Rigel a fierce but fearful look, then scrambled to his feet and ran away.

Short of breath and with scraped knees, Rigel bent to pick up what he had reclaimed.

The scratches were painful, but he didn't pay them any attention. All he needed was a glimpse of her from afar and he would no longer feel his knees burning.

And that evening, he saw her appear in the doorway of the dormitory. For the last few days, her hand hadn't stopped wiping away her constant tears.

All of a sudden, Nica lifted her eyes to her bed at the far end of the room and her girlish face lit up. Her shining smile made the whole world glow. Through the windows, Rigel watched her run to her bed and throw herself onto her pillow.

He watched her cuddling her caterpillar plushie, the only thing she had left to remind her of her parents. Rigel had noticed how threadbare and tattered it was. Its seams had burst during the tussle with the other boy, and its stuffing was poking out like a puff of foam.

But she just narrowed her eyes and smiled through a stream of tears.

She clutched it to her chest as if it was the most precious thing in the world.

Rigel watched her silently as she cuddled her little treasure. Stood there, hidden in a corner of the garden, immensely relieved, he felt buds blooming amongst all the thorns in his blackened heart.

★ ★ ★

'How are you feeling?'

Curtains full of sun and soft light.

Anna was standing with her back to me. She asked the question with a unique grace.

Rigel was sitting at the table in front of her and just nodded without meeting her eyes. He had been off school for two days with the fever.

'Are you sure?' she asked softly.

Concerned, she brushed aside a lock of his hair, revealing the cut on his brow.

'Oh, Rigel . . .' she sighed with a hint of exasperation. 'How did this happen?'

Rigel looked sideways and didn't say a thing. There was a silence between them which I didn't understand and Anna didn't ask any other questions.

I didn't know why I lingered to watch them. Anna's behaviour pulled at my heart; I was entranced by her maternal care. But every time I saw her and Rigel speaking, I got the impression I was missing something.

'I don't like the colour of this cut,' she said, turning her attention to his brow. 'It could get infected. You haven't cleaned it, have you?' She made him tilt his face a little. 'We'll need . . . Oh, Nica!'

I jumped as she noticed me. I was instantly ashamed of how I had been watching them secretly, stealing looks.

'Can you do me a favour? Upstairs, in the bathroom, there's disinfectant and cotton balls – could you go and fetch them?'

I nodded, avoiding looking at Rigel. I hadn't spoken to him since the conversation in the kitchen.

I was surprised to find that I had been watching him more and more often, the worst part being that I hadn't even noticed that I was doing it.

There was something hanging in the air between us and I couldn't stop thinking about it.

A few minutes later, I returned with the things Anna had asked me for. I found her dabbing at Rigel's cut with a napkin. I anticipated her next request and doused a cotton ball with disinfectant.

When I held it out to her, she moved a little to one side, still concentrating on the cut. I realised she was making space for me, and hesitated. Did she want me to clean it?

I moved forward tentatively and edged around Anna so I was facing Rigel.

For a fleeting moment, his eyes were on me. On my hands, my hair, my face, my shoulders. And then, just as suddenly, he tore them away and stared in another direction.

As I drew closer to him, I accidentally brushed against his knee and thought I saw a muscle twitching in his jaw. Anna tilted his head back again.

'Just here,' she said, pointing.

Rigel seemed to be putting in a huge amount of effort to not recoil as sharply as he wanted to. He didn't flinch, but I could tell that it took him a tremendous amount of self-control.

I carefully dabbed his brow. I was tense, partly because I was scared of hurting him, partly because I was closer than he normally allowed me to be.

His throat seemed tight. He stared fixedly off to one side, his hand gripping his knee so forcefully that his knuckles looked like they might burst through his skin.

I knew that he didn't like being the centre of Anna's attention. He had never wanted to be cared for and looked after. It irritated him. Even when we were children, when everyone else was begging for a cuddle, Rigel had never been interested in affection.

Not like me. I would have given anything to be on the receiving end of all this tender, loving care.

Suddenly, the landline rang.

Anna spun around so quickly that I jumped.

'Oh . . . you carry on, Nica, I'll be right back.'

I threw her an imploring look, but it was no use. Anna left, leaving me alone with Rigel.

Trying not to let anything show, I carried on doing just what she had asked me to, but it was impossible not to notice Rigel's hand. His fingers dug into his own flesh as if this closeness to me was more than he could bear.

My heartbeat slowed.

Did he really hate the idea of being close to me so much? Did it really disgust him so much?

Why?

I was overcome with sadness. I had really hoped that things would change, but there was an abyss between us. An unbridgeable void.

And it didn't matter how hard I hoped, it didn't matter how much things had changed for me. That invisible wall was still there, and always would be.

He would always push me away.

He would always shatter my every hope.

He would always be distant and unapproachable.

I looked down at Rigel one last time, clawing for confirmation of that sadness. Maybe I just wanted to feel upset enough that I would abandon all hope, as if that was the only way I'd be able to accept it . . .

Instead, my heart skipped a beat.

Rigel's shoulders were no longer a bundle of tension. His fingers had loosened on his knee, as if he'd been gripping for too long and no longer had the strength. And his face . . . his features were calm, and he was no longer staring with stubbornness, but with *resignation*. At my touch, his languishing eyes filled with a suffering that somehow seemed to give him some sort of relief.

I looked at him in shock, incredulous. He looked exhausted, worn out, as if he had given in. He looked so changed, like a different person altogether. I trembled at the sight of him. My heart raced, beating so hard it hurt.

Rigel sighed, keeping his lips shut, as if he didn't want anyone to hear, not even himself. I fell to pieces.

There was more. I looked at him. I wanted to tell him that it didn't have to be this way, that we could be a different fairy tale, if he wanted.

I looked at him with sad, silent eyes, wishing I could understand him.

And instinctively . . . my fingers slid over his skin and slowly stroked his temple.

He seemed so vulnerable with that tormented expression that I didn't even realise what I was doing.

Rigel jumped. His eyes shot daggers. He froze when he saw that I was watching him, *that I had been watching him all this time*.

He grabbed my sleeve and jumped to his feet.

Before I knew it, my arms were over my head, his gaze pinned to mine, his body towering over me. I stared at him breathlessly, rooted to the spot. His eyes flashed with unstoppable emotions. His warm breath tickled my cheeks, which suddenly burned.

'Rigel . . .' I whispered faintly, afraid.

He slowly loosened his grip on my sleeve. His fingers released the fabric and his eyes fell to my lips. My throat went dry. He sucked all my energy and I felt suddenly weak.

A quivering silence shattered that moment into fragments. My heart shuddered, thundered, begged for just a single breath . . .

And then, Rigel released me.

It was so sudden that for a moment it felt like the ground had dropped out from under my feet. I stumbled, and in that deafening confusion, heard footsteps.

'It was just some friends. They were calling to ask if . . .'

Anna halted in the doorway. She blinked several times as Rigel moved past her to leave the room. She turned to face me.

'Is everything all right?' she asked.

I couldn't find the words to answer her.

Later on, trying to study, I couldn't think straight.

My thoughts kept buzzing around Rigel like bees to pollen. I blinked, trying in vain to shoo them away, but they persisted, like the lingering traces of a harsh light stared at for too long.

I came back to my senses as a message flashed on my phone screen.

I put my pencil down and checked it. It was Billie, sending me another goat video. She'd been sending me a load of these recently. I didn't know why goats scream like that, but whenever I opened one, I couldn't stop watching. Only yesterday she had sent me a video of a llama frolicking about and, just like that, I'd lost half the afternoon.

I sighed with a little smile. It was childish, but . . . those videos gave me a sense of tranquillity. I cherished Billie like a gem. I was grateful that there was someone who thought of me, who didn't need any special reason to send me a message, who trusted me and considered me a friend. It was all new for me.

Suddenly, my phone rang.

I looked at the screen and hesitated before picking up.

'Hello? Oh . . . Hi, Lionel.'

He'd been ceaselessly trying to speak to me the past few days: on the phone, at school between lessons, but seeing him gave me a strange, almost uneasy, feeling. I didn't want to push him away, but after what happened with Rigel, his face just reminded me of the attack. Part of me wanted to erase that memory, push it away and pretend it never happened . . .

But as soon as I'd begun to avoid him, Lionel had started messaging me more and more insistently. He asked me if Rigel had tried to defend himself with lies and false excuses.

I had denied it, and he seemed reassured.

'Look out the window,' he urged me. When I did so, I was surprised to find him there.

He waved hello, and I waved back, uncertainly.

'I was just passing by,' he explained with a smile. 'Why don't you come down? We could go for a walk.'

'I'd love to, but I have to finish my homework . . .'

'Oh, come on, it's a beautiful day, let's go,' he insisted brightly. 'You don't really want to stay shut up inside?'

'But I've got a physics test on Friday . . .'

'Just a quick walk round the block, come on.'

'Lionel, I'd love to,' I said, holding the phone in both hands. 'But I've really got to study . . .'

'You think I don't have to too? It's just a walk. Fine, if you really don't want to . . .'

'It's not that I don't want to,' I hastened to say.

'So what's the problem?'

I watched him through the window, and wondered if he'd always been so pushy. Maybe I was just being more evasive than usual . . .

'Okay,' I finally gave in.

Just a quick walk round the block, he had said, right?

'I'll put my shoes on. I'll be down in a sec.'

He smiled.

I grabbed a jacket and slipped on my sneakers. I looked at my reflection in the mirror and made sure the red mark on my neck wasn't visible. It was still there, like a reminder that wouldn't fade away. The thought that it came from Rigel's lips made my skin tingle. I decided to hide it with a bottle-green scarf and went downstairs.

I told Anna that I was going out, but then stopped and doubled back to grab something from the kitchen.

'Hi,' I greeted Lionel at the front gate. I tucked my hair behind my ear and held out a popsicle. 'Here.'

Lionel looked at it, then at me, and I smiled warmly.

'It's got a crocodile inside.'

He gazed at me, dumbstruck. His smile was triumphant.

He was right, it was a beautiful day.

We licked our popsicles as we walked along the road. I listened attentively as he told me about his dad's new car. He didn't seem happy about it – he complained about his father's choice several times, even though it seemed like it was a very expensive model.

It was only after we had walked a fair distance that I realised that we were no longer on the familiar leafy streets of home.

'Hold on, wait . . .' I looked around, disorientated. 'We've gone too far. I . . . I don't recognise this area.'

He didn't seem to have heard me.

'Lionel, we've walked out of my neighbourhood,' I tried to tell him, slowing to a stop. He carried on walking until he noticed that I was no longer with him.

'What are you doing?' he asked, looking at me. 'Oh, don't worry. I know this area well,' he added calmly. 'Come on.'

I watched him with a twinge of an emotion I couldn't explain. He noticed it too.

'What's up?'

'It's just that we said we'd go for a quick walk around the block . . .'

When would he realise that we'd gone too far?

'We've just gone a bit further,' he replied as I slowly approached him. He looked me in the eyes, then glanced down. 'I actually live around here . . .' He kicked a stone. 'Five minutes away.' He threw me a look, then looked at his feet again. 'As we've come this far, we could drop by.'

I noticed his slight embarrassment and softened. He wanted to show me his house. I was just as fond and proud of where I lived, and I hadn't lost any time in inviting Miki over. It must have been the same for him.

'Okay,' I smiled.

Lionel seemed pleased. He looked at me brightly, then straightened up and scratched his nose.

When we reached his house, I noticed that it was very well kept. The garage had an automatic door with a shiny handle. Perfectly level pebbles formed a carpet that went all around the house. In the back garden, I glimpsed a basketball hoop and a very new, red-hot lawnmower. Perfectly precise lines of violets bordered the garden. I couldn't help but think how different they looked to the lively, untamed gardenias that adorned our picket fence.

As the door opened, a clean, open space unfolded before my eyes. The floor was marble, white curtains filtered the sunlight and not a sound broke the silence.

It was a beautiful house.

Lionel dropped his jacket on an armchair, and seemed to find it unusual that I wiped my shoes carefully on the mat before stepping in.

'I'm so thirsty! Come on, there's no one home.'

He disappeared through a door. I followed him, and found it led to the kitchen.

He was standing by the fridge, holding a bottle of water and a glass, from which he was drinking large gulps.

It was only when he put the bottle back in the fridge that he noticed I was watching him.

He blinked at me for a moment. 'Oh, yeah . . . do you want some water too?'

I tucked my hair behind my ear, pleased by his kind offer.

'Oh, thank you.'

He held out a glass with a proud smile and I lifted it to my lips, grateful for how cool and refreshing it was. I would have liked some more, but Lionel had already put the bottle away.

He showed me every corner of the house, top to bottom.

I took note of several framed photos scattered here and there on sideboards, tables and shelves. Lionel was in almost all of them, at different ages, always holding either an ice cream or a toy car.

'I won this last month,' he announced proudly, showing me his latest tennis trophy. I congratulated him and he seemed intensely pleased. He showed me his medals, and the more I admired his trophies the more he seemed to glow with pride.

'There's something I want to show you,' he smiled at me slyly. 'It's a surprise . . . come on.'

I followed him through the house until he stopped in front of a closed door off the beautiful living room. He turned towards me and I looked up at him, my eyes curious and clear.

'Close your eyes,' he told me with a devious smile.

'What's in that room?' I asked, looking at the mahogany door.

'It's my father's study . . . Go on, close your eyes,' he laughed.

I found myself smiling instinctively and closed my eyes, intrigued.

I heard the door open. He led me forward and together we entered the study.

His hands turned my shoulders around so I was facing a specific direction. He squeezed me just before letting me go, as if he wanted to imprint something onto me.

'Okay . . . open your eyes.'

I opened my eyes.

The study was beautiful, but that wasn't what stunned me. It was the wall in front of me, which was covered with frames of all shapes and sizes, and the *exorbitant* number of insects peering out from behind the glass.

Dozens of shining beetles, golden chafers, chrysalises at every stage of their cycle, bees, multicoloured dragonflies, praying mantises, even a collection of snail shells neatly arranged in a line.

I found myself staring at the display, frozen as if someone had preserved me too.

'Do you see?' Lionel asked proudly. 'Go and have a closer look!'

He dragged me over to the frame of butterflies. I stared aghast at their beautiful, immobile wings and their minute, pinned abdomens, and Lionel pointed at a sample near the bottom of the frame.

'Have a look at what it says.'

Nica Flavilla, read the elegantly handwritten caption next to a graceful, bright orange butterfly.

'It's got your name!' Lionel beamed at me proudly, as if he had shown me something so incredible that I should have been flattered.

I felt the blood draining away from my face. All I could see was drawn wings and pierced abdomens. Lionel misinterpreted my silence.

'Crazy, right? My dad collects a load of stuff in his free time, but I think he's particularly proud of these. I think he prepared them all for display himself, when he was . . . Oh, Nica . . . Are you okay?'

I had crumpled against the desk. I clamped my lips shut. It felt like I might vomit the popsicle back up onto the marble floor.

'Do you feel ill? What's wrong?'

He assailed me with questions and I swallowed again, feeling something wobble inside of me.

'Wait here, okay? I'll go and get you some more water. I'll be right back.'

He left the study and I tried to calm down. It was just the shock. I tried to take deep breaths. I knew I was especially sensitive, but that was the last thing in the world I had been expecting.

Lionel hurried back with the bottle of water.

He handed it to me, but only when I took it did he realise that he had forgotten a glass.

'Hold on.' He disappeared again and I closed my eyes, taking a deep breath in.

The room had stopped spinning. Soon, Lionel returned with a glass and I thanked him.

'Are you feeling better?' he asked, once I'd finished drinking.

I nodded, trying to reassure him.

'It's passed . . . I'm fine now.'

'Sometimes our emotions can get the better of us,' he smiled, amused. 'You weren't expecting that, were you?'

I smiled nervously, then changed the subject by asking what his father did. I learnt he was a notary, and for a while we carried on chatting.

'It's getting late,' I said at some point, looking outside. I still had a heap of homework to get through.

We left the study and Lionel insisted on walking me back home. 'If you want to freshen up before going, the bathroom's through there . . .'

I froze.

Lionel followed my eyes, and when he saw that I had stopped in front of a door which had been left ajar, he smiled.

'Mom keeps her stuff in here,' he explained, pushing the door open all the way. Long sticks with brightly coloured ribbons appeared before my eyes.

'She's a rhythmic gymnastics instructor,' he told me as I walked in, entranced.

A large mirror filled the far wall, next to some strange, skinny bowling pins.

'They're clubs,' he explained. 'She won a lot of medals in her time. She was good. She just teaches now.'

I looked at a collection of photos on another wall with bright, shining eyes. So vivid, so graceful! She looked like a multicoloured swan, radiating harmony, softness, enchantment.

'It's so beautiful,' I breathed sincerely, glowing.

I turned towards him and smiled with shining eyes.

Lionel stared at me with mild enthusiasm. He smiled back at me, with the same glint in his eye that he had in all the photos where he was holding his trophies.

He picked up one of the sticks and a long ribbon swirled through the air. I watched the flickering strip of pink in awe and laughed, spinning around as Lionel made it spiral above my head.

I spun around a few times, trying to follow the ribbon with my eyes. Lionel was just a blurry smile beyond the flashes of silk.

Then, suddenly, the ribbon started to wind tightly around me. My smile became strained.

'Lionel . . .' I let out.

My arms got caught in the ribbon, and I was overcome by a visceral terror. I was suffocating. My body twisted, my heart reared up and my fear burst out with a terrible scream.

The stick crashed to the ground.

I stepped back under Lionel's stunned gaze. I was shaking violently as I tore the ribbon off me, gasping so desperately I couldn't breathe. My blood pounded in my temples and my mind flooded with vivid nightmares, interspersed fragments of darkness and memories of a closed door and a flaking ceiling.

'Nica?'

I gripped my elbows, hugging my arms tightly around me, and gasped for breath.

'I . . .' I gasped, weak and trembling. 'I . . . sorry . . . I . . . I . . .'

Tears of powerlessness stung my eyes. The need to hide pushed me back into myself with a nauseating urgency, and the feeling of Lionel's eyes on me corroded my stomach. Collapsing into my terrors, I felt like a little girl again.

I shouldn't let myself be seen.

I wanted to cover my arms, to disappear, become invisible. I wanted to rip my skin off just to divert his attention.

'You know what will happen if you tell anyone about this?'

I wanted to scream, but my throat closed up and I couldn't utter a word. I turned and sprinted out of the room.

I found the bathroom and locked myself inside. Writhing with nausea, I threw myself towards the sink. I put my wrists under the spurt of cold water gushing from the faucet, and stayed like that as Lionel kept banging insistently on the door, calling for me to open up.

Some wounds never stop bleeding.

Some days, they burst open and Band-Aids aren't enough to make them heal. For me, these were moments when I realised I was just as naïve, childlike and fragile as I used to be. I was a little girl in the body of a young woman. I looked at the world with hopeful eyes because I couldn't admit to myself that life had let me down.

I wanted to be normal, but I wasn't.

I was different.

Different from all the others.

When I eventually got home, it was getting late.

The asphalt was bathed in the light of the sunset filtering through the trees.

Lionel walked with me in silence up until the picket fence.

After an endless time in the bathroom, I eventually came out and apologised profusely. I tried in every possible way to downplay what had happened, telling him that I had just got a bit frightened, that it was nothing, that there was no need to worry. I knew how ridiculous my excuses sounded, but that didn't stop me from hoping he'd believe them.

Lionel was very unsettled by my reaction. He was worried he'd done something wrong, but I assured him that it was fine, that it was nothing. I didn't look him in the eyes and he said nothing. I wanted more than anything to erase the incident from his memory.

'Thanks for walking me home,' I murmured. I didn't have the courage to look him in the face.

'Don't mention it,' was all he said, though I could tell from his tone of voice that he was still disturbed.

I found the strength to look up and give him a gentle smile, with a tinge of sadness. Lionel tried to do the same but something about the house caught his attention.

'See you soon,' I said, but his hand held me back.

Before I could move, Lionel leant down and planted a kiss on my cheek.

I blinked and saw the corner of his mouth curling up in a smile.

'See you, Nica.'

I put my hand to my cheek in befuddlement as I watched him walk away, then I went inside.

The house was enveloped in calmness. I took my jacket off and hung it up, then dashed across the hall to go upstairs. I froze when I sensed the presence of someone else. In the dying light, I noticed the room with the bookshelves was occupied by a silent figure.

Rigel was sat at the piano.

He was immersed in total silence. One of his fingers brushed lightly over the surface of the keys. There was a faded, elegant charm about him and a shiver came over me.

After a while, he looked over his shoulder at me.

My soul quivered deep inside of me. He was looking at me in a way he never had before, his gaze somehow burned me and froze me at the same time. It was bitter. Powerful. It shook me to my core.

Rigel looked away from me and stood up.

Before he could leave, however, I heard myself gasping, 'What happened between you and Lionel?'

I'd never been good at giving in or letting go, I didn't have it in me.

I took a step forward.

'How come you ended up fighting?'

'Why don't you ask him?' Rigel spat, so venomously I flinched. 'He's already told you all about it, hasn't he?'

'I want to hear it from you,' I said feebly.

Rigel tilted his face, his lips shining with a cruel smile that didn't reach his eyes.

'Why? You want to hear how I *smashed* his face in?' he asked with a biting resentment.

I didn't understand. My gaze fell on the window that looked out over the front garden.

Had he seen?

He made to go, leaving me there, and before I had a chance to think, my body moved.

Not this time.

In a leap of courage, I blocked his path. A shiver ran down my minute body as I looked up. Rigel was towering over me, his hair set ablaze by the sunset. I instantly regretted having acted so rashly.

Looking at me uncertainly, in a strangely hoarse voice, he whispered, 'Move.'

'Answer me.' My voice was thin, it sounded like I was begging. 'Please.'

'Move, Nica,' he reproached me, stressing each syllable.

I moved my hand. I didn't know what it was that always made me want to look for a closeness with everyone. But when it came to Rigel, I couldn't help myself. After the night I had looked after him, I was no longer scared of the invisible wall between us. In fact, I wanted to bridge it.

That gesture was enough to provoke a reaction. I felt a stab of disappointment. He stopped me from getting any closer. He moved away and shot me a look of ice and fire. His breathing was laboured. It seemed like an involuntary reflex, but that didn't make his flinch away from such an innocent gesture any less hurtful.

But he let Anna touch him. And Norman. And he had no problem touching anyone who picked a fight with him . . . He only flinched away like that . . . from me.

'Does it bother you that much when I touch you?' My hands were shaking. I felt a sharp stab in my heart. 'Who do you think looked after you when you had a fever?'

'I didn't ask you to,' he spat out stonily.

He was acting as if I had cornered him. My eyes opened wide.

I saw the image of my hands supporting him, the effort it took to get him up the stairs, the care and attention with which I had stayed with him all night. Had that just annoyed him?

Rigel clenched his fists and tightened his jaw. Then he moved past me as if he couldn't wait to get away from me.

By that point, my body was shaking so violently that I could hardly recognise myself.

'I can't touch you but you can touch me, is that it?'

I stared at him, my eyes shining with fury. Then, with my heart burning like a volcano, I tore the scarf from my neck.

'This doesn't count for anything, does it?'

His eyes dropped to my throat. Rigel stared at the red mark and I pursed my lips.

'*You* did this,' I burst out. 'When you had a fever. You don't even remember.'

Something happened that I'd never seen before. There was a flash of dismay in his eyes and for the first time, I saw Rigel's confidence crumble before me.

His perfect mask wavered. His gaze went cold, and something akin to fear made its way across his face. It was so fleeting that I thought maybe I was mistaken.

Something suddenly flashed through his eyes and his tight smile returned quicker than ever, so full of fierceness that it chased away any sense of vulnerability.

I suddenly understood. Rigel was about to *bite me*.

'Well, you can't exactly say I was feeling myself . . .' he sneered, looking me up and down. He looked at me sarcastically and clicked his tongue. 'You didn't *really* believe I'd want to do that *to you*? I was having a lovely dream before you interrupted . . . Next time, Nica, don't wake me up.'

He smiled a devilishly charming smile, then gave me a scornful look. He was used to using his power like that to put that invisible wall between us.

He turned his back to leave, but he can't have been expecting what tumbled out of my mouth next.

'It's just a shield,' I said quietly. 'Your spite. It's like someone hurt you and you don't know how else to protect yourself.'

He froze. My words had hit their target.

I no longer believed in his mask. The more Rigel wore it, the more I knew he just didn't want others to see what lay beneath.

He was abrasive, sarcastic, complicated and unpredictable. He didn't trust anyone.

But he was more than that.

Maybe one day I would understand the complicated inner workings of his soul.

Maybe one day I would be able to crack the mystery that would explain all of his actions.

But there was one thing I was absolutely certain of.

Tearsmith or not . . . No one made my heart quiver like he did.

17. Gravy

You can recognise those who are different immediately.
In their worlds, it's others whose eyes see.

That day, we were due to have guests from just outside the city. Some old friends of Anna and Norman were coming for lunch.

When I found out, something inside of me started vibrating, pushing away all other thoughts. I was anxious to make a good impression.

I smoothed down my dress. It was very simple, white, with a ruched bust and straps that left my shoulders exposed. I looked at my reflection in the small, silver-framed mirror in the hallway and felt my stomach twisting with an unfamiliar emotion. I wasn't used to seeing myself like that, like a doll, so smart, polished and groomed.

If it wasn't for the Band-Aids on my hands and my mother-of-pearl eyes, I wouldn't have recognised myself.

I made sure that the side of my neck was covered by my braid. The mark had been fading over the past few days, but I didn't want to risk it.

'Oh, it's so hot today!' I heard a woman's voice exclaiming from the front door. 'If only I'd known. There's not a breath of wind here with you!'

Mr and Mrs Otter had arrived.

The woman who had spoken was wearing a beautiful, cobalt blue overcoat. Anna had told me she was a tailor. She kissed both her cheeks with genuine affection.

'Is the car all right there in the driveway? George can move it if it's in the way . . .'

'It's absolutely fine, don't worry about it.'

Anna kindly took her hat and invited her in.

They walked arm in arm and Mrs Otter put a hand on her wrist.

'How are you, Anna?' she asked, almost apprehensively.

Anna responded by squeezing her gently, but I noticed that she was looking at me as they walked through the hall. Mrs Otter was too busy searching Anna's eyes to notice me.

When they eventually stopped in front of me, Anna said with a smile, 'Dalma, this is Nica.'

Here we go . . .

I tried to contain my trepidation and smiled.

'Hello.'

Mrs Otter didn't reply. She gazed at me, her mouth slightly open and her face full of confusion. She couldn't believe her eyes. She blinked and looked at Anna.

'I don't . . .' She seemed to be lost for words. 'How . . .'

I also tried to catch Anna's eye, almost as shocked as Mrs Otter was, but at the next moment, she looked at me with a completely new sort of astonishment. She seemed to have only just realised the reason for these introductions. Anna's hand was still holding hers.

'I'm so sorry . . .' She seemed to have recovered, but was still breathless. 'I was caught by surprise.' Her lips melted into a shy, slightly incredulous smile. 'Hi . . .' she exhaled earnestly.

I couldn't remember anyone ever having greeted me like that before. It felt like she had caressed me, without even touching me.

What a miraculous feeling, the feeling of someone looking at me like that . . .

Satisfied, I thought I could safely say that I'd made a decent impression in that white dress.

'George!' Mrs Otter called, waving a hand behind her. 'Come here.'

Her husband, who had a bushy moustache, was congratulating Norman on the conference. When Anna introduced us, he was just as astonished as his wife.

'My goodness,' he said out of nowhere. Anna and Norman laughed.

'It was a surprise,' Norman murmured, awkward as ever. Mr Otter took my hand.

'Pleased to meet you, Miss.'

I offered to take their jackets, which they seemed to appreciate. Dalma clutched Anna's arm and turned to her to ask, 'Since . . . since when?'

'Not that long ago, actually,' she replied. 'You know when we spoke the time before last? They arrived that week.'

'They?'

'Oh, yes. It's not just Nica . . . There's two of them. Norman, dear, where's . . .'

'Upstairs, still getting changed,' he replied readily.

Our guests exchanged a tentative look but said nothing. Anna turned to them. 'What about Asia?'

I imperceptibly furrowed my brow.

Asia?

The front door opened again. I blinked in surprise as someone else came in. A willowy, backlit girl, phone in one hand and handbag in the other.

'I'm sorry, I had to take a call,' she said. She wiped her feet on the doormat, dropped the car keys in the key bowl and smiled.

'Hi.'

Suddenly, everyone turned their backs to me. Anna approached her with open arms and such a radiant smile I was floored.

'Asia, sweetheart!'

They embraced each other tightly. She was very tall, and her clothes looked tailor-made for her. She looked a few years older than Rigel and I.

'You're looking good, Anna . . . How are you doing? Norman, hi!' She hugged him too – *Norman,* the maximum amount of physical contact I'd seen him engage in was a pat on the back – and planted a kiss on his cheek.

Now everyone was smiling at her.

I observed how close they all seemed. Their familiarity seemed to shine with an alien, inaccessible light.

Anna hadn't told me that Mr and Mrs Otter had a daughter.

'Come in,' Anna welcomed her, while Asia cast her eyes around looking for someone.

'Where's Klaus? That old cat better come and say hello to me . . .'

'Asia, this is Nica.'

She didn't notice me straight away. She blinked, then looked down and saw me. I lifted a hand to wave.

'Hello, lovely to meet you,' I said with a smile, under Anna's affectionate gaze. I looked at the girl and waited for her to reciprocate.

But Asia didn't move a muscle.

She didn't even blink. Her eyes stayed so motionless that I started to feel uneasy. I felt like a butterfly on display, pierced by invisible pins.

Asia turned to Anna.

She looked at her as if she was her mom, her gaze hiding some need.

'I don't get it,' was all she said. It seemed like she hoped there had been some sort of misunderstanding.

'Nica's staying here with us,' Anna explained delicately. 'She's . . . on a pre-adoptive placement.'

I smiled. 'Shall I take your jacket? I'll hang it up for you.'

Once again, it seemed as if Asia hadn't heard me.

Her eyes were glued to Anna, as if she had stopped the world and was holding it calmly in her hand, a calmness that Asia couldn't accept.

After a while, she mumbled, 'I don't think I understand.'

'Nica's going to be part of our family. We're adopting her.'

'You want to . . .'

'Asia,' Mrs Otter murmured, but her daughter was still staring tremulously at Anna.

'*I don't . . . understand,*' she whispered again. But it wasn't the explanation that she didn't understand. It was that Anna's calm gaze had now turned to me.

I got a sudden, strange, icy feeling that I was out of place. It felt like I had somehow done something wrong, just by living under that roof.

'Norman and I were feeling a bit lonely,' Anna explained after a while. 'We wanted . . . a bit of company. Klaus . . . well, you know how he is, he's never been all that sociable. We wanted to wake up and hear someone else's voice.'

Anna and Asia exchanged a meaningful glance.

'And so here we are,' Norman intervened to dissipate the tension. Anna moved away to check on the roast and Asia watched her go, her eyes full of dismay and other emotions I couldn't comprehend.

I took a step towards her and smiled.

'I can take your jacket for you if you want . . .'

'*I know* where the coat rack is,' she snapped.

I fell silent and she went to hang her jacket up herself.

I clutched the skirt of my dress. Every inch of my body felt out of place. Anna announced that lunch was almost ready.

Dalma approached me and asked kindly, 'Nica, I haven't even asked how old you are.'

'Seventeen,' I replied.

'And the other girl? Is she the same age as you?'

'There's another girl?' Asia asked slowly.

'Oh no,' Anna replied. Those two words made everyone freeze. The guests stared at her. I couldn't understand what had just happened. 'To tell the truth . . .'

'Sorry I'm late.'

Everyone turned around.

Rigel had entered the room.

His alluring presence filled the living room, drawing every last shred of attention to him. He was wearing a light-coloured shirt, one I was sure Anna had insisted on, and he was still buttoning up the cuffs. I couldn't imagine any piece of clothing looking more perfect on him.

A lock of hair hid the cut on his brow and lent him a mysterious charm. He looked up, and everyone was bewitched by his dark eyes.

The guests stared at him, flabbergasted.

I knew how destabilising Rigel was, but their reactions still seemed unusual. They seemed even more incredulous and taken aback than they had been with me.

His lips formed a smile so persuasive that I felt my guts squirm, even though he wasn't even looking at me.

'Good morning. My name is Rigel Wilde. It's a pleasure to meet you, Mr and Mrs Otter.'

He shook both their hands and asked how their journey had been. They were like putty in his hands.

Asia was as still as a stone. She was staring at him with a disturbing intensity. Rigel slid his eyes to meet hers.

'Hello,' he said, impeccably politely.

Silence ensued.

I was still clutching the skirt of my dress.

'Well, um . . .' Norman started. 'Shall we sit down to lunch?'

As I sat down to Norman's left, I felt Asia's gaze piercing my skin.

I wondered if she had wanted to sit there, but then she sat down next to Anna and dragged her into a whirlwind of chatter.

Watching the two of them laughing, I realised with a stab to my chest that for Anna, she was much more than a friend's daughter. Asia was beautiful, sophisticated. She was at college. They seemed in perfect harmony. She seemed to know Anna in ways that I couldn't understand.

I looked away from them to the other side of the table.

Rigel was sat as far away as possible from me. When the rest of us had sat down, he had looked at the empty chair next to me, but then chosen the seat opposite.

He hadn't so much as glanced at me since he had come downstairs.

Was he deliberately ignoring me?

Just as well, I told myself.

The thought of his proximity gave me an empty feeling in my stomach. I swore I wouldn't look at him. The last moments we had shared tormented me enough.

'Nica, do you want some meat?' Norman asked, proffering the platter. I served myself with a smile.

'Have some gravy, too,' he advised kindly, then turned to Mrs Otter.

The gravy boat was on the other side of the table, of course, right next to Rigel. I gazed at it despairingly, before noticing that Asia was examining him with an unsubtle, intense interest. As she lifted her fork to her mouth, I let my gaze run over her hands, her hair, her perfect face. Why was she staring at him like that?

Rigel flashed a smile at Mrs Otter and I looked away.

I shouldn't look at him.

But the gravy . . . Anna and I had made it together . . . it made sense that I wanted to taste it, didn't it?

I stole another furtive look at the gravy boat and decided not to worry about it. Rigel poured some for himself, then placed it back on the table, still holding the serving spoon.

Then, noticing he had got some on his thumb, he lifted his hand to his mouth and placed his thumb on his lower lip. He closed his mouth around the tip and then slowly slid it back out, licking off the gravy. As he lowered the serving spoon, he lifted his deep, dark, narrow eyes to me.

'Nica . . . are you all right?'

I startled and turned towards Mrs Otter. She was staring at me, dumbfounded.

'You've gone red, dear . . .'

I glanced away. I felt almost feverish. 'The mash,' I croaked. 'It's . . .' I swallowed. 'Spicy.'

I felt *his* eyes boring across the table.

My stomach was radiating a strange hotness all through my body. I tried to ignore it, but it spread through me with a crawling sensation. I had to concentrate on the lunch. Just the lunch . . .

After a while, I noticed Norman looking at my plate.

'Oh, Nica, are you not having gravy?'

'No,' I replied shortly.

Norman blinked, and I realised how tersely I had answered him.

I felt my cheeks burning with shame and hurried to put things right. 'I just . . . prefer it like this, thank you.'

'You're sure?'

'Yes, certain.'

'Oh, come on, pass the gravy boat.'

'I don't *like* gravy!' I burst out.

It was, to say the least, *tragic,* when I noticed Anna opposite me, staring, stunned, with her fork halfway to her mouth.

'It . . . it's not that I don't like it!' I bleated desperately, leaning forward and clutching my knife and fork. 'I love it, it's delicious! I've never tasted any better, it's so flavourful and . . . and . . . *full-bodied*. It's just that . . . well, I've just already had so much of it that . . .'

'So, Rigel!' Mr Otter interrupted.

I jumped as if I'd been struck by lightning. Hot and embarrassed, I hurried to pull out a strand of my hair that had ended up in my mash. Asia looked at me across the table with narrowed, critical eyes.

'Your name is very unusual. If I'm not mistaken, there's a constellation that . . . well, that has the same name?'

I froze at that question. Rigel stared at the table and took his time before replying. His smile was with us, but his eyes seemed elsewhere.

'It's not a constellation. It's a star,' he replied calmly. 'The brightest star in Orion.'

Mr and Mrs Otter seemed enthralled.

'How fascinating! A boy named after a star . . . Whoever named you made a very intriguing decision!'

Rigel's smile sparkled enigmatically.

'Oh, undoubtedly,' he said with a hint of sarcasm. 'It certainly helps me keep in mind my distant origins.'

His answer stabbed me right in the chest.

'Oh . . .' Mr Otter stammered, panicked. 'Well . . .'

'That's not why.'

I bit my tongue. Too late. I had spoken out loud.

Everyone turned. Their attention crashed down on me and I looked down.

'She chose that name . . . because when they found you, you were about a week old. *Seven days old* . . . And Rigel is the seventh brightest star in the sky. And that evening it was shining brighter than ever.'

There was a moment of silence, and then a cascade of admiring comments. Everyone started talking at once, and Anna told Dalma with a hint of pride that we had been 'very close' at the institute.

I looked up at Rigel. He hadn't moved. His gaze slowly slid over the table and then lifted to my face. There was a hint of shock in his eyes.

'I didn't know that,' Anna smiled at me in surprise. 'The matron didn't tell us . . .'

I glanced away. Words tumbled out of my mouth almost automatically.

'It wasn't Mrs Fridge at the time. It was the matron before her.'

'Really?' she asked, wondrous. 'I didn't know that either . . .'

'I get it now,' Dalma said with a smile. 'A young man so . . . he must have caught your eye straight away.'

Anna squeezed Norman's hand, and something in the air shifted. Everyone noticed.

It was then that I understood. Maybe I had always known. Something else was going on. Anna gave a slight smile.

'Rigel. Would you . . . please?'

There was an eerie silence. Rigel placed his napkin on the table and got to his feet. The guests watched him uncertainly, and with every step their awareness seemed to grow and grow.

The sounds of the piano floated through the house and Mr and Mrs Otter froze. Asia suppressed a shudder and gripped her napkin.

He played. Everything else disappeared. Nothing else mattered.

A cold raindrop trickled down my thigh. I hugged my knees to my chest, wiggling my toes in the wet grass. Rain pitter-pattered down around me.

'Maybe they liked me . . .' I murmured like an insecure child. I tore up handfuls of grass. 'I've never been good at this . . . at making people like me, I mean. It always feels like I'm getting something wrong.'

I looked up and sighed pensively, looking at the drizzle above me.

'Anyway . . . it's not as if I can ask them, can I?'

I turned my head. The mouse next to me carried on cleaning her damp fur, paying no attention to my presence.

I had found her stuck in the wire netting, thrashing about desperately. When I managed to free her, I noticed she was injured, so I spread some honey on her little leg with a toothpick. Honey had soothing, medicinal properties.

I stayed there with her, and without realising, went into my own strange little world. I started talking to her as though she was listening. It was the only way I knew how to open up. I came from a place where I had never been able to.

No . . . I had never been *allowed* to.

It might have looked like madness to other people. But . . . it had always been my only way to feel less alone.

A cool raindrop fell on my cheek and I scrunched up my nose. Deep down, I felt like smiling. I was soaking wet, but I loved how that felt. It felt like freedom. And now my skin smelt that way too.

'I've got to go. They'll be back soon.'

I got to my feet. My wet dress stuck to my skin. Anna and Norman had gone out for a walk with the guests and would be home any minute.

'Take care, okay?'

I looked at the little creature at my feet. She was so tiny, soft and clumsy that I couldn't understand how anyone would be scared of her.

Her round ears and pointy nose gave me a tender feeling few people would have shared.

When I got back inside, I realised what a state my hands were in. The different coloured Band-Aids – yellow, green, blue, orange – on my fingers were smeared in honey and wet with rain.

I went to my room and replaced them all, one by one.

I checked they were all attached properly then headed to the bathroom to quickly dry myself off.

'So,' I heard someone whispering. 'Can you tell me what's wrong?'

I froze.

The hallway was empty. The whisper was coming from the stairs. Who was round the corner?

'You can't do that,' I heard. 'You didn't say another word.'

'I can't bring myself to,' the other person whispered resentfully.

I recognised the voice. It was Asia.

'I can't bear it. They . . . how can they stand it?'

'It's their choice.' This voice sounded more and more like her mother. 'It's their choice, Asia . . .'

'But you saw it! You saw it too, what that boy did!'

. . . *Rigel?*

'Meaning?'

'*Meaning?!*' she repeated in disgust.

'Asia . . .'

'No. Don't say it. I don't want to hear it.'

I heard footsteps and jumped.

'Asia, where are you going?'

'I left my bag upstairs,' Asia replied, horribly close.

My eyes opened wide. She was coming towards me. I was sure that I shouldn't have overheard that conversation. I seized the nearest door handle – the bathroom.

I snuck inside and leant against the door, closing my eyes with a sigh.

They hadn't seen me.

When I opened my eyes, I noticed something strange. The room was filled with dense steam.

My heart stopped.

Rigel was staring at me, wearing only a pair of trousers. His hair was dripping, water running down him in transparent rivulets, making the natural contours of his body glisten spectacularly in a way I could never have imagined.

My throat went dry; my mind went completely blank.

I stared at Rigel, unable to breathe. It was the first time I had seen him topless, and the sight of it shook me to my core. His powerful, muscular shoulders looked like marble. Prominent veins ran up his thick forearms. The bones of his pelvis formed a perfect V above the waistband of his tracksuit and the half-moons of his pecs carved his broad, solid, manly chest.

He was a masterpiece.

'What are you . . .' Rigel started, but his voice faltered when his eyes landed on my body.

I suddenly remembered the state I was in.

My wet dress was clinging to the curve of my hips, to my cold-stiffened breasts, my drenched thighs. The fabric was almost transparent. I panicked.

I stared at him wide-eyed. I could have sworn he was staring back at me in the same way.

'Get out.'

His eyes flashed. His usually deep, silken voice was a hoarse growl.

'Nica,' he said through clenched teeth. '*Get out.*'

My brain screamed at me to obey. I wanted to get as far away from him as possible.

But I couldn't move. Asia and Dalma were just a few steps away from us, I could hear their voices clearly through the bathroom door. I couldn't leave, not yet. What would they think if they saw Rigel and me together, him half naked and me soaking wet, shut in the bathroom together?

'I told you to get out,' he snarled. 'Now!'

'Wait . . .'

'*Move it!*'

He took two strides towards me and then I did something stupid.

I stepped to the side and blocked the door handle with my body as his shadow engulfed me.

My movement made the steam swirl around us.

The next moment . . . I was standing with both hands gripping the door handle behind me.

Before my eyes, occupying my entire field of vision, was *just* him.

In front of my face, his chest rose and fell with his deep breathing. His hands were placed on the door behind me, either side of my head.

The heat emanating from his body penetrated my soaking skin. I was breathless.

My heart was beating so violently that it chased all thoughts from my mind.

Rigel was breathing heavily with his teeth clenched. His hands were still pressed so forcefully against the door that I could almost sense them shaking.

'*You* . . .' he murmured with a hint of bitterness. 'You're doing it deliberately.' He clenched his fists in frustration. 'You're *playing* with me.'

His lips, teeth and tongue were just there, just a breath away, bare, wet and dominating. It was too much. I stopped thinking straight, and wondered what would happen if I tried to *touch him*. Right there, right then . . . Brush his skin, feel its warmth, its energy, its firmness . . .

Would he let me?

No. Probably he'd pin my hand to the door, above my head, like the last time.

I thought I was dying when, an interminable moment later, Rigel brought his face close to my hair, behind my ear and . . . took a deep breath in.

His chest expanded as he inhaled my scent.

When he breathed out, my blood roared in my ears and his boiling hot breath flooded my throat.

My heart was now thumping so desperately it hurt.

'*Rigel.*' His name slipped out of my mouth like a plea. I wanted to ask him to move away, but all I could manage was that imploring whimper.

He clenched his jaw. Suddenly, he grabbed my hair and tilted my head backwards. I gasped in surprise.

Our eyes were pinned on each other. I was panting. I hadn't even realised. My cheeks were burning, my eyes were straining, my heart was racing.

'How many *times* . . . do I have to tell you to stay away from me?'

It took him such a large effort to say those words that I felt shaken to my core.

I looked at him, my eyes full of desperate emotion.

'It's not my fault,' I whispered, quieter than a breath.

It was his.

He was the one who was stopping me from keeping my distance.

It was his fault.

Destiny had bound us together so tightly that I was unable to form a thought that wasn't about him. I couldn't even run away when he was about to bite me.

It was his fault, and his alone, because he had left marks inside of me that I wasn't able to erase.

Sensations that I couldn't control.

Turmoil that I didn't want to ignore.

I had abided by the rule, because it never changes: you have to get lost in the woods to vanquish the wolf.

I had met the wolf. But I had got lost in his contradictions.

They had become a part of me. Each one of them was like a shudder that Rigel had painted on me, making me less grey.

I was chained to him in ways I couldn't explain.

How could I find the words to make him understand?

Suddenly, a lock of his wet hair fell over my face.

Trembling, I closed my eyes. When I opened them again, it was stuck to my cheek. It ran down my face like a teardrop.

Rigel watched, and a light in his eyes went out. They clouded over like dusty diamonds.

We were children again.

I saw that moment replaying in his eyes. Me, at various ages, in front of him, crying tears that he had brought about.

Slowly . . . he let me go.

He turned his back and moved away like an inevitable wave. With each step he took, I felt the thread that connected us growing tenser and tenser until it hurt.

'Get out.'

There was no harshness in his voice. Just a bleak firmness.

Never before had I felt so rooted to the spot. I felt like I was crumbling. My hands were shaking.

I looked at the floor, full of contradictory emotions. Then, coming to my senses, I clenched my eyes shut, turned around, and opened the door.

There was no one there.

I walked along the now empty landing, trying not to slip.

Suddenly, the floor seemed to transform into a treacherous forest path beneath my feet, like the one from the stories.

I was running through a forest of shivers.

I was walking through the pages, on a paper path.

I'd spent my whole life running away from him. I had prayed for an escape from the condemnation of his gaze.

But there was no way out.

His eyes shone like stars.

Lighting up the way . . .

Towards the unknown.

18. Lunar Eclipse

I looked at love, and was afraid.
His blood vessels and moles bloomed with roses,
like unfinished, unspoken sentences.
He was more me than I had ever been.

After that afternoon in the bathroom, Rigel did everything in his power to avoid crossing paths with me.

It wasn't that we shared all that many moments together, in truth, but those that we did withered away almost to nothing. It was typical of Rigel to be so distant and avoidant, silent, discreet and indifferent.

He avoided me during the daytime. In the mornings, he would make sure to leave before me.

Walking to school by myself, I remembered all the times in which I had walked a short distance behind him, never daring to be next to him.

I couldn't make sense of the feelings he provoked in me.

Wasn't this what I'd always wanted? For him to be far away from me?

Even when I'd arrived here, I wanted nothing more than for him to disappear.

I should have felt relieved. And yet . . .

The more his eyes evaded mine, the more I couldn't stop seeking them.

The more he ignored me, the more I couldn't help but constantly wonder why.

The more Rigel kept his distance . . . the more I felt the thread that bound us tensing, as if it was an extension of me.

That's how it was in that moment. I was walking down the landing, thinking about him. I had just got back from school, but as usual, I was lost in thought, cut off from the world, so I didn't immediately notice the floorboards creak. Then, I realised that the creaking was coming from the room nearest to me.

I momentarily put aside what was on my mind and my insatiable curiosity led me to poke my head around the door.

I froze in surprise.

'Asia?'

She turned around.

What was she doing there?

She was standing silently right in the middle of the room. She was holding a scarf I had seen her with before, but I didn't have the slightest idea what she was doing in our house. When had she got here?

'I didn't know you had dropped by,' I said, seeing as she didn't pay me any notice. Her gaze slid over the walls as if I wasn't there. 'What . . . what are you doing in Rigel's room?'

This was apparently the wrong thing to say. Her angry glare became as sharp as a thorn. I was forced to step aside as she walked past me without a word.

'Asia?' Anna called from the stairwell. 'Is everything all right? Have you found it?'

'Yes. I'd left it on the bench in your room. It was on the floor. Thanks for letting me check.' I followed her out of Rigel's room and onto the landing as she closed the door behind us. She waved the scarf then stuffed it in her bag.

Anna came up and brushed her arm with a smile that radiated a warmth destined just for her.

'It's no bother at all,' she was saying sweetly. 'You know you can come by any time you want. We're on your way to campus, come and drop in to say hello every now and then . . .'

For no apparent reason, insecurity clawed at my chest. I tried to subdue it, but it slithered through my heart, tainting everything with spite and wretchedness.

Suddenly, every detail seemed amplified to the utmost degree. Anna's gaze was *shining* when she spoke with her. Her fondness for this girl was deep and maternal.

She smiled at her, cuddled her. She treated her like a daughter.

At the end of the day, who was I, compared to her? What could my few weeks count for, in comparison with a lifetime?

I began to feel familiar sensations of alienation. I balled my fists and struggled not to compare myself to her. It wasn't like me to make comparisons like that. I had never had a competitive streak, and yet . . . My heart was racing. I plunged into my anxieties. There was no escape. The world went dark.

Maybe I would never be enough.

Maybe Anna had realised . . .

What if she realised she had made a mistake?

If she had seen how dull, strange and broken I was?

My temples throbbed. Irrational fears crawled over my skin and my mind tormented me with images of The Grave, the gates sliding open again for me.

I'll be good.

Anna laughed again.

I'll be good.

My throat went tight.

I'll be good, I'll be good, I'll be good . . .

'Nica?'

I swear.

Anna was watching me, her brow slightly furrowed. There was a hesitant smile on her lips.

'Is everything . . . okay?'

My blood pounded in my head. I hid my face behind my hair and forced myself to nod. I froze.

'You're sure?'

I nodded again and hoped she wouldn't press. Anna was caring and attentive, but her soul was too pure to doubt my sincerity.

'Okay, well, I'll take Asia downstairs . . . I brought some flowers from the shop for her to take home . . .' I could hardly hear what she was saying, and missed the last few words.

It was only once they had moved away that I was able to breathe again.

I unclenched my fist and stretched out my fingers. I often had moments like these, it was impossible to fight them. I was used to unfounded panic, to sudden moments of intense anxiety, to the disorientating sensation that I was stuck in a suffocating bubble. One too many remarks would provoke uncontrollable anxiety, one too few would feed my monstrous insecurities.

Sometimes I would wake up in the middle of the night and be unable to fall back to sleep. In my nightmares I would relive an anguish that I had hoped, futilely, to forget.

It was rooted deep inside me, lurking in wait for the right moment to wield my vulnerabilities against me.

I had to hide them. Hide myself. Anna and Norman would only keep choosing me if I appeared perfect. That was the only way I could flee from the past, the only way I could have a family, the only way I'd get another chance . . .

I went into the bathroom and splashed cold water on my wrists. I breathed slowly, trying to dispel the venom that had invaded my heart. The sound of running water didn't do anything to change my reaction, but it did calm me down. I remembered that my skin was free, intact, unconstrained, that I didn't need to feel like a frightened little girl any more.

She was no longer imprinted on my body.

Just on my mind.

When I was sure the feelings had passed, I went downstairs.

Norman was home for lunch that day. I was comforted that he welcomed me with a smile, sat in his normal place.

I realised how unfounded my reaction had been. We were building something together, and Asia couldn't take that away from me.

I noticed then that someone was already sitting in the seat next to mine.

Rigel totally ignored me. His elbow was leaning on the table and he was looking down at his plate. I only noticed a moment later that there was something different about his silence.

He seemed . . . vexed.

'It's just a grade,' Anna said calmly, cutting her chicken. She tried in vain to meet his eyes. 'It's nothing, you don't need to worry about it.'

I suddenly got the impression that I had missed something important.

Sitting down, I tried to catch the gist of the conversation. I was stupefied.

Had Rigel . . . done badly in a test?

His irritated expression indicated that he hadn't been expecting it either.

Rigel always considered every action, every consequence, he never left anything to chance. But this . . . he hadn't expected this. He couldn't bear to appear weak, or to be at the centre of Anna's attention. His teacher must have been concerned about the unexpected test result too, and insisted that Rigel discuss it at home.

'Why don't you study together?'

I froze, my fork halfway to my mouth. Anna looked me in the eyes.

'What?'

'It would be ideal, wouldn't it? You said you did well in the test,' she smiled proudly at me. 'Maybe you could do a couple of exercises tog—'

'That's not necessary.'

Rigel had sharply interrupted her. It was completely unexpected to hear him reply to her like that, and, when I looked at her, I noticed that her hands were tenser than normal. She looked surprised and a little sad.

'I can't see what harm it would do,' she said cautiously. 'You could both help each other . . . after all, it's the same subject. Why don't you give it a try?' She turned to me. 'What do you think, Nica?'

I looked at Anna's face. I wanted to make her happy, but I couldn't deny feeling very uneasy. Why did I always find myself in these situations? It would have been easier to reply if Rigel hadn't been avoiding me like the plague.

'Yeah,' I murmured, trying to give her a smile. 'Okay . . .'

'You'll help Rigel with a few exercises?'

I nodded, and Anna seemed pleased. She smiled and served everyone another portion of stuffed peppers.

Next to me, Rigel remained shrouded in that indecipherable silence. And yet, it seemed as though he was gripping his cutlery with more force than was necessary.

An hour later, I was looking around my room.

Anna had suggested that we study upstairs, because that afternoon she was getting some flowers delivered and the noise might disturb us. I didn't need to look at Rigel to know there was no chance we would be using his room for our study session . . .

I moved my desk into the middle of the room, grabbed another chair and positioned it next to mine.

Why were my palms sweating?

The question answered itself. I couldn't imagine myself helping Rigel with exercises, or even just explaining something to him. It was surreal. He had always been a step ahead of everyone else . . . When had he ever let anyone help him?

Neither of us had uttered a word to one another in days. If it hadn't been for Anna and Norman, we probably would have even avoided each other at mealtimes.

Why? Why was it that every time it seemed we'd taken a step forwards, he took five steps back?

I jumped when I eventually noticed his presence behind me. He was standing in the doorway, tall and silent.

The sleeves of his sweater were pushed up to his elbows. In one hand, he was holding a couple of books. His eyes were unperturbed, and staring at me as if he'd been there for a while.

Be calm, I ordered my heart, as Rigel looked around warily.

'I've already got the books out,' I stuttered.

He stepped cautiously into the room.

I wished I could say that I was used to him, but sadly that wasn't true. Rigel wasn't one of those boys that typically you can get used to. His narrow, panther-like eyes were simply destabilising.

His slender presence filled the room. He came towards me and I realised that this was the first time he had been in my room.

For some absurd reason my nervousness grew.

'I'll grab my notebook,' I said faintly.

I went to go get my stuff out of my backpack then walked to the door and made to close it.

'What are you doing?'

His steely eyes were pinned on me.

'The noise . . .' I explained. 'It might disturb us . . .'

'Leave the door open.'

I slowly withdrew my hand. Rigel threw me a lingering glance before turning round. I couldn't understand why he'd insisted on that.

Did it bother him *so much* to be in the same room as me?

I felt a prick in my chest.

Without a word, I went and sat down. I kept my eyes on the text-book, kept turning the pages until I heard him coming to sit down next to me.

That peacefulness was unusual for us, but I had to keep going. At the end of the day, it wasn't complicated, it was just a study session.

I decided to steel myself, strengthened my resolve, and pointed at one of the exercises in the textbook.

'Let's start with one of these.'

There was a moment of silence and I felt the tension rising immeasurably. Had he noticed the tremble in my voice? I kept my eyes fixed on the problem I'd picked out, incapable of lifting my gaze.

Then, to my surprise, wordlessly, Rigel started writing.

I didn't move as he wrote down figures and solutions in intent silence. My astonishment grew. Experience had led me to believe that he would give me his usual impudent, hurtful sneer, poke fun at me and leave.

But instead, he was here.

He hadn't left. He was still next to me, writing . . .

I jumped when, after a while, I noticed that he had stopped. I stared at him, wrongfooted.

'Have you f . . . finished already?'

I leant over to look at his notebook. I was stunned. He had solved the problem, rigorously and precisely. His hand lay still next to his workings.

How long had it taken him? Three minutes?

'Okay . . .' I acknowledged, embarrassed. I found some more complicated problems. 'Let's try these ones.'

I pointed at several exercises with the end of my pencil, and he proceeded to solve them all meticulously, one by one. I was entranced by the fluid movement of the pen in his hand. He wrote in an elegant cursive, without any unnecessary flourishes. It seemed like the handwriting of a boy from long ago.

I noticed that he had a very masculine grip. His wrist had well-defined bones and tight nerves. His long, strong pianist fingers turned the page of his notebook and he continued writing.

My gaze slowly moved up his arm.

His veins stood out against his skin, his powerful bone structure emanated strength and security.

The top three buttons of his blue sweatshirt were undone, exposing the base of his neck, which pulsed slowly with the rhythm of his breaths.

How tall was he? Was he still growing? Even sitting down he would have towered over me if he leant over.

His head rested on his half-closed hand in a relaxed, concentrated pose. His soft, black hair fell over his eyes, perfectly framing his elegant features.

He was so enchanting he made me shiver.

He had the power to bewitch my heart.

To rip out my soul and charm it like a snake.

Rigel was like a perfect symbiosis, a lethal fusion of silk and shadow.

He was terrible, irreverent, but also the most gorgeous creature I had ever seen . . .

I jumped.

The bubble of my thoughts suddenly burst under the intensity of his eyes, which were no longer looking at his notebook. They were looking intently at me.

'F . . . finished?' I croaked. My voice was verging on ridiculous. Had he noticed me gazing at him, wonderstruck?

Rigel examined my face, then nodded. The hand his head was resting on was pulling one of his eyelids slightly to one side, making his gaze look like a cat's.

I felt feverish.

What was happening to me?

'Okay . . . Let's try something different.'

I turned the page, trying to hide how nervous I was. I decided to get straight to the point, and pointed at one of the exercises we'd been set in preparation for the test. Still stubbornly silent, Rigel set about tackling the problem.

This time I concentrated on his calculations. *Just* his calculations. I followed his workings carefully, making sure that everything was correct. After a while, something caught my eye.

'No, Rigel . . . Hold on.'

I peered closer and saw his hand stop.

'No . . . not like that.' I looked closely at his workings. His logic was faultless, but this wasn't how this problem got solved.

I flicked through my notebook and somewhat hesitantly showed him the pages on vectors.

'See? It says that the magnitude of the difference between two vectors is always *equal to* or *greater than* the difference between the magnitude of the two vectors taken individually . . .'

I tried to explain to him in words what the textbook only expressed in formulae. I pointed at the exercise with a finger wrapped in a Band-Aid.

'So, we need to write out the magnitude like this . . .'

Rigel looked at my notes with a different sort of attention. He really was listening to me.

He continued with the exercise more slowly. I watched him go, line by line.

'Okay . . . That's it. Now the arithmetic. Exactly . . .'

Step by step, we reached the solution. For the first time in my life, I noticed a hint of uncertainty in him, but that just spurred me on.

When he finished the exercise, I checked that everything had been carried out correctly.

'Good . . .' I said, as he carefully studied the solution. 'Let's try another one.'

We tackled exercise after exercise. The minutes rushed by like the wind, the silence only interrupted by my occasional murmurs.

After around an hour, a fair few problems had been ticked off by my pencil.

Rigel was finishing yet another exercise and we were both immersed in deep concentration, together.

'Okay . . .' I reached over the desk to add a little arrow that he had forgotten onto a vector. 'The S vector is on the x-axis . . . exactly . . .'

My elbows were leaning on the table. I was so absorbed that I hadn't realised I was sitting on the edge of my seat.

'The vector forms a 45-degree angle with the x-axis . . .'

I checked all his workings carefully.

They were all correct. This exercise, too, was perfect.

Had I succeeded? Had I really been able to help Rigel with something?

And had he, for once . . . really let himself be helped?

I felt a vivid, profound happiness.

I swiftly turned to give him a radiant smile, my eyes like glowing half-moons.

'You got it . . .' I breathed softly.

But whatever I had been about to say next . . . lost all meaning.

We were close. A breath away.

I had been concentrating so hard that I hadn't realised how I had been inching towards him, leaning over the desk, my hair falling down my back.

I turned my head and found his eyes boring into mine.

I saw my reflection in those black depths and found myself unable to breathe.

And Rigel, his head still resting on his hand, stared at me with slightly widened eyes and a cool expression.

My eyes in his, like a lunar eclipse.

★　★　★

Nica's eyes.

He didn't move. His heart had stopped.

Everything suddenly froze, the moment her smile lit up the world. He knew it. He knew he shouldn't have gone.

He knew he shouldn't have let her get so close.

And now it was too late. Nica had looked at him, smiled at him, and torn away another shred of his soul.

On the desk, his hand was crushing the pen. Fierce tremors came from within him, from hidden ravines that she, so close and bright, had awakened.

She drew back, and every second of that movement gave him a sense of relief so strong it was almost painful.

'Rigel . . .' she murmured, almost fearfully. 'There's something I want to ask you.'

Nica looked down at her soft hands clasped in her lap, depriving the world of light, just for a moment.

'It's something . . . that I've been wondering about for a while.'

She looked up at him, and Rigel desperately hoped that she wouldn't see his hand trembling right in the middle of the table. She was staring at him in that way of hers, with those large eyes and eyelashes curled like daisy petals.

'What did you mean? When you said I was the Tearsmith?'

Rigel couldn't even remember how many times he had imagined her asking this question, in a thousand different scenarios – it always came when he was feeling the most exhausted and destructive, when he was at his limit, when he was clamouring for redemption.

He gave her back everything he had never been able to put into words. He threw the truth right at her, and bled with every thorn he pulled out. And it was a pain that transformed into relief, as a warm light radiated through all the holes, all the wounds those thorns had left behind.

She was his redemption.

But in that moment . . . in that moment when Nica had really asked him and *waited* for his answer, Rigel felt nothing but a visceral terror. And so, before even giving himself a chance, he heard his own voice replying: 'Forget it.'

Nica looked at him, confused and painfully beautiful.

'What?'

'I said *forget it*.'

Her face fell.

'Why?'

She knew, she had realised this was important. You can't just make certain accusations then hope they'll be forgotten. He could see it in her eyes.

Her gaze, for him, was something akin to hell.

He would always wonder why those eyes seemed so disappointed by his actions, his silences. For the rest of his life, he would constantly wonder about that wound dripping from her silvery eyes.

Those eyes would always torment him.

And Rigel only knew one way to protect himself against torment.

'Don't tell me you really believed it?' he said sarcastically. 'You didn't really think I was being serious?'

He flashed her a provocative smile.

'Have you been thinking about it all this time, *little moth*?'

Nica winced. He noticed the curve of her neck behind her hair and his insides started writhing.

'Don't do that.' Her voice hardened.

'Don't do *what*?'

'That,' she looked at him stubbornly. 'Don't do it.'

Hearing her speak with such determination pushed him towards her.

He was so fatally attracted to her when that side of her came out. For all her sweetness, Nica was capable of a tenacity that made him lose his mind.

'*That's* just what I'm like,' he said, leaning towards her tiny body.

'No. *That's* just how you behave.'

Now she was leaning towards him, and Rigel recoiled, with his body, and his heart.

'What did you mean?' she insisted. 'Rigel . . .'

'Forget it,' he spat through gritted teeth.

'Please . . .'

'*Nica.*'

'Answer me!'

Nica's hand grabbed his bare wrist and he felt his heart burning.

He jumped to his feet and tore away from her.

The violence of the action reverberated in Nica's eyes. He saw her wavering, upset, and the whole room started to tremble.

Rigel found himself battling to control the writhing in his chest. He clenched his fists, trying to hold them still, and she looked at him with large, fearful eyes.

'Don't . . .' He took a deep breath, trying to control himself. He was burning so intensely he was worried Nica could feel it. 'Don't touch me.' He hurried to put on a smile, masking himself behind a cruel smirk that almost hurt. 'I've told you before.'

He didn't have time to see the flash of hurt in her eyes. She charged towards him, her eyes glinting with anger.

'*Why?*' she asked loudly, her voice cracking. She was like an injured animal, folded over in pain. 'Why not? Why can't I touch you?'

Rigel stepped back, bowled over by her anger.

And God, *she was so beautiful,* her cheeks flushed and her eyes shining with determination. God, it hurt him so much, how forcefully, irresistibly attracted he was to her.

It was too much, even for him.

Don't touch me, he wanted to tell her again, *wanted to beg of her again*, but Nica came closer, shattered his defences, her little fingers still burning his skin.

His tortured soul ruptured in astonishment.

The next moment, all he could hear was his teeth grinding and her sharp breath in.

★ ★ ★

The movement took my breath away.

A moment ago, I had been gripping on to his arm. The next thing I knew, my back was against the wall.

Rigel's eyes swallowed me up like sinkholes.

His chest was rising and falling with his heavy breathing and his forearm was over my head. His body loomed over me, so close I could feel his heat like a scorching sun's.

I shook like a leaf. I looked into his eyes, breathless, my voice reduced to a rattling gasp.

'I . . . I . . .'

He grabbed my jaw and tilted my face upward towards his.

His fingertips were burning against my skin. I couldn't breathe.

Silent hurricanes roared in his eyes. He was so close I could feel his breath tickling my cheeks.

I was gasping for breath, my cheeks were so hot I felt my whole body burning under his touch.

'Rigel . . .' I whispered, confused and frightened.

A muscle in his jaw twitched. His thumb slid lightly over my mouth, as if to still the whisper that had made my lips tremble.

Slowly, he brushed my lower lip. His thumb sunk into the yielding flesh of my mouth, rubbing it, *burning it*, making it throb.

My knees gave in when I saw that his eyes were fixed on the point where he was touching me.

'Forget it.' His lips moved hypnotically.

All I could hear was him. The sound of his voice shot straight into my veins.

'You've got to . . . forget it.'

I tried, in vain, to make sense of the glint of bitterness in his eyes.

In his eyes raged hurricanes and storms, dangers and forbidden places . . . but my desire to explore them grew day by day. My heart was thumping. That realisation frightened me.

Getting lost in the woods meant finding the path.

But getting lost in the wolf . . . meant being lost forever.

Why did I so badly need to touch his world, to understand it?

Why couldn't I just forget it all, like he asked me to?

Why did I see galaxies in his eyes, and in his solitude a soul to touch with caution?

After a moment, I noticed that his hand was no longer on my face.

I felt an inexplicable loss when I realised that he had already walked away. I blinked as I watched him stride out the room, clutching his book in whitened fists.

Rigel was running away. Again.

This realisation disturbed me. When had our roles swapped? Since when had he run away from me?

Since always, I whispered to myself. *He's always been running away from you.*

Maybe it was a seed of madness that had sprouted inside of me.

I didn't know how else to explain it. I disobeyed him and my own senses, steeled myself and ran after him.

19. Underneath

I can defend myself against everything.
Everything except sweetness.

'Rigel!'

I followed him across the landing, determined to make him hear me. He threw me a nervous look, but I was forced to keep tailing him as he didn't stop. He was striding with an excessive urgency, as if he was desperate to get away from me.

'Please, wait. I want to speak to you . . .'

'About *what*?' He suddenly turned to face me, grinding his teeth menacingly. He seemed tense, almost . . . scared.

About you, I wanted to burst out, but I stopped myself, because that would be madness. I now understood that Rigel was like a wild beast who, when cornered, lashed out with aggression.

'You never answer my questions,' I said instead. 'Why?'

I hoped that this would draw him into a discussion, but I knew it hadn't worked when his gaze slipped away from me. Rigel's eyes were the windows to his soul, a clear surface, the only place in which he couldn't hide away. They were as black as ink but, deep down, they shone with a light that few people would have been able to discern. As he started walking away again, I felt the need to leap forward and grasp that light with my hands.

'Because you ask questions that are none of your business,' he murmured in a near-indecipherable tone.

'They would be my business if you . . . if you let me understand you.'

Maybe I had gone too far, but I got what I hoped for: Rigel stopped. I hesitated, but then cautiously stepped towards him. He seemed to be listening to every one of my footsteps. He turned around and finally looked me in the eyes. The way he was looking at me made me think of a hunter and defenceless prey. But I was the hunter, and he was my prey, staring down the barrel of my gun.

'I just want to understand you, but you don't give me the chance.' I fixed my eyes on his, trying not to let my sadness show. 'I know you hate it when people pry,' I added quickly. 'And I know you don't wear your heart on your sleeve, but maybe if you tried talking about your emotions, the world might feel a bit lighter. You don't have to always be alone. You might find it's worth your while to trust someone.'

He held my gaze.

'Sometimes . . .' I whispered, drawing even closer to him, 'you might find that people are happy to listen to you.'

Rigel's gaze was so steady that it was as if he was trying to hide how much he was trembling inside. One by one, vivid, unfamiliar emotions flashed through his eyes. My heart beat irregularly, deliriously. I had been wrong. Rigel's gaze wasn't cold and empty, but so full of multiple different hues at once that it was impossible to separate them. His eyes were like the northern lights, reflecting his inner state, and at that moment he seemed taken aback, confused and frightened by my behaviour.

Then, all of a sudden, Rigel closed his eyes. In a quiver of nerves, I studied his face. His jaw was clenched, a vein on his temple was bulging and his beautiful face had turned frighteningly stony.

I didn't know what was happening, but suddenly he took a step backwards to put more distance between us. We lost eye contact, and all my hard-won little triumphs slipped away.

Had I done something I shouldn't have?

'Rigel . . .'

'Stay *away*,' he spat out, as if the words were burning his tongue.

I felt the harshness of his tone like a stab in the chest. Suddenly, he gave me a frenzied look.

He was gripping his bedroom door handle. I stepped back as I noticed his white knuckles. I stared at him, hurt and confused, unable to understand the reaction I had provoked in him, and the next minute, Rigel disappeared from view. The door slammed behind him.

It felt like a boulder had fallen on my heart.

Why had he reacted like that?

Was it . . . *my fault*?

Had I done something wrong?

I wanted to understand, but I couldn't make sense of it.

Why could we not communicate?

I plunged into an ocean of questions. My insecurities paved a dead-end road.

I had to resign myself to the fact that Rigel didn't want to share anything with me. He was a puzzle without a solution, an impenetrable fortress. A black rose that protected its vulnerabilities by scratching and stabbing with its thorns.

Disheartened, I trudged downstairs and lingered outside the dining room. A wonderful fragrance billowed around me like a cloud, lifting my spirits for a moment.

Anna was checking the flower delivery. The floor was carpeted in ribbons and waxy paper. The whole room was filled with huge vases of tulips that Anna would spend the entire afternoon making sure looked perfect. Carl, her assistant, was minding the shop while she was away.

I watched her from the doorway. Her hair glowed golden in the sunlight and her lips formed a slight smile. She was so beautiful and bright when she smiled like that. She was my real-life fairy godmother.

'Oh, Nica!' she burst out, happy to see me there. 'You've finished already?'

I looked down, feeling a pang in my chest. I didn't want her to see the disappointment sullying my heart. I wanted to tell her all my worries and let her tend to my fears and insecurities, but part of me just couldn't, part of me was too scared. I had been taught that weaknesses were for hiding, disguising, being ashamed of. Anna would find out that I was a broken, tattered doll, when I wanted her to always see me as a perfect young woman who was full of light and deserved to stay with her forever.

I wanted her to embrace me and wipe away my sadness, in that kind, tender, maternal way of hers.

'Has something happened with Rigel?'

I realised that she had come closer. I didn't reply, and she gave me a heartfelt smile.

'You're like an open book,' she said, as if that was a good thing. 'Your face is as clear as the surface of a still lake. You know what they say about people like you? That you've got an honest heart.'

She tucked my hair behind my ear, and every piece of my soul clung to that gesture. I loved it when she touched me that tenderly, as if I was one of her flowers.

'I'm maybe starting to get to know you both a little better . . . Rigel's a complicated character, isn't he?' She gave me a bittersweet smile. 'But I popped my head in earlier. You were working well together. I'm sure he understands a lot better now, thanks to you.'

I had never had much faith in myself, but I couldn't pluck up the courage to show her how happy her words made me. I was utterly despondent, and I couldn't hide it.

Anna didn't try to break the silence. She seemed to accept and respect it. She softened, and to my surprise, asked, 'Do you fancy giving me a hand?'

She took my hand in hers. My heart skipped a beat. Suddenly, the little girl in me stirred, confused by the intensity of my emotions. I let her lead me to a beautiful bunch of tulips that needed to be tied with ribbon.

I was lost for words. I watched her graceful movements. She held the stems together in a tight bundle then wound a ribbon around them. She showed me how to curl the ends of the ribbon. I was enraptured by the care she took over every stage of the process.

We arranged the bouquet together. The tulips created a beautiful mosaic of shades of pink and white. We stood back to admire our work.

'It looks good . . .' I said, entranced. I had recovered my voice.

Anna smiled, and brandished a tulip under my nose. I held it gently and stroked the petals with a finger free from Band-Aids. It was wonderfully soft.

'Do you like them?'

'A lot . . .'

She took an intensely pink tulip and enthusiastically plunged her nose into it.

'What do they smell like?' she asked.

I stared at her, confused. 'What?'

'What do you think they smell like?'

I looked at her, bowled over, eyebrows raised.

'Like . . . tulips?'

'Oh, no, no, come on . . . Flowers never smell just like flowers!' she reproached me playfully. Her eyes were shining. 'What do they smell like?'

I smelt it deeply, holding her passionate gaze.

It seemed . . . *It seemed . . .*

'Candy . . . raspberry candy,' I said. Anna's eyes lit up.

'Mine smells like tea bags and . . . lace . . . Yes, newly made lace!'

I hid a smile behind the flower. *Lace?*

I took another sniff, watching her with bright, lively eyes.

'Soap bubbles.'

We watched each other, both our noses buried in petals.

'Baby powder,' she suggested.

'Forest fruits jam . . .'

'Powder puffs!'

'Cotton candy.'

'Cotton candy?'

'Yeah, cotton candy!'

Anna beamed at me, then burst out laughing.

Her laughter caught me by surprise. My heart leapt in wonder and I stared at her, my chest constricting. When her bright eyes looked at me and I realised the reason for my sudden joy, a burning love replaced my incredulity. I wanted to make her laugh again, I wanted to feel her gaze on me every day, I wanted to let my heart feast on it.

It was like a fairy tale, Anna's laugh. It was like a not-too-distant happy ending. It was one of those laughs that made you feel the lack of something you never even had.

'You're right,' she admitted. 'It smells just like cotton candy.'

I felt my soul melt when she placed a hand on the top of my head. Her kindness was contagious, I laughed alongside her among tulips that now smelt like a thousand different things, but no longer simply of tulips.

We passed the time arranging the other vases, and then I went back upstairs.

I felt light, cleansed and carefree. Anna had a tremendous power over me: she could make my heart soar.

I bumped into Klaus on the landing. I decided to play with him for a bit, but a short while later, unfortunately found myself running round the house trying to get away from him.

He chased after me with warlike meows, biting at my heels like he was possessed. I dashed back downstairs.

I rushed into the living room and jumped onto the armchair. Klaus dug his claws into the arm. I stared at him with raised eyebrows as he poked his nose around and swiped his evil little paws at me.

Eventually, he seemed to decide that he had tormented me enough, turned his back and strutted disdainfully away.

I strained my neck to make sure that he wasn't lurking around the corner, waiting to ambush me.

Well . . . at least I had managed to get his attention . . .

My phone started vibrating. I pulled it out of my jeans pocket. It was a message from Billie. With a surge of pleasure, I read: 'Grandma says you haven't been over in ages. Why don't you come and study over here tomorrow?'

As usual, she had also sent a goat video.

It was about time I got used to the idea that Billie thought of me as a friend, but the feeling of being appreciated was so new for me. I started to prepare a reply, hoping I wouldn't come across too over-joyed, but a rustling sound disturbed my thoughts.

I looked up.

The couch against the wall was occupied by a perfectly still figure.

His head was on the armrest and his dark t-shirt blended into the upholstery. As I became aware of Rigel's presence my heart stopped.

One arm was resting on his chest, the other was folded behind his head. His soft, white fingers were curled into a gentle half-fist that dangled in mid-air. He was asleep.

How had I not noticed him?

It was unusual for him to be sleeping in the afternoon. Something inside of me was drawn to the sight of him, but my conscience brought my feelings to the fore and told me I should leave. I didn't want to stay there, not after what had happened. His mere presence troubled me.

I got to my feet and threw one last glance at his peaceful face.

I looked at his serene features, his dark eyelashes shadowy brush-strokes on his graceful cheekbones. His black hair framed his face and spilled onto his forearm like ink. He was so peaceful he looked almost vulnerable.

He was painfully beautiful. My heart hurt. It was . . . it was unbearable.

'It's not fair,' I whispered.

It was his fault. Someone should take responsibility for that painful, heart-wrenching, angelic beauty.

'You act like a monster to keep the world at bay and then . . . then you lie there like *this*,' I accused him, disarmed by how innocent he looked. 'Why? Why do you always have to mess everything up?'

I wanted to forget it, but I couldn't. I knew that there was something bright and fragile inside of Rigel, and now I'd seen it, I couldn't give in. I wanted to extract it from the mystery that enshrouded it, bring it to the surface and watch it glowing in my hands. I really was like a moth. I'd get burnt flying close to that flame.

I suddenly froze. I could count his eyelashes. I could see the tiny mole by his lips . . .

Stunned, I straightened and quickly moved back, my heart thudding against my ribs. I stared at him, shocked at myself. *When had I got so close to him?*

I was still holding my phone, and instinctively gripped it tighter. My fingers slipped accidentally and the video Billie had sent me started playing. The goat started screaming at the top of its lungs and I almost dropped my phone.

Heart in my throat, I scarpered out of the room, just before Rigel woke with a start, his eyes wide open in alarm at the goat's screaming.

I bolted to my room but tripped over something at the top of the stairs. Before I could understand what was happening, there was a ball of fur on top of me, biting at my shins.

I had been right . . . Klaus had been waiting in ambush for me.

I was so embarrassed.

The shame hung over me into the evening.

I'd have rather buried myself in the ground than find Rigel there in front of me. Luckily, he claimed he had a headache and didn't come down for dinner.

I suspected that it was my fault. It would shatter anyone's nerves to be woken up like that.

Being alone with Anna and Norman was something I had always wanted, but my eyes kept being drawn to the empty chair next to mine. I couldn't stop thinking about it. It was as if my desires had been transformed and I no longer fit in that family portrait.

After I had helped Anna clear the table, I withdrew to the room with the bookshelves to read for a bit. I let my gaze wander over the titles, trying to find one that would distract me from my thoughts. My attention was caught by one book in particular: *Myths and Legends from Across the World*.

I was instantly drawn to it. I stroked a finger down the spine, then slid it off the shelf and turned it over admiringly in my hands. It was leatherbound and the cover was embossed with interwoven flowers. It was beautiful.

I settled into the armchair and started flicking through it. I was curious to read different fairy tales to the ones that I had been raised with. What legends did other children grow up with? Did they really not know the story of the Tearsmith?

I looked for a contents page, but couldn't find one. But several of the titles had intrigued me, so I started to read.

'I'm starting to think you're getting a taste for it.'

I jumped.

I got a strong sense of déjà vu. I gripped the book, a fair chunk of which I had already read, and looked up to find someone staring at me intently.

'For what?' I asked, shocked by his presence.

'For waking me up at the worst moments.'

He'd got me. My cheeks immediately started burning. I stared at Rigel guiltily.

Had he come all this way just to say this?

'It was a mistake,' I replied. I lowered my gaze, not brave enough to look at him. 'I didn't know you were there.'

'That's strange,' he retorted. 'You seemed quite . . . close.'

'I just came into the room. It's you who were sleeping at weird times.'

Rigel kept staring at me with those eyes that plundered my soul, and I regretted my choice of words. I was scared of annoying him, that he'd lose his temper or his mood would sour again.

More than anything, I was scared he'd run away.

When did I become so contradictory?

'I'm sorry,' I whispered, because, after all, I was. I was still upset about how things had gone that afternoon, but it wasn't like me to be vindictive. I hadn't woken him up deliberately, and I didn't want him to think that I had.

His presence hurt me, but I wanted us to be able to pick up the conversation exactly where we had left it. But there was no chance of that, and I knew it . . . And so, I adopted an alternative tactic.

'You said once that fairy tales are all the same. That they follow a standard format . . . the wood, the wolf, the prince . . . But that's not always the case.'

I opened the book to the first page of Andersen's *The Little Mermaid*.

'In this one, there's the sea and a girl who's in love with a prince. But there are no wolves. It doesn't follow the rules. It's different.'

'And is there a happy ending?'

I hesitated, because it seemed like Rigel already knew the answer.

'No. In the end he falls in love with someone else. And she . . . dies.'

I suddenly wondered why I had embarked on that conversation. I had just proved his point.

We had been in this room the last time that Rigel had spoken about the compromise of happy endings – if the rules are disturbed, then so is the 'happily ever after'.

'That's the point of them,' he said cynically. 'There's always something to fight. It's just the monster that changes.'

'You're wrong,' I whispered, determined to make my words count for something. 'Fairy tales don't teach us resignation. They urge us to not lose hope. They don't just tell us that monsters exist . . . but also, that they can be overcome.'

I suddenly remembered what he had told me, in front of these very bookshelves . . .

'And you, you're so desperate for your happy ending, but are you brave enough to imagine a fairy tale without a wolf?'

It hadn't been a meaningless question. It was impossible to have a direct conversation with Rigel, there were always allusions, hidden meanings in his words. You just had to have the courage to grasp them.

'I'll take it. I'll take a fairy tale without a wolf.'

He was determined to be the villain of the tale, as if some things could never change. But I wanted to make him understand that he was wrong. Maybe that way, he'd stop thinking it was him against the world.

And against himself.

Rigel stood still, staring at me. Without knowing why, I got the feeling he didn't believe me.

'And then?'

I was taken aback.

'Then?' I repeated uncertainly.

He scrutinised me.

'And then what? What's the ending of this tale?'

I was silent. Because I hadn't been expecting that question, but mostly, because . . . I wasn't sure of the answer. I wanted to say something to surprise him, but my silence was enough to make his eyes cloud over, as if it was confirmation enough.

'Nothing quite meets your rosy expectations, does it?' he murmured. 'Everyone's got their place in your perfect world. Just as you want them. But you can't see beyond that.'

His face fell as if I had contradicted him again. No . . . *hurt* him?

'Maybe reality isn't like that. Have you ever thought about that? Maybe it's not how you think, maybe it doesn't all work out like you want it to. *Just maybe*,' he said with merciless emphasis, 'there are people who don't want to live in your perfect dream. And you don't know how to accept that. You want answers, Nica, but the truth is you're not ready to hear them.'

His words struck me like a slap in the face.

'It's not true,' I said, my heart racing at top speed.

'Oh, no?' he hissed. I stood up.

'You can take your armour off. You don't need it.'

'What do you think you'd see underneath it?'

'*Enough,* Rigel!'

Irritability stung my eyes. I couldn't bring myself to talk to him, I couldn't think straight I was so frustrated.

We couldn't understand each other because we didn't speak the same language. Rigel was trying to tell me something. I heard him, but he was speaking in a language he had never taught me. A scathing language, full of meanings that I couldn't interpret. I had always been as transparent as spring water, but he was like a dark ocean of uncharted depths.

I wrapped my arms around myself as if to protect myself from the strange glare in his eyes.

'You're not making any sense,' I told him. He was making me lose my mind. 'You talk about fairy tales as if they were just nonsense for children, but the truth is that you grew up at The Grave too, you believe in them too.'

Every child at the institute believed in the stories we were told, and every child left the institute carrying those stories within them. Ours was a different world, a world that made us incomprehensible. But it was our truth.

Rigel didn't reply. He stared at me in a way that assailed my heart, then glanced down to the book I had left on the armchair.

I wanted to make him see the light, but he seemed a prisoner of his own shadows.

I wanted to reach my hand out towards him, but I was tired of always getting scratched.

But nothing broke my heart as much as seeing the spark that I had been looking for die in his eyes.

I finally understood that I wasn't battling against him, but against something that couldn't be seen.

Rigel wasn't just cynical and recalcitrant. He was disillusioned with life. There was something raw and visceral in him that I had never seen in anyone else. It made him refuse to delude himself, to push everyone away, to see the world with such disappointment that it almost burned his stomach. *What was it?*

'Myths, legends, fairy tales . . . they're all based on the truth.'

I shuddered at how low and sincere his voice sounded.

226

'Myths are about the past. Legends teach us about the present. And fairy tales . . . they're the future, but only for a few of us. A rare few. Fairy tales are for those who *deserve* them, while the rest of us are doomed to dream about an ending we'll never get to see.'

20. A Glass of Water

> *You cannot hide*
> *A heart that trembles.*

The room was messy and dusty as always.

The desk would have been handsome without all that chaos and the sticky rings of brandy stains. But it didn't matter.

He kept his eyes lowered.

By now, Rigel knew the grain of the floorboards by heart.

'Look at him. He's a disaster.'

It had always been like this. Two adults in the room speaking about him as if he wasn't there.

Maybe that's just how you speak about problems. As if they aren't there.

'Look at him,' the doctor said again to the woman. His voice reverberated with a hint of pity. This time, Rigel hated him with every fibre of his body.

He hated him for his sympathy. He didn't want it.

He hated him because he made him feel even more wrong.

He hated him because he didn't want to hate himself more than he already did.

But most of all, he hated him because he was right.

The disaster wasn't in his dirty fingernails. It wasn't behind his eyelids, that sometimes he wanted to tear away. It wasn't in the blood on his hands.

The disaster was within him. It had taken such deep root that it was incurable.

'You don't have to accept it, Mrs Stoker. But the boy is clearly showing the early symptoms. His incapacity to relate to others is just one of the signs. And as for the rest . . .'

Rigel stopped listening, because it was the 'rest' that hurt him the most.

Why was he like this? Why wasn't he like the others? These weren't questions for a child, but he couldn't help but ask them.

Maybe he would have been able to ask his parents. But they weren't there. And Rigel knew why.

Because no one likes disasters.

Disasters are inconvenient, useless and burdensome.

It's easier to get rid of broken toys than keep them.

Who would ever want someone like him?

★ ★ ★

'Nica?'

I blinked in surprise.

'How have you translated number five?'

I searched through my translations, trying to concentrate.

' "He said goodbye",' I read from my notebook. ' "He said goodbye before leaving." '

'See!' Billie said triumphantly.

Next to her, Miki stopped chewing gum and looked at her sceptically from under her hood.

'And who told you otherwise?'

'You got it wrong!' Billie accused her, pointing at her notebook. 'Look!'

Miki stared stonily at the page.

'It says "good buy". Not "goodbye".'

Billie scratched her head with the end of her pencil, doubtful.

'Oh,' she said, after some thought. 'I thought . . . Your handwriting's atrocious! Look at this, is that meant to be an *e*?'

Miki closed her eyes and Billie beamed at her.

'Can I copy your other answers?'

'No.'

I watched them squabbling, letting myself get lost in my thoughts again.

We had got together for a study session, but for some reason I couldn't concentrate. My mind floated away at the slightest distraction.

I knew, really, that the distraction had eyes as dark as night and an impossible personality.

Rigel's words were stuck in my head, and showed no sign of leaving.

Suddenly, the door to the porch opened and Billie's grandma, covered in flour, made a grand entrance.

'Wilhelmina!' she boomed, making her granddaughter jump. 'Did you forward that message about Saint Bartholomew that I sent you on your phone?'

Billie hid her face, trying not to show her exasperation.

'No, Grandma . . .'

'What are you waiting for?'

I didn't understand what they were talking about, but when she saw my confused expression, Billie started to explain.

'Grandma's still convinced that chain messages bring you the saints' protection . . .'

Billie jumped as her grandma, chest heaving, commanded, 'Do it!' She brandished the rolling pin at Miki. 'Miki, you too! I've just sent it to you!'

'Oh, come on, Grandma,' Billie complained. 'How many times have I told you that they don't work?'

'Baloney! They protect you!'

Billie looked up at the ceiling, then gave in and picked up her phone.

'All right . . . Can we have a snack then though?'

Her grandma's scowl melted into a smile.

'By all means!' She assumed an almost martial pose, slapping the rolling pin into her palm.

Billie, meanwhile, started texting fervently.

'Okay, I've sent it to a few people . . . Oh, Nica, I'll send it to you, too! That way we'll all be safe and sound!'

Her grandma's gaze whipped over to me and I winced, my shoulders hunching up to my ears.

'To me?'

'Yeah, why not? You've got to forward it to fifteen contacts,' she explained and I swallowed, still in her grandma's firing line.

Fifteen contacts? I didn't even have fifteen contacts!

'Done!' Billie announced, and mine and Miki's phones both vibrated. Her grandma looked at us proudly, her apron fluttering in the breeze.

'I'll go make you a snack,' she said, turning back inside. Then she seemed to have second thoughts. 'By the way, did you hear back from them?'

Billie glanced up, her shoulders slumped. 'The call dropped again,' she mumbled, and I realised that she was speaking about her parents. 'But I think I heard a camel. They're still in the Gobi desert.'

Her grandma nodded, and looked at her softly before heading back inside.

Silence fell over us like dust.

'Any news?'

The question surprised me. Maybe because it had been Miki's ever-indifferent voice which was asking it.

'No.'

Billie didn't look up. She was doodling listlessly on the corner of a page.

'They postponed again. They're not coming back at the end of the month any more.'

Suddenly, the image I had of Billie became nuanced. Her back was curved and her curls tumbled down her back like a trailing plant. The light that was always shining in her eyes had become but a glimmer trapped in her dulled gaze.

'But . . . Dad told me that they'd take me to a wonderful photography exhibition. He promised. And a promise is a promise . . . right?'

She looked up at me.

'Right,' I said clearly. Billie tried to smile, but it seemed to be a huge effort. She blinked as Miki shoved her notebook under her nose. She glanced at her, then muttered, 'Didn't you want to copy the others?'

Billie looked at her for a moment, and slowly smiled.

Later on, Billie tried to contact her parents again. The call dropped a few times, but in the end, just as she was losing hope, someone picked up. Her face lit up with an incomparable joy when she heard her dad's voice down the line.

Unfortunately, the call was interrupted, but she wasn't disheartened as I had feared. She flopped backwards onto the bed, ecstatic, fantasising about all the exotic wonders her parents had told her about.

'Such amazing places . . .' she murmured, eyes closed. 'One day I'll go too! To watch the sunset from the tent, to see the dunes, the palm trees . . . together . . . to photograph the world . . .'

Her voice faded away into a whisper, and then into just a movement of her lips, and finally into nothing.

Just like that, Billie fell asleep, in the middle of the afternoon, her phone still in her hands and hope behind her eyes, lost in a cloud of curls.

I slid the phone from her hands and placed it on the bedside table, watching her sleep.

'They seem like good people,' I noted, speaking about her parents.

She had put them on loudspeaker, and they had said hello to us enthusiastically. I could see where Billie got her bubbliness from.

'They are.'

Miki wasn't looking at me. Her eyes were planted on her friend's sleeping face.

Her gaze was as impenetrable as ever, but seemed to hold a tinge of melancholy.

'She misses them more than she lets on. She's only brave enough to admit it at night.'

'At night?'

'When she calls me,' she murmured. 'She dreams that they come back . . . Then she wakes up and they're not there. She knows she overreacts sometimes. She knows it's for work, that they're, well . . . She'd never tell them, but she misses them. They've been away for a long time.'

Miki is really so sweet, I remembered Billie saying. *So sensitive.* Up until that point, I hadn't been able to see it. But I pictured her, in the dead of night, after a day barricaded behind her poker face, falling asleep with her phone beside her, waiting for the moment when it would light up and she would become the only witness to the instances when Billie didn't have the strength to smile.

Miki . . . was her family.

'She'll never be alone.' I met Miki's eyes and smiled sweetly. 'She's got you.'

Miki watched as I tucked Billie in.

'I'm going to go get a glass of water,' I announced, getting to my feet and straightening my rumpled top before tiptoeing out of the room. I hoped I wouldn't inconvenience anyone by getting a glass from the kitchen, but then I remembered that Billie's grandma had gone out to play bridge with friends.

Before heading down the stairs, I turned back and reopened the door to Billie's bedroom.

'Miki, sorry, did you also want a glass of –'

I didn't finish the sentence.

The words withered in my mouth.

My eyes opened wide. A cascade of black hair intermingled with Billie's curls. Miki was leaning over her, her lips on hers.

Time stopped.

I froze.

I stared as Miki slowly straightened up. Her eyes were so full of shock that they looked wild. Under the shadow of her hood, her lips were parted but her jaw was tense.

'I . . .' I stammered, trying to find the words. I opened my mouth several times, panting, but I couldn't finish the sentence. Miki crashed towards me and pushed me out of the room.

She closed the door behind her and her eyes glinted threateningly like embers in the light of the landing. It seemed like they pierced me.

'*You,*' she hissed through gritted teeth, jabbing a finger in my chest. Her voice caught in her throat in a way I'd never heard before. 'You . . . saw *nothing*.'

I was speechless. I closed my mouth and looked at the door behind her, the door to the room where Billie was sleeping. I looked back at her, standing stiffly in front of me.

Then, without batting an eyelid, I shrugged and said calmly, 'Okay.'

Miki's eyelid twitched.

'. . . *What?*'

'Okay,' I repeated simply.

She stared at me, torn between anger and shock.

'What do you mean, "okay"?'

'I didn't see a thing.'

'*Yes, you* did *see!*'

'See what?'

'You know what!'

'Nope.'

'Don't . . .' she burst out, about to explode. She was still pointing at me and her face was red. 'You . . . you didn't . . . *you* . . .'

She gritted her teeth, balled her fists and let out an angry cry.

I waited in silence as Miki burned with a frustration that made her hands shake. For an interminable moment, the only sound was our breathing.

I really would pretend I hadn't seen anything, I thought. If that was what she wanted, that was what I would do.

Miki was refusing to look at me, glowering with the expression of someone who would do anything to erase that moment. But, for the first time since I had met her, Miki didn't leave. She had just snarled at me, and even though I knew it was only because she was having some sort of internal struggle, *she was still there*.

I couldn't ignore her. Not like she wanted me to. Even though it might make her hate me, I asked, 'Miki . . . do you like Billie?' My voice was delicate and clear as water.

It was a stupid question, but I asked it all the same, because I wanted her to realise how straightforward this was.

Miki didn't answer. Bitterness clamped her lips shut and knotted her throat.

'There's nothing wrong with it . . .' I said softly, very softly, as if my vocal cords were shaping glass. I looked at her with clear eyes. 'It's a beautiful thing . . .'

'You *don't* understand,' she spat out.

Frustration dripped from her eyes like wax, reaching her balled fists like a silent prayer.

I fell silent again, because maybe I really didn't understand.

But Miki was there, and I had never wanted so much to catch a glimpse of her eyes from under her hood. I wanted them to show me some emotion – something I'd never before had the courage to ask for.

'Maybe not,' I murmured, lowering my gaze. 'But if you . . . if you want to tell me . . . if you let me understand . . . you might find it's simpler than you think . . . you might find that there's nothing bad, inexplicable or wrong about it. Some things it's better to talk about, some things make us feel better when someone else hears them.'

Miki pursed her lips. I looked at her with sincere eyes, my palms open towards her, my hands covered in Band-Aids.

'If you want to explain, I promise I'll try to understand. I'll listen, in silence, without interrupting you, for as long as you want. If you *try* . . . I promise I'll make it as easy as breathing, or drinking a glass of water.'

I looked at her earnestly, and her bright eyes flickered.

'Miki . . .' I whispered softly. 'Do you fancy a glass of water?'

Miki and I sat on the ground near the French doors in the kitchen for a couple of hours. Even though there were chairs a few metres away, which would definitely have been more comfortable than the floor, we sat there with our glasses of water, in silence, watching the dappled light through the trees outside.

She didn't say much. No soliloquy burst forth from her lips. She kept it all bottled up inside of her. We just sat next to each other quietly, keeping each other company.

'It's you . . .' I said simply. 'That white rose every Garden Day . . . that's you.'

She said nothing.

After a while, I asked, 'Why don't you tell her?'

'She doesn't feel the same way.'

Miki stared at the ceiling.

'You can't know that . . .'

'I don't need to,' she said sourly. 'She doesn't like . . . girls.'

I looked down. My relaxed, outstretched legs contrasted with hers, which were huddled to her chest.

Miki broodingly stubbed out yet another cigarette in the ashtray.

'I can't imagine what she'd think of me.'

'She loves you. Nothing will change that.'

But she shook her head. She stared at the wall in front of her with despairing, hopeless eyes.

'You don't get it. That's the whole point. I'm her best friend,' she murmured, as if it was a condemnation that made her feel better and worse at the same time. 'Our relationship . . . it's important. It's the most stable thing in both of our lives, it's something we can both rely on. And if I told her the truth . . . it would disrupt all that. It would be impossible to go back to how we were before. I can't bear to lose that. To lose her. I can't . . . do without her.'

It was as if Miki was watching Billie from the outer wall of a fortress. A little door through which all she could glimpse was barbed wire. Whereas I saw a meadow of flowers wherever I looked.

I looked down at my hands. Silence fell between us, slow and unrelenting.

'There's a type of caterpillar,' I said after a while. 'A caterpillar which is different from all the others. Sometimes you see it on acanthus plants. You know . . . caterpillars know that they have to transform. There comes a moment when they spin their cocoons and turn into butterflies. Right? It's simple. But this caterpillar . . . well, it doesn't realise. It doesn't know that it has to become a butterfly. If it doesn't feel like forming a chrysalis, if it doesn't . . . well . . . *if it doesn't believe enough* . . . there's no transformation. It doesn't spin a cocoon. It stays a caterpillar forever.'

I stared down at my ruined hands.

'Maybe it's true that Billie doesn't like girls. But . . . maybe she might like you. Sometimes, there are people who touch us so deeply that they stay within us, despite their . . . outer shell. They're important, and can't be replaced by anyone.' I gazed calmly at the wall. 'Maybe Billie hasn't thought about you like that . . . maybe she never will, but . . . you're the only person she wants by her side forever. And if you don't tell her . . . if you don't even try, Miki . . . you won't ever find out if she feels the same way. And then nothing will change. And then Billie will never really see you. And then you'll stay a caterpillar . . . forever.'

My words snuffed out like a candle flame.

I turned my head, and found Miki gazing at me, exposed and intent like I'd never seen her before. It was as if I'd somehow managed to breach her outer walls.

She looked away and tried to hide a little sniffle, but I heard it quite clearly.

'You're the last person,' she muttered, 'I ever thought I would tell.'

It didn't sound like an insult. It sounded like she had just lost a small battle with herself. I felt like she had accepted me.

'You've both always been alike in that way,' she mumbled.

'In what way?'

'You and her . . . the way you see the world. You . . . you remind me of her sometimes.'

Miki shook her head with a little sigh. Then she lowered her hood and her face came into the light.

Her eyes were smudged with make-up and her black hair framed her angular face. I couldn't help but notice the harmony of her high cheekbones and full lips.

Beneath her cargo pants and oversized hoodies, there was an unexpected beauty.

She noticed I was watching her, and threw me a wary look.

'What?'

I smiled.

'You're beautiful, Miki.'

Her eyes opened wide. She quickly looked away, closed her mouth and hunched her shoulders. She wrapped her arms around her knees, fed up, but I thought I saw her cheeks flush an unusual pink for her complexion.

'You and your . . . *caterpillars*,' she muttered, surly and embarrassed. I couldn't help but smile.

I laughed gently, my head leaning back against the wall and my eyes closed. I was sure I glimpsed Miki's face next to me relax into a serene expression.

'Hey . . . What's up?'

We turned around. Billie was in the doorway, rubbing her eyes with her hand.

'What are you doing there?' she asked sleepily.

Miki looked down. She seemed almost on the verge of saying something, but stayed silent. I needed nothing else.

'Don't worry,' I smiled at Billie. 'We're just having a glass of water together.'

I spent the rest of the day at Billie's.

Nothing seemed to have changed. Even though I now knew Miki's secret, it didn't stop her rolling her eyes when Billie started teasing her. I was sure that she liked their way of being together. That was why she couldn't do without her.

I had got a few messages while we were studying.

'Who is it?' Billie asked curiously, straining to look.

It was Lionel.

When I had been told to send the chain message to fifteen contacts, I had struggled a little.

I had sent it to the few people I had saved in my contacts: Anna, Norman, Miki and Billie again, the customer service number for my phone network, but then I came up short. I still needed to send it to ten more people, and my heart fell at the thought of disappointing Billie's grandma. And so I had sent it to Lionel ten times in a row.

He was surprised, to say the least, by my religious devotion.

'So?' Billie asked, curious as a cat. 'Who's messaging you so often? Come on, give us a look!'

'Oh, no one new . . .' I replied. 'It's just . . . Lionel.'

'Lionel? Oh, from lab . . . God! Do you chat?'

'Well . . . yeah, every so often.'

'Every so . . . how often?'

'I . . . I don't know,' I replied. She was now watching me with fervent interest in her eyes. 'Often, I'd say.'

Billie put her hand to her mouth emphatically and I jumped.

'*He's flirting with you!* He is, isn't he? God, it's obvious! Miki, did you hear?' Billie nudged her sharply. 'And you? Do you like him, Nica?'

I blinked at her candidly.

'Well, yeah.'

Billie's jaw dropped and she brought her palms to her cheeks. Before she could trill anything, however, Miki shoved her pencil between us.

'She meant do you *like* like him,' she clarified, pointing at my phone. 'If you're interested in this guy.'

I looked at her questioningly. When I finally understood, my eyes opened wide, my cheeks burned, and with a gulp I hurried to shake my head.

'Oh, no, no, no!' I corrected myself hurriedly. 'No, I . . . I don't like Lionel like that! We're just friends!'

Billie looked at me wordlessly, her hands still planted to the side of her face.

'. . . Just friends?'

'Just friends.'

'And does he know that?'

'Huh? What do you mean?'

'Oh, come on, let me see!'

She snatched my phone. With a genuine curiosity, she started to read my messages.

'Wow,' she exclaimed. 'You speak almost every day! He messages you a lot . . . and here . . . here he's messaged with some stupid excuse . . . ooh, and here . . .'

'I'm *sorry*,' Miki suddenly interrupted her. 'But all this guy does is talk about himself.'

I was surprised to see that she had also leant over to read through the messages with a raised eyebrow. She gave me a sceptical, enquiring look.

'Does he at least ask you how you're doing?'

The question confused me.

'Well, if I bump into him at school . . .'

'Does he ask?' she interrupted.

'No . . . but I'm fine,' I replied, not understanding what the issue was. Miki gave me a dark look before lowering her gaze back to my phone, arms folded across her chest.

'He's very proud of his achievements,' Billie said slowly, scrolling through the messages, and I understood from her tone that something in our conversation hadn't been what she was expecting.

'Yeah,' I agreed. 'He is . . .'

'Just to be clear,' Miki burst out, once and for all, 'do you talk about anything other than his tennis tournaments?'

I looked at them both, one of them suspicious, the other still holding my phone.

In truth, I couldn't remember a single occasion when we hadn't ended up chatting about something to do with him. I rifled through all my conversations with Lionel, our walks and the popsicles we'd shared, but I couldn't find an exception.

Miki shook her head. 'You're too naïve. Can't you see?'

Billie gave me my phone back with a hesitant, almost apologetic smile.

'We don't want to stick our noses in . . . I hope it doesn't come across like that. But it's only right that he asks how you are, don't you think? Even though we don't see each other every day, even I ask you that, because I care about the answer. Miki's right on this one.'

'He's using you to flatter his ego,' Miki declared, scowling. 'And you're so kind you don't even notice.' She hissed an insult as Billie elbowed her playfully.

'Excuse her, Nica, she gets awfully grouchy in moments like these. It's just her way of being worried about someone.'

Miki glared at her. Those words echoed around my head. I looked silently at Miki, brimming with emotion. *Miki was worried about me?*

'Are we studying or not?' she grumbled, lowering her head over her book again. Billie smiled.

'Were there lots of sourpusses like her at your institute?'

Miki glowered and tried to give her a kick, while Billie playfully tried to hug her. I couldn't remember anyone having been worried about me before.

Only one name came to mind. A dim candle that had been there ever since she went away.

Adeline.

Adeline, and her hands braiding my hair and cleaning my grazed knees. Adeline, who had always been a little bit older than me and the other children . . .

I smiled in an attempt to lighten the atmosphere.

'No, no one who defended me quite so vehemently.'

I realised that I might not have expressed myself clearly when I saw the unspoken question on Billie's face. I knew that she'd been wanting to ask me about the institute for a long time, but had always worried it wasn't the right time.

'What was it like?'

I hesitated. Billie seemed to instantly regret having asked such a direct question, as if it might offend me.

'If . . . if you want to talk about it,' she said, giving me a chance to avoid the subject.

She looked a little embarrassed, and I realised that she didn't want to upset me.

'It was . . . fine,' I said reassuringly. 'I was there for a long time.'

'Really?'

I found myself nodding. One question after another, I began to paint a picture of the big gates, the overgrown garden, the occasional visits and the life I had lived there, alongside children coming and children going.

I hid the greyer details, burying them like dust under the carpet. In the end, all that was left was a rough and slightly shabby existence.

'And you'd been there for twelve years? Before . . . Anna?' Billie asked. Miki was listening attentively but silently.

I nodded again.

'I was five when I arrived.'

'Was your brother there for a long time as well?' Billie pursed her lips. 'Sorry. I know you don't like him being called that. I said it automatically . . . Rigel, I mean.'

'Yes,' I murmured, lowering my gaze. 'Rigel . . . was there before me. He never knew his parents. It was the matron who named him.'

Billie looked at me in surprise, as everyone did when they found that out. Even Miki, who up until that moment had had nothing to do with the conversation, was now looking at me with a note of curiosity.

'Seriously?' Billie was stunned. 'He was there before you? You must know him really well.'

No. I didn't know him.

But I knew everything about him.

It was a paradox.

Rigel was rooted in me, like a scent that lingers all your life.

'It must have been hard for both of you,' Billie murmured. 'Your matron must have been very sad to see you go.'

A light breeze blew through my hair. I looked up at Billie. She was smiling gently.

'She must have been really sad to say goodbye, no? After all, she watched you grow up, she'd known you practically your whole lives!'

I looked her in the eyes. They seemed bigger than normal. I could just about feel the breeze on my bare arms.

'No,' was all I said. 'Mrs Fridge . . . hadn't known us for all that time.'

Billie blinked, confused.

'Sorry . . . didn't you say she named Rigel when he arrived?'

'No,' I replied mechanically. I felt again the urge to *scratch*, but my fingernails were still. 'That was the matron before her.'

Billie was amazed. Miki, next to her, stared at me. She was watching me carefully. I could feel her eyes piercing the distance between us, boring into my skin, imprinting onto my flesh.

'The matron before her?' I heard Billie saying. The breeze became a biting wind.

'There were two matrons?'

I dug my fingernails into my thighs.

'You never told us!'

Billie leant forward, her eyes large. I felt the pain from my fingernails sinking into my skin. Miki's eyes were like two monstrous, insatiable bullets, devouring me bit by bit.

'So,' I heard again, my blood pounding in my ears. 'You weren't raised by Mrs . . . Fridge. That was her name, right? It was the woman before her?'

All my senses roared. My skin was tense and shaking. I felt cold and clammy. Thorns were stuck in my vocal cords. All I could do was nod, mechanically, like a lead soldier.

'And how old were you when Mrs Fridge arrived?'

'Twelve.' I heard the answer as if it hadn't been me who voiced it.

It was as if I wasn't there, everything was amplified, all I could feel was my body on the brink of explosion. Then came the sweat, the anxiety, the rasping, the tearing at my heart, the terror that took my breath away. I withdrew, withheld, and swallowed, begging that someone would make everything stop, but Miki's eyes were staring at me and I was crushed by dread. The thorns in my throat grew sharper, I was suffocating, my pupils dilated. Everything was pulsating and again, I heard that voice clawing monstrously at my soul.

'*You know what will happen if you tell anyone about this?*'

Billie leant forward again, yet another question on her lips, but at just that moment, Miki accidentally knocked over her glass of juice.

It spilt all over the table, and Billie held back a yelp and leapt out the way. She grabbed the biology textbook before it got wet and scolded Miki for her clumsiness.

The conversation was over.

It was only then, when I was no longer at the mercy of their attention, that I lifted my hands and saw the marks my fingernails had left on the fabric of my pants.

That night, the house was quiet. It was just me and the glass in my hands.

'Nica?'

Anna's hair was a bit dishevelled. She held her bathrobe closed around her.

'What are you doing here?' she asked, coming into the kitchen.

'I was thirsty.'

She gave me a long look, and I lowered my face.

She came up to me, slowly and silently. I tried not to look up at her, because I was scared of what she might see in my eyes. There was no light in my gaze, just the darkness I would never be able to get rid of.

'It's not the first time you've been awake in the middle of the night,' she said softly. 'Sometimes, when I go to the bathroom in the nighttime, I see a light on in the landing, coming from under your door. I sometimes hear you going downstairs . . . and fall back to sleep before you come back up.'

She hesitated, looking at me tenderly. 'Nica . . . are you having trouble sleeping?'

There was kindness in her voice, but I couldn't let it touch me.

I felt sore where her eyes fell.

I felt wounds that wouldn't stop bleeding.

I felt nightmares where others had dreams, dark rooms and the smell of leather.

I felt that I had to *be good*.

I looked up to meet her eyes, then gave her an artificial smile.

'It's all okay, Anna. Sometimes I can't sleep. There's nothing to worry about.'

Good children don't cry.
Good children don't talk.
Good children hide their bruises and only lie when they're told to.

I was no longer a child, but some part of me still spoke in the same, childish voice.

Anna stroked my hair. 'You're sure?'

I clung to her affection so desperately I shook. All it took was that sweetness for me to fall to pieces. I nodded, trying to smile more convincingly, and she started making chamomile tea. I declined when she offered me some. Eventually, I decided to say goodnight and return upstairs.

I felt the weight of my body with every step. I got to my room and reached for the door handle when a voice made me freeze.

'I know why you can't sleep.'

My empty gaze stayed fixed on the door. I didn't have the strength to confront him, not at that moment.

I turned around, with dull eyes and the resigned calmness of someone who knows their demons and no longer tries to hide them.

'You're the only one who doesn't know.'

Rigel was watching me from the doorway to his room, cloaked in darkness. He looked down.

'You're wrong.'

'No,' I whispered harshly.

'Yes . . .'

'She *loved* you!'

My throat burned with the effort of raising my voice. I realised my fists were clenched, and my hair was falling over my face.

The reaction was so unexpected, I wondered how it could have come from a gentle soul like mine. From me, who lived by tenderness, who caved in to fear in a frightening manner.

It was because of those memories. It was because of *Her*. It was because of the cracks with which she had marked my childhood, and the childhood of many others. The childhood that she gave to Rigel, the son of the stars, at the expense of everyone else.

'You've *never* understood.'

At that moment, I wanted to hate how bound I felt to him. How he infected my thoughts. That feeling of sweet agony. I wanted to hate how I let him see me as no one else did, so vulnerable and covered in scratches that, for other people, I covered in Band-Aids.

He would never understand.

I went into my room and closed the door, as if I hoped to shut out all my pain.

As if I hoped to be able to shut it out again and again.

Hiding it, concealing it. Covering it with a smile.

I didn't yet know that the following day . . . all my shields would shatter for good.

21. Without Speaking

Skin cannot heal
A wounded soul.

That day, it was raining.

The sky was the colour of dirty metal. The fragrance of the apricot tree was so intense that you could smell it from inside the house.

Asia's voice was ringing through the air.

Dalma had dropped by to say hello, bringing a cake to thank Anna for the beautiful flowers she'd given her. Asia had also popped in on her way back from lectures and was chatting with them in the living room.

She hadn't so much as said hello to me.

She had brought a packet of Norman's favourite almond cookies. She left her bag on the couch, hung her jacket up and came into the kitchen where Anna and I were preparing tea.

'Asia!' Anna kissed her on both cheeks. 'How were lectures?'

'Boring,' she replied, sitting at the kitchen counter.

I no longer expected her to acknowledge my presence.

Anna was placing the teapot on the tray when the doorbell rang.

'Nica, could you bring the tea through, please?' she said, before going to open the door.

I arranged the cups and saucers on the table in the living room, where Norman was saying hello to everyone. Dalma asked if we were expecting anyone.

I didn't know who it could be. Between the clinking of the cups and the chatter, all I could make out was a man's voice.

'Mrs Anna Milligan?' he asked.

After a few moments, I heard footsteps. The stranger came in, and I was surprised to hear Anna stammering, confused. Norman got to his feet, and I followed suit.

A tall, well-dressed man appeared on the threshold. I had never seen him before. He was wearing a jacket that squared his narrow shoulders and I glimpsed suspenders over his shirt. He wasn't wearing a tie, and his face was inscrutable.

Everyone turned to look at him.

'My apologies for the interruption,' he said, noticing he wasn't the only guest.

There was something professional about his way of speaking.

'It was not my intention to disrupt a social gathering. I won't take too much of your time.'

'Excuse me, but who are you?'

'Norman,' Anna stammered. 'He . . .'

'You would be Mr Milligan?' the man deduced. 'Good afternoon. I apologise for any inconvenience. I must ask for a few minutes of your time.'

'Of . . . our time?'

'Well, no, not of yours,' he corrected himself. 'I have a few questions for the young people who live with you.'

'What?'

'The young people in your care, Mr Milligan.' The man was extremely diligent. He looked around the room. 'Are they home?'

A heavy silence fell. Then Asia and Dalma turned to me.

I was standing up, my back to the kitchen, so surprised that I was struggling to stifle the sound of my breathing.

The man's eyes fell on me.

'Is that Nica Dover? The girl who lives here?'

'But what do you want from her?' Anna asked courageously. He ignored her, his gaze fixed on me.

'Miss Dover, I have a few questions to ask you.'

'But,' Norman burst out, 'who are you? And what are you doing in our house?'

The man looked icily at him, then slid a hand inside his pocket.

He looked at him gravely, then pulled out a shiny police badge. 'Detective Rothwood, Mr Milligan. Houston Police.'

Everyone stared at him in dismay.

'W . . . what?' Norman stammered.

'There must have been some mistake,' Anna interrupted. 'Why on earth would you want to interrogate . . .'

'Rigel Wilde and Nica Dover,' the man read from a little card he'd pulled out of his pocket. 'Resident at 123 Buckery Street, with Anna and Norman Milligan. That's this address.' Detective Rothwood slipped the card back inside his jacket then looked up at me. 'Miss Dover, if you'll allow it, I'd like to speak to you in private.'

'No, no, wait a moment!' Anna looked at him, determined, putting herself between us. 'You can't just turn up and demand to ask questions without any explanation! They're minors, you can't discuss anything with them if you don't tell us why you're here!'

Detective Rothwood glanced sideways at her. For a moment, I thought he was annoyed, but then I realised he had understood. Anna's behaviour was the closest thing to maternal instinct that I had ever seen.

'The information I require concerns a rather delicate matter that has recently come to our attention. An investigation has been opened, I am here to take statements and try to shed a little light on the matter.'

'What matter?'

'Certain incidents concerning Sunnycreek Home.'

I heard him as if from behind glass.

I froze. A terrible foreboding made its way inside me, and a high-pitched screeching sounded in my ears.

'Sunnycreek?' Anna frowned. 'I don't understand. What sort of incidents?'

'Incidents dating back several years,' the detective specified. 'My intention is to confirm their veracity.'

The feeling of foreboding became a mole, then a bruise, then a stain, and finally, gangrenous. It seeped through me like ink, and I felt something *scratching* relentlessly.

It was my fingernails.

'It's a very serious matter. It is precisely in light of this that I am here.'

Something was wrong with the room, the walls were distorting, folding over me: a slow collapse, the loss of colour, the walls filling with cracks and cobwebs.

A small, dark room.

The detective's eyes fuelled that ruin, as if I had feared this verdict my whole life.

Anna ushered me, Norman and the detective into the kitchen and quietly closed the door as the detective began to speak again.

'Miss Dover. What can you tell me about Margaret Stoker?'

My throat closed. Alarm bells rang through my entire body. Reality started to derail.

'Who is this woman? Why should they know her?' demanded Anna.

'We understand that Mrs Stoker was director of Sunnycreek Home before Angela Fridge. After several years of continuous service, however, she left the institute. The circumstances around her dismissal are unclear. Miss Dover, do you remember anything . . . in particular, about Margaret Stoker?'

'Enough!'

Anna's voice cut through the air. My heartbeat was deafening. Familiar reactions started coursing through me at a nauseating speed. I saw Anna standing in front of me, as if to shield me.

'We want to know what's going on. Enough with these meaningless answers! What's this all about? Tell us, once and for all!'

Detective Rothwood was still staring at me. His gaze pierced me, stripped me, he seemed fixated. When I looked away, I could still feel it jabbing into me like a scalpel left by a surgeon.

'A few days ago, a charge was brought to Houston Court by Peter Clay, an ex-resident at Sunnycreek Home, now an adult. The charge in question relates to several forms of punishment not in line with the institute's directives.'

'Punishment?'

'Corporal punishment, Mrs Milligan.' Detective Rothwood gave her a steely look. 'Torture and brutality against children. Margaret Stoker is accused of mistreatment and aggravated abuse of minors.'

I didn't hear anything else.

Peter throbbed in my mind. *It was Peter.*

The room spun violently around me.

Peter spoke. He had shattered the vase, and now the darkness was spilling everywhere, swallowing everything around it.

Icy, deranged feelings coursed through me, freezing my heart and crushing my stomach. The anxiety, the sweat, the suffocation. The nausea. The air pounded me as if it was alive, and my heart palpitations intensified to the point of hurting, of bursting through my chest.

Peter spoke, and now everything would come out. I had to hide, to find cover, to escape, but my legs were like lead and my body had turned to stone. Memories flooded my mind – the sound of metal, the feeling of leather – *and fingernails mercilessly scratching and scratching and scratching.*

My vision shook.

'You can't be serious . . .' Anna murmured, as my tremors became ever more violent. 'That . . . that's inconceivable . . . Nica, she . . .'

She turned around. And she saw me.

She saw me, saw that I was a heap of shudders, my eyes devastated by a truth kept hidden for too long.

Me, a tangle of cold and sweat, anxiety and fear.

Me, trembling uncontrollably.

Her mouth fell open. Her gaze became incredulous and dismayed. Her voice made me want to disappear.

'Nica . . .' she whispered, distraught.

Terror roared in me like a monster. My skin cracked apart, my heart was racing at over a hundred beats a second, and feverish anxiety took my breath away. I was full of shivers, it felt like I was being crushed again – *the belt, the powerlessness, the dark, the screams.*

I took a step backwards.

Everyone was staring at me in horror and dismay, and *No, no, no, don't look at me like that, I'll be good,* the little girl inside of me screamed, *I'll be good, I'll be good, I'll be good, I swear.*

Now they knew how ugly, broken, useless and ruined I was, and suddenly everyone was looking at me like *She* looked at me, everyone had her eyes, her gaze, her condemnation and her scorn. I saw her face, I heard her voice, sensed her smell, felt her hands on my bruises, and it was too much. It was unbearable.

My heart burst.

'Nica!'

I fled, my pupils dilated and my lungs full of panic.

I ran through the kitchen, but quickly collided with something. I looked up, my eyes stinging with tears, and with a violent shudder saw that he had heard everything.

Rigel's gaze was the final blow. His eyes were dim, full of what we had both always known. They shattered me for good.

I stepped around him and ran out the back door. Voices called after me as I dove outside, the rain getting into my throat. Like never before, I needed the sky, the open air, to get away from bricks and mortar, to know they were as far away as possible.

I fled because that's what I had always done.

I fled because their looks were more than I was able to bear.

I fled, because I wasn't brave enough to see myself in their eyes.

As I ran, my lungs at the point of collapse, the storm pouring down on me, I realised that no matter how far I got from The Grave, it would always follow me.

She and that dark room would never leave me.

I would never truly be free.

Desperation made me run faster and faster. I tore through a world of rain and the image of Anna's disappointed face clawed at my soul until I collapsed into the mud in the park near the river.

My clothes were soaked through. I hid away there, under the shelter of a bush, like I did in the grounds of The Grave, trying to escape from *Her*. I looked for green, for peace, for silence, and prayed that she wouldn't find me.

The cold bit at my skin. Water soaked through my shoes and my breath became a feeble rattle.

I lay there until the cold seeped into my bones, freezing everything. Slowly, my vision clouded over.

As everything dimmed and faded around me, I heard footsteps slowly coming towards me through the torrential rain. They stopped in front of me. Breathing ever more slowly, I glimpsed a pair of shoes before everything went dark.

As my senses left me, a pair of arms lifted me off the ground. They enveloped me and I recognised a familiar smell, a scent that broke something inside me. It smelt like home. I dissolved into his warm embrace, burrowing my face in his neck.

'I'll be good,' I whispered feebly.

And then the darkness swallowed me up.

22. I'll be Good

Only those who have known darkness
Grow up seeking the light.

I had never been strong. I had never been able to be.

'*You're like a butterfly,*' my mom would say. '*A sky spirit.*' She had called me Nica because she loved butterflies more than anything else in the world.

I had never forgotten it.

Not even when her smile faded from my memories.

Not even when all that I had left of her was *tenderness*.

All I had ever wanted was a second chance.

I loved the sky for what it was, a clear surface and white clouds. I loved it, because it was always calm, even after a storm. I loved it, because when everything else crumbled, it always stayed the same.

'*You're like a butterfly,*' my mom would say.

For once, I wished she was wrong.

I remembered that face like skin remembers a bruise. A stain in my memories that would never go away.

I remembered it, because she had engraved it too deeply into me for me to ever be able to forget.

I remembered it, because I had tried to love her, as if she was my second chance.

That was my biggest regret.

I loved the sky, and she knew it. She knew it, just like she knew that Adeline hated loud noises and that Peter was afraid of the dark.

It was where we were most broken that she would push the hardest. She used our weaknesses, the areas in which even the oldest of us were still childlike. Our fears were like seams that she would unpick, as if we were dolls to cut apart, bit by bit.

She punished us because we misbehaved.

Because that was what naughty children deserved. It was penance for our sins.

I didn't know what my sin had been. Most of the time I couldn't understand why she did it. I was too young to understand, but I remembered each of those moments as if they had been tattooed on my memory.

They never left.

When one of us was punished, the rest of us all huddled into our seams, praying we wouldn't be next.

But I didn't want to be a doll. No, I wanted to be the sky with its clear surface and white clouds, because it didn't matter how many rifts ran across it, how much thunder and lightning marred the calm, it always stayed the same, never breaking.

That's what I dreamt of being. Free.

But I always returned to porcelain and rags when her eyes landed on me.

She dragged me onwards, and I saw the cellar door, the narrow stairs leading down into a dark abyss. That bed without a mattress and the belts she constrained my wrists with all night long.

My nightmares would always look like that room.

But her . . .

She was my worst nightmare.

I'll be good, I said to myself when she passed by me.

I was too small to be able to look her in the face, but I would never forget the sound of her footsteps. It terrified us all.

'I'll be good,' I whispered, wringing my hands, wishing I was invisible, a crack in the plaster.

I tried to be obedient, I tried to give her no excuses to punish me, but I was like a butterfly, with the tenderness my mother had left me. I cared for lizards and injured sparrows, got my hands dirty with earth and pollen, and she hated imperfection almost as much as weakness.

'Cut it out with those Band-Aids like a little street urchin!'

They're my freedom, I wanted to tell her. *They're all the colour I have.* But she would drag me onwards and all I could do was clutch at her skirts.

I didn't want to go down there, to spend the night there.

I didn't want to feel the iron bedframe scratching my shoulder blades – I dreamt of skies and a life away from there, someone who would hold my hand instead of grabbing my wrist.

Maybe that someone would arrive one day, with blue eyes and hands too gentle to bruise. My story would no longer be one of dolls, but something else.

A fairy tale, perhaps.

With golden flourishes and that happy ending I'd never stopped dreaming of.

The bed shook with the clanging of the woven steel.

My legs were shaking and the darkness fell like a curtain around me.

The belts around my wrists creaked as I thrashed and flailed, feverishly scratching at the leather.

My eyes were burning with tears and my body writhed for a crumb of her attention.

'I'll be good!'

My fingernails scraped and snagged in my desperation to free myself.

'I'll be good! I'll be good, I'll be good, I swear!'

She left through the door behind me, and darkness swallowed the room.

All that was left was a sliver of light on the wall opposite, then darkness within darkness, and the echo of my screams.

I knew . . . I knew I could never speak of it.

None of us could, but there were times when light seeped even through the walls of The Grave. There were times when keeping quiet seemed like an even worse nightmare.

'You know what will happen if you tell anyone about this?'

Her voice, a whisper like nails down a blackboard.

'Do you want to find out?'

Her fingernails, plunged deep into the flesh on my elbow, asked this question. I lowered my face, as I did every time I couldn't bring myself to meet her gaze – because there were abysses in her eyes, dark rooms and fears that I didn't have the courage to see.

'You want to know what happens to *disobedient* children?'

She tightened her grip on my arm until my skin cracked open.

The familiar feeling of my heart plummeting, the belts constraining me, *crushing* me, the noise of the leather under my fingernails, the plunge of panic. I shook my head, stitched my lips, wide eyes promising that I'd be *good, good, good* just as she liked.

We were a little institute on the periphery of a city that had forgotten us. We were nothing in the eyes of the world, and nothing to her either.

She was supposed to be more kind, more patient and more loving than a mother, but it seemed as though she did everything possible to be the exact opposite.

No one realised what she was doing.

No one saw the suffering on our skin.

But I preferred smacks to the cellar. I preferred blows to the leather on my wrists. I preferred a bruise to that iron cage, because I dreamt of freedom, and bruises don't get inside, bruises stay outside and don't stop you from flying.

I dreamt of a good world, and I saw light even where there was none. I searched the eyes of others for what I had never found in her, and silently whispered prayers they couldn't hear – *Choose me, please, choose me. Look at me and choose me, choose me for once.*

But no one ever chose me.

No one ever saw me.

I was invisible to everyone. I wished I could be to her, too.

'What have I told you?'

My wet eyes were pointed downwards at her shoes, I was incapable of looking up.

'Answer me,' she hissed. 'What have I told you?'

My trembling hands held a lizard to my chest. I felt so small, with my short legs and pigeon toes.

'They wanted to hurt her . . .' My little voice was always too weak. 'They wanted . . .'

A violent yank tore the words from my mouth.

I tried to keep hold of the lizard but it was no use: she wrenched it from me. My arms were outstretched, my eyes open wide.

'No . . .'

The burning of skin on skin, her palm on my cheek, the blast of her slap. Scorching, smarting, like a swarm of wasp stings.

'You remember what you told me?'

In the shadow of the storm, Adeline's eyes were the only colour in a sea of grey.

'What your mom said to you . . . do you remember?'

I nodded and she took my hand. I felt her gaze on my jagged fingernails, that I'd snagged desperately scratching on the leather belts.

'You know how we can make everything disappear?'

I lifted my swollen, tearful eyes and Adeline gifted me one of her smiles. She kissed each of my fingertips.

'See?' she said, leaning over me. 'Now they don't hurt any more.'

She knew that in reality they'd never stop hurting. We all knew it, because our seams all bled the same.

Adeline hugged me, held me against her too big, shabby clothes. I let her warmth envelop me, as if it was the last bit of sun in the world.

'Never forget it,' she whispered, as if that memory of my mother belonged to her too.

I dug in my memory and clung to it as tenderly as I could.

'You're a sky spirit,' I repeated to myself, like a dirge. 'And like the sky, you can't be broken.'

'Was it you?'

I trembled, paralysed with terror.

A stray dog had got into the institute and had wrecked her office, scattering her papers everywhere.

Nothing scared me more than when she was angry. And at that moment, she was furious.

'Did you let it in?'

'No,' I whispered anxiously. 'No, I promise . . .'

Her eyes glared frightfully. Fear overcame me. My breathing quickened, my heart surged, and everything crumbled dreadfully around me.

'No, please . . .' I whimpered, stepping backwards. 'No . . .'

Her hands shot forwards. She made to grab me and I turned around, trying without success to escape. She caught me by my top and hit me quickly and brutally, her fist like a stone in the small of my back. I lost my breath and my vision went hazy.

I collapsed to the floor, a searing pain in my kidneys ricocheting through my entire body.

'You and your disgusting habits!' she shouted, towering over me.

I couldn't breathe. I tried to stand up, but I was too dizzy. Unbearable stabbing pains brought tears to my eyes, and I wondered if I'd find blood in my urine that evening. I covered myself with trembling hands and prayed I'd become invisible.

'This is why no one wants you,' she hissed. 'Disobedient, dirty little liars like you stay here!'

I bit my tongue and tried not to cry, because I knew how much that incensed her.

She was breaking something inside of me, something that instead of growing up, would stay small forever. Fragile, childlike and ruined. Something desperate and naïve that would make me look for the good in everyone, just so I would not have to see their bad side.

It's not true that children stop being children when they become disillusioned.

Some have everything taken from them.

And stay children forever.

'Choose me,' I would beg when someone came to visit.

'Look at me. I can be good, I swear, I know how to be good. I'll give you my heart if you choose me, please, choose me.'

'What have you done to your hands?' a woman asked one day, looking at my jagged fingernails.

For a mad moment, the world stopped and I hoped against hope that she would see, would understand, would say something. For a moment, we all froze, holding our breath and our eyes wide.

'Oh . . . nothing.'

The matron approached, her smile like a sore that turned your blood to ice.

'You know, when she plays outside all she does is dig about in the dirt. She digs and digs and uproots the grass looking for stones. She likes it a lot, don't you?'

I wanted to scream, to confess, but her glare sucked out my soul. All my bruises throbbed. My heart shrivelled. She was inside me, the terror was devouring me, making me nod. I was scared I wouldn't be able to get out, I was scared of what she'd do to me if they didn't believe me.

That night, the bed jolted as I thrashed against the belts constraining my wrists. The darkness fell over me again, punishing me for having attracted attention. The tears and the screams would stay inside there forever.

'I'll be good! I'll be good! I'll be good!'

I would have screamed until I lost my voice, if it hadn't have been for . . . that touch.

That unique touch.

Every time, the door quietly opened, and a slice of light glided into the room before narrowing the next moment. In the dark, footsteps approached the bed. Warm fingers touched my hand, held it gently, and a thumb traced comforting circles on my palm that I would never forget.

And then, nothing . . . Then, the pain would dissipate in my tears, my heart would slow, my rasping gasps would become gentler breaths and I would try to make out a face to put to the only gesture that had ever brought me comfort.

I never glimpsed anything.

There was just that caress.

That sole relief.

23. Little by Little

And the girl said to the wolf:
'What a big heart you have.'
'That's just my anger.'
And so she said:
'What a big anger you have!'
'It's to hide my heart from you.'

I was lying down.

I felt my arms beside my body, my legs were outstretched and my head was heavy.

I tried to move, but couldn't. Something was holding me back, pinning me to the mattress.

I tried to lift my hands, but they were stuck.

'No . . .' came out of my mouth, my lungs swelling with panic. Stress made my heart pound frantically against my ribs.

I tried to get up, but there was something stopping me.

'No . . .'

Everything started pulsating again, like an endless nightmare. My fingers started squeezing, scraping, digging. I couldn't move.

'No, no, no!' I screamed. *'No!'*

The door burst open.

'Nica!'

Different voices filled the room, but I carried on thrashing about, not seeing anyone. I was blinded by panic. All I could feel was my immobilised body.

'Doctor! She's awake!'

'Nica, calm down! Nica!'

Someone cleared a path through them and wrenched me free.

I gasped and frantically scurried to huddle up at the head of the bed. Distressed, I squeezed the fingers of the hand I found next to me. The person who had freed me stiffened as I gripped them with everything I had in me. Trembling, squeezing my eyes shut, I put my forehead to their wrist.

'I'll be good . . . I'll be good . . . I'll be good . . .'

Everyone was watching me breathlessly.

The hand I was holding closed into a fist, and I prayed they wouldn't let me go. It was only when I opened my eyes a few moments later that I realised whose hand it was.

Rigel looked at me, his jaw clenched. He planted his eyes on Dalma and Asia – and a man I had never seen before – and stonily ordered: '*Out.*'

There was a long moment of silence in which I didn't look up. Then, I heard the sound of their footsteps slowly walking away.

Anna came towards me.

'Nica . . .'

She placed her palm on my face. I felt her warmth on my cheek. This was my bed, my room. I was no longer in The Grave. I realised that what had been constraining me before were just the bedcovers, someone had tucked me in too tightly.

There were no belts, nor woven steel.

'Nica,' Anna whispered, desperately. 'Everything is okay . . .'

The mattress sank under her weight, but I couldn't bring myself to let go of Rigel's wrist. I gripped it until Anna's fingers delicately slid into mine and loosened their grip.

She slowly stroked my hair, and I heard Rigel walking away. When I looked up in search of him, I just saw the door closing.

'The doctor's through there.' Anna watched me, shaken. 'We called him as soon as you got home . . . I'd like him to take a look at you. You might have a fever, or light-headedness . . . I changed your clothes, but maybe you're still cold . . .'

'I'm sorry,' I interrupted her with an exhausted sigh.

Anna stopped talking. She watched me, mouth open, and I couldn't manage to hold her gaze.

I felt empty, broken and flawed. I felt destroyed.

'I wanted to be perfect,' I confessed. 'For you. For Norman.'

I wanted to be like the others. That was the truth.

But I was still naïve and fragile. I repeated *I'll be good* to myself because I had the constant fear of making a mistake and being punished.

The feeling of the belts on my skin had scarred me to the point that sometimes even too tight a hug, not being able to move or simply the feeling of powerlessness could trigger panic attacks.

I was ruined, and I always would be.

'You *are* perfect, Nica.'

Anna stroked me slowly, shaking her head. Her eyes were full of anguish.

'You're . . . the sweetest and kindest person I've ever had the good fortune to meet . . .'

I stared at her, my heart empty and heavy. But in Anna's gaze . . .

In Anna's gaze there was no blame or condemnation. There was just me. And in that moment, for the first time, I realised that Anna's eyes were the colour of the sky.

With that clear surface and those white clouds, with that freedom I'd sought in so many different faces, I saw my reflection in her eyes.

There was the sky I'd always been looking for. It was in Anna's eyes.

'You know what struck me the first time I saw you?'

Tears stung my eyes. She smiled a slightly broken smile.

'Tenderness.'

My heart broke with a soft, boundless pain.

A pain so bad it was good. Her face blurred through my tears.

'Tenderness, Nica,' Mom smiled at me. 'Tenderness, always . . . Remember that.'

I saw them both, as if they were inside of me. Mom passing me that blue butterfly, Anna handing me a tulip.

Both of them with that passionate look, both of them with shining eyes.

Anna taking me by the hand, and Mom leading me onwards. *Mom laughing and Anna smiling,* alike and different, a single entity dwelling in two bodies.

It was that tenderness that united us, that kept us together . . . The tenderness that Mom had given me was what had allowed me a second chance.

I leant forwards and plunged into the arms of the woman in front of me. I no longer held myself back, hugged her tightly, no longer scared of being overly familiar or being rejected, and her hands held tightly, protectively, on to me.

'No one will hurt you any more . . . *No one* . . . I promise . . .'

I sobbed in her arms. I let myself go. And in that desperate embrace, in that sky I could finally touch, I felt my heart confess what I'd never had the courage to tell her.

'You're . . . my happy ending, Anna.'

Later, after the doctor's visit, she was still there.

I listened with deep affection to her heartbeat as she stroked my hair.

'Nica . . .'

I sat up just enough to be able to look her in the face. She looked tentatively at my reddened eyes and tucked a lock of hair behind my ear.

'What do you think about the idea of talking about this . . . with someone?'

Anna now knew why I couldn't sleep at night, how terrible my childhood had been. But the thought of confiding in someone else twisted my guts to the point that I couldn't breathe.

'You're the only one . . . I could talk about it with.'

'Oh, Nica, I'm not a doctor,' she said, as if she wished she was one just for me. 'I don't know how to help you . . .'

'You're good for me, Anna,' I confessed in a little voice.

It was true. Her smile reassured me. Her laughter was like music. Her affection made me feel loved like I never had before.

I felt better when I was with her. I felt protected, wanted. I felt safe.

'Do you still want me?' I whispered, frightened. I needed to know, but I was afraid to hear the answer. I would never see my dreams in the same way without her.

Anna inclined her head, distraught. Then she clutched me to her with all her strength.

'Of course,' she admonished me. I loved her even more madly.

I wanted to keep her close, always. Every day, every moment, for as long as she'd allow.

'I wanted to understand you better,' she said, her voice sounding more fragile.

Then, I noticed that she was wearing a leather strap around her wrist, next to her watch. I hadn't noticed it before. It seemed incongruous for a woman like her, more suitable for a teenager.

'Nica . . . there's something you should know.'

I instantly realised what she was about to tell me. I listened in silence.

'You and Rigel . . . you're not the first to have lived here.' She waited a moment, then said, 'Norman and I had a son.'

She looked up to see my reaction, but I gently held her gaze, calm and aware.

'I know, Anna.'

She stared at me in surprise. 'You already knew?'

I nodded and looked down at her leather bracelet.

'I realised.'

From as soon as I had arrived.

The dark t-shirts I sometimes saw Rigel wearing that weren't his. Klaus sleeping under his bed. The place at the table next to Norman, where the wood was slightly worn. The empty photo frame on the table in the hall, an absence that Anna hadn't been able to completely erase.

I didn't need to ask why she had kept him secret. She had done everything she could to make us feel like it was our home.

'That day, at the institute,' she said quietly, 'the day we brought you home . . . it was a bit like a fresh start.'

I understood, because it had been the same for me. It had been like saying goodbye to a different life, and clutching at a second chance.

'We wanted you to feel at home,' she swallowed. 'We wanted to feel . . . like we were a family again.'

I slid my hand slowly into hers, my colourful Band-Aids against her skin.

'You are the best thing that's ever happened to us,' I told her. 'I want you to know that. I . . . can only imagine how much you miss him.'

Anna closed her eyes. My words seemed to furrow lines into her face. A tear rolled down her cheek and her voice cracked as she said, 'There's not a day when I don't think of him.'

She went to pieces like I'd never seen before. I pressed closer to her and leant my head on her shoulder, hoping to give her some warmth. My heart ached with hers. I felt her pain like a warm wave.

'What was his name?' I asked softly after a while.

'Alan.'

I felt her looking down at me.

'Do you want to see him?'

I sat up, and Anna brought a hand to her chest. She slipped off her long necklace with a round, shining, inlaid pendant. I couldn't remember ever seeing her without it.

She opened it as if it was a golden, tiny book.

There was a photo of a boy inside. He must have been a little older than twenty. He was sitting at the piano in their house. His black hair framed his kind, smiling face and his eyes shone sky blue.

'He's got your eyes,' I said in a whisper, and Anna, despite everything, smiled tearfully.

'He was the only person that Klaus ever liked,' she said, still with that shaky smile. 'It was Alan who found him, one day on his way back from school, as a boy. Oh, you should have seen them. It was pouring with rain. Alan was holding him as if he'd found hidden treasure. They both looked so small and soaked.'

Anna gripped the photo, not brave enough to stroke it.

I wondered how many times a day she held that pendant in her hands. How many times her heart broke behind those eternally smiling eyes.

'He loved playing the piano . . . He *lived* for that piano. In the evening, he'd get home, and no matter what time it was, he'd be there. He'd say, "You know, Mom, I can only speak through these keys and chords, and you understand me all the same." *And he was right . . .*' she whispered through her tears. 'He could only speak through the piano. He wanted to be a musician, before the accident . . .'

Her voice faded and she swallowed.

That little pendant seemed incredibly heavy. I took her hand in mine, helping her to bear its weight.

'I'm sure he'd have made it.' I closed my tearful eyes. 'I'm sure Alan would have become a great musician . . . and I'm sure he loved the piano as much as you love your flowers.'

Anna lowered her head, and I held her to me, letting our wounds join hands. As if that was the only way we'd find a cure, crying and bleeding together.

'I never wanted to take his place,' I whispered. 'Rigel and I . . . no one could ever replace him. But the truth is . . . the people we love never really leave us, you know? They're inside of us, and then one day we realise they've always been there, we can find them just by closing our eyes.'

Anna collapsed against me. I wanted to carry on, to tell her that our hearts are boundless, that they only know how to love, scars on scars, bruises on bruises. That I would have been happy to take that place next to Alan, however small and worn out it was. That I would be happy to fill it with all the colours I could . . . and to let myself be loved for what I was, exactly how I loved her, with my butterfly heart.

'Let's choose a photo together,' I said. 'That frame downstairs shouldn't be empty any longer.'

A few hours after that conversation, I decided to get up.

I left my room, wrapping my hoodie around me, and glimpsed someone on the landing.

I didn't know she was still there, but decided not to ignore her.

'Asia.'

She stopped. She didn't turn towards me. She never did. She had never pretended to accept my presence, and she wouldn't start now.

'I'm sorry about what happened to you,' she said, somewhat flatly. I couldn't work out if she was being sincere.

She started to walk away but I moved in front of her.

'Asia, I'm not going to give Anna up.'

She came to a slow stop again. Something about the way she was standing gave away a hint of surprise.

'What did you say?'

'You heard me,' I replied calmly. 'I'm not going anywhere.' There was no hesitation in my tone, just a composed firmness. 'You can't know how much I've wanted a family. Now I've got one . . . Now I've got this chance with Anna and Norman . . . I'm not giving it up.'

I waited for a reply, but none came. Asia didn't move.

'I know you know what I mean,' I carried on, my voice softer. I didn't want to be domineering, I just wanted to make her understand.

I approached her slowly, trying to get my good intentions across. 'Asia, I . . . don't want to take . . .'

'*Don't,*' she interrupted icily. 'Don't say it. Don't you *dare* say it.'

'I don't want to take Alan's place.'

'SHUT UP!'

I jumped. She turned towards me and her eyes glowered. They were full of a pulsing suffering, a suffering that had never stopped bleeding.

'Don't you dare,' she glared at me fiercely. 'Don't you *dare* talk about him.'

I noticed something possessive about her tone. It was different to Anna's bare grief.

'Do you think you know anything about him? Do you think you can come here and wipe out everything there was of him? No photos, no memories, no nothing! You know nothing about Alan,' she snarled. '*Nothing!*'

Her face was twisted with anger, but I didn't react. I looked at her with calm eyes and a truthful heart.

'You were in love with him.'

Asia's eyes opened wide. I had hit the nail on the head. I should have stopped there, not said anything else, but instead I added, 'That's why you can't stand seeing me here . . . Because I remind you of him, and he's not here any more. Anna and Norman have moved on in their own way, but you haven't. That's it, isn't it? You didn't tell him,' I whispered. 'You never told him how you felt, he never knew. He was gone before you found the courage to tell him. That's your biggest regret . . . that's what you're carrying inside, Asia. You can't accept that he's no longer here, and that's why you hate me. But you can't bring yourself to hate Rigel,' I finally shot at her, 'because he reminds you too much of him.'

It happened in a flash.

Anger got the better of her. She refused my words, refused to admit it to herself, so much so that her rage exploded and her hand lashed through the air. I saw her rings glinting and then her slap clapped like thunder.

I had closed my eyes, but suddenly realised that her slap hadn't landed on me. Someone had pulled me out of the way and taken the hit.

I looked up, and was dismayed at what I saw. Under a wave of black hair, Rigel's face was turned to one side, his normally poised shoulders now hunched.

Asia and I both stared at him, incredulous.

He straightened his head as his black eyes drove icily into Asia. Through gritted teeth, his voice dripping with a slow, chilling menace, he spat, 'I want you . . . *out* . . . of here.'

Asia pursed her lips, her face a blotchy red. I detected a hint of shame in her eyes, which then flew to look over Rigel's shoulder. Further down the landing, a dismayed face was watching her wordlessly.

'Asia . . .' Dalma murmured, disappointed by her daughter's unexpected behaviour.

Asia clenched her fists, trying to suppress her angry tears. Then, with a swish of hair, she disappeared down the stairs.

Dalma, aghast, put her hand to her face and shook her head.

'I'm sorry,' she sobbed. She seemed mortified. 'I'm so sorry.'

She looked away and followed Asia down the stairs.

At that moment, I noticed that the shadow that had engulfed and protected me was no longer there.

I turned and saw Rigel walking away. I felt disorientated, shaken and confused.

As he disappeared around the corner, a call, prayer-like, left my mouth: 'Wait . . .'

I wouldn't let him leave this time.

Despite the feverish shivers running down my spine, I followed him. My bare feet pounded the wooden floorboards and I regretted not putting socks on.

Without realising what I was doing, I stretched out my hand and grabbed his t-shirt with the little strength I had.

'Rigel . . .'

Almost imperceptibly, he tensed and clenched his fists. He still had his back to me, standing tall and stiff, but being so close to his body made me feel strangely safe.

'Why?' I asked. 'Why did you take that slap for me?'

All of my senses were directed towards him. All I could hear was the sound of his breathing.

'Go and rest, Nica,' he told me in a deep, measured voice. 'You can hardly stand up.'

'Why?' I insisted.

'Did you want to take it?' he retorted, his voice harsher.

I bit my lip and fell quiet. I tightened my grip and then, eyes lowered, said, 'Thank you. For talking to the detective . . . Anna said you told him everything.'

I still couldn't believe it.

Anna had reassured me that I didn't have to answer any questions, because Rigel had done so for me.

He'd told him everything: the screams, the slaps, the smacks, when *She* punished us by refusing us food. When she tied us up in the cellar, when she had smashed Peter's fingers in a door just because he'd wet the bed.

He'd told him everything, not missing out a thing. Then, the detective had asked him if the matron had treated him the same way.

And he had said no.

Then, Detective Rothwood had asked if she had ever touched him in a different way to how she touched the others, in a way that wasn't appropriate for children. Rigel, again, had said no.

And I knew that this was the truth.

Because the detective couldn't understand.

The detective had never seen the matron moving his little fingers over the piano keys, with a light in her eyes that never shone for anyone else.

He had never seen them together, sat on the piano stool, his legs dangling off the floor and her giving him a cookie every time he played the right chord.

'You're the son of the stars,' she would whisper to him, in a voice that didn't seem like hers. 'You're a gift . . . a little, little gift.'

The detective couldn't know that the matron couldn't have children, and Rigel, so alone and abandoned, was the only thing she ever felt could be just hers.

Not like the rest of us, who came from broken families, who already had parents behind us. Not like us, who were just a heap of used dolls.

'I hated her.'

I had the impression that this was the first time he had ever confessed this to anyone.

'I hated what she did to you,' he said slowly. 'I couldn't stand it. Every single day . . . I heard you . . . I heard *all* of you.'

'*I know why you can't sleep,*' he had said to me, and I had replied to him unfairly. I had always thought that Rigel enjoyed the attention, that he didn't care what she was doing to us. He had always been in her shrine, safe from everything else.

But it wasn't really like that. Not at all.

It was as if someone had finally given me a light to shine through the fog. I better understood his looks, his behaviour, I understood why he always seemed so faded when he played the piano.

It was sadness.

He carried within him a piece of *Her,* a fragment of her sewn under his skin that he would never be able to discard. As much as he might have despised her, as much as he might have wanted to erase her, he would always have something of hers. I wondered if it was better to be hated or loved by a monster.

Why hadn't he left, if he hated her? Why did he choose to stay?

I wanted him to speak again. To open up and explain that piece of his past that I had never been able to understand. How little did I know of him?

'I know it was you who brought me home.'

Rigel stiffened, as if waiting for something.

'It was you who found me . . .' I said, a weak smile softening my lips. 'You always find me.'

'I can only imagine how that distresses you.'

'Turn around,' I whispered.

His masculine wrists emanated strength and tension, his tendons visible. I had to ask him a second time before he decided to listen to me. The fabric of his t-shirt fell from my fingers, and very, very slowly Rigel turned to face me. I felt a pang in my heart when I saw his face.

He had a nasty scratch on his cheekbone. His skin was red. It must have been from Asia's rings when she'd slapped him.

Why?

Why did he hide his pain and let no one get near?

Instinctively, I raised my hand. From under his black hair, his eyes flitted warily towards it, as if he understood and was scared of my intentions.

Rigel seemed to suppress the instinct to recoil. Fragile but determined, I moved slowly, held my breath, and went up onto tiptoes. My heart brimming with hope, with all the tenderness I could, I stroked his cheek.

As I touched his skin, his vulnerable, lost eyes darted down to me.

Again, I saw that explosion of emotion. Again, I was dazzled by unfamiliar galaxies. Still holding my breath, still holding his gaze, I let my palm lie flat against his cheek.

It was warm. Soft and firm.

I was afraid of scaring him, that he would push me away. But he didn't. I lost myself in his eyes, drowning in that deep, black ocean.

The next moment . . . his fists slowly unclenched. His knuckles relaxed, he became less tense. We looked each other in the eyes, and his face looked so docile it broke my heart. He let out a sigh through his nose, so soft and woeful that I could barely hear it.

With that expression of gentle resignation, Rigel let himself be touched. It was as if I had defeated him with a single touch.

He lowered his gaze and, with a gentle pressure that shook my soul, pressed his face against my palm.

My heart was beating desperately. A glorious, destabilising sensation flooded me, engulfed my soul, making it shine like the sun.

Rigel turned to meet my gaze. I wanted this moment to last for an eternity, for nothing to ever move again, for him to keep looking at me like that forever . . .

'Nica!'

The moment shattered in an instant. Rigel leapt away from me, and being separated from him felt like the worst thing that could ever happen to a person. The next minute, Anna appeared behind me on the landing, looking shocked and upset.

'What happened with Asia?'

I didn't have time to reply before Rigel stepped between us. My eyes darted to him and I felt an uncontrollable impulse to stop him.

My mind was spinning. I was going mad.

Anna told me that Dalma had told her what she had seen, but I couldn't concentrate on what she was saying. Thoughts of his dark eyes, his cheek, him yielding to my touch whirled like a roaring universe inside me. But the central force that held everything together was moving away from me . . .

'I'm sorry, Anna,' I whispered, before turning around and following him.

I couldn't think clearly. I ran down the stairs, stupidly risking dizziness from the fever.

I needed to speak to him. To ask him questions, to get answers, to understand his actions, to tell him that . . . *that* . . .

I saw the front door open and Rigel was there, on the sidewalk. There was someone with him, but his name was already on the tip of my tongue.

'Ri—'

I broke off as something – one singular thing, one *familiar* thing – caught my eye.

The world stopped still.

With wide eyes, I stared at her. Disbelief took my breath away.

I would never forget that cascade of blonde hair.

Never.

Not even after all that time.

It wasn't possible . . .

'Adeline . . .' I whispered, astounded.

And then, Adeline stood up on her tiptoes and planted a kiss on Rigel's lips.

24. Constellations of Shivers

It's not the wicked who roar.
It's those who are bleeding,
and have no other way to hide their pain.

'I know it's you . . .'

Adeline noticed my little hand holding her t-shirt. She turned and found me standing beside her.

'What?' she asked, confused.

'Keeping me company. I know it's you, down there, holding my hand when she punishes me.'

That comfort in the dark could only be her.

Adeline looked at me for a while, and then . . . she understood. Her eyes looked to the end of the corridor, towards the cellar door.

'What if she sees you . . .' I watched her, small and worried. 'Aren't you afraid she'll find out?'

She looked down at me again. She stared at me for a moment, then her face softened into a smile.

'She won't find out.'

She took my hand, being careful of my broken nails, and I squeezed hers back with all the affection coursing through my body. I drew her arms tight around me, letting her soft hair envelop me. I loved her fiercely.

'Thank you,' I whispered tearfully. 'Thank you . . .'

Adeline.

My heart was pounding in my ears.

Chaotic images flashed through my mind – Adeline smiling, comforting me, blue eyes and hair as bright as the sun; Adeline crying, hiding in the shadows of the ivy, wrapping her arms around one of the other children, braiding my hair in the grounds of The Grave, as if we could build ourselves a happy ending, just the two of us.

Adeline, there. Adeline, kissing Rigel.

Frozen, I watched as Rigel shoved her away and shot her a glare that made her laugh lightly.

I couldn't breathe. I felt a stab in my heart as Rigel's suddenly urgent eyes noticed me. I stared at him with that silent scream stuck in my chest.

Then, Adeline noticed where he was looking and turned around. Her eyes landed on me . . . and her smile vanished.

I saw her eyes widen slightly, as though she couldn't believe what she was seeing.

'Nica?' she gasped incredulously.

The next moment, as if she had been struck by a sudden realisation, her gaze fell on the house behind me. Then, she turned to Rigel and gave him a look that I couldn't quite decipher but that was disturbingly intimate.

'Oh . . .' Adeline turned back to me, emotional. 'Nica . . .'

'Nica!' Anna was running towards me, alarmed. She wrapped a blanket around me as I continued to stare wide-eyed at Adeline.

'Nica, you've got a fever! You can't stay outside like this! The doctor said you need to rest!'

Anna looked up, and met Adeline's gaze. They looked at each other for a while, and then Anna put an arm around my shoulders.

'Come inside,' she said, trying to lead me in. 'You shouldn't get cold again . . .'

The blanket tight around me, I reluctantly complied.

'Adeline . . .'

'I'll visit,' she promised, stretching towards me. 'Don't worry. You . . . rest. I'll come and see you in the next few days, I promise!'

All I could do was nod before Anna took me back inside.

I looked for Rigel's eyes. With a tinge of sadness, I saw they were no longer looking at me.

★ ★ ★

'Oh, Rigel . . .' she murmured. 'What have you done?'

Rigel couldn't bring himself to look at her. He felt too dejected for the tone of resignation in her voice.

She was stuck in his eyes, like a burn that would never fade.

'Why are you here?' he spat out, disgruntled and taking his frustration out on the girl next to him.

Adeline hesitated before replying.

'Do you think I've forgotten what day it is, the day after tomorrow?' she said, almost sweetly. He shot down her attempt to ease the tension with a glare.

She lowered her gaze.

'I heard about Peter,' she admitted. 'A policeman came to ask me questions . . . He asked me about Margaret. He said that they're tracking down all of us who were at the institute before she was fired. It was him who told me you weren't at The Grave any more. And now I know why.'

A silence fell. It was a silence full of blame, countless mistakes, and to Rigel it felt inevitable.

'Does she know?'

'Know *what*?' he hissed cagily, but his venomous anger just crashed impotently against the wall of painful truth in her eyes.

Because Adeline knew. Adeline had always known.

Because Adeline had always been interested in him, in a way that he could never reciprocate, doomed as he was to an eternal, indestructible love.

Because she had always looked for him at the institute, only to see him look for Nica.

'That you made yourself be chosen so you could stay with her.'

Rigel ground his teeth in anger. His body was tense and rigid. He wasn't looking at her, and didn't say anything, because replying to her would be equivalent to admitting to the only allegation he couldn't deny.

The writhing inside was killing him. He was tormented by the thought of Nica seeing Adeline kiss him. He remembered how she had stroked his cheek, how she had brushed it so gently, and it was even more painful when he realised that inside him there was a glimmer of *hope*. Hope that, somehow, she could want him, that she could reciprocate his desperate feelings.

'Don't breathe a word to her,' he ordered stringently. 'Stay out of it.'

'Rigel . . . I don't understand you.'

'You can't understand me, Adeline,' he snarled in an attempt to defend himself, to protect everything right and wrong that he knew was inside of him. She shook her head and threw him a look that for a moment reminded him painfully of Nica.

'Why? Why won't you tell her?'

'*Tell her?*' he repeated, stifling a derisive laugh, but Adeline wasn't discouraged.

'Yes,' she replied with a simplicity that annoyed him even more, if that was possible.

'Tell her *what*?' he snarled, like an injured beast. 'Have you seen where we are, Adeline? Do you think that, even if we weren't stuck here, she'd ever look at me?'

Rigel hated those words, because he knew they were true.

Those eyes would never look for him, with need, desire or love.

Not a disaster like him.

And he was too disillusioned to admit that he would have given anything to be wrong.

'Someone like *her* could never want someone like *me*,' he spat bitterly, with all the pain that he was constantly trying to subdue.

Adeline stood watching him, with sincere, earnest eyes.

And he would remember that moment forever . . .

The exact, tragic moment in which his only hope came alight within him, to torment him every single day, to make every single thing he thought he knew tremble.

'If there's anyone able to love that much . . . If there's anyone in the world with a heart that big, it's Nica.'

* * *

'Is there anything else you want to tell me?'

I shook my head.

The social worker gave me an understanding look. She was extremely kind, professional, highly discreet and attentive. Only a day had passed since the incident, and though her visit had been scheduled for the following week, it had been brought forward because of what had happened. Her task was to assess the foster care and check that no problems or incompatibilities had arisen. She had asked about Anna and Norman, school and how living together was going. Before speaking to me, she had asked Rigel the same questions.

'All right. In that case, I'll write up the first report.'

She stood up. I did the same, wrapping the blanket around me. My temperature was still coming down to normal.

'Ah, Mrs Milligan,' she reached out towards Anna. 'This is a copy of their medical files. If you ever consider contacting a psychologist, I think these might be useful for you.'

Anna took the slim, organised files. The documents were in a turquoise folder. She slowly looked through them, carefully and respectfully.

'It is also my duty to inform you that social services can provide psychological support in the event that . . .'

'And who wrote these reports?' Anna interrupted her. I glimpsed the words *Psychological and Behavioural Diagnoses* on the sheet of paper she was looking at. I thought I saw a photo of Rigel on it too.

The woman's answer was pragmatic, 'A medical specialist, during the years in which Mrs Stoker was director of the institute.'

'Oh,' Anna remarked shortly. 'So I imagine there won't be anything about the panic attacks and trauma due to the violence and abuse.'

There was an icy silence.

I stared at Anna, taking a while to process what she had said. Where had that cutting tone come from?

The woman seemed incredibly embarrassed.

'Mrs Milligan, I don't know what impression you've formed of us. What has come to light about Margaret Stoker . . .'

'I don't care,' Anna shot her down. 'All I know is that woman was fired when she ought to be in jail, serving time for what she did.'

I remembered the day that Margaret left. Some visitors had noticed our bruises and had informed Social Services. Margaret had been fired immediately and the nightmare ended overnight, like a bubble suddenly bursting.

I would never forget the others' eyes. It was like seeing the sun after a lifetime underground. They all had dulled faces and faded eyes, as if they hadn't seen the light in so long that they no longer believed in it.

Some nightmares you never really believe can end.

'Where were the inspections?'

There were inspections. But they were too sporadic, unfocused and superficial.

'How is it possible that no one ever realised?' Anna continued, irate.

Because *She* was good.

She was good at leaving bruises where they wouldn't be seen.

She was good at hurting us in the most hidden places.

She was good at turning us into broken dolls who wouldn't breathe a word.

She was good, and in the meantime the world forgot about us, entrusted us to a woman who would become the mother of our nightmares.

I knew that this was what often happened to broken things. They get shut away, far from everything, just so they don't have to be seen any more. We were different, alone, problematic, children of no one. Those they didn't know where to put.

Sometimes I wondered what would have become of me if I hadn't ended up at The Grave, but in a different institute. A place that was regulated, safe. A place where there weren't any beds in cellars or dead-end roads. A place without *Her*.

'I just wonder how it can have gone on for years,' Anna said icily. 'I wonder how you can have managed not to see it, not to know. I wonder . . .'

'Anna.' I put a hand on her arm and looked at her, a silent request in my candid gaze.

I shook my head.

She was arguing with the wrong woman. It wasn't the social worker's fault that Margaret was a monster. It wasn't anyone's fault.

Someone should have protected us. Someone should have seen, should have known, it was true, but the past can't be changed. Raking it all over would only hurt me.

I didn't want to feel more anger.

I didn't want to feel more hate.

It just reminded me of how much anger and hate I'd received as a child . . .

'My job is to oversee the adoption process. I will do everything I can to make it work out.' The social worker looked at us with a sincere determination. 'I want Nica and Rigel to have a family, a peaceful life and a stable future as much as you do.'

Anna made a sign of assent, accepting her task. Then we both showed her out.

'Goodbye.' The social worker opened the door, and Klaus darted outside. Surprised, she stepped backwards and bumped into Anna, making her drop the medical files. The folders opened and papers scattered everywhere.

I knelt down to help her and, suddenly, I found myself holding a sheet of paper with a photo of Rigel.

Unintentionally, my eyes glimpsed terms like 'symptoms', 'incapacity', 'rejection', 'solitude' and . . .

'Thank you, Nica.' Anna took the paper from me and put it back in the file.

I stared at her hazily. I didn't even respond. Those words were whirling around, causing tumult inside of me.

Incapacity. Rejection. Solitude . . . Symptoms?

What symptoms were they talking about? And why were there so many pages in his file?

Thoughts were spinning around my head. I couldn't think straight. Those details spoke to me. Each one was a piece of the puzzle that was Rigel. Maybe, if they were put together correctly, they'd finally form a picture of his soul that, perhaps, I might eventually be able to make sense of . . .

Adeline came to see me that afternoon.

I opened the door and she stepped inside respectfully. It was so strange to lead her through the house that I had to turn round and look at her face.

I couldn't believe it was her. That she was there.

I stopped in the living room, feeling a bit awkward. She looked at me, her eyes suddenly charged with emotion.

'Do you . . . want something to drink? Anna's made tea,' I murmured, wringing my hands. 'I know that . . . well, you used to really like tea. If you want, I can . . .'

I broke off as Adeline rushed to embrace me. I was stunned. I sunk into her unexpected warmth and the feeling of her hands gripping my shoulders abruptly set my chest aflame. In her arms, a sudden yearning exploded within me. I found myself hugging her back tightly, as if she was a piece of me, as if without her I'd never been complete.

'I wasn't expecting to find you here,' she whispered shakily.

I realised how much I had missed her. It was as if someone had just returned an essential part of my heart.

The day that Adeline was moved to another institute, my world lost its last flicker of light.

'How you've grown . . .'

She pushed my hair away from my face to get a better look at me. I couldn't help but think the same about her.

She was an adult. She was only a few years older than me, but I realised with a twinge of sadness that I'd never imagined her looking so grown-up.

But that was still her smile. Those were still her eyes, her blonde hair, her soft and reassuring voice . . .

'How are you feeling?'

I felt like crying.

'Better,' I replied, trying to contain my emotions. I ushered her to the couch then went to fetch the tea.

'I didn't . . . I didn't know that you'd left The Grave.' Her hand slid into mine and she looked around, emotional and admiring. 'It's so lovely here . . . this house seems tailor-made for you. They seem like really good people.'

'What about you?' I asked tentatively. 'Are you with a family? Do you live nearby?'

Adeline's smile faded.

'I'm still there, Nica,' she said warily. 'In the institute I was transferred to. I've come of age, so I should move on, but . . . I haven't got a job,' she smiled sadly. 'I come into town every now and then . . . I found a job in a small bookstore, but it closed last month.'

I felt a pang in my heart.

I knew I had been lucky, I knew I had been an exception, but that news still saddened me.

'Adeline, I'm . . .'

'It's okay,' she interrupted me calmly. 'It's been a long time now. It's all right.'

She gave me a weak smile then looked down at Klaus, who had started to nibble at the edges of my blanket. 'I heard about the detective . . . are you all right?'

'Anna thinks I should speak to someone about it,' I confessed after a moment. 'She thinks . . . it could help.'

'I think she's right.' Adeline shrugged and sighed. 'You can't heal from things like this on your own.'

'Have you gone?'

She nodded slowly.

'A couple of times. I went under my own steam. The owner of the bookstore was very nice, and he had a friend who was a psychologist. I didn't . . . tell him about *Her*. I didn't tell him about Margaret, exactly, but it helped to talk, in some way.' She shook her head slowly. 'But Nica . . . you were very young when you were first subjected to all that. We all take on our experiences in different ways, especially when they're traumatic. We all experience them in our own way. Take Peter, for example . . . He never got over it.'

I nervously nibbled at my Band-Aids. I knew Adeline was right. *She* had never left. She was still so vivid in my mind.

We hadn't all suffered the same trauma, but none of us had ever been the same again.

'You can't heal from things like this on your own.'

But the question was, could you ever heal from things like this?

Adeline gently pulled my fingers away from my mouth and smiled softly.

'You're still in the habit of nibbling your Band-Aids when you're nervous.'

I blushed, embarrassed, and looked down. It was a bad habit from childhood.

'Is that why you came?' I asked. 'Because you heard about what happened?'

Adeline glanced away. She suddenly seemed uneasy.

'No . . . Actually, I came for another reason. I remembered last week . . . and I thought about coming. For Rigel.'

My stomach turned.

'For . . . Rigel?'

'Don't you remember? It's his birthday tomorrow.'

I was taken aback. Speechless.

Rigel's birthday.

March 10th.

How could I have forgotten?

I let it sink in, still staring at Adeline.

It wasn't actually the day he was born, but the day he'd been found outside The Grave. They had never been able to work out the exact date of his birth, and so they had chosen that day to mark it.

I remembered his birthday because it was the only birthday that the matron ever celebrated. I remembered Rigel, his face lit up by a candle on a birthday cake, sat alone in the cafeteria . . .

'I wanted to surprise him,' Adeline murmured. 'But I should have realised that he wouldn't react as I expected.'

The memory of their kiss was like a punch to the heart. I glanced away, unable to look at her. I didn't realise that I was gripping my knees tightly.

'It's never been a day to celebrate for him. Rigel . . . has never liked the attention,' I said quietly.

'No, Nica . . . that's not why.' Adeline looked down sadly. 'It's because of what he went through.'

I glanced at her furtively, shocked, and she looked at me sadly.

'You really never thought about it?'

I was trapped in Adeline's gaze. Then . . .

Then I realised. I realised how stupid I had been.

What he went through . . . *being abandoned by his parents.*

'His birthday . . . the day they found him, reminds him of the night his family abandoned him,' Adeline confirmed.

I had always misunderstood. I had always seen him inside Her bright, perfect shrine. I had associated suffering with what *She* did to us, and knew that he couldn't understand.

But me? What had I understood about him?

'Rigel isn't like us.' Adeline looked at me urgently. 'He never has been . . . We lost our families, Nica, but they didn't want to leave us. We can't understand what it's like to be rejected by our own parents and left inside a casket without so much as a name.'

Constant distrust. Disillusionment.

The lack of connection, defensive shields for pushing the world away.

His aggressive, suspicious personality.

Incapacity, solitude, rejection. Symptoms.

Rigel had abandonment issues. It was a trauma he had always carried. He had grown up with it, and it had become his reality.

The signs had always been there. I had just never been able to see them.

Adeline seemed to understand. 'He'll never show how much it hurts,' she said. 'Rigel masks everything . . . He always holds back, but inside . . . his soul is so open to pain and feelings it's scary. Sometimes I don't know how he doesn't go mad. I'm sure he hates even his own name,' she concluded. 'Because the matron gave it to him, and because it's the symbol of his abandonment.'

Suddenly, everything I knew about Rigel took on a different hue. Rigel pushing me away; Rigel not letting me get close; Rigel as a boy, staring at a birthday candle all alone.

Rigel picking me up in the middle of the park, letting himself be touched for the first time, surrendering like someone who still believes they're injured . . .

'Don't leave him, Nica. Don't let him destroy himself.' Adeline looked at me, distressed. 'Rigel condemns himself to being alone. Maybe because he thinks that's what he deserves . . . He grew up knowing he wasn't wanted, and he's convinced that's how it will always be. But don't leave him alone, Nica. Promise me you won't.'

I wouldn't.

Not any more.

I wouldn't leave him alone, because he'd been alone for too long.

I wouldn't leave him alone, because fairy tales are for everyone.

I wouldn't leave him alone, because you can't appreciate life by yourself, only with someone at your side, hand in hand, with strong hearts and bright faces.

I wouldn't leave him alone, because I wanted to talk to him, listen to him, to hear him for a long time to come. I wanted to touch his soul. I wanted to see him smile and laugh, his face light up. I wanted to see him happy more than I'd ever wanted anything before.

I wanted all this and more, because Rigel had carved my heart into the rhythm of his breathing, and I no longer knew any other way to breathe.

I wanted to scream, right there on the couch, shout all of this to the world. But instead, I let my heart speak, and held the rest back for myself.

'I promise.'

The following afternoon, I was walking briskly around the neighbourhood holding a small package.

I was slightly late. I looked up and glimpsed the ice cream kiosk on the other side of the street.

I crossed the road and looked around for a familiar face.

'Hi,' I said to Lionel. 'Sorry I'm late. Have you been waiting long?'

'No, don't worry about it,' he replied, starting to walk. 'I've grabbed us a table. Actually, I have been waiting a while, yes, but it's no big deal.'

I apologised again and offered to get him an ice cream. He accepted immediately, and I went up to the kiosk to get two cones.

When I came back, I noticed he was looking at me. I held out his ice cream and felt his eyes running up and down my bare legs.

'What's up?' I asked once I'd sat down.

'That's a nice dress,' he said. He looked at the red and white polka dot fabric fluttering in the wind and enhancing my complexion, and the brown cross-body bag that Anna had given me. 'It suits you. You look really pretty.'

My cheeks flushed pink and I raised my eyebrows. I looked away, and thought back to the conversation at Billie's house.

'Thanks,' I replied, hoping he wouldn't notice my embarrassment.

'You didn't need to wear it to come here.'

'Huh?'

Lionel smiled breezily.

'Not that I don't appreciate it . . . but there was no need to put on such a pretty dress just to get an ice cream together. You really didn't need to. It's just an ice cream.'

'Oh, no, I . . . I know. I'm wearing it for dinner afterwards. You know, to celebrate. It's Rigel's birthday today.'

Lionel was still for so long that his ice cream started to melt and drip down his finger.

'Ah,' he said, staring at me flatly. 'Today's his birthday?'

'Yeah . . .'

He was quiet. He started eating his ice cream again while I smiled at a ladybug that had just landed on the back of my hand.

'So you put it on for him?'

I looked at Lionel, who was now polishing off his ice cream with the little spoon, too engrossed to look at me.

' "For him"?'

'For your *dear* sweet brother,' he clarified with indifference. 'You dressed up so prettily for his birthday?'

I looked at him, confused. I wasn't wearing the dress for anyone . . . just for myself.

I wanted it to be a special occasion. It was me who had told Anna and Norman, and knowing how little Rigel enjoyed parties, we had chosen something simple, with just us, and Adeline, too. For once, I had wanted to wear something different.

'We're having a special dinner at home,' I said quietly. 'I thought it would be nice . . .'

'And you put on a dress for dinner at home?'

'Lionel . . . is there something you want to tell me?'

I didn't understand. Hadn't he just said that the dress suited me?

'Forget it,' he murmured, shaking his head. He saw my upset expression and added, 'I didn't mean anything. It seemed strange, that's all.' He bit into the wafer and tried to smile at me.

We finished our ice creams in silence.

'What's this?' he asked after a while, shaking the packet I had placed on the table. 'This is why you were late, isn't it?'

'Yes,' I replied, tucking my hair behind my ear. 'I saw it and stopped to buy it, I'm sorry . . .'

'What is it?'

'It's a present for Rigel.'

Lionel immediately stopped turning it over in his hands. He held it and slowly turned to me.

'Can I see?'

I nodded, and he slowly unwrapped it.

Out came a little glass sphere. It had a black silk string and was filled with coloured sand in such a way that a beautiful starry sky was drawn across the glass surface. The grains sparkled in the light, twinkling like little stars.

It was Orion, etched onto the glass like a web of extremely fine diamonds.

I didn't even know what it was. A keyring, maybe. I wasn't sure. But when I'd stumbled across it in a little store selling blown glass ornaments, I couldn't help but think it would be perfect for him.

Some part of me imagined him fiddling with it absentmindedly as he read . . .

Lionel turned it over in his hands. I got up to throw my spoon in the trash.

'It's handmade,' I told him. 'The woman in the store said it was the last one. She paints the sand on herself! She wears some kind of monocle, and sits on a stool arranging the grains with a long needle so that . . .'

The shattering of glass made me jump.

At Lionel's feet, broken shards of glass sparkled in the middle of a ring of sand. I stared at them, breathless.

'Oh,' Lionel said, scratching his cheek. 'Whoops.'

He apologised and I knelt down, picking up the shards of glass.

That carefully chosen gift was now in pieces.

Why? Why did anything to do with Rigel always have to end up in pieces?

Shaking with frustration, I gripped the shards and looked up at Lionel. My eyes were shining with an unfamiliar emotion.

He apologised again, but this time I didn't reply.

I returned home with a heavy heart. I had really wanted to see Rigel accept my gift, and now some part of me would always wonder whether he would have.

'Oh, Nica, you're back!' Anna was busy laying the good tablecloth.

'Could you take this box upstairs while I finish laying the table? It goes in the room at the end of the landing.'

I searched her face and gave her a knowing look as she handed me a key. The room at the end of the landing was where Alan's stuff was kept. I headed upstairs.

I turned on the light and put the box down next to a wardrobe. In that room there were clothes, boxes, old CDs and rolled-up posters. There were also books. I looked closer, and saw that they were university textbooks.

I discovered that Alan had studied Law, like Asia.

I carefully took down a particularly large book and opened it. I wanted to feel closer to him, to understand more about him. I wanted to ask Anna to talk about him, but I didn't know whether she would have been happy to do so.

I flicked through a book called *Criminal Law,* amazed at the excessive number of pages. I noticed how clean and neat it was. Alan must have taken great care of his textbooks.

Absentmindedly, I read through the titles of the chapters:

Child Abuse . . .

Bigamy . . .

Domestic Violence . . .

Incest . . .

I frowned. One word caught my eye – *Adoption.* I read intently.

'In many states, *adoption* constitutes a binding familial relation. Through the adoption process, the *adoptee* legally becomes part of the *adoptive* family. Therefore, they are to be considered a full member of the family for all intents and purposes.

'Section Thirteen A of the Alabama Criminal Code: Any relationship or marriage between family members, whether consanguineous or adoptive, is considered incest under the law.

'This includes: parents and children by blood or through adoption; brothers and sisters by blood or through adoption; half-brothers and half-sisters.

'Incest is a Class C felony. Class C felonies are punishable by imprisonment for up to . . .'

I stopped reading. I closed the book and moved away as if it had burnt me. My ears were buzzing.

I stood still, staring at the cover without really seeing it. Something silently lurched within me, a stormy sea. I didn't understand that feeling of emptiness. I didn't understand what was happening.

I slammed the door shut, bewildered. As I retreated, it felt as if the walls were moving away from me. Everything suddenly seemed out of place, strange, as if my bearings had shifted.

I pushed the feelings away and locked the door before going back downstairs. I tried to focus on the evening ahead, and to ignore the strange emotion that wouldn't leave me alone.

It was a peaceful dinner.

I could finally introduce Adeline to Anna and Norman. They offered her the gravy, asking if she wanted more.

I kept glancing at Rigel to see if he was enjoying himself. Unfortunately, Adeline stopped me from seeing him clearly.

There was cake, there were presents. I cringed a little when I remembered I had nothing to give him.

Eventually, when darkness had long since fallen, Adeline decided it was time to go.

Norman offered to give her a lift home, but she declined politely. Anna gave Rigel a kiss then went upstairs to bed. Norman followed after wishing us goodnight.

'Thanks for a lovely evening,' Adeline said breathily.

She hugged me goodbye, then approached Rigel, who was still sitting down. I almost winced as she bent over to embrace him.

'Think about what I said the other night,' I thought I heard her whisper.

Rigel turned his head, as if he both didn't want to hear her words and at the same time couldn't get them out of his head. With a sigh, she left.

It was just the two of us.

Silence fell, and Rigel glanced towards me. When he saw that I was watching him, his eyes darted away and he got to his feet.

'Rigel.'

I approached him from behind, stopping before I reached him.

'I bought you a present today . . . I didn't forget. But I wasn't able to give it to you.'

'It doesn't matter,' he murmured.

I looked down.

'It matters to me,' I replied sadly.

I wanted that evening to be special for him. I wanted him to feel how much those around him cared about him, even if he couldn't see it. I wanted him to know that he wasn't alone.

'I'm sorry,' I said in a little voice.

I took hold of the back of his t-shirt, feeling the need to be closer to him.

'I cared about it. And now I want to . . . I want to make up f—'

'Don't say it,' he interrupted me. His hands were stretched out, as if making an urgent plea. *'Don't say it . . .'*

'I want to,' I murmured stubbornly. 'Let me make it up to you. There must be something you want . . .' I tightened my grip, looking for his face. 'Anything at all . . .'

Rigel inhaled slowly. He was silent, but then, with an incredibly slow, deep voice, he asked, 'Anything at all?'

I remembered how he had held me in the rain. The slap he took for me. The scratch on his face . . .

'Yes,' I whispered, without hesitation.

'And if I asked you . . . to stay still?'

'What?'

Rigel turned slowly. His dark eyes were planted on me.

I was hardly breathing. In his eyes I saw the reflection of my red and white dress and my mouth hanging open under my silvery eyes.

'Still,' his lips whispered, sending me adrift. *'Stay still . . .'*

I froze. Rooted to the spot by the sound of his voice.

Tall and imposing, he looked at me through his eyelashes. It was only then that I noticed there was a smear of icing sugar on the corner of my mouth. I tried to wipe it off, but I couldn't. Rigel's fingers circled my wrist, holding my hand away. His silky touch exploded on my skin and my breath shook.

He was touching me.

I didn't move as he slowly brought my arm back down, trapping me in his gaze.

'Stay,' he swallowed, *'still . . .'*

I was hypnotised.

I looked at him with powerless eyes, burning with uncontrollable emotions.

His eyes searched my face. Then, he slowly leant over me.

His masculine musk invaded my nostrils. My heart was pounding in my throat.

I felt his breath on me, and . . . his lips landed on the corner of my mouth.

I held my breath.

His hot tongue brushed against the edge of my mouth. My heart tightened, my knees trembled. As Rigel licked the icing sugar from my lips, I found myself gripping the skirt of my dress as if it was my only anchor in that madness.

I could no longer understand a thing.

My breathing deepened, our breath mingled and the smell of him got into my throat, blurring my mind like the sweetest of poisons.

My heart was about to burst. My head was spinning and I forgot how to breathe.

He was killing me.

Soundlessly.

I sensed his fingers trembling around my wrist . . .

He pulled away, licking away the sugar from his bottom lip. I stared at him, bewildered, boiling, overcome with shivers.

I was frightened of what was stirring within me. Terrified by how my skin had reacted.

His breath destroyed me.

His eyes were burning on my lips.

His breath swept over my cheeks.

I closed my eyes and . . .

★ ★ ★

Nica's lips.

Rigel couldn't see anything else.

His blood was throbbing in his temples. His mind was hazy. His heart was on the verge of breaking through his chest.

She hadn't moved.

She had stayed still.

Without realising what he was doing, he gently pushed her

287

backwards against the table. Breathing heavily, he found himself running his hands up and down her forearms, and then he grabbed her wrists.

He was dying to kiss her.

The writhing feeling within him roared. The taste of her honey-like skin was still on his tongue, a condemnation that would burn him forever.

He had to get away from her. Before it was too late.

He had to let her go, to snarl at her, to push her away, to never look at her again . . .

But Nica was there, and *God*, she was the most sinfully beautiful thing he had ever seen. With that dress that clung to her breasts, her long, chestnut hair, her lips, glossy and parted, the breaths he wanted to snatch from them.

She was gorgeous, irresistible.

He lunged forward, inhaling her sweet scent. He couldn't stop himself. He stroked the hot skin of her wrists and felt her hold her breath. His heart thumped against his ribs, an unbearable torture.

Her scent was going to his head. He could understand nothing, he was losing contact with reality. There was no comparison for the effect Nica had on him.

And he wanted . . . *In that moment, he just wanted* . . .

She shuddered.

Rigel looked up.

He saw her swallow, her eyes clenched shut. She looked shocked. Her cheeks were flushed and her knees were trembling. She was shaking so much she couldn't breathe, even her narrow wrists were trembling in his hands.

She couldn't even look at him.

And again, destructive feelings were triggered in him: terror, rejection, devouring passion, those feelings that suffocated him, crushed him, an eternal condemnation. Anguish and frustration returned. Rigel wanted to scrape them away with his fingernails, tear them off him and no longer feel so dark, desperate and wrong. He was tired of feeling like that, but the more he tried to resist, the more his heart withdrew into his chest like an injured beast.

He just wanted to feel right. He just wanted to touch her, to feel her.

He desired her with everything he had, but everything he had was stings, thorns, pain and a soul full of suffering.

And she couldn't even bring herself to look him in the eyes.

'If there's anyone able to love that much . . .' As Nica trembled before him, those words died inside him.

And Rigel thought that there was a terrifying sweetness in the way that a lifetime of looking at her had made his soul crumble between his bones.

★ ★ ★

He let me go.

Rigel moved away and I tumbled back into reality.

No, my heart screamed painfully.

I felt like I was going mad. I could no longer tell up from down. I was no longer myself: all I could feel was an invisible force binding me to him.

I was about to stop him, but just at that moment, the doorbell rang.

I jumped, and in front of me, Rigel turned, his eyes shooting towards the front door.

Who could it be at that time of night?

'Don't go,' I begged him. My voice sounded anguished. 'Don't leave. Please . . .'

I bit my lip, hoping to convince him to wait for me, for once, not to disappear.

Maybe I'd succeeded, because Rigel didn't move. I threw him one last glance before heading into the hall. I was sure I could feel his eyes following me.

I glimpsed someone through the obscure glass. Someone who was hammering on the door as if it wasn't the middle of the night.

I peered through the peephole. My eyes flew open.

I stared at the door, astounded, then reached out to open it.

'Lionel,' I said breathlessly.

He stared at me, his hand still outstretched, his eyes distraught. He looked as though he'd been running.

'What are you doing? Why are you here at this time of night?'

'I saw lights on,' he said hastily, stepping towards me. The frantic look in his eyes frightened me. 'I know, it's really late, I know, Nica, but . . . I couldn't sleep . . . I couldn't . . .'

'What's happened? Are you all right?'

'No!' he replied, beside himself. 'I can't stop thinking about it, I've reached the limit. I can't stand this, I can't stand that . . . you're here, that . . .' he bit his lip, utterly bewildered.

'Lionel, calm down . . .'

'I can't stand you living here *with him*!' he finally spat out.

My stomach turned.

I threw an alarmed look over my shoulder. Lionel's words had reverberated through the silence like a cannon shot.

I slipped out and closed the door behind me. Lionel stepped backwards and my eyes fell on the open gate behind him.

'It's late, Lionel. Maybe you should go home . . .'

'No!' he interrupted frantically, raising his voice. He didn't seem himself. 'I won't go home. I can't pretend any more! I can't stand knowing he's always around you, acting like an untouchable bastard and you with that . . . *dress*!' He was gesticulating wildly, looking me up and down. When he looked up at my face, there was a sinister glint in his eyes.

'You've been together all this time! Haven't you? What did he ask you to give him for his birthday, huh? *What?*'

'You're not yourself,' I replied, my chest tight.

'You won't tell me?' He was breathing heavily. His eyes frantically searched my face. 'You still don't get it, do you?'

I stepped towards him.

'Lionel . . .'

'*No!*' he erupted, out of his mind, and moved a few steps backwards. 'How can I make you understand? Huh? How?' He ran his hand through his hair. 'Are you really that naïve?'

I flinched as he clenched his fists.

'I can't go on like this, it's absurd! How long have we been chatting? *How long?* But you still don't seem to get it! What do I have to do for you to understand? What? God, Nica, open your eyes!'

Impulsively, Lionel took my face in his hands and kissed me. My eyes flew open. I instinctively pushed him away.

I staggered backwards, disconcerted. He stared at me, dumbfounded. Then he looked over my shoulder.

I shuddered when I saw two black eyes staring at us from the front door. In the shadow of night, they were two lightless, ruthless chasms.

They landed on me. Rigel stared at me as I heard the world scream. Then he turned around and disappeared.

'Rigel!' I called. I was about to follow him, but Lionel grabbed on to my arm.

'Nica . . . Nica, wait . . .'

'*No!*' I burst out, raising my voice. I yanked my arm free, and Lionel stared at me in dismay before I turned and ran inside.

★   ★   ★

His nerves felt like they were about to explode.

A dull pain devoured him as he strode – or maybe fled – from that scene. He had a lethal desire to shatter him, to smash that moron's face and tear him away from her. Seeing them together felt like going mad.

His mind was spiralling down into the dark.

He had always known that Nica would never see him as she saw the rest of the world, not him, not his dirty, dilapidated heart.

He had made himself too hateful. Even to her.

His blood went to his head. His fists were clenched. The sight of them tormented him, he felt an irrepressible urge to break something.

No one would ever want him, *no one*, because he was broken, different, wretched, a *disaster*.

He kept the world at a distance.

He ruined everything he touched.

There was something wrong with him, and there always would be.

He didn't know how to feel normal emotions, he couldn't even feel something as sweet as love without scratching it to shreds in his attempt to push it away.

Attachments meant suffering. Attachments meant abandonment, fear, solitude and pain. And Rigel didn't want to feel those any longer.

Love hurt him. It had Nica's eyes, her bright smile, her innocent sweetness that broke his heart.

His temples pulsed, white dots erupted behind his eyelids and he felt something rising within him, a cruel and burning anguish.

'No . . .' His muscles contracted. He pushed away the pain that threatened to make him lose his mind. He clenched his eyes shut, scratching, torture.

In a blind fury, he kicked his backpack and sat on the bed. He crazily grabbed handfuls of his hair as if he was about to tear them out of his scalp.

'Not now . . . *not now* . . .'

⋆ ⋆ ⋆

'Rigel!' I called.

I reached the first floor and went to his room. The door was ajar. I pushed it gently.

He was there, sat on the bed, immersed in the darkness.

'Rigel . . .'

'Don't come in,' he hissed, making me jump. I stared at him, distressed by his menacing tone.

'Go . . .' He ran his hand through his hair. 'Go, now.'

My heart was pounding madly, but I didn't move.

I had no intention of going anywhere.

I moved slowly towards him, noticing his shallow breaths, but Rigel gnashed his teeth.

'I told you *don't come in*,' he snarled angrily, sinking his fists into the mattress. His pupils were incredibly dilated, like a wild beast's.

'Rigel . . .' I whispered. 'Are you . . . okay?'

'Never better,' he hissed. 'Now go.'

'No,' I insisted. 'I won't go . . .'

'Out!' he exploded with a frightening violence. 'Are you deaf or what? *I told you to get out of here!'*

He snarled terribly. I stared at him, distraught, my eyes wide, and I saw a devastating suffering hidden like a shard of glass in all that anger. It knotted my throat, and pricked even the inside of me.

He was pushing me away again, but this time I could see his desperation.

'Because Rigel condemns himself to being alone,' I heard as he suffered before me.

'Did you hear? GO, NICA!' he spat at me, in a way that would have scared anyone. For once, I followed my heart instead of my reason.

I reached out, put my arm around his head and pulled him towards me.

I held him.

I held him so that I'd break with him, without knowing why I was going to pieces too.

I held him with all the strength I had, and his hands grasped for my dress, as if he was going to push me away.

'You won't be alone any more . . .' I whispered in his ears. 'I won't leave you, Rigel. I promise.' I sensed his shuddering breaths against my stomach. 'You won't feel alone ever again. *Ever again* . . .'

And as I said those words . . . he violently clutched the fabric of my dress. And then . . . he pulled me towards him.

Rigel clung to me. He pressed his head against my stomach.

His breath caught in his throat, shattering my soul, as if that confession had been all he needed to hear.

An earthquake rumbled through me. My eyes widened and my hands dug into his hair as if my soul was being uprooted from myself.

He clung desperately to me, as though I was the thing he desired most in the world . . . and my heart exploded.

Erupted like a newborn galaxy.

My soul expanded and wrapped around Rigel, merging with his breath. I felt the urgent need to have him there, close to me, united like two parts of the same spirit. United by the heart, two fragments that had spent a lifetime chasing each other to become one whole.

I shivered and my eyes filled with tears. I clung to him, untethered, and once and for all, realised the truth.

It was too late.

I was full of him, inside. He had left his mark all over me.

All I wanted, all I desperately wanted was him, clasping me in his arms as if that would save the world. As if that would save him . . .

Him, who I had known all my life, that boy at The Grave with dull, black eyes – *Rigel*, every fibre of my being screamed, *Rigel, and no one else*.

It felt like he had always been within me, bringing meaning to my silences, holding my dreams when they were too frightening. I was living off his heartbeat, that unsteady, clashing rhythm that had imprinted directly on my heart.

I belonged to him with every glimmer of my soul.

With every thought.

And every breath.

We were the end and the beginning of a single story – eternal and inseparable, Rigel and I, a star and a sky, scratches and Band-Aids: *together, a constellation of shivers.*

Together . . . right from the start.

And as I fell apart, and sewed myself back together out of pieces that screamed nothing but his name, as everything disintegrated and he became a part of me, I understood that my heart would always and only ever belong to him.

25. Collision Course

My heart is full of bruises,
but my soul is full of stars,
because some galaxies of shivers
only shine under the skin.

Time stopped.

The world stopped turning.

There was just *us.*

Inside me, universes colliding had reshaped everything I thought I knew.

I couldn't move. My eyes were fixed and staring. But inside . . .

Inside, I was no longer myself.

My soul shook. Emotions burst out of everywhere, I couldn't stop them. My feelings spiralled down, with increasing speed, increasing momentum – *No, no, wait,* I wanted to shout at my heart, *please, wait, not like this . . . not like this . . .*

But there was no respite.

It was crazy to think that the world was oblivious to the explosion that had just taken place within me. It was like a special torture, just for me, silently digging deeper and burning with every breath.

Rigel's fingers clutched at the dress at my hips. His hands slowly worked their way up my body, rumpling the fabric. I didn't dare to breathe. I wanted to feel them every day.

Suddenly, his mouth landed on my stomach.

He kissed my skin through my dress.

I held my breath. I was in disarray. Hypersensitive and burning, I didn't have the presence of mind to react. Another kiss, higher up this time, on a rib that would burn forever more. I shivered. His hands drew me closer to him.

'R . . . Rigel,' I stammered, as he left a long, burning kiss on my breastbone. He seemed lost, bewildered by my warmth, my scent, my body so close.

My heart pounded in my stomach, rising to meet the caress of his lips. I clutched his hair in my hands and his breath made my head spin.

He kissed the bare skin of my chest, slowly, in that way that was uniquely him, with teeth and lips. His hot tongue traced the contours of my breasts as they rose and fell with my gasping breaths. His fingers crept along my thigh and squeezed, drawing it to him. My heart couldn't resist.

I tried to ignore the sweet tension that was rising in my stomach, but it was impossible. It felt like it was twisting my heart. I felt hot, wet, trembling. The situation was getting out of hand. I didn't recognise any of these sensations, and yet they all belonged to me.

I let out a soft moan.

Unrestrained, he pulled me closer to him and possessively pressed my thigh against his side. He sunk his mouth into my throat, biting it, torturing it, taking that tension to the limit. My breathing accelerated.

His teeth probed the curve of my neck, savouring it like a forbidden fruit. My legs went weak, my heart took up all the space in my body.

I couldn't think.

I felt my ankles shaking, the bones of his pelvis cutting into my thighs, my hands firm against his shoulders to keep him close to me. He had become the centre of my universe. He was all I could see, all I could feel, every inch of my body trembled at just the thought of him.

He kissed the artery in my throat where my pulse was pounding. I was hardly breathing, overwhelmed by violent sensations. He squeezed my breast. A powerful, frightening shiver gripped my stomach.

Suddenly, reality crashed over me like a bucket of freezing water. I jumped, the tension broke and the fear of how real and true my feelings were overcame me.

'No!'

I detached myself from his body and moved away.

Rigel was staring at me, petrified, with dishevelled hair, and every step away from him I took was like a stab in the heart.

'We can't,' I murmured disjointedly. 'We can't!'

I wrapped my arms around myself and he saw the flash of terror in my eyes.

'What . . .'

'It's *wrong*!'

My voice echoed around the room. That one word broke something within both of us.

Something shifted in Rigel's eyes. I had never seen them look as bright as they did in that moment.

'It's . . . *wrong*?' he repeated quietly. It didn't even sound like his voice. Incredulity morphed into hurt and his eyes dimmed as if his soul was shrivelling. 'What? What's wrong, Nica?'

He already knew the answer, but he wanted confirmation.

'This . . .' I replied, not brave enough to name what was inside of me, because defining it would have been equivalent to admitting it, and therefore accepting it. 'We can't! Rigel, we . . . we're about to become brother and sister!'

Saying this caused me excruciating pain, but that's what we would be in the eyes of the world. *Brother and sister.* The relationship I had always refused now seemed like eternal condemnation.

I remembered what I had read in Alan's book. It burned like a scorch mark that would never go away.

It was a mistake, we shouldn't, *we couldn't* – my soul screamed, and the injustice of it took my breath away. Our fairy tale grew thickets of thorns, its pages rotted, and the more Rigel looked at me, the more I felt the childish desire to smash myself in two.

My heart hung in the balance of two shining globes.

On the one side, light, warmth, wonder and Anna's eyes. The family I had always wanted. The only hope that enabled me to survive the matron hitting and hurting me.

On the other, dreams, shivers and universes of stars. Rigel. Everything he had painted within me. Rigel and his thorns. Rigel and his eyes that pierced my soul.

And me, there in the midst of that chaos, crushed between two conflicting desires.

'You're still lying to yourself . . .'

Rigel was still looking at me. But now . . . now he was light years away from me.

His eyes were no longer open wounds, but deep, distant chasms.

'You're deceiving yourself . . . you want to believe in the fairy tale, but we're broken, Nica. We're splintered. It's in our nature to destroy things. *We* are Tearsmiths.'

'*You've destroyed me,*' Rigel's eyes seemed to whisper. '*Yes, you, so fragile and soft, you are destruction personified.*'

I felt tears stinging my eyes.

We spoke a language that others couldn't understand, because we came from a universe that was ours alone. Those words scratched me, they pierced my soul, like nothing else in the world.

'I can't lose all this,' I whispered. 'I can't, Rigel . . .'

He knew it. He knew what it meant to me. He stared at me, his gaze burning with pain, fighting a battle he knew he couldn't win.

I saw the light in his eyes fading.

I wanted to grasp it, but it was already too late.

★ ★ ★

'*Go then,*' he hissed.

Nica jumped, tears in her eyes. He felt like dying.

His mind was all black and screaming. Pain gnawed at his heart. He knew how important it was for her. He knew how much she yearned for a family. He couldn't blame her.

But her promise to never leave him had given him a hope that he hadn't even had time to hold on to before she snatched it away from him. His destructive thought patterns started tearing everything to shreds, ripping him to pieces.

'Please . . .' Nica shook her head. 'Rigel, please, I don't want this . . .'

'And what do you want? What do you want, *Nica*?'

His frustration exploded. He got to his feet, towering over her, and burned under those eyes that he dreamt of every night.

'What do you want from me?' he asked, exasperated.

The writhing inside him rose up, urging him to touch her, to kiss her. He clenched his fists, powerlessly. For a moment, he wanted to rip his heart out and throw it away. He knew that he only had himself to blame. This, at the end of the day, was the painful punishment for his own mistake.

Playing the piano, that day at The Grave.

Making Anna and Norman choose him.

Staying with her.

It had been an act of pure selfishness, a desperate attempt not to lose her. And now he'd forever be paying the price.

'I don't fit into your perfect fairy tale,' he whispered with a painful bitterness.

He wished he could hate her. He wished he could tear her away from his soul, free her from him, stop *hoping*.

But she was etched on his heart.

He had tried to give in to love, but he realised that he only knew how to love in that desperate, draining, fragile and twisted way.

Nica's shining eyes looked at him, destroyed, and Rigel knew she would never be his.

He would never hold her.

He would never kiss her, feel her, breathe her in.

She would always be unreachable, but close enough to hurt him.

In that moment, he realised that there would never be a happy ending. Not for him. He realised, with a painful pang, that he had to hurt her, so she would go away, far away from the disaster that he was. He had to hurt her, because inside he hurt too much to admit to himself how much he wanted her to choose him.

He wanted her with all his being. But more than anything, he wanted to see her happy.

And so if it was a family that would make her happy, he would make that decision easier for her.

'Go. Go back to your little friend. I'm sure he can't wait to pick up from where you were interrupted.'

'Don't.' Nica clenched her eyes shut. 'Don't try to make me hate you, you won't succeed.'

Rigel burst into hateful laughter, trying to make it sound believable. Fuck, it hurt him to laugh like that. It was like being devoured by pain.

'You think I want you around? You think I want your stupid *kindness*?'

He'd never be able to stand having her near him as a sister. Never.

'I don't know what to do with your promises,' he snarled, injured.

Nica looked away, guilty and distraught. She couldn't see the sickening sadness in his black eyes.

Rigel felt yet another scar when he saw tears rolling down her cheeks. He stood still, his fists trembling at his sides, and realised that standing firm before her was the bravest thing he had ever done.

And then she left. Again.

He went back to being the wolf.

They were retracing the same steps. Walking along the same path.

But hurting more, this time. Struggling more.

It would never be like before.

Nothing would ever be the same again.

★ ★ ★

'I'll never leave you alone again.'

I felt my promise infecting my soul as I ran away.

From him. From myself. From what we were.

It was all wrong.

Me. Rigel.

The reality that bound us together.

What I felt.

What I *didn't* feel.

All of it.

I went downstairs, into the kitchen and out the back door into the garden. I always looked for nature, fresh air and green when I felt myself suffocating. It was the only way I could breathe.

The darkness of the night enveloped me. I leant against a wall, sliding slowly to the ground.

All I could see were his eyes. His dark eyes, the way he looked at me. My promise shattering in his gaze, that light going out . . .

And yet, I would say the same thing again. I would swear it, forever, because some part of me knew I would never be able to lie to those eyes.

How would I be able to look at him, from here on in?

How would I bear to be near him, without touching him?

Without dreaming of him, holding him, wanting him?

How would I be able to see love in others, when his crumpled heart was the only one I wanted?

How would I be able to think of him as a brother?

I felt split down the middle.

I was lost.

I buried my head between my knees, wretched. It felt like life was making fun of me.

Which piece of your heart will you choose? it seemed to whisper. *You can only live with one, because the other will inevitably die. Which piece will you choose?*

I felt confused, fragile, stricken.

I was past the point of no return. It was too late to turn back.

I hadn't even realised that my phone was vibrating. I slipped it out of my pocket.

An extremely long message filled the illuminated screen. Through bleary eyes I just about managed to unlock it.

It was Lionel, apologising for what had happened, for having come to my house in the middle of the night.

The message was far, far too long. I couldn't manage to grasp even a single word. I was exhausted.

I was staring at the screen when he called. I saw his name flash up on the screen, but didn't have it in me to pick up.

I didn't want to speak to him. Not then.

'I know you're there,' he wrote, when he saw that I was online but not answering his call. 'Please, Nica, pick up . . .'

He called me again. Once, twice. On his third try, I leant my head backwards and closed my eyes. I accepted the call with a sigh.

'Lionel, it's late,' I whispered, worn out.

'I'm sorry,' he said immediately, maybe scared that I'd hang up.

He seemed desperate and sincere.

'I'm sorry, Nica . . . I shouldn't have behaved like that. I was thoughtless, and I wanted to tell you that I'm sorry . . .'

It wasn't the right time to talk about it. I couldn't think straight. There was a world in pieces whirling inside of me, and I couldn't see beyond it.

'I'm sorry, Lionel. I don't feel up to talking about it now.'

'I don't regret what I did. It maybe wasn't the right way to go about it, but . . .'

'Lionel . . .'

He fell silent. He was upset, I could tell, but at that moment I was incapable of giving him my attention.

'Tomorrow evening . . . my parents are away. I'm having a party and . . . I'd like you to be there. We could talk about it.'

I swallowed. I had never been to a party in my life, but I was doubtful that I was in high enough spirits to participate. I stared hazily at the garden.

'I'm . . . not sure I'm in the right mood.'

'Please come,' he begged. Then he seemed to regret the outburst and moderated his tone. 'I want us to talk about it. And then . . . it'll make you feel better, won't it?'

He didn't even know why I sounded so tearful. He hadn't even asked.

Did he think it was because of him?

'Promise you'll come,' he insisted.

Suddenly, I realised how much simpler things could be with Lionel. It could be normal.

It could be as simple as possible.

If it weren't for my soul.

And my mind.

And my heart.

If it wasn't for the starry sky inside of me . . .

I clenched my eyes shut.

I'll be good, the little girl inside reminded me. I pushed her away. I didn't want to listen.

I was protecting my dream. Feeling loved by a family. That was what I had always wanted.

So why did it hurt so much?

The next day I was woken up by my phone ringing.

I had slept terribly.

'Nica!' a voice trilled. 'Hi!'

'Billie?' I murmured, covering my eyes with my hand.

'Oh, Nica, you won't believe it! Something incredible has happened!'

'Mm . . .' I mumbled drowsily.

My heart was heavy. My cooled emotions and memories from the previous night were like smouldering ruins.

'I swear, I thought it was going to be a morning like any other . . . who would have thought? When Grandma told me I had three lucky stars on my horoscope, I never thought I would be *that* lucky!'

I tried to sit up as Billie kept jabbering on.

'Why don't we hang out tonight? Then I can tell you everything! Do you want to come to mine . . . We can order chicken wings and do those rhubarb face masks I got in the cereal . . .'

'This evening?' I murmured evasively.

'Yeah, are you busy?' she asked, a little disappointed.

'Well . . . there's that party . . .'

'A party? At whose?'

'Lionel's,' I replied after a moment. 'Last night . . . he asked me to go.'

There was a moment of silence. I glanced down at my phone screen to check that Billie was still there.

Her voice exploded in my ear.

'*Oh my God!* Are you joking? He invited you officially?'

I moved the phone away from my ear, dazed.

'I don't believe it! So you like him? Oh wait, has he told you that he's interested?'

'It's just to chat,' I explained, but she wasn't listening.

'What are you wearing? Have you already decided?'

'No,' I replied uncertainly. 'To tell the truth I haven't given it a thought . . . But really, it's just to chat,' I clarified. That was the truth, at the end of the day. Lionel had asked me several times, making it clear how important it was to him.

'I've got another idea!' Billie exclaimed. 'I'll help you choose! I'm meeting Miki today, why don't you come too? Grandma gave me a load of make-up that I haven't used yet, and then I can also tell you what's happened!'

'But . . .'

'Come on, it's perfect! We'll come and get you in a bit, bring something to change into for tonight! I'll call Miki and let her know. Later!'

She hung up before I could say anything else.

I stared at the phone, open-mouthed. I flopped back onto the mattress and held back a sigh.

I didn't share Billie's enthusiasm about the party. I had only accepted Lionel's invitation so I could chat with him and clear things up. But a little later, I left my room gripping my backpack and looking only a little faded.

When I found myself on the landing, I realised I couldn't lift my gaze.

His door . . . was there. Just a few metres away.

Before something inside me could start stirring in that painful way again, I headed downstairs. I made for the front door, my face downturned because everything made me think of him.

I felt him around me.

He was in the air, like something invisible and fundamental.

I glimpsed the piano out of the corner of my eye and immediately looked away. I got to the door, for the first time impatient to leave that house, but it opened under my nose.

'Nica!' Anna blinked. 'Oh, sorry . . . are you heading out now?'

I hurried to let her pass.

'Are your friends already here?'

I had told her that I was going out, so I nodded. I helped her with her bags and she smiled.

'Thank you.'

Before I could cross the threshold, she planted a delicate kiss on the top of my head. I looked at her, bewildered, and she smiled at me sweetly. I felt suddenly overcome by a desperate, guilty feeling: Anna didn't know how much I felt torn asunder. She didn't know what I was giving up because I needed her . . .

I looked down, biting my lip.

'I'm off,' I murmured, feeling awkward.

I rushed out of the house, trying to swallow those pieces of my heart.

'We are Tearsmiths . . .'

I urgently drove the thought away as I walked along the street. But his voice remained in me, in my blood, a whisper that would never go away.

I looked for Billie's grandma's car, but I couldn't see it. I did notice, however, a car with its engine running. I headed towards it, but stopped when I saw a man behind the wheel that I'd never seen before.

'Nica! It's us! Get in!' Billie waved from the window. 'You took your time,' she reproached me, as I timidly sat down.

Miki, next to the window, gestured hello.

'Sorry,' I replied. The car set off, and I leant towards the driver's seat with a hesitant smile. 'Hi . . . I'm Nica.'

The man behind the wheel glanced at me in the rear-view mirror then turned his attention back to the road. I sat back, confused, and Billie waved her hand.

'He never talks while he's driving.'

I threw Miki a cautious look.

'I'm sorry I made you wait. Is he your grandad?'

Billie burst out laughing, making me jump. I looked at her, dumbfounded, and then realised that instead of heading south, as I had thought we were, the car was driving towards the north of the city.

I knew very little about Miki. She always got picked up from school somewhere no one could see her, maybe because there was something about her family situation that embarrassed her. I had assumed that she felt inferior to the rich girls at school, but when the car eventually pulled up in front of her house . . . I realised I had got it completely wrong.

'Here we are!' Billie chirped.

Before me rose an enormous villa in all its grandeur.

Massive, dazzlingly white columns supported a circular terrace, in perfect Art Nouveau style. A wide set of steps led onto an avenue lined with cypress trees. The entrance was guarded by two silent, proud lion statues. Jubilant flowers burst out all around in the magnificent garden.

'Do you live here?' I croaked, as Miki got out of the car, chewing gum and her hands deep in her hoodie pockets.

She nodded, passing by me. I stared at her, stunned. A short distance away, a gardener was trimming a hedge in the shape of a rearing colt.

'Come on!'

Billie dragged me up the shining white steps. The solid walnut front door opened before Miki could touch it.

'Welcome back, Miss.'

We were welcomed by a kind-mannered woman to whom Billie trilled a greeting.

I was gobsmacked by the entrance hall. A large crystal chandelier dominated a room with a shiny granite floor.

The woman helped me take my jacket off. I stared at her, confused, as Miki took off her tatty hoodie and held it out to her. This time I stopped myself from asking if it was her grandma.

'Who's that?' I asked Billie in a whisper.

'Her? Oh, that's Evangeline.'

'Evangeline?'

'The housekeeper.'

I watched the woman move away, blinking.

'Are you an only child?' I asked Miki as she led the way. The opulence surrounding us made me feel as small and insignificant as a bug.

She nodded.

'Her family has generations of nobles behind them,' Billie told me. 'Even though there's no such thing as nobility any more . . . her great-grandparents were the real deal. Look, here they are!'

She looked towards a portrait of a couple, the woman wearing velvet gloves, the man with large sideburns, both of them with severe, haughty expressions.

Then I glimpsed a painting that was, to say the least, enormous. It portrayed three people – a man with a severe face and two glacial eyes that seemed to burn through the canvas; next to him, less severe but just as refined, in a dress that flattered her raven hair and fair complexion, a beautiful woman gave a slight smile; and in front of them, sitting down, was Miki.

It was really her, in an organza dress and her hair tidily brushed down over her shoulders.

'They're your parents,' I noted, looking at the portrait of the serious, noble-looking couple.

Her father, in particular, looked more like a marble statue than a man. He seemed unspeakably austere – intimidating, even. I swallowed. All that solemnity made me feel uneasy.

Suddenly, the door opened behind us. All three of us turned around, and before us loomed a great, big mountain of a man. He was wearing an elegant, haute couture suit; his face was refined and aristocratic; his dark hair was streaked with grey, and his sharp jawline bore a meticulously groomed beard, above which shone two predatory eyes.

There was no doubt about it. This was Miki's father.

His eyes landed on us and I shuddered. I felt like shrivelling under his gaze.

He puffed out his chest, and then . . .

'*Little duckling!*' he cooed, beaming.

He ran towards us, arms open wide.

I stared at him, shocked, as he gave Miki a crushing hug, spinning her around like a little girl. He smiled, thrilled, and his large hands stroked her head lovingly.

'My sweet little duck, how are you? You're back!' He rubbed his cheek against hers. 'How long has it been?'

'Since breakfast, Dad,' Miki replied, wearily, like a worn-out doll. 'We saw each other this morning.'

'I missed you!'

'And we'll see each other again at dinner . . .'

'I'll miss you!'

Miki patiently endured her father's affections, while I stared disconcerted at the man who up until a moment ago had terrified me with just a look. The same man who was now fussing his daughter with the same voice Norman used when he wanted to pet Klaus.

'Oh, Marcus, let her breathe!'

A magnificent woman was proceeding towards us, with an elegance that couldn't be captured in a portrait.

Miki's mom was a woman of rare finesse. Her movements were like liquid silver; she glided along the floor like a perfume, silky and beautiful.

Miki looked a lot like her.

'Wilhelmina,' the woman smiled at Billie. 'Hello, how wonderful to see you again.'

'Hello, Amelia,' my friend replied.

Miki took the opportunity to introduce me.

'Mom, Dad, this is Nica.'

They turned scorching smiles on me.

'It's not often we get the chance to meet new friends,' her mom said. 'Makayla is always very reserved . . . It's a pleasure to meet you.'

Makayla?

She turned towards her.

'I'd like her to wear new clothes every once in a while, but she insists on these bulky hoodies . . . Oh, honey, not that tatty rag again?'

I realised she was referring to Miki's Iron Maiden t-shirt. It was the same t-shirt that I had fixed. The panda was still there, embroidered on the fabric. Miki hadn't unpicked it.

'I've had it for years,' Miki argued. 'Don't touch it.'

'Makayla loves this scrap of cloth she insists on calling a t-shirt,' her mom told us. 'Sometimes she's so scared I'll get rid of it that she even sleeps in it . . .'

'Dad, can Nica get a lift later? She's got to go somewhere.'

'Of course, anything for my little duck,' her dad replied proudly.

I felt even more like a fish out of water when the man who had driven the car appeared in the room carrying a tray and wearing white gloves. I noticed that he had an incredibly aquiline nose. Miki's dad's expression immediately changed. He approached him conspiratorially.

'Hey, Edgard . . .'

'Yes, sir?' asked the butler.

'You made sure no *men* got in?'

'Yes, sir. Not one adolescent male has come through that door.'

'You're certain?'

'Absolutely.'

'Good,' Marcus proclaimed triumphantly. 'No man will get near my little duckling!' It was a good job he wasn't looking our way, because Miki's expression was priceless.

'We're going upstairs,' she croaked, already climbing the stairs.

We waved goodbye to her parents, and they did the same.

Miki's room was in complete contrast to the rest of the house. Her desk was littered with books and violin sheet music, the walls were covered in band posters, cuttings from magazines and photographs. A panda plushie was sat on a chair in the corner of the room.

'Your parents are incredible,' I said. 'They seem so present.'

'Yeah,' she replied. 'Too present sometimes . . .'

I had thought that Miki didn't get enough attention from her parents, and I was pleased to learn that wasn't the case.

'Ready?' Billie turned her bag upside down and out fell a bewitching cascade of shiny tubes and tubs.

'Right, sit here,' she said, settling me into a chair.

'And now . . . close your eyes!'

'A bit of this one . . .'

A tingling sensation on my cheeks.

'And a bit of this one . . .'

It was the first time I had worn make-up. It was a completely new experience for me.

At the institute, I had looked admiringly at the women who came to visit or who were in the newspapers that the matron would throw away. At the time, I was just a little girl with a grey face and big eyes, wondering what it would be like to shine like that. Now, however, I was probably too shy to ask Anna if we could buy some make-up together.

'Here we are!' Billie announced triumphantly. 'Done!'

I opened my eyes and looked at my reflection in the mirror.

'Oh . . . wow,' I gasped, bowled over.

'Wow, yes,' she commented.

Miki was standing behind me with her arms outstretched, her nostrils flared and a twisted frown.

'What on earth have you done to her?'

'What?' Billie asked, bringing her face next to mine.

I gazed at my reflection: peacock eye shadow, fiery red lipstick that was a little smudged around my mouth, pink blusher like two round apples on my cheeks.

'Yeah,' I said. 'What?'

We both stared at her like two owls and she put her head in her hands.

'You two . . .' Miki growled, shaking her head. 'Give me strength . . .'

'You don't like how I've done her make-up?'

'Since when have you known how to do make-up? You've never held a make-up brush in your life! Give it here!'

She grabbed the brush and make-up remover wipes. She vigorously wiped my face clean to start again, while Billie pouted and crossed her arms.

'Fine, you do her make-up if you're so good at it . . .' she conceded. 'I'll help her choose an outfit!'

She held out my backpack with both arms.

'Are the clothes you brought in here?'

I nodded, and Billie unzipped the bag and took out my clothes, as curious as a cat. She rifled through skirts and blouses with a concentration that made me feel a little uneasy.

'This is cute . . . Oh, and this . . .' she murmured, as Miki drew two thin lines over my eyelids with something cold and wet.

'I like this . . . No, not this . . . *Oh God!*' Billie yelped. I jumped and Miki swore.

'This! Absolutely! Nica, I've found your dress!'

She lifted it victoriously and something twisted inside me. It was the dress I had bought with Anna, the one with the little buttons down the chest and the sky-blue fabric.

'No,' I heard myself murmur. 'Not that one.'

I couldn't even remember putting it in the bag. I had just shoved in a load of folded clothes.

'Why not?' Billie asked, dismayed.

In truth . . . I didn't even know myself.

'It's . . . for special occasions.'

'And this isn't a special occasion?'

I twisted my fingers. 'I told you . . . I'm only going because Lionel asked me. I have to speak to him.'

'So?'

'So . . . I'm not going to get involved.'

'Nica, it's a party!' Billie burst out. 'Everyone will be dressed up for . . . *for a party*! And this dress must look amazing on you, really amazing . . . What better occasion to wear it?'

'There's no need . . .'

'There is though,' she replied with newfound determination. In her eyes I saw the affectionate gleam of someone who wanted me to shine. 'Everyone should see you wearing this, Nica . . . You won't look out of place, trust me . . . And if you really want to you can wear it for other occasions too, but today . . . today is definitely one of those occasions. You won't regret it, I promise . . . Do you trust me?'

She smiled and laid the dress out on the bed. I realised she wanted to give me a unique, different and exciting evening. I had never been to a party, I had never worn a dress like this, I had never dressed up and worn make-up, and I suspected that Billie knew this. She was doing this for me. To brighten me up and make me feel special.

And yet, seeing that gorgeous dress waiting for me on the bed, all I could do was look down and feel, deep down, even more wrong.

I knew who it was I wanted to wear that dress for, and he wasn't going to be at the party.

Miki lifted my chin with her finger, and without meaning to, I met her gaze. I quickly glanced away before she could see the distress in my eyes.

'Look what I've found!'

Billie poked her head out of the wardrobe. When had she opened it?

She showed me some light-coloured, slender sandals, with a thin strap that fastened around the ankle. They were very cute. And they were still in the box.

'Are they yours?' I asked Miki.

She smirked. 'A gift. From distant relatives. They aren't even my size . . .'

'But they're your size!' Billie held them out to me, beaming.

I looked uncertainly at the little heel.

'I've never worn heels before . . .'

'Try them on, come on!'

I slipped my feet into them and Billie and Miki made me stand up.

They suited me. I teetered after just a few steps, but they didn't seem to think that was a problem.

Billie waved a hand. 'Don't worry about it, you've got all afternoon to practise walking in them!'

That is how I spent the rest of the day.

Eventually, once I'd put on the dress and my make-up was finished, they said I could look in the mirror.

I obeyed. And . . .

I was speechless.

It was me. But it didn't look like me.

My eyelashes were thick and black, making my grey eyes look dazzling. Whatever Miki had put on my lips made them look like two luscious petals. My cheeks were rosy and full, and my skin, usually grey and a little dull, shone under my freckles like iridescent velvet.

A white silk ribbon held half of my hair up off my face, while the other half tumbled softly down my back.

It was really me . . .

'You'll give him a heart attack,' Billie burst out with glee and pride.

I looked at her, my cheeks burning. She yelped, 'If I had my camera with me, I'd take a photo of you! You're . . . *God,* you look . . . you look like a doll!'

She smoothed the fabric over my hips, looking at me with bright, admiring eyes.

'Holy cow, just wait for them to see you! Miki, what do you think?'

'I'll tell Edgard to drop you off right outside the house,' Miki said, looking at me sideways. 'So you're not roaming the streets looking like that.'

Billie laughed and looked at me euphorically. 'It'll be like a fairy tale, you'll see!'

A fairy tale . . .

Right . . .

I looked at my reflection with dull eyes, trying to feel the same euphoria as Billie, but I couldn't do it. Inside me there was just an expanse of arid emptiness. And it whispered *his* name.

'Oh Nica, before you go, I've got to tell you what happened today!'

She flapped her hands excitedly. I realised that she'd been waiting to tell us all day.

'What's it about?' I asked, giving her my entire attention.

'You won't believe it!'

We gathered around her, inviting her to speak. Billie kept us on tenterhooks for a little longer, but it was clear that she was champing at the bit to tell us. Finally, she burst out, 'I found out who gave me the rose!'

Silence fell.

I stared at her, my mouth open in alarm. Miki, next to me, was petrified.

'What?' I swallowed.

'I've worked it out!' she replied happily. 'I went out this morning to do some shopping, and as I was crossing the park this sausage dog almost tripped me up . . . Heavens! This guy arrives, and basically, with one thing and another, we get talking . . . and I find out he's at the same school as us! The point is that we were chatting all morning, he even came with me to do the shopping. And we're laughing and joking, and then you know what he says to me? He says he's happy that it was me that Findus, his sausage dog, tripped over, because it gave him an excuse to talk to me . . . He says he's been wanting to for ages, but that he's been too shy . . . And then, well, I had a lightbulb moment!' Her eyes were shining. 'I asked him if he was the one who sent me the rose. I got straight to the point, basically! So he said, "What rose?", and I said, "The white rose, the one I get anonymously every year,". . . and, well, what did he say? You know what he said? *He said yes!*'

The joyful reaction Billie had been expecting was not forthcoming.

I couldn't see the expression on Miki's face. I cleared my throat and said, 'You're . . . sure? You're definitely sure that . . .'

'Yes! Without a shadow of a doubt! You should have seen how embarrassed he was, he couldn't look me in the face!' She waved her hands, her hair static with excitement. 'Can you believe it? It's him! Would you ever have guessed that I'd practically fall ov–'

'No.'

Next to me, Miki was still completely motionless. And yet something within her must have just snapped.

'It's not him.'

'I can hardly believe it either! I swear, I never would have thought that such a cute guy . . .'

'No,' Miki said again. 'He lied to you.'

'*Mm mm,*' Billie shook her head with a smile. 'No! He said it loud and clear . . .'

'And you believe him? You believe a stranger?'

'Why shouldn't I?'

'Maybe because he told you exactly what you wanted to hear!'

Billie blinked. She hesitated before replying. '. . . And so what if it was?' she asked quietly. 'What harm does it do?'

'*What harm does it do?*' Miki repeated through gritted teeth. 'As ever, you're too naïve to realise when you're being made fun of!'

'What do you know? You don't even know him!'

'Oh, and you do?'

'Well, a bit, yeah! We spent all morning together!'

'And so now you believe whatever bullshit he tells you?'

Billie jerked her chin back with a frown. 'What's your problem? I wouldn't have told you if I'd have known you'd react like this . . .'

Miki clenched her fists, shaking with frustration. 'How were you expecting me to react?'

'I was expecting you'd be happy for me! Nica's happy for me!' She turned towards me. 'Aren't you?'

'I . . .'

'I'm supposed to be happy that you let the first guy to pass by take the piss out of you?'

I didn't like the way things were going. There was something nasty crackling in the air.

'He wasn't taking the piss out of me! He said . . .'

Miki raised her voice. '*It's not him!*'

'*Yes, it is!*' Billie burst out, throwing her hands up in the air. 'Stop making out as if you're always right!'

'And you stop believing any old bullshit!'

'Why?' Billie dug her heels in. Her tone had changed. 'Is it so difficult for you to accept that someone might be interested in me?'

'You're so obsessed with your own loneliness you can't see beyond the end of your nose!'

Miki realised she had gone too far when her best friend's eyes flashed with surprise.

I stared at them, breathless, feeling an earthquake beneath my feet that I was unable to stop.

'That's how it is, is it?' Billie whispered, looking hurt. 'And you don't need anyone or anything. Your parents are so *present* that you can treat everyone else badly?'

'What's that got to do with it?' Miki retorted, red in the face.

'You always do this! *Always!* You can't even be happy for me!'

'It's not him!'

'That's what you want!' she shouted, spewing resentment. 'You *want* it not to be him! You want me to be alone like you, because there's no one else who can stand you!'

'Oh, I'm sorry,' Miki shouted, infuriated. 'I'm sorry if you haven't got anyone else to call at four in the morning! It must be hard for you, to have to confess everything to me when you feel a bit lonely!'

'You're happy that there's *anyone* calling you,' Billie erupted tearfully. 'You enjoy it, it's the only consolation you have for your repulsive personality! *No one* wants anything to do with you!'

'IT'S NOT HIM!'

'Stop it!'

'It's not him, Billie!'

'Why?' she screamed.

'Because it's me!'

Billie's face twitched. She stared at her friend, stunned and speechless.

'What?' she dared to ask after a while.

'It's me,' Miki spat out. She couldn't even bring herself to look at her. 'It's always been me.'

Billie looked at her, aghast, in a way I had never seen before.

'It's not true,' she murmured after a moment. The incredulity on her face hardened. 'It's not true, you're not telling the truth . . .'

'Yes, I am.'

'No!' she burst out, shaking. 'You're lying!'

Miki said nothing, and her silence turned the certainty in Billie's eyes to ashes. Slowly . . . she started to shake her head.

'No, I don't believe you . . .' she whispered, as if she was trying to convince herself. 'Why did you do it? Why . . . why did you . . .' She narrowed her eyes. 'Out of pity?'

'No . . .'

'To punish me? Is that it?' Tears were streaming down her face. 'Because I was too affectionate?'

'No!'

'So I'd stop complaining how lonely I was? Is that it?'

'Stop it!'

'Tell me the truth! Once and for all!'

It was the only way that Miki could express what she was feeling. In an act of desperation, she grabbed Billie's face and kissed her on the lips.

It was too sudden. Billie's eyes flew open, full of horror and dismay, and she pushed her away as hard as she could.

She staggered backwards, her wrist to her lips, shaking and shocked. The way she was staring at her best friend was nothing like how you would look at someone you've known your whole life, someone with whom you've shared years of smiles and tears.

I heard the thunder of Miki's heart breaking apart.

Billie turned and ran away.

'Billie!' I called after her, distressed. I stopped outside the room and saw her disappearing at the end of the landing.

Miki bumped into me as she ran the other way, holding back her tears.

'M . . . Miki . . .' I held out a hand to her and turned from one to the other, upset, not knowing who to run after.

I had never seen them argue like that, never. They had said terrible things to each other, things they didn't even really think. I knew that anger could bring out the worst in even the best of people.

I thought about Miki, and everything that was surely tearing her to pieces. And yet, she had endured the loneliness of her feelings day after day and had managed to hold it together.

Billie, on the other hand, must have been distraught.

I turned and ran to her.

I opened the doors one by one until I found her in what must have been a tea parlour.

She was crouched on the ground with her arms around her knees.

I approached her cautiously, and realised that she wasn't just shaking . . . she was sobbing.

My heart ached. With all the tenderness in the world, I placed a hand on her shoulder, and knelt down to hug her from behind.

I hoped she didn't think I was being intrusive, but that worry vanished when she tightened her grip on my arms, accepting my presence.

'You don't have to stay here,' she whispered tearfully. 'Don't worry about me . . . Go, otherwise you'll be late for the party.'

But I shook my head. Without hesitation, I slipped off my sandals and sat down next to her.

'No,' I replied. 'I'll stay with you.'

26. Fairy-Tale Beggars

'It doesn't matter if you are destroyed.
It doesn't matter if I am.
Mosaics are made out of shattered shards of glass,
and look how wondrous they are.'

Billie was silent for a long time. She stared blearily through her thick tears into the middle distance.

I couldn't imagine how she must be feeling. It probably felt to her like a lifelong friendship was slipping away.

I wanted to comfort her. Tell her that it would all go back to how it was before.

But maybe the truth was that there are some things that are destined not to remain the same, despite our best efforts. Things that will inevitably change, because life follows its own course.

'It's okay,' she said, when my touch reminded her I was still there. As much as I tried to believe it, I knew she didn't even believe it herself.

'I know it's not,' I replied. 'You don't have to pretend it is.'

Billie closed her eyes. She shook her head slowly, like a broken puppet.

'I . . . I can't believe it.'

'Billie, Miki . . .'

'Please, I . . .' she interrupted, distraught. 'I don't want to talk about it.'

I looked down.

'She didn't do it out of pity,' I whispered all the same, without looking at her. 'The rose . . . She wasn't just being nice. You know she wouldn't have done that.'

'I don't know . . . anything any more.'

'What's happened doesn't have to put your whole friendship into question.' I tried to meet her eyes. 'Your relationship has always been true, Billie . . . Truer than you can believe.' I saw her swallow and added, 'She loves you . . . so much . . .'

'Please, Nica.' Billie pressed her lips together as if every word could hurt her. 'I need . . . a moment. To process. I know you don't want to leave me alone, but . . . you don't need to worry about me. I'll be okay . . .' She noticed my apprehensive look and seemed to want to calm me down. 'I just want to be on my own for a bit.'

'Are you sure?'

'Yes, absolutely . . .' She tried to smile. 'Really, it's . . . all okay. And you've got a party to go to, haven't you?'

'No, it doesn't matter. It's late now . . .'

'But what about all this?' she asked. 'You don't mean to tell me that we spent all that time getting you ready for nothing? I won't accept it . . . And I'm sure Lionel must be waiting for you . . .'

I tried to say something, but she got in first. 'You should go. You look amazing . . . this is your evening. Don't ruin it because of me.'

'What about you?' I asked, looking for a reason to stay. 'What will you do?'

'I'll be all right. I told you . . . it's all okay. I've already asked Grandma to come and pick me up. She'll be here any minute . . .'

I told her that I had already decided to stay, but she dragged me to my feet, smoothed my dress down and reassured me that I didn't need to worry. Before I could insist, she pushed me gently out the room.

'Go,' she smiled sadly. Before I could answer back, she added, 'Enjoy yourself . . . for me. We'll speak tomorrow.'

I found myself on the landing. As soon as the door closed behind me, instead of doing as Billie had told me, I headed in the opposite direction.

I looked for Miki behind every door.

When I found the last bedroom with a closed door, I knew she must be there. I knocked.

I called her name several times before whispering that I was sorry about what had happened. I told her I didn't want to pry, that she could let me in even if she didn't want to talk.

That I'd stay there, next to her, for as long as she wanted.

But she didn't reply.

Miki left the door closed. I stood there, staring at the handle, needing to see her.

'Miss,' a voice called.

I turned. Evangeline was looking at me, displeased.

'The car is waiting to take you wherever you wish to go.'

The anguished look I threw her was a silent plea that I could not suppress.

'I want to see Miki . . .'

'She isn't disposed to see anybody at the present moment,' she replied slowly, giving me a look that said a thousand words. 'She told the driver, however, to take you wherever you desire to go. The car is waiting for you in the avenue.'

I didn't want to leave like this, without even having seen her.

Evangeline folded her hands over her stomach, troubled. 'I am sorry.'

I looked down before giving a last lingering, powerless look up at the closed door. Then I gave in and followed her down the stairs.

Evangeline held out my jacket and I balled it up against my chest. Eventually, after having wished me a good evening, she walked me to the door and ushered me towards the car.

Edgard opened the door for me. I thanked him and got into the back seat. The crunch of gravel accompanied us as the car drove down the drive to the gates.

I turned around for one last glimpse at the house, before it suddenly disappeared behind the cypress trees.

I was clutching my dress when we arrived at Lionel's house. The music was so loud it made the car shake. I found myself staring at the people crowding the garden, unable to move.

'Is this the correct address?' Edgard asked.

'Yes . . . yes, it's this one.'

I felt pinned to the seat, as if my heart had put down roots. But Edgard's expectant look made me feel just enough embarrassment to open the door. I stepped out into the dark street, lit by streetlights.

People were thronging on the sidewalk and the music was so loud I could hardly hear my own thoughts. Surrounded by bare-chested boys, crates of beer and shouting, I felt out of place in my meticulously put together outfit.

I was as still as a statue, and the longer I stayed put, the more something inside of me recoiled.

What was I doing?

I had only just arrived and I already wanted to leave. I should have made my way through the crowd to find Lionel, but the feeling of being in the wrong place slowly crept over me.

Suddenly, I became aware of what I was feeling.

It wasn't right.

Something was painfully out of place.

Something couldn't adapt, couldn't fit in.

It was me.

It was all of me, body and soul.

I looked at my reflection in a car window. The dress made me look like a doll.

But inside, I was ash and paper.

Inside, there were stars and wolf eyes.

My soul was torn in two, but without the other half, not even breathing made any sense.

I had gone there hoping to forget, and maybe, to find in Lionel a reason to stay. But I had been deluding myself.

You cannot deceive your own heart, shouted the universes I had enchained. And in my sad eyes, I saw all the unrelenting, inconsolable need I felt for *him.*

Rigel.

Rigel, who had taken root within me.

Rigel, who had anchored himself in my bones with the destructive grace of dying flowers.

Rigel, who was my constellation of shivers.

There are no fairy tales for those who beg for a happy ending. That was the truth.

And in that moment, I admitted it to myself. I didn't know what I was doing there.

I had nothing to do with that party.

It wasn't my place.

It wouldn't make me forget the feelings I carried inside. It would only fill them with thorns.

I decided to leave. I'd find another opportunity to speak with Lionel. I just wanted to go home.

But before I could start making my way, I was swept off my feet.

I held back a scream. I had been lifted off the ground, flipped over and hoisted like a sack of potatoes. My bag was tangled all around me.

'Hey, I've got one too!' the stranger holding me announced, and with horror, I saw that one of his friends was doing the same with a giggling girl.

'Now what?' one of them asked, excited.

'Let's throw them in the pool!'

They let out a loud whoop and charged madly towards the house. I thrashed about and begged him to let me go, but it was useless. He was holding me so tightly I was sure his hands would leave marks on my legs.

It was only once we'd got inside that they both checked their madness and looked around, confused.

'Err, there's no pool here . . .' one of them stammered.

I seized the opportunity to wriggle free and run away before he could catch me again.

It was hell inside. People were shouting, dancing, making out. A guy was draining a keg of beer through a tube, cheered on by a small crowd. Another was waving his cap about and moving jerkily as if he was riding a bucking bronco, which, when I looked closer, I realised was Lionel's red lawnmower.

Dismayed, I looked for the door, but I was too short to see over all those heads.

I slipped through the crowd, looking for the exit, but suddenly someone whammed into me and I almost crashed to the floor.

'Sorry!' a girl said, trying to pull her friend to her feet.

Why had they all gone crazy?

'Forgive her, she's drunk too much . . .'

'He was stunning!' The other girl screeched, as if she had seen an extra-terrestrial. 'He was hot as hell, fuck, but you don't believe me! *You don't believe me!*'

I tried to help her to her feet and she clung on to me.

'He was the most beautiful guy I've ever seen!' she wailed at me, her breath stinking of alcohol.

'Yeah, yeah, okay . . .' her friend muttered. 'Otherworldly, tall, gorgeous, with eyes "darker than night", sure . . .'

'It was enough to give you *a heart attack*!' the girl howled. 'It's not safe for someone that hot to be out in public! I had to try and touch him, you know? His skin was so white it didn't seem real . . .'

I froze. Petrified, I surprised myself by gripping her arm with more force than was necessary.

'The boy you saw . . . did he have dark hair?'

Her face lit up hopefully.

'You saw him too! I knew I wasn't dreaming!'

'Where did you meet him? Was he . . . here?'

'No,' she whined, pointing to her right. 'I saw him outside . . . One moment he was there, walking along, and I tried to get near him . . . God . . . then the next moment he was gone . . .'

I turned round and barged towards the door. My heart was pounding.

It was him. I felt it in every single atom of my body.

But fate was against me. I was almost at the exit when suddenly, someone grabbed my wrist. I spun around and was confronted with the only face I absolutely didn't want to see.

'Nica?'

Lionel was looking at me as if I wasn't real.

'Y . . . you're here,' he stammered, stepping closer. 'I didn't think I'd see you . . . I thought . . . I thought you wouldn't come . . . but . . .'

'Lionel,' I muttered, mortified. 'I'm sorry, I'm really sorry, but I've got to go . . .'

'I'm so happy you came,' he slurred close to my face, making me flinch away. His breath reeked of alcohol and I couldn't really hear him over the noise.

'I . . . I've got to go.'

The music was too loud. He took my hand and gestured for me to follow him.

He led me towards the kitchen, where we found two people rummaging in the fridge for beer. When they left, laughing, Lionel closed the door so we could talk.

'I'm sorry I didn't get in touch . . .' I said sincerely. 'I should have said something. But, Lionel . . . I wasn't sure I was going to come and now I . . .'

'It's enough that you're here,' he murmured, slurring his words.

He gave me a clear, distant smile and filled a red plastic cup with punch and held it out to me.

'Here.'

'Oh . . . No, thanks . . .'

'Try it,' he insisted, beaming, before taking a big gulp in my stead. 'Come on, just a sip.'

I decided to indulge him. I was about to head home, what did it matter? I tried the drink and screwed my eyes up. I curled my lips and he seemed satisfied.

'Good, right?'

I forced a cough. I realised that the drink must have been swimming in alcohol.

'I really thought I wouldn't see you,' I heard him say. I looked up and realised he was dangerously close. 'I thought you wouldn't come . . .'

I felt the need to be honest, to look him in the eyes and tell him I couldn't stay.

'Lionel, I want to explain . . .'

'No need, I understand completely,' he interrupted, almost falling over onto me.

I let go of the cup and held him up, teetering on my heels.

'Are you all right?'

He snickered. 'I've just . . . drank a bit . . .'

'Seems a bit more than a bit,' I murmured.

'I didn't see you arrive . . . I thought you'd stood me up . . .'

I expected him to snicker again, but he didn't. Instead, there was a long, lingering silence.

The next moment, I felt his hand sliding along the kitchen counter next to me. I met his eyes and he swallowed, his face tilted down towards me.

'But you're here now . . .'

'Lionel,' I whispered, and felt his hand sliding onto my wrist.

'You're here and you're . . . more *beautiful* than ever . . .'

I tried to step backwards but my back was against the counter. I pushed against his chest with one hand. The other, unfortunately, was trapped in his grip. I stared at him, alarmed.

'You said we should talk . . .' I started, but his body sidled up against my dress.

'Talk?' he whispered, pressing himself against me. 'There's no need to talk . . .'

I turned my head, trying to hide my face against my shoulder, but it was no use. His lips found mine all the same, his wet mouth completely covering mine. He kissed me against the kitchen counter. The taste of alcohol mixed with my breath. I was almost suffocated, and my attempts to make him stop were to no avail.

'No . . . Lionel!'

I pushed against his chest, struggling to squirm free, but his hand came up to my face so he could kiss me more deeply. His fingers wormed their way into my hair to hold me still. I couldn't move.

'Please . . .'

He didn't listen. He did the one thing that could break me. He seized both of my wrists. And gripped.

Reality crashed around me.

A shock ran down my spine, a deep-rooted, visceral terror made my heart thump against my ribs. I wheezed.

Constriction, panic, belts on my wrists, my arms trapped. The dark cellar. My body contracted; my soul rose up.

There was a loud crunch when Lionel let me go. He was drenched in an orange liquid. The plastic cup was rolling on the floor, cracked in a few places. I had torn one hand free and lunged for the closest thing and thrown it in his face.

I stared at him, wide-eyed and distraught, before running away.

I fled the kitchen and barged through the crowd to get away from that house, away from that terror that had stuck to my bones. My heartbeat was deafening. I felt frozen, clammy and slippery.

Reality was throbbing around me, anxiety closed my throat, poisoning me with familiar feelings.

I felt like I was suffocating with all those bodies pressing against me. Suddenly, a startling scream tore me from myself.

I turned around, along with everyone else. I froze.

A dark shadow was flitting about the room.

A little bat had got in through the open window and was now darting over everyone's heads, blinded by the light and noise. Some of the girls were screaming, terrified; others covered their hair with their hands.

I stared at the bat, my heart racing. He flew into a lampshade, dazed, trying to find a way out. A cup tore through the air and hit him full on, sending him to the wall.

Someone laughed. Voices were raised.

Another cup flew through the air, and when it crashed against the wall there was more laughter. Their fear soon turned to fun.

Suddenly, everything started flying: aluminium foil balls, cigarette butts, bottle caps and pieces of plastic. A deluge of trash rained upon the bat, tearing my heart to shreds.

'No!' I shouted. 'No! Stop it!'

He fell in a bowl of punch, his wings getting doused in alcohol. The laughter intensified and I grabbed the arms of the people nearest me.

'Enough! Stop!'

But no one was listening to me. They kept urging each other on, shouting, entertained. It was unbearable.

The truest part of me took over. I barged my way through the crowd until I had got through the throng of bodies. I saw him crouching against the wall, and all I could do was throw myself on him and cup him in my hands.

Balls of paper were raining down. Someone threw a cigarette at me.

I clutched the bat to my chest, trying to protect him, and felt him desperately clinging to me, his little claws scraping my skin. I looked around, terrified, and felt again that shudder inside of me, that terror that cut my breath into gasps.

I saw arms raising all at once – *and the matron raising her voice, raising her hands, clenching and pushing and cracking ribs* – and my panic screamed louder still.

I pushed back through the throng, not caring who I knocked over.

I finally found the exit, tumbled out onto the sidewalk and tore like a maniac away from that hell. I almost stumbled in my heels, but I didn't stop. I ran, muscles aching, until the noise faded behind me, until I got home.

I only calmed down when I glimpsed the picket fence in front of me. I caught my breath and glanced anxiously over my shoulder. Then I looked down at the warm body that was tickling my neck. The bat was still there, clinging to me and trembling. I tilted my cheek towards his little head, gently nuzzling the small, misunderstood creature.

'It'll be okay . . . .' I whispered.

He looked up, and I met his bewildered gaze. Two black eyes, like shiny little marbles, pierced my heart.

There was nothing in the world that reminded me of Rigel more than that little creature of the night, all claws and fear, held tight in my arms. I wanted to go back, to hold him, to stay with him. To tell him he had left me everything. That inside I was full of him, his disasters and his shivers.

I didn't know how to live without him any more.

I swallowed and opened my hands to let the bat fly away. He clumsily scratched my skin before managing to take flight.

I lingered, watching him for a moment, but then heard footsteps behind me. Just as I glimpsed the bat disappearing into the darkness, a hand grabbed my shoulder and turned me around.

I met a pair of distressed eyes and jumped.

'Nica?' Lionel was panting in my face. 'What . . . what are you doing?'

'Let me go,' I muttered, trying to shrug him off. The feeling of his hand on my skin alarmed me, immediately awakening unpleasant sensations.

'Why did you leave like that?'

I stepped back, freeing myself from his grip, but he grabbed me again. I knew he wasn't being himself, I knew that Lionel wasn't like this, but I was still frightened.

'What does this all mean? First you come, but then you go like that?'

'You're hurting me.' My voice sounded higher. Fear and a sense of powerlessness ballooned inside me. I tried to push him away but he wasn't having it: he grabbed me by the shoulders, frustrated, and shook me angrily.

'Fuck, stop this and look at me!'

All of a sudden, Lionel's hands flew off me.

He staggered backwards and his body crashed to the ground so forcefully that all the breath left his lungs.

The only thing I could make out through my tears was a tall, fearsome silhouette slipping into the space between me and him. The clenched fists at his sides were burning with a motionless, dangerous calm.

Rigel stared down at him with that cruel, dark, devilish beauty, the veins in his wrist bulging.

'Don't you . . . *touch her*,' he hissed slowly, his eyes glinting with a terrifying, icy fury.

'You!' Lionel spat with a blind hatred, crawling forward on his elbows.

Rigel raised an arched eyebrow.

'*Me*,' he agreed derisively, before stamping forcefully on Lionel's hair, pinning his head to the asphalt. He writhed on the ground, wheezing.

I wasn't breathing. Rigel's eyes shone with that ruthless violence that consumed any glimmer of light.

He turned to look at me over his shoulder, his gaze piercing my soul.

'Go inside.'

I opened the gate with trembling hands, a lump in my throat. I thought he would have unleashed all of his fury, but he very, very slowly let Lionel go. He threw him an intimidating glare then made to follow me. But Lionel groaned and grabbed him by the hem of his jeans. He dug his fingernails in, trying to hurt him any way he could.

'You think you're a hero, do you?' he screamed, beside himself. 'Is that what you think? You think you're the good guy?'

Rigel froze.

'The good guy?' It was a low, sinister whisper. 'Me . . . *the good guy?*'

In the darkness, his pale lips curled upwards.

He was smiling. It was that dark, monstrous sneer that had so often made me quake.

Rigel crushed the hand that had grabbed him under his shoe. At his feet, Lionel writhed in pain. Rigel stamped brutally on his hand until each of his fingers had become swollen.

'Do you want to see *inside me*? You'd piss yourself before you could take a look,' he hissed icily. I thought he'd break his wrist. 'Oh, no, I've never been the good guy. You want to see how *bad* I can be?'

He stamped again, so hard I heard bones snapping.

A little sob burst out of me. Rigel clenched his jaw and his deep, narrow eyes flashed towards me. He seemed to have only just remembered that I was watching.

He stared at me in a way I couldn't interpret, clenched his fists, and abruptly set Lionel free. He jerked his hand away, moaning and rocking back and forth in the street. Rigel turned his back on him, once and for all, and walked like a terrible angel towards me.

The sound of the front door opening broke the silence.

My eyes adjusted to the darkness. Slowly, the outline of Rigel appeared. He was leaning against the door, his dark hair covering his face, and his jaw in the darkness looked sharp like a sickle.

I shuddered, hearing him breathing. That intimacy reignited

everything I had desperately tried to suppress. I was a statue of flesh and desire that was struggling not to fall to pieces. For the first time, I wondered if there would ever be a way for us to live together without hurting. Would there ever come a day when we would stop wounding each other?

'You're right. I'm . . . deluding myself.'

I looked down, no longer able to lie to myself.

'I've always wanted a happy ending . . . I've looked for it, every single moment of my life, hoping that one day it would come to me. I've wanted it ever since *She* . . . the matron . . . how she treated us meant all I could do was hope for a better future. But the truth . . .'

I pressed my lips together, defeated, surrendering completely.

'The truth is that you, Rigel . . . you're part of the fairy tale.'

Tears blurred my vision.

'Maybe you always have been. But I've never had the courage to see it because I was scared of losing everything.'

He stood still, enveloped in silence. I looked to one side, trying to control the emotions that would give me no peace. My heart exploded, I was on the verge of breaking into tears.

I saw the piano, gleaming in the faint light. I stared at it for a moment before my legs carried me towards it.

I brushed my fingers over the white keys as if I could still feel his hands there. I felt sad about what he had said to Lionel.

'It's not true that you're bad. I know what you're like, inside . . . and there's nothing bad, or scary. You're not like that,' I whispered. 'I see in you . . . all the goodness that you can't see.'

'That's what you're like,' he said after a while, behind me. 'You always look for the light in everything, like a moth.'

He was standing in the doorway. The shadows made his face painfully beautiful, but his gaze was dull and lifeless.

'You look for it even where it doesn't exist,' he said slowly. 'Even where it's never been.'

I looked at him with defenceless, yielding eyes and shook my head.

'We all have some light, Rigel . . . inside us. I've always looked for goodness. And I found it in you. It doesn't matter what the truth is, because the only light I see now is you. Wherever I look, at any moment, I only see you.'

I saw his eyes shining in the darkness. I would never forget his gaze.

I saw his heart in his eyes.

I saw how much he was crumpled, wrecked and bleeding.

But also radiant, alive and desperate.

We were something impossible, and we both knew it.

'There are no fairy tales, Nica. Not for people like me.'

There we were. The final reckoning.

There were no more pages that would continue our story of silences and tremors. Our souls had chased after each other for our entire lives, and now we'd reached the end of the line.

We didn't fit in with other people, because we were different. We spoke in a language that no other could understand.

A language of the heart.

'I don't want anything without you in it,' I found the strength to admit, once and for all, out loud.

I had just whispered the unspeakable, but it didn't matter, because it was the truth.

'You were right. We're broken . . . We're not like other people. But maybe, Rigel, we're shattered, in pieces, but we can put ourselves back together again, better this time.'

No one knew my demons better than he did.

No one else knew my scars, my traumas, my fears.

And I had learnt to see him as no one else did, because in his unique heart I had found my own.

We belonged to each other in a way that no one else would be able to understand.

And maybe it was true, maybe it was in our nature to destroy things. But in that *destructive, destroyed* way, we were something that was ours alone.

Terror and wonder. Shivers and salvation. We were a frenzy of notes that made up a jarring, otherworldly melody.

He had pulled at my soul so subtly that our destiny had written itself, as if on a blank page. And it had taken me so long to realise, it felt like a lifetime to take even the first step.

I moved towards him in the darkness. His eyes gleamed as if the whole sky was in the room. He carefully watched my every movement, as if what I had just admitted had pinned him to the spot with a force that was stronger than his will.

Holding his gaze, I held out my hand to brush his. Under his eyes, I felt minute and dangerous at the same time. He was tense all over, as if he wanted to resist . . . but armed with my tenderness, I wrapped my fingers around his wrist and pulled him towards me.

I lifted his hand to my face.

A muscle in his jaw twitched. His touch warmed my soul and I sighed. It felt like I could sense his pulse. One of my tears fell on his hand, which was still half-closed, as if something inside him still didn't dare to touch me.

He stared at me as if I were incredibly fragile, as if I might shatter under his touch.

'Before, you were afraid of me,' he whispered.

'Before . . . I hadn't learnt to see you yet.' Tears rolled down my cheeks, and I remembered the moment when I had shattered everything. 'I'm sorry . . .' I breathed. 'Rigel, *I'm sorry* . . .'

We were seeing each other for the first time.

Then, like a slow miracle . . . his hand unfurled on my cheek.

Rigel touched my face, and the warmth of his fingertips melted my heart.

His thumb lightly touched the corner of my mouth, stroked it as if that caress held all the impossibility of what we were.

'I'm not one of your creatures, Nica,' he murmured sadly. 'You can't . . . fix me.'

'I don't want to,' I whispered.

He had left roses inside of me, he had left petals and a trail of stars where once I had been a cracked, parched desert. We shared something, in that silence, in the shadow of our shortcomings.

Rigel was a wolf, and I wanted him for exactly what he was.

'I want you . . . as you are. I promised. And I haven't stopped believing it . . . I won't leave you alone, Rigel. Let me . . . let me stay with you.'

Stay with me, my heart prayed. *Stay with me, please, even though I'm scared, even though I don't know what will become of us.*

Even though we'll never be right together, you and me, because although there's a story for everything, there are no fairy tales about wolves and moths.

But stay with me, please, because if we're broken together, then it's the rest of the world that's wrong, not us.

If we're broken together, then I am no longer scared.

I slowly kissed his hand.

His muscles tensed, he was holding his breath and it seemed as if his chest was about to explode.

I wanted everything about him: his bites, his mistakes, his chaos and his caresses.

I wanted his vulnerabilities. His authentic self. I wanted his untameable heart. I wanted the boy without the happy ending, who had been unjustly abandoned under a sky full of stars.

I leant forward and he suddenly stopped breathing. I clasped his hand against my face and stood up on my tiptoes. With all the tenderness I had, I closed my eyes and gently pressed my lips to his.

My heart was pounding against my ribs. Rigel's mouth was warm and velvety soft. With a gentle smacking sound, I pulled my lips away. Rigel was dangerously still for a long moment. I couldn't understand his reaction.

The next moment, he pushed me backwards into the piano. My heart in my throat, Rigel slid his fingers into my hair and tilted my head back.

He was breathing heavily, staring at me, wide-eyed, as if I had done the last thing he ever would have expected me to. I was scared he'd push me away, but he pulled me close and his lips slammed against mine.

A universe of scratches and stars exploded in my clenching heart.

I clung to him with shaking hands, overcome by an unbearable passion. Our heartbeats accelerated, our breath mingled, I felt my entire being screaming his name.

Rigel kissed me . . .

He kissed me as if the world was about to fall down around us.

He kissed me as if his life depended on it, as if it was the only thing that could take his breath away.

His trembling fingers moved through my hair down to my shoulders, behind my neck, gripping me tightly as if I might dissolve at any moment. I squeezed his wrists so he knew I wouldn't leave any more, that however much the world shouted *no*, we belonged together, until our last breath.

I touched him, shyly and hesitantly, and the innocence of my touch seemed to drive him mad. He gasped and grabbed my hips, ruffling the fabric that clung to my body. He pressed me to him possessively, and his hot, eager mouth kissed me ardently. I felt his teeth on my lips, on my tongue, every kiss was a bite that sent shivers through my stomach.

I was breathless, my heart beating like mad, and I felt like I was about to explode.

Rigel slipped a knee between my thighs, wedging me against him, and his kiss became powerful, terrifying, divine.

I wanted to tell him that it didn't matter if there weren't fairy tales for people like us, that it didn't matter if we'd never be right together. As long as we stayed together, the future could not scare me.

We were exiles from the realm of fairy tales.

But maybe, after all, we could be our own fairy tale.

A fairy tale of tears and smiles.

Scratches and bites in the darkness.

Something precious and ruined, where we were the only happy ending there was.

I clenched my thighs around his knee, and something in Rigel ignited. He seemed unable to think, to control himself, to hold back. He grabbed my legs to lift me up, my sandals slipped off, and I trembled as our heartbeats collided like twin worlds.

'*Together* . . .' I whispered into his ear like a plea.

Rigel tightened his grip on my thighs until it hurt. There was a dissonant, clashing sound as my body slipped onto the piano keys.

The more I touched him, the more his body went wild against mine. I was subjugated by him, unable to move. But I realised that even though he was holding me so tightly I couldn't move, I wasn't frightened. Because Rigel knew what I had gone through.

He knew my nightmares better than anyone else.

He knew all of the places I was cracked, and there was something protective and desperate about the way he touched me. Something that seemed to both desire and protect my vulnerabilities. I knew he wouldn't hurt me.

As I held him in my arms, giving him all my sweetness, I knew that whatever dark disaster his heart was, I would always keep it with me. Forever.

And ever.

And ever . . .

'Nica?'

A light turned on upstairs. The sound of footsteps.

Anna's voice.

I opened my eyes wide. Rigel abruptly pulled away from me and I felt as though I'd just been uprooted.

Anna came into the room, wrapped in her bathrobe, and found me standing near the piano all alone. I stared at her like a fawn in the headlights, my fingers fidgeting nervously.

'It's you, Nica . . .' she mumbled sleepily, looking at my bare feet. 'I heard a sudden noise . . . the piano . . . Is everything all right?'

I nodded, my lips pressed tight together, hoping she wouldn't notice my flushed face.

'What are you doing here in the dark? Are you having trouble sleeping again?'

'I . . . I just got home,' I squeaked, almost ridiculously, before swallowing hard. 'I'm sorry for waking you . . .'

Anna relaxed and glanced at the front door. I took the opportunity to hurriedly readjust a strap on my dress.

'Don't worry about it, it's fine. Come here . . .'

She reached out a hand towards me with a smile.

I bent down to pick up my sandals, and went towards her so she could accompany me upstairs. But before I crossed the threshold into the hall where she was waiting for me, I glanced sideways . . .

He was there, in the darkness, leaning against the wall, his chest heaving with heavy, silent breaths. His lips were still moist and swollen and his hair tousled by my fingers.

Rigel looked at me like the living sin he was.

I felt both peace and torment . . . relief and corruption.

Bright flashes and storms in the dark.

I felt a storm looming over us, laden with thunder.

'*Well . . .*' a voice inside me whispered, counting the purply, starry universes he had left inside me, '*. . . look at all these beautiful colours.*'

27. Tights

*Desire is a flame
that extinguishes the mind
and ignites the heart.*

'Nica?'

I blinked, coming back to reality.

Norman was looking at me, slightly worried.

'Is that okay for you?'

He and Anna were watching me.

'I'm sorry, I got distracted,' I stammered.

'The psychologist, Nica,' Anna replied patiently. 'You remember we spoke about it? We said that maybe talking with someone would help make you feel better,' she continued delicately. 'Well, my friend has given me the number of a very good one who is available in the next few days.' She looked at me closely. 'What do you think?'

A feeling of anxiety pricked at my stomach, but I tried not to let it show. Anna wanted to help me, she just wanted what was best for me. Knowing that eased my discomfort, but it didn't make it disappear. Her encouraging look, however, made me take heart.

'Okay,' I replied, trying to trust her.

'Okay?'

I nodded. I could at least give it a go.

She seemed happy to finally be able to do something for me.

'All right then. I'll call the practice later to confirm.' She smiled at me and stroked my hand, then looked over my shoulders with a bright expression. 'Oh, hello!'

Every inch of me tensed as Rigel came into the kitchen. My skin became sensitive to his presence and my stomach filled with sparks. It took all my strength not to look up and plant my eyes on him.

What had happened the previous night was still aflame inside of me. *His lips, his hands . . .*

I felt them all over me. I would have thought I had dreamt them if I couldn't still feel them burning against my skin.

He sat down opposite me and I dared a glance at him.

His dishevelled hair framed his attractive face. He lifted a glass of juice to his mouth, his eyes pinned on Anna and Norman, who were telling him something.

He seemed . . . normal. Not like me. I was a ball of nerves.

He ate breakfast, apparently calm, and his eyes didn't glance towards me once.

Images of our bodies clinging to each other flashed through my mind and I gripped my mug tightly.

He didn't mean to ignore what had happened . . . did he?

At some point, he took an apple with a lazy smile and said something that made Anna and Norman burst out laughing. He lifted the fruit to his mouth and, while they were distracted, his gaze fell on me.

Rigel plunged his teeth into the apple in a long, deep bite, locking me in his gaze. He licked his upper lip and slowly looked my body up and down.

It took me a moment to realise that the ceramic mug was burning my fingers.

'It's raining,' I heard Anna say, as if from another world. 'I'll drive you to school today.'

'Are you ready?' she asked a little later. She slipped her coat on while Rigel was coming down the stairs. 'Have you got an umbrella?'

I shoved a small one inside my backpack, trying to fit it in among the books. In the meantime, Anna went outside to bring the car around.

I moved closer to the front door. There was that scent of freshness in the air that I really liked. I reached my arm out to open the door and leave, but something stopped me.

Rigel had reached his arm over my head and was holding the door closed.

'You've got a ladder in your tights.'

His deep voice so close made me shudder.

'Did you know?'

His tall, dominating presence loomed over me.

'No,' I said faintly, sensing him come closer. 'Where?'

His warm breath caressed my neck. The next moment, he reached round and I felt his finger burning my skin, just below the hem of my skirt. He pressed his fingertip on it, turning his face up towards me.

'Here,' he said slowly, through his teeth.

I looked down and swallowed.

'It's only little . . .'

'But it's still there,' he said in a gravelly murmur.

'It's almost covered by my skirt,' I replied. 'You can hardly see it . . .'

'You can see it enough . . . to wonder where it goes.'

There was something suggestive in his tone. I felt myself blushing.

'I can always take them off,' I said without thinking. Rigel's breathing became heavier.

'*Take them off?*'

'Sure,' I cheeped. His chest pressed against my back. 'I always carry a spare pair with me . . . I can change them.'

'*Mm . . .*' he murmured on my skin, as if lost in me, and that simple sound made my stomach burn.

His attention made me melt like wax, and at the same time, I felt alive, electrified and feverish.

I was lost in him, in the tension radiating off him, in his heat, his silence, his breath . . .

The sound of the car horn tooting brought me back to reality. Anna was waiting for us.

I bit my lip as Rigel moved away and the heat of his body disappeared.

He moved past me through the door. Lingering in the slipstream of his scent, I let out a sigh that I could never let the rest of the world hear.

Billie's yellow raincoat was the first thing I glimpsed on that drizzly morning. She was standing on the wet asphalt by the gates, her face downturned. She gave me a faint smile of relief, and I realised that she had been waiting for me because she didn't want to go in alone. She tried to ask me about the party, but I wanted to find out how she was doing. Judging by the bags under her eyes, she hadn't slept well.

'You . . . haven't called her, have you?' I asked cautiously as we approached the lockers.

Billie didn't reply, which saddened me.

'Billie . . .'

'I know,' she whispered sorrowfully.

I didn't want to insist. But even though I knew that forcing the matter wouldn't achieve anything, there was still some part of me that couldn't let it be.

'You need time,' I murmured, 'and that's understandable. But if you told her that . . . if you spoke to her.'

'I can't,' she swallowed. 'It's all so . . . so . . .'

She froze, torment flashing through her pale eyes. I didn't have time to turn around before she picked up her backpack and headed straight to class.

Miki, behind me, slowed down. She watched her go with a dull, wounded expression.

'Miki,' I gave her a smile that I hoped was supportive. 'Hello . . .'

She opened her locker without replying. She looked as bad as Billie, as if that rift in their relationship had broken them both.

I looked down.

'I wanted to say thank you,' I said after a moment. 'For yesterday. For having me over, and helping me with my make-up.' I stared at my hands and continued. 'It was really nice to meet your parents. And I know you maybe don't want to hear this right now but . . . despite what happened, I had a nice afternoon. It was nice spending time all together.'

Miki had frozen. She wasn't looking at me, but after a while, she spoke. 'I'm sorry I didn't reply,' she murmured quietly.

I knew she was talking about the messages I had sent her asking how she was.

'It's okay,' I replied. I touched her hand and she looked down. 'If you want to talk about it, I'm right here.'

She didn't reply, but her eyes, when they looked up at me from under her hood, said more than she ever would have.

'Hey, Blackford.'

Out of nowhere, a hand landed on Miki's locker. It was a boy with thick brown hair, Miki's classmate. I recognised him as we had had a few classes together.

He flashed a cocky smile that made many girls giddy.

'The weather's matching your mood today?'

'Go fuck yourself, Gyle.'

Gyle threw a cheerful glance at his friend.

'I need science notes,' he said, not beating about the bush. 'Well, who doesn't . . . that sicko Kryll is giving us a test next week. He's hysterical about these jars of creatures that keep going missing from his lab . . . You've got all the notes, right?'

She ignored him. He tilted his head.

'Well?' He smiled unpleasantly. 'I know you can't wait to do me this favour. After all, you must be pleased someone's deigning to speak to you.'

Miki was silent. He looked her up and down.

'If you didn't always wear those trampy hoodies,' he insinuated, leaning over her, 'you know what other *favours* you could do me?'

Both he and his friend burst out laughing. Miki elbowed him sharply in the ribs. I threw an uneasy glance at my friend, and Gyle's cocky look turned to me.

'Hey, little Dover. You've got a ladder in your tights, did you know?'

I opened my eyes wide. He looked at me as though I was a little mouse.

'How intriguing . . .'

'Beat it, dickhead,' Miki growled. I tried to pull my skirt down to cover the ladder, but my efforts just seemed to amuse him.

Gyle leant over me, smirking.

'You know what they say,' he whispered in my ear. 'Some things are best left to the imagina—'

He was shoved forcefully into the row of lockers. A hand was gripping his arm.

His stupefied expression soon turned to anger. He spun around to glare furiously at the culprit. But he froze when he realised who it was.

Rigel slowly turned. His naturally predatory eyes fell on Gyle, and he looked at him for a long moment before languidly parting his lips.

'Whoops.'

Gyle didn't react. Even his friend behind him had stopped laughing. He seemed to find his voice only when Rigel started moving away.

'Watch out,' he murmured quietly, threateningly. He was maybe hoping that Rigel wouldn't hear, but those feline eyes swivelled back to him, as if Rigel had been waiting for precisely that.

' "Watch out",' he repeated with a cutting sneer. Something glinted in his black eyes, a sort of dark amusement. 'For who? *For you?*'

Gyle nervously looked away. His cockiness had disappeared. He suddenly seemed like he wanted to eat his words.

'It doesn't matter.'

Rigel gave him a lingering look. The entire corridor was coursing past him, a river of adoring and hostile looks. He stood tall and cruelly gorgeous in the middle of the flow. A masterpiece of fangs and ink.

Then, for a fraction of a second, his gaze fell on me. My heart leapt, but then Rigel turned and walked down the corridor.

'Arrogant bastard,' Gyle hissed, when he was out of earshot.

I watched as Rigel took a book out of his locker.

'I'm not sure about him.'

I blinked and turned towards Miki. She was holding a book and looking away from me.

'About who?' I asked, perplexed. Then it dawned on me. 'Rigel?'

She nodded. 'There's something . . . *strange* about him.'

'Strange?' I tried to understand, opening a bottle of water and lifting it to my lips.

'Yes. There's something about him. His behaviour.'

'In what way?'

'I don't know how to explain it . . . maybe it's just a vibe . . . but sometimes he looks at you as though he wants to *devour* you . . .'

I choked on my water. I coughed loudly, thumped my chest, and hoped that she wouldn't notice my unease.

'What are you talking about?' I swallowed, as my eyes looked everywhere but at her. I suddenly felt as nervous as a spider. I started tidying my notebooks in my locker in an attempt to seem busy. I thought I could feel Miki looking at me closely, but then Gyle decided to remind her of his existence.

'So?' he insisted again. 'You'll lend me your notes?'

'No,' she shot back bluntly. 'Deal with it.'

'Oh, come on!' Gyle argued.

'I said no.'

'You want something in exchange, is that it? You think maybe a good fuck would do you good?'

'I swear, Gyle, I'm going to clobber you over the head with this violin,' Miki snarled. 'Piss off.'

'What about you, Dover?'

I jumped. Helpless, my eyes darted to Gyle. He smirked at the look on my face.

'Do you have the notes?'

'I . . .' I stammered, as his gaze fell to the ladder in my tights and then ran up my thighs.

'You could let me see . . .'

I felt myself burning with shame when I noticed that Rigel had looked up from the book he had been flicking through and was staring at us.

'Have you got a knack for anatomy?' Gyle came closer to my face. 'I bet you have . . .'

Something struck his head with force.

The violin resounded in its case and he lifted a hand to his head, rubbing it with a grimace.

'Don't try to use your brain, dickhead,' Miki spat through gritted teeth, putting an end to the conversation.

Billie had told me never to believe corridor gossip, as most of the time it was made up. I left the classroom with the excuse of needing to go to the bathroom, hoping she was right.

My hurried footsteps echoed down the empty corridor. I slipped past the row of lockers and saw that the white door at the end was ajar. Plucking up my courage, I peered inside, then pushed the door fully open, slipped into the room and closed the door behind me.

Two eyes lifted to me.

Rigel was sat right in the middle of the infirmary.

'I heard what happened,' I said, getting straight to it. I immediately noticed a red mark and a cut on his white cheekbone.

Are you all right? I wanted to ask, but instead, a nasty sense of foreboding made me say, 'Is it true?'

Rigel stared at me, his face downturned.

'What?'

'Rigel . . .' I sighed wearily. It was always like this with him. Every word was a convoluted insinuation. 'You know what. Is it true?'

'It depends,' he replied, with a show of nonchalance. 'Which part are you referring to?'

'The part where you broke Jason Gyle's nose during baseball.'

According to the gossip, Gyle had had the misfortune of finding himself in Rigel's path when Rigel was hitting the ball during practice. Too bad that it had been Gyle who had thrown him the ball. And that Rigel had smacked the bat into it so forcefully that it was sent right back at Gyle's face fast enough to break the sound barrier.

'It wasn't Rigel Wilde's fault,' the girls in his class had protested. 'He didn't do it deliberately, he's innocent.'

Rigel clicked his tongue.

'Some people would do better to not play if they don't have a sporting attitude,' he joked. 'It was a *tragic* accident.'

'That's not what I heard,' I murmured.

His eyes glinted. He looked at me in that shadowy, mischievous way he'd had since he was a little boy.

'And what did you hear?'

'That you provoked him.'

I had seen Miki between classes. Thunderstruck, she swore she had glimpsed Rigel hiding a twisted smile after the 'accident'.

At that point, the teacher had clearly seen Gyle jump onto Rigel like a ferocious animal. Rigel had stayed still just long enough to let his face be ruined by a punch, then he had unleashed a devastating flurry of blows.

That was why I had come to find him. It was Miki who had told me where he was.

'*Provoke* him? Me?' he repeated in a light drawl. 'What hurtful slander . . .'

I shook my head, exhausted, and came closer to him. His eyes seemed more alert.

'How is it you always end up in fights?' I asked him.

Rigel tilted his head to one side and smiled, unabashed.

'Are you worried about me, Nica?'

'Yes,' I whispered without hesitation. 'You always end up getting hurt. The last thing I want to see is you with more wounds.'

The tone of the conversation shifted as if I had said something important. I didn't want to joke about this. Rigel was watching me now, without any games or pretence.

'The wounds you can see are the only ones that go away,' he replied, with a seriousness that made my chest tighten.

'Not everything has to hurt forever, Rigel,' I told him. 'Some things can heal. Even if it takes time, even if it doesn't seem possible . . . sometimes they can. Sometimes . . . even just a little part of us can heal.'

He watched me for a long time.

Those rare moments when Rigel had such a *docile* expression gave me shivers. I wanted to touch him.

My fingers brushed against his neck and then his jaw.

'What does that mean . . . "heal"?' he asked, without taking his eyes off me.

He seemed like a wild but submissive beast in my hands.

'Healing means . . . touching with kindness something that was touched with fear.'

I touched the cut on his cheekbone, and thought I felt him trembling.

Suddenly, my heart leapt as he touched me.

I held my breath as he squeezed my knees, his fingers pressing against the tender, supple flesh revealed by the hole in my tights.

His fingertips left burning traces up my thighs. He pulled me closer to him and I suppressed a shiver.

'Rigel . . .'

'You're still wearing those tights,' he remarked, noting that I hadn't changed them. His fingers slowly squeezed and my heart thumped against my ribs.

'Rigel, we're at school . . .'

'I told you, Nica,' he growled. 'That tone of voice just makes matters worse . . .'

Suddenly, the sound of footsteps came from beyond the door. I froze.

The door handle turned.

Without thinking, overcome by panic, I pulled him to his feet and shoved him into the storage closet before diving in after him.

The space was ridiculously small, and I suddenly realised what a stupid thing it was to have done. Rigel didn't need to hide. He could have stayed there.

The door opened, and through the keyhole, I saw the nurse come in.

'Wilde?' The woman called.

I stopped breathing when I saw that the principal was with her.

'He was just here,' she declared, then they started to discuss what had happened.

I tried not to make any noise as their voices filled the room.

Behind me, Rigel also didn't make a sound. If it weren't for the pressure of his chest against my back, I would have struggled to believe that he really was there behind me, so meek and compliant. But feeling his controlled breathing reminded me of all the times our bodies had touched.

I brought my face closer to the keyhole and dared a careful look at the two women. How long would they stay there for?

I felt Rigel's warm breath tickling my neck. His lips parted and the gentle sound they made slipped directly into my brain, causing a hot shiver. I tried to turn around, but his face was already there, against my neck, in that tiny space. His silky hair brushed against my cheek and my nostrils filled with his powerful musk.

'*Rigel* . . .'

'*Shh* . . .' he whispered in my ear as his hands pressed around my hips.

My heart beat faster and faster.

Before I could do anything . . . Rigel bit my neck.

My eyes opened wide and my fingers rushed to grab his wrists. What was he doing?

He planted a long kiss on my throat and I swallowed. The feeling of my fragile, delicate body quivering against his made him hold back a gasp.

He pulled me even closer to him, his hands setting my insides aflame.

'*Stop . . .*' I whispered faintly.

All I got in response was a deep breath that shuddered down into my vertebrae.

His fingers ran down my thighs, then up into the hollow between my breasts, savouring the furious pounding of my heart. He took my face by my chin and tilted it to one side.

I panted, wide-eyed, as his burning lips closed around the curve of my neck, igniting me.

My ankles were tingling, I couldn't breathe. Languidly, his mouth teased my tender skin, as if he wanted to taste me.

With his other hand, Rigel found the ladder in my tights. He nibbled my neck, tasting me, then, he slipped his finger through the hole.

His fingers slithered over my bare skin, numbing it. All I could feel was the violent thumping of my heart, his hot breath, his firm body against mine, and his finger, reaching, and then . . .

The two women left, and I tumbled out of the closet. The atmosphere suddenly shifted.

I turned around, my eyes wide open and my face flushed. Rigel was staring at me from the shadows, licking his swollen lips as if I was a delicacy. I stammered incoherently, and then a cold draught on my leg made me look down.

It had been little, but now the ladder was gaping; a splash of milky flesh shone through the tights. My mouth fell open and I was sure I saw him smile.

'Oh . . .' Rigel murmured. 'Now you've *really* got to change them.'

It had been mad to risk that.

No one could find out what was happening between us. No one could know, or we would lose everything. I wouldn't be able to stand never seeing Anna and Norman again. Not now that they had become such an important part of my life.

I knew that I was being contradictory, but I also knew, deep down, that I would never want to destroy what we had built together.

He didn't seem to realise the gravity of the situation, and this worried me. From the perspective of everyone else, we were about to become a family. For some people, we already were.

We had to be careful.

But while I was acutely aware of this, I also couldn't stop thinking about the feeling of his hands. I hardly recognised myself.

The more he touched me . . . the more I felt like I was going mad.

My heart shuddered.

My hands shook.

His touch moulded me and my chest filled with delirious ecstasy.

The more pieces of my soul I gave him, the more I became his.

How could I manage all this?

'Nica, you've got a visitor.' Norman poked his head into my room, interrupting my thoughts.

I looked at him, confused. When I went downstairs, I glimpsed two vivid blue eyes in the doorway and broke into a smile.

'Adeline!'

Her eyes softened as soon as she saw me.

'Hi,' she greeted me warmly.

She was wearing a beanie and rain boots to keep her dry. She was like a ray of sunshine in the eye of a storm.

'I hope I'm not disturbing you,' she apologised. 'I was in town and I . . . saw they've opened a new bakery. I thought of you,' she said, slightly embarrassed. 'They'd just baked these pastries, and I know how much you like jam . . .'

She held out a packet and I felt a warm sensation in my throat, as sweet as honey.

'Adeline, you shouldn't have . . .' I took the bag and looked up at her with a smile. 'Why don't you stay? We could eat them together . . . it's no bother,' I anticipated, before she could say anything. 'We've got that tea you really like, and it's raining so much, come on.'

She wiped her boots on the mat and gave Norman a grateful smile as he took her coat and hung it up.

'Make yourself at home,' I welcomed her. 'I'll make some tea and be right with you.'

She did as I had told her and after a while, I came into the living room carrying a tray with a steaming teapot.

She was standing up with her back to me.

I was about to call to her, when I realised that there was someone else there too. At the far end of the room, shrouded in his usual silence, Rigel sat reading, oblivious to the rest of the world, his skin bathed in the light coming through the window.

The world stopped.

I saw something I maybe hadn't wanted to see.

Adeline . . . Adeline was looking at Rigel as if nothing else existed.

With whispering eyes.

And silent lips.

With a broken heart, the sort of longing you have for something you've always gazed at from afar.

Adeline was looking at Rigel in exactly the same way that I looked at him.

28. A Single Song

When you cannot see the light,
let's look together at the stars.

'Adeline . . . Do you have feelings for Rigel?'

Adeline lowered her cup. I saw surprise in her eyes.

'Why are you asking me that?'

Maybe Anna was right about me: my heart was very transparent, and I couldn't lie. I had never been good at hiding my emotions, and this was no different.

'Nica,' she whispered, 'if you're talking about that kiss . . .'

'I want to know,' I said, bluntly. 'I . . . I need to know, Adeline. Do you feel something for him?'

I knew I couldn't tell anyone about Rigel and me. Even though Adeline had known us our whole lives, since long before we had been taken in by Anna and Norman, this just wasn't something I could tell her.

If it got out, the consequences would be disastrous. But I had to ask her.

She looked down. 'I've known you both a long time,' she whispered. 'We grew up together. Rigel . . . is also part of my childhood. And even though I've never been able to understand him, I've learnt to not judge his behaviour.'

I got the feeling that I was missing something, again. I didn't understand. I had never seen them together at the institute, but Adeline seemed to know him in a way I couldn't interpret.

'Rigel has taught me a lot. Sometimes, the greatest sacrifice comes not in our words, but through what we leave unsaid. He taught me that there are some opportunities you have to seize, and others when all you can do is . . . step aside. We have to accept that there are some things we can't change, and the measure of our love is how much we are prepared to sacrifice to protect them from a distance. He taught me that we have to have the courage to let go of the things we care about the most.'

Adeline looked up, piercing me with her sky-blue eyes.

I did not fully understand her words. I did not grasp their hidden meaning. It would only become clearer at the very end.

Her eyes glistened, a labyrinth of things left unsaid. Maybe she, too, had desires that she had learnt to restrain, choosing silence over speech.

'Believe me, Nica,' she smiled gently. 'All I feel for Rigel is a deep, deep fondness.'

I chose to believe Adeline.

Maybe I hadn't understood everything she had said, but there was one thing I was absolutely certain of: I trusted her, and knew she would never make fun of me.

I wanted to be open with her, to confess what bound Rigel and I together, but I couldn't. I needed to share my fears and insecurities with someone, but I knew I had to keep them inside.

I was alone with those feelings.

Alone with him.

'So?'

I blinked. Billie was looking at me with a concerned expression.

'Sorry, my head was in the clouds,' I apologised.

'I asked if you want to study together,' she said flatly. 'If you want to come over to mine after school.'

'Oh, I'd love to, but I can't today,' I replied regretfully. 'Anna's got me an appointment at the doctor's.'

Billie looked at me for a moment, then she nodded slowly. She had not seemed at all herself the last few days. The dark circles under her eyes made them look shiny and sunken, and she seemed so tense and dull, so different from her usual bubbly self.

I knew why: she and Miki hadn't said a word to each other in days.

However straightforward the solution seemed, I knew that it wouldn't be enough for her to simply grab the phone and make up with her best friend. Something had broken that afternoon. What they said to each other had shaken the most fundamental aspects of their relationship, and the more time passed, the more the rift between them seemed to deepen.

'I'm sorry, Billie,' I said sincerely. 'Maybe another time . . .'

She nodded again, without looking at me. She let her gaze wander over the hustle and bustle of students. When her eyes came to a stop, I knew who she had seen.

Miki was walking along the corridor, her backpack slung off one shoulder and her hood lowered. I realised then that she wasn't alone. She was walking alongside another girl. It must have been one of her classmates. I had previously seen her saying hello to Miki a few times, so I wasn't that surprised to see them together. I noticed a hint of uncertainty in Miki's eyes. She hesitated for a moment, then came towards us.

I was so happy to see her approaching that I couldn't help but smile sweetly.

'Hey,' I greeted her happily.

Miki looked down, which I interpreted as a greeting.

'I found it,' was all she said, holding out a small backpack to me. It was the one with the clothes I had left at her house the afternoon of the party.

'Oh,' I replied, surprised. 'Where was it?'

'Evangeline had put it with my things.'

'Just think . . . well, thanks. Oh, yeah!' I looked for something inside my backpack and held it out to her. 'Here . . . these are for you.'

Miki reached out a hand to take the cookies, perplexed.

'Anna wanted to thank you for your hospitality. And for the lift, the make-up and the sandals . . . so we made cookies together.' I scratched my cheek. 'Yeah . . . the ones I made don't look that pretty,' I admitted, looking at the ugly shortbread bears with their lumps and deformities. 'But I've tried them, and . . . after the first few bites . . . if you chew for a bit . . . they get a bit softer.'

Miki's friend smiled at me. 'They don't look all that bad.'

'I hope so,' I said, appreciating her intervention. Billie, behind me, was watching us wordlessly.

'You shouldn't have.' Miki seemed lost for words. 'There was no need.'

'Come on . . . is that all you've got to say?' Her companion laughed, giving her a playful nudge. 'She baked them for you! You can at least say thank you!'

Miki gave her a gruff look, but I saw her blushing under her make-up.

'Of course,' she stammered, in that slightly crabby way that made me realise how much she actually did appreciate the cookies. 'Thank you.'

'Always as surly as a bear,' her friend good-naturedly teased her. 'Like when you don't have your coffee. Did you know that Makayla is *impossible* if she hasn't had her beloved caffeine?'

'It's not true . . .' Miki grumbled.

'Oh, but it is! She's a beast, I swear,' she laughed. 'If I didn't know what she's like . . .'

'What do *you* know about what she's like?'

We turned around.

Billie's arms were crossed, her hands were clasped a little above her elbows. There was a hostility glinting in her eyes that I had never seen in her before. She seemed to realise what she had just said only as we all turned around to look at her. Instinctively, she clamped her lips shut and walked away, her arms still tightly wrapped around herself so she wouldn't fall apart.

'Thanks for the cookies.'

Miki lifted up her hood and left in the other direction.

Her friend watched her go. When our eyes met again, neither of us could think of the right thing to say.

The rift was getting wider.

Ever wider.

In the end, it would swallow everything: dreams, memories and happy moments.

Nothing would be left.

Just ruins.

Just emptiness.

The waiting room in the psychologist's office was simple and elegant. A tropical plant broke up the cold tones, and on the anthracite-coloured walls, there were several abstract paintings that, despite my patient efforts, I couldn't reach an interpretation of.

I risked a little glance at the person next to me.

Rigel's arms were folded, his ankle was resting on his knee and his mouth was creased in a scowl.

He was irritated. Very irritated.

His body was seething with the annoyance of being there. Anna had convinced him by saying, 'Seeing as Nica's going . . . why don't you give it a try too? You might find it useful . . .'

I could imagine how he was feeling. Rigel, sitting down to talk about himself? Rigel, who had built himself such a thick mask that it even covered his heart? It was so absurd it was almost inconceivable.

I examined the profile of his face. His manly jaw was tense, his upper lip slightly curled. He was as magnificent and captivating as ever, despite his extreme irritation.

At that moment, I noticed the girl sat at the far end of the waiting room. She was holding a magazine in front of her face, her legs were crossed, and her eyes were practically glued to Rigel. She was staring at him so intensely that I was surprised his skin wasn't melting off his bones. As Rigel inclined his head, she crumpled the cover of the magazine in her hands.

I looked at her more closely . . . She had shining brown eyes and an extremely delicate face. She was pretty. Very pretty.

Feeling an emotion I didn't know how to describe, I wondered whether he had noticed her.

I turned around.

Rigel's head was leaning against the wall, his face turned to one side.

And his gaze . . . his gaze was planted on my hand, next to his leg. I hadn't even realised that I had brushed his knee. He seemed enraptured, as if, despite his irritation, that touch had been enough to enchant him.

'Goodbye!'

A well-dressed man appeared in the doorway in front of us. He held it open to let a man in his forties walk out.

'See you next week, Timothy,' he said. 'So, the next appointment is . . .'

He let his gaze wander until it landed on Rigel and me.

'Oh, you must be Mrs Milligan's children,' he burst out. I saw a muscle twitching in Rigel's jaw. 'You're already here, excellent . . . Miss, would you like to go first?'

I nibbled the edges of my Band-Aids, nervous, and got to my feet. He smiled, letting me pass.

'Anna isn't actually our adoptive mom yet,' I corrected him faintly.

The doctor looked at me, realising his mistake.

'I apologise,' he said. 'Mrs Milligan told me about the adoption. I didn't realise the process was still ongoing.'

I wrung my hands. My palms were sweating. He noticed my jitteriness. His gaze was deep and perceptive, but the attentive way he looked at me didn't make me feel intimidated. It was just unexpectedly sensitive.

'Would you like to talk to me?' he asked.

I swallowed. I felt my body trembling, whispering *no*, but I tried to pay it no attention.

I wanted to do this for myself.

I wanted to try.

Even though my guts were twisting with terror and reality was crashing down on me.

Slowly, I nodded. It took me an enormous effort, maybe the most effort anything had ever taken me.

An hour later, once again I walked through that door.

I felt clammy, tense and shaky. I had told him a little bit about my childhood, but I hadn't been able to tell him about my traumas, because every time I tried to open the doors to that part of my mind, my anxieties were there, ready to ambush me. I had gotten upset, frozen and fallen silent many times. I had only managed, with difficulty, to tell him a few things, but he reassured me that I had been good. It was my first time.

'We can meet again, if you'd like to,' he said gently. 'No rush. Next week, maybe.'

He didn't force me to reply. Instead, he let me process in silence. Then he looked up at Rigel.

'Your turn,' he said, as I sat back down. 'This way, please.'

I realised that Rigel hadn't moved an inch from where I had left him.

He looked at me closely, as if to check if I was all right. Then, after a moment, he unfolded his arms and decided to get up and cautiously walk into the psychiatrist's office.

* * *

He walked through the door with measured steps, but his first thought was that he didn't want to be there.

Lately . . . he was always feeling in a strange frenzy.

It was a sizzling sensation that ignited his blood. It was visceral, like a poison. Twisted and delicious.

It was her.

Impulsively, he spun around to seek her eyes. He met her shining gaze just for a moment, just long enough to imprint the image of her on his mind.

It was as if he had to keep looking at her, to see her, to make sure that she wasn't a dream.

That if he turned to look at her, she would meet his eyes.

That if he touched her, she wouldn't be frightened.

That if he ran his hand through her hair, she wouldn't fade away like a dream, but stay there, in his hands, her eyes locked on his.

She was real.

She was so real she made his blood shudder.

The disaster was roaring inside of him. It was scraping and scratching the walls of his heart, asking if he was mad, if this was just another illusion. Rigel turned to look at her, desperately searching for her eyes and desperately, urgently clinging on to them.

He imprinted her inside him, her and her pale eyes. And that light that flooded everything.

And even though his heart was still delirious, inside him, something was pulsating with tenderness.

Something that knew how to be gentle, that warmed him, that lay in the shadows of his thorns and placed colourful Band-Aids between the cracks in his soul.

For a moment, as the door closed on Nica, so small, light and *real*, he reminded himself that even if he couldn't see her, she would still be there . . .

'Okay, Rigel. Rigel, right?'

The doctor's voice tore him away from his thoughts.

He had almost forgotten him. Almost.

'I understand this is also your first time,' he heard him say, as he appraised the office. Something on the desk caught his attention. They looked like cards, but they were as large as the pages of a book. They were arranged in two neat rows, and on each of them was a series of black dots that formed vague shapes.

'Interesting, aren't they?'

Rigel's eyes flitted back to the doctor. He was standing near him, staring at the pages with the dots.

'It's the Rorschach test,' he informed him. 'Contrary to what most people think, it's not a tool for evaluating mental instability. It's used to show how the subject perceives the world. It aids in assessing personality.' He moved some of them aside, revealing ever more abstract designs. 'Some people see anger, lack, fear . . . Others see dreams, hopes. Love.' The doctor looked up at him. 'Have you ever been in love?'

Rigel felt like laughing, in that exaggerated, malicious and unrestrained way that made people see him as a wolf.

He and love had a lifelong battle. They tore each other to pieces. But neither of them could survive without the other.

But for once he didn't laugh. Instead, Rigel found himself staring at those meaningless blots. He had always heard people speak of love as a sweet, tender feeling that lightened the heart. No one ever spoke of thorns, no one spoke of the cancer that was longing, or the torment of an unrequited glance.

No one spoke of how much it hurt, love, when it devours you until you can't breathe.

But he knew he was different. He wasn't like other people.

He sensed the man watching him intensely, as if curious about the various emotions flitting through his eyes.

'What is love, for you?'

'A writhing,' Rigel murmured. 'Bites that never heal.'

By the time he realised he had opened his mouth it was too late. He had been speaking to himself, not to the psychiatrist. It was a thought he had always kept inside.

But now, the doctor was staring at him, and Rigel felt every molecule in his body protesting against his gaze. He found it repellent, oppressive, something to shrug off as soon as possible.

For a moment, he had got lost inside himself, and Nica had pulled the unspeakable from him. He promised himself it would not happen again.

He looked away, and started to pace around the room like a caged animal.

'I know about your condition.'

Rigel froze. Immediately.

'My . . . *condition?*'

So Anna had spoken about him. He slowly turned around.

'Have no fear,' the doctor said calmly. 'Do you want to take a seat?'

Rigel didn't move. His stare glinted with a light as sharp as a pin.

The doctor gave him a reassuring smile.

'You can't imagine how good it feels, to talk. You know what they say? Words let us read the soul.'

Read the soul?

'Everyone's a little nervous their first time . . . it's normal. Why don't you settle down on this armchair here?'

Read . . . the soul?

He turned and looked at the doctor. He flashed his black, shark eyes at him. Then, out of nowhere . . . he smiled. His lips parted to reveal his teeth, one of his finest masterpieces.

'Before we get started, there's something I'd like to ask you.'

'Excuse me?'

'Oh, I'm sorry,' he began, stepping closer. 'It's first-time nerves, you know how it is. Essentially, doctor, I've always been a little wary of the confessional approach. You know, because of my . . . *condition.*'

The doctor looked at him in surprise when, instead of the arm-chair, he gracefully sat down in the chair in front of him.

'It's just out of curiosity,' he said, polite and innocent. 'You don't mind, do you, *doctor*?'

The man laced his fingers together under his chin, and accommodated Rigel's request. 'Go ahead.'

Rigel gave him a measured smile, like a tamed beast, and asked, 'What is the aim of these sessions?'

'To facilitate an improvement in psychological wellbeing and to help you in your personal growth,' the doctor replied calmly.

'And so you take it for granted that your . . . . *clients* are in need of help.'

'Well, if they come to me of their own free will.'

'And if they don't come to you of their own free will?'

He gave him a calm, shrewd look.

'Is this your way of telling me that you did not choose to come here?'

'It's my way of trying to understand your approach.'

The doctor seemed to consider.

'Well . . . sometimes, people find it helps them feel better. Sometimes, people construct realities in which they believe they are healthy. They think they do not need help. But inside, they feel empty, useless, like a broken frame or a shard of glass.'

'If they do not think they need help, how can the opposite be true?' Rigel asked, enigmatically.

The doctor pushed his glasses up his nose.

'That's just how it is. The mind works in complex ways. We cannot understand everything. Rorschach himself once said that the soul needs to breathe too.'

'Even yours?'

'Excuse me?'

'You are human, doctor, like everyone else. Does your soul need to breathe, too?'

The doctor looked him in the eyes, as if seeing him for the first time.

Rigel smiled ironically, but his gaze remained icy.

'If I were to tell you that in those designs I saw desires, traumas or fears, you would find some way to analyse me. If I were to tell you, on the other hand, that I saw nothing, or that I think they're just meaningless blots, you would interpret that just the same. Perhaps as a refusal. Or evasion. Am I wrong?'

He waited for a reply that did not come.

'Whatever I say, you would find something to correct. No matter the situation, anyone who walks through that door is destined for a diagnosis. Maybe the point, doctor, isn't how people feel, but how you make them feel. The point is your conviction that there must be something that is not right, that they need to be fixed, because they are useless, empty and wrong . . . like a broken frame, or a shard of glass.'

The man stared at him, and Rigel held his gaze, unmasked now.

'Go ahead, doctor,' he said sourly, looking at him from under his black eyebrows. 'Isn't this the moment where you try to *read* my *soul*?'

From the silence that ensued, he surmised that he had been success-ful. Like hell he'd let himself be psychoanalysed. He'd had enough of that as a child. He didn't need to hear again that he was a disaster. He knew that full well. No chance he was going to let another shrink near his brain.

The way the man was watching him, as if he actually had already understood everything about him, filled his stomach with irritation.

'You have a strong defence mechanism there, Rigel,' he said shrewdly. It wasn't a compliment. 'Today you have decided that there is nothing I can do to help you. But one day, maybe, you might realise that instead of protecting you, this defence mechan-ism is devouring you.'

★   ★   ★

I lifted my gaze from the mug in my hands to the silent figure before me.

Rigel was sat at the piano. His hair was falling over his face and his hands were moving slowly, distractedly, over the keys.

His soft melody was the only sound throughout the whole house.

He had been like this since we got home.

When the office door had opened, the first thing I had seen was the psychiatrist's unsmiling face. The second was Rigel's icy, shadowy expression.

He had not said a word. I knew that it wasn't like him to babble meaninglessly, but I could tell from his silence that the meeting with the psychiatrist had not gone as planned.

I stepped closer and placed the steaming mug down next to him, making my presence known.

'Is everything okay?' I asked gently.

He didn't turn to look at me. He just nodded.

'Rigel . . . what happened with the doctor?'

I tried to be as delicate as possible. I didn't want to pry. I was just worried about him, and wanted to comfort him.

'Nothing important,' he replied tersely.

'You seem . . . upset.'

I tried in vain to catch his eye. He was staring at the white keys as if there was a world in front of him that I could not see.

'He thought he could come in,' he murmured, as if I was the only one who could understand. 'He thought . . . he could see inside me.'

'And was that his mistake?' I whispered.

'No,' he replied, shutting his eyes. 'His mistake was thinking that I'd let him.'

I wished I didn't feel that stinging emptiness inside my chest, but I couldn't control the emotion.

It was my mistake too, I wanted to admit, but I was too frightened of his reply.

Rigel was introverted, complicated and averse to affection but, above all, he was unique. I had known for some time now that he had built a barrier between himself and the world, a barrier that was rooted in his heart, lungs and bones, that was a part of him.

But I also knew that, beyond that barrier shone a universe of shadows and velvet. And it was precisely that rare and beautiful galaxy that I wished I could enter.

Slowly, tenderly.

I didn't want to hurt him.

I didn't want to change him, or worse, to *fix him*. I didn't want to wipe away his demons, I just wanted to sit with them and silently count the stars above us.

Would he ever open that door for me?

I lowered my gaze, defeated by my fears. Even though we had become closer, there were still moments in which we were too far apart to understand each other.

I turned around, thinking to give him some time alone, but something stopped me from leaving.

A hand around my wrist.

I slowly looked up. His eyes met mine and, after a moment, I granted his silent request. I turned around and sat next to him on the piano stool.

Before I knew what was happening, Rigel slid a hand under my knee and pulled me towards him.

The feeling of his body against mine sent a staggering shiver down my spine. The next moment, I was enveloped in his warmth and felt such a vibrant, intense happiness my head spun.

I still wasn't used to being able to touch him. It was a strange, wonderful sensation, always new, always powerful, a rush of dizziness.

I nestled my head into the crook of his neck, snuggling into his warm torso, and he sighed softly, relaxing.

For a moment, I thought that, maybe, if he was as affectionate as I was, he might have lowered his face and rested his cheek on my head.

'What do you think about when you play the piano?' I asked after a while of listening to his slow, melodious chord progressions.

'I try not to think.'

'And can you, not think?'

'Never.'

I had always wanted to ask him that. I had never heard him play anything happy. His hands always conjured wonderful, angelic, but heartbreaking melodies.

'If it makes you sad . . . why do you do it?' I found myself asking, looking up at him. I was entranced by the sight of his lips parting as he started to speak.

'There are some things that are out of our control,' he replied enigmatically. 'Things that . . . belong to us, that we can't get rid of. Not even if we want to.'

A sense of foreboding crept over me.

I stared at his fingers sliding slowly over the keys, and it suddenly dawned on me.

'Does it remind you of . . . *Her*?'

The memory of the matron still fed the monsters of my nightmares. Rigel had told me he hated her, and yet somehow, he had carried her with him since childhood.

'It reminds me . . . of what I've always been.'

Alone, I could almost hear him saying. *Abandoned, left by a closed gate.* I suddenly wanted him to stop playing.

I wanted to tear her from his soul, wipe him clean of every trace of that woman.

I wanted her far away from Rigel.

The idea that she had loved him, with her violent hands and her eyes tainted with anger, tormented me.

She was an illness. Her love was a bruise that she had inflicted on his heart for so long that just the idea of it revolted me.

'Why then?' I asked quietly. 'Why do you still play?'

I didn't understand. It was like picking a scab, knowing that it would bleed again.

Rigel was quiet for a moment, as if he was gathering a reply inside himself. I loved his silences as much as they scared me.

'Because *the stars are alone,*' he recited bitterly.

I tried to make sense of those sad words, but it was impossible.

I knew that Rigel was trying to give me a reply, in his own way, but for the first time I wanted him to unlock the doors to his heart and finally give me the keys to understand his secret language.

I wanted to know everything about him. Everything. Every thought, dream and fear. Every worry, desire and ambition.

I wanted to enter his heart like he had entered mine, but I was scared of losing my way.

Maybe Rigel knew no other way to express himself.

Maybe this was the only way he could, giving me pieces of his puzzle bit by bit, hoping that I would be able to fit them all together.

I wished I was up to the task. To make him see how wonderful, extraordinary and intelligent he was. And beautiful, for those who knew where to look, because a soul like his shone only for a few.

'You know what I say to myself when I feel sad?' I looked down at my Band-Aids and smiled. '*It doesn't matter how much it hurts. You can put a smile on a scar.*'

I gently placed my hand on top of his.

Rigel's hands stopped when he felt my skin on his. Initially, he didn't seem to understand, but then he started playing again. Together, our fingers lowered, danced over the keys, and as melodies came to life under our united hands, my heart swelled with emotion.

Together, we played. Slow and uncertain. Awkward and slightly faltering. But together.

And then, suddenly, increasingly lively and imperfect notes tumbled over one another. I found myself smiling as my hands clumsily followed his, trying to keep up, our wrists one on top of the other.

Our hands chased each other over the keys, brushing against each other, and I heard my laughter accompanying the notes.

I laughed. My heart laughed, my soul laughed, all of me laughed.

Together, we wiped away the sadness of the music.

We wiped away Margaret.

We wiped away the past.

And maybe, from now on, Rigel wouldn't think of *Her* when he played the piano.

But of us.

Our hands united.

Our hearts intertwined.

Our melody, full of clashes, mistakes and imperfections.

But also laughter, wonder and happiness.

He would remember my Band-Aids on his fingers, my weight in his lap and my scent on his skin.

We would defeat her together. Without even speaking.

Music, after all, is harmony born from chaos.

And we were the only song, the most spectacular and secret of all.

Rigel stopped.

He lifted his fingers to my neck and wove them through my hair. Slowly, he tilted my head backwards and looked into my face.

And I looked back at him, my cheeks hot and my eyes shining like laughing half-moons. The smile on my lips glowed with all the warmth exploding in my heart.

His eyes absorbed every detail of my face.

He looked at me as if there was nothing else in the world that was worth looking at that way.

★ ★ ★

There was a beauty in fragile things that he would never understand.

There was something that made them ephemeral, rare, to be enjoyed only while they lasted.

That was how Nica was.

He would never understand.

He would never understand how something so delicate could crack him, rather than getting cracked herself.

He would never understand how she managed to get inside, even when he was buried deep within himself.

She was beautiful. Her innocent eyes and her rosy cheeks, her sweet smile and that laugh, which simply shattered his soul.

She was smiling at him.

He wondered if there was anything in the world more powerful than Nica smiling at him.

Than Nica in his arms, letting him touch her, blowing away his every thought just by looking in his eyes.

She didn't cast away his torments. She took them by the hand. Even though they were twisted, extreme and wrong.

Even though they tried to ruin her.

She tamed them with a gentle touch, astounding them every time.

And Rigel knew why, even if he didn't understand how: even his torments were in love with her.

He wanted her with all his soul, even if that soul was a disaster.

He swallowed, and found himself tightening his grip on her hair. It was stronger than he was, his desire to hold her, to feel her, to fill his hands with her. He had never been tender, the only tenderness he had inside him bore her name.

Nica leant her temple against his arm, more calm and peaceful than he had ever dreamt of seeing her.

She looked him in the face, fearless.

And as that smile brought him to his knees again, Rigel realised that there were no words strong enough to express how he was feeling.

She was the most beautiful thing that he had ever had inside him. And he just knew that whatever the cost, he would protect her. At every moment. Every instant. For as long as he could.

★ ★ ★

Rigel's mouth closed on mine and a sweet shiver swept through my body. I melted against his warmth as he held me in that embrace, his fingers still entwined in my hair.

My fingers brushed along his clavicle then curled loosely around his neck. I moved my lips against his, responding gently, drawing a sigh from him.

I wanted to tell him that I loved it when he sighed like that, so quietly, almost secretly, as if he didn't want anyone to hear, not even himself.

He tilted my head further back, bending me to his will, and I let him. I was like putty in his hands.

His breathing was heavy, controlled, and his hands were touching me as if they wanted to probe even my soul, but at the same time were scared to.

I didn't understand why there was always that trembling in him. Trying to transfer my calmness to him, I stroked his neck gently and sweetly sucked his lip.

He tightened his grip on me. The wet smack of his kiss, his hoarse, hot breath on my swollen mouth, the taste of him stupefied me. His tongue was a blaze of heat.

Rigel wasn't kissing me. He was slowly devouring me.

And I was letting myself be devoured, because that was all I wanted.

Overcome, I recklessly nibbled his lower lip, and he let out a guttural moan. He grabbed my thigh and I found myself straddling him, his fingers pressing behind my knee and his other hand clenched against my side, urging my hips against his.

I was breathless.

I tried to catch my breath, but his hot, insatiable mouth seized mine, stunning me, bending me, biting me possessively.

I clung to him, trying to follow his rhythm. He pushed me against his crotch with such desire that my breath caught.

My head was spinning, my breathing ragged.

He rubbed me against him and the friction between our bodies was earth-shattering. I felt something close to panic, but hotter, more viscous, more urgent.

I tried to move, but he gripped my hips so fervently it was as if he wanted our bodies to fuse together. Our bodies were burning together, and when he bit me, I couldn't hold back a moan. I clung to his shoulders and squeezed my knees around him, my thighs trembling against his sides.

Everything narrowed to him.

His hands on my body.

The pressure of his pelvis.

Lips, breaths, tongues, hands . . .

I couldn't imagine what would have happened next, had we not been interrupted.

There was a knock at the door and I jumped abruptly.

His mouth moved away from mine. I realised I was short of breath, my cheeks flushed and my hands trembling.

Rigel lowered his face, panting slightly in the hollow of my throat. His hands were still gripping the curve of my hips and his muscles were slightly quivering, as if strained. He had more self-control than I did, more experience. His powerful body shook in a restrained manner, not like mine, which seemed wracked with destabilising sensations.

I couldn't detach myself from him, but when there was a second knock at the door, I realised I had no choice.

Rigel reluctantly let me go. I got up, my cheeks burning, and with my heart in disarray, ran to the door.

'Anna!' I exclaimed, finding her struggling with an enormous bunch of flowers. I took them off her, intoxicated by their fragrance.

I carried them into the kitchen and she placed the shopping bags on the counter, exhausted.

'It was so busy!' she burst out. 'I haven't had a minute's peace all day.'

I put the flowers in a vase and admired them. As always, they were wonderful. She noticed me looking and smiled radiantly.

'You like them?'

'They're gorgeous, Anna,' I said, entranced by their beauty. 'Who are you sending them to?'

'Oh, no, Nica. These aren't for delivery. They're for you.' She beamed at me, then announced, 'Your boyfriend sent them.'

29. Heart Against Heart

I was not a princess.
I would have sacrificed the fairy tale
to save the wolf.

'What?' I asked, incredulously.

Anna smiled as if to reassure me.

'The boy outside gave them to me,' she explained gently. 'He said they're for you . . . He was so awkward! I asked him to come in but he didn't want to. Maybe he was worried about being a bother,' she added, seeing my wide eyes.

At that moment, I noticed something white sticking out of the bouquet.

A note. With a drawing of a snail on it.

'Nica, you don't need to keep it a secret from me. It's not a problem if you have a boyfriend . . .'

'No,' I said urgently. 'No, Anna . . . you've got it wrong. He's not my boyfriend.'

She frowned gently. 'But he told me to give you these.'

'It's not what you think. He's just . . . just . . .'

A friend, is what I would have said before, but I was speechless. After what he had done, I could no longer call Lionel a friend. I bit my lip, hard. Anna must have sensed my discomfort.

'I must have got the wrong end of the stick then. I'm sorry, Nica. It's just that you've seemed so wistful lately, and then this boy turns up at the door with these wonderful flowers and I just thought . . .' She shook her head, smiling gently. 'Oh well. In any case, it's a beautiful bouquet. Don't you think so, Rigel?'

I felt a painful tension when I turned around.

Rigel was standing in the doorway. His face was expressionless and he didn't reply. He stared at the flowers, his eyes like bottomless pits. He looked away from them as Anna approached him, lowering his dark gaze to her as if she had torn him away from something silent and icy.

'Can I . . . have a word?' she asked him.

I didn't know why, but I noticed a flash of annoyance on his face. As if he already knew what she wanted to speak to him about.

He nodded and they moved away together.

'The doctor's called . . .' I heard Anna saying as they went up the stairs.

As I turned back around, my eyes fell on the note. I hesitated, before reaching out to read it:

> *I've wanted to write to you many times, but this seemed the best way to do it.*
> *I don't remember clearly what happened the other night, but I can't shake the feeling that I scared you. Did I? I'm sorry . . .*
> *When can we talk? I miss you.*

My hands were shaking. Every moment of what had happened flashed before my eyes like a scar: his lips, his hands, his arms constraining me, holding me still, my voice pleading with him.

In a sudden impulse, I tore the flowers from the vase, moved to the sink and flung open the cupboard underneath. I paused, holding the bouquet in midair, staring at the trash with trembling hands.

I gripped the stems, pressed my lips together. My throat tightened. I couldn't do it.

Those flowers didn't deserve it.

But there was something else.

Something, within me, the most ruined part of my heart, the part that the matron had deformed, couldn't bring myself to hate him, destroy him, wipe him away.

I saw his drawing of the snail sticking out through the petals and couldn't find the strength to chuck them.

I should have torn up that piece of card and thrown it away, but I couldn't.

I had never known how to tear things.

Not even with all the *tenderness* in the world.

More wonderful bouquets arrived over the next few days, each one of them with the same little note with the drawing of a snail.

Anna put them in a vase for me for when I got home.

One afternoon, there was also a packet of crocodile-shaped gummies. I found myself squeezing it in my hands before shoving it in a drawer to get it out of my sight. The next day, there were more lying on the table, wrapped up with ribbon.

'They're from an admirer,' Anna whispered one evening to Norman, who gave a conspiratorial 'Ooh'.

Klaus, on the other hand, did not appreciate all the commotion. He hissed at the vases that Anna left on the furniture, and nibbled those that weren't lucky enough to be placed out of harm's way. He seemed to understand that they weren't from Anna's shop, but from someone else.

One evening, I heard a rustling in the kitchen. I turned the light on and found his yellow eyes staring at me, a white petal sticking out from under his whiskers.

'Klaus,' I murmured, exasperated. I approached, and he turned his ears back, continuing to munch defiantly on the flower. 'Come on . . . You want another tummy upset?'

He wriggled away before I could lift him off the counter. For him, being picked up was probably a lot worse than an upset tummy.

I sighed quietly, looking at the bunch of white roses. I pulled out the flower that he had destroyed and turned it over in my hands. I already knew what the little note would say. I had stopped reading them because they just upset me.

I saw Rigel standing in the shadows near the door when I turned around. His black eyes, dark diamonds, fell on the white rose in my hands.

He hadn't said a thing the last few days. But I knew what this meant. Getting closer to him had meant learning to interpret the silences he wrapped himself in.

'This doesn't mean anything,' I whispered, before he could turn around. I didn't want his traumas and suspicions to make him withdraw from me, but I knew they had marked his heart ever since he was a child.

'But you haven't thrown them away.'

He turned his back on me and I bit my lip, wishing I could tear down all the walls that still existed between us. Sometimes, they

366

seemed like an endless staircase, full of cracks and broken steps designed to make me fall.

Sometimes, when I paused, exhausted, and looked up, I couldn't see the top.

But I knew that he was there.

Alone.

And I was the only one who could reach him.

'Nica?' I heard a knock on my door the following morning. 'Can I come in?'

Anna came in and found me still in my nightshirt. She smiled, said good morning, then took the hairbrush off me. She sat on the bed and started to brush my hair.

I felt an immeasurable love warming my chest. Her hands touched me carefully, comfortingly, making me dream of a life of caresses and smiles. It was the most wonderful feeling in the world.

'I've got a very important client next week,' she started to tell me. 'He wants me to supply the flowers for an event he's organising at the Mangrove Club. There'll be lots of people, and seeing the name of my shop among the suppliers will be like a dream come true.'

Her touch became uncertain, and she hesitated.

'But, well . . . the client in question is a friend of Dalma's. This wouldn't have been possible if she hadn't given them my name.' Anna lowered her voice. 'She's helped me so much. I want to be able to thank her. I'd have never gotten such a big opportunity without her.'

I turned.

She was waiting for my reply, but as I stayed silent, she continued.

'I haven't forgotten what happened,' she said sadly. 'I haven't forgotten what happened with Asia . . . There's not a day when I don't think about it. But they are important to me and Norman, Nica . . . They've shared moments with us that we'll never forget.' I sensed Alan's shadow reflected in her eyes. 'And so I wanted to ask you . . . I'd like to invite them over for . . .'

'Anna,' I interrupted her. 'It's fine.'

She stared at me with her piercing blue eyes.

That conversation made me realise how much she cared about me.

But I bore no grudge against Asia. Despite what had happened, what I felt towards her wasn't anger, but more a deep sorrow.

I didn't want to compromise her relationship with Anna. I had never wanted that. I knew how much they loved each other and I didn't want that to change because of me.

She held my face. 'Really?'

'Really.'

'You're sure?'

I nodded slowly. 'I'm sure.'

Anna exhaled shakily and her face broke into a smile. She stroked my cheek and I smiled back at her, basking in the glory of her touch.

She finished brushing my hair, asking my opinion on what she should cook. I told her that Norman would surely appreciate her famous gravy.

'I'll go and call Dalma,' she announced as we got up, and she ushered me down to breakfast.

I headed downstairs. I felt light, fresh and bright. I felt happy. Those moments with her did my heart good. I loved the fact that she always asked my opinion.

My spirits raised, I lingered in the doorway to the kitchen, and my heart soared even more when I saw Rigel sitting at the table with a book and a mug. His head was resting on his knuckles and his dark, dishevelled hair around his face stood out against the soft morning light. His eyes silently scanned the words on the page in front of him. Anna told me that he had woken early because of a headache.

I lingered in silence to watch him without him noticing me. I loved doing that. He was simply himself in those moments. Parts of himself that he usually kept hidden became visible. Once again, I was entranced by his delicate yet fierce looks. His pure, white skin, the sharp line of his eyebrows, his sculpted cheekbones and wild eyes. His careless gestures, those lips that dispensed bites and stinging smiles to whoever dared to come near.

He turned the page, and I wondered where such a masterpiece could have come from.

I came closer, trying not to distract him. I circled the table, and took advantage of there being no one else there to lean over and plant a kiss on his cheek.

Without warning.

When I straightened up, I saw he had frozen, his eyes startled.

He blinked and turned his face to me, surprised.

'Good morning,' I whispered tenderly. I gave him my sweetest, brightest smile, then picked up the coffee jug and moved towards the cabinet.

I felt his gaze still burning me.

'Would you like more coffee?' I asked.

Rigel stared at me for a moment, then nodded. I noticed his eyes looked more alert.

I moved back towards him and filled his cup. His eyes slid up my body to my face.

'Here,' I said softly.

I turned around, and his gaze fell on the silky reflection of my nightshirt.

I reached to get a cup for myself, but the shelf was empty. I stretched for the shelf above, but it was too high.

I stared at the row of cups, frowning, thinking about getting something to stand on, but the noise of a chair caught my attention.

Rigel stood up and approached me. He easily reached for a cup, taking his time to look down at me. His eyes fell on my face, lingering on my mouth and my wide, shining eyes.

'Thank you,' I smiled.

He held out a hand and I made to take the cup, but suddenly he seemed to change his mind. Lazily, he retracted his hand and hid the cup behind his back.

I stared at him, speechless.

'Rigel . . .' I pleaded. 'Can I have it?'

I traced the outline of his arms with my fingers, trying in vain to reach the cup. I looked up at him again. Maybe it was just the reflection of the sun, but I thought I caught a glint of entertainment in his eyes.

I smiled indulgently, and he asked, in a low voice, 'You want this?'

'Yes, please . . .'

I reached round and drummed my fingers on his wrist, but he showed no sign of giving it to me. I placed a hand on his side and he watched me with his feline eyes.

'Won't you give me something in exchange?' he murmured, hoarse and low.

His breath was warm and tempting. His body was hot under my fingers.

Since when had he been so playful?

This development excited and softened me. I tilted my head and brought his hand to my lips, without breaking eye contact. I kissed his skin. His fingers slowly rubbed against the mug.

Rigel stared at me with deep, liquid eyes. His fingers, still under mine, slid to my cheek. He stroked my lips with his thumb, and I slowly, sweetly kissed his fingertip, still looking at him, exposed and sincere.

He came closer, watching me with a burning attraction, as if he wanted to absorb everything about me – my scent, my lips, my eyes, my hands, even my innocence . . .

A loud noise made me jump.

We both froze.

Anna's voice broke the spell that was between us. 'Can someone get that?' she shouted. 'I think it's the mailman!'

Rigel had closed his eyes; his face had turned to stone. When he opened them again, I felt a powerful, icy chill.

I went to answer the door. His arm blocked my way, pushing me back again. He overtook me and headed decisively towards the front door, dropping the cup on the table as he went.

The delivery boy pulled up the visor of his cap when Rigel opened the door. He must have been new: he looked uncertainly at the little card he was holding and scratched a pimple.

'Hello . . . I have a delivery for this address,' he announced. The little card with the snail poked out of a beautiful bunch of flowers. 'Can you sign here?'

Rigel stared down at Lionel's little drawing with cutting eyes. Then he looked back up at the delivery boy and moodily muttered, 'I think there's been a *mistake*.'

'I don't think so,' the boy retorted. 'It's for Nicol . . . no, Ni . . . ca . . . Dover.'

Rigel flashed him a smile so polite it was frightening.

'Who?'

'Nica Dover . . .'

'Never heard of her.'

The boy lowered the hand holding the flowers, blinking, bewildered.

'B . . . but . . .' he stammered. 'The label on the mailbox says "Dover and Wilde" next to "Milligan".'

'Oh, them? They're the previous owners,' Rigel replied. 'We've just moved. They don't live here any more.'

'Where do they live now?'

'The cemetery.'

'The . . . *oh* . . .' The boy's eyes opened wide. His glasses almost fell off. He pushed them up his nose and they fogged up.

'Quite.'

'Holy smoke, I didn't know . . . Jeez, I'm sorry . . .'

'They were elderly,' Rigel informed him, clicking his tongue for dramatic effect. 'Over a hundred, both of them.'

'Ah . . . Well, good for them . . . Thanks all the s—'

'*You're welcome.*'

He slammed the door in his face.

And no pretentious bunch of flowers managed to cross the threshold.

That day, at least.

The evening when the Otters were coming for dinner came in the blink of an eye.

Anna was exuding an almost tangible cheeriness.

She looked at the tablecloth I was putting out, satisfied, then told me that she had bumped into Adeline on her way home.

Anna was very fond of her. She loved her kind manners and her sincere smiles. She knew how close Adeline and I were, and I got the impression that she was upset when Adeline had told her she was still looking for a job.

'Such a sweet girl,' she said, sliding the pie into the oven. 'I lent her my umbrella because she was getting soaked – she didn't even have a coat!'

She closed the oven door and adjusted the temperature, then took off the oven gloves, seeming somewhat troubled.

'Where did you say she lives?' she asked me.

'At Saint Joseph's,' I replied. 'She's been there since she was transferred. Now that she's of age she should leave, but until she finds a job . . .'

'I've invited her over for dinner too,' Anna said, slicing the bread. Still holding the cutlery, I looked up at her.

'I know it was just supposed to be us, but I couldn't help it. She's always so nice . . . and I know how close you are. It took some convincing for her to accept that it wouldn't be a bother, but in the end, she said she'd come.' She smiled gently. 'Are you pleased?'

My heart would have said yes if my thoughts hadn't betrayed me. Something inside me was still burning from the last time we had seen each other. On the one hand, hearing her say she felt nothing for Rigel had reassured me, but on the other, I feared this was not the truth. I had chosen to believe her, but the doubt still nagged at me.

Anna looked up at the clock. 'Oh, I didn't realise it was so late! Nica, you go and get ready, I'll finish up here.'

I nodded and went upstairs, letting my hair down.

I picked up my bathrobe and clean underwear and went into the bathroom, where I got undressed and turned on the shower before stepping under the hot water.

I washed carefully and used scented shampoo on my hair, enjoying all the foam.

After rinsing myself off thoroughly, I got out, careful to not get the floor wet. I put on my bathrobe and fastened it around my waist. It was a bit small even for me, but it was a lilac colour that I'd always really liked.

I slipped on my panties, hopping on the spot. I tilted my head and looked at the white lace tracing the curve of my pelvis. This was the first time that I had worn underwear that wasn't just plain cotton. It felt so soft against my skin.

Starting to rub my hair dry, I heard a voice calling me from downstairs.

'Oh, Nica, I forgot the lacy placemats! Could you fetch them? They're in the dresser in my bedroom!'

I rubbed the sleeve of my bathrobe over my forehead and heard Anna add, 'The bottom drawer!'

Without a second thought, I tightened the bathrobe around my waist, left the bathroom and retrieved what she had asked for. I held them out to her, halfway down the stairs.

'Sorry, I didn't realise you were still in the shower! Thank you! Yes, these are perfect. Now, go and get dry, sweetheart, or you'll get cold . . .'

She was worrying I'd get ill, so I went back into the bathroom, finding the door wide open.

I suppressed a little shiver and wrung my hair to get the remaining water out. As I started to brush my hair, I noticed the clean and neatly folded shirt next to the sink.

A black, button-up shirt.

A man's shirt.

I blinked at it, speechless. It hadn't been there before.

After a moment, I eventually noticed the presence behind me and whirled around.

I almost dropped the hairbrush.

Rigel was in the doorway. Immobile.

Under his dark hair, his black eyes were literally *planted* on me. In one hand he was holding his towel, and I realised he must have gone back to his room to fetch it, thinking that the bathroom was free.

'I . . . I . . .' I stammered, cheeks burning. 'I hadn't finished . . .'

I saw his hand slowly gripping the towel. My throat went dry, and I saw a glint of something raw in his eyes as they burned up my entire body: they slid over my trembling ankles, my wet thighs, the curve of my breasts and the exposed skin at my throat.

The sound of him taking a deep breath made my blood quiver. He looked me straight in the eyes and I swallowed under his white-hot gaze.

'Rigel, the guests are arriving. Anna's about the house and . . .' I gripped the hairbrush. I peered around him into the landing, and suddenly realised that we were facing one another, predator and prey. 'I need to leave,' I blurted out.

Rigel was staring at me, a storm churning in his eyes, as if his mind was working at breakneck speed.

We seemed to have gone back to the beginning, back to when I was too scared to pass near him for fear he might maul me. Even though now it might be for different reasons . . .

'Rigel,' I tried to reason with him. 'I need to get through.'

I hoped my voice didn't sound too feeble and intimidated; he'd already told me what effect that had on him. But he just slightly squinted his eyes and then . . . smiled.

In such a calm, relaxed manner that it was frightening.

'Of course,' he said, his voice controlled. 'Be my guest.'

I won't do anything to you, he seemed to be promising, but his gaze made me feel like a little mouse facing a panther.

I swallowed hard.

'If I come . . . you'll let me through?'

Rigel licked his lips, letting his eyes wander, and he seemed more like a beast standing guard outside its lair than ever before.

'*Mm . . .*' he agreed.

'No, say it . . .' I stammered.

'*What?*' He laughed, amused.

'That you'll let me through.'

He blinked with an innocence that, if it was possible, made him seem even more dangerous.

'I'll let you through.'

'You promise?'

'I promise.'

I looked at him for a moment, uncertain, before deciding to approach.

And Rigel did, in fact, keep his promise.

He let me through.

He let me through, but then . . . he grabbed me so impetuously that it took my breath away.

He swept me off my feet. Literally.

I heard the door slam shut. My back against the wall, his body towering over me, I opened my eyes wide and Rigel slid his hand through my hair, bringing his lips to mine.

He kissed me with a wild, overwhelming fervour.

I tried to breathe, to keep hold of my ability to think clearly. I tried to push him away, to disentangle myself, but he trapped my lip between his teeth and sucked it until my legs went soft.

He trapped me against him, with his wolfish ways and his scorching lips, and I felt suddenly powerless.

Reality throbbed, blurred. I felt like I was losing my mind.

I should have been rational, understood the risk, but my feelings for him were too strong. They shattered me, suffocated me, melted me. I stroked his throat and responded with all the desperation coursing through my body.

Rigel grabbed my thighs and lifted me up. The bathrobe came loose and slid off my shoulders. I curled my toes as he bit the curve of my neck, tasting my fresh skin like it was forbidden fruit, sweet and juicy. My slender body tensed under his teeth. My legs trembled.

I was still so unused to being able to touch him, and letting him touch me, that at the slightest touch I trembled and my cheeks burned. I felt weak, hot and electrified.

Rigel sought my mouth again, I couldn't keep up with him. As he parted my lips, I welcomed him with a little moan, and when his hot tongue entwined with mine, an ardent heat blazed from my stomach to my toes.

I didn't understand how he could drain my energy like that, and at the same time make me feel so alive. His wild desire and his musk were completely intoxicating.

Suddenly, his hands slipped under my bathrobe, and I tensed. Without realising, I tilted my head and pulled away.

His mouth was just a breath away from mine. I gasped, my eyes half-closed, dazed, my heart about to burst from my chest.

Rigel licked his swollen lips. His hair shadowed his face. He seemed to realise he had scared me, because he pressed his cheek against mine, trying to control himself. In that moment, I noticed the trembling way he was holding me close to him.

His touch was rough, boisterous, wild. But also fearful of hurting me.

I loved that contrast in him, because even if he seized me like a beast, sometimes he seemed to understand me like no one else. Rigel was not violent or tyrannical, he was just a little gruff. He was made that way, but that didn't make him wrong for me.

He gave me a long, gentle kiss on my neck, where my pulse was racing. His thumbs traced delicate circles on my skin and my body relaxed.

I leant my head against his with a sigh.

I calmed down, my mind languidly slipping into delirium.

I sought his lips again, and we plunged into a spiral of hot, deep kisses.

His tongue moved slowly now, sensually, and his fingers on my hips tightened passionately, unconsciously mirroring the rhythm of his tongue.

The taste of him went to my head. His hands sank into my flesh, rubbing me lustily against him. My cheeks flushed again, my breathing became laboured. A strange pressure pulsed in my lower stomach, sweet and unbearable.

His tongue set my mouth on fire. I found myself sucking it gently, almost shyly, making his fingers clench, digging deep into my skin.

I jumped. His fingertips trailed up my thighs, brushing against the lace of my panties. I clamped my legs around him until our breaths became synchronised again.

Rigel left my lips to bite my jaw, and then my neck, then my shoulder. He seemed lost, hungry, greedy for me. His hands squeezed my hips again, as if he craved the feeling of my flesh trembling, yielding, and moulding to his touch. I suppressed a moan of pain and arched into him. His fingers swept up my back, clutching my shoulder blades while his mouth stamped kisses on the sensitive skin behind my ear. My thighs tensed, my muscles quivered.

Rigel tilted me backwards and, pressing into my pelvis, put his lips to my breast.

I couldn't breathe.

My head was spinning.

He was driving me crazy, tormenting me. He was making me explode, making me pant, making me alive.

He annihilated me with a kiss, made me part of himself.

And I let him do it, because I desired no other wolf but him.

The feeling I experienced was so strong that it made me tremble. I wished it didn't always feel like we could be torn away from each other at any moment. As if there was never enough time, or words, nothing that we could experience fully.

I wanted to enter his heart and find out if he also felt this need that rendered everything else meaningless.

To belong to each other.

To stay together.

To hold each other tight.

Soul against soul.

And heart against heart.

For our cracks to converge, until there was no more fear . . .

The sound of the door handle came from far away.

Too far.

The door cracked open, and my soul jumped, my breath froze.

Quickly, I placed my hand on the door and pushed it back forcefully.

I held my breath as I heard Norman's voice through the door. 'Oh . . . Um . . . is there someone in the bathroom?'

I abruptly pulled away from Rigel and felt him resisting, trying to hold on to me.

'Oh, Norman, Nica was taking a shower!' Anna's voice approached and terror overwhelmed me. 'She might not have finished yet . . . Nica?' She knocked. 'Are you still drying off?'

I panted, terrified, realising I was a disaster. There were bite marks on my chest. I feebly closed the bathrobe around me, throwing an anxious look at Rigel. He was still watching *me*, as if nothing else mattered.

Anna knocked again. 'Nica?'

'Y . . . yeah,' I said shrilly. As Rigel licked his lower lip, I added, 'I . . . I haven't finished yet.'

'Is everything okay?'

'Yeah!'

'Okay, I'm coming in . . .'

'*No!*' I shouted in panic. 'No, Anna . . . I . . . I'm not dressed yet!'

'Don't worry, Norman's left! You've got your bathrobe on, right? I wanted to show you something.'

I was struggling to breathe. I bit my lip, hard, staring at the door, trying to think.

Very slowly, I lowered the handle and opened the door just enough to peer through the crack.

'Oh, Nica, you're still all wet,' she remarked. 'And your face is all red . . . Are you sure you're all right?'

I swallowed, trying to divert her attention to something else. I noticed then she was holding something.

A dress.

'Dalma made it,' she announced happily, seeing where I was looking. 'It's for you. A little gift, to make up for what happened . . . I know how much you like bright colours but . . . she thinks that a darker shade, with your complexion, would look magnificent. And . . . here . . .'

It was black.

The soft fabric looked like a glistening ink stain in her hands. I couldn't see it all, but I saw enough to grasp that it was nothing short of stunning.

'Do you like it?' Anna asked.

'It's beautiful, Anna,' I whispered, almost speechless. 'I . . . I don't know what to say. Dalma is inc—*Oh!*'

I flushed and pressed my hand over my mouth. Behind the door, Rigel had just pinched my damp thigh.

Anna looked at me, confused and concerned, and I nudged her back with trembling hands. I guided her down the hallway, urging her to move with me.

'I want to try it on right away! Dalma will be pleased . . . What time are they coming? Gosh, it's so late . . .'

I kept talking and pulling her along, not giving her a chance to look back and discover . . . *him*.

The dress from Dalma was perfect. It fit me like a glove, clinging to my curves as if it had been stitched onto me. The sleeves covered my arms down to my fingers, but left my shoulders exposed.

Flustered, I smoothed the dress over my hips, looking at my reflection in the mirror.

The subtle shine of black complemented my complexion. Far from making me look dull, it provided a rare contrast that made me feel as special as a star in the night sky.

It was wonderful.

I would never get used to seeing myself like that. To always smelling nice, to wearing clean clothes every day. To being able to take a shower whenever I wanted, to taking as long as I needed to warm up, to seeing myself in a mirror without cracks.

To feeling that sensation on my skin, as if I was something beautiful and worthy of admiration.

Inside, I was still a little girl who rubbed flowers on her clothes and patched them up herself. Some things I would never be able to wash off.

I slowly brushed my hair, and found myself thinking about how long it had grown. When I was little, every breath of wind had puffed it up, and I dreamt of flying free like a dragonfly. I was just a child at the time, but that didn't stop me from dreaming big.

I gathered my hair to one side and tried to braid it, but it kept snagging on my Band-Aids and got into such a messy tangle that I gave up. I left it loose and tidied it down my back.

When I went downstairs, the Otters had already arrived.

Norman was holding a bottle of wine and wearing a cheerful red sweater. He was telling them about a colony of mice he had found in some woman's attic. I greeted George, who smiled at me from behind his large moustache.

Dalma was in the kitchen with Anna. As soon as she saw me, she froze with a thrilled expression on her face.

'You've put it on . . .' she murmured, looking at me as if I was the one who had given her a gift. 'Oh Nica . . . You look amazing.'

She seemed almost moved when I went up to her and kissed her on the cheek.

'It's a special occasion,' I replied, looking at Anna, who smiled at me, touched. 'Thank you, Dalma . . . I don't know what to say. It's such a beautiful gift.'

She blushed happily. It was only then I noticed the figure behind her.

'Hi, Asia.'

Asia looked as smart and sophisticated as ever. Her hair was in a ponytail and the way she moved made her look like a princess, but my greeting was met by an awkward silence. She looked away from me, towards the ground.

'Hi,' she murmured, not looking at me.

For the first time, she didn't seem haughty, but almost . . . embarrassed.

'I'll put these in the car,' she said, gesturing to several packets of dried lavender and jasmine that smelt incredible. They must have been a gift from Anna.

'Do you need a hand?' I asked, following her, but her reply was rather brusque.

'No.'

I stopped, letting her continue.

Her slender legs carried her to the front door and she pulled out the car keys. But something caught her attention. Asia froze, and I knew why.

The framed photo of Alan was gleaming on the table in the hall. The glass needed replacing, there was a small crack towards the bottom. Her eyes lingered on the crack, over which was carefully placed a small, blue Band-Aid.

Blue like Alan's eyes.

Asia slowly looked up at me. Her gaze wandered to my hands, covered in colourful Band-Aids, and then she looked me in the face. For a moment, I saw something gentle, fragile in her eyes, something that she had never conceded before.

Remorse, and pain, but also . . . resignation.

She turned and went outside.

I watched her disappear through the front door and headed back into the kitchen.

I was filling the gravy boat when the doorbell rang.

'Here we are.' Anna lifted her wrist to her forehead because of the heat from the oven. The pie looked amazing. 'Nica, can you go and check that everything's ready, please?'

I reached the dining room to make sure that everything was in order, but froze when I passed the door to the hall.

It hadn't been Asia who had rung the doorbell, but Adeline.

Her soft blonde hair brightened the hall. She must have just taken her coat off, but I couldn't see her clearly just by peering through the doorway.

'You keep looking at me like that.'

'Like what?' a deep voice pressed her. Inexplicably, I tensed.

It was Rigel. He had opened the door for her, and now was look-ing at her, haughty and suspicious.

'Like . . . as if I was always in the wrong place,' she said with a dented smile. Her pale eyes looked at him in a uniquely knowing way. 'You asked me to stay out of it, and that's what I'm doing. That's what I've always done . . . Am I wrong?'

What did she mean?

Out of what?

They exchanged a long look before Rigel glanced away. I saw something flash through Adeline's eyes that I couldn't put my finger on. Something too full of need, warmth and compassion, that he let slip over him, or simply didn't notice.

But I did. And once again I got the impression that I was missing something, that I was lagging behind, that I didn't know what they were talking about . . .

There was a world behind those black eyes that I couldn't touch. A soul that Rigel had never let anyone see.

So why?

Why was she speaking as if she understood him?

As if she knew him?

Suddenly, they noticed me.

Adeline's eyes flashed and met mine, and I exchanged glances with Rigel. He seemed to be so focused on figuring out what I had over-heard that I felt even more out of place.

'Nica.' Adeline smiled at me hesitantly. 'Hi . . .'

'Hi,' I said, dazed and confused. She pulled a packet out of her bag.

'I brought some dessert,' she said, embarrassed. 'I wanted to bring flowers, but seeing as Anna sells them it seemed a bit dumb . . .'

She came closer, looking at me, then smiled sweetly. 'You look beautiful,' she whispered, as if the most beautiful flower was me.

I watched her go as she walked past me. As I turned back around, Rigel came towards me.

My mind went blank. I was lost for words.

He was wearing a pair of dark pants and a white shirt that fit his chest impeccably. The light-coloured fabric did not clash at all with his appearance, but made his eyes look like two magnetic, dangerous chasms. His dark hair and his sharply defined eyebrows stuck out more than usual. His seductive allure was shattering.

I stared at him, wide-eyed and pink-cheeked, taken aback.

He stopped in front of me, perfectly at ease in his ruthless beauty. I felt overwhelmed by how intensely he was looking at me. He tilted his face to one side and studied my outfit, how the dress hugged my gentle curves. For a moment, it seemed as if he was about to say something, but then, as if in some internal battle he had learnt to lose, he swallowed his words.

I wondered why he always looked at me like that. It was as if he was shouting something at me, but at the same time, praying that I wouldn't understand it. I despaired in my attempts to understand him, but, however much I had learnt to read his silences, his glances remained an impossible mystery.

What did Adeline know?

And why had he opened up his secret world to her?

Did he not trust me?

My insecurities assailed me. I tried to pay them no attention, but they crawled over my skin. I stared into Rigel's eyes and my heart screamed with the desire to bind him to me, to be important, to enter into his soul as he had entered mine.

What was I to him?

'Oh, here you are!' Norman appeared in the doorway and smiled at us. 'We're ready! Do you want to come through?'

The dinner was warm and lively.

The table was beautifully laid with the good cutlery and the serving dishes steaming in the centre, amongst the clinking sounds of the crockery and delicious aromas.

Adeline had sat on the other side of the table, deliberately leaving the seat next to Rigel free for me.

I stole glances at her, feeling a sheen over my heart. Seeing her sitting amongst the people I loved made me feel tender, conflicting emotions. I felt an immense fondness for her, but also a lot of uncertainty.

'Would you like some gravy?' she asked Asia, who looked at her with suspicion.

In response, Adeline smiled and kindly poured her some. Asia gave her a wary look as she also took a piece of bread for her and placed it next to her plate.

'There's such an incredible smell in this house!' George announced. 'I can almost taste the flowers!'

'Is there maybe something we don't know?' Dalma said in turn.

They turned to look at Anna, who chuckled. 'Oh, no, don't look at me! This time I've got nothing to do with it.' She looked at them one by one, then added excitedly, 'They're all for Nica.'

I choked on my pie. I swallowed with effort as everyone turned to me.

'For Nica?' Dalma stared at me with warm, wondrous eyes. 'Nica . . . is someone sending you flowers?'

'She's got a secret admirer,' Norman said awkwardly. 'A boy who sends her bouquet after bouquet, every day . . .'

'A *suitor*? How romantic! Who is he? Do you know him?'

I swallowed, extremely uncomfortable, and fought the urge to nibble my Band-Aids at the table.

'He's a classmate.'

'He's such a nice boy!' Anna intervened excitedly. 'So attentive . . . A cup of tea seems the least we could offer him in exchange for all these gifts! He's the same boy you went to get an ice cream with, right? Your friend?'

'He . . . yes . . .'

'Why don't you invite him over one of these days?'

'I, well . . .'

I jumped, my entire body tensing.

Under the table, a hand had landed on my bare knee.

Rigel's fingers were touching my skin. I stiffened.

What was he doing? Had he gone mad?

I clenched my napkin and tensely stared at everyone around the table, one by one.

Dalma was right next to me.

Had she seen?

She turned to look at me and I felt my heart jump to my throat.

'Not every boy sends flowers. It takes a particular sensitivity . . . don't you think?'

'Yeah . . .' I swallowed, trying to seem normal, but at my reply, Rigel's fingers clenched my knee. I couldn't hold back a shudder.

When Dalma turned away, I seized the moment to grab his wrist and tear his hand away. I shifted to one side, my cheeks tingling.

Everyone misunderstood my blush.

'I bet he's handsome . . .'

'Handsome and in love!'

'In . . . in love?' I stammered feebly.

Anna smiled at me. 'Well, he wouldn't send all these flowers to just anybody, would he? Lionel certainly feels something very deeply for you . . .'

I wanted to say something, but they all started speaking at once, bewildering me. They all spoke over each other, my thoughts got muddled and I couldn't understand a thing.

'How long have you known him?'

'What a charming boy . . .'

'We were in love at their age, too, weren't we George?'

'Nica,' Anna burst out, 'why don't you invite him over tomorrow afternoon?'

The abrupt noise of a chair made me jump. In the excitement, almost no one noticed Rigel leaving, slipping through the door, followed by my and Adeline's eyes.

My heart felt frozen and constricted, a feeling that grew stronger as I noticed that Asia was still staring at his empty chair. Slowly, she looked up at me.

It suddenly felt as though I was sitting on pins and needles.

I lowered my gaze and, murmuring some excuse, left the room full of chatter behind me. They paid almost no attention, and for once I was grateful.

I looked for Rigel, and suddenly heard a noise from the room at the end of the hall. I hurried towards it, and when I got to the doorway, my eyes opened wide. He was there, tearing to pieces each of the flowers that Lionel had sent.

'No! Rigel! Stop it!' I grabbed his wrist and he jerked away from me so abruptly that petals swirled down around him in a silent spiral. His eyes pierced mine and I trembled.

'*Why?*' he demanded angrily. 'Why didn't you say anything?'

I stared at him, wide-eyed, but didn't have time to reply before he took a step towards me.

'What do you feel for him?'

A dull, heavy sensation made me incapable of tearing my eyes away from Rigel.

'What?'

'What do you feel for him?'

His voice was a growl, but there was something vulnerable pulsing in his eyes, like a wound. I stared at him incredulous, because that question shook all the trust we had struggled to build together.

'Nothing . . .'

Rigel looked at me with a burning bitterness. He slowly shook his head, as if he was facing a truth he didn't want to accept.

'You can't do it . . .' he burst out. 'After everything he's done . . . after how pushy he was, after he almost laid his hands on you, you *still* can't bring yourself *to hate him*.'

It was as if his words scratched me. They struck me, penetrated my skin, because . . . they were the truth.

I couldn't deny it.

It didn't matter how much I got hurt. I could not hate . . . try as hard as I might.

And yet I had been taught hatred. The matron had imprinted it on my skin in a way that I would never be able to forget.

She had broken me, stamped on me, deformed me. Pummelled me and cracked me. She had bent me so far that I would always be like that, warped and fragile like a child.

That was what she had left me. A faulty heart, that looked in others for the goodness it couldn't find in *Her*. A moth that pursued the light in everything, even if it meant getting burnt.

I stretched out my hand. I looked at Rigel with dull eyes, and shook my head too, swallowing that awareness.

'It's not important,' I said quietly.

'*Not* important?' Rigel repeated, his black eyes full of hurt and anger. 'Oh, it's not? So what is actually important for you, Nica?'

No.

Anything but that.

I clenched my fists shakily.

He was the last person who could say that.

'I know what's important,' I whispered, my voice not even sounding like my own. I felt my blood boiling under my skin and looked up at him, my gaze watery and shiny. 'I'm the only one who seems to have grasped what really matters.'

A hard look flashed across his face.

'What?'

'*It's you!*' burst out of my mouth. 'You're the one who has never cared about anything or anyone, you haven't even realised the way that Adeline looks at you! You're behaving as if this was nothing, as if there weren't any risks! You know what will happen if we're found out, Rigel? Do you even care?'

My insecurities got the better of me. I tried to push them away but they poisoned my heart, reminding me that I was fragile, soft and frightened. For the first time, my fear of not being enough was projected onto Rigel.

'You're just playing with fire, it almost seems like you're enjoying it. Even at the table, in front of other people, you're there tempting fate, and then you dare to suggest that it's *me* who doesn't care?'

I wasn't myself, but I couldn't stop. I couldn't stand it.

For us, I had had to make compromises with myself, and lie to the only person who had ever truly loved me. The only person I never wanted to deceive: Anna.

I had chosen him, but that choice had broken my heart.

I'd make that choice ten times over, then a hundred and then a thousand, if it meant staying with him.

It would break my heart every time, but I would still choose him.

I would always choose him.

But I couldn't say if it was the same for Rigel.

He had never given me a single assurance.

I had told him that I wanted him by my side, I had opened up my most intimate and fragile side to him, exposed myself to his silence.

'I'm risking everything. Everything I care most about. But you don't even seem to realise. Sometimes you act as if you don't care, as if this was just a ga—'

'*Don't,*' he interrupted me sharply, closing his eyes. 'Don't say it.'

He opened his eyes, and I saw something trembling furiously in his gaze.

'Don't *try* to say it.'

I looked at him, my gaze dull, and this time it was me who shook my head.

'I don't know what this is for you,' I whispered bitterly. 'I never know what you're thinking . . . or what you're feeling. You know me better than anyone else, but me . . . I know hardly anything about you.'

Suddenly, it seemed as if we weren't in the same room, but light years apart.

'I told you that I wanted you for what you are . . . as you are . . . I told you the *truth*. I never expected you to say the same, nor that you'd suddenly open up to me overnight. The truth,' I whispered shakily, 'is that I'd be fine with whatever. All I want is to understand you. But the more I try to do that, the more you push me away. The more I try, the more I get the feeling you want me far away. Far away from you. Farther than anybody else . . . And I don't know why. We're broken together, but you never let me in, Rigel. Not even for a moment.'

I felt completely drained.

Rigel's eyes were an impenetrable black.

I wondered where he was, behind those eyes.

If he felt the same pain that I did, the need for me to be part of his world as he was part of mine.

My heart ached even more. My vision blurring, I looked down. His silence was yet more proof that I did not have the strength to listen.

★ ★ ★

His fists were trembling.

The writhing inside him rose up like a monster.

He couldn't do it any more, he couldn't carry on being himself . . .

He had never felt so trapped inside his own body, never wanted so badly to be someone else, anyone else.

She wanted to *come in*.

It would just hurt her.

She thought there was something in there, something soft and right, but there wasn't. Inside, there were just remnants, fear and a soul oozing with torment. Scratches and anger. Pain and a sense of powerlessness.

Inside, he was a disaster.

He had learnt to shun connection, affection, everything. He had even tried to shun her, had pushed her away, scratched her, tried to tear her away from him. Nica had taken everything from inside him. With her shining smile and her tenderness. With her unique light he had never been able to understand.

He had always prayed that she would look at him, because the whole world seemed to shine in her eyes.

In Nica's eyes, not even he appeared quite so wrong.

But now she was finally looking at him . . . he was wracked with fear.

He was scared she would see how wrong he was, how worn out, rotten and beyond repair. He was scared of not being understood, of being refused, of seeing her realise that she could have better.

He was scared he would be abandoned again.

That was why he could not let her in.

One part of him wanted to keep her with him always. Another part, the part that loved her more than he loved himself, couldn't shut her in that cage of thorns.

Nica looked down sadly.

And Rigel said nothing, because, even though she didn't know it, that silence cost him more than any words.

He was disappointing her again. Why was it that the more he tried to protect her from himself, the more he ended up hurting her?

Nica left, taking all the light with her. Watching her disappear, Rigel felt his heart tighten and *all* his thorny regrets bury deeper into him, one by one.

30. Until the Very End

I do not want the happy ending.
I want the grand finale.
Like in those magic shows
that leave you open-mouthed
and believing, just for a moment,
that magic is real.

No one was breathing.

Rigel watched them all, in a line, standing stock still next to one another.

He wasn't with them. As ever.

The matron's shadow paced in front of their little bodies like a black shark.

'Today, a woman told me that one of you was making signs to her from the window.'

Her voice was like slow, screeching glass.

Rigel watched the scene from a distance, sat on the piano stool. He hadn't missed the glare of pure hate that Peter had thrown him.

He never got punished with them.

'She told me that one of you was trying to tell her something. But she didn't understand what.'

No one breathed.

She looked at them, one by one, and Rigel saw her fingers closing around the elbow of the girl next to her.

Adeline tried not to stiffen, not even when the matron started crushing her arm in a slow, violent grip.

'Who was it?'

They were all silent. They were scared of her, and that was enough to make them guilty in her eyes. That was how she saw them.

Adeline's skin turned purple. She was gripping her so hard that he felt his own gaze was screaming with her pain.

'Ungrateful brats,' the matron hissed with inhuman hatred.

Rigel instantly understood what the reddish glare in her eyes was. It was a flash of violence.

Everyone started trembling.

Margaret let Adeline go. Then, she mechanically unfastened her leather belt.

Rigel saw Nica, at the end of the line, trembling more than all the others. He knew that belts terrified her. Something scratched inside of him as he watched her, like fingernails scraping against his skin. He realised his heart had frozen and his palms were sweating.

'I'll ask again,' the matron said, walking slowly up and down the line. 'Who. Was. It?'

He saw them shudder. He could say that it was him. After all, he had taken the blame for something he hadn't done before. But it wouldn't work this time. He had been with her all day.

And Margaret was too angry. When she was this angry, someone always had to suffer the consequences.

She wanted to inflict pain.

She wanted to beat them.

Not because she was sick, or disturbed. But just because she wanted to.

And Rigel couldn't expose himself, couldn't take all the blame, or she would stop trusting him, and giving him more freedom than the others, and then he wouldn't be able to protect Nica.

'Was it you?'

She stopped in front of a girl with quaking knees, who frantically shook her head, looking down. She was wringing her hands so tightly that her fingers had gone white.

'And you, Peter?' she asked the little red-haired boy.

'No,' he replied feebly.

That frightened cheep had always been his condemnation. The leather in the matron's hands creaked.

Rigel knew it wasn't Peter. He was too scared to do anything.

Peter was tender, delicate and sensitive. That was his only fault.

'Was it you?'

'No,' he repeated.

'No?'

Peter started to cry because, like all the others, he sensed she wanted to let off steam.

She grabbed him by the hair and he held back a yelp. He was little, scrawny, with dark shadows under his eyes that dug into his cheeks. He looked pathetic, his nose running and his eyes full of fear.

Rigel glimpsed the disgust in the matron's gaze, and wondered if there was a single crumb of humanity in that woman.

Once again, he swore to himself that he would never become attached to her, not even if she cuddled him, cared for him like a mother and told him he was special. Not even if she was the only one who ever gave him a crumb of affection.

He could never forget her other face.

She did not usually punish them in front of him. She would always make sure that he was in another room, as if he didn't know what she did, what a monster she was. But this time, it was different. This time, she had flown into such a rage that all she could think about was beating them.

'Turn around,' she ordered.

Peter's eyes filled with tears. Rigel hoped he wouldn't wet himself again, or she would make him regret staining the carpet.

The matron made him turn round and he lifted shaking hands to his head to protect himself, whispering prayers that would never leave that room.

The noise was so loud that everyone held their breath. She lashed him on his back and on the backs of his thighs, where no one would see the marks.

His tiny body crumpled under the thundering strike, and she seemed to despise him even more, just because he had reacted to the pain.

How could he do it? How could he be loved by such a monster?

Why was the only person who gave him affection so inhuman?

He felt even more wrong. Twisted. Inadequate.

Rejection pushed inside him until it broke him apart. Even more.

He couldn't become attached. He couldn't feel love. Love was wrong.

'I want to know who it was,' the matron hissed, the veins on her temples throbbing with fury. She hated not finding the culprit.

She prowled around the children, the belt clenched in her fist. She came up to Nica. With horror, Rigel saw that she was convulsively nibbling her Band-Aids. She did this when she was nervous, and the matron knew it.

She stopped in front of her, her cruel eyes lit up by a sudden realisation.

'Was it you?' she whispered menacingly, as if Nica had already confessed.

Nica stared at the belt in her hands. She was pale, little and trembling. Rigel felt his heart pounding in his ears.

'*Well?*'

'*No.*'

She slapped her so hard that her little neck cracked. Rigel felt his fingernails digging into his palms as Nica turned around. A tear fell down her cheek, but she didn't even dare to wipe it away.

The matron wrung the belt in her hands, and Rigel felt his heart racing – he could see her anger, her mad eyes, her hand raising, hitting, the belt flashing through the air – and something screamed inside of him.

Panic overcame him.

He did the only thing that came to mind. He looked around and grabbed the scissors the matron had used to cut the sheet music. Then, in a sudden, crazy gesture, instinctively, feverishly, he sunk the blade into his palm.

He regretted it immediately. Pain exploded furiously and the scissors clattered to the floor, making everyone turn around.

Red droplets stained the carpet, and when the matron noticed, the hand that was about to strike Nica lowered. She ran towards him and cradled his palm as if it was an injured sparrow.

It was only then that Rigel met Nica's eyes. They were scared, fragile, distraught.

His vision went hazy with the pain. But he'd never forget her gaze.

He'd never forget her eyes, as pale as freshwater pearls.

That light would stay inside him forever.

★ ★ ★

The smell of the river was fresh and strong. The noise of the road-works on the bridge was lost in the distant churning of water.

I stared at the workmen without really seeing them. They were redoing the bridge parapet and for several weeks, instead of a railing there had been an orange net that obscured the view.

I had gone there to feel the grass under my feet and the reassuring embrace of fresh air, but my heart was throbbing like a wound. It was all I could feel.

When I got back home, a voice welcomed me. 'You're here!'

Anna had her coat on, ready to leave, and I nodded slowly. I saw her eyes searching my face, but I hid behind my hair.

'There's cake through there,' she said in that soft voice I loved so much. 'Do you fancy something to eat?'

I replied that I wasn't very hungry. I felt slack, extinguished. Her forehead wrinkled with worry and I tried to smile.

'Nica . . . I'm sorry about last night.' She gave me an embarrassed look. 'I realise that . . . I might have gone too far. All that about Lionel and the flowers. I'm sorry.' She tucked my hair behind my ears. 'I'm just so happy that there's someone who appreciates you for who you are. Making you uncomfortable was the last thing I wanted.'

I put my hand on hers, and whispered, 'It's all okay, don't worry.'

'It's not,' Anna murmured. 'You seem so despondent. Ever since you came back to the table last night . . .'

'It's nothing,' I lied, finding my voice. 'It's . . . I'm just a little tired, that's all.' I softened my gaze. 'You don't need to feel guilty, Anna. You didn't do anything to upset me.'

'You're sure? You would tell me, wouldn't you?'

I hoped she couldn't sense my heart tremble at that question.

'Of course. Don't worry.'

In moments like those, I couldn't work out what hurt me the most. What I felt inside, or having to hide from her what I couldn't tell a soul.

Anna's eyes were understanding. But she was the last person in the world I could confess my feelings to.

'Put a scarf on.' I smiled at her. 'There's a bit of a breeze.'

She thanked me. I waited for her to leave, said goodbye, but as soon as she had gone, the same feeling of emptiness returned.

I slowly walked to the living room and sat down on the couch, wrapping my arms around my knees.

I wondered if this was how Billie and Miki were feeling, as if something fundamental was off kilter. I just wanted to talk to someone about it.

'I thought it would come from outside.'

Klaus, curled up on the couch next to me, stared at me with an eye half open. At that moment, he seemed like the only one I could confide in.

'When it all started . . .' I whispered. 'I thought that any obstacle that would come between us would come from the outside. That we'd somehow . . . tackle it together.'

I turned towards him, feeling my eyes mist over.

'I was wrong,' I murmured. 'I didn't take the most important thing into account.'

Klaus watched me in silence. I slipped down, huddling into myself as if to protect myself from the world.

I let tiredness take over my thoughts. I fell asleep, but not even in sleep was I able to find the peace I hoped for.

At a certain point, I thought I felt someone touching my face.

Fingers . . . brushing my cheek.

I'd recognise that touch among a thousand others.

'I want to let you in,' I heard. 'But I'm a path of thorns inside.'

It was as if he knew no other way to say it. His melancholic tone burned my heart. I tried to cling on to reality, to struggle to stay awake, but it was in vain. His words drifted away with me and vanished.

It was evening by the time I woke. As I opened my eyes, I felt two things weighing down on me.

The first one was those words, which I was sure hadn't been a dream.

And the other . . .

The other was Klaus, curled up on my chest, snoozing with his nose tucked in my neck.

The next day, Rigel didn't come to school with me.

When Norman came downstairs, he told me with an awkward smile that he would give me a lift, that Rigel wasn't feeling well, his headache from the previous day hadn't passed yet.

I wasn't able to pay much attention in class that day. My mind kept wandering to the previous afternoon, to the few words he had whispered when he thought I was sleeping.

When I left school, under a drizzly sky, I glanced around, hoping I wouldn't bump into Lionel. So far, I had managed to avoid him. Even during lab I had sat as far away from his desk as possible.

'Are you heading home?'

Billie looked at me from under her mass of curls. I met her lingering, opaque gaze and wrinkled my brow in a contrite smile.

'Yeah . . .' I murmured softly.

She nodded silently. The dark circles under her eyes were visible even in the shadow of her hood.

'Okay,' she whispered.

I realised she was feeling the same loneliness as me.

Billie needed me. She needed a friend . . .

As she was turning away, I grabbed her hoodie.

'Wait,' I stopped her. She turned and met my gaze. 'Do you fancy . . . going to grab something to eat?'

I saw her hesitate. 'Now?'

'Yeah . . . There's a café at the crossroads, just by the bridge. Will you come with me?'

Billie looked at me for a moment, uncertain. Then she looked down and took her phone into her shaking hands.

'I . . . I'll tell Grandma that I'm staying out . . .'

I smiled at her softly. 'Okay. Let's go.'

I spent the whole afternoon with her.

We ate sandwiches and sat on the little couches in the café, sipping chocolate frappés as the rain fell outside.

Billie spoke to me about a lot of things. She told me that her parents were supposed to be back by the end of the month, but by now she had given up all real hope.

I listened to her patiently, never interrupting her. I had thought that she wanted to vent, but I realised that she just needed some company.

When we parted ways towards evening, she still seemed a little dispirited, but her eyes were flickering with a silent relief.

'Thank you,' she said.

I gave her an encouraging smile and squeezed her hand.

I walked home as the first streetlights came on, and suddenly my phone rang. I pulled it out of my pocket and checked who it was before answering.

'Anna? Hi . . .'

'Hi, Nica, where are you?'

'I'm on my way,' I replied. 'Sorry, I'm running late. I should have told you.'

'Oh, honey . . . I'm not at home,' she sighed. I pictured her with her hand on her forehead. 'This event at the club is driving me mad! I've still got deliveries to check, I really can't put them off until

tomorrow . . . No, Carl, those don't go there,' I heard her saying to
her assistant. 'No, dear, those go with the begonias by the entrance,
over there . . . Oh, I'm sorry, Nica, but I really don't know what time
I'll finish tonight . . .'

'Don't worry, Anna,' I reassured her. 'I can make something warm
for Norman when he gets home . . .'

'Norman's having dinner with colleagues this evening, remember?
He'll be back late, that's why I've called you . . .'

I heard her sighing as I opened the gate.

'Rigel's been alone all day . . . Can you go and see how he's doing?
Just to make sure he hasn't got a fever,' she said anxiously.

I recalled the time I'd had to call her when they were at the conference, ages ago, when Rigel was so ill. Anna was always worrying.

I bit my lip, then nodded. I remembered she couldn't see me, and
as I entered the house and dropped my keys in the bowl, replied that
it was all fine and she didn't need to worry.

'Thanks,' she murmured, as if I was her guardian angel. Then she
said goodbye, and I hung up.

I took my soggy shoes off so I wouldn't get the floor dirty and
went to go find him. I couldn't see him anywhere, so I deduced he
must be in his room and walked upstairs.

But I hesitated outside his door. My heart was thumping in my chest.

The truth of the matter was that I had been thinking about him all
day, and now it came to it, I was scared of confronting him.

I steeled myself, lifted my hand and knocked.

I went in. The dim light coming through the window marked out
the edges of the room.

Rigel was enveloped in shadows. My chest tight, I saw the silhouette of his body, and for a moment, listened to him breathing.

Outside it was raining, but the smell of the rain wasn't enough to
mask his musk, which diffused into my blood and reminded me how
deeply he had penetrated my soul.

Tenderly, I approached and placed a hand on his face. It was hot,
but fortunately not feverish.

I sighed. I let my fingertips brush against his skin, giving him a
hidden caress, then turned around. I had already reached the door,
but stopped at the sound of his voice.

'I can only hurt you.'

I froze. I heard those words as if, deep down, somewhere, I already knew.

'That's who I am . . .' he murmured, disillusioned. 'And it's all I know how to be.'

I stared ahead, my eyelids drooping, my expression flat, as if my heart was a dusty diamond that had stopped shining.

Slowly, I turned around. Rigel was sitting up, his hands gripping the edge of the bed, his face downturned, shadowed by his hair. It was as if he didn't want me to see him.

'That's the truth . . .'

'I can sleep at night,' I interrupted him, drained but determined. 'I don't need to keep the light on any more. I'm not staying up because I'm scared to fall asleep. The nightmares haven't gone away . . . but they're fading. They're fading, because in that blackness, I don't see the cellar, but your eyes. You're healing me, Rigel. And you don't even realise it.'

He had filled me with stars. And he couldn't see it.

'Healing *is possible* . . .' I whispered, really believing it.

At that point, however, Rigel looked up. And I understood that whatever truth his gaze held was out of my reach. He had never let anyone see him.

'Something in me is broken . . . and won't ever heal.'

'*The stars are alone*,' he had said to me some time ago in the same cryptic tone.

I realised that he was telling me something important, that he was trying, in his way, to make me understand.

The door to Rigel's heart no longer seemed like a portcullis outside an impenetrable fortress, but like the entrance to a dense thicket of thorns, etched in crystal, ready to collapse in on itself.

'There are some things you can't fix, Nica. And I'm one of them. I'm a *disaster*,' he whispered adamantly. 'And I always will be.'

'I don't care,' I whispered sincerely.

'No, you don't care,' he repeated, almost harshly. 'Nothing is ever too far beyond repair for you. Nothing is ever scary, dark or bad enough. That's how you are.'

'You're not beyond repair,' I replied.

Why did he keep condemning himself to loneliness? It hurt me, because he wouldn't let me stay with him through that pain.

He stared at me with a bitter, contemptuous irony.

'Every tale has a wolf . . . Don't pretend you don't know what part I'm playing in this one.'

'Enough!' I stubbornly protested. 'Is that what you think you are to me? The monster that ruins the story? Is that how you want me to see you?'

'You have no *idea* how I'd like you to see me,' he whispered.

I stared at him, stricken. I tried to hold his gaze, but he clenched his jaw and turned away, seeming to regret what he had said.

'Rigel . . .'

'You think I don't *know*?' he interrupted angrily. His eyes shot daggers at me.

For a moment, the burning, submissive look he gave me made me think of a wolf looking up at *his* moon.

'I know how much it's costing you. *I know.* I can read it in your eyes, every single day. All your life, that's all you've ever wanted. A family.'

I froze. I hadn't realised I had come closer to him.

'This situation is suffocating you. You don't want to lie, but you're forced to every day.' And then, centring in on my heart, he added, 'You'll *never* be happy like that.'

A boiling sensation gripped my throat. Tears were blurring my vision, affirming my vulnerabilities.

Rigel was reading my soul.

He knew what drove my most shining desires.

He knew my dreams, my torments, my fears.

I had been a fool to think he hadn't realised.

I could not hide.

Not from him.

His gaze was the condemnation I had never stopped dreaming of.

His voice was a wound that I would carry inside forever.

But his scent was like music.

And in his eyes, I found my salvation.

I was his.

In a strange, mad, painful and complicated way.

I was his.

'I chose you . . .' I breathed, disarmed. 'Over everything else . . . I chose you, Rigel. You'll never understand it, because you only see things in black and white. I have always wanted a family, *that's true*,' I stressed in a whisper. 'But I chose you because we belong together. Don't push me away . . . Don't keep me at a distance. You're not a price to pay. You're what makes me happy . . .'

I clenched my eyes shut in anguish.

'I want to come in . . . even if you're a path of thorns inside.'

His eyes flashed, and I seized the moment to stretch out my hand and hold his face.

I was still scared that he would flinch away, that he would recoil from my touch, but Rigel just lifted his eyes to me, two shining black galaxies.

I looked at him imploringly, and for a moment swore that he was staring back at me in the same way.

Why?

Why couldn't we stay together?

Why couldn't we be together like everyone else?

'I want you,' I told him again, looking him straight in the eyes. 'You, and only you. Whatever you are, however you see yourself . . . I want you as you are. You're not taking anything away from me, Rigel. Nothing . . .'

I stroked his cheek, clinging to his dark gaze, and prayed he would believe me. I wished I could give him my eyes so he could see himself as I saw him, because I loved his complexity more than anything else.

'If I let you *in* . . .' he whispered slowly. 'You'll get hurt.'

I smiled sadly and shook my head. Showing him all my Band-Aids, I said, 'I've never been scared of getting hurt.'

He clenched his eyes shut, defeated. Before he could do anything else, I lifted his face and closed my lips over his.

I didn't know how else to let my heart speak. I anchored myself to that kiss as if my life depended on it.

His hands grasped my sides and my tears fell on his cheekbones.

We anchored ourselves to each other, clinging on, chaining ourselves, knowing we would sink. That we would forever be lost, because in the ocean of reality there was no place for us.

We were shattered, broken, ruined.

But the light within us shone with the power of a hundred stars.

He had the strength of a wolf.

And I had the tenderness of a butterfly.

And I couldn't believe that something so beautiful and sincere could also be wrong.

I kissed him, almost with despair, clinging to him with such passion that we fell backwards. His shoulders touched the mattress and I kept on holding his face, not letting him go.

I felt his pulse pounding against my stomach. Rigel traced my back with his fingers and then gripped, almost as if he couldn't think straight. His hands were shaking, as they did every time he touched me. I thought that I never wanted to be touched by anyone else.

He was one of a kind.

The only one.

The only one who could send me to pieces.

The only one who could put me back together.

The only one who could floor me with a smile and destroy me with a glance.

Rigel, my soul cried out. I clasped him to me, my Band-Aids snagging on his shoulders, my hands refusing to ever let him go.

You're not alone, my every kiss shouted, and his fingers closed in my hair, grasping tightly. I let him embed himself into me, up until the last shiver.

Rigel gripped my hips, and the next instant, it was my back against the mattress.

He pressed me into the bed. I felt his muscles trembling, as if they needed some release, to explode, to let themselves go. I slipped my hands through his hair and kissed him passionately. My tongue tangled with his and something within him gave in.

He impulsively pinned my wrist above my head and grabbed my thigh, pushing it possessively against his side. His fingers left rough half-moons on my flesh, and my back involuntarily arched. My lips parted in a silent gasp.

Rigel froze, panting, and looked me in the eyes. He seemed to realise only then how forcefully he had grabbed me, holding me in that constricting position.

I sensed the constant effort he was making to keep that part of himself at bay.

I watched him, my heart in my throat, powerless in his grasp. He had me in a vice-like grip, but he was shaking as much as I was. I looked at him because, even though he had never been tender, when I was held in his gaze I was not scared.

I had known those eyes all my life.

They were eyes that had cradled me when I couldn't sleep at night.

Eyes that had always been with me, tattooed on my soul.

They would never hurt me.

Slowly, I intertwined my ankles behind his back, with all the tenderness I had, defenceless and disarmed. Rigel looked at me, his jaw tense. As a tear dripped down my forehead, I reached up and stroked his cheek.

'You're good like this,' I whispered to him. 'You're my beautiful *disaster . . .*'

He looked at me, a silent emotion in his eyes. A powerful, inscrutable emotion.

My heart panged as he lifted the hand that he had gripped and brought it to his mouth. His lips landed on my soft wrist and kissed it slowly. His face among my Band-Aids was the sweetest, most impossible and desirable thing I had ever seen.

There he was, Rigel, touching my mistakes. He kissed my fingertips one by one, and I felt my eyes brim with tears until my vision burned.

He *was not* my most beautiful mistake.

No.

Rigel was my destiny.

He was my broken, crumpled, beautiful finale.

And he always would be.

I wrapped my arms around him and pulled him down to me. Our lips were consumed in kisses, and his hands slipped under my dress.

I jumped when I felt his hot fingers.

Rigel breathed slowly, then traced the curve of my pelvis as if he had desired it all his life. My heart drummed furiously against my abdomen.

He caressed me deeply, touching nerves I didn't even know I had.

His hands slipped down between my shoulder blades, and the next moment, my bra came undone, revealing my back.

I held my breath.

Before I could take one, Rigel slipped his finger inside my bra and touched my bare breast. He squeezed, and I felt my cheeks flushing, my breath accelerating. I was burning with incredible, completely new emotions. He touched a nipple, tweaking it, twisting it with his fingers. A strange hotness spread out from my breast to my stomach.

My heart leaping, I noticed my arms lifting. My dress almost ripped as he pulled it over my head with my bra.

The air in the room whipped my skin, I was totally exposed. Instinctively I tried to cover my chest with my arms. I looked for his eyes, and found them already on me, two chasms of terror and wonder.

I felt inadequate, small and fragile. I felt vulnerable, so much so that I found myself resisting when he took my wrists to move my arms.

Extremely slowly, he opened my arms, holding my hands in place, level with my head.

Then he looked at me. All of me.

His eyes slid down my body, devouring me as if I wasn't real.

When he looked at my face again, I glimpsed in his eyes a heat I had never seen before.

Powerful. Extreme. Burning.

Something incomprehensible made my breath shudder.

Rigel leant over me and his lips closed around my nipple. I opened my eyes and tried to move, but his hands were pinning my wrists to the mattress, holding me still. He sucked through his teeth and a sweet tension flooded my lower stomach, becoming boiling and unbearable. I felt my body writhing, curling, imploring, but all I could do was desperately squeeze my thighs around his leg.

'Rigel . . . please . . .' I panted, without knowing exactly what I was begging for.

In response, his teeth clamped down around my nipple and the sensation grew stronger. My back arched and my lips shuddered, the tension in my abdomen got so intense it took my breath away.

I was too sensitive. My body was ice and fire, something I could hardly recognise. It was so strong my eyes half-closed.

Then, Rigel lifted himself off me and took off his t-shirt.

He seemed to be burning with the need to feel contact between our bodies. The rustle of fabric mixed with the sound of my breath and his dishevelled black hair fell over his face.

I shivered again, faced with the masterpiece he was.

His pale skin made his wide shoulders look as if they had been sculpted in marble. His defined chest seemed made to be touched, felt and admired, but his raw, exaggerated beauty intimidated me so much that I again clasped my arms to my chest, unable even to touch him.

I stared at him, my cheeks burning, lifting my fingers to my swollen lips, my gaze trembling. His face, a dark angel's, was full of disbelief.

He was my fairy tale. I was sure of it.

But he was also my greatest shiver.

My wildest fear.

The only nightmare I never wanted to stop having.

When he kissed me again, I exploded.

His skin burned on mine, and the feeling that flowed through me was so intense I gripped his shoulders tightly. I felt my bare breasts against his chest, the friction of his skin on mine was incredible.

He positioned himself between my legs, and his burning fingers touched me all over, as if he wanted to absorb, to take everything from me, even my soul. Suddenly, it seemed as if everything in his body was screaming for me to touch him.

Uncertain, I placed my fingers on his skin, because I didn't know where else to put my hands.

Slowly, I traced the outline of his arms and his strong shoulder bones. Once again, I felt small, insecure and even more fragile than I was.

The next moment, his spine tensed. I realised he was reacting to my touch, however hesitant it had been. With more courage, I ran my fingers up his chest, caressing him up to his neck before sinking my fingers into his hair.

His mouth left mine to leave a trail of burning kisses down my body. Rigel sunk his lips into my stomach, biting and caressing with his tongue, before continuing downwards.

I was breathing heavily, desperately, and gripped my fingers in his hair. My blood was pulsing under his lips like a mad symphony of tremors.

He kissed my inner thigh, the softest and most sensitive part. Then he lifted my trembling leg and continued that torture until I couldn't think clearly. He nibbled my ankle, and his black eyes looked up at me, burning me.

He was panting, kneeling on the mattress, his lips swollen and his eyes shining. The spectacle of him took my breath away.

The bones of his pelvis traced his lower abs and his broad chest emanated a seductive, infernal heat. He was gorgeous and terrifying. I couldn't take my eyes off him.

My cheeks were burning, and while my legs were closed and trembling, my heart was a wide open, pulsing flower.

The next moment, his hands reached my pelvis. Reality was pounding around me, but nothing felt as real as his fingers on the edge of my underwear.

Breathing quickly, Rigel stopped and lifted his eyes to mine.

I became definitively aware of what was about to happen.

This was the point of no return.

Slowly, waiting for me to say no, Rigel's fingers tucked inside the waistband of my panties. Then, he pulled them down.

I felt my heart stop. My breathing ceased.

Every nerve in my body became aware of the fabric sliding down my legs and disappearing.

I was panting, fragile and bewildered. Rigel's eyes slid down to where I was now exposed.

I squeezed my thighs. Like never before, I wanted to escape from the condemnation of his gaze. Like never before, I wanted to hide and disappear. I tried to huddle up into myself, but before I could, his fingers moved down between my thighs.

He touched me where no one had ever touched me before. As he touched that soft flesh, my surprised moan made him hover over me again. He leant down and sucked my breast. The reaction that came over me was so intense it floored me.

He tantalised, massaged, and my breath became erratic. It felt like I was losing my mind. I trembled, my cheeks became furnaces. One part of me wanted it to stop, because the other part wasn't able to withstand that raging fire.

I found myself clutching him, incapable even of speaking, and a moan broke from my lips.

'Rigel . . .'

In response to that imploring moan, his fingers between my thighs moved with increased vigour and the caresses of his tongue intensified.

My back arched and my eyes opened wide. I dug my nails into his back.

I felt my limbs shake convulsively. The room started spinning. My legs were trembling and a tingling sensation grew in me. I couldn't breathe. It was the most consuming feeling in the world.

His hands closed around my hips, pulling me towards him. I startled when I felt his desire between my legs. I was so hypersensitive by now that it took nothing at all to make me tremble.

There was nothing, now, between us. My heart thumped violently, my gaze quivered.

'Look at me,' I heard him whisper.

I met his eyes.

Rigel looked at me . . . He looked at me in a way that, until the end, I would never understand. Infinite emotions burned in his gaze, I chased each and every one of them until they were imprinted in my memory.

Until they were mine.

Mine and mine alone.

Then he pushed inside. I stifled a moan of pain and felt my muscles tensing, burning. My body stiffened and a piercing feeling made its way inside of me as he slowly advanced, trying not to hurt me.

I took a breath in, feeling a tear roll down my temple. Rigel didn't break eye contact, not even for a moment. His deep, dilated pupils remained anchored in mine, as if he wanted to engrave every single nuance of that moment into his soul.

Every single nuance of me.

And I let him.

I let him take everything.

Everything I could give him.

We fit together . . . like broken pieces of a single soul.

And for the first time in my life, for the first time since I was a little girl, every part of me seemed to find its right place.

Without cracks or chips.

Rigel fused with me, his hand clutched my ribs as if he wanted to reach my heart. He put his other hand on the headboard, tilted his face, and placed his forehead against mine.

Maybe because he also wanted to tell me something without words.

Maybe because, *even though he had never been tender,* he was choosing to give me the softest part of himself.

And as the world reduced to nothing but us, I wanted to tell him that it didn't matter if he was a disaster inside. With the ink that he had given me, we would write something that was just ours.

And maybe he would stay as impenetrable as the night, as multi-faceted as a vault of stars, but in that single song, our hearts beat as one.

We would find a way.

Together.

We would find it. Even if it didn't exist, we would write it with what we had.

With our souls.

And with our hearts.

With secret melodies and constellations of shivers.

With the strength of a wolf, and the tenderness of a butterfly.

Hand in hand . . .

Until the very end.

31. Closed Eyes

I love you as only the stars can love:
From a distance, in silence, without ever going out.

I didn't have bad dreams that night.

No cellars.

No belts.

No spiral staircases into the darkness.

The whole night . . . I thought I could feel someone watching me. When my nightmares came knocking, I thought I heard a whimper escaping from my lips, but the next moment . . . they would vanish. Something enveloped me, sending them away, and my limbs sunk into oblivion, cradled by a reassuring warmth.

I opened my eyes, slightly fuzzy-headed.

I didn't know what time it was. Outside the window, the sky still held the faint darkness of night. It must have been a few hours before daybreak.

Gradually, my eyes focused. I realised that my pelvis hurt, and the muscles in my leg felt slightly stiff. I moved my thighs under the covers, and couldn't help but notice the gentle burning coming from below.

I lowered my eyes. A well-defined wrist was resting on my side. I looked at its strong, angular contours before looking up at the boy beside me.

Rigel's other arm was folded under the pillow. His breath was light and steady. His lowered eyelashes emphasised his elegant cheekbones, and his black hair fell over his pillow like liquid silk, soft and messy. His lips were swollen and a little chapped, but still gorgeous.

I loved watching him sleep. There was a surreal beauty about him. His relaxed features made him look . . . enchanting and vulnerable.

I felt my heart thump in my chest.

Had it really happened?

I stretched out my hand and there was a rustling sound. I hesitated, and then cautiously touched his face, feeling its warmth under my fingertips.

He was really there.

It really all happened . . .

An uncontainable happiness filled my heart. I half-closed my eyes, inhaling his masculine scent, then silently slid forwards, drawing closer to him.

Sweetly, I planted my lips on his. The slow, gentle sound of that kiss reverberated through the silence. As I pulled back to look at him, I realised his eyes had opened. They shone out from under his dark lashes. I felt them on me before I could meet them, black and incredibly deep.

'Did I wake you up?' I whispered, wondering if I hadn't moved tenderly enough.

His eyes remained fixed on mine, but Rigel didn't reply. I relaxed against the pillow, enjoying the feeling of his gaze on me.

'How are you feeling?' he asked, looking at my body wrapped in the covers.

'Good.' I looked for his eyes, feeling happiness warming my cheeks. 'Better than ever.'

The thought of Anna and Norman came to my mind, and I remembered that I'd better go back to my own room.

'What time is it?' I asked, but Rigel seemed to have already guessed what I was worrying about.

'They won't be awake for another few hours yet,' he said, and I heard *you can stay, for a little longer,* with no need for him to say it.

I wanted to look into his eyes, but I was so peaceful I contented myself with the feeling of his body close to mine. Tiredness lingered on my skin but, after some time, instead of closing my eyes I whispered, earnest and heartfelt, 'I've always loved your name.'

I didn't know why I chose that moment to tell him. I had never told him this, not once. But now my soul felt connected to his like never before.

'I know you don't think the same way,' I added slowly, as he looked at me again. 'I know . . . what it represents for you.'

His gaze was alert now. There was a remote light shining deep in his eyes that I simply contemplated without trying to grasp.

I spoke to him softly, sincerely.

'It's not like you think it is. It doesn't connect you to the matron,' I murmured.

Rigel continued looking at my eyes and lips, lying with his hair spread out over the pillow. The intimacy of our conversation reverberated in his inscrutable gaze.

'And what does it connect me to?' he asked, his voice slow and hoarse, as if he didn't really believe me.

'Nothing.'

He looked at me without understanding, and I softened my gaze.

'It doesn't connect you to anything. You're a star in the sky, Rigel, and the sky can't enchain you.'

I stretched out a hand towards him. I brushed the skin on his shoulders and under his eyes with my fingertip . . . I traced a line from a mole to his clavicle, and then to the three little points of the belt below. In silence, I drew the constellation of Orion on his skin.

'Your name isn't a burden . . . it's special. Like you, it only shines for those who know where to look. Like you, it's silent, deep and complex as the night.' I added an invisible trail to the three points at the bottom. 'You ever think about that?' I smiled. 'I'm named after a butterfly, the most ephemeral creature in the world. But you . . . you've got the eternal name of a star. You're rare. And people like you shine with your own light, even if you don't know it. Rigel makes you . . . exactly what you are.'

My finger lingered on his chest, just above his heart. Just there, at the furthest point of the invisible constellation, where the star he was named after must be.

With a rustling of the bedsheets, I turned over and looked for my dress on the floor. I rummaged through the pockets and then turned back to him.

Rigel looked at the small purple Band-Aid I was holding. Tiredness wrapped around my limbs, but before he could understand what was happening, I unwrapped it and placed it over that point on his heart.

'*Rigel*,' I whispered, pointing at the Band-Aid, his star.

Then I took an identical one, the same colour, unwrapped it and put it over my heart.

'*Rigel*,' I concluded, pointing at my skin, then covering it with my palm, as if sealing a promise inside.

Even though sleep was slowly overcoming me, I managed to feel his hand gripping the bedsheets wrapped around my hip.

'The stars are *not* alone. You are not alone,' I smiled at him sweetly, slowly closing my eyes. 'I'll always . . . carry you with me.'

I didn't wait for his reply.

I slipped peacefully into sleep, because I had learnt to respect his silences.

Because I had learnt that I couldn't demand answers when I

knocked on the door to his soul. I had to enter slowly, sit carefully in that crystal rose garden and wait patiently.

And the whole time, I felt his gaze lingering on me, though I didn't understand the *real* meaning of it. Not until the right moment arrived would I understand it.

I slipped into the comforting warmth of his breath and fell asleep. When I woke up, later . . . he was gone.

It was mild that afternoon.

The wind was picking up and rustling the leaves in the trees, carrying the fresh fragrance of the clouds. Taking deep breaths in, it felt as if I could rise up with the breeze and walk in the sky.

A week had passed since that morning.

My calm, measured footsteps beat on the asphalt of the sidewalk. There was no one around us; we were alone.

'Look,' I whispered in the breeze. My backpack gently jostled against my back as I came to a stop.

The sunset illuminated the river, making it gleam like a treasure trove of minerals. The places where they were redoing the parapet on the bridge were still surrounded by orange netting, but beyond that you could see the shadows lengthening on the leafy branches. Under the bridge, the water was glistening with bright, sparkling reflections.

A step ahead of me, Rigel's profile stood out in the rosy light. He was looking in the direction I had indicated, his black hair dancing around his head. The light was so warm it made his eyes look even more brilliant.

Coming home from school with him was now one of the moments that I loved the most. They were not particularly special occasions, but there was a peace in the way we were not scared to be seen beside each other. We were far enough away from everyone and everything; we could put the world to one side for a moment.

'Aren't they beautiful? All those colours,' I murmured as the water rushed beneath us, glistening like honey.

But I wasn't watching the river. I was watching him.

Rigel realised. Slowly, he turned towards me.

He met my eyes, maybe because he too had come to understand something about us, that there was something in our glances that others couldn't see. Our silences spoke words that no one else could hear, and that was where we were destined to meet each other: between things unsaid.

He waited for me to slowly come beside him, with all my usual tenderness. I stopped at what could be considered an acceptable distance. Even though there was no one around, even though the workmen had already gone, we were in public and there were limits I could not forget.

'Rigel . . . is there something worrying you?'

I held his gaze, and saw something in his eyes that made me persevere.

'You seem distant. The past few days it's felt as though there's something bothering you.'

No, bothering wasn't the right word. It was something much deeper. It was something I didn't recognise; it gave me no peace.

Rigel slowly shook his head, looking away from me. He looked into the distance, to where the river vanished into a vague ribbon between the trees.

'I've never got used to it,' he admitted in a faint voice.

'To what?'

'That way you have,' he said, in an unusual tone of voice, almost surrendering, 'of always seeing what no one else does.'

'So there is something then?' I looked for his eyes, sensing that my hunch was correct. 'Something wrong?'

He was quiet. I spoke more softly. 'It's the psychologist . . . isn't it? I saw you speaking with Anna, this morning . . . I remember she wanted to speak to you after the appointment that day. And the day before yesterday . . . you were out all afternoon.'

I gently brushed his hand, and his eyes shuddered away from the horizon to focus on that touch.

'Rigel,' I said softly. 'Do you want to tell me what's going on?'

Slowly, his eyes lifted to my face.

He looked at me in that way again. The same way he had looked that morning a week ago, like a mark that nothing could wipe away.

Suddenly, something extraordinary happened. I would never have been ready for it.

For a moment that left me confused and breathless, the defences in

Rigel's eyes all crumbled and a wave of emotions flooded out and crashed into me like a tsunami.

Remorse, desperation and an uncontainable heat burst from his eyes. I trembled, wide-eyed, assaulted by such powerful emotions that I felt my knees buckling.

My shocked heart tore open, and I took half a step backwards.

'Rigel . . .' I whispered faintly.

I was incredulous, I didn't understand what had just happened. Before I could do anything, however, he leant over and gave me a long kiss on the corner of my mouth.

When he pulled away, I looked at him with a bewildered urgency in my eyes, confused by that storm of emotions and devastated by that reckless kiss.

What did it mean?

I was about to ask him, but the world came crashing down around me.

I glanced over Rigel's shoulder. *And I saw him.*

A few metres away, someone was standing in the now howling wind, staring blankly at us.

But it wasn't just anyone.

No.

Lionel.

My heart plummeted with a silent sob. Seeing the scream in my wide-open eyes, all Rigel could do was turn around. His eyes immediately darkened when they landed on the boy behind him.

Lionel was clutching a beautiful bunch of flowers, identical to the ones that were crowding the house. Flashing through his confused, bewildered eyes, I saw every part of what had just happened. Of the truth.

My fingers wrapped around Rigel's. The intimacy of our breaths. The proximity of our bodies. *His lips on mine.*

After weeks, after all that time . . . all it had taken was a moment.

He realised.

And that realisation, for him, was like slipping on ice.

Lionel was looking at me in a different way, his gaze was burning with a thousand emotions: dismay, incredulity, defeat and devastation.

Slowly, he lowered the hand that was holding the flowers. Then, like a gush of acid, his eyes slid spitefully to Rigel.

'*You* . . .' he hissed, in a voice I barely recognised. The bunch of flowers was shaking in his hand, and an unnatural fury made his features look sharper. 'You've finally done it. You've finally put your *filthy* hands on her.'

'Lionel,' I stammered, but suddenly Rigel interrupted me.

'*Oh,* another bunch of flowers,' he said scathingly. '*How original.* You can leave them in the porch, I'm sure someone will go to the bother of taking them in.'

His voice was shining with an excessive, repressed anger, and Lionel's eyes spurted fire. He charged towards him, devouring the asphalt.

'You've always been a *piece of shit,*' he accused him, his throat going dangerously purple. 'I knew you were an arrogant bastard, right from the start! You had to get your fucking hands on her, *didn't you*? You had to, what else would a *son of a bitch like you* do!'

'Maybe she wanted *my fucking hands on her,*' Rigel retorted, his lips twisted into a cruel smile. 'Much more than she wanted *yours.*'

'Rigel!' I implored him, wide-eyed, but Lionel came up and screamed in his face. 'Are you happy now? *Huh*?' His voice was burning with nervous tension. 'Happy now that you've felt her up good and proper? You satisfied? You don't deserve her!'

Rigel narrowed his eyes, a terrifying earthquake, burning like a wound.

'*You,*' he spat out with pure fury, '*you* don't deserve her!'

'You *disgust* me!' Lionel gave him a look full of hate. I tried to calm him down, but his eyes burned me too, and he screamed, 'You both disgust me! You think you'll get away with it? You really think so? Well, think again. Your dirty little show ends here!' Lionel's eyes, brimming with contempt, shot daggers at Rigel again. 'I'll tell everyone! Everyone will know what you get up to at home, what *type* of family you are – everyone! Then we'll see what people have to say.'

My eyes opened wide. I felt panic squeezing my throat.

'Lionel, please . . .'

'*No,*' he spat out vindictively.

'You have to understand, please!'

'I've understood well enough!' he burst out, repulsed. 'It's all quite clear. So clear I could vomit.' He clenched his teeth. 'You've chosen to screw your future adoptive brother, Nica. Nice one. You've chosen to let yourself be touched by him, a sick bastard who lives with you and should just see you as a sister. A sister, don't you get it? All this is indecent!'

'Why don't you send *me* a nice bunch of flowers,' Rigel shot back, scathingly. 'Then we can kiss and make up.'

Lionel was on him in an instant.

Everything happened all of a sudden. The flowers fell to the ground in a monstrous explosion of violence. Fists, punches and snarls filled the air and my eyes opened wide in horror.

'No!' I shouted with trembling lips. 'No!'

In a mad impulse, I threw myself on them to try to stop the fight. My hands scraped at their arms, panic swelling in my voice.

'Stop it! I'm begging you, no! Stop –'

My words stuck in my mouth. My head whipped to one side and my hair lashed my face. The world spun around with a nauseating violence and I crashed to the ground.

The impact with the asphalt knocked the air out of my lungs. I felt my cheek scraping and a burning stinging my right eye, making me clamp them shut. A dull pain throbbed between my temples like a drum.

I leant on my wrists, unstable, and the iron taste of blood filled my mouth. My eyelids were burning. With shaky, tearful eyes I looked up at the person who had struck me.

Lionel was staring at me with a devastated expression. His bewildered gaze harboured a look of pure horror.

'Nica, I didn't . . .' He swallowed, beside himself. 'I swear, I didn't mean to . . .'

Lionel didn't see Rigel, standing still, his black hair covering his face. He didn't see his face turned to one side, towards me, looking as if it had been him, rather than me, who had got hit.

He didn't see the ice in his eyes, as sharp as needles, staring to one side with incredulous brutality.

He didn't see any of this.

No . . .

All he saw was the flash in his burning, black eyes, shooting daggers at him, searing furiously through the air.

Rigel grabbed him by the hair and hit him so hard that his lip burst open. Lionel let out a moan of pain as a siege of punches rained down on him. Blinded with rage, Rigel pounded him, crushed him, bent him, bombarded him. Lionel reacted by trying to hit him in any way he could. He managed to scratch his face. The fight became so violent it was unbearable.

'Please! ENOUGH!' Tears burned my eyes. '*I beg you!*'

A fist pounded into Rigel's temple, splitting his eyebrow.

'No!'

My knees burning, my bones trembling, I dragged myself to my feet and threw myself on them again.

I had just been thrown to the ground by doing this, but not even the taste of blood in my mouth could stop me.

Not even the pain in my cheek. Nor the punch that had felled me.

Not fear, nor the knot in my throat.

Nothing could stop me, *because* . . .

Because, I, after all . . . had a moth's heart. And I always would have . . .

Because it was in my nature to get burnt, just as Rigel had said. And I wouldn't understand the consequences of this decision until it was too late.

My vision clouded with tears, I threw myself on them, grabbing on to what I could. I grabbed wrists and arms without even knowing who they belonged to. I was pushed back several times as I grabbed, scraped and begged with no restraint.

'Enough! Rigel, Lionel, *enough*!'

It all happened too quickly.

A shove caught me off guard and my body was thrown backwards. I stumbled, and crashed into something that buckled under the impact of my body.

A terrifying creak resounded through the air, a noise that stopped time.

Under my sudden weight, the orange netting that was replacing the parapet gave way.

My eyes flew open. I was unable to comprehend what was really happening. I tried to grab on to something, to push myself forwards, but the weight of my backpack on my shoulders dragged me backwards and I lost balance.

My eyes silently screaming, I managed to glimpse, as if in slow-motion, Rigel's face turning, his hair slapping his face.

His eyes were tormented, full of a blind terror that I would never see in him again.

He was the only handhold in a world that was slipping away.

In a heart-wrenching sequence of images, I saw his body leap and stretch out towards mine. His arm stretched out so far it almost pulled out of its socket and his shadow swallowed me up just as I tumbled over into the void.

Rigel seized me and the air screamed monstrously around us as we went into free fall, a shrieking creature that tore tears from my eyes.

As we fell from that dizzying height, his body shielding mine and his arms wrapped protectively around me, all I could feel was the incredulity of death.

And him.

The pressure of his hands, clutching me to his chest as if to dissolve me into his pulse.

Before the impact, before we were swallowed up into a violent black, before everything tore into ice, I noticed his lips near my ear.

The sound of his voice was the last thing I heard.

The last . . . before the end.

With the howling wind . . . the world tragically dimming around us, darkness obliterating us both, all I heard was his voice, whispering feebly:

'*I love you.*'

32. The Stars are Alone

Everyone assumes that death is an unbearable pain.

A sudden and violent emptiness . . . a fatality in which everything becomes nothing.

They don't know how wrong they are.

Death . . . is nothing like that.

It is perfect peace.

The end of all senses.

The erasure of all thoughts.

I had never considered what it meant to stop existing. But if there was one thing I had learnt . . . it was that death doesn't let you go without asking for a compromise.

I had already brushed against death once in that accident, when I was just five years old.

It had let me go, but in exchange it had taken my mom and dad.

It wouldn't spare me. Not this time.

I was there again, on the other side of the scales to life.

And in the balance was a price I could *never* pay.

There was a piercing sound.

It was the only thing I could make out.

Slowly, out of the nothingness, something else emerged. An aseptic, pungent smell.

As it became more intense, I started to perceive the shape of my body, bit by bit.

I was lying down.

Everything weighed on me so heavily that I felt pinned. To what, I still didn't know. A few moments later, I realised that something was biting my finger.

I tried to open my eyes, but my eyelids were as heavy as boulders.

After many attempts, I managed to summon enough strength to open them.

The light was as sharp and merciless as a blade, piercing my vision.

I clenched my eyes shut again. As soon as I was ready to take on that intensity, all I was able to see was . . . white.

I focused on my arm, outstretched over an immaculate bedcover. On my index finger there was some sort of little clamp that pinched my fingertip and pulsed with my heartbeat.

The smell of disinfectant was nauseatingly strong. I felt weak and bewildered. I tried to move, but it was impossible.

What was happening?

I made out the shape of a man sitting in a chair next to the wall. I stared at him through my eyelashes, and after a while, found the strength to open my mouth.

'Norman . . .' I breathed raggedly.

It was a barely audible whisper, but Norman jumped. His eyes darted to me and he leapt to his feet, spilling his little plastic cup of coffee on the floor. He rushed towards my bed, tripping over his own feet, and stared at me, his face purple with emotion. The next moment, he turned back towards the doorway.

'Nurse!' he shouted. 'Call the doctor, quick! She's awake, she's conscious! And my wife . . . Anna! Anna, come, she's awake!'

Hurried footsteps resounded through the air. Suddenly the room was invaded by nurses, but before anything else, the figure of a woman appeared in the doorway. She grabbed on to the door jamb and tears welled up in her eyes.

'Nica!'

Anna made her way through the people to get to me, gripping on to my bedcovers. Her wide eyes stared feverishly at my face and an inconsolable despair distorted her voice.

'Oh, thank God, *thank God* . . .' She cupped my head with a shaking hand, as if she was scared of breaking me, and tears gushed down her reddened face.

Despite feeling so slow and sluggish, I realised that I had never seen her look so distressed.

'Oh, honey,' she stroked my skin. 'It's all okay . . .'

'Ma'am, the doctor is on his way,' a nurse told her, before raising my pillow in a practised motion.

'Can you hear me, Nica?' a woman asked me clearly. 'Can you see me?'

I nodded slowly, and she came around to examine the IV drip and check my vitals.

'No, no, slowly,' Anna whispered when I tried to move my left arm.

It was only then that I noticed how much every single movement hurt. An atrocious stabbing pain pierced my chest and something stopped me moving.

A bandage.

My arm was folded against my chest and bandaged up to the shoulder.

'No, Nica, don't touch it,' Anna admonished when I tried to rub my eye, which was burning terribly. 'A capillary's burst, your eye's red . . . How's your chest? Does it hurt to breathe? Oh, Doctor Robertson!'

A tall, greying man with a short, well-groomed beard and a snow-white shirt came up to my bed.

'How long has she been conscious?'

'A few minutes,' a nurse replied. 'Her heartbeat is regular.'

'Blood pressure?'

'Systolic and diastolic both normal.'

I didn't understand a thing. My mind was blank and confused.

'Hi, Nica,' the man said, clearly and carefully. 'My name is Doctor Lance Robertson, I'm a doctor at Saint Mary O' Valley Hospital and I'm the head of this department. I am now going to check your reactions to stimuli. You might feel a little light-headed and nauseous, but that's completely normal. Relax, okay?'

The backrest started to lift.

As soon as I felt the weight of my head on my shoulders, an excruciating dizziness made my guts twist. I gagged and folded forwards, but from my empty body all that came out was a burning, hacking cough that made my eyes water.

Anna immediately ran to help me, holding my hair off my face. I gripped the covers as once again, I retched ferociously, my body twisting over itself.

'It's all okay . . . These are normal reactions,' the doctor reassured me, supporting my shoulders. 'Don't be scared. Now, I'm going to sit here . . . Can you turn towards me without moving your legs?'

I was too dazed to understand what he meant. It was only then that I noticed a strange swelling sensation in my foot. But the doctor had already straightened my chin with his finger.

'Now, look at my finger.'

He pointed a little light into my eye, but when he switched to the other one, it burned so much I had to squeeze it shut. Doctor Robertson said that it was all okay, and I struggled on with the exercise until he seemed satisfied.

He turned off the little light and leant towards me.

'How old are you, Nica?' he asked, looking me in the face.

'Seventeen,' I replied quietly.

'When is your birthday?'

'April 16th.'

The doctor checked my records, then looked at me again.

'And this lady,' he pointed at Anna. 'Can you tell me who she is?'

'She . . . she's Anna. She's my mom . . . well . . . my future adoptive mom,' I stammered, and Anna's eyes brimmed with tenderness. She pushed my hair off my face, stroking my temples as if I was the most fragile and precious thing in all the world.

'All right. No obvious neurological trauma. She's well,' the doctor announced to general relief.

'What . . . happened?' I finally asked.

On some level, I already knew. A violent confusion was raging through my disastrous, beaten-up body. And yet, tears closing my throat, I struggled to recall what had happened. I met Anna's eyes and absorbed the anguish on her face.

'The bridge, Nica,' she helped me remember. 'The netting broke and you . . . you fell . . . into the river . . .' she struggled to say, destroyed. 'Someone saw you, and called an ambulance . . . We got a call from the hospital . . .'

'You've cracked two ribs,' the doctor intervened. 'And when they found you, your shoulder was dislocated. We've put it back in, but you should wear the brace for at least three weeks. You've also sprained your ankle,' he added. 'Undoubtedly as a consequence of the impact. Considering what you've gone through, you've got off practically unscathed.'

He hesitated, serious. 'I don't think you realise how lucky you are,' he added, but I was no longer listening.

A feeling of terror gripped me.

'That boy was with you,' Anna continued. 'Lionel . . . do you remember? He's here too. It was him who raised the alarm. The police have asked him some questions, but they'd like to know . . .'

'*Where is he?*'

She jumped.

My heart thumped in my throat so violently I felt suffocated.

Seeing me like this, Anna almost broke down.

'He's in the waiting room, just outside . . .'

'Anna,' I begged shakily. 'Where is he?'

'I told you, just outs—'

'*Where's Rigel?*'

Everyone turned to look at me.

In Anna's eyes, I saw an indescribable anguish.

Norman squeezed her hand. After what seemed like an endless moment, he gripped the curtain around my bed . . . and then pulled it aside.

Next to me, the devastated body of a boy was lying immobile.

A violent vertigo came over me, and I gripped the bed railing, trying hard not to fall apart.

It was Rigel.

His face was falling sideways off the pillow. His skin was devoured by bruises and his head was swathed in an excessive number of bandages, from which locks of black hair poked out. His shoulders were held in a single, complicated bandage and two plastic tubes went into his nostrils, supplying oxygen to his lungs. What destroyed me the most was seeing him breathing so slowly that he seemed motionless.

No.

I retched again, my throat tight, ice rushing into my bones.

'I wish I could say he was as lucky as you were,' the doctor whispered. 'But sadly that is not the case. He's broken two ribs and cracked three others. His collarbone is fractured in several places, and the iliac crest in his pelvis is slightly fractured. But . . . the problem is his head.

The head trauma caused him to lose enormous amounts of blood. We believe that . . .'

The doctor was cut off by a nurse calling him from the doorway. He excused himself and walked away, but I didn't even see him go. My gaze was fixed on Rigel, dripping with a dull devastation that my heart could not bear.

His body . . . he had protected me with his body . . .

'Mr and Mrs Milligan,' Doctor Robertson called, holding files in his hand. 'Could you come here for a moment?'

'What's happening?' Anna asked.

He looked at her in a way I couldn't explain. And she seemed to immediately understand. Instantly, the eyes that I had learnt to love crumbled in desperation.

'Mr and Mrs Milligan, it's arrived. The confirmation from Social Services . . .'

'No,' Anna shook her head, pulling away from Norman. 'Please, no . . .'

'This is a private hospital, as you know . . . And he . . .'

'Please,' Anna begged, tears in her eyes, clinging to his shirt. 'Don't transfer him. Please, this is the best hospital in town, you can't send him away! Please!'

'I'm sorry,' the doctor replied regretfully. 'It's not my decision. We understand that you and your husband are no longer the boy's legal guardians.'

It took my brain a moment to process that information.

What?

'I'll pay for everything!' Anna feverishly shook her head. 'We'll pay for the hospitalisation, the treatment, whatever he needs . . . Don't send him away . . .'

'Anna . . .' I whispered, demolished.

She gripped the doctor's shirt, begging him. *'Please . . .'*

'Anna . . . what's he saying?'

She trembled. After a few moments, as if admitting a painful defeat, I saw her slowly lower her head. Then she turned to me.

As soon as I saw her crushed eyes, the abyss inside me deepened.

'He asked,' she confessed, with palpable pain. 'It was what he wanted . . . he was adamant. Last week . . . he asked me to call off the adoption process.' Anna swallowed, slowly shaking her head. 'We concluded it all these last few days. He . . . didn't want to stay here any longer.'

The world had reduced to a suffocating throbbing and I hadn't even realised. In my heart, a dull emptiness was making everything meaningless.

What was she saying?

It was not possible. Last week we . . .

An overwhelming sense of foreboding knotted my chest.

Had he asked after we had spent the night together?

'You'll never be happy like this.'

No.

No, he had understood, I had explained it to him.

No, we had knocked down the walls between us, and looked inside each other for the first time, and he had understood, *he understood . . .*

He couldn't have. He couldn't have given up on a family, gone back to being an orphan . . .

Rigel knew. He knew that those who were sent back were never sent to The Grave. They were considered problematic, and as such were sent far away, to other institutes. And I would never find out where he had gone for confidentiality reasons. I would never find him again.

Why? Why hadn't he said anything?

'I thank you for your trust in our hospital,' Doctor Robertson said to Anna. 'However, Mr and Mrs Milligan . . . I have to be honest and tell you that the boy's condition is critical. The head injury is deep, and Rigel is dangerously close to what is called a Stage Three coma. It's also known as a deep coma. And at the moment . . .' He hesitated, looking for the right words. 'The likelihood of him waking is slim. Maybe, if it weren't for his pre-existing condition, the clinical outlook might not have been so serious, but . . .'

'Condition?' I whispered feebly. 'What condition?'

Anna's eyes flew open and she turned towards me. But what shocked me most wasn't her falling silent in a way that was almost like giving up. It was how the doctor looked at me, as if I didn't even know the boy next to me.

'Rigel suffers from a rare disorder,' Doctor Robertson said. 'A chronic condition that has alleviated over time. It's a neuropathic disorder that manifests in attacks of pain in the fifth cranial nerve. In particular . . . the temples and the eyes. Patients are born with it, but over time they learn, in some way or another, to live with it . . . Unfortunately, there is no cure, but it can be managed with medication, and over time the attacks become less frequent.'

Time was passing, but I no longer existed.

I was no longer there. I was not in that room.

I was outside that reality.

My soul screaming in disbelief, all I could feel was my gaze slowly turning to Anna.

That was all it took. She went to pieces, bursting into tears in front of me.

'I'm sorry, Nica!' she sobbed. 'I'm sorry . . . He . . . he didn't want anyone to know . . . He made us promise not to tell you . . . from the first day . . . he made us swear. Mrs Fridge had informed us, but Rigel made us promise . . .' She clenched her eyes shut, sobbing. 'I couldn't say no . . . I couldn't . . . I'm sorry.'

No.

A deafening roar was shaking within me.

This wasn't real.

'When you found him on the floor that night we were away . . . I was scared to death . . . I thought he must have had an attack and fainted . . .'

No.

'I spoke to the psychologist about his condition, to help him . . . He must have told him, and Rigel reacted badly . . .'

'No,' a whisper left my lips. Nausea was pounding in my temples; it was all I could feel.

It wasn't true. If he was ill, I would have known. I'd known Rigel his whole life. *It wasn't true* . . .

A sudden memory snuck up on me.

Him sitting on the bed. The look he had given me that evening, when he said, 'Something in me is broken . . . and won't ever heal.'

The world exploded. I shattered and every piece of the puzzle finally slotted into place.

The repeated headaches.

Anna's excessive worry when he had a fever.

The knowing looks they exchanged that I had never understood.

Rigel, on the evening of his birthday, in his bedroom, his fingers gripping his hair and his pupils dilated.

Rigel with his clenched fists, screwing his eyes shut as he backed away from me.

Rigel with his back turned on the landing. His snarl, *'You want to fix me?'*, like an injured beast.

I tried to resist the invasion of memories, to refuse them, push them away, but they clung to my ribs, blurring my vision. With a brutal force, the last piece of the puzzle wedged into my mind.

Rigel at The Grave, when we were children.

Those little white candies that the matron gave only to him.

They weren't candies.

They were pills.

My throat brutally closed. I hardly heard the doctor as he started to speak again.

'When patients with prior neurological conditions suffer injuries of this nature, the brain tends to try to protect the whole system. The states of unconsciousness into which they fall, in the majority of cases, degenerate into . . . irreversible comas.'

'No,' I swallowed. My body was shaking violently. Everyone turned towards me.

He had thrown himself off that bridge for me.

To save me.

For me.

'Nica . . .'

'No . . .'

I doubled over retching again, and this time bile burned my throat, corroding what remained of my body.

Someone came to help me, but jumped when my hands pushed them away.

I was wracked with a mad pain, and lost the last glimmer that anchored me to reality.

'No!' I shouted, becoming even more distraught. My eyes were consumed by tears and I lunged towards him, trying to reach him.

This couldn't be the end, we had to stay together. *Together,* my soul screamed, twisting around on itself. Voices tried to calm me down but the devastation inside me was so violent it blinded me.

'Nica!'

'*No!*'

I pushed Norman's arms away and threw back the covers. The beeping became alarmingly rapid, my cracked ribs throbbed and the air filled with panicked shouts. They tried to hold me back, but I writhed as much as I could, my screams filling the room.

The bed shook and the metal bars clanged.

I flung my arm out and the needle of the IV drip tore out of my skin with a burning sting as I thrashed, kicked and feverishly clawed at the air, Band-Aids tearing across my vision.

Hands grabbed my wrists, trying to keep me still. In the madness of pain, they became *leather belts inside a dark cellar.* Terror exploded and I was plunged headlong into my nightmares again.

'*No!*'

My back arched.

'*No! No! No!*'

I felt a sharp prick in my forearm and gritted my teeth so tightly that the taste of blood filled my mouth.

Darkness swallowed me up.

And in the dark, I dreamt only of black, of a starless sky and wolf eyes that would never open again.

'She's had a shock. Many patients have breakdowns, it can happen . . . I know what you saw was upsetting, but you shouldn't worry. She just needs rest.'

'You don't know,' Anna's voice was shaking with distress. 'You don't know what she's like. If you knew Nica, you wouldn't say this is normal.' With a sob, she added, 'I've never seen her like this.'

Their voices faded, sounding like they were coming from a distant universe.

I sunk once again into a dense, artificial sleep. Time slipped away with me.

When I opened my eyes, I had no idea what time it was.

My head was unspeakably heavy, and a sharp pain was stabbing behind my eyes. I opened my swollen eyelids, and the first thing I noticed was a golden light.

It wasn't the sun. It was hair.

'Hey . . .' My eyes focused on Adeline. She was squeezing my hand and her lovely lips were ruined from crying. Her hair was in a braid, as she used to wear it when we were at The Grave. I had always loved her because she, unlike me, shone even between those grey walls.

'How . . . how are you feeling?' The distress on her face was evident, but she still sweetly tried to reassure me despite her pain. 'There's water, if you want . . . Can you take a sip?'

I tasted bile in my mouth, but I didn't move, silent and drained. Adeline pressed her lips together, then tenderly slipped her hand into mine.

'Here, hold on . . .' She reached out towards the bedside table and I noticed a second glass of water next to my bed.

Someone had placed a little dandelion in it.

It was like the ones I had collected as a child, in the yard of the institute. I would blow on them, wishing I could leave and live the fairy tale I had always dreamt of.

I knew it . . . She had brought it.

Adeline adjusted the backrest so I could drink more easily. She put the glass back on the bedside table, and something in her crumpled to see me so lifeless. She arranged my bedcovers and her gaze fell on my arm, on the scratch that had been left when the IV drip had been torn away. Her eyes brimmed with tears.

'They wanted to restrain your wrists,' she whispered. 'To stop you writhing and hurting yourself . . . I asked them not to. I know what it evokes for you . . . Anna was against it too.'

Adeline looked up, her eyes dripping with pain.

'They're not going to transfer him.'

She burst into tears, sobbing hoarsely, and hugged me. For the first time ever, for as long as I had desired human affection, I stayed as limp as a doll.

'I didn't know either,' she confessed, holding me so tight it almost hurt. 'I didn't know about his illness . . . believe me . . .'

Her sobs rattled her breath. I let her tremble against me, scratching and weeping, I let her hurt as she had always let me. And as her body crumbled against my exhausted chest, I wondered how similar our pain was.

'Nica . . . there's something I need to tell you.'

A tear fell from her face, dropping to the floor. The sadness of her words was so intense that I looked up at her.

Adeline took something out of her pocket. Then, with trembling fingers, she placed it on the bed.

Lying crumpled on the bedcovers was my polaroid.

The photo that Billie had taken of me, the one I couldn't find and was sure I'd lost.

It was there.

'They found it in his wallet,' Adeline murmured. 'In an inside pocket. He always . . . carried it with him.'

The world crumbled definitively around me.

I felt a truth growing in me that had been kept hidden for a long time.

A truth of secret glances, unsaid words, years of silenced feelings in the deepest depths of the soul.

A truth . . . that I had never been able to see, but that her heart had guarded silently every single day.

'It wasn't me, Nica,' I heard her say, from a world that was falling apart. 'At The Grave, when Margaret shut you in the cellar . . . It wasn't me who held your hand.'

My face furrowed with tears, the pain shattered me, everything was burning, and I finally understood what I had never before been able to understand.

All those words, and behaviours.

I felt the truth coming into me, becoming part of me, melding with my soul and making *all* my thorns of regret tremble, one by one.

'For all this time . . . For all his life . . . He has always . . . always . . .'

*　★　★*

He had always known there was something wrong with him.

He was born knowing it. He had felt it for as long as he could remember. That was how he had justified it to himself that he had been abandoned.

He wasn't like other people.

He didn't need to see the matron's glances, or the way she shook her head when families said they wanted to adopt him. Rigel watched them from the garden, and saw on their faces a pity he had never asked for.

'Well?'

The man shining a light in his eyes did not reply. He tilted back Rigel's childish face, and he saw sparks exploding.

'Where did you say he fell?'

'Down the stairs,' the matron replied. 'It was as if he hadn't even seen them.'

'It's because of the illness,' the doctor pulled his eyelid open, inspecting him. 'When the pain is very strong, the dilation of his pupils causes disorientation and a sort of hallucination.'

Rigel didn't understand much of this, but still he didn't look up. The doctor examined him, and he sensed within his gaze an unbearable knowledge.

'I think that you should get him an appointment with a child psychologist. His condition is very unique. It's related to his trauma . . .'

'Trauma?' the matron asked. 'What trauma?'

The doctor gave her a look halfway between puzzlement and indignation.

'Mrs Stoker, the boy is showing clear signs of abandonment issues.'

'That's not possible,' the matron hissed in that voice that made the other children cry. 'You don't know what you're talking about.'

'You said yourself that he was abandoned.'

'He was still in a swaddling blanket! He can't remember what happened, he was a newborn baby!'

The doctor gave her a stoic look of extreme self-control.

'He's perfectly capable of understanding now. Children this young feel the lack and tend to blame themselves, project it onto themselves and think they are responsible for it. It is possible that he has convinced himself that the condition he was born with is the reason that they . . .'

'He doesn't suffer from anything,' the matron snapped, her eyes full of stubborn anger. 'I give him everything he needs. Everything.'

Rigel would never forget the doctor's look. It was the same that he had glimpsed on many other faces. That sympathy made him feel, if it were possible, even more wrong.

'Look at him . . . he's a disaster,' he heard him murmur. 'Denying the evidence won't help him.'

The attacks never came in the same way.

Sometimes they just felt like an irritation behind his eyes, other times they were absent for days and then exploded with an unexpected ferocity. Those were the moments he hated the most, because as soon as he started to hope that he had got better, they returned even stronger than before.

And so Rigel would scratch his eyelids, scratch his clothes, grip whatever he was holding until he tore everything to shreds. He would feel his heart racing in his throat with a horrendous, jarring sound, and out of fear that someone could see him, he would flee far away and hide.

Due to his size, he could hide in tiny places like a baby animal. He would squeeze in, because in the darkness he felt the most intensely what he had always been: alone.

Alone, because he hadn't been enough for his mother, and he never would be enough for anyone else.

It was always the matron who found him.

She would gently pull him out of his hiding places and take him by the hand, not caring about his blood on her fingers.

She would sing him soft songs about the stars, distant, lonely suns, and he would try not to look at her skirt, crumpled by whoever she had punished last.

This was how the disorder grew in him: over time, he learnt love and affection can't exist, because the stars are alone.

He had always been different.

He didn't work like other people. He didn't *see* like other people — *he saw her as the wind tousled her long brown hair, he saw bronze wings on her back, fluttering, then fading away, as if they'd never existed.*

The doctor had warned him that seeing things that weren't really there could be a consequence of the pain. He knew this full well, but still Rigel hated this more than any other weakness.

It was as if the illness was making fun of him, and every time the sparks obscured his vision, he saw *a radiant smile and grey, warm eyes that would never look at him.*

He saw dreams. Illusions.

He saw her.

And maybe he wouldn't have felt so flawed, deep down, if there was at least one part of him that wasn't twisted, extreme and wrong.

But as that awkward love grew ever stronger, Rigel stared at the grooves his fingernails left in the earth, crevices dug by a wild beast.

'It will get better with time,' the doctor said.

The other children stayed far away from him, they looked at him fearfully, having seen him suddenly scratch at the piano keys and tear the grass from the ground in crazy outbursts.

They didn't come near him because they were scared of him. But, this suited him. He couldn't stand their pity. He couldn't stand those looks they gave him, throwing him into the trashcan of the world. He didn't need to be reminded of how different he was. Certain condemnations aren't chosen: they are our silences and the invisible pain of our shortcomings.

But maybe that was his most painful shortcoming: silence. He would not realise this until one summer afternoon, when he stood up on his tiptoes, stretched out his little arm, and was blinded by a stabbing pain before he could reach the glass near the sink in the laundry room.

Pain exploded like a cluster of thorns and he gritted his teeth. The glass shattered in the sink, and all Rigel could do was grip, grip, grip until he felt the shards cutting his skin.

Red droplets marked the porcelain – *and Rigel saw flowers of blood and hands of a beast, fingers curled like claws.*

'Who's there?' a little voice asked.

He felt his stomach tightening with a burning sensation even before he jumped with surprise. Nica's footsteps pounded the floorboards and that sensation transformed into a wild terror.

Not her.

Not those eyes.

Even though he had always been the first to push her away, he couldn't stand the thought of her seeing him for the broken, bloody beast he was.

Maybe because Nica would have pitied him, and found a chink in his armour, and then he wouldn't have been able to keep her out.

Or maybe because looking in her eyes . . . was like looking inside himself, and seeing himself for the disaster he knew he was.

'Peter, is that you?' she whispered, and Rigel ran away before she could see him.

He hid in the bushes, seeking solitude, but the pain returned and he collapsed on the grass.

He clenched his eyes shut, scratching at the stalks of grass with agitated fingers. He didn't know how else to relieve the excruciating pain.

'It will get better with time,' the doctor had said. And for the first time, his temples still throbbing, Rigel found himself smiling. But it was that bitter, cruel smile, that smile that almost hurt. That smile that had nothing joyous about it, because he knew, deep down, that if it came from within him, it couldn't be anything but *twisted, extreme and wrong*.

He wondered if this was how wolves laughed: empty, hissing, tense-jawed.

And yet, despite how hopeless he felt . . . Rigel couldn't stop thinking about her.

With her clear gaze and her freckles, Nica pushed back the darkness, found a place between the rot and the ink. Despite everything, she was always smiling, she had a light he would never be able to understand.

'There's a fairy tale for everyone,' he had heard her say once, a daisy in her wind-tousled hair.

Rigel was watching from a distance, as always, because there is nothing so scary, and yet also so attractive, to the dark as light.

Nica, tiny and fragile, had her arm wrapped around a younger child.

'You'll see . . .' She smiled, her eyes red from crying, but still as hopeful as the dawn. 'We'll find ours.'

Rigel wondered whether there could be something, somewhere,

for him, too. Something lost in forgotten pages. Something good and kind, that could touch him carefully, without necessarily wanting to fix him.

Watching her, always from too far away, Rigel wondered if, maybe, she was that something.

'You should tell her,' a voice whispered one evening.

Rigel had closed the door to the cellar, where Nica, finally, had fallen asleep. He didn't turn around.

He knew who had discovered him. Those blue eyes followed him everywhere.

Adeline, behind him, clutched the hem of her grey dress before whispering, 'She thinks it's me who holds her hand.'

Rigel looked down and thought of Nica, behind that door. She, who loved fairy tales, who dreamt so desperately of living in one.

'Whatever,' he replied. 'Let her think that.'

'Why?' Adeline looked at him with a hint of desperation. 'Why don't you tell her it's you?'

Rigel didn't reply. Then, in silence, he placed his hand on the door. The hand that, only down there, in the darkness of broken dreams, could find the strength to touch her.

'Because there aren't any fairy tales where the wolf holds the girl's hand.'

He always hated looking her in the face.

Just as he loved it, every inch of it, with excruciating desperation.

Rigel had tried to weed out that love, he had purged every single petal with hands that had been learning to tear things apart since childhood.

But after one petal, there was another, and then another immediately after, and in that infinite spiral staircase, he plunged so deep into Nica's eyes that it became impossible to resurface.

He drowned in them. Hope touched his heart.

But he didn't want to hope. He hated hoping.

Hoping meant deluding himself that one day he would get better, or that the only person who loved him was not a monster who beat the other children until they bled.

No. It wasn't for him.

He wanted to erase it, push it away, tear it off him.

To free himself from those feelings, because they were *twisted, extreme* and *wrong,* just like he was.

But the more time passed, the more Nica burrowed into his heart.

The more the years changed them, the more he scratched at the thorns of that love without end.

And as the days became years, as she continued to smile, Rigel understood that in her sweetness, there was a strength that no one else had.

A strength like no other.

Having a soul like Nica's meant knowing how harsh the world could be, but deciding, day in day out, to love and to be kind.

Without compromises. Without fear.

Wholeheartedly.

Rigel had never dared to hope.

But he fell desperately in love with her – she who was hope embodied.

'Have you got all your things?'

Rigel turned around.

The woman was standing in the doorway to his room. She had said her name was Anna, but Rigel had hardly listened to what she and her husband had just been saying.

He had seen her throwing a look at the empty bed that used to be Peter's.

'When you're ready . . .'

'She's told you, hasn't she?'

She lifted her eyes, but his were already there, fixed on her face, inscrutable.

'About what?'

'About the illness.'

He saw her stiffen. Anna stared at him wordlessly, maybe surprised that he spoke about it with that cold terseness.

'Yes . . . she told us. She said that the attacks have gotten better over time . . . but she gave us the list of the medicines you take.'

Anna looked at him with a sensitivity that didn't even touch him.

'You know . . . it doesn't change anything,' she tried to reassure him, but Rigel knew they had seen the note about him, and that, on the other hand, changed a lot. 'For me and Norman, it's . . .'

'I have a request.'

Anna blinked, shocked at the interruption.

'A request?'

'Yes.'

She must have wondered if he was the same polite and affable young man who, a moment ago, down in the living room, had introduced himself with the most charming of smiles.

She furrowed her brow, uncertain.

'Okay . . .' she murmured.

Rigel turned. Through the dusty window, he saw Nica placing her cardboard box into the trunk of their car below.

'A request about what?'

'About a promise.'

If you grow up with a wolf's heart, you learn to recognise sheep.

He had always known, long before Lionel had grabbed Nica in the street and shaken her, trying to get his own way.

As he had thrown him to the ground, he had felt the sadistic satisfaction of inflicting the same physical pain that he had endured his whole life. Lionel's pathetic anger only fed the darkness within him.

'You think you're a hero, do you?' Lionel had spat. 'Is that what you think? You think you're the good guy?'

'The good guy?' he'd heard himself whisper. 'Me . . . *the good guy?*'

Rigel had wanted to throw his head back in cruel laughter.

He had wanted to tell him that wolves don't *hope*. They have too much rot inside for such a sweet, light emotion.

If it was true that there is a fairy tale for all of us, his had got lost in the silence of a broken boy with muddy hands.

'Do you want to see inside me? You'd piss yourself before you could take a look.'

He had squashed Lionel's hand to the ground, savouring his pain.

'Oh, no, I've *never* been the good guy,' he'd hissed with a raw sarcasm that came from the soul. 'You want to see how *bad* I can be?'

He would happily have shown him, but he'd remembered that Nica was there.

He'd turned, looking for her.

She was watching.

And in those shining eyes, Rigel had failed, yet again, to see himself for the monster he was.

There was a suffering worse than the pain attacks.

And she was the only one capable of inflicting it.

'We're broken together,' Nica had whispered. 'But you don't let me in, not even for a moment.'

Rigel saw again the broken glass, the cuts on his hands.

He saw the torn-up grass and the blood on his fingers.

He saw himself, so dark and alone, and he couldn't stand the thought of letting her into that disaster that even he would never be free from. Of seeing her touch that naked, angry part of him, that slaughtered his soul and screamed in pain like a living creature.

So he stayed silent. Again.

And her disappointed look scarred his heart.

He wanted to love her. To be with her. To breathe her in.

But life had only taught him how to scratch and tear.

He would never know how to love tenderly. Even her, who was tenderness incarnate.

And seeing those beautiful eyes fill with tears, Rigel knew that if there was a price to pay, to save her from himself, he would give everything he had. Every single petal, for that love with no end.

That moment would have come sooner or later.

Rigel had always known it. But he had been blinded by the hope that he would be able to stay with her forever, that he would no longer be alone. He had found solace in his wishful thinking.

He had seen her lying in his bed, her bare back poking out between the sheets. Then she had opened her hand. Seeing the purple Band-Aid that she had put on his chest, he knew what he had to do.

He clenched his fists and, closing the door behind him, went downstairs with only one aim in mind.

The writhing feeling seized his heart, trying desperately to stop him, but Rigel pushed it back down inside himself with all his remaining strength.

He had looked for his fairy tale, and found it in Nica's eyes.

He had read it on her skin, in her scent.

He had embedded her in his memories of that night, and now he knew that he would never forget her.

Downstairs, the light in the kitchen was already on, even though it was very early, and everyone else was still asleep. He was certain he knew who he would find there.

Anna was wrapped in her bathrobe and her hair was dishevelled. She was busy making tea, but it didn't take her long to notice him standing in the doorway.

'Rigel . . .' She put a hand to her heart in surprise. 'Hi . . . how are you feeling? It's very early . . . I was just about to come up and see how you were doing . . .' She gave him a worried look. 'Are you feeling better?'

He didn't reply. He stared at Anna with those eyes that would hide no more. Now that he was letting *her* go, he no longer needed to pretend.

She looked at him, confused.

'Rigel?'

'I can't stay here.'

He spat out those words as if they were venom.

Anna, on the other side of the room, didn't move.

'. . . What?' was all she managed to whisper after a while. 'What do you mean?'

'Just that. I can't stay here any longer. I have to go.'

He had never found it so difficult to talk. Or so painful. His heart was refusing to leave her.

'Is this . . . some sort of joke?' Anna tried to smile, but all she managed was a pale grimace. 'Some sort of game I'm not aware of?'

He looked her in the face. He didn't need to speak. His eyes would express how firm he was in his decision. She had to understand.

437

Slowly, all traces of colour drained from her face.

'Rigel . . . What are you saying?' Anna looked at him with disconsolate eyes. 'You can't be serious, you can't . . .' She clung to his gaze as disappointment flattened her voice. 'I thought you were doing well here, I thought you were happy . . . Why are you saying this? Did we do something wrong? Norman and I . . .' She paused, before whispering, 'Is it because of the illness? If . . .'

'The illness has *nothing* to do with it,' he hissed. It was always a raw nerve. 'It's just my decision.'

Anna looked at him, anguished, and Rigel held her gaze with all the resolve he had.

'Ask to cancel the adoption.'

'No . . . You can't be serious . . .'

'I've never been more serious in my life. Ask. Today.'

Anna shook her head. Her eyes shone with a maternal obstinacy he had never seen before.

'You think they'll accept it just like that? Without any justification? This is serious. It doesn't work like that, they'll want specific reasons . . .'

He interrupted her.

'There's the note.'

Confusion crept over her face.

'The note?' she repeated, but Rigel knew that she knew what he was talking about. That indelible clause in the Foster Care Placement Order, made just for him.

'The note about *me*. If my attacks interfere with family harmony and degenerate into violent episodes, the adoption process can be suspended.'

'That note is an aberration!' Anna burst out. 'I have no intention of using it! That line about violent episodes refers to the adoptive family, and you've never hurt any of us! The illness isn't an easy way out, if anything it's a reason for you to *stay* here!'

'*Oh,* come on,' he spat back with a sarcastic smile. 'You've always only wanted me because I remind you of your son.'

Anna stiffened.

'That's not true.'

'Yes, it is. Isn't that what you thought when you saw me there, playing the piano? Don't pretend it's not the case. You were never there for me.'

'You don't . . .'

'*I'm not* Alan,' he hissed, making her jump. 'I never have been. And I *never* will be.'

There he went again. Looking in those drained eyes, Rigel got yet more confirmation that there was nothing he could do better than lash out and hurt others.

For a moment, all Anna could do was absorb the harshness of his words. When she looked down again, he was certain he saw her hands shaking.

'You've never been his replacement. Never. We've grown fond of you . . . for who you are. Because of who you are.' Her lips twisted into a bitter smile as she shook her head. 'I would like to think . . . that you've grown fond of us too.'

He didn't reply. The truth was that he had realised he could either love desperately, or feel nothing at all, and in the abyss between those extremes, there was no room for fondness.

The matron's fondness for him had made him reject any feelings of attachment that might spontaneously sprout within him.

'I can't do that. Even if it's what you want . . . I can't send you back there.' Anna looked up, her eyes wounded but bright. 'How can you want to go back there? To that horrible place . . . *No*,' she cut him off before he could interrupt her. 'You think I haven't grasped what sort of a place it is? Do you really need to leave here that badly?'

Rigel clenched his fists. The writhing feeling was twisting through him, tearing and scratching, its screams a desperate condemnation.

'There must be some other way. Whatever it is, together, we can find a solution, we can . . .'

'I'm in love with her.'

Rigel would always remember how that confession had burned. It was so private that he hadn't even voiced it to himself, and saying it aloud in front of someone else was intolerable.

His words resounded through the glacial silence.

'In love with her,' he spat through gritted teeth, 'to the *bone*.'

He felt Anna's gaze on him, and he didn't need to meet her eyes to know that they were frozen with disbelief. Rigel dug his fingernails into his palms and lifted two deep, knowing eyes to her face.

'You get it now? I will *never* see her as a sister.'

There was nothing Anna could do, nothing but stare at him as if she was seeing him for the first time.

Rigel let her.

'This isn't the right place for me. As long as I stay . . . she will never truly be happy.'

As he lowered his face, thinking of her smiling at him with that Band-Aid on her chest, Rigel realised once and for all that if there was a finale, for those like him . . . it had been within him since the very beginning.

'The stars are alone,' the matron had told him once. *'Like you. They're distant, some of them have already gone out. The stars are alone, but they never stop shining, even when you can't see them.'*

Rigel had understood it then, in that moment when Nica traced constellations on his chest.

He had understood, after having watched her sleep all night long, never closing his eyes for an instant.

He had understood that somewhere, deep in his heart, she would always be with him.

'You are not alone.' Nica had said, *'I'll always . . . carry you with me.'*

Because the stars are alone, but they never stop shining, even when you can't see them.

Rigel knew that he would always shine for her, even if he could no longer see her.

She was his star, she had always been the most precious thing his gaze had ever touched.

He would look at her from his cracked heart, and would know that wherever she was, Nica was happy. With a real family, the fairy tale she had always wanted.

'She deserves . . . everything you can give her.'

'Rigel . . . do you want to tell me what's going on?'

He would never forget her eyes. Nica's eyes, where he had lost himself when he was just a boy.

Rigel had looked into those Tearsmith eyes and known, again, that he couldn't lie to her.

'What's happening is that I'm leaving you,' he would have said, if he wasn't the way he was. *'For the first time since you took everything from me, I'm letting you go.'*

But he couldn't bring himself to say it. Not even at the end.

So he did the only thing he had never allowed himself to do.

He lowered all defences.

He looked at her, and that burning love gushed from his eyes like a river bursting its banks.

She had gasped, unable to understand, and he burned her into his memory all over again, every last bit of her.

'Rigel . . .'

He couldn't have anticipated what happened next.

He couldn't have known that they would never get home, that those unsaid words would stay stuck in him like his last regrets.

He would always remember the frozen scream in her eyes.

He would never forget the terror he felt at that moment, his heart thudding to his throat. The netting giving way and Nica falling backwards.

Rigel lunged forwards and adrenaline dilated his pupils. Nica's hair spread out behind her and he saw her *moth wings unfurling in the sunset, an angel about to take flight*.

Another of his hallucinations. The last.

Rigel grabbed her. Moving his body beneath hers was instinctive, born from the need he had always had to protect her. Even from himself.

He felt the writhing. He screamed, thrashed, clutched her feverishly to himself. He felt himself closing around her like a flower, his thorns standing up all together to protect her from the impact.

And before he even realised it was the end, Rigel heard those words bursting from his mouth, the redemption of his whole existence.

'I love you.'

Nica was trembling in his arms, like a butterfly held for too long.

And as that whisper left him, for the first and last time in his life, Rigel felt . . . peace.

An eternal, sweet relief, the almost exhausting abandon he had always fought against.

He would never be alone.

No.

Because Nica was within him. With her innocent eyes and heart-breaking smile . . . She, who would never leave him, who would always be an *eternal star* in his heart.

And as the world tore away the last page of this story without an end, Rigel buried his face in her neck, just like a wolf, and held her to him with everything he had.

With all his strength and all his breath.

With every word unsaid, and every crumb of regret.

With all of his petals.

And all of his thorns.

With everything he had . . . for that love without end.

> *'Farewell,' the robin said to the snow,*
> *Loving it for the last time.*
> *'I was cold, but you tried to cover me,*
> *And now you've got into my heart.'*

Which piece of your heart would you choose?

You can only live with one, because the other will inevitably die.

Which piece would you choose?

'You,' Rigel would reply, eyes closed.

Always, and no matter what, 'I would have chosen you.'

33. The Tearsmith

And so, Love was born. He started to wander
the world, and one day met the Sea.
The Sea was enchanted, and gave him his tenacity.
He met the Universe, who gave him his mysteries.
Then he met Time, who gave him eternity.
And finally, he met Death. He was fearsome,
greater than the Sea, the Universe and Time.
He prepared to face him, but he gave him a light.
'What's this?' Love asked.
'It's hope,' Death replied. 'So I can see you
from afar, and will always know you're on your way.'

When I was a child, they said that it was the truth that brings colour to the world.

That is the compromise. Until you know the truth, you can never see reality in all its colours.

Now that I knew everything I had never realised before, I should have been able to see all the world's brilliant hues, with the eyes of someone who finally understood.

And yet . . . everything had never looked so grey.

The world, reality, even me.

When I was a child, they also said that you cannot lie to the Tearsmith. Because he can read the depths of your soul . . . there are no emotions you can hide from him. He is the one who instilled in you all your desperate, agonising, heart-wrenching feelings.

When I was a little girl, I was scared of him. I thought he was a monster. For me, he was exactly what they wanted us to believe: a bogeyman who would come and take you away if you told lies.

I still didn't know how wrong I was. I would only realise at the very end.

Only with my eyes full of that truth would I finally understand that fairy tale I had carried with me all my life.

Adeline told me everything.

Through her words, I reconstructed that solitary life lived parallel to mine.

Each piece, each scrap of paper . . . everything fell into place, forming the pages of a story that, finally, I could read.

From that moment on, the only thing that dwelled in my eyes was the awareness of an ending I never could have predicted.

The next day, a police officer came to ask me some questions. He asked me to tell him what had happened, and I answered his questions in a monotone. I told him the truth: the meeting with Lionel, the fight, the fall.

Eventually, after having jotted down a few notes, the man looked me in the eyes and asked if Lionel had deliberately pushed us off the bridge.

I was silent. My mind replayed every moment of what had happened, his anger, his vindictive fury, his face twisted in disgust. Then, once again, I told the truth.

It was an accident.

The man nodded, and left as he had arrived.

When they heard about the accident, Billie and Miki rushed to the hospital.

Miki arrived very early. She waited outside on one of the chairs in front of my room, and only got up when Billie ran breathlessly into the corridor, her eyes full of tears.

They looked at each other as the nurses bustled by, one with lips tight with stress, the other with a face red from crying.

The next moment, Billie threw her arms around Miki and sobbed.

They held each other tighter than they ever had before, clutching on to one another, and their embrace radiated with all the warmth of reunited love. They stayed in each other's arms for an eternity, then slowly pulled away, looking each other in the face. The look they gave each other before coming into my room promised light and clear skies after a terrible storm.

They must have spoken.

A lot. At length.

They still had time.

'Nica!'

Billie ran to my bed. She threw herself on me in a hug. My cracked ribs throbbed painfully, but I just half-closed my eyes without making a sound.

'I can't believe it,' she sobbed. 'When I heard the news I couldn't . . . I swear I couldn't breathe . . . *God,* how awful . . .'

She gently wrapped her fingers around mine.

Miki squeezed my hand, her eyes stained with smudged mascara.

I couldn't summon the strength to tell Billie that she was hurting me.

'If there's anything we can do . . .' I heard her murmur, but her words got lost in the black hole that was my heart.

At that moment, Miki turned towards Rigel. I remembered when she told me there was something about him she wasn't sure about. Like everyone else, she had seen the wolf, and hadn't been able to glimpse the soul that flickered beneath.

'Oh, my photo . . .' Billie smiled, drying her tears with her hand. 'You kept it . . .'

The polaroid was there, flimsy and crumpled, tethering me to reality with its unbearable, banal light-heartedness.

I felt my heart rotting against my ribs as she whispered, touched, 'I didn't know you kept it . . .'

I wanted to tell her what that photo meant for me. I wanted her to feel the excruciating pain devouring my insides. It was killing me.

Maybe one day I would tell her.

One day, I would tell them that not all stories are contained in books. That there are invisible, silent and hidden tales that live in secret and die unheard. Fairy tales without an ending, destined to always be unfinished.

Maybe, one day, I would tell her ours.

They looked at me, uncertain, looking for any remnant of my usual carefree self. When I did not move, they decided to leave me in peace.

It was only when they were at the door that I heard myself whisper quietly, 'He protected me.'

Miki, behind Billie, stopped and turned around.

I did not look up, but felt her gaze on me. After glancing at Rigel one last time, she turned around again.

Alone, my attention fell to my hands.

They were both completely white. My skin was bare from my wrists to the ends of my fingernails. On my fingers were constellations of red marks, little cuts and scars.

I slowly looked up. A nurse was arranging Rigel's IV drip on the other side of his bed.

'My Band-Aids,' I murmured mechanically. 'Where are they?'

She noticed I was watching her. Seeing a strangely bright flash in my pale, stagnant eyes, she hesitated.

'You don't need them any more, don't worry,' she replied gently.

My expression didn't change. She came closer to me, and lifted my hand to show me my fingers.

'See? We've disinfected all the cuts. They're clean.' She tilted her head and smiled at me. I didn't smile back. 'Were you doing gardening? Is that how you got all these scratches?'

I stared at her silently, as if she hadn't spoken. Maybe she noticed that I was still looking at her with serious, destroyed but shining eyes.

'I *want* . . . my Band-Aids.'

The woman looked at me, taken aback, not knowing what to say. She blinked a few times, not understanding.

'You don't need them,' she repeated, maybe wondering whether my senseless request was just a consequence of shock.

After I had lost my mind, shouting and scratching and tearing the IV drip away, the nurses on the ward had kept looking at me warily.

The woman seemed very relieved when someone else came in. She turned slowly and disappeared, forcing me to open my eyes.

But I wished I hadn't.

The air froze around me, trapping the saliva in my throat.

Lionel was warily coming in, invading the room. His eyes were haggard and his lips bitten, devoured by stress. That was all I could see, because my eyes mechanically moved away from him to the wall.

I wanted to stop him, to tell him not to come any closer, but I realised that my throat was so tight I couldn't make a sound. He stopped next to my bed and more than ever I smarted from how powerless I felt.

For what seemed like an eternity he sat next to me, in a silence he didn't know how to break.

'I know I'm probably the last person you want to see.'

He couldn't even look at Rigel. The idea that he was lying behind him, hanging on to life by a thread, made my stomach twist like a cigarette being stubbed out.

'I . . . I hear you spoke to a police officer. I know that . . . you told him it was an accident. I wanted to thank you for telling the truth.'

I stared numbly off to one side. Lionel kept trying to meet my eyes, as if urgently seeking atonement.

'Nica . . .' he whispered imploringly, reaching for my hand. 'I never wan—'

He jumped as I forcefully jerked my arm away. The tubes of the IV drip flashed and I looked up at him, my eyes wide and white-hot like never before. My hands shook as with a glacial slowness I enunciated, 'You cannot touch me again.'

Lionel looked at me, hurt by my unexpected reaction.

'Nica, I didn't want this,' his voice was a remorseful lament. 'Believe me, I'm sorry . . . I shouldn't have said those things to you . . . I wasn't myself . . . and the punch, Nica, I promise I never wanted to hit you . . .' He looked at the capillary he had burst in my eye and bit his lip, looking down.

He still couldn't look at Rigel.

'I won't tell anyone. About the two of you . . .'

'It doesn't matter any more,' I breathed.

'Nica . . .'

'*No,*' I whispered, inconsolable. 'Nothing matters any more. I thought you were my friend. My *friend,* Lionel . . . do you even know what that means, *friendship*?'

My voice was unrecognisable, an icy hiss.

This wasn't me. I was always gentle and tender. I had a smile for every occasion. There were crystals of wonder set in my eyes and my fingers were always covered in colourful Band-Aids.

But in that moment, I was the result of a tale torn in two.

The result of a birthday present shattered next to an ice cream kiosk.

Of fleeing from a party. Of shuddering gasps of fear when his hands had grabbed me. Of the disappointment that had stung my heart when he spat out all his disgust and anger and threatened to condemn us.

No, this wasn't me.

Parched, ashy pages scratched my throat as I said, 'I would have forgiven you for everything. *Everything* . . . but not this.'

I knew it wasn't his fault. And yet, looking back on the sequence of events that had started with a little snail, I wondered if Lionel had ever cared for me with the pure and unconditional selflessness that I had felt towards him.

'Leave.'

He swallowed his distress.

It was true that I had a moth-like heart.

It was true that I pursued the light until I got burnt, because what I had gone through as a child had broken me, beyond repair. But even though the most ruined parts of my soul tried to persuade my eyes to meet his, nothing could convince me to forgive him.

He had torn away half of my soul.

Lionel pursed his lips, and tried to say something that wilted away into silence. There was nothing he could say that could bring back what he had taken from me.

In the end, defeated, he lowered his face. He turned and slowly walked away. I called after him.

'Lionel.'

I lifted my faded eyes and finally met his gaze. 'When you walk out that door, don't ever come back.'

He swallowed in dismay and threw me one last look. And then he left.

Not even then did he look at Rigel.

Maybe, people like Lionel can never see reality's true colours. They don't have the courage to face the truth, to see it inside themselves.

Even if they did everything in their power to bring out the darkest shades, if they tore and scratched to let the ink spill out.

In the end, all they can do is walk away, not brave enough even for one last glance.

It was difficult to eat.

I never had an appetite, and sometimes I left the trays they brought me untouched. Anna tried to encourage me to eat, but there was a discomfort in her gaze that made all her efforts fruitless.

I could see it in her eyes that evening too, as she helped me to get into a position in which my cracked ribs wouldn't hurt.

'How's that?' she asked. 'Does that hurt?'

I shook my head, almost imperceptibly.

After a while, Anna put her hand on my face and I looked up. I saw a trembling, sorrowful love in her eyes.

She caressed me for an extremely long moment. She examined every inch of my face, and I sensed what she was going to say before she said it.

'I thought I'd lost you too.'

She looked in my eyes and the furrow in her brow deepened.

'For a moment . . . I thought you'd vanish like Alan.'

She tried to hold herself together, but couldn't stop her eyes brimming with tears. She lowered her face, squeezing my hand in her lap.

'I don't know what I would have done . . . without your sweet smile. I don't know how I would have managed, not finding you in the kitchen in the morning, saying hello, looking at me like you do. I don't know what I would have done without your happy face reminding me that it's a lovely day even when it rains, or that there's always a reason to overcome sadness. I don't know what I would have done without you . . . without my Nica . . .'

Her voice broke and I felt her breaking through the numbness inside of me.

I moved my free hand to put it on hers, which was warm and trembling.

Anna looked up and I saw in that sky I loved so much the reflection of my tearful eyes.

'You are the sun,' she whispered, looking at me like a mother. 'You've become my little sun . . .'

I wrapped my arm around her as tears streamed down her exhausted face. Anna desperately held me close to her and I closed my eyes, cradled like a child.

Our hearts laden with sorrow, burning together like a single flame, I shared the sobs shaking her chest, and she shared mine.

Like mother and daughter. United. Close.

Anna tilted her head and her eyes slid to the side. She looked at Rigel with the same desperate love that she showed for me. Then . . . she pulled away and looked me in the eyes, in that deep and knowing way that adults have. No, actually . . . that only mothers have.

And I realised. There, in the silence of the hospital, I realised that she *knew*.

In that instant, my heart collapsed like a house of cards.

'I didn't know how to tell you . . .' I whispered, annihilated. 'I couldn't . . . I didn't know how to show you that lying to you broke my heart. You're the most wonderful thing that has ever happened to me . . . I was scared of losing you.'

Hot streams of tears rolled down my cheeks. I was in pieces.

'My heart was torn in two. I waited for you for so long, Anna, longer than you can imagine, but Rigel . . . Rigel is everything I have. Everything. And now he . . .' I wiped my bony wrist over my eyes, burning with tears.

Anna hugged me but said nothing. Even she knew there was something unbreakable in the bond between us.

And yet . . . she didn't make me feel wrong.

'Rigel told me,' she whispered, and something in my heart jammed like a rusty gear. I trembled in disbelief, overcome with confusion. All I could do was hug her tighter and wait for her to continue.

'I know now that he would never have told me if he had any other choice. He knew that otherwise I would never have agreed to what he asked me. He . . . wanted you to have a family, more than anything.'

Anna held my face and looked for my eyes, only to find them lowered above my trembling, chewed lips. She leant her forehead against mine, holding me until I stopped crying.

'The doctor didn't tell you because he didn't want to give you false hope,' she whispered after a while. 'But . . . he told me that hearing the voices of loved ones can sometimes help.'

I lifted my dull eyes and she continued. 'It stimulates the consciousness, he says, and the long-term memory. None of us would have the power to make a difference. But you . . .' Anna looked down and swallowed. 'You have that power. He might hear you.'

That night, when the hospital fell as silent as a sanctuary, my heart was still quivering. For I don't know how long, Anna's words carved channels within me, echoing through my despairing mind.

I stared into the darkness. The only thing I could make out was an immense void that made every breath meaningless.

He was there, a few steps away. And yet . . . he had never been so distant.

'You wanted to leave,' I whispered into the darkness.

He didn't move. I could hardly see him, but I would have been able to trace the outline of his face even with my eyes closed.

'You wanted to leave without saying anything to me . . . because you knew that I would have done anything to stop you. You knew that I wouldn't have let you.' I stared at him blankly. 'We have to stay together. But maybe that's always been the difference between me and you. I've always deluded myself. But you . . . never have.'

My throat closed slowly, but I didn't take my eyes off him. I felt something inside, pushing to escape.

'The rose was yours,' I continued. 'You tore it to pieces because you didn't want me to understand. You've always been scared I'd see you for what you are . . . But you *were wrong*,' I whispered, my voice breaking. 'I see you, Rigel. And my only regret . . . is not having been able to sooner.'

I didn't want to feel tears burning my eyes again, but it was inevitable.

'I wish you'd let me understand you . . . but every time you pushed me far away. I always thought you couldn't quite trust me, that you couldn't give me a chance . . . It wasn't like that. It wasn't me you didn't give a chance to, but yourself.'

I clenched my eyes shut.

'You're unfair, Rigel.'

There was a silent earthquake trembling inside me, and everything became harsh and boiling.

'You're unfair,' I accused him through my tears. 'You've never had the right to make decisions for me . . . to keep me far away. And now you're about to leave me again . . . Always alone, even at the end. But I won't let you,' I insisted. 'You hear me? I won't let you!'

I tore the bedcovers away. I reached my hand out towards his immobile body, burning with desperation when I realised he was out of reach.

I slipped off the mattress, and my feet shook as they touched the floor. My ankle hurt, stiff and swollen, and I gripped the bar of the bed as hard as I could, but it was a pathetic gamble. My legs gave way and I collapsed to the ground, falling on my free forearm with a searing pain. My cracked ribs screamed under my flesh and a rush of pain took my breath away.

I couldn't imagine what people would think of me, if they saw me then. I was a pitiful spectacle, pressing my lips together, tears splashing onto the tiled floor. But in some way or another, I managed to find the strength to crawl to his bed.

I took his hand and struggled to pull it towards me. I held it, as he had held mine so many times, in that dark cellar when we were children.

'Don't leave me alone again,' I begged, on my knees, my eyes ruined by tears. 'Please, don't . . . Don't go where I can't follow you. Let me stay next to you. Let me love you for who you are. Let's stay together forever, because I can't stand a world where you're not with me. I want to believe, Rigel . . . I want to believe that there's a fairy tale where the wolf holds the girl's hand. Stay with me and we'll write it together . . . Please . . .'

I pressed my forehead against his hand, bathing his knuckles in tears.

'*Please* . . .' I repeated, my voice twisted with sobs.

I don't know how long I stayed there, wishing I could meld with his soul.

But something changed that night.

If it was true that he could hear me . . .

I would give him everything I had.

The next day I asked the nurses to no longer close the curtain that separated me from Rigel. Not in the morning nor the evening: at every moment, I wanted to be able to see the face of the boy in the bed next to me.

When Anna arrived at the hospital, she didn't find me with dull eyes and a blank expression as she had the previous days.

No.

When she arrived, I was already awake, sat up in bed, my gaze alert and attentive.

'Hello,' I greeted her, before she could say anything.

She stared at me in surprise, blinking, and when I realised Adeline was with her, a wave of warmth softened my gaze.

'Hi,' I said quietly. Speechless, she glanced at Anna and then looked back at me with a heartfelt expression.

'Hi . . .'

A little later, as she braided my hair, I ate a spoonful of apple sauce.

Relentlessly, the days went by, one by one. As my medical situation stabilised, I spent every free moment making sure Rigel might hear me.

I read him books and stories, tales of the sea. I read whatever Anna brought me, and my words accompanied the silence until evening fell.

Doctor Robertson came by regularly to check on me. He looked at the book I was holding, and when his eyes moved to Rigel, the world suddenly stopped and I felt a suffocating hope take my breath away.

I froze and stared at the doctor with a burning hunger, as if he might glimpse in that immobile body some detail that others hadn't been able to see. Some movement . . . or reaction . . . anything that could catch his professional attention.

Each time, when Doctor Robertson left, my heart ached so much that I had to bite my lips so as not to ruin the pages of the book with my fingernails.

The darkness of the previous days was fading.

I had asked them to always keep the curtains open so that Rigel could sense the sky. Or so that I could see it for him, and tell him about it.

'It's raining today,' I told him one morning, looking out the window. 'The sky is glistening . . . It's like a sheet of metal, dripping water.' Then I remembered something, and meekly added, 'Like when it used to happen at The Grave. Do you remember? The other children would say it's the colour of my eyes . . .'

As always, my words were met with no response. Sometimes that silence stirred in me a desire so absurd that I imagined I could hear him reply. Other times, the suffering was so heavy that it seemed like a battle I could never win.

And the more time passed . . . the more the hopes that he would wake diminished.

The more the days relentlessly went by, the more my frustration seemed like a venom that took away my hunger and the flesh off my bones.

Billie and Miki tried their hardest to stay with me, and Anna sought out countless ways to comfort me – she brought me the mulberry jam I so loved and sometimes she pushed me around the ward in a wheelchair.

One day, the nurse called her and she left me for a moment next to the coffee machine, promising she'd be right back. She must have been frightened when she came back and didn't find me where she had left me. She looked all over the ward for me, worried to death, and it was only when she passed by our room that the panic gripping her throat finally lifted. I was there, next to Rigel's bed, my hand on his, my shoulders hidden by the back of the wheelchair.

'You have to eat,' she whispered, after throwing away the Melba toast with jam that I had refused to touch. I didn't reply, trapped in an impenetrable world of my own, and all Anna could do was lower her face, vanquished by my silence.

She helped me wash. As I unbuttoned my shirt, in the bathroom mirror I saw all the sharp edges of my body, evidence of the loss of all the lifeforce I had tried to transmit to Rigel. If there was a price to be paid to give him all I had, it was in the dark circles that encroached on my protruding cheekbones.

I couldn't sleep at night. Wrapped up in the bedsheets, I counted the sharp *beeps* of Rigel's heartbeat, the only sound in the darkness, praying I wouldn't hear them stop. I was crushed, suffocated by the terror of falling asleep and no longer hearing that sound when I woke up.

When the nurses noticed the stress on my face, they gave me drugs to help me sleep, but I persistently struggled against them, bringing my body close to exhaustion.

'You can't go on like this,' Doctor Robertson said to me one evening, when I had reached my limit.

I was verging on a breakdown, and my healing progress had taken a terrifyingly sudden dip.

'You need to eat more and rest, Nica. You won't get better if you don't sleep.'

He looked at me, dwarfed under the bedsheets, as slender and frail as a chrysalis. He seemed to have reached the end of his tether.

'Why? Why are you struggling against the drugs to sleep? What are you fighting?'

I slowly, torpidly turned my face to his, and saw my ghostly reflection in his eyes.

My grey eyes overwhelmed my emaciated face, shining with a mad determination.

'Against time,' I confessed without blinking.

My voice was as soft as a silk thread.

All he could do was look at me, defeated and knowing.

'Every day takes him further away.'

Billie and Miki came often to see how I was doing, and Adeline was there every day, taking care of me and braiding my hair as she had done when we were girls.

By now, I was used to visitors. But I never would have dreamt that one afternoon, I would see Asia walk in.

Initially, I was certain I must have been mistaken. But when Adeline got to her feet, surprised to see her there, I realised that my eyes were not deceiving me.

Although there was no trace of make-up on her face, I couldn't help but notice that she still looked clean and tidy. Her hair was held back in a ponytail and she was wearing a grey hoodie that did nothing to detract from her sophisticated charm.

Asia looked around warily, like an animal in an unfamiliar environment, and for a moment I wondered whether she was just looking for Anna.

Then our eyes met. A moment passed before she looked at me fully. Her gaze ran over my thinned face, then to my body wrapped in the baggy shirt.

Adeline interlaced her fingers then said meekly, 'I'll leave you alone for a little while.'

'No,' Asia retorted, stopping her. In a softer tone, she added, 'Stay.'

When she got to my bed, she didn't sit down or come any closer to me, and I couldn't imagine what had brought her there.

She stared at the IV drip that ran into my arm. Then, without me saying a thing, her eyes moved slowly to Rigel. She stared at him for an extremely long time. When she finally spoke, I noticed she was biting her lip.

'I've often felt jealous of you,' she murmured out of nowhere, without taking her eyes off Rigel. 'We haven't had much chance to get to know each other. But it's always been clear you have no idea what it means to give up. You never stopped trying to build a relationship with me . . . even though I always pushed you away and treated you like an obstacle. Even though I didn't know you well, it didn't take much to realise that you don't know how to give up.' She turned slowly to meet my gaze, her eyes brimming with accusation. 'But look at you now. You've stopped fighting.'

No, I wanted to say to her, that was exactly what I *hadn't* done. There was an uncrushable tenacity within me that was sapping the breath from my lungs. I was reduced to this precisely because I couldn't give up.

But . . . I said nothing. I kept still, and my lack of reaction provoked something that I never would have expected.

Sadness. For the first time since I had met her, Asia seemed to understand. More than anyone else.

'You can't help him if you don't help yourself first,' she whispered in a completely new, heartfelt tone of voice. 'Don't do as I did . . . Don't let pain destroy you. Don't let yourself drown in regret. You've got something I never had. Hope. If you throw it away, I'll never forgive you.'

She stared at me harshly and I saw her trembling, but in that tremble I glimpsed how she was trying to break through the wall I was wilting behind.

'You can't fight death with sacrifices. But with life. You made me realise that. She's still in this room – the girl who went through hell and then looked me in the eyes to say she wouldn't step aside, wouldn't give Anna up. *Come on,*' she growled, 'let her out. You won't save him by effacing yourself . . . You have to give him a reason to wake up. To make him see that you're here, that you're well, that you're fighting to stay alive, even though living right now is killing you. Don't let suffering turn you into someone you're not. Don't make the mistake I did . . . We don't choose pain, but we can choose how to live with it. And if living means enduring, then do it for him. Give him your strength and courage. He's there, life is still beating in his chest, and you've got to grab on to it with everything you've got.'

By the end of that speech, she was out of breath, tears in her eyelashes and her hard eyes welling with emotion.

She had never looked at me like that. Never. Not once.

And yet . . . . I would remember her gaze forever.

Asia looked away, maybe annoyed at herself for that outburst of emotion. Even Adeline, behind her, was staring at her, speechless. Asia hid her face from me and once again her shining eyes fell on Rigel.

'You still have a chance,' she said quietly. 'Don't throw it away.'

I watched her turn to leave as abruptly as she had arrived, her fingers tight around her bag and her shoulders stiff.

'Asia.'

She stopped. She conceded me a glance over her shoulder, and found me between the covers, my face gaunt and my eyes glimmering with a fragile light.

'Come back and see me again.'

Something shone in her eyes. The next moment, she left, after giving Adeline one last look.

Nothing had changed. But in that moment, it felt like I could see the world more clearly.

'Adeline . . . can I ask you a favour?'

She turned to look at me expectantly.

I looked up at her.

'My Band-Aids. Could you bring them?'

For a very long moment, Adeline stared at me wide-eyed, as if she had grasped the meaning of my words.

Then . . .

She smiled.

'Of course.'

★

457

When my Band-Aids were back on my hands, bringing colour to that white room, I felt something within me fall back into place. I chose the colours carefully, and started to feel more like myself again.

One yellow, like Klaus's eyes.

One sky-blue, for Anna and Adeline.

One green for Norman, subdued like his smile.

One orange for Billie's bubbliness, and one sea-blue for Miki's depth.

One red, for Asia, for her fiery personality.

And finally . . .

Finally a purple one for Rigel, like the one I had put on his chest that night in his bedroom.

Looking at them all together on my hands, I realised that even though love has many different colours, they all pull at the same strings – the heartstrings. Together, they are a unique, invisible force that only the soul can feel.

Those days were difficult.

My stomach was a bitter knot that refused all food. My insides twisted with the need to vomit and Anna ran to me, pulled back the covers and helped me lean over to regurgitate the meal onto the floor.

But, slowly, slowly, I started to eat again, with more determination than before.

Soon, I started to walk again. My ankle healed, and my ribs no longer stabbed like shards of glass when I stood up. Slowly, food started to stay in my stomach and my healing process got back on track.

Asia came to see me again as I had asked her to. She didn't seem convinced, to start with, but when she saw I had regained some colour and was doing better, a little edge in her gaze softened.

Day by day, my face filled out, and the bones of my shoulders vanished back under my skin. The brace was taken off my arm and I slowly started to be able to move again.

But as my body got back on track . . . Rigel's remained exactly the same, immobile, trapped by his feeble heartbeat.

Wake up, throbbed in my chest, as slowly I came back to life.

He was still hardly breathing. Nothing seemed to alter his precarious condition.

'*Wake up,*' I murmured under my breath, as the nurses changed his bandages.

But his face just became thinner, the veins in his wrists stood out even more.

The shadows under his eyes got deeper, and the more I held his hand, the more his skin felt limp under my fingers. The more I watched him sleeping, the more he seemed to fade away under my eyes.

I told him old legends, tales of wolves coming home, but while in the daytime, I fought with light and hope, at night the desire to see him opening his eyes overwhelmed my soul.

'*Wake up,*' *I implored him, prayed, in the darkness. 'Wake up, Rigel, please, don't leave me — I can't carry on living without your eyes. My moth-heart can't warm up without you; all it can do is burn and flutter. Wake up and hold my hand, please, look at me and tell me that together, we're eternal. Look at me and tell me you'll stay with me forever, because the wolf dies in all the stories but this one . . . In this one, he lives, and he's happy, and he walks hand in hand with the girl. Please . . . wake up . . .*'

But Rigel didn't move, and in my pillow, I stifled the sobs I couldn't let him hear.

'*Wake up,*' I whispered until my lips cracked.

But he . . . didn't wake up.

I was discharged a few days later.

The doctor's encouraged eyes shone with the relief of seeing me on my feet, healthy, ready to leave. He couldn't know that my heart was bleeding and tormented, just as it was on the first day, because I was leaving a piece of me behind in that room.

Slowly, I started going back to school.

The first day, just like those that followed, it was impossible not to notice people's eyes always on me. Whispers followed me wherever I went, and everyone was still talking about the accident.

That same day, I learnt that Lionel had moved to another town.

My life went by, dull and ordinary, but there was not a single day I did not go and visit Rigel.

I brought him new bunches of flowers to replace the old ones. I kept telling him stories and did my homework on a chair next to the wall. I went over geography and biology with him, and together we studied literature.

'Today the teacher asked us to write an essay on a classical work of our choice,' I announced one evening. 'I chose *The Odyssey*.'

I flicked through the pages of the book, his heart monitor still sharply beeping.

'In the end, Odysseus makes it home,' I said quietly. 'After many difficulties . . . After having overcome unspeakable trials . . . Odysseus makes it. In the end, he comes back to Penelope. And discovers she's waited for him. For all that time, she waited for him . . .'

Rigel, dull, white, didn't move. His eyelids were pale and thin; they looked like a shroud. Sometimes I found myself wondering how much it would cost him to lift those two thin veils covering his eyes.

I stayed there as long as I could. The nurses tried to send me home, to push me away from those four white walls, maybe more out of concern for my wellbeing than because of the hospital's regulations. But when they found me there one evening, trying to sleep huddled up on the metal chair in the corridor, for once they didn't scold me. But the head nurse told me that in the evening, at least in the evening, I had to go home.

But I didn't want to . . .

I wanted to stay with him.

Because every night, Rigel became paler and more distant, and my soul gnawed away at my bones every moment I was not clutching his hand, trying to pull him out of that abyss.

Every day I arrived at the hospital earlier and earlier, and spoke to him for longer and longer. At the weekend, I drew his curtains and whispered good morning to him, always bringing a new bunch of flowers with me.

But at night . . .

At night I dreamt of his white hands, and his eyelids opening onto starry galaxies.

I dreamt of him looking at me with those unique, deep eyes, and in every dream . . . Rigel smiled at me.

He smiled at me in a sweet, sincere way I had never seen him do . . . In an honest way, that carved an excruciating longing within me.

And when in the morning I realised that it had all been a dream, when I realised he wasn't really there, my chest broke in half and all I could do was sob into my pillow, tasting tears in my mouth.

But the next day, I would always be there with him in that white room, with my flowers and my shattered soul.

'Oh . . .' I exhaled one morning, seeing the sun finally break out after a storm. The light broke into a million pieces and a shimmering rainbow appeared.

'Look, Rigel,' I whispered gently. A sad smile tightened my throat. '*Look at all those beautiful colours . . .*'

My hand shook. A few moments later, I was leaving the room with my lips tense and my fingers over my eyes.

There was something desperate about life continuing onwards, despite my grief, coursing on like a relentless river.

It didn't matter how much I wanted it to slow down.

It didn't matter how much I prayed for it to stop, to look at what it was leaving behind.

The world didn't wait for anyone.

Holding the string of a balloon, dressed in a rib-knit dress, that spring day I stared at his bed from the doorway.

My hair was falling down the sides of my face. There was still that same beep echoing through the silence that the room had been suspended in for so long.

I slowly approached his bed and summoned the courage to look him in the face.

It had been almost a month since the accident.

'It's from Billie,' I whispered quietly. 'She brought me a few, actually. She says that a birthday without balloons isn't really a birthday.'

I lowered my face, as fragile as a leaf. Then I reached over and tied the balloon to the metal headboard. Seeing that balloon so close to his immobile body made my heart ache.

I sat on the bed.

'Anna made a cake with strawberries. It was perfect . . . The cream melted in your mouth. I've never had a birthday cake before . . . But maybe, now that I think about it, you wouldn't have liked it. I know you don't really have a sweet tooth.' I looked at my palms in my lap. 'Klaus is still sleeping under your bed, you know? Even though you never got on . . . I think he misses you a lot. And Adeline does. She doesn't say so, she's trying to keep my chin up, but . . . I can tell from her eyes. She cares an awful lot about you. She just wants you back.'

With my hair covering my lowered face, my eyelashes poking through the locks, I sat there listening to the sound of the heart monitor for what seemed like an eternity.

'You know, Rigel . . . this would be a good time to open your eyes.'

My throat was burning and I swallowed, trying not to crumble. Slowly, I looked up at him.

The light coming through the window kissed his closed eyelids. It had been a week now since they removed the bandages from his head, and the doctor said that as he wasn't moving, his ribs were starting to heal.

But his mind had never been so far away.

Looking at him, I couldn't help but admit that even touched by death, Rigel was still heart-stoppingly beautiful.

'It would be an unforgettable birthday present.' I felt tears welling up. 'The best present you could give me.'

My hand slipped into his, and I wanted him to squeeze it like never before. I wanted him to crush my fingers until they went numb. I felt again that shattering sensation, the sense of foreboding that I was about to go to pieces.

'Please, Rigel . . . There are still so many things we have to do together . . . that I have to tell you . . . You've got to grow up with me, graduate, and . . . have so many more birthdays and you have to . . . you deserve so much happiness . . .' Tears blurred my vision. 'I can give you that. I will do everything to make you happy. I promise you . . . it's all I want. Don't leave me alone in this world. We're broken together . . . and we . . . we fit together. We fit together so beautifully . . .'

My tears fell on the back of his hand. My heart floundered and once again, I felt hopelessly his.

'You're my light. I'm lost without you. I'm lost . . . Please, look at me . . . If you can hear me, please, come back to me . . .'

Something moved inside my hand.

A twitch.

It took a moment for me to register it . . . and the world turned upside down.

He had moved.

A violent emotion seized my throat. I was breathless for so long that my voice failed me.

'D . . . doctor!' I managed to cough.

Gasping, I stumbled off the bed and ran shakily to the door.

'Doctor!' I shouted. 'Doctor Robertson, come! Quick!'

Doctor Robertson rushed towards me, and seeing the expression on his face, I realised that my unexpected shouting had broken through even his professional demeanour.

'What happened?' he asked, hurrying to check Rigel's vitals on the screen.

'He . . . reacted,' I blurted out frantically. 'He reacted to what I said to him . . . He moved . . .'

The doctor stopped looking at the monitor and turned to look at me. My eyes were red and my fingers interlaced, slender and trembling.

'What did you see?' he asked, more warily now.

'He moved,' I replied again. 'I was holding his hand and he moved his fingers . . .'

Doctor Robertson threw another glance at Rigel's vitals, then he shook his head.

'I'm sorry, Nica. Rigel's unconscious.'

'But I felt him,' I insisted. 'I swear, he squeezed my hand, I didn't imagine it . . .'

The doctor sighed, then plunged his fingers into the pocket of his shirt and pulled out something that looked like a metal pen. He turned it on and a very narrow beam of light came out of it, which he pointed into Rigel's eyes after having pulled up his eyelids.

There was no reaction.

The world slowly crumbled around me. All I could do was stand there staring at him, fragile and useless.

'But I . . . I . . .'

'It's not unheard of for patients in a comatose state to twitch every now and then,' the doctor told me. 'They can have spasms, contractions . . . Sometimes they even cry. But that . . . doesn't mean anything. His movement was probably just a reflex, an involuntary reaction to the drugs.'

He looked at me with an embarrassment that broke me even more. 'I'm sorry, Nica.'

For the first time, I felt something much more painful than tears burning in my eyes: disillusionment.

I understood, like never before, how destructive it could be to cling on to hope.

Doctor Robertson put a hand on my shoulder before leaving. I knew that if I had the strength to look at him, I would see the pain he felt for tearing away yet another dream.

I spent my eighteenth birthday there, with my heart pounding against my ribs and that balloon hovering over his immobile body.

When I was a child, they said that it was the truth that brings colour to the world.

That is the compromise. Until you know the truth, you can never see reality in all its colours.

But some of those colours can destroy us.

Some truths have stories that we're not ready to let go of.

I wasn't ready to let go of mine.

But I had no more smiles to show Rigel. I had no more fairy tales to tell him.

I just had an empty heart, eroding me from the inside like a foreign object. There were times when I felt it slipping out of my chest and thudding to the ground under my blank gaze.

In times like those, I thought that if my heart really did fall out, I would kneel down to gather it up without batting an eyelid. All I could feel was pain.

As I stayed there with him that evening, not even the nurses came in to tell me to leave.

Maybe because they had seen my glassy eyes and hadn't been able to tear me away. That bed that seemed to keep not only one, but two hearts beating.

It had been several days since my birthday, and still nothing had changed. He was still there. I was still there.

Maybe we would be there forever.

I had run out of stories, and every light I tried to give him had flickered out like a match behind his closed eyes.

There was nothing left.

My soul was just a deep emptiness, from which resurfaced words that I had carried all my life.

'Once upon a time, in a distant, far-away place, there was a world where no one could cry.'

My voice was a shaking whisper.

'Emotions didn't burn, and feelings . . . didn't exist. People's souls were empty, stripped of all emotion. But hidden far from everyone lived a little man cloaked in shadows and boundless solitude. A lonely artisan, with strange, incredible powers and whose eyes, clear as glass, could produce crystal teardrops.

'One day, a man turned up at his door. He saw the artisan's tears and, spurred by a desire to feel a shred of emotion, asked if he could have some. Never, in all his life, had he wanted anything more than to be able to cry.

'"Why?" the artisan asked him, in a voice that sounded unlike a voice.

'"Because crying means feeling," the man replied. "Because tears encapsulate love and the most heart-wrenching of farewells. They are the most intimate extension of the soul. More than joy or happiness, it is tears that make us truly human."

'The artisan asked if he was sure, but the man begged him. So he took two of his tears, and slipped them under his eyelids.

'The man went away, but many more came after him.

'Each one of them asked for the same thing, and one by one, the artisan fulfilled this desire. And so it came to be that they learnt to cry: with anger, desperation, pain and anguish.

'Excruciating passions, disappointments and tears, tears, tears – the artisan corrupted a world of purity, tainting it with the deepest and darkest of emotions.

'And humanity dispersed, to become what we are now.

'That is why . . . every child must be good.

'Because anger isn't in a child's nature, nor jealousy, nor spite.

'Every child must be good, because tears and tantrums and lies are not in their nature.

'And if you lie, he will know. If you lie, it means you're his, and he sees everything, every emotion, every shiver of your soul. You cannot deceive him.

'So be good, child. Be obedient.

'So don't be naughty, and above all, remember: you cannot lie to the Tearsmith.'

My words faded into silence. Now they were there, glistening in ink, it seemed as if they had been waiting for this ending all along.

'That's how he always was for me,' I confessed. 'He was always what they wanted us to believe. A frightening monster . . . But I was wrong.'

I looked up at him, my eyelids heavy with tears.

I had looked for our fairy tale for so long, without knowing it had been inside me from the very beginning.

'Look, Rigel,' I whispered eventually, destroyed. 'Look how you make me cry. The truth is . . . You are my Tearsmith.'

I shook my head, utterly shattered.

'I realised too late. Each one of us has a Tearsmith . . . A person who can make us cry, make us happy or destroy us with just a glance. A person who's inside us . . . who's so important they can make us despair with just a word, or thrill us with a smile. And you can't lie to them . . . You can't lie to this person, because the feelings that connect you to them are always stronger than any lie. You can't tell someone you love that you hate them. That's how it is . . . You can't lie to the Tearsmith. It would be like lying to yourself.'

I was overcome with anguish, every inch of my being was suffering. I knew that if there was an ending to this story, it would always be with that dark-eyed boy I had seen many years ago on the threshold to The Grave.

'I wanted to look you in the eyes when I told you,' I sobbed, clutching his bedcovers. 'I wanted you to see it in my eyes . . . but maybe it's too late. Maybe our time is up . . . and this is my last chance . . .'

I lowered my forehead to his chest. And as the world faded around me, I confessed to him the words I had been saving for our ending.

'*I love you,* Rigel,' I whispered, my heart in pieces. 'I love you like loving freedom from a dark cellar. Like loving a caress, after years of bruises and punches . . . I love you more than I've ever loved any colour in all my life . . . and I love you . . . as I can love *only* you, you who hurts me and heals me more than anything else, you who are light and dark, the universe and the stars. I love you as I can love only you, you're my Tearsmith . . .'

My body was wracked with sobs and I clutched on to the pages of our story with everything I had.

With every desperate shred of me.

With every tear, and every breath.

With all my Band-Aids, and my soul that would never be able to feel again.

And for a moment . . . I swore I could feel his heart beat harder. I wished I could take it in my hands and hold it to me, to take care of it forever. But all I could do was look up at his face, like I had done every single day.

All I could do was muster the courage to look at him again.

And this time . . .

This time, when my heart fell out my chest . . . I heard the thud. But I didn't bend down to pick it up.

No. I stayed still.

Because my eyes.

My eyes were looking straight into his eyes.

Tired, weary eyes . . .

Black eyes.

The emotion that overcame me was so visceral and incredulous that for a moment I ceased to exist. I was too terrified to hope.

My vision drowning in tears, I stared at that thin gap between his eyelids. I was unable to move. I felt like if I dared to breathe, that moment would shatter like glass.

'. . . *Rigel* . . .'

But his eyes . . .

His eyes were still there.

They didn't disappear, like in dreams.

They didn't evaporate, like an illusion.

They stayed right in front of me, fragile and true, exhausted wolf eyes that reflected my own image back at me.

'Rigel . . .' I shivered violently, too destroyed to believe it.

But I wasn't imagining it. Rigel was looking at me.

This wasn't a dream.

Rigel had opened his eyes.

My forehead furrowed, his name erupted on my lips. I eventually let myself go and that consuming void burst free from me in an earthquake of pain and anguish.

My body was overcome by such an intense joy that my breaths became shuddery gasps. My head collapsed on his chest, drained of energy. His eyes were the most beautiful miracle ever.

More beloved than any sky.

More desired than any fairy tale.

It is true that there is a fairy tale for everyone. It is true, but mine was not a tale of sparkling worlds or golden flourishes. No . . . Mine had spiky rose gardens and eyelids opening on starry galaxies.

It had constellations of shivers, and thorns of regret, and I clutched at them desperately, hugging each of them one by one, every last spine.

I put a hand on Rigel's cheek, sobbing, and he continued staring at me as if, despite his state of deep confusion, my face was stirring a deep and boundless feeling in him.

And I . . . I didn't take my eyes off his.

Not even for a moment. Not even as I stretched my hand out and pushed the button to call the nurses . . . Nor when they ran in, and incredulous voices burst out.

Not even when the whole ward was suddenly plunged into commotion.

I stayed with him the whole time, chained to his gaze, body and soul.

I stayed with him, just as I had every night in my dreams, every day of every week.

I stayed with him, never leaving, until . . .

Until the very end.

It was a little while before Rigel could speak.

I had always assumed that when people woke up from a coma, they were immediately lucid, or at least in control of their body. I discovered that this was not the case.

The doctor told me that it would take a few hours before he would regain complete control over his movements, and that after more than two weeks in a coma, most patients fell into a vegetative state. He was happy that after so many complications Rigel had at least been spared that.

He also explained that after waking up, some people could be agitated and aggressive because they didn't recognise where they were. Because of this, he urged me to speak calmly when I went back to him.

Before he left me alone with him again, Doctor Robertson placed a hand on my shoulder and gave me a smile so full of hope I felt my chest swelling.

When he left, I tucked my hair behind my ear, turning towards the boy lying in the bed. Seeing him so peaceful gave my heart an immense sense of relief.

I ran my fingertips over his face, tracing his features, and beneath my touch, Rigel opened his eyes.

He slowly blinked, still too weak to move, and his eyes focused on the outline of my face.

'Hi . . .' I whispered, softer than ever before. The line on the monitor that pulsed in time with his heartbeat showed two palpitations in quick succession.

Hearing his heart so present, my throat tightened with tears of uncontainable joy. He recognised me and his eyes anchored in mine like binary stars.

I tenderly brushed several strands of hair off his face, convincing myself I wasn't dreaming.

'You've come back,' I breathed. 'You came back to me.'

Rigel looked deep into my eyes, and even though his body was visibly worn out, I thought he had never looked so wonderful.

'. . . Like in your stories,' he blurted out hoarsely. I trembled with a burning love when I heard the sound of his voice again. Tears brimmed in my eyes like old friends. I let myself be overcome with weeping, too shocked to struggle against it.

'You . . . heard me?'

'Every single day.'

I smiled through my tears, feeling them stream down my cheeks. Everything I had told him, whispered, confessed – he had heard it all.

He knew that I'd never let him go. Not for any reason in the world.

'I waited for you a long time,' I exhaled, my fingers interlocking tightly with his.

We held hands, wolf and girl, and in our united palms I found all the light I had never stopped looking for.

'Me too.'

34. Healing

There is a force that cannot be measured:
The courage of those who don't stop hoping.

Rigel's recovery took time.

It took several days before his sleep cycle completely stabilised, and several more for him to regain control over his body.

He recovered full lucidity, and despite the physical impediments that kept him pinned to the bed, it didn't take long for the more intractable sides of his personality to re-emerge.

If there was one thing he had never been able to stand, it was being cared for and worried about, in any shape or form. Maybe, because of his illness, he had spurned this so much that he was now repulsed by the idea of anyone having any sort of concern for him. And so, while he struggled to get better, he wasn't dealing very well with the prospect of being subject to the loving care and attention of complete strangers.

In particular, the nurses.

Over the last few weeks, they had all fallen for that alluring, angelic boy sleeping an unnatural sleep and fighting for his life. They had all tended to him carefully, changing his bandages and looking at him like a dream that was too fragile to last.

Now that he had opened his magnetic, disdainful wolf eyes, the air seemed to crackle with electric excitement.

As was easy to imagine, neither the doctors, nor the head nurse, nor Rigel appreciated this.

'Miss Dover?' I heard one afternoon. I was a step away from the door to his room, and turned around to find the head nurse coming towards me.

'Oh, hello!' I gripped the flowers and the book I had brought with me. 'How are you?'

She was a large, matronly woman with a hefty bust and strong arms. She put her hands on her hips and looked at me with an expression that was far from friendly.

'There have been some *altercations* . . .'

'Oh, erm . . . again?' I stammered, trying to lighten the conversation with a laugh, but she didn't seem in the right mood, so I just gave a somewhat forced smile.

'I imagine . . . yes, that there was some . . . *disagreement* . . .' I tried. 'But try to understand, this isn't easy for him. He hasn't got bad intentions . . . He's a good boy. He barks but he doesn't bite.'

Then I thought for a moment and corrected myself. 'Well, he does actually bite, now and then . . . but that's more in defence . . .' I shook my head gently. 'And you know . . . he finds this situation stressful.'

'*Stressful?*' she repeated, offended. 'He gets all the care and attention he needs!' she retorted. 'And more!'

'Exactly . . .'

'*What?*'

'I'm sure he does,' I hurried to add. 'It's just that he, well . . . how can I put it . . . he's a little *wild*, but . . . I assure you, he can be civil. You'd be amazed to know how polite he can be. He just needs to get used to it . . .'

She was still looking at me with a deeply furrowed brow so I pulled a marvellously fragrant lily out of the bunch of flowers and held it out to her with one of my sweetest smiles. She softened and took it with a murmur. I was satisfied.

'Don't worry. Trust me. I'm sure that he'll be able to behave in a way more appropriate for . . .'

'What are you doing?'

I whirled around. That alarmed voice had come from Rigel's room.

Without thinking, I rushed inside. The nurse at his bedside was red and agitated.

471

I moved around her, and only then saw him.

Bathed in the sunlight illuminating the white curtains, there was a complex bandage around Rigel's chest and the bedcovers were pulled down to his pelvis. His cheeks were shadowed, and he flashed his mesmerising, dark eyes at the nurse next to him.

'What's happening?' I asked, when I saw that he was sitting up, leaning on his arm. He was gripping the bedcovers as if they were imprisoning him.

'I told him he can't get up,' the nurse said. 'But he won't listen . . .'

'It's all fine.' I smiled politely at the woman, putting a hand on his shoulder to guide him back down. I felt his muscles struggling not to rebel. 'There's no need for alarm . . .'

She slipped away, taking his lunch tray with her. I watched her disappear through the door, then turned back to him with a sweet smile.

'Where did you think you were going?'

Rigel shot me a glare like a captive beast, but that was all.

I calmly arranged the flowers, as if I hadn't just caught him disobeying the doctors again. 'How are you today?'

'Marvellous,' he spat out bitingly. 'They'll put a sign outside my room soon, like in a zoo.'

He wasn't in a very good mood. Having been caught trying to sneak off probably didn't help.

'You've got to be patient,' I said gently, reviving the petals with my fingers. 'You're in capable hands, you know? And being *nice,* once in a while, wouldn't hurt. Or at least not hostile. Could you try, at least?'

Rigel stared at me, his upper lip slightly curled, and I gave him an indulgent look.

'They told me you were rude to a nurse. Is it true?'

'She wanted to shove plastic tubes up my *nose,*' he hissed, deeply indignant. 'I politely told her she could put them up her —'

'Oh, Nica, how lovely to see you again!'

Doctor Robertson came into the room, his shirt fluttering and a little card under his arm. He came up to us and with a delighted expression, said, 'Hello Rigel, how was the soup?'

Rigel smiled politely.

'It was *pitiful.*'

'We're in a good mood today, I see,' the doctor observed, then asked him the normal, routine questions.

He asked him if he had any lethargy or light-headedness to report. He asked him if his headaches were frequent and Rigel gave him the necessary answers, as if responding to his questions was an obligation he could not avoid.

'Good,' Doctor Robertson announced. 'I'd say that your recovery is proceeding well.'

'When can I get out of here?'

The doctor blinked and stared at him, wide-eyed.

'*Get out?* Get out . . . Well . . . The microfracture on your pelvis has healed. As for the collarbone . . . that will take a couple of weeks yet. And your ribs still haven't healed. You can't really expect to just ignore life-threatening injuries, can you?'

Rigel gave him a piercing glare, but Doctor Robertson held his gaze, unwavering.

'Remember, as well, that however unpleasant hospital food might be, it's important that you eat. It's necessary for your health to get back on track.'

I found my gaze flitting between them, trying to read the palpable tension in the air. Rigel seemed to be putting in a huge amount of effort to do as I had told him and not say anything *uncivil,* and, after promising he'd be back later in a satisfied tone, Doctor Robertson strutted triumphantly from the room.

Rigel sank back onto the pillows with a sigh so resigned that it almost sounded like a snarl. He lifted his arms, and crossed them over his face.

'If I stay here any longer . . .'

It was unusual for him to speak so much. But what we had gone through had knocked down the wall which had always hidden his soul. It was as if, after what I had said and done for him, Rigel had finally understood that he couldn't hide from me any longer.

'You were in a coma for over a month,' I reminded him, sitting down on his bed. 'Don't you think that all this is . . . appropriate?'

'I would *appreciate it,*' he enunciated through gritted teeth, 'if they didn't come to change my bandages when there's no need.'

'Can't you enjoy being cared for, every once in a while?'

He froze. He moved an arm, and looked at me as if I had said the most ridiculous thing in the world.

'*Being cared for?*' he replied sarcastically.

'Yes, cared for . . .' My cheeks went pink. 'I don't know, you could, you know . . . relax. I know it's not easy for you . . . but every now and then you could try to let someone look after you. Enjoy the attention for a bit,' I stammered, glancing at him. His arms were still raised, crossed over his face, but his eyes were fixed on me.

I got the impression that he was still thinking intently about the idea of being cared for, but understanding it in a very different way to me . . .

Before he could say anything, I got up carefully. I smoothed my shirt and tucked my hair behind my ears.

'Where are you going?' he asked, as if I was leaving for the ends of the world.

I turned and realised he was still watching me.

'I'm just going to the vending machine,' I replied, then I laughed. 'Where are you worried I'll go?'

Rigel gave me a sideways glance, maybe scared that if I left him at the mercy of the doctors, someone would take advantage of my absence to lock him in that room.

It was unusual to see him so vulnerable and nervous, trapped in an environment that in his twisted mind felt hostile. So I smiled at him sweetly and brushed his dark hair off his face.

'I'm going to get some water. I'll be right back . . . Look at that book I brought you, it's the one on the mechanics of stars you asked me for.'

I gave him a lingering look before leaving.

I walked along the corridor towards the lobby and pulled out some change for the vending machines.

'Oh, you're here!'

I turned to see that familiar shock of golden hair.

'Adeline!'

She smiled, radiant, and I moved my hair behind my shoulders. She was wearing a flowy, indigo blouse that looked amazing with her eyes.

'I've brought you the house keys . . . Anna said you forgot them.'

She held out the keys with their butterfly keyring, and I took them.

'Oh, thanks, I hope it wasn't a bother . . .'

'Don't worry, I was coming this way . . . Asia's outside, she drove by the shop and she's going to give me a lift home. Did the lilies go down well?'

'They've got such a strong scent,' I thanked her happily. 'You were right.'

In her shining eyes, I saw that light we had in common.

Adeline was no longer looking for a job. The event at the Mangrove Club had been a big success. Everyone had loved Anna's flower arrangements so much that in the following days she got constant phone calls. She got bookings for event after event, each one more important than the last, and her shop finally got the chance she had so hoped for and so deserved.

And that wasn't all. Her eyes brimming with fondness, Anna had offered Adeline the job she had spent so long seeking.

When Carl, her assistant, had seen her come through the shop door, his jaw almost dropped to the floor. He immediately offered to help her, not knowing that Adeline had always had a rare sensitivity. She was capable of bringing light even to my greyest days. I wasn't surprised to learn that she had a particular affinity with flowers that made her a perfect fit for the job.

And there were no words that could express how I felt when I went into the shop to see Anna and Adeline there together, laughing and chatting.

I had always wanted Adeline to stay in my life. Now I knew that she would.

'Is Asia not coming in?' I asked, looking towards the entrance.

'Oh, no, she's waiting for me in the car,' she smiled, shaking her head. 'You know how impatient she can get.'

An unexpected friendship had formed between them during my convalescence. When Asia came back to visit me, Adeline had done everything she could to involve her. They would sit behind me, each holding a section of my hair, and as Asia would mumble indignantly that it was impossible, Adeline giggled softly and showed her how to do a fishtail braid.

Over time, Asia came back even without me asking her.

'She's not that bad,' Adeline joked.

'No,' I agreed. 'She can be a bit difficult but . . . she's a good person. All she does is tell me I'm stubborn.' I smiled, remembering what she had said. 'Pig-headed, incorrigible and as constant as hope.'

'It's true. You are. You're like hope.'

I raised my face and looked Adeline in the eyes. Her tone wasn't casual like mine. No . . . she was being sincere.

'I'd never manage to do what you've done.'

'Adeline . . .'

'No,' she said, her voice clear. 'I couldn't do it. Staying by him every day without ever losing heart. Waking up every morning with the strength to smile. You gave him all of yourself . . . You spoke to him every day, and every night. You were strong enough to continue even when you were fading away . . . You never gave up. It's true what the doctor says. It's only a light as powerful as yours that could bring him back.'

Embarrassed, a warmth spread through my chest and I smiled gently.

'The doctor never said that . . .' I mumbled, but Adeline gave me the same fragile smile.

'He told me in confidence.'

I looked down at my fingers. My Band-Aids were a reassuring riot of colours.

'Asia helped me. As I was fading away, she helped me find my way. I know now why Anna is so fond of her . . . She was right about her.'

Adeline touched my arm encouragingly.

'Oh,' she burst out as a car horn honked from outside. 'I've got to go . . .'

'Aren't you coming to say hi to Rigel?'

'Oh, I'd love to, but Asia's waiting for me! Maybe tomorrow, after my shift . . . will you be here?'

I nodded happily. 'Of course.'

She smiled at me. Then she said goodbye and turned around in a swirl of golden hair.

I watched her run outside, and glimpsed her opening a car door. Asia lifted up her sunglasses, grumbling reproachfully, and I saw

Adeline chuckling as she put her seatbelt on. A few moments later, the car darted away.

I turned around, a smile on my lips and my hair swishing down my back.

When I got back to Rigel's room, he was no longer alone.

Next to his bed was a tray and the nurse who had brought it was arranging his bedsheets, careful not to tangle the wires of his IV drip. I realised that I had already seen her there many times. It was often her who changed his bandages. She was very young, and as delicate as a fawn. When she touched Rigel's skin, I felt an itch in my stomach.

Rigel seemed to realise that she was stealing glances at him. He was about to shoot a glare at her, but at the last minute, something else flashed in his eyes. He glimpsed at her name badge and then pulled himself up, leaning towards her with a persuasive smile.

'What do you think, Dolores, would it be possible to get something *decent* to eat?'

She blushed and her eyes widened. She tried to reply, but faced with those eyes, all that came out of her mouth were disconnected words.

'I'm sorry but I'm not . . . not . . .'

'*Erm.*'

The nurse jumped as if something had exploded. She turned around and found me standing in the doorway. Her cheeks on fire, she moved away and disappeared behind me.

I stared at Rigel, pouting slightly with a frown. I got to his bed and put the bottle of water on his bedside table, as he watched his chances for a better lunch vanish.

'Could you try not to . . . corrupt the nurses?' I grumbled, slightly sulkily.

Rigel stiffly rearranged himself between the covers.

'I was trying to be *polite* . . .' he joked through gritted teeth, not even trying to be believable. I stared at him, slightly reproachfully.

'You're not supposed to get up,' I reminded him, looking at the complicated bandage on his collarbone. 'The doctor said that you've got to keep your arm as still as possible . . . It hurts, doesn't it?' I whispered, seeing his tense jaw, 'Oh, Rigel . . . You know you shouldn't force it . . .'

Rigel didn't even care about his broken ribs, but I remembered well the stabbing pains every time I moved. Even breathing had hurt. I was sure he must have been in pain.

'If you want to get out of here, you have to take it easy, follow their advice, and above all . . . eat,' I concluded, as my gaze fell on the tray they had brought him.

Rigel gave me a hostile glare but I reached out to take the tray and put it on my knees, looking at the contents. A glass of water and fruit, which, for convalescents, consisted of apple sauce.

I took the plastic tub and turned it over in my fingers before opening it. I put the spoon down and held the tray out to him.

'Come on, eat.'

He glowered at the apple sauce as if it could poison him. I got the impression that moving was really hurting him now. He had seriously overdone it, even though he would never admit it.

'No, thanks,' he murmured, in a tone of voice that would have made anyone desist. Except me.

Carefully, I took the tub and held it in my hands. I rearranged myself then plunged the spoon into the golden pulp.

'What are you *doing*?'

'The more you stay still the better it is . . . That's what the doctor said, right?' I smiled tenderly. 'Come on, open up.'

He stared at me, the spoon in my hand, struggling to understand. When he seemed to realise that my intention was exactly as he had suspected – to *spoon-feed* him – a wild, indignant look sharpened his eyes.

'*No way.*'

'Come on, Rigel, don't be a baby . . .' I breathed, coming nearer. 'Open up . . .' I placed the spoon close to his mouth, and flooded him with my most innocent look.

He clenched his jaw, staring at me, his lips pressed tight shut. It was as if the urge to throw the tray up in the air was fighting furiously against the fact that it was me coaxing him.

'Come on . . .' I wheedled.

Rigel clenched his teeth. He seemed to be straining to not say whatever was caught in his throat. Then, seeing my sweet, keen expression . . . and my encouraging, imploring eyes . . . after what seemed like a genuine internal struggle, he finally decided to open his mouth a tiny crack.

I softly guided the spoon between his lips, and he stared at me, his eyes so burning they almost consumed me. Finally, his gaze full of bitterness, he swallowed.

'Well, was that so bad?'

'Yes,' he spat out petulantly, but I had already prepared a second spoonful. For a moment, I thought he would break it with his teeth. With good will and a lot of patience, I convinced him to eat more than half the tub.

At a certain point, some of the sauce dribbled out the corner of his mouth, and without thinking, I collected it with the spoon. He saw my eyes brimming with tenderness and couldn't take it any longer.

'*That's enough*,' he hissed, snatching the tub and the spoon from me. He dropped them on the bedside table, and before I could protest, the tray suffered the same fate.

'Oh, well,' I said in a little voice. 'We almost . . .'

His arm wrapped around my waist and he pulled me towards him.

I tried to not fall on top of him but it was useless: he was too strong, I couldn't extract myself.

'Rigel,' I stammered, caught off-guard. 'What are you doing?'

I tried to pull back, but he held me tightly against his body. Before I could say anything, he moved his lips to my ear and growled flippantly, 'You wouldn't deny me a moment of being. . . *cared for*. . .'

I flushed. The heat of his skin reminded me how much I had missed him. My breath shook, and Rigel buried his face in my neck and inhaled my scent, encircling me with his arm. I felt him take a deep breath.

'Rigel, we're in public . . .' I stammered, blushing.

'*Mm* . . .'

'What if someone comes in . . .' His fingers slowly probed under my denim shirt, finding a way to touch the skin on my waist. He gripped my hip and I held my breath.

'R . . . Rigel, you don't want to make the head nurse angry again . . .'

I jumped and my eyes flew open, shocked, bringing a hand to my neck.

He had just bitten me.

'*Rigel!*'

Time healed more wounds than one.

I was most relieved about Billie and Miki.

What had happened to me had made them think about how life is too short and unpredictable to waste time on misunderstandings. They finally had a conversation, and even though neither of them told me what was said, I understood that the storm had passed.

One day, I even saw them arriving at school holding hands. Looking in their clear eyes, I knew their friendship had been repaired. Scrutinising Miki's face, I couldn't find any trace of melancholy or disappointment. I knew that for her, as well, the fact of having someone so important back by her side superseded any of her heart's other desires.

Their relationship probably wouldn't go back to what it was like before . . . but watching them holding hands, I understood they too would gradually work out a way to stay together.

Until the very end.

I picked an afternoon to ask them over to do homework together. That same day, I took my heart and opened it like a book.

I told them everything.

From losing my parents, to finding myself on the doorstep of the institute at five years old, alone and with nothing left. I told them about when my days at The Grave became years, and about the matron, the pages that she had torn out of the story of our lives.

And then I told them about Rigel.

I told them everything, not missing anything out. All his biting and teasing; every secret and word left unsaid; every single moment that had tied us together with a thread stronger than destiny.

I told them our story, not changing a single comma.

Even though it was so imperfect and destroyed, even though in many people's eyes it would have been incomprehensible . . . it was the only story I wanted.

At the hospital, things got better. Rigel's bandages were taken off and he started rehabilitation. The complete recovery of his faculties was far from problem-free, and I don't know how many flowers I had to give to the head nurse for the various *disagreements* that arose.

Then . . . there was the question of the adoption.

As soon as Rigel was no longer a member of the Milligan family, he would have to go back to an institute, but Anna did everything in her power to stop him being sent far away. She made many phone calls, went in person to the offices of Social Services to explain that, given Rigel's illness, keeping him nearby would allow him to keep in contact and therefore to maintain a mental stability that was critical for his condition.

With help from the doctor, Anna also attached medical reports that stressed the correlation between Rigel's psychological state and his pain attacks: it had been demonstrated that a peaceful environment made them less severe and frequent, while stress and anxiety just made them worse.

In the end, to all our surprise and relief, they decreed that he should be transferred to the Saint Joseph Institute. The same as Adeline.

The Saint Joseph was so much closer than The Grave, just a few bus stops away. The director was a stocky, burly man, and Adeline assured me that despite his grouchy personality, he was a good person. Looking into her sincere eyes, a part of me felt relieved that Rigel wouldn't be alone.

As for school, on the other hand, Anna had already paid the fees for the whole year, and so he would graduate with me.

As I walked along the deserted hospital corridor late that afternoon, my footsteps echoed against the walls as they had done countless times. It was difficult to imagine that the next day I would not be back.

I came to a stop in front of his room as always.

The bed was made, the chair against the wall was no longer there. The bedside table was cleared, there were no more flowers to break up all the white.

The moment of his discharge had come.

Standing still on the threshold to the room, I admired his backlit silhouette.

Outside there was a stormy sunset, still beaded with raindrops. The clouds were illuminated by a flaming red and the light that shone through the air seemed capable of anything.

Rigel was standing by the window. His black hair framed his face and his strong shoulders stood out against the glass. One hand was slid into his pocket in a way that made him look tragically enchanting.

I took a moment to watch him in silence.

I saw him as a child again, with that angelic little face and his eyes so black.

I saw him at seven years old, with grazed knees and my ribbons in his hands.

I saw him at ten years old, a candle in front of him, staring into nothingness.

I saw him at twelve years old, his eyes wary and his chin lowered, and then at thirteen, fourteen and fifteen, with that unscrupulous beauty that never seemed to change.

Rigel, who never let himself be touched, whose intelligence made everyone fall quiet, who threw his head back in joyless laughter. Rigel, cheekily clicking his tongue, terrifying people with just a glance – Rigel, watching me from a distance, hidden, with the eyes of a boy but the heart of a wolf.

Rigel, so rare, twisted, shadowy and alluring.

I saw him, through and through, and couldn't believe that he was . . . mine.

That inside him, that wolf heart silently carried my name.

I would never let him go again.

★ ★ ★

'Here we go then,' he heard a voice.

Rigel turned his head and saw Nica approaching, her hands clasped behind her back. Her long hair was fluttering, and there was something utterly brilliant in those springs of stars she had for eyes.

She stopped near him, next to the window.

'So, Rigel? Do you agree to stop running away?' Nica asked him. 'To give yourself up to me?'

'Will you give yourself up to me?' He repeated the question back to her, his voice husky and calm. He looked at her deeply and whispered, 'Will you give yourself up . . . to what I am?'

The corners of Nica's mouth curled. She looked at him in that way that melted his soul between his bones and replied, 'I already have.'

And Rigel knew it was true.

It had taken a lot for him to realise. To accept it.

It had taken all her praying.

It had taken tears. And shouting. It had taken her anguish at seeing him leave for a place where she couldn't reach him.

It had taken those words she had whispered to him that last night, to make him understand once and for all.

For a moment, he wondered what would have happened if things had been different. If they had never fallen from that bridge. He would have left, to save her from himself, and Nica would have never learnt that every single choice he had ever made, in his whole life, revolved around one single thing.

Her.

Maybe, one day, even if they could never know when, they would have found each other.

Or maybe not. Maybe they would be lost forever, and he would have lived an entire life imagining her growing up.

Instead, she was there, after weeks of crying.

And looking into those eyes he had carried inside him since childhood, Rigel heard his heart whispering . . .

This is the only way I could understand it.

Hearing you next to me every day.

And listening to you cry every night.

I never really believed that you could want . . . me. And now you know the disaster I am, you can understand why.

I always thought you would be happier if I let you go. I don't know how to be like other people, his desperate heart wanted to tell her. *I never have, and I never will.*

But you made me see that I was wrong.

Because now you know everything, you see me for what I am. But despite this, you don't want to change me. Despite this, you're not afraid. Despite all this, what you want is . . . to stay with me.

And in the end, after all these unspoken words, after everything he had always been, Rigel slowly closed his eyes and just sighed . . .

'I give myself up.'

Her smile was shaking and bright.

'Good,' she breathed, with an emotion that seemed to split her chest asunder. Her look seemed to say, *'We've got time to combine our flaws to make something beautiful.'*

She was so damned irresistible that Rigel wondered how he was managing to suppress the urge to touch her. Before he could give in to the impulse, Nica brandished under his nose what she had been hiding behind her back.

He was speechless.

It was a black rose. With many leaves and a stalk riddled with thorns.

It was like the one that he had given to her long ago, and that he had then torn to pieces in a burst of anguish.

'Is that . . . for me?'

'*Me?*' Nica raised an eyebrow playfully, 'Did *I* give *you* a flower?'

Rigel turned his head, about to frown. He was starting to furrow his brow when something completely unexpected happened.

An invisible force curled his lips, and for the first time he felt something sincere and spontaneous being born within him.

Not the smirk which masked his pain. No . . .

What he saw in the reflection of her eyes was a mercilessly radiant smile.

Nica stared at him, holding her breath. Her eyes were still a little shiny, but now they were wide open and expressionless as he'd never seen them before.

Rigel wanted her to look at him like that forever.

'I like it when you smile,' she whispered, smiling too. Her hands were trembling now, and seeing her like that, her cheeks flushed and her eyes emotional, the urge to touch her became unbearable.

Rigel slipped a hand into her hair and pulled her towards him.

He tried not to hurt her as he embraced her tightly.

God, her hair . . . her scent . . . her shining eyes looking at him without fear, expectantly, even as he held her so tightly.

She was his star.

He bent down to her ear, wrapping his free hand around hers, which was still holding the rose.

As the writhing feeling within him urged him to kiss her inviting lips, Rigel thought he could tell her anything he had been carrying inside, right there and then.

Right at the end of everything.

That he had loved her every day, since she was just a child.

That he had hated her, because he didn't know what love was, and then he had hated himself for exactly the same reason.

That she was so good for him it almost *hurt*, because every flower within him stabbed with thorns, just like that rose she was holding.

He could have whispered so many things, right there, into her ear.

He could have told her, 'I love you, to the bone.'

Instead, clutching her hair, he chose to say . . .

'You are . . . *my* Tearsmith.'

And Nica, so sweet, small and fragile, smiled. Smiled through her tears.

Because it was as if he was telling her . . .

You are the reason I can cry, and the cause of my happiness.

You are the reason my soul is full, and feels, feels everything it can feel.

You are the reason I can withstand any pain, because seeing the stars makes it worth slipping into the night.

You are all this for me, and more than I can say.

More than anyone could ever know.

He kissed her, losing himself in her mouth. He devoured her lips slowly, gently, finding them so soft and sweet it was maddening.

Nica took his face between her hands and for the first time, Rigel found relief in that unbelievable pain that only she could inflict on him.

Because those petals and thorns would always be part of him.

From the beginning to the end.

Whether it was the rose she was holding, or the roses he carried inside . . . it didn't matter.

The flowers she had given him, after all, were all the same.

35. A Promise

There are three invisible things,
with an extraordinary power:
music, fragrance, and love.

The June sun was shining in the sky.

The air was warm and light, like touching a petal.

In the school yard, among the happy chatter of hundreds of voices, crowds of families and students were celebrating.

It was graduation day.

Proud grandparents hugged their grandchildren, while parents took photos for posterity and a light, pleasant music played through the loudspeakers, providing a backing track for every word.

It was one of those days that seemed impossible to forget. There was something magical, different and special in the air, that would lodge in your memory forever.

'Smile!'

A flash lit up our smiles. Anna had a hand on my arm and Norman had his arm around my shoulders as I held my certificate, delighted. My graduation robe brushed against my ankles and the mortarboard on my head looked more funny than serious.

'That one's come out really well!' Billie exclaimed, victorious, and the golden tassel on her cap swung in the air.

'You really are an expert photographer,' Norman remarked, shy and smiling, maybe because she had already taken so many shots of us.

She grew even more excited. 'We should take one of us all together!' she said exuberantly. 'I want to hang it up in the hall at home!'

She gave us the happiest smile I had ever seen. Her eyes were shining like jewels. She turned and ran to where Miki and her parents were standing with two other adults.

Billie's mom and dad were laughing animatedly, and stuck out in the crowd like a pair of multicoloured exotic birds. He was wearing a Hawaiian shirt and she had a head of curls and a pair of extremely showy earrings, a gift from an Amazonian tribe. When Billie had introduced me to them, they had taken my hand in both of theirs and looked at me with the same fervent enthusiasm that I had seen so many times in the eyes of my friend.

I really liked them.

I knew how important it was to Billie that they were there to see her graduate. But seeing how much they doted on her, I knew they wouldn't have missed it for the world.

They were in the middle of telling some lively story, that from their gestures seemed to be something to do with a monkey chase. Miki's parents, as impeccable and composed as royals, were listening with subtle smiles, their hands lightly placed on their daughter's shoulders.

It was all going well.

There was light in my life.

This was a day of immense happiness for me, a moment of pure joy. For a fraction of a moment, my thoughts went to mom and dad.

I wished they were there . . .

I wished they could see me.

In my most treasured memory, I was walking behind them, stopping to look at everything. Dad was the most hazy of the two of them, an outline blurred by time, but I remembered Mom like a light you can't forget.

I lingered behind, ever curious about the world, and she, enveloped in light, always turned around to find me. She looked towards me, smiling, holding a hand out towards me through the sunbeams.

'*Nica?*' was all she said. Her voice was the sweetest sound in the world. '*Come.*'

Someone touched my face.

Norman was carefully rearranging the tassel on my cap. I met his eyes, and he gave me a little smile. His thoughtfulness soothed my heart.

'They've arrived!'

A chorus of excited voices rose around us. Some people turned around to look. Several pairs of girls and boys were advancing across the lawn with large baskets dangling from their arms.

'What's happening?' Anna asked, trying to see.

'It's for the graduates,' I replied, my face breaking into a smile. 'I didn't think they would, but . . .'

I knew that previous years they had prepared a small play, but this year was different. The same committee who organised Garden Day had thought of something that could be both funny and celebratory.

Everyone's mortarboards were replaced by flower crowns: white lilies for the girls, and, for the boys, wreaths of forest green leaves adorned with small, midnight-coloured berries.

It was certainly an unusual choice – maybe even a strange one – but it brought a smile to people's faces to see all those young students walking around proudly with buds and berries on their heads.

Anna brought a hand to her heart and laughed.

Before I could move, someone took off my mortarboard and replaced it with a flower crown. I turned around to see Billie giggling happily and then turned towards Miki, who blew on a lock of black hair that had slipped from under her lily crown. She glowered at Billie, grabbed a wreath from a basket and brandished it like a blunt weapon.

'If I catch you . . .' she threatened.

There was no point trying to intervene. I watched them as Miki ran after her and shoved the flower crown on her head as if trying to knock her out.

I looked happily at Anna and Norman, then, ecstatic, grabbed a wreath for boys and set off. I moved through the teeming crowd of happy faces, as the fragrance of the flowers started to diffuse through the air. I stopped when I found who I was looking for. A short distance away, a beguiling young man was speaking with the principal.

Rigel's gown was hanging open, he was wearing elegant pants, his mortarboard was under his arm and his hands were in his pockets.

I cautiously approached, not wanting to interrupt an important conversation, but at that moment, they started to walk off. I decided to run after them.

I stopped behind him and drew his attention by clearing my throat.

Rigel turned around. His eyes fell on me, but when he saw my mischievous expression, there was a hint of discomfort in his voice.

'Not more photos . . .'

In reply, I gleefully showed him the wreath. His gaze fell to it and he arched an eyebrow.

'You're joking,' he said flatly, but I sensed a note of uncertainty in his tone, as if over time he had learnt when I was being serious.

'You fancy putting it on?' I asked.

'I'd *happily* give it a miss,' he joked dryly, adorable even when he was being a party pooper.

'Come on,' I urged him, coming closer and smiling. 'Everyone else is . . .'

'No . . .'

I interrupted him with a little jump, reaching up and sliding it onto his head. A couple of berries fell and bounced off his chest. Rigel blinked, stiffly, as if he couldn't believe I'd just put a flower crown on his head.

Before he could react, however, I took his chin in my hand and stood up on my tiptoes to kiss his jaw.

He scowled, and I smiled at him angelically.

'It suits you.' I rocked back and forth gently, found his hand and interlaced my fingers with his. Rigel sensed that I was trying to calm him down, and my heart leapt when I thought I saw the corners of his lips curling upwards.

You can smile, I wanted to tell him, my heart racing. *You can smile. For real, nothing will happen . . .*

'You don't say.'

He slowly brought our clasped hands behind my back. He slotted me to him, his eyes staring at me from under his eyelashes.

That wreath really did look good on him. He looked like a prince of the forest.

'Satisfied?' he murmured.

I nodded, radiant, and a lily petal fell over my eyes. He looked at my face as I touched his cheek with my free hand.

'I dreamt of this day.' My eyes rose languidly to his face. 'I dreamt of seeing you here. Of seeing you graduate with me.'

The sweetness of my voice made his gaze deepen. He knew I was referring to when I thought I'd lost him. He was silent, letting me touch him, and he looked down at my lips.

'What happens now?'

'Whatever we want,' I replied softly, because I wasn't scared any more. 'This is just the start.'

I closed my eyes, relishing his closeness, and nestled my head into his neck. I let myself be enveloped by his warmth and wanted him to feel the joy my heart was trembling with.

I was full of life and I was happy. Happy to see him there, with that crown on his head, happy to be with him at the beginning of a wonderful new journey.

I was ready.

'Hey!'

Billie was waving her camera about.

'We should take a photo all together!'

Luckily, she was too far away to hear Rigel's less-than-kind comment. The others joined us, and after a countless number of photographs, we continued with the celebrations.

By the end of the day, the yard was strewn with petals and berries. I said goodbye to Rigel when he had to go, probably to continue the conversation with the principal, and it was just us left in the yard.

It had been an unforgettable day.

I felt someone touch my hair.

It was Anna. She carefully tidied a lily on my forehead and looked at me sweetly.

'I'm so proud of you,' she said, with a tenderness that I engraved in my memory. Those heartfelt, sincere words had me pinned under her gaze.

There was something I wanted to ask her. It had actually been a while that I'd wanted to, but I hadn't found the courage. In that moment, facing her, I realised I couldn't wait any longer.

'Anna,' I breathed. 'I'd like to go and visit Alan.'

My voice was soft but determined. I felt her hand pause in my hair.

'I wanted to ask you before,' I admitted, choosing my words carefully. 'But it never seemed like the right moment. I didn't even know whether it was right to ask you. But I'd like to . . . I'd really like to.' I looked at her with sweet, clear eyes, holding her gaze. 'Do you think we could visit him?'

There was an emotion on her face that I had never seen before.

I had always been scared of being intrusive, inappropriate and indelicate. I had always been afraid of being too much, because affection was a gift that I had always longed for from afar.

Only with time had I learnt that you cannot be overbearing in love. In love, there is only sharing, and reciprocity.

Anna tilted her face, and in her gaze, I saw a reply that had no need for words.

We went straight there that afternoon.

I was still wearing the lily crown.

It was late, and the marble headstones were bathed in the light of the sunset. There wasn't anybody else in the cemetery, and a sense of stillness hovered over the epitaphs, mingling with the warm fragrance of early summer.

Alan was at the end, in the shade of a birch tree.

When we reached him, I noticed that someone had left flowers. They were fresh and full. They can't have been there for longer than a day.

'Asia,' Anna murmured with a bittersweet smile.

There was no moss at all on the headstone. She must have come by often to check that it was always clean and cared for.

Norman knelt down and left a bunch of blue flowers on the grass in front of the headstone. He took a very long time arranging the paper, making sure there were no creases, that it was perfect, every fold and every corner.

When he stood back up, Anna came nearer and touched his shoulder. She leant her head against his while I looked at Alan's grave. The wind was the only sound around us.

I wanted to tell him so many things.

To talk about me, about him, the person he had been. To tell him that, even though I had never heard the sound of his voice, in a strange, vague and impossible way, I felt close to him.

I wanted to fill that silence, to give him something in exchange, something that I couldn't express, because my presence was only due to his absence.

I wanted to find a way to speak to him with my heart, but as Anna and Norman turned around, silence enveloped me as I stood there before him.

I heard them walk away slowly, their shoes resounding against the cobblestones.

I didn't move. I carried on looking at the words inscribed in marble, unable to see anything else.

Slowly, I raised my hands and lifted the flower crown off my head. I knelt down before him and placed it beneath his name, holding it for a moment in my hands, covered in Band-Aids.

'I'll take care of them,' I whispered, letting my heart speak. 'I will try to live up to two such extraordinary people. I promise.'

The breeze carried the fragrance of nearby flowers.

I got up, my hair fluttering around my head. My promise lodged itself into the depths of my soul. I wanted to keep it with everything I had, every day, as long as I could.

Forever.

'Nica?' I heard.

I turned. Everything was bathed in warm sunbeams. Norman and Anna were there waiting on the path for me. She smiled, surrounded by light. Then she held out her hand.

And, in the depths of my heart, I heard the sweetest voice in the world calling:

'*Come.*'

36. A New Beginning

*Every ending is the start
of something exceptional.*

Three years later.

A pleasant warmth came in through the open window.

The rustling of leaves and the spring birdsong floated through the peaceful neighbourhood.

'So . . . leptospirosis is an infection with biphasic symptoms . . .' I chewed the end of my pen, concentrating. I licked my lips and noted down the information, refining the paper that I had to hand in the next week.

Klaus was snoozing on my crossed legs. I stroked him distractedly, flicking through the volume on Infectious Diseases to the appendices.

I was in the third year of Veterinary Medicine, a degree I had chosen with my heart and soul. I found every element of the course fascinating, but it was still challenging, and even though this was a special day, I couldn't avoid studying . . .

'Nica! They've arrived!'

A voice called me from downstairs and I suddenly glanced up. My lips parted in a smile and I dropped the pen on the bed.

'Coming!'

I was so excited that Klaus woke up indignantly. He jumped down off my legs, vexed, just as I got up.

I ran to my bedroom door, but at the last moment stopped in front of the mirror, noticing the state I was in. I tidied my tight, striped shirt and brushed the cat hair off my denim shorts.

I looked a little dishevelled, but that didn't bother me. I looked at my reflection and saw the fresh, bright face of a young woman, not the grey, gaunt face that had crossed the threshold of this house for the first time four years ago.

In the mirror, I saw a girl with a healthy, rosy complexion, with freckles brought out by the sun and a slender but full face. Graceful, no longer bony wrists, and a bright gaze that reflected a soul made of light. More gentle and pronounced curves completed the body of a twenty-one year old. Well, an *only just* twenty-one year old . . .

I smiled and blew on the stray strand of hair over my forehead, then ran out the room.

There were only three colourful Band-Aids on my hands. I looked at them passionately, noting how they had become fewer and fewer over the years.

Who knows, maybe one day I would no longer need them . . . I would look at my bare hands, knowing that all the colours were inside me. I smiled. *Only inside me . . .*

On the landing, I bumped into Klaus, who was still upset about having been disturbed, and as I passed I gave him a little tap on his rump.

He startled, outraged, and I took advantage of the fact that he was still sleepy to start running. He was thirteen now, and spent more time sleeping than anything else, but he could still be quite energetic and run about like a whirlwind.

I laughed as he chased me down the stairs, and in that moment of total euphoria my thoughts flew momentarily to *him*.

When would he call? Was it possible he still hadn't found a moment to write to me?

I reached the ground floor and jumped to one side. Klaus, on the other hand, ran straight ahead without managing to catch me in time. I walked into the dining room, smiling.

'Here I am,' I announced, hearing him mewling angrily from a distance.

Anna turned and smiled at me. She was radiant, dressed in a cotton shirt with puffball sleeves and midnight blue pants. She seemed the bright dream I had wanted ever since I was a child. And that wasn't all . . .

The room was an explosion of carnations. Their fragrance wafted into my nostrils. I approached Anna, paying attention to the vases on the floor. She passed me one of the flowers as I stepped over a red bouquet. I took it in my hands, we exchanged a knowing look and plunged our noses into the petals.

'Bread!'

'Fresh laundry and . . .'

'New paper!'

'Apple peel . . . no, actually . . . ginger . . .'

'It's definitely bread. Freshly baked!'

'I've never heard of a flower that smells of bread!'

Like every time, I couldn't help but laugh. I plunged my nose into the carnation and gave an entertained giggle which she shared.

This would always be our game.

Even though many things had changed, Anna and I would always look at each other like that.

After the success of those years, her business had grown so much that she hadn't only significantly expanded the shop, but now had two more. One had already been going for two years, and the other was almost ready. Anna seemed to have exclusive rights to flower arrangements in town, and bookings kept coming in.

Now there was a state-of-the-art television shining in our living room, and the couches were brand new. The ceilings had all been repainted and there was a lovely red car in the refurbished driveway. But it was still our house, and I wouldn't have changed it for anything in the world.

I liked it like this, with the wallpaper and narrow staircase, the smooth parquet flooring that Klaus skidded on and the copper pans glistening in the kitchen light.

And Anna too . . . despite her sophisticated clothes and her elegant silver hair clip, she still had the same eyes that I had first seen at the foot of the stairs, that morning at The Grave.

She had become my adoptive mom.

After a year of foster care, she and Norman had confirmed my adoption and we had become a family.

Now, I was Nica Milligan.

Even though, to start with, I was scared to change my surname, over time I became convinced I had made the right decision. There was nothing nicer than seeing my name and reading within it the union of the four people who thought of me as a daughter.

'I'd best get them out of the way by tonight, or we won't have room to eat,' Anna noted lightly.

'We could eat like this, Adeline and Carl wouldn't mind . . .' I turned the carnation and then asked nervously, 'Do you think Carl will ask her to marry him? I know it's maybe a bit soon, but he's twenty-eight . . . and sometimes when I try to ask Adeline, she blushes furiously and hides her smile behind her hands . . .'

'That girl doesn't tell us everything,' Anna chuckled, admiring the flower.

I heard my phone ringing and looked up, my hair swishing.

It was him!

I stammered to Anna that I had to pick up and dashed out of the room. I was sure it was in my room, but judging by the sound of the ringing, I must have left my phone outside. Having a little snack whilst barefoot in the garden, with the sun and fresh air, had become a habit that was hard to break.

I rushed out onto the porch but nearly tripped over someone.

'Oh, Nica, careful!'

'Sorry, Norman,' I said, pushing back the hair that had fallen over my face.

He held out my phone that I had left on the wrought-iron table, and I beamed at him.

'Thanks.'

He smiled, then leant over to give me a kiss on the cheek. He was still a bit awkward, but that was one of the things that I liked best about him.

'Happy birthday again,' he said, still wearing his work cap. 'See you this evening?'

'Of course.' I put my arms behind my back and rocked back and forth happily. 'We'll be waiting for you. And . . . please, have mercy on those little mice . . .'

'No mice, it's another hornets' nest . . .'

'Well, they've got reason to exist too,' I replied frankly, tilting my head. 'Don't you think?'

'You explain that to Mrs Finch,' Norman said, looking at me with a telling expression, as if I was being a bit cheeky.

We had always had different opinions about his job, and I didn't miss an opportunity to remind him of what I thought. A few years ago, it wouldn't even have occurred to me, but growing up, for me, had meant gaining confidence, strengthening my convictions and learning not to fear the judgement of my family.

I tilted my head and said goodbye to him, before turning towards the still-ringing phone with trepidation.

It wasn't him.

It was Billie.

A drop of disappointment tarnished my heart. There was nothing I liked better than hearing from my friends, but still, I couldn't suppress a feeling of disappointment that it wasn't *his* name flashing up on the screen.

Had he forgotten?

He wouldn't forget such an important day . . . would he?

I swallowed my disappointment and urged myself to pick up.

'Hello?'

'HAPPY BIRTHDAY!' The words burst so loud in my ear that I almost staggered backwards.

'Billie!' I laughed, confused. 'You've already said happy birthday, we spoke this morning!'

'Have you opened our present?' she asked, curious, referring to the parcel that she and Miki had sent.

'Oh, yes,' I replied, pacing up and down the porch. 'You're . . . crazy!'

'So you like it?'

'A lot,' I whispered sincerely. 'But you shouldn't have. Who knows how much it cost . . .'

'I got dad to advise me,' she ignored me, excited. 'He says it's one of the best on the market. It takes amazing snapshots, and what a colour palette! Have you tried it yet? We put some film in there for you, did you see?'

'Yeah, I've already taken one,' I pulled a photo from my jeans pocket, looking at it tenderly. Anna and Norman, in our dining room, with their arms around each other, smiling. 'It came out well,' I said happily. 'Really . . . thank you.'

'You're welcome!' she burst out, gleeful. 'It's not every day you turn twenty-one! It's an important milestone . . . almost more important than coming of age! It's worth a significant present . . . So, what about this evening? All confirmed? We're coming over to yours for dinner?'

'Yep, Sarah's bringing cake, she said, and Miki wine.'

'Let's hope Miki loosens up a bit,' she confided hopefully. 'At least tonight . . . you know, Vincent's trying his hardest to get her to like him, but . . . well, Miki is Miki . . .'

I sighed, understanding.

I remembered when we were just girls. The time after the accident had been something of a new beginning for everyone.

It hadn't been easy initially. Billie was jealous about everything Miki did without her. I found her behaviour confusing, and more than once I had found myself thinking that maybe, deep down, she shared Miki's feelings after all. I soon learnt this wasn't the case.

Miki was a fundamental part of her life, and over time, Billie had matured enough to realise that being apart sometimes wouldn't mean losing her. She had understood that she couldn't suffocate her with all the affection she felt for her, and when Sarah arrived in Miki's life, she had done everything she could to make her feel at ease.

Miki had met Sarah at an Iron Maiden concert two years ago. When they got together, Miki's father had been gobsmacked to learn that all his efforts to not let *males* into the house had been for nothing.

'Vincent's a great guy,' I tried to reassure her. 'Miki just needs time. You know how she is . . .'

'Right,' she muttered down the line.

Vincent was Billie's boyfriend of several months. He was an unaffected, awkward guy. He made me think of how Norman must have been when he was young.

He knew how important Billie's relationship with Miki was to her, and he always tried to involve her. He always left her the best place at the table, and tried as hard as he could to entertain her with his jokes, trying to get her to accept him. She made him work hard.

Miki had never been good at making new friends. And Vincent . . . well, he wasn't a friend, but Billie's boyfriend. And even though that special place in her heart now belonged to Sarah, maybe out of some sort of . . . protective instinct towards her best friend, Miki had never let down her defences.

Their relationship had always been very exclusive. Maybe that was why it was so complicated.

'Give her time. It'll all be fine tonight, you'll see.'

'It's just that . . . I want her to like him,' she sighed. 'It's very important for me . . . to know that the people I love like him,' she moaned. My eyes narrowed in understanding. We were very similar in that respect.

'I'm sure she does like him. It's just that she needs time to show it. And anyway, Sarah loves Vincent . . . she'll manage to soften her, you'll see. Don't worry.'

Billie sighed again, but this time I was sure she was smiling.

'Let's hope the wine has its effect,' she joked, and I hid a smile.

We chatted for a while longer and then I said goodbye, promising her we'd be in touch later to agree on timings for dinner.

When I hung up, the mild sense of disappointment hadn't gone away. My heart stung a little, as if someone had poked it with a needle.

It was a special day, and even though I had never had many expectations, things had changed. We had grown up and I couldn't help but think that no one could begrudge me wanting him to wish me a happy twenty-first birthday.

All I wanted was to hear his voice caress my ears, and to look into those dark eyes where I had left my heart. *I wanted him there,* quite simply, and even though I had told him that I had an assessment to hand in, I couldn't accept the thought that we would be apart, especially today.

That he wouldn't call, especially today.

That he was busy with who knows what university thing, especially today.

Given the excellent grades he had left high school with, Rigel had been given a generous bursary to study at Alabama State University.

I had always thought that he would gravitate towards degrees that were more . . . philosophical or literary, given the boundless knowledge he had of these subjects. Instead, Rigel had chosen to study Engineering. And of all the available subdisciplines, he had decided on aerospace.

It was one of the most difficult and complex degrees, and many students would throw in the towel without completing even the first year. But towards the end of high school, I had realised that he was fascinated by everything to do with the universe.

In hospital, all he had done was read books about the mechanics of celestial bodies. The more texts he discovered on stellar kinematics, the more sleepless nights he spent learning about their laws and theories.

In all honesty, I never thought that he would be so interested in space. Probably because of the complex relationship he had always had with his own name, and everything that the solitude of the stars meant for him. But maybe, in some way, constellations and galaxies had become so much a part of him that his desire to understand their secrets had transformed into a profound, boundless interest, so much so that he had actually chosen them.

We are scared of the unknown, I had read once. Rigel had chosen to no longer let himself be dominated by what had always marked him, but rather to study it until he had analysed it, understood it, and made it his. Perhaps the stars had always been written in the story of his life, ever since they had watched over him, that night, wrapped in a basket in front of the gates to The Grave.

The lecturers constantly told him how brilliant he was, that he had a dazzling career ahead of him.

However, while I was happy for him, his studies took up even more of his time than mine did. And as if that wasn't enough, ever since his freshman year, Rigel had made use of his knowledge to give private tutoring.

It was wild how many students despaired about exams, especially for a difficult major like his. Some people offered him an exorbitant amount of money to help them; others needed to overcome one last hurdle to get their degrees and seemed up for anything.

For that reason, lately I had hardly seen him. He was busy with assessments, and private tutoring took up a large part of his time. It was almost as if he had some specific goal in mind.

Rigel certainly wasn't someone who would go out of his way to help others. He only did so if there was a motive. I knew he needed the money for something, because he didn't spend money as lightly as others did.

It was a mystery that he had not revealed to me.

Despite the time that had passed, he still had secrets from me, and knowing that just increased my unease.

Once again, I was surprised by the phone.

It was a message.

From him.

My heart thumped, but fell speechless when I opened the message. It wasn't what I had hoped for.

He had sent me an address.

Underneath, the only words he had added were: 'Come here.'

I stared at the message, expecting to find something else, maybe a happy birthday, but I was disappointed. There was nothing like that.

I read the address he had sent me again, but I didn't recognise it. I guessed that it was somewhere in the town centre, but I didn't recognise the name of the street. There was nothing special about his message, nothing out of the ordinary.

A tinge of disappointment in my heart, I lowered my eyes and went back inside to fetch something I had been meaning to give to Rigel.

Half an hour later, I had arrived at my destination. I looked around for him, and when I couldn't see him anywhere, I assumed he hadn't got there yet. I sent him a quick message to let him know I was there.

Suddenly, my phone screen lit up. Two green eyes shone from the video call request icon.

'Hi, Will,' I said, getting my face into frame.

A boy with chestnut hair greeted me enthusiastically and said, 'Happy birthday, silver eyes!'

I smiled gently and shook my head, embarrassed.

'Thanks . . .'

'So? How does it feel to be old?'

'Still snowed under with studies,' I replied jokingly. 'I've still got to finish the paper on Infectious Diseases. Where are you at with it?'

'I started it, but . . . Oh, come on, I don't want to talk about that.'

Will was a veterinary student like me. We followed the same courses, and we often discussed the subjects and exchanged notes for exams. He was a dishevelled, sporty-looking guy, with bright green eyes. Recently, he had started saving me a seat next to him in the third row of the lecture hall, even though I hadn't asked him to.

We chatted for a while and his dazzling smile kept me company as I walked along the sidewalk in the afternoon sun.

'. . . It makes me nervous. Lab, I mean . . . I want to be good, but using the scalpel always . . . has a certain effect on me. I know it will be our job, and that we'll be doing good work, but I'm just not very good at it . . .'

'You are, though. You're a lot more delicate than the others. It took you an entire year to muster the courage . . . and you're so careful . . . it's crazy. Do I have to remind you that the lecturer used you as an example in the last lab?'

I bit my lip and brushed away a strand of hair that had fallen into my eyes. Will's eyes watched the movement of my fingers.

'You know, Nica, I was thinking . . .' he said, a subtle change in his tone of voice. 'Well, there's a really great bar in the centre of town . . . Do you know it? The one on the corner of the park. Now that you can drink, well . . . you've got no excuse not to come. I could come and pick you up this evening . . .'

I looked him in the eyes, but the intention I saw shining there implied something that made me look away.

I shook my head and licked my lips. 'I've got plans . . .'

'Oh, yeah, your boyfriend, right?'

The thought of Rigel dazzled me. I felt bewildered and vulnerable for a moment, but long enough for Will to notice.

'Oh, don't tell me . . . your boyfriend has forgotten your birthday.'

I smiled with a hint of pity, unable to believe what he had just said. 'It's not like that at all.'

He didn't know Rigel. He didn't have the slightest idea what we had been through and what it was that tied us together. No one apart from us could read the scars we shared and understand how deeply we were bonded.

We were chained together in a way that no one else could understand. Not even time could draw us apart . . . We had conquered it together, three years ago.

'He's just . . . very busy. That's all.'

'You seem very sure,' Will noted, looking at me carefully. 'But . . . you never talk about him.'

That observation struck me. I thought about it, and after a while I realised that he wasn't wrong.

It was true . . . I spoke very rarely of Rigel. I guarded every page of our story far away from prying eyes; it was a labyrinth to which only I had the keys. I couldn't talk normally about our relationship. It would be like trying to explain the ocean to someone who had never seen it, reducing it to an expanse of water, without considering the beauty of its blue depths or the massive creatures that swam down there with majestic levity.

Some things can only be understood if seen through the eyes of the soul.

Will looked at my thoughtful face and interpreted my silence as hesitation.

'You know, *silver eyes* . . . I'd never forget your birthday.'

I blinked and looked into his eyes, finding them steadfast and determined. He smiled lazily through the screen.

'If, instead of pining after your absent boyfriend, you fancy coming for this beer with me, you'd soon forget about being so callously neglected . . .'

I noticed as he was still speaking, recognised *that* feeling only too late, a diamond blade cutting through the air to the back of my head.

I turned around, my heart in my throat.

He had always sent a shiver down my spine . . . a tingling feeling that was both glacial and boiling.

A young man had appeared on the threshold of a building.

His painfully unmistakable black hair caught the light of the sun. His pale wrists stood out clearly against his broad, strong chest. Magnificently tall, leaning against the door jamb and wearing a studded leather jacket, he looked dangerously attractive.

His explosively beautiful face no longer had the beguiling charm of a boy, but the assertive power of a man. His jaw had lost all trace of childishness and his black eyes under his arched eyebrows contrasted with his pale skin in a bewitching, breathtaking way.

Rigel was staring at me, arms crossed over his strong chest, his head at an angle and his narrowed eyes venomously magnetic.

I felt a burning joy tightening my throat. My heart shook with excitement and my body tensed. I was almost standing on tiptoes, but when I noticed the combustive way he was looking at me, everything abruptly froze.

Speechless, I suddenly realised that he must have heard every word.

'Rigel,' I swallowed. Although I felt an uncontainable happiness, my eyes shone with trepidation: that lethal gaze did not portend the fairy-tale reunion I had hoped for.

'What's up?' Will asked. He hadn't seen what was happening.

My tongue was tied, so I decided to lift the phone so he could see for himself. I framed the boy behind me. His infernal allure was evident even from this distance. I tried to smile as Will turned into a pillar of salt.

'Rigel, have you . . . have you met William?'

'Oh, I don't think I've had the *pleasure*,' he hissed, looking down and cracking his jaw. His deep voice made the walls of my stomach tremble, along with Will on the screen.

The problem was that when he became angry like this, he became, if possible, even more attractive. And decidedly too unpredictable.

Catlike, Rigel stalked away from the doorway towards me. His every step was fluid and precise; he moved like a merciless predator. Having him there made my skin crackle. Even though the emotions emanating from him were anything but positive, I felt the world bending under his feet to frame him.

Will paled as I continued to tilt the screen to get Rigel's height in frame.

'H . . . hi, I'm Will. One of Nica's classmates. You . . . yeah, you're her . . .'

'*Boyfriend,*' Rigel emphasised, coming closer. '*Partner. Lover.* You pick which you like best.'

There was a profound discomfort in Will's eyes.

He must have had a very different idea of what Rigel was like to what he was seeing now.

Rigel stopped behind me, and even I found myself swallowing. Then he bent over, pinned his gaze on Will and hissed, 'You were saying?'

'I . . . I was just saying . . . well, I was asking Nica if she wanted, we could all go out together to celebrate, I dunno . . . somewhere . . .'

'Well, what a *delightful* suggestion,' Rigel drawled. There was nothing *delightful* about his tone. 'How thoughtful. Because, you know, for a moment, dear William . . . I was under the rather distasteful impression that you were asking her out.'

'No, I . . .'

'*Oh,* of course, I must have *misheard,*' Rigel snarled, ripping him apart with his glare. 'A clever boy like you wouldn't make a mistake like that. Would you?'

'Rigel,' I whispered, tense, trying to calm him down, but I jumped as he snatched the phone from my hands. My mouth fell open, but before I could grab it back, he lifted it up out of my reach.

'Rigel!'

'Now that I think about it, *William,*' he clicked his tongue as I chased after him, 'I think we'll have to decline your *kind* offer.

Actually, I've got a better idea. Why don't you go by yourself to get that beer you're so keen on. Maybe then you can have a little think about *being so callously neglected.*'

Will stared at him, disturbed. He must have thought Rigel was deranged as he gave him a creepy sneer.

'Enjoy yourself. It's been a pleasure to meet you . . . *Oh,* one last thing . . .' He lowered his voice so I could hardly hear him. 'The next time you call her *silver eyes,* I'll give you a reason to call yourself *black eyes* . . .'

He abruptly ended the video call.

I stared at him, open-mouthed, gobsmacked. He didn't even deign to turn around to look at me as I gasped, wide-eyed.

'No . . . You . . . Did you just threaten him?'

'No,' he replied without missing a beat. 'I gave him some advice.'

Before I could say anything, he turned around. His face was hard with a burning irritation.

He handed me back my phone, glaring at me from under his dark hair.

'*Just as well,*' he hissed bitterly, 'that you told me he didn't hit on you.'

'He hasn't hit on me . . . Until now he hasn't . . .'

'Yes, I imagine in a class of eighty people, he saves you a seat because he feels *lonely,*' he snarled, prowling around me.

I felt him touch my back, and a shiver bit into my skin. His body was towering over me, waking a deep sense of belonging within me.

'At least he called me . . .' I whispered before I could stop myself. I felt that sentence burning my lips and regretted it instantly.

Rigel came to an abrupt stop.

'*Excuse me?*'

I pulled my sleeves down over my hands, aware that I couldn't take back what I had already said. I decided to take action on the nagging thought that had been eating away at me for hours.

'Not one word. No sign of life . . . It's half five in the afternoon, Rigel. You make me come to this address with no explanation and then turn up like this, angry and abrasive . . .'

In reality, it thrilled me beyond words that he had *turned up like this.* Just being around him made my soul glow deliriously bright. But I couldn't pretend I wasn't hurt by the fact that he had ignored me all day.

'Is this because I was *impolite* to your little friend?'

'I don't want to talk about Will. He doesn't matter right now!' My voice hardened and my eyes narrowed.

My legs were tense and I was almost standing on tiptoes, my hands clenched and my hair brushing against my sides.

'It matters that . . . on such an important day, you . . .'

'Did you think I'd forgotten?'

The slowness with which he pronounced this question made me look up at him. Suspended galaxies whirled in his eyes, so familiar that I softened, but also so boundless that I flinched. I felt a little pinch of guilt.

'No,' I replied, lowering my voice. 'But you're always so busy that . . .' I left the sentence hanging, and couldn't help but glance away.

I bit my lip, feeling foolishly vulnerable under his gaze, as if I had offered him an exposed flank.

I knew he had his own things to do and his time was taken up with his own affairs, and yet . . .

Was it possible that that boring private tutoring was more important to him than spending time with me?

I turned around, and driven by who knows what impulse, walked away from him. I didn't know why I felt almost ashamed . . . misunderstood, childlike, despite my twenty-one years. I knew that he had his projects, his plans, and the last thing I wanted was to come between him and his future.

I had just reached the kerb when two hands grabbed my waist.

Rigel pinned my back to his chest, and held me so vigorously I was thrown off centre. Those fingers that could so agilely run over piano keys plunged into the soft flesh of my body. His masculine scent completely astounded me.

'You think I'm too busy to remember *you*?'

I shivered as his hot lips brushed my earlobe. My breath shook and when I looked down I could see his shoes behind mine. His presence was a burning pressure behind me.

'Is that what you think?' he whispered hoarsely. 'You think that today . . . you didn't cross my mind?'

I tried to turn around, but Rigel held me like that, pressing me forcefully against him.

'Or that,' his breath slid on my neck, 'I haven't spent all day . . . waiting for when I could finally . . . *touch you?*'

His lips and teeth brushed against my neck, and every inch of me burned with his breath. He was only holding me by my hips, but I could feel goosebumps on every nerve.

I jumped as he pressed his mouth against my ear, whispering so softly that he seemed to be suppressing the urge to bite me.

'You think I haven't been dying for the smell of you? Or for the taste of your mouth? You think that . . . I don't fall asleep every night . . . picturing *having you*,' he possessively squeezed my sides, 'in my arms?'

I was hardly breathing. Rigel bent towards me.

'You're cruel, *little moth.*'

My pulse raced, my heart pumped shocks down my nerve endings. I breathed slowly, almost in secret, as if I might let on how deeply his presence overwhelmed me.

'Little moth?' I murmured. 'I didn't think you'd call me that again . . .'

Rigel nuzzled my cheek, and I almost stopped breathing as his hands slowly slid over my stomach, pressing me against him.

'But you're *my* little moth,' he whispered with a boiling sweetness. 'My . . . *sweet* little moth.'

I wavered, completely bewildered by that tone of voice he had never used before, and he seized the opportunity to ask persuasively, 'Don't you want to hear what I've got to tell you?'

Every shred of me answered *Yes,* because that was what I had been craving all day. I stayed still, in a silence charged with expectation, and Rigel understood without me needing to speak.

I sensed him slipping his hand into his jacket pocket. I heard a rustling of fabric, and then he brought his face to mine again.

His soft hair brushed against my temple when he whispered slowly in my ear, 'Happy birthday, Nica.'

He slid something cold and metallic around my neck.

I blinked, surprised, and looked down. When I saw what it was, my mind went blank.

It was a slender, silver necklace with a drop-shaped pendant. The crystal it was made of was so beautifully chiselled that it looked like a white star.

And then I understood.

It was a teardrop.

Like the Tearsmith's.

'Now do you want to know why I asked you to come here?'

I turned around, still shaken by that gift, whose deep meaning belonged only to us. Rigel slowly pulled me towards him, but I knew he was just ushering me towards the door he had emerged from.

I didn't understand until my eyes followed his, which were planted on the intercoms. On the third row, a new nameplate read 'Wilde'.

I looked up, stunned, speechless.

'It's my apartment.'

'Your . . .'

Rigel looked at me with his deep, black eyes.

'I've been saving up since the start of university. The private tutoring meant I'd be able to pay rent, once I'd found a place. And I found one.'

My heart was thumping so loudly I was staggered. He murmured, 'You remember that girl who was struggling with that last exam for a year? She graduated, because of me. And to thank me for being such a *great teacher*,' he smirked, 'she offered me a nice apartment in town at an exceptional price. I wanted it to be a surprise.'

I stared at him, wide-eyed, my heart quivering. He tucked my hair behind my ear, tilting his attractive face.

'I'm not asking you anything,' he whispered, looking me in the eyes. 'I know your home is where you are now. I know you're finally enjoying everything you have. But if you want to come over every now and then . . . and stay over . . . with me . . .'

I couldn't take it any longer. My chest exploded, radiating a heat that cancelled out even the light of the sun. I threw my arms around his neck, clutching him to me with all the strength I had.

'It's amazing!' I shouted, making him stagger. I clung to his body and he held me. 'Oh, Rigel! I can't believe it!'

I laughed, burying my face into his neck, excited that he no longer had to stay in the institute, that he had a place to call home, *his* home, excited about his freedom. Excited that he was so unique and surprising, that we no longer had to be so far apart from each other. I couldn't wait to spend whole days and endless nights with him. To wake up next to his face in the morning, to spend the weekends together, drinking coffee in bed on Sunday mornings.

It was the most wondrous birthday present I could have ever wished for.

I took his face in my hands and kissed him, insanely happy, giggling against his lips as he moaned passionately.

Rigel was holding me so tightly I could feel his heart. I heard it beating just like mine, in exactly the same jarring, mad way.

We were still broken, and that wouldn't change.

We were destroyed, and we would be forever.

But in that fairy tale that bound our souls together, there was something raw and indestructible.

Powerful and everlasting.

Us.

And, about to turn our last page, I realised that eternity *does* exist, for those who love beyond measure, even just for an instant.

Because no ending is ever an ending.

Every ending is just . . .

A new beginning.

37. Like Amaranth

I don't want you without your demons,
without your faults or your darkness.
If our shadows can't touch,
then our souls can't either.

After quickly popping into a gift shop round the corner, I followed Rigel up to his apartment on the third floor.

There was no elevator, but the stairs were as polished as pearls. The stairway was well-lit and led to a large, dark wooden door. On the wall opposite, a brass nameplate shone with his name.

At least that was what I saw before he covered my eyes with his hand.

'Are you peeking?' he asked.

'No,' I replied, earnest as a child. I wished I could control my enthusiasm better. I was sure it was seeping like liquid light from my pores.

'Don't cheat,' he admonished me, his shiver-inducing voice in my ears.

I smiled as he tickled me. I loved it when he let himself be playful and genuine. In those moments, Rigel showed me a side of himself that drove me crazy.

I searched for the keyhole with my fingers, with no help from him, but when I found it I had no difficulty in sliding in the key that he had passed me.

I opened the door and a burst of light filtered through his fingers.

'Are you ready?'

I nodded, biting my lips, and then he lifted his hands away from my eyes.

Before me appeared a welcoming, bright room with a contemporary charm. The furniture was modern and simple, with cream tones that contrasted captivatingly with the shiny, dark wooden floor. Everything, from the window frames to the cushions on the couch matched the coffee-coloured parquet flooring in an elegant, deliberate style. I cautiously stepped inside, letting my eyes explore.

It smelt new and fresh. I glimpsed the door to his bedroom at the end of a small hallway, and my footsteps rang through into the kitchen, my favourite place in any house. For me, it was a room for sharing, chatter, guests and warmth. The bright colours complemented the natural light of the apartment. There was a spacious counter and the steel sink and stove gleamed with a delicate brightness.

It was stunning. It didn't seem at all like a student apartment.

I turned towards Rigel with shining eyes, and only then noticed that he had been silently watching me all that time. Even though he was sure of himself, cutting and intimidating, in that moment he just seemed to want to hear my judgement.

'It's stunning, Rigel. I'm speechless. I love it so much,' I smiled, enraptured. He looked at me with a strange emotion in his eyes.

My cheeks were tingling with happiness, and I started exploring the rest of the apartment, curious and excited. I could already picture him in those rooms, a book in one hand and a cup of coffee in the other. I moved over to an elegant sideboard under the window and from the paper bag I had brought with me from the shop I pulled out a small plant with clusters of red flowers.

I knew that Rigel didn't particularly like plants. He frowned at it.

'What's that?' he asked, with a hint of displeasure.

I smiled, sensing that he found it unusual and a bit ugly.

'Don't you like it?'

From the sceptical way he looked at it, I knew the answer was *No*.

'I haven't got time to look after it,' he replied, avoiding my question, and still a little put out at my sudden departure earlier. 'It will die.'

'It won't die,' I reassured him with a smile. 'Trust me.' I came closer to him, looking at him brightly. 'Now . . . close your eyes.'

Rigel tilted his head and looked at me, intrigued, studying my every movement. He hadn't expected that, and he was normally too suspicious to take orders from anyone. However, when I stopped in front of him, he decided to comply.

I lifted up his hand and opened his silky fingers. Then I placed in his hand a small, shining object, just as he had done with me.

Now it was my turn.

'Okay, you can look now.'

Rigel opened his eyes and looked down.

In his hand there was a little wolf, carved out of a material as black and shiny as obsidian. It glistened in the light like an iridescent gemstone. There was something wild and special about that slender, running wolf. It was refined, unique. It had literally been love at first sight for me.

'It's a keyring. You could use it for your apartment keys,' I told him.

'A . . . wolf?'

I couldn't tell whether he liked it or not.

'It's wild, solitary, and linked to the night. It's wondrous, mysterious and strong. It made me think of you.'

Rigel lifted his eyes to me. My cheeks were burning, and I wondered whether maybe I had gone too far with my sincerity and naïve sweetness. But I had wanted him to see that, despite how he felt in that contentious role, I loved his wolf-like ways more than anything else.

Slightly embarrassed, I opened my handbag and pulled out a picture frame.

It was a photo of the two of us, on graduation day. I was hugging him, a smile bright in my eyes, and he must have been caught off guard because instead of looking at the camera, his eyes were lowered to look at me.

I loved that photo so much I had got it framed.

'It's my favourite photo,' I stammered, blushing childishly. 'But you don't have to put it up, if you don't want to. I thought you might like to have something of us to . . .'

'Stay over tonight.'

His body invaded my space. His scent was intoxicating as he towered over me. I looked up to find him close, burning and bewitching.

'Stay over . . .' he repeated in a low whisper. 'Fill the sheets with your smell. Leave your things about.' His voice got deeper. 'Put your shower gel in the bathroom. I want to find you there when I wake up . . .'

I was struggling to breathe. He put his hands on the sideboard behind me, trapping me. Even with time, I still hadn't learnt to get used to him. He was no longer a boy, and it seemed as if nature had a precise plan to transform him into a bewitching, otherworldly angel. Sometimes I wished he would stop ageing, because the older he got, the more he held himself with a dominating self-assurance that could make any woman pale . . .

'I promised Anna I'd go home for dinner with her . . .' I whispered, as he slowly bit the skin under my jaw. He sucked gently and my body melted.

I sighed, forgetting what I had been saying, and Rigel put a hand on my throat, tilting my head to allow him to deepen the kiss.

Being shut in an apartment with him certainly wasn't something I could complain about, but his intoxicating presence made it harder to keep my promises.

'Rigel . . .' I pursed my lips as he pressed even closer into me. His mouth moved slowly, burningly, behind my ear and his fingers slid into my hair, bending me to his will.

He was good at that.

Both what he did and what he said were very persuasive. And unfortunately he knew all too well how to use these powers to his advantage . . .

At that moment, I heard my phone ringing and jumped. Instinctively, I put my hands on his chest and Rigel stifled a husky, disgruntled moan.

He didn't like it when someone interrupted his plans to slowly devour me.

'I'll bring my things over,' I assured him sweetly, touching his neck. Rigel pulled away from me and I smiled. 'But give me time.'

I left the photo frame in his hands. He looked at me with a frown, then lowered his black eyes to the photo of the two of us. Before I ran to pick up the phone, I saw him contemplating it in silence.

I rummaged in my bag, but by the time I had found my phone, it had stopped ringing. I saw there were three missed calls from Adeline, one after the other.

I wondered why she had been so persistent. That was unlike her. I checked to see if she had written a message, but seeing that she hadn't, I decided to call her back.

I lifted the phone to my ear, but only had time to hear the first dial tone before a loud crash made me jump, my heart leaping to my throat.

I got a tremendous fright. Breathless, I dropped the phone and ran into the other room, where my eyes opened wide.

Rigel was leaning against the wall near the window, his muscles quivering and a chair upturned at his feet. He was violently gritting his teeth and his uncontrollably shaking arms were a tangle of nerves on the verge of exploding.

I stared at him, breathless and frightened.

'What . . .' I started to ask. I saw his clenched fists, his fingers gripping the photo frame violently. He was giving off a burning, neurotic tension. I gasped.

He was having an attack.

Rigel clenched his eyes shut, that invisible pain sending him into a terrifying frenzy. He fell to his knees, the glass shattered in his hands and the shards cut his skin, drawing blood. He put his head in his hands, convulsively digging his fingernails into his black hair. I trembled before him.

'Rigel . . .'

'*Stay away!*' he screamed with a terrifying ferocity.

I stared at him, my heart in my throat, distressed by that reaction. His pupils were dilated, his face was so screwed up he looked almost unrecognisable.

He didn't want me to see him in that state, he didn't want anyone to see him, but I would never have left him alone. I tried to take a step towards him, but he screamed again.

'I told you to stay away!' he snarled like a beast.

'Rigel,' I whispered, defenceless and sincere. 'You won't hurt me.'

His feral eyes stared at me from under his dishevelled hair. In his pained, brutal gaze, I saw a screaming suffering that broke my heart.

I knew that his attacks could be dangerous for those around him, but I wasn't scared for my safety. I slowly approached him, trying to show him I was defenceless, and he stared at me, panting. I was terrified of scaring him, of triggering an even more violent reaction, but slowly, the tremors waned, a sign that the attack was passing.

I had never seen one like this.

I reached him and sat down next to him. He avoided my gaze. I saw the nerves in his tense jaw, the vein throbbing in his temple, and imagined that his head was exploding.

With cautious, very gentle movements, I let my hands slide around his chest and hugged him from behind.

His heart was pounding madly. He was still shaking.

'It's okay, I'm here,' I said, as softly as possible, knowing he found that tone of voice calming and reassuring.

He was digging his fingernails into his palms. I was scared he had hurt his head, but I didn't move to check, not yet. He needed stillness and silence.

On the floor, the photo of us lay among bloody shards of glass. It was scratched and ruined. Rigel stared at the broken frame and shattered glass for a moment that seemed like an eternity.

'I'm a disaster.'

'A wonderful disaster,' I specified.

I pressed my cheek against his back, radiating all my warmth to him.

'You're not a bad person. You're not . . . don't think that, not even for a minute,' I said sweetly, and when he didn't respond, I continued. 'You know what the plant I brought you is? It's an amaranth. Its name means "the unfading flower". It's immortal. Like my feelings for you.'

I smiled, closing my eyes.

'It's different from other flowers. It needs very little care, it looks unusual and it's very enduring. It's strong, just like you. And it's unique, exactly like you.'

I didn't know whether my words got through to him, but I wanted to make him see that, even though I couldn't feel that pain with him, maybe it would be less unbearable if we faced it together.

'Stop trying to make it out to be something special. I'll never work well,' he admitted to himself.

I knew how much his illness affected his psyche. The attacks didn't only shake him physically, but they also damaged his mind. They twisted it. They generated resentment, feelings of inadequacy, and such an intense frustration that it made him renounce himself.

'It doesn't matter.'

'Yes, it does,' he whispered resentfully.

'No, it doesn't. And you know why?' I asked softly. 'Because I think you're perfect as you are. I want every part of you, Rigel . . . even those you keep trying to hide. The most fragile and freakish parts. You're not a bad person. You're my adorable, complicated wolf . . .'

I was being over the top again, but seeing him so vulnerable made me want to protect him. I remembered when he was eighteen, the accident had almost taken him away from me. I had let myself fade away, unable to accept the thought of losing him. At the time, I was too young to realise how wrong that had been, but at that moment, I realised that I was prepared to give everything I had for him.

'I'm here for you. I'll always be here for you . . .' I looked up and planted a kiss on his shoulder, before resting my chin there. Then, after one last glance, I went into the bathroom and returned with what I needed.

This time I sat in front of him. I moistened some cotton balls with disinfectant and then tenderly saw to the cuts on his hands. I cleaned his skin, careful not to hurt him, and his eyes followed my every movement. Finally, after having disinfected the cut along his index finger, I pulled out the Band-Aids from my pocket and put one on his finger.

I chose a purple one, just like the one I had put over his heart many years ago. Maybe Rigel noticed, because he looked up into my eyes.

I smiled at him sweetly.

'Let me see for you, because you don't know how to see yourself.'

I kissed his hand, and before he could react, I came closer and nestled into his chest.

Rigel didn't hold me. His hands were still shaking.

But his heart was with me.

Beating against mine.

And amidst those broken shards of glass, our souls took each other by the hand and walked under the stars.

Once again.

I stayed with him that night.

I told Anna what had happened and confessed that I didn't want to leave him alone. The whole night, rather than sleeping, I stroked his hair and waited for his headache to subside. I suspected that that sudden attack was because of the stress of the last few months. What with private tutoring, his studies and other projects, Rigel had put himself under a lot of pressure that had repercussions on his health. That suspicion tormented me until the morning, when I went home, still infested by the thought of him.

I made myself some lunch, unable to stop thinking about the image of him with his head in his hands. I wished I could have reset my mind, rewound it like an old film, but I was destined to relive that moment and wonder what it must have been like for him to endure that pain all his life.

The doorbell rang, tearing me from my thoughts. I went to open the door, assuming it was Norman home for lunch, but I soon realised I was wrong.

It was Adeline. I instantly remembered the missed calls, and that I hadn't called her back.

She stared at me, short of breath, and I brought a hand to my forehead.

'Oh, Adeline, I . . .'

I was about to apologise, but there was an expression on her face I hadn't seen in a long time. Too long. Something visceral and ancient resurfaced within me before she could even say anything.

'Nica,' she announced. 'Margaret's back.'

I must have been in another dimension. Everything suddenly seemed to stop existing. The air, the ground, the sun, the wind, my hand still on the door handle.

'. . . What?'

'She's back.' Adeline came in and closed the door behind her. 'They arrested her at the airport. She's here, Nica. Since two weeks ago.'

After Peter had denounced her three years ago, it had come to light that Margaret had left the country long ago. More precisely, when she had been fired from The Grave, without any investigations into her violent conduct.

At the time, we were scared that she had escaped prosecution, but Asia assured us that for serious crimes, such as abuse, the State of Alabama had no statute of limitations.

Margaret had not only committed a heinous crime, she had done it many times over several years, with extreme cruelty, causing lasting psychological damage. It didn't matter how many years had passed. She had abused, humiliated and beaten children in her care, and not even time could erase what she had done.

'She thought she could come back as if nothing happened. She didn't know that someone had denounced her. As soon as she arrived, they arrested her.'

Adeline was speaking feverishly, but I could sense something underlying her agitation that I felt too: a mix of bewilderment, paralysis, vengeance and terror. I let her get it all out, because I was too overwhelmed to react.

She paced up and down the room, then turned to look at me, her heart in her eyes.

'The trial is in a couple of days.'

I couldn't process that information. I couldn't believe I was there, experiencing this. I felt detached from it.

'They need as many witnesses as possible. Unfortunately, after all these years, not everyone is traceable. Many of us are adults now, some can't be found, others won't come.'

Adeline paused, and in an instant, I understood what she was about to ask me.

She looked at me with her large blue eyes, then with a soft but determined voice, she said, 'Come to the trial, Nica. Give testimony with me.'

That request triggered an irrational panic. I should have been happy about this news. I wanted justice, but the thought of *Her* being so close to my present situation shook me to the core.

And I knew why. I was still going to the psychologist. My fears had diminished, but they hadn't gone away. I still couldn't wear belts. The feeling of leather nauseated me. And in some situations, my terrors came back like monsters gnawing at my soul.

I was not healed. Sometimes, I still sensed her there, like a presence that had never gone away. Sometimes, in the nighttime, I could hear her horrible voice whispering in my ear, *'You know what will happen if you tell anybody?'*

'I want to forget it too, Nica.' Adeline half-closed her eyes, delicately clenching her fists. 'Me too . . . There's not a day that passes when I don't wish I had a different childhood. A happy childhood. Without *Her*. But this is the moment, Nica . . . our moment is here, finally, someone is ready to listen to us. It's our turn now. We can't stay silent, we can't stay out of this, not now . . . For me, for you, for Peter and all the others. She deserves to pay for what she did.'

Adeline was staring at me, short of breath and her eyes full of tears, but there was a steely determination on her face. She was scared to death. I could see it in her eyes.

None of us wanted to see her again.

None of us wanted to face her again.

But we all carried the same scars.

The same desperate desire.

To close that nightmare forever.

I looked at that girl who I had considered a part of myself ever since we were little girls, and in her, I saw the two of us, small and covered in bruises, supporting each other through everything.

'I'll give testimony.'

I clenched my hands so she wouldn't see them trembling. In her gaze there was a flickering but powerful light.

'But you have to promise me one thing,' I continued. 'Rigel can't know anything about this.'

Adeline didn't move. A look of shock and confusion passed through her eyes, making me look away. I didn't need to look at her to know that she had thought I would feel supported by Rigel's presence, that he would have given me strength and courage.

'Is it because . . .'

'I don't want him there,' I interrupted her, more resolute than ever before. I clenched my hands and looked up at her, allowing no discussion. 'He can't come.'

On that fateful day, I wore a pair of dark, tight-fitting pants. My long hair brushed the hem of the little grey vest I wore over a white silk blouse. It felt as though that little piece of cloth was suffocating me, and I couldn't stop fiddling with it. Anna had asked whether I wouldn't prefer to wear a jacket over the blouse, but the idea of something around my wrists was enough to make my stomach turn.

Outside the courtroom, the stately marble floor resounded with the footsteps of elegantly dressed men and women. There was a sophisticated, solemn atmosphere. The ceilings were so imposing that I felt awestruck and insignificant.

'It will all be okay,' Anna's voice whispered.

Adeline, next to her, swallowed almost imperceptibly. Her blue eyes were like an agitated, murky winter sea. She was pale, and there were dark circles under her eyes. I hadn't been the only one who had had sleepless nights leading up to that day. Carl hadn't been able to come, and she was missing him.

'I'll be there with you, in the gallery,' Anna continued. 'We've just got to wait . . . Oh, here she is!'

I turned towards the figure walking up the wide stairs.

Asia came towards us, dressed in a dark skirt and a petrol-blue satin halter-neck blouse. She wasn't wearing heels, which made her look younger, but her determined aura made her seem in perfect harmony with that distinguished, formal environment.

I was surprised to see her there. I knew that she had graduated in Law and that she wanted to become a civil rights attorney, but I hadn't been expecting to see her.

What was she doing there?

'Sorry,' she said in a resolute tone. 'I missed the time change.'

Adeline's eyes filled with something tremulous and shining. I realised she had asked her to come. Asia came up beside her, and held her gaze with a silent strength.

She had come to support us.

I was happy she was there too.

'We've got to go in,' she informed us pragmatically. 'Anna, you go and sit in the gallery. You two, you'll have to sit in the waiting room until they call you up. The attorney general will ask you to introduce yourself at the witness box.' Asia looked us in the eyes firmly. 'Try not to get agitated. Nervousness won't help you. The defence attorney could try to persuade the jury that you're lying. Respond to the questions calmly, as clearly as possible. No one will rush you.'

I wrung my hands, trying to memorise her words, but I had the unpleasant feeling that I had already forgotten all her advice. I had to speak candidly before an audience about something that, despite how much time had passed, still twisted my stomach. I tried to remind myself why I was there, why I was doing this, and summoned my courage.

When we went into the courtroom, I was surprised by how respectfully silent the crowd of people was. Several journalists, over to one side, were waiting for the judge's arrival, hoping to publish the story in the evening papers.

Anna turned towards us, giving us an encouraging look which I clung to with all my heart. Then she went to sit in the gallery. I followed her with my eyes and we sat down near the wall.

I wished there was someone tall and reassuring, with unmistakable black eyes, sitting next to me.

Looking at me in that profound way that only he could.

Holding my hand with his silky fingers.

Defying everyone with his gaze, because I was nervous and scared.

Reminding me that it didn't matter how dark my nightmares were, because that was where I could see the stars . . .

No, my soul decreed. *No, he could not be there.*

He had to stay far away.

In the dark.

Safe.

The judge came in, announced by a court official, and everyone got to their feet. When we sat back down, the clerk of the court announced, 'The State of Alabama against Margaret Stoker.'

A sudden realisation gripped my throat.

She was there.

Suddenly, I no longer felt comfortable in my own skin. I started to sweat. I nervously scratched my palm with my index finger until it became red. I felt sticky, stiff, clammy.

I wanted to scratch myself until I bled, until I got scabs, and then to pick them off, but Asia took the hand I was scraping with and pulled it into her lap, holding it in an iron grip. I didn't have the strength to turn and look at her. Adeline was holding my other hand, gripping on to me, and I clutched back so hard it must have hurt.

'Thank you, Your Honour. Members of the Jury,' the attorney general declared, after having introduced the case and the bill of particulars. 'With your permission, I will commence the examination in chief.'

'Proceed, attorney.'

The man nodded thanks to the judge, then turned to the audience. 'As first witness, I call Nica Milligan to the stand.'

A charge ran through my body. I jumped.

It was me. I was the first.

I got up with a tremor and walked through the silent court as if my skin was not my own. The air felt barbed. I tried to ignore all the looks around me, the faces following me like mute dummies. The witness box was screaming at me, dominating all other thoughts.

Within a few moments, I moved past the gallery and the legal official swore me in, then pointed to the witness box, where I went to sit down under the gaze of the jury. The vest was suffocating me. My hands were sweaty.

I sat on the edge of the seat, my knees tight together and my fingers interlaced, a tangle of nerves. I didn't dare look around.

'Please state your name for the record,' the prosecutor instructed.

'Nica Milligan.'

'And you live at 123 Buckery Street?'

'Yes . . .'

'Your adoption process was completed two years ago. Is that correct?'

'That is correct,' I replied in a tiny voice.

'And can you confirm that your previous surname was Dover?'

I gave another affirmative response, and he took several steps forward, continuing with the examination.

'And so, at the time in which you responded to the name of Nica Dover, you were one of the children entrusted to Sunnycreek Home?'

'Yes,' I murmured.

'And was it Mrs Stoker here who directed the institute, at that time?'

I froze. Time stopped.

A visceral force made me look up and face reality.

And I saw her.

Sat in the dock, like an old photograph. I looked at the woman who had torn away my childhood dreams. Time seemed to turn back years.

She hadn't changed. It was still *Her*.

Margaret stared at me, her eyes as sharp as thorns, her grey, stringy hair hanging down to her shoulders. She was older, her bulldog face was marked by cigarettes and alcohol, but that darkened appearance just made her gaze look even more hollow and ferocious. She still had those burly forearms, those big, nervous hands that more than once had cracked my ribs.

I looked at her. I could still feel her hands on my skin.

Her eyes slid over me, looking at my clean clothes and my healthy, grown-up appearance, as if she didn't recognise me at all. She seemed to not believe that the gremlin with the hands covered in Band-Aids and the dirty face had transformed into the smart, nourished young woman before her.

A strange madness overcame my heart. My temples throbbed, my pulse started to gallop. It felt like someone had just turned my soul over on itself.

'Miss Milligan?'

'Yes,' I whispered, my voice unrecognisable. My fingers were trembling uncontrollably but I tried not to let it show. The attorney brought his hands behind his back.

'Answer the question.'

'Yes. She directed the institute.'

Something within me shrieked, writhed, threatened to choke me. I resisted those feelings, forcing myself to stay present, to not throw to the winds all the efforts I had made with my psychologist. We had confronted the matron many times in my imagination, but having her there before me was a nightmare turned into reality.

The attorney proceeded with the questioning. I responded slowly, fighting against my insecurities, the words that got stuck, my voice that gave way, without ever stopping.

I wished I could look her in the eyes, proudly, and make her see the woman I had become.

I wished I could make her see that I had followed my dreams, just as when I was a child I had followed the clouds in the sky. Without ever giving up.

And I wished that she would see me for what I was, that she would see the strength in my bright eyes, the determination, even though inside it was still that moth-heart that shone.

And yet, I couldn't bring myself to look her in the face.

'Good. I have no further questions, Your Honour.' The attorney general sat back down, satisfied with my statements. Then, it was the defence attorney's turn.

He started to cross-examine me, trying in vain to lead me astray. I didn't contradict myself, I didn't retract my statements, because each memory was still vivid in my head, alive on my skin.

I remained firm in my testimony, further corroborating the charges, and as such, the defence decided to withdraw.

'That'll do, Miss Milligan,' he declared.

I had done it.

I looked up.

A multitude of emotions hung over the faces of the otherwise composed jury members: coldness, tension and incredulity.

I had just finished recounting the details of when she tied me up in the cellar and left me to writhe in terror. Of when my lips cracked from screaming and thirst. Of when she threatened to pull my fingernails out, so I'd stop scratching at the leather belts.

I shifted my gaze and met Margaret's dark, searching eyes. It was as if she had finally recognised me.

Then she smiled.

She smiled like she smiled when she closed the cellar door behind her. Like she smiled when I clutched at her skirts. She smiled in that twisted, repulsive way, a triumphant smirk.

A red, brutal emotion took hold of my throat.

I rushed to my feet and under the request of the judge, left the witness box, clammy and feverish. I was trembling uncontrollably. I crossed the room, temples throbbing, but when I got to the end of the room, instead of sitting down again, I suddenly grabbed the door handle and threw myself out of the room. Bile rose to my throat and I only managed to find the restroom by the skin of my teeth. I grabbed the sink and vomited up all the trauma corroding my soul.

My skin was crawling with sweat, my insides were writhing. I winced as strained tears blinded my eyes: I saw her there, with that mocking smirk and all the pain she had caused me.

In front of *Her* I wasn't a twenty-one-year-old woman.

I was still the dirty little girl, praying I could *be good*.

Hands tried to touch me, but repulsion assailed me and my brain refused that touch. I pushed away the fingers that were trying to help me, and a familiar voice urged me to think straight.

'Leave it . . . No. Stop . . .'

Asia tried to calm me down, fighting against the slaps with which I tried to push her away. Maybe I hurt her, but I wasn't myself. She managed to take me by the shoulders. I trembled.

'It's all okay. You were good. You were good . . .'

I tried to move away from her, but she stopped me, holding me strangely, a little stiffly. And yet warmly.

I tried to struggle free, but in the end, her grip won over my resistance.

Her hands weren't soft like Anna's, nor familiar like Adeline's.

But they held me.

And, even though we came from different, separate universes, I unleashed my tears and let her, for once, touch that childlike heart that I kept hidden from everyone.

That evening, I stood in the shower for what felt like an eternity. I washed away the sweat, the trauma and the shivers that had stuck to my skin. I washed away the smell of fear, the scratches on my wrists and everything that remained from that day.

Then, I went to Rigel's apartment, with a crumpled soul and empty eyes.

My life seemed smeared, like something rubbed out with an eraser. The truth was that I needed to breathe for a while in his presence, to be with him, because he was the only light that could bring me comfort in that darkness I sometimes plunged back into.

He didn't even know what power he had over me.

Rigel took the darkness and transformed it into velvet. He touched my heart, and suddenly, everything seemed to work again, as if he knew the secret melody to make its complex gears turn. He had paradise in his eyes and hell on his lips. He was the only truth that managed to make everything else pale into insignificance.

I slid the key into the lock. I should have at least knocked, but when I smelt his scent in the air, I silently entered the apartment without even thinking about it.

I dropped my bag on the couch and slid off my jacket, noticing a lamp shining on a table in the other room. I expected to see him there, but all I found was a book open on a page about the movement of satellites, a glass of water, a plate with a few crumbs on it and a few pages of notes in his elegant handwriting.

I touched the pen in the groove between the pages and imagined him there studying, his gorgeous face lit up by the lamp and that concentrated expression he always had when reading.

The next moment, I sensed a silent presence behind me.

I turned around. I knew he had the perennial habit of moving about like a predator in the darkness.

'*Perhaps,* you want to explain.'

He was standing in the doorway, magnificent and terrifying. His eyes bored through the darkness in that way that had made me tremble so often. He was holding the evening newspaper. It was rolled up in his hands, but I knew what was written there.

Everyone was talking about the case of the Sunnycreek children.

He came closer and slapped the newspaper down on the table, his stormy gaze still pinned on me. His familiar scent awakened my heart. His eyes were pushing me away and crushing me like black holes, but I felt my body reacting to his closeness, as if it belonged to him more than ever before.

'*Why?* Why didn't you tell me?'

He was angry.

Very angry.

He wanted to have been there. He didn't like what I had done, and the idea of not having been with me for the trial went against his heart's most primordial instincts.

I just wanted to dive into his arms, to feel held, to feel safe, but I knew I couldn't avoid this discussion. Rigel deserved an explanation.

'If I had told you, you would have come,' I whispered. 'And I tried to stop that happening.'

'You tried to . . . *stop that happening*?' His eyes narrowed into two thundering slits. 'And for what reason, Nica?'

There was a flash of realisation in his eyes, destructive, hostile, as if I was his enemy.

'What is it, did you think I was too *weak* to come?' He took a step towards me, oozing anger and pain. 'Is it because of what you saw the other day? The attack?'

'No.'

'Then *what*?'

'I didn't want her to see you,' I whispered with disarming honesty. Rigel didn't move, but something crystallised in his eyes.

'I couldn't stand the thought of her eyes on you again,' I confessed. 'That seeing you would awaken something in her. I wouldn't have been able to bear it. I hate how obsessed she was with you, that sick affection she forced on you. I can't breathe when I think about it. I wanted her far away. I wanted to protect you from her, even if it meant facing it alone!'

My fists shook and my throat burned. I felt tears threatening to burst forth again. I couldn't help but cry; I had reached my limit.

'I'd do it again,' I hissed through gritted teeth, thinking about that smirk, the way she had destroyed me. 'I'd do it a hundred times to keep her away from you. I don't care if you think it was stupid. I don't care if you're angry with me. I don't care, Rigel, I would do anything, *everything*, to stop her seeing you again!'

I clenched my eyes shut, and a desperate force exploded from me like a star.

'So be angry. Shout at me!' I incited him, reeling from the stressful day. 'Tell me I was wrong not letting you come, tell me I made a mistake! Say whatever you want, but don't ask me to apologise, don't, because the only thing that brings me any comfort in all this mess is knowing that for once, just for once, I was able to do something to prot—'

His hands grabbed me and he pulled me towards him.

I collided with his chest with a gasping sob. His warmth enveloped me like a glove and the world trembled in his arms, silenced by an invisible, sweet and incredibly powerful force.

I trembled, sobbed my heart out, my strength falling away from me.

'Fool,' he whispered gently in my ear.

I closed my eyes. God, that was all I wanted to hear. I wanted Rigel to erase Margaret forever, just with the sound of his deep voice.

His hand rose up my neck, trying to cradle me, and I clung on to that gesture with a feeling of desperation. I let him touch my heart, in his own way. He knew how to put me together, just by holding me like that, and I loved him all the more for it.

'You don't need to protect me,' he murmured, so softly it pulled at my heartstrings. 'You don't need to defend me against anything. That's . . . my job.'

I buried my face in his clean, fragrant sweater. I shook my head, moaning against his chest.

'I'll always protect you,' I confessed, as small as a child, because I didn't know how else to be. 'Even if you don't think you need it . . .'

Rigel held me tighter and I let him engulf me, utterly, inch by inch, until I became one with his warmth. He knew I was like that, that we were like that, stubborn and impossible until the very end.

We would carry on sacrificing ourselves for each other.

We would carry on protecting each other, in our own way, choosing silence over words, gestures over anything else.

We would carry on loving each other like this, in that excessive, imperfect way, full of mistakes but as sincere as the sun.

I looked at him with languishing, destroyed eyes, and he tilted his head, looking back at me, calmly and deeply.

My heart pulsed, thrilled once again by his face, by everything he meant for me, and Rigel lowered his lips to kiss me.

His soft mouth gave me a warm, tingling feeling in my stomach. I lifted my arms to his shoulders and pulled him to me with a burning desire.

I interwove my tongue with his, and Rigel gripped my hips, trying to hold me back, slow me down. He was trying to contain the feral passion that was threatening to consume me, but I pushed my fingers into his shoulders and pressed myself against him.

'I need you,' I begged. 'I need this. Please . . .'

Rigel was breathing heavily, his chest heaving, his hair falling into his eyes. I held his face and sunk my soft, needy lips against his.

His muscles tensed. His breath rose to his throat.

I felt his composure crumbling. I kissed him more insistently, and the pressure of my slender body finally made him give in.

He seized my neck and his mouth landed on mine, devouring me with fiery kisses. His tongue invaded my mouth and his confidence stunned me, sending an intense shiver down my spine. I slid my hands through his hair and kissed him with a bewildering passion, drawing a husky moan from his chest.

His breathing became eager, impetuous. Rigel pushed me back until I banged into the edge of the table, which he cleared with an abrupt sweep of his arm. The glass and plate shattered and leaves tumbled to the parquet flooring as he grabbed my body and laid me down.

With trembling fingers, I tried to take his sweater off. Rigel sent it to the floor along with his shirt, burning like a raging fire. His dark hair fell like a soft halo on his strong shoulders. I had no time to admire him before he unzipped the fly of my pants, abruptly lifted my pelvis and slid them down my legs. My breathing became laboured. My cheeks were burning and I found myself lifting my arms up as his tough hands almost tore my hoodie off me.

There was no calm. No patience. We were throwing ourselves at each other like animals.

My skin went numb; it felt frozen and boiling at the same time. My bare shoulder blades collided with the table and Rigel closed his hand around the curve of my neck, squeezing until my nerves burned. I writhed under his touch and my heart beat like crazy as he plunged his fingers into my thigh, and then sunk his teeth into the inside of it, where my flesh was softer and more sensitive. I clenched my eyes shut and a charge ran through me, making me grip the sides of the table.

My body began to quiver, and I let Rigel take me completely, take everything, fill me up with him.

I didn't care if he left marks.

I wouldn't stop him.

I needed this. His red-hot touch, his bites, his dark love.

I needed to lose myself in his soul, because it was the only place I would never be scared.

My hands shook, my muscles tensed. Rigel tore away my panties with conviction, the waistband dug into my skin, taking my breath away. Then, with no tenderness, he grabbed my ankles and pulled me along the table towards him until I was against his crotch. His body was burning with tension, with cravings, with the need to taste me, tear me to pieces, make me his.

And I wanted him for what he was. I didn't want him to be anything other than himself.

A beautiful demon. The only angel that dwelled in the darkness of my soul.

I was hardly breathing as his possessive touch burned my skin. His fingers worked their way up my thighs, and then he squeezed, feeling my velvety flesh moulding under his fingertips. His hands were full of me, it hurt, and a slight gasp escaped from my lips.

That sound made him grip harder. I narrowed my eyes and arched my ankles. Rigel bent over to press his burning lips to the intimate part between my thighs. When he bit me, my eyes flew open and I gasped.

I instinctively flinched, but he gripped my hips, holding me in a tight, vice-like grip. He started to torture me with his mouth, kissing, licking and sucking impetuously, a merciless storm that made me clench my eyes shut. I moaned. I couldn't feel my legs, my lower stomach was pulsating hard.

His thirsty tongue kept caressing me, unrelenting, and his teeth stimulated nerves that sent shocks over my skin.

My breathing became erratic, I trembled, my cheeks burned. I gripped his hair in my fingers, but Rigel didn't stop, he twisted his tongue around the sensitive area and then sunk his teeth in more forcefully than before. I bit my lip and his fingers clawed at my skin, holding me still while those hot strokes teased me with a sweet cruelty, smashing my muscles to pieces.

When he straightened up, I was unable to speak, exhausted and trembling. My brain was buzzing. Rigel licked his red, swollen, violent lips, then, giving in to the impulse which was devouring him, he lowered his pants.

He seized my pelvis and lifted it, taking my breath away again. He had never been delicate, and I wouldn't expect him to make an exception for me. Rigel always tried to control himself, to contain himself, as if he was constantly scared of breaking me. He was ravenous, wild and impetuous. I wanted him to continue sculpting my soul, casting the world far, far away with all his usual roughness.

I felt his hardness pushing between my legs. My heart missed a beat. My blood was trembling, my body boiling and my heart shuddering to breaking point. I was glad I was on the pill, as there was no time for any other protection.

I wanted to tilt my head, to look in his eyes, but the sensation as he pushed decisively inside me was so unexpected and intense that my toes curled and my spine arched.

My thighs were trembling, as if I would never be able to get used to him. I dug my fingernails into the wood of the table and Rigel breathed in that low, virile way, enjoying the hot, yielding feeling enveloping him. I bit my lip, small and trembling, but instead of continuing, he put a hand to my cheek and pinned my eyes in his gaze.

Time stopped.

My chest exploded with an uncontainable emotion, and I clung to those eyes I loved so wildly, pouring all my feelings into them.

That was where our souls met.

That was where they gave each other everything.

His eyes tied to mine, Rigel started to move inside me. He pushed deep inside me, powerfully pinning me to the edge of the table, gripping my body, making my bones ache.

His breath filled the air.

The world went away.

It became his eyes.

It became his skin, his scent, his vigour and his strength.

It became him.

And the darkness turned into velvet.

Stars bloomed among the shadows.

Rigel leant over me and I met his demanding thrusting with numb legs and trembling ankles. His grip on my pelvis hurt, but I plunged my fingernails into his back and kissed him back with all the sweetness trembling through my body.

Because we were a galaxy of stars, me and him.

A magnificent chaos.

A delirious shining.

But it was only together that we could glow.

And we would always be like that.

Difficult to understand.

Imperfect and unusual.

But immortal . . .

Just like amaranth flowers.

38. Beyond all Measure

Let's wear the stars.
And walk among dreams.
We'll be celestial bodies.
You will wear my love like an eternity.
And any moon, seeing you so resplendent,
will want the love of a sun
to make it shine the same way.

A ring.

Carl had given Adeline a ring.

The news of their engagement had shocked and delighted everyone. Anna had brought her hands to her heart, emotional, and I had thrown myself at her in such an enthusiastic hug that we both fell onto the couch.

I felt a joy I couldn't explain in words, that filled my heart with music and light. I loved her deeply. She deserved happiness.

Anna decided to organise a little party at our house to celebrate and invited all our friends. After all, Adeline was part of the family now.

'You'll be on time, won't you?' I typed on my phone as my footsteps pounded along the sidewalk.

I was walking briskly along the street, my hair fluttering behind me in the breeze.

'Yes,' was Rigel's only reply, concise as ever. He never wasted words, not even in messages.

I knew how busy he was with his studies and all the rest, but I hoped he'd be on time, especially that evening.

'See you at eight, then,' I wrote, happy and light.

That day I had another reason to be in a good mood: after weeks of studying, I had passed the Infectious Diseases exam with full marks. It wasn't an easy subject, and I had immediately called Rigel to let him know how happy I was, because he knew how enthusiastic I was about my studies. He was always the first person I called after an exam, and the only one who would give me a compliment that made me smile gleefully like a little girl.

'Have fun with the others,' he replied, unusually attentive.

I was going for a beer with some classmates before dinner. According to them, we should celebrate such an important exam, and I thought it was a really nice idea. I had gone home to get changed, dressing for the evening so I wouldn't have to excuse myself later when guests were over.

'Thanks,' I messaged, smiling at the screen, then I put my phone away and hurried to the bar.

It was well-lit, sophisticated and inviting. Through the window, I glimpsed leather couches and rows of lights hanging from the ceiling like the branches of a weeping willow. It had a friendly, relaxed atmosphere.

Will was already there. He was waiting outside the bar, but he didn't notice me until I was right behind him.

'Hi! Have you been waiting long?'

'Hey. No, I just got here . . .' he said softly, turning to face me.

He looked down at me, and I checked my reflection in the bar window to make sure nothing was out of place.

I was wearing high heels, some tight-fitting pants and a short blazer that came down to my waist. Underneath, I had chosen a pearly grey top that matched my eyes. It was a sophisticated, feminine corset top with long, puffy organza sleeves. My hair was loose and around my neck was the beautiful tear-drop necklace that Rigel had given me for my birthday.

I had also put on some light make-up for the evening. My eyes were shining, and soft lipstick accentuated the softness of my lips, making them look fuller and bringing out the rosy complexion of my cheeks.

After having overcome challenges and gaining confidence, several years ago, Anna and I had shared one of those mother–daughter moments I had always dreamt of. We went shopping for beauty products together, and she had taught me how to do my make-up. Slowly, calmly, carefully and patiently. It had been a very intimate and important moment for me, one that I would remember forever.

Norman, on the other hand, had taught me to drive, and thanks to him I had got my licence. He had come to the test with me, and despite how nervous I was, he calmed me down with his usual awkwardness. After I passed, I came out of the building waving my licence, and he had given me a soft, proud and awkward hug, laughing behind his thick glasses.

I guarded these moments in my memory, like a treasure chest of precious wonders.

I noticed Will looking at my legs. Billie had told me that those pants showed off my curves more than my other clothes, but I had chosen them because they were extremely comfortable and I felt good in them, not because I wanted to attract attention.

'So,' I said, biting my lip and looking around. 'Are the others coming or . . .'

'They're coming.' Will looked me in the eyes. 'You know they're always late. Even to class.' He smiled and his green eyes shone.

He was attractive. His athletic physique and smile won the hearts of many women. It was one of those sunny, contagious smiles that I often found myself light-heartedly reciprocating. Each time I did, however, he became pensive, as if he saw in my spontaneous, genuine smile something that wasn't there in the adoring looks of others.

'You did well today, in the exam,' Will murmured warmly.

He had come closer. He let his eyes wander over my face, and I smiled with relief.

'Thanks. You too. I was a bit nervous at the start . . . I'm happy it went well.'

'We could study together next time,' he suggested, without taking his eyes off me. He gazed at me, enchanted. 'We could meet up after class . . . You know, I don't live too far away from campus. You could come over to mine . . .'

'Guys! Hey!'

Two of our classmates joined us, interrupting the conversation. Will bit his lip. I looked up at them and smiled in greeting. I really hoped that he was inviting me over just as a friend, but I feared this was not the case. I drove away those thoughts and concentrated on the two girls who had just arrived. We didn't often go out together, but I liked them. We spoke about our shared passion and keen interest in our studies. Another couple were supposed to come too, but couldn't make it in the end because of a time clash.

'So . . . is it just us?' Will asked and the girls nodded, at which point he looked back up at me. His eyes lingered on me for a moment before he added, 'Let's go in then . . . .'

'I've heard lots of good things,' I smiled happily, gesturing to the bar. 'Two good friends of mine came here and said that their craft beers are really good! They also serve these sandwiches with a special sauce with the drinks, and fries that are to d—'

I was cut off by someone coming up behind me, spinning me around and lifting my face up, crushing his lips onto mine.

My heart leapt as I recognised the scent of Rigel. His fingers held my jaw as he gave me such a heated and unexpected kiss that it took my breath away. He devoured my lips so demandingly that my slender body almost gave way under his fiery passion.

I gripped his arm, and Rigel planted his narrowed eyes on Will, firing him an incandescent look while still kissing me. I squeezed his leather jacket, certain I had no more breath left in my lungs, and he decided to withdraw.

Scarlet and shaken, I tidied my hair, and Rigel put an arm around my shoulders before turning with casual, false innocence towards my speechless companions.

'Oh, *William*,' he said, clicking his tongue. 'You're here too. What a scatterbrain I am, I didn't see you *at all*.'

Of course he had seen him. He had glared furiously at him.

Will stared at him, petrified, and the girls gaped at him with bewildered expressions.

He had certainly made a dramatic entrance, but I knew that wasn't the only reason his appearance had caused such astonishment.

Rigel wasn't the sort of guy you expected to just bump into on the street. He was terrifying and enchanting. He gave off a masculine authority which, combined with his sculpted physique, made him seem a born predator.

'Do . . . do you think that's appropriate?' I stammered, indignant and still shaken.

'Now, don't tell me you didn't like it, *little moth*,' he hissed in my ear, with that gruff, amused tone of voice that inflamed my stomach.

I frowned at him reproachfully, still as red as a tomato.

'So you're the mysterious boyfriend,' one of the girls burst out, encouraged by her friend. They looked at him admiringly.

He gave them a shrewd look and a half-smile and told them the name of his star. 'I'm Rigel.'

He had never been very forthcoming, and that wasn't about to change, but I knew all too well how skilfully he could make people like him if he wanted to. I was sure that was what he was doing now.

'Oh, Nica is always so secretive about you,' she reproached me affectionately. 'She never opens up! She told us that you're studying engineering and you play the piano, but as for the rest, she always seems . . .'

'What have you done to your hands?' Will interrupted her. He was staring at Rigel's hands, which were covered in red cuts and scratches.

They were wounds he had got during the attack at his apartment, the ones I had tended.

'Oh, nothing,' he declared calmly, a glint in his eyes. 'A fight.'

That wasn't true!

Will had a wary expression.

'A . . . fight?'

'No, he just cut himself,' I tried to downplay it, but Rigel curled his lips into an effortless smile, knowing he didn't need to raise his voice to be intimidating.

'Some dude got on my nerves. Maybe I should have listened to my psychiatrist when he told me I've got *serious problems* with anger management and a strong inclination for *personality* disorders . . .'

He burst out laughing, shaking his head, as Will stared at him, wide-eyed.

I smiled nervously.

'He . . . he's joking . . .'

The girls relaxed, getting his strange sense of humour, but Will froze, as if my boyfriend was even worse in the flesh than he had imagined.

'So, shall we go in?' Rigel suggested nonchalantly, utterly

formidable. His arm was still around my shoulders, as if the situation was enormously relaxing for him. I thought I glimpsed Will swallow.

'You're . . . coming too?'

'Oh, did the invitation not extend to me? I don't think that's what you said the other day, on that video call . . .' Rigel let it go, piercing Will with a glare that evoked all the friendly *advice* he had dispensed during that conversation.

Will seemed to get the gist. He turned around and hurried into the bar, as if there was nothing he wanted more than to be swallowed up by the revolving doors. My classmates followed him, chatting breezily about how fancy the bar was.

'You know,' Rigel murmured sourly when we were alone, 'you've got a strange knack for attracting imbeciles.'

'Can you stop terrorising him?' I glanced at him sideways.

'That hasn't even crossed my mind,' he hissed into my ear, squeezing my arm. The compact heat of his body tested my good will. I suspected he was aware of this.

'Is that why you came? Because of Will?' I asked, an edge of hardness in my voice, as we slipped together through the revolving doors. His broad hand touched my face. I wanted to grab hold of it. Just a bit.

'You've been wanting me to meet your friends for ages . . . Right?'

He was putting his spin on the situation again. It was true that I had often expressed that desire, but I also knew him well enough to know that he hadn't come just because he suddenly *fancied* a bit of socialising.

Rigel stopped the door with a hand. He tilted his face and looked at me. 'Aren't you happy I'm here?' he asked in a low voice, his black, velvety eyes swallowing up my resolve.

I looked at him, my throat tight, my eyes shining and my cheeks still slightly scorching, because in truth, I was incredibly excited he had come, more than he could imagine. He stared at my eyes and lips, and my heart melted with a sigh.

'Will you behave?' I asked quietly.

He raised an eyebrow with a hint of mirth, putting on that angelic act that made him seem like the worst of devils.

'Don't I *always*?'

I shot him a knowing look, but Rigel pushed me through the door into the pleasant warmth of the bar. It was even nicer inside – the little lights created a pleasant, relaxed, almost festive atmosphere. I noticed a load of young people sitting around tables and at the bar. It must have been a popular student bar.

We found the others at the back, sat on couches around a circular table. We sat down. Rigel kept his jacket on, but I took mine off and put it on the couch next to me. I looked around with bright eyes, enchanted. I slowly tucked my hair behind my ears, and only noticed then that Will, on the other side of the table, was furtively looking at me in my glossy organza top.

He quickly glanced away towards the bar as I smiled at my friends, nodding in agreement with their comments about the bar.

Next to me, Rigel leant back and stretched an arm behind me. I sensed his gaze following the little line of buttons down to the small of my back, but I kept talking to the girls.

I was feeling a strange sort of euphoria. Adeline was getting married, university was going well, I had a special, loving family . . . those emotions all melded together into a mix of happiness that made my face glow and my eyes shine.

While the others were distracted, Rigel leant over me and moved his burning lips to my ear.

'You know, I've been *thinking* . . .' he whispered, breathy, smooth, venomous. The words slid on his tongue like silk.

I drew closer, smiling, and asked lightly, 'About what?'

'About all the things I'd like to *do to you.*'

I choked. I blushed, wide-eyed, and I saw Will on the other side of the table watching us with a hesitant expression. I thought of the things that he usually did to me, and blushed even more.

Rigel buried his face in my hair, burning my skin with his breath. He wasn't being good, he was being as bad as he could. It already hadn't been easy to control my reactions to having him close, and hearing him speak to me so intimately, brazenly, definitely didn't help.

I jumped when I felt his phone vibrating.

Rigel pulled away from me slightly reluctantly, and smoothly pulled it out of his pocket. I surmised that it was one of the many people who contacted him about private tutoring. He got up to go and have the conversation outside, away from the chatter and background noise.

I watched him disappear through the crowd, which unconsciously parted to let him through. It was strange to see him there, he was like a colour that always clashed with the others.

He always seemed out of place. Everyone else looked identical next to him, like stones next to a diamond. Of course, everyone had their nuances, their peculiarities, but Rigel was more complex than everyone else. His many facets gleamed like the stars. He had a cutting personality and a mineral heart; a soul like his shone only for a few.

And I would hold it tight. Forever.

'Good evening,' a young waitress smiled at us kindly, clicking her pen. 'What can I get you?'

We greeted her and ordered from the menu. She quickly jotted our choices down on her pad. I chose a porter for Rigel, one that wasn't too smoky. I really hoped he'd like it. The waitress left us.

I joined in with the others' conversation about university, our courses, the afternoon labs, and by the time our drinks arrived after a few minutes, Rigel still hadn't come back.

I looked around for him. I didn't want to be too anxious, or clingy, but because of his illness I was always worried that he'd have an attack and feel ill. Even though there was nothing I could do, short of helping him take his medication, the idea that something could happen to him at any moment distressed me.

I got to my feet, promising I'd be right back, and went to go look for him. I just wanted to make sure he was all right, even if I just glanced outside. But there was no need to head towards the exit. To my surprise, I found him standing near the bar, holding his phone, and facing a . . . *group of people*?

'Rigel?'

I took his hand and he spun around, staring at the fingers covered in Band-Aids that had interlaced with his. He calmed down when he realised that it was me. Even after all these years, he still wasn't used to some spontaneous gestures.

He was with three boys and a girl I had never seen before.

'Hi,' I said, surprised and confused, then I looked up at him, searching for his eyes. 'I didn't see you come in . . .'

'That's our fault,' one of the boys said amicably, his hands in his jacket pockets. 'We happened to bump into each other.'

I gave him a curious look, but noticing my confused expression, the girl gave a tight smile and with a hint of satisfaction announced, 'We're in the same faculty.'

'Oh!' I smiled, an intense warmth spreading through my chest.

It was the first time that I had had the opportunity to meet his classmates and I was very happy about it.

'Pleased to meet you! I'm Nica.'

'Are you . . . a friend of his?' one of them asked tentatively. I realised that Rigel's solitariness, his wariness about any sort of intimacy, was the reason for their uncertainty.

'I'm his girlfriend,' I replied calmly, to a shocked reaction.

They all smiled at me with a new awareness, as if my happy, bubbly presence made Rigel seem more approachable.

'Oh, wow . . .' the guy who had spoken before remarked, winking at the others.

'You didn't tell us you were seeing anyone, Wilde,' the girl smiled, making sure I heard her. 'You never mentioned it, not once . . .'

She glanced at me as if she was expecting me to be upset, but my face was clear and serene.

I didn't need to know why he hadn't said anything. Rigel was reserved, closed and introverted. He definitely wasn't the sort to tell others about himself. I knew what he was like, and I didn't suspect him of anything.

What we shared was indestructible. It went beyond our souls and was stronger than any words.

She, however, interpreted my silence as a victory. I saw the satisfaction on her face when I just smiled before looking up at Rigel.

'I just wanted to tell you that the drinks have arrived,' I told him softly, intending to give him space. 'I got you a porter.' Then I turned back to the others and smiled at them kindly. 'It's been a pleasure. Have a lovely evening.'

They also said goodbye, and that they hoped to see me again, but the girl stayed silent, biting the inside of her cheek with a hint of irony. She shot me a contemptuous look, then looked hungrily up at Rigel, which was the last thing I saw before turning away.

I made to leave, but suddenly had second thoughts and turned back around. Determined, I grabbed Rigel's face and pushed my lips against his.

I clung to him, overwhelmed him with a breathtaking kiss, plunging my fingers into his hair. I kissed him so passionately that I surprised even myself. I took his mouth, his strength, his heart, everything, and eventually, I pulled away with a sonorous smack, leaving his lips red and swollen.

There was total silence.

They stared at me, stunned, some of them with their eyebrows raised, some with silent approval on their faces, but I didn't turn around.

Immobile in my arms, Rigel looked at me, his eyes slightly widened with shock and his hair dishevelled. It was such an unusual and adorable expression that I smiled at him sweetly.

'I'll see you at our table.'

I planted another, softer kiss on his lips and walked away, completely at ease, feeling his passionate gaze and the girl's baffled glare on me as I left.

When he came back to us, sitting in the same seats as before, I sensed a subtle vibration about him that no one else seemed to notice. I got confirmation of it only later, in the street, when we left the others to get to the party.

'What was that about?' he whispered insinuatingly in my ear, sliding his arm confidently around my shoulders.

I noticed his mocking tone of voice and glanced quickly up at him.

'*Don't tell me you didn't like it . . .*' I murmured, too embarrassed to look at him.

Rigel bit his lip, and a rare burst of low, gruff laughter burst from his chest, vibrating in my bones. I looked at him, a little bewildered and blushing, and suddenly my chest swelled with a burning love.

I should have been used to seeing him smile and being himself, but I wasn't. It was almost . . . strange to see him like this, lit up by bright colours. It was strange, but not unpleasant. No, it was strange and *beautiful*, wonderful and stunning, breathtaking. A strangeness that bewitched your heart and soul, like a flash of lightning in the dark.

That was what Rigel was like, for me.

My light in the darkness.

A flash of a tempest, shining brighter than the sun.

'*Touché . . .*' he drawled, his smile still gleaming on his teeth.

My soul drenched in his laughter, I huddled in and leant my head back, chortling gently against his arm.

There was always something unique and special in our normality.

And that . . . that would never change.

'Congratulations!' I burst out, hugging Adeline tightly.

She looked radiant in her pastel-coloured dress, and even before I saw her face I could tell her cheeks were flushed. She pulled away and smiled at me with bright eyes and two pearl earrings framing her rosy cheeks. I thought she looked incredible. Carl, beside her, greeted me, his ears red with emotion.

'His parents are here too,' Adeline told me, indicating Carl's family amongst friends and loyal clients of the shop. She insisted that I meet them, and introduced me to them with the sort of soft pride reserved for family members.

I said hello to Dalma and George, who were holding glasses of champagne. Asia was with them too. I stopped and gave her a hesitant smile charged with a thousand meanings. She tilted her head and gave me a deep smile back, upon which, maybe, one day, we would be able to build many things.

I would never forget what she had done for me several days ago, at the trial.

The doorbell suddenly rang. Guests were still arriving. I looked up at Rigel and told him that I'd go to greet them. He nodded, and Asia's parents approached to say hello to him and have a little chat. I left them and went to open the door.

A girl with an impish face and her hands on her hips appeared before me.

'Is the party here?'

'Sarah!' I smiled, and she lifted a hand to her face, looking at me excitedly.

'What a lovely neighbourhood, Nica, it's adorable! All these flowers, the picket fence . . .'

'Are you going to get out the way?' someone grumbled behind her.

Miki barged past her, giving her a grouchy look. I admired the angular, attractive face of the woman she had become.

Her long black hair rippled down her back, and there was still chewing gum in her lovely, full mouth. She was wearing tight black pants, a pair of platform combat boots and a pale, baggy sweater that hid her figure. Miki had always had generous curves, but she had never shown them off. She always felt more at ease in soft, comfortable clothes, and even though she had matured over time, her style hadn't changed.

'I'm happy you're here,' I greeted her happily, but she shot me a look that was far from conciliatory and turned to take her jacket off. I looked at her, somewhat alarmed, and moved towards Sarah.

'What happened? Why is she in a bad mood?'

'What do you think happened? As we were filling up the car some moron whistled at her . . . you know how she takes that sort of thing . . .'

Miki glowered at her.

'You could at least have not joined in,' she snapped. Sarah snickered.

'We were just showing our appreciation . . .'

At that moment – luckily – someone else knocked at the door. I opened, and was suddenly blinded by a powerful flash.

'*Bam!*' Billie burst out, ecstatic. 'Ah, that's a really nice one . . . I'll call it *The Panther's Assault* . . .' She looked at Miki's heavily made-up eyes caught on screen and nodded approvingly. Then she looked up, smiling gleefully. 'Hi!'

Ever since she had got her hair cut, her blonde curls were all over the place, but I thought the cut flattered her. It suited her bubbly personality.

'You've come at just the right time!' I greeted her, letting her in. 'Norman's pouring the champagne.'

Behind her, a very tall, slightly gangly boy stepped forward timidly. He immediately took his cap off, as if he was entering a church.

'Hi, Nica . . . thanks for inviting me. I've . . . I've brought this bottle of wine . . .'

'*Vince!*' Sarah burst out, smiling, spreading her arms out wide as though her team had just won.

'Oh, hi, Sarah . . .'

'What are these muscles? Incredible! Look at this!' She whistled, touching his skinny arms, and Vincent blushed, flattered.

'Well . . . Yeah, you know, I've started working out and . . . Oh, hi, Miki,' he stammered quickly.

Miki responded in her usual manner, without looking at him, and Vincent wrung his cap in his hands, stealing glances at her.

He was trying as hard as he could to win a crumb of approval from her, but he didn't seem to be having much success. But Vincent was so shy and awkward it was impossible not to like him, and I was sure that Miki too, under that hard outer layer, knew this very well.

'Come on in,' I invited them. 'Anna's just got the appetisers out the oven . . .'

I knew that the party was for Adeline, but I had taken the liberty of inviting my friends too. I adored surrounding myself with the people I loved. It made me feel like I was in a warm, pleasant and enveloping bubble. I wished they could always be here, at home, maybe because I had had nothing of my own as a child, and so I had grown up believing that happiness was to be shared.

Sarah wasn't drinking, but Vincent soon returned holding two champagne flutes. He held one out to Billie, who smiled sweetly under her mass of curls.

'Thanks, honey.'

I thought the other one was for him, but instead he held it out for Miki. She stared at it, unwavering.

'I don't like champagne,' she muttered, looking away.

'I know . . .' Vincent replied awkwardly. 'I got you some white wine . . . I know it's your favourite . . .'

Miki looked up at him. Behind her back, Sarah gave him an enthusiastic chef's kiss and a triumphant thumbs up.

Billie was watching her best friend slightly apprehensively. She sighed in relief as Miki decided to take the glass that Vincent was holding out for her.

She held it to her chest with a surly expression, not knowing how to respond to someone being nice to her. She met Billie's hopeful eyes and muttered, 'Thanks.'

Vincent blushed and took a step backwards. Then he realised his hands were empty and bumbled off to go and get more drinks.

'I adore him,' Sarah said, as he bumped into Norman, one more awkward than the other.

Billie's eyes softened in gratitude. Those words brought her comfort; they were all she wanted to hear.

A little later, when the party was in full swing, I saw Vincent gesticulating in the middle of an animated conversation.

Rigel, next to him, had his arms crossed over his chest, a glass of champagne in one hand and his face slightly lowered, in shadow. Under his sharp eyebrows, his eyes were looking off to one side. He was visibly suspicious about how familiar Vincent was being, but at the same time he was sufficiently *contained* that Vincent didn't notice.

I tried in vain to hide a smile.

Vincent loved space, cosmology and quantum theory, and he seemed to hold Rigel in very high regard. Even though Rigel's silences and wary glares made Miki seem like a charmer, Vincent seemed pleased to see him.

And, even though they were so different, Rigel tried to be . . . *nice* to him. Or at least civil.

At that moment, I noticed that a little distance away, Anna was watching him. In her slightly sad gaze, there was a fondness that Rigel would never be able to reciprocate.

'*I can't . . . form attachments,*' he had whispered to me once.

We had been taking a walk after dinner with Anna and Norman, and that flat admission had broken the silence. I had immediately known what he was referring to, because his tone of voice changed when he was speaking from the heart.

I had looked up at him, his hands in his jacket pockets, his black hair mingling with the night. It was always too direct for him, in moments like those, to look me in the eyes.

He couldn't grow fond of them.

He couldn't grow fond of anyone. That was the truth.

His abandonment issues and the psychological burden of his illness had left him, since childhood, seriously emotionally insecure.

And his relationship with the matron had only made things worse. As a child, Rigel had had a desperate need for affection, but getting it from a woman like her had pushed him to refuse the only form of love he had ever received. Margaret was a monster, and he knew it.

That had led him to reject affection, to grow up without attachments, to push them away. Solitude, frustration and a lack of reference points for a normal relationship had seriously undermined his ability to form emotional attachments.

It wasn't his fault. He had protected himself as if from an illness, producing the antibodies that would stop him getting sick.

In that dark street, I had accepted his silence and taken him by the hand. I couldn't tell him how much Anna and Norman really loved him. Deep down, I was sure that the boy he once was long ago would have wanted to reciprocate their love.

The doorbell rang again.

I put down my glass and headed straight to the door, but before I could get there Klaus wriggled between my legs. He stopped and glared at me indignantly, put out by having all these people in the house. I picked him up and kissed his head, scratching behind his ears as he liked, and smiled as purrs escaped from him. I stroked him gently then put him on the first step of the stairs. He looked at me resentfully, probably offended I hadn't kept fussing him as he deserved.

'Coming . . .' I said as I opened the door.

I froze.

The past reappeared under my eyes, momentarily tearing me from the present.

The boy before me turned around. As soon as I looked him in the face, I felt my heart disappear. Time stopped.

'. . . Peter?' I whispered feebly.

He stared at me. I remembered those eyes perfectly.

'Nica . . .'

I felt my heart swell. I couldn't breathe. Without thinking, incredulous, I stretched my arms forward and hugged him. His red hair brushed my cheek.

I was too overcome by intense emotion to immediately notice that Peter was stiff and trembling.

I remembered him as a skinny child with persistent dark circles under his eyes, who always cried more than everyone else and hid behind whoever he could. He had never known how to defend himself against cruelty. A gentle soul like his didn't even have the strength to protect itself.

'I can't . . . I can't believe it . . .' I gasped, pulling away from him. I felt my eyes brimming. It was only then that I noticed how drastically pale he was and the tense nerves in his neck. It took me a moment to realise that it was me who had caused that reaction.

'Yeah . . .' Peter tried to smile, but the corner of his mouth twitched strangely. His lips seemed to be constantly tingling. My heart faded into confusion, and then it dawned on me: I had scared him.

I had overlooked something fundamental. Peter was like me. But much more so.

He too had stopped growing.

Adeline had told me, long ago, he had never gotten over what happened.

'Adeline invited me,' he swallowed. I saw that, slowly, he was calming down. 'She knew I was here . . . for the trial. I saw you, that day,' he confessed. 'I saw both of you. I was there too. I listened to what you said in the witness box, Nica. I wanted to say hello but I couldn't find you afterwards.'

I had run away, that was why.

I gave him a shaky smile that I hoped conveyed everything.

'If I'd have known you were there, I would have found the strength to stay.'

Peter's eyes convulsively flicked to one side for a fraction of a second, and I sensed this was his way of showing unease and embarrassment.

'It was very brave,' I said more softly. 'What you did. Without you . . . she would never have been convicted.'

Margaret would not torment us any longer. With the various testimonies, the overwhelming evidence and the medical reports of the lasting psychological damage she had caused, the court had not only found her guilty, but had also given her a sentence that meant she would never be able to harm anyone else.

She would not infest our future.

Only our past.

I wondered what she had thought, when she found out that it had been Peter who had triggered it all. The only one who had never been strong enough to react, the only one who was always too little and terrified of her to do anything.

'Come in,' I invited him warmly, moving aside to let him pass. I stayed an acceptable distance from him, and hoped he would understand that I would not invade his personal space without consent again.

Peter came in warily, and I let him take his own jacket off. It was strange to see him there, in my present. The first thing I thought was that I wanted to introduce him to Anna and Norman.

I settled him down on the couch, and asked if I could bring him anything to drink, but he declined. I noticed he had a little twitch on his left eyelid and he kept looking around nervously.

He still had the same carrot-coloured hair, the same pale blue eyes above his long nose. His face was more freckles than anything else, and although he was now a young man, his skinny build had not changed at all. He still seemed small, fragile and scared. Like a little boy.

'So . . . is this your home?'

'Yes,' I replied softly, slowly sitting down near him. 'I met the Milligans when I was seventeen. They came to The Grave . . . They're very lovely people. I'd like to introduce you to them, if you'd like.'

I didn't want to be too much. He had just got here, and I didn't know how comfortable he was with strangers. Maybe Adeline hadn't told him there would be so many people. His gaze kept darting around, as if he wanted to have a pair of eyes on everyone in the room.

'I know you were adopted when you were moved to Saint Joseph.' I tried to meet his eyes, tucking a strand of hair behind my ears, and he nodded. Peter had left at the same time as Adeline. He, however, hadn't stayed in the new institute for long.

'The Clays,' he announced, showing me a photo of a happy,

smiling couple with dark skin on his phone. In the photo, Peter looked peaceful with his arms around their son, a young boy whose fingers were held up in a V sign.

Seeing me smile, he seemed to relax a little.

'They came when I was thirteen,' he explained. 'That day . . . well, I tripped over the carpet. I wanted to make a good impression, but instead I broke a plant in the hall. Straight away, they decided they wanted to get to know me. They thought I was . . . nice, I think.'

I laughed, bringing my hand to my mouth, and Peter gave a slight smile. He told me about them, about school, about how it had felt to leave the institute to be welcomed by a family. I related strongly to what he was saying, and was happy to learn a little more about what had become of his life.

Suddenly, however, Peter froze. His face turned to stone, and his eyes hardened with shock. I stared, confused at that unexpected shift, and instinctively turned around to see where he was looking.

My heart plunged when I realised.

Rigel.

He had seen Rigel, on the other side of the room.

Adeline was talking to him animatedly, and even though his pale lips were sealed in their usual hermetic expression, his black eyes were paying attention to her. She smiled and gave him a playful nudge. He said something that made her burst into bright laughter.

'*Him* . . .' Peter gasped, his voice unrecognisable. 'What's . . . he . . . doing here . . .'

'It's not what you think, Peter,' I hurried to say.

I remembered the role Rigel played in our childhood memories. The *violent* and *cruel* monster who Peter himself had warned me against.

'There are things you don't know,' I continued gently. 'Rigel . . . never had anything to do with the matron. Believe me.'

Maybe if he had seen him at Margaret's trial things would be different, but Rigel hadn't been there that day.

'I should have known that sooner or later I'd see him again. *Look at him*,' he spat out bitterly. In Peter's eyes, Rigel was an impeccable, shining young man, while he would always carry the signs of that abuse. 'He hasn't changed at all.'

'He's not the person you think he is,' I declared, somewhat sourly.

His body was tense, the twitch in his eyelid indicating he was getting increasingly stressed. I wanted to take his hand, but I knew that wasn't a good idea.

'Peter,' I whispered. 'Rigel is very different from the boy you imagined . . .'

'Are you defending him?' His incredulous eyes slid into mine. 'After *everything* he did to you?'

He looked at me as if I was an alien. Suddenly, something murky and venomous darkened his face.

'Of course. After all, he's always been good at that. At *manipulating* people . . . That must be why Adeline invited him. Even after all this time . . .'

There was a hint of jealousy in his eyes as he looked at them again. I sensed he was repressing some feelings towards Adeline.

And yet, even though I knew that Peter had always disliked Rigel, he seemed more jealous of him than of Carl.

'You're wrong,' I said, softly and sincerely. 'Adeline loves him. She cares about him . . . like a brother.'

'Oh, but that didn't stop him *screwing her*,' he hissed acidly.

I stopped breathing.

I stared at Peter, unable to move, as if my heart had stopped.

'What?'

'What's wrong? Didn't you know?'

I stared at him, frozen, and instinctively my gaze was drawn to Adeline. I saw her there, smiling, happy, madly in love with her fiancé. Peter's words gnawed at my brain.

'I shared a room with him,' Peter reminded me. 'I know what I'm talking about. I used to have to get up and leave when she came over . . . Every *damned* time . . . She didn't see anything but him. Always and only him. As if he didn't already have everyone else's attention . . .'

He glared daggers at Rigel, full of hate. 'I'm not surprised he's here, he probably wants to remind her of the effect he had on her. Or that he *still* has . . .'

'Rigel's here with me,' I burst out, almost automatically. My brain was scrambled, there was a strange feeling in my chest, but those words still found their way out of my mouth. 'We . . . we're together.'

Peter looked as if I had just told him something abominable, abhorrent. Dismay created a strange contrast on his face – he had the eyes of a child, but the incredulous fury of an adult.

'You're . . . *together*?' he repeated, as if I had gone mad. '*You* are going out with him? Have you forgotten how he treated you? He hated you, Nica!'

'He didn't hate me, Peter,' I whispered. Even though Rigel was a tale others could not understand, Peter was a part of our past, and I felt the need to change his mind. 'Quite the contrary . . .'

'Of course,' he burst out sarcastically. 'He was in love with you but repeatedly fucked *another girl*.'

I jumped. Those words struck me right in the heart, like a well-placed kick. I fell silent, and Peter shook his head, now with a hint of pity.

'You were always too naïve, Nica.'

Something deep inside my chest stirred, burned, became persistent, and I couldn't stop my eyes from looking at Rigel.

His obsidian gaze cut through the room. Adeline was no longer next to him. Instead, his attention was completely devoted to the boy sitting on the couch next to me. He stared at Peter with immobile eyes, with the same glimmer of recognition that I had had when I had seen him standing in the doorway.

After a moment, his gaze met mine.

In that moment, the thought that he and Adeline had touched each other, been together as we had, eroded me from the inside.

I now understood the kiss she had given him when she came back, years ago. She and Rigel had already shared many kisses.

The thought of it twisted my stomach. I got up, looking away, and made my excuses to Peter before leaving the room.

I knew now that I wouldn't be able to make him change his mind: he was too steadfast in his beliefs, in his past, to be able to re-evaluate everything. His mind would not be changed, and my need to get away from there was too strong. The image of Adeline was stuck in my mind, and despite how I was feeling, I didn't want to ruin her moment.

I walked down the hallway and into the room at the end. My hair brushed against my cheekbones as I came to a stop in the middle of the room, far away from the noise and people's looks.

I heard someone close the door behind me, and turned around, certain I already knew who it was.

'Were you and Adeline together?' I demanded, unable to hold back, as if those words had burnt my lips.

Rigel gave me a long look, his face lowered, a cautious expression darkening his gaze.

'Is that what Peter told you?'

'Answer me, Rigel.'

Silence was the only response I got. And I had learnt to interpret the absence of words much better than their presence.

I looked away, disheartened, and then turned back towards him.

'When were you thinking of telling me?'

'What did you want to hear, *exactly*?'

'Don't change the subject. You know how important you both are to me. The idea of the two of you . . .' I tried to find the right words, but bitterness closed my throat.

It shouldn't have mattered. It happened before Rigel and I discovered that we belonged together, what did it have to do with the two of us? Nothing.

And yet the thought gnawed at my insecurities, gave me no peace.

Adeline had told me that it was him who held my hand when Margaret punished me, that it had been him who had protected me every time, that his behaviour had always been motivated by something unique and profound, from the beginning. But now, those words seemed hollow, distant.

Had she been lying?

'That's why you were always so tense when I tried to speak to you about the past. You were scared I'd find out.'

I had to be rational, but the idea that they had kept me in the dark tormented me. The fear that there was something between them had overwhelmed me too often, I had tried to remember how their relationship had started too often. But only because they had not been honest with me.

Why did they always have to put me to one side, protect me, make decisions for me?

Could they not have told me the truth?

'It happened a long time ago,' Rigel replied thunderously, as if those words were costing him something. 'No, I didn't want you to find out. What choice did I have?'

'You chose to not tell me,' I replied quietly. He scowled, hearing the bitterness in my voice. He took a step towards me, frustration in his eyes.

'Is that how it is? Peter turns up and we sink back down to where we started?'

'Leave Peter out of it,' I whispered categorically. 'He's the only one who's been honest with me.'

'Peter knows *nothing*,' he snarled angrily, towering over me. 'After all this time, it's him who you're choosing to believe?'

'That's not the point . . .'

'*And yet* it's enough for you to lose trust in me!'

'I'd trust you with my life!' I raised my voice, my eyes open wide in a defenceless, fragile expression. 'Don't you get it? I trust you as I trust myself – you're the one who chose to keep quiet about something like this. You know what you and Adeline mean for me . . . You know I think of her like a sister . . . How many other things haven't you told me?'

I was maybe overreacting. Maybe I shouldn't have said that. But the fact that they had decided to hide this from me gave me an ill-defined feeling of disillusionment.

Maybe, some other girl in my shoes would have preferred not to know.

Maybe, some other girl would have preferred to stay in the dark, happy and oblivious.

But not me.

I was an open book with Rigel. I trusted him more than anyone else, but I needed him to trust me too. I needed him to tell me things, rather than keep them from me out of fear of losing me.

He wouldn't lose me, I just wanted the truth. Did he really think that I would leave him for something that happened years ago?

I sighed gently and shook my head. I lowered my arms slowly, looking at him sadly.

'You can tell me anything,' I whispered faintly. 'And it hurts me when you choose not to. If you don't want to talk about Adeline, then I'll never know what there was between you. Fine . . .' I whispered, in spite of my feelings. 'But sometimes I just want you . . . to let me understand how you're feeling. I know you, Rigel, but I can't read your thoughts.'

I wrapped my arms tight around myself, looking down, letting the most delicate part of my heart speak. 'You can . . . trust me,' I said sincerely. 'You don't have to be scared of hurting me. And if you don't want to talk about this . . . If . . . if you don't want to talk about Adeline . . . then I won't ask you about it. Whatever there was between you, if you can't tell me . . . I accept it.' I swallowed quietly. 'I won't doubt you . . . But I wish you'd have done the same. That you felt free to talk to me . . . to be honest with me. I'm hopelessly in love with you,' I admitted, subdued. 'And that won't ever change.'

I looked up, surrendering completely. My attempts to smile were counteracted by the bitterness in my gaze. I looked away and sighed gently.

'Let's go back,' I murmured, moving past him.

I got to the door and opened it, ready to go back and chat at the party, ready to go back to a reality that was proceeding without us. But I couldn't do it.

A hand landed on the door and closed it firmly shut.

I could feel Rigel's breath on my neck, his warm chest pressing against my back.

I didn't move when I felt his solid body against mine. I stayed still, trapped in his heat. He was my end and my beginning.

I would always remember the silence of that moment.

'I've loved you since I was five years old.'

Rigel's voice was a hoarse, barely audible whisper. His lips gently brushed against my ear, as if those words were an unspeakable secret. I wasn't breathing.

'I tried to stop it as hard as I could,' he continued, the words pouring out of his mouth. 'But you didn't give me any choice. You broke through everything. You took everything from me, and I hated you for that. I was with her, because I looked for you in everyone else . . . but no one ever had enough freckles, no one ever had your hair or eyes that were pale enough.'

There was another pause. His body was still close against mine, his hot breath against my neck. I sensed how difficult it was for him to say this.

'I never knew how to love,' he confessed, embittered and defeated. 'I can't take care of people, I can't be nice. I don't believe in emotions, because I'm not capable of forming attachments . . . But if love exists, then it has your eyes, your voice and your damn Band-Aids on its fingers.'

He lifted my hand.

He took from his pocket one of the Band-Aids that I had left at his apartment, opened it and then put it around my finger.

Like a ring.

'This is all I've got to give you. And if one day you'll marry me, Nica . . . everyone will see that you're mine, that you have been, silently, since the beginning.'

My eyes opened wide. Boiling tears trembled on my eyelids, flooding my vision. I couldn't believe what I had heard, I couldn't believe he had really said that. My chest was pounding as if someone had just inflicted a brutal wound.

Slowly, trembling, I turned towards him. Rigel met my eyes, and held my gaze with everything he had.

'You have the eyes of the Tearsmith, for me,' he murmured. 'And you always will.'

A hot, violent wave crashed into my chest. Boundless feelings exploded out of me, burning everywhere, flooding my soul with a light that no one else would be able to give me.

Tears ran down my face. He touched my cheek, stroking it slowly, and I didn't see the wolf, but something else.

He was the boy who had seen me for the first time, on the threshold to The Grave.

His was the hand that had found the courage to hold mine in the cellar.

Those were the arms that had lifted me, protected me.

The face that had taken a slap for me.

The heart he had never had the courage to give me.

But that, with everything, screamed my name.

He held it out to me, his hands covered in scratches. Even though he had never known how to love with tenderness, he was showing me the most fragile and vulnerable part of himself.

For the first time in his entire life, Rigel confessed the words I had unconsciously been wanting to hear for years.

That I had been waiting for, hoping for, loving in secret.

And, even if I never heard them again, even if he stayed the boy who only spoke with his eyes, my heart would always, forever, be full of that love.

Because it was not true that we were a disaster. No.

We were a masterpiece.

The most beautiful and spectacular of all.

I put my hand on his and smiled. I smiled at him with all my heart, my soul, my tears and that Band-Aid around my finger.

I smiled at him like the woman I was, and the little girl I always would be.

And he smiled back, with all the deepness of his eyes.

Those eyes that I would always be madly in love with.

I threw myself into his arms, plunging into his embrace like never before. I clung to him with every shred of myself, and Rigel bent over me, holding me as if I was the smallest, most fragile and precious thing in the world. He lifted me in his arms and I latched myself to his heart like a butterfly.

I leant my forehead against his and kissed him, again and again and *again,* and each kiss was a smile, each kiss was a tear that would unite us forever.

And on the brink of our finale, I understood that if there was a moral to this story . . . *it was us.*

Yes, us.

Because our souls shone with the force of a thousand suns.

And just like thousand-year-old constellations, our story was written there.

In that infinite sky.

Amid hurricanes of misfortune, and clouds of stardust.

Eternal, indestructible.

Beyond all measure.

Epilogue

The fairy lights on the beautiful Christmas tree sparkled like fireflies, casting a golden light even into the furthest corners of the dim, decorated living room. I advanced across the shining marble floor, trying not to make a sound.

A little girl was curled up asleep on the couch in front of the fireplace, totally blissful, her little face resting on the chest of a handsome man. A strong forearm was loosely wrapped around her.

Rigel's head was tilted to one side; his eyes were closed.

At thirty-four years old, he was even more attractive than ever before. There was the shadow of a beard on his jaw, and every muscle in his body seemed honed towards his natural instinct to protect. His broad shoulders and defined wrists lent him a beguiling air of self-assurance that was perceptible as soon as he walked into a room.

I carefully took the girl, careful not to wake him, and lifted her into my arms.

They had spent the whole day together.

When she had arrived in our life five years ago, Rigel had confessed his fear to me: he was scared that he would be unable to love her, as had been the case with everyone else.

But I was sure that fear would vanish as soon as he saw her in my arms, small and defenceless, with jet black hair just like his.

Delicate, precious, innocent . . . a black rose.

Earlier that afternoon I had leant in the arched doorway to the living room and found them there, sitting on the piano stool. She was in his arms, wearing a velvet dress.

'Daddy, tell me something I don't know,' she had asked, looking at him adoringly, as she always did.

She loved him madly, and never stopped saying how her daddy was the best of all, because he sent satellites into space.

Rigel, thoughtful, had tilted his face, his eyelashes brushing his elegant cheekbones. Then he had taken her little hand in his, palm against palm.

He had never been tender with anyone. But with her . . .

'Many of the atoms you're made of, from the calcium in your bones to the iron in your blood, were created in the heart of a star that exploded millions of years ago.'

His slow, deep voice caressed the air like a wonderful symphony.

I was sure she hadn't understood, but nevertheless, her mouth fell open into a little O. Rigel said she was the spitting image of me when she had that expression.

I had made my presence known at that point.

'Her kindergarten teacher said something interesting,' I burst out. 'Apparently, our daughter won't let any little boys near her, because someone has convinced her that they spread diseases. Do you know anything about that?'

Rigel gave me a piercing look as the little one played with his shirt collar. Then he clicked his tongue.

'Absolutely no idea,' he declared.

She looked up at him, her little face crumpled into a concerned expression.

'I don't want boy disease, Daddy. I won't let them get near.'

I watched her hug him, my arms crossed and eyebrows raised.

Rigel smirked.

'She's a sensible girl,' he murmured, pleased with himself.

I smiled again as I remembered this.

I suddenly felt her murmuring against my throat.

'Mommy . . . ?' she said, rubbing her eyes on my skin.

'Go to sleep, honey.'

She wrapped her little hands around my neck and her soft hair tickled my chin. I inhaled the fragrance of her cherry shower gel and cuddled her as I climbed the stairs.

'Mommy . . .' she whined again. 'Was Daddy sick earlier? Did he have a headache again?'

I nestled my head against hers, cradling her against me.

'It happens sometimes. But then it passes . . . It always passes. He just needs to rest. Your daddy is very strong, you know?'

'I know,' she replied, determined.

I smiled as we reached her bedroom, where I lay her down in bed. I turned on the nightlight that projected stars onto the ceiling and carefully tucked her in. She clutched my caterpillar plushie, completely resewn and repaired for her. I noticed she was staring at me with her large, grey eyes. Her sleepiness seemed to have completely vanished.

'What is it?' I asked softly.

'Will you tell me a bedtime story?'

I stroked her black hair.

'You should go to sleep, Rose . . .'

'But it's Christmas,' she objected in a little voice. 'You always tell me a wonderful bedtime story at Christmas . . .'

She looked at me hopefully, with her tiny little nose, her skin as white as a doll's. I couldn't find a reason to say no to her.

'All right,' I agreed and sat down next to her.

Rose smiled happily, and in her eyes shone the reflection of a thousand little stars.

'What story do you want me to tell you?'

'The story of you and Daddy,' she replied immediately, excited. I rearranged the bedcovers on her chest. 'Your story.'

'Again? Are you sure? I tell that one every year . . .'

'I like it,' she replied simply, as if that was enough to settle the matter.

I smiled, sitting more comfortably on her little bed.

'All right . . . Where do you want me to start?'

'Oh! From the beginning!'

I narrowed my eyes, looking at her sweetly. I reached my arms out to arrange her pillow, making sure she was warm and comfortable.

'*From the beginning*? Okay . . .'

I leant back on the mattress, propping myself up with a hand. I looked up at the stars above us, and slowly, softly, started the tale . . .

'We had many stories at The Grave. Whispered tales, bedtime stories . . . Legends flickering on our lips in the glow of a candle.'

I looked sweetly into her eyes and smiled.

'The most famous was the one about the Tearsmith.'

Acknowledgements

Until the very end . . .

And so our journey draws to a close . . .

It seems unbelievable that we have reached the end of this story.

Thank you to everyone who has got this far.

Thank you to Francesca and Marco for the wonderful opportunity.

Thank you to Ilaria Cresci, my editor on the long journey of bringing this novel to life. She has been beside me day and night, shared moments of anxiety and joy, with professional dedication and devoted friendship. I am grateful for everything I have learnt from her.

Thank you to my family who, without knowing it, gave me the strength to follow my dream. Thank you to my best friends, for how enthusiastically they embraced this news and how deeply they believed in it. They are my strength.

And finally, thank you to all my readers, who dreamed, flew and imagined along with me. They believed in this story from the beginning and waited patiently for it every day, supporting me in every choice and always being by my side.

This is all for you.

I dedicate these last words to you, because you are the essence of this book, the soul of this story and the pulsing heart of this project.

I hope you know that . . .

Crying is human. Crying means feeling, and there's nothing wrong with that. There's nothing wrong with collapsing and letting go. It doesn't mean we're weak, it means we're *alive,* that our hearts are beating, worrying and burning with emotions.

I hope you know that . . .

You don't need to be scared of not being perfect. No one is perfect, and fairy tales are also for those who don't think they deserve them, even for those who think they're too different and broken to want one at all.

Look for them.

Do it. Don't give up. They're not always easy to find. Sometimes they're hidden in a person, in a place, in a feeling, or inside you. Sometimes they're a bit worse for wear, but they're there, before your eyes, waiting to be discovered.

And I hope you know that . . .

We all have our Tearsmith. And all of us, in turn, are someone else's Tearsmith. Let's not forget the power we have over the people who love us. Let's not forget that we can hurt them, that our words and actions can have a profound impact on their heart. That sometimes, a smidgen more tenderness can make a difference.

It's sad, isn't it?

To have reached the end.

But when all is said and done . . . every ending is just a new beginning.

I hope that Rigel has taught you that silences can hold the depths of the universe, and that through Nica you have realised that there is a Band-Aid for our every endeavour. We should put them proudly on our fingers because we should admire those who, despite their wounds, keep on trying and never give up.

Wear them with pride. Always.

And don't stop trying. Ever.

Do it. Okay?

I . . . I have to go.

Our time is up, but . . .

Remember: you cannot lie to the Tearsmith.

And if anyone tells you that fairy tales aren't real . . .

Tell them there's one they don't know.

One they've never heard.

And if they want to hear it . . . come back here.

Give me your hand.

Hold tight and follow me.

There are dark paths ahead, but I know the way.

Are you ready?

Good. *Here we go . . .*

ERIN DOOM is an Italian author whose debut novel, *Fabbricante di lacrime* (*The Tearsmith*), shot to the top of the charts in 2022 and has since sold more than half a million copies. Her second and third novels, *Nel modo in cui cade la neve* (*The Way the Snow Falls*) and *Stigma* (2023), are also bestsellers. Doom studied law and currently lives in Italy.

ABOUT THE TYPE

This book was set in Bembo, a typeface based on an old-style Roman face that was used for Cardinal Pietro Bembo's tract *De Aetna* in 1495. Bembo was cut by Francesco Griffo (1450–1518) in the early sixteenth century for Italian Renaissance printer and publisher Aldus Manutius (1449–1515). The Lanston Monotype Company of Philadelphia brought the well-proportioned letterforms of Bembo to the United States in the 1930s.